Eden's Gates

Eden's Gates

by

Charles Roberts

Strategic Book Publishing and Rights Co.

Strategic Book Publishing and Rights Co.
12620 FM 1960, Suite A4-507
Houston, TX 77065
www.sbpra.com

ISBN: 978-1-60911-804-4

This book is dedicated to the memory of The Old Place

Ere I made my escape from Eden,
And my heart was bound in chains,
As I hungered for its freedom,
I sought release from its pains,
I cried to God in Heaven,
"From my captors set me loose!
And from my prison rescue me
With peace and love and truth."
And when He opened Eden's Gates
And my heart set free to fly,
I found the truth my greatest pain,
My jailor, Lord, was I.

— Edna Clemens Austen
A Collection of Victorian Verses

Part One

Chapter One

The hard-packed earth felt cold to Henny's bare feet as she searched the dirt floor for her slippers. Jolted from a restless sleep that April morning in 1853, the little black girl sat in the darkness and moved her feet back and forth beneath her bed. Dread that she would be beaten made the nine-year-old girl's heart pound in her chest like the dasher in an empty churn. She tried not to think of being whipped, but her fear was as real now that she was awake as it had been in the fitful dreams of her sleep.

When her toes struck her slippers, she slipped them on her feet and felt her way in the darkness until she found her dress hanging on a peg on the door. No hint of light shone through the cabin's single window, yet she feared lighting the rag in the tallow dish would alert anyone outside that she was awake.

Shivering in the cold Virginia air, she allowed her fingers to linger and lovingly caress the dress's delicate Alençon lacework. She slipped the dress, unlikely clothing for a slave, over her head and smoothed the tiers of lace cascading down her thin body. With shaking hands, she tied a bow in the white satin sash attached to the waist and quickly checked to make sure the red velvet ribbons were still attached to the ends of the dozen short plaits sprouting all over her head.

Tiptoeing to the door, Henny listened. When she heard no shuffling feet, or crying child, or squeak of the water pump, she eased open the door and slipped outside. Relieved that she had not slept past the darkness that concealed her, she crept toward the edge of the cabin's narrow porch and looked up and down the lane that passed through the slave quarters of Hawthorn Hill Plantation.

Moonlight bathed the whitewashed cabins in silver, and a chilling breeze seemed to stir the doubts challenging Henny's mission. Shivering in the ghostly glow, she eased toward Old Sheba's cabin next door. When she did not hear the rumble of the old woman's snore, she stepped from the porch and heard her voice.

"Whar you goin'?"

Henny whirled toward the sound from between her cabin and Old Sheba's.

"I say, why you up 'fore the mornin' bell ring?"

Henny searched the darkness for the old woman and the sound of a streaming liquid striking the ground.

"You goin' up there?" The voice was raspy from age and a night unused.

"Yes," Henny said, her tone determined, yet still a whisper. She looked down to see Old Sheba squatting between the cabins.

"You get whipped if you do!"

"And you get whipped for what you doin', too. You 'sposed to go to the privy for that."

"Nobody whip me. Privy too far and I too old. I just makin' water."

The splatter stopped and with a grunt and the crack of resisting joints, the old woman struggled to her feet.

Old Sheba was the oldest person, black or white, on Hawthorn Hill Plantation. Henny had been told she was over two hundred years old and saw no reason to doubt it, or the claim the old woman could foretell the future—about which Henny had consulted her the day before.

"Ain't I talked no sense in you yet?"

Henny stiffened. "You not know to give me that fortune if I not tell you what I studyin'."

"Be the same fortune whether I knows it or not. You get whipped either way."

Old Sheba hobbled from between the cabins, her deep-set eyes glaring at Henny from above sharp cheek bones covered with black, leathery skin.

"I don't believes in you fortunes no more," Henny said.

The old woman angrily shook her tiny, nearly bald head dotted with patches of white, wool-like hair. "I whip you myself if I has to. That make my fortune come true mighty quick."

Henny's determination wavered only a moment before she broke into a run down the lane. "I's goin' anyhow!"

"You goin' to get a lickin'!" Old Sheba called after her. "And when you does, don't come back here wantin' me to loves you and 'tend the stripes on you legs. I done told you!"

Henny pressed her hands against her ears to shut out Old Sheba's warning and ran on. Yet she could not so easily flee the shadow of failure and punishment the old woman's prophesy cast on her plan. Concealed by darkness and the morning fog, only the whiteness of her dress and the satin sash whipping after her revealed Henny as she raced past the sleeping cabins and turned up the path to the big house.

As she approached the gate to the kitchen yard, she saw Aunt Beck emerge from her cabin just outside the fence. Henny quickly veered to one side of the path and pressed her thin frame against the wall of the smokehouse as the ruler of Hawthorn Hill's kitchen trudged past her. Aunt Beck's short, rotund figure listed from side to side, so close Henny could hear the old woman's wheeze and the soft tread of her steps.

Aunt Beck was followed by her husband, Uncle Lemiel, a dignified, white-haired old gentleman, only a little taller than his wife. When they passed through the noisily squeaking gate, Aunt Beck went to the kitchen while Uncle Lemiel approached a tall pole and pulled a rope attached to a large brass bell mounted at the top.

The bell's slow, monotonous toll officially announced another day at Hawthorn Hill Plantation. For fifty years, Uncle Lemiel and his bell had roused the plantation awake in the morning and signaled the end of labor in the evening. It was as if no rooster could crow, nor bird sing, nor the sun itself could rise until Uncle Lemiel summoned the day with this morning ritual. Black and white alike responded to its call, and one by one, flares of light could be seen in the cabins as lanterns were lighted and the people rose from corded beds and corn-husk mattresses for the day's labor.

When the final peal of the bell had melted into the silence of the foggy morning, the old man lumbered up the steps to the covered passage linking the kitchen to the big house. Only house servants and yard workers were allowed to enter the yard, yet Henny eased toward the gate and was about to open it when she heard footsteps.

Glancing behind her, she recognized the rail-thin figure of Piney, the kitchen girl. Henny sniffed in disgust and quickly retreated into hiding, again pressing herself close to the smokehouse wall. She stiffened with resentment as the thin, thirteen-year-old Piney approached.

Piney was an enemy of long standing. Carrying a pail of milk still warm from the cow, and butter, cooled by the waters of the spring house, Piney passed inches from Henny. Her antagonism stirred, Henny thought how easy it would be to extend her foot and trip her old enemy, causing her to fall and spill the milk. But she wisely resisted the temptation. Piney would only wail and create a scene, expose Henny, and destroy her goal, which remained preeminent, even when weighed against so pleasing a sight as a raging, humiliated Piney sprawled on the ground in a puddle of milk.

Once Piney had passed, Henny ran her fingers down her dress, remembering the origin of the girl's hostility when two years earlier they had fought bitterly for its possession. Sent from the big house to the quarters with other hand-me-downs, Henny and Piney had both claimed the dress. Although four years older and a foot taller than Henny, Piney had retreated from the determination and fury of Henny's flying fists and surrendered the dress. But the resentment and rancor of the battle remained.

Henny again savored her victory in possessing the finest garment in the quarters, so unlike the broadcloth and gingham clothing worn by the other slave children. Although two sizes too large for her, and further emphasizing her thin, bony frame, she wore the dress proudly, oblivious to its beginning signs of shabbiness.

Suddenly, the kitchen door swung open and a splash of yellow light spilled down the steps and across the ground.

"Get on in here. Does I has to come fetch you myself to get you here on time?"

Henny caught her breath at the sound of the angry voice. It was Emma, the ill-tempered housekeeper, the person Henny most feared would discover her. Emma's switches, brooms, cane, or any other weapon at hand, had often struck those violating the rule against trespassing in the yard.

"I comin'," Piney said, her stick-thin form lurching to one side as she balanced the heavy bucket of milk. "That cow mighty slow givin' down this mornin'. It lak she holdin' on to ever drap she can."

Emma, stooped by age and rheumatism, and silhouetted against the light from the kitchen, looked like a giant black bird, crouched and waiting to pounce on her prey. Henny was relieved to see she did not carry the leather strap rumor had was her favorite weapon.

"Mr. Lionel be gettin' home any day now," Emma said. "We got cakes and custard to make. You bring eggs?"

"You never told me to."

"How we gonna make custard with no eggs? You goin' to have to go back and get 'em."

"We don't know for certain just when Master Lionel comin'. That custard spile if you makes it today!"

"Hush your mouth. I decide when the custard spile!"

Emma was a matriarch of enormous power on the plantation. She ruled both black and white alike with unquestioned authority and even dominated Master Lionel whenever she could. She had been the master's wet nurse and Mammy, and reared him since infancy. Even now, she exercised powerful prerogatives that long-ago position earned her. The master loved the domineering old woman like a mother and tolerated her bullying with amused indulgence. To incur Emma's displeasure was unwise, and, because Master Lionel often defended and upheld his Mammy's unjust and ruthless tyranny, the old woman was feared and appeased at every turn.

Piney entered the kitchen and returned with a basket as Emma's tirade continued, the head of her black, bird-of-prey silhouette bobbing angrily. "And don't you rob the nest. I know you been too sorry to leave a nest egg. You not leave a nest egg and I'll cut the blood out of you. You don't and I wear you out. And don't you brang no less than a dozen. And make sure they good size."

Piney, her head lowered in sullen, resentful obedience, approached the gate while Emma continued to storm. "And then you go to the spring house and brang me some more butter."

The angry black bird disappeared with the slam of the kitchen door. Piney, muttering bitterly to herself, stomped through the gate.

Henny eased around the smokehouse and carefully lifted her dress to protect it from being snagged by weeds and dampened by the morning dew. Cautiously, as if she feared Emma could hear her footsteps on the grass, she crept toward the gate and reached out to open it.

Caution stilled her hand, but summoning her courage, Henny pushed the gate. It screamed at her touch, the hinges crying out as if to alert Emma of her presence. She snatched back her hand and tried again, pushing the gate slowly, only an inch at a time, to mute the cry of the hinges. Once she had made an opening through which her thin figure could pass, she slipped into the yard and carefully, silently, eased the gate back into its closed position.

Keeping close to the fence, Henny hurried along the edge of the yard toward the corner of the house.

The horizon was faintly pink now with the promise of sunrise, but the air, still cool in Virginia in the early mornings of April, cut through the porous lace of her dress. Henny shivered and clasped her arms around herself to create warmth.

At nine years of age, Henny's life of servitude was just beginning. Her work so far—weeding the vegetable garden, assisting in the wash house, and helping Old Sheba care for children too young for the fields—had been easy. But as the years of her childhood receded into the past, Henny knew more strenuous labor awaited her in the future.

With the arrival of spring, planting was almost upon them and the full tobacco season would begin in Virginia. In May, when the threat of frost was past, carefully prepared plots of earth would be burned free of weeds, parasites, and disease that might have survived the freezing tidewater winter. Then tobacco seeds would be planted and the beds covered with canvas to protect them. When the plants were mature and sturdy enough to survive in the fields, they would be set in long rows in countless acres across Virginia, tended, and nurtured until the broad-leafed plant reached waist-high to a man. At summer's end, the plant would be harvested and hung in barns and smokehouses to cure for the market.

Henny knew she would eventually find herself with the other blacks, laboring under the blistering sun, hoeing, weeding, worming, cutting, staking, and hanging the plant in barns. Any day now, Master Lionel or Cyrus Mudley, the overseer, would assign her to the fields.

But a single hope remained to redirect her fate, and today that hope would become a reality or earn her the whipping Old Sheba had predicted. Henny had decided to even risk the agony of the lash to pursue her dream.

Just as she reached the side porch, a hand reached out of the darkness and seized her by the arm. Henny cried out in fright and jerked free of the hand.

"Mornin', haint," a voice said.

Henny found herself before a friendly face, barely discernable in the darkness, grinning with satisfaction and pleased at having frightened her.

"I ought to knock your head off," Henny said, angry at the scare, but relieved it was only fourteen-year-old Reuben, the stable boy. "And I ain't no haint."

"You sure look like a haint to me. I seen you clear down at the cabins with that white dress shinin' in the dark. Look just like a ghost with you dress floatin' in the air all by itself like a haint wearin' it."

"Hush. Ol' Emma hears you."

"Let's go down to Miss Lavinia's flower garden," Reuben said. "They can't see us there."

Fearing discovery in the unprotected openness of the yard, Henny followed Reuben to the flower garden opposite the side porch. Barren since winter, a boxwood hedge framed the area and partly obscured the wooden bench to which Reuben guided her. Henny kept her eyes on the house.

"Set on this bench. They can't see us here," Reuben said.

"Seat wet," Henny said, feeling the dew as she ran her hand along the seat. "I get my dress wet."

"I dries it off for you." Reuben slid down the length of the bench. "There. I done soak it up with my britches. Don't bother me none."

Henny felt the bench, found it sufficiently dry, and sat down, her attention drawn to a lighted window on the second floor.

"Look! They somebody up already," Henny said. She pointed toward one of the tall, dimly lighted windows on the second floor. Shadowy figures moved about the room.

"That Miss Lavinia's room," Reuben said, plopping down beside her. "Now, what you doin' up here?"

"Ain't none of your business."

"I makes it my business. You tells me this minute or I fetch old Emma."

"She just lay you out, too. You ain't 'lowed in the yard neither."

"Oh, yes, I is. I is to come to the front of the house whenever I hear Master Lionel's hounds bark so if it company, I can fetch they horses to the stables."

"They ain't no hounds barkin' this mornin'."

"That 'cause Miss Vinny tells Mr. Mudley to lock 'em up yesterday. Right after her ride, she sends me to fetch Mr. Mudley and tells him the master's hounds is diggin' up her flower bubs."

"Miss Lavinia ain't got no flowers yet. Won't have none till summer time."

"That what she say just the same. Mr. Mudley tell her Master Hawthorn cut a shine the last time she has his hounds put up—he say it kill they keen—but she says he not cut no shine on her and to locks 'em up anyhow."

"If the hounds up, why you up here?"

"Me and Pa been catchin' fishin' worms. Mr. Lionel be back any day now and apt to want to go fishin'. All this rain makes them worms just come right on out of the ground and we got nigh a bucket full."

Unimpressed, Henny snorted and continued to watch the upstairs window where the shadowy figures rushed about in her mistress's room.

"Now what you doin' up here?" Reuben said. "You tell or I calls Emma."

"I come to see Miss Vinny," Henny snapped. "I got to talk to her 'bout somethin' before she go ridin'. She always go to the stable by the side porch."

"You addled? Miss Vinny don't take her ride till full daylight and the sun ain't even rise yet."

"I has to come 'fore daylight so Emma not catch me," Henny said. "Light's gone out!" She jumped from the bench and dashed to the edge of the hedge. The second floor window was dark now and the house barely discernable against the sky.

"What you want Miss Vinny for?" said Reuben.

"Angelica's leavin'. They sendin' her to Richmond next week."

"Everybody know that. She done been down to the quarters tellin' us all 'bout it and sayin' 'bye for over a week now. First she cry then she act happy. How Angelica goin' to Richmond your business?"

Henny said nothing. Her eyes searched the hulking shape of the house for lights.

"You know why they sendin' Angelica to Richmond?" Reuben asked.

"Reckon she havin' a baby."

"How you know?"

"That what Piney tellin' ever body. Reckon she hears it at the big house. And folks in the cabins sure surprised with Angelica bein' sich a good Christian and all."

"It ain't the truth. Angelica ain't married and you know Miss Lavinia don't 'low people ain't married to has babies."

"Don't care one way or the other. I is sick of hearin' about Angelica. That's all folks talk about in the quarters—wantin' to know if Angela got a baby comin', who done it, and why Miss Lavinia sendin' her off to Richmond."

Reuben broke into a grin and his words flowed like molasses. "She in love. She and Big Gabriel from over at the Wroughton place been in love most a year now." The boy shook his head in mystification. "Pappy say they wants to get married but old man Wroughton won't let his people marry off the place."

"I's seen her in church sittin' with a big man that wasn't our people," Henny said.

"Pappy say Miss Vinny and Master Lionel don't care they marry or not and Master Lionel, he try over and over again to get old man Wroughton to sells Gabriel to him, but he won't do it for no price at all. So they can't get married. Pappy say Horace Wroughton not sell him to nobody for nothin'."

"Gabriel that great big fellow?" Henny asked absently, her attention still fixed on the darkened house. Horace Wroughton she had heard of. He owned the neighboring plantation and his brutal treatment of slaves was well known to the black population and often talked about in the quarters. The name Wroughton had become a touchstone of fear among the people, adult and child. A threat of "Horace Wroughton git you" or "I'll have Master Hawthorn sell you to Horace Wroughton" guaranteed fearful obedience to any request.

"You don't know who Gabriel is?" Reuben asked incredulously.

"Don't care who he is."

"Why, Gabriel the best runner in the county. And last year he whip Big Andrew from the Dabney place in the wrestlin' contest. They say he lift up a whole horse one time when it mire-up in the swamp and able to lift a whole cow just by hisself."

"I know who he is. I seen him in church holdin' hands and grinnin' at Angelica."

"That him."

"Aunt Beck and Old Sheba say it shameful the way they acts in church, holdin' hands and lookin' at each other like they goin' to eat each other up and not pay no mind to the sermon. I think it awful, too."

"And they does more than that down at the fence line," Reuben said.

Henny twisted her face in disgust. "I knows it. They kisses and nuzzles, 'cause I seen them do that, too."

"Ever body see 'em." Reuben's grin widened. "That what people in love does. Old Sheba tell my mammy she hear ol' Mr. Wroughton threaten to whip Gabriel for courtin', and won't let him work no field next to ours no more, 'cause all he do is hangs over the fence kissin' and holdin' hands with Angelica, and not get no work done a tall," Reuben said. "Miss Vinny get plum wore-out with how Angelica cry and go on 'bout it and say her and Mr. Lionel done everthang they could do to get Wroughton let'em marry, but he won't for nothin', so she sendin' her to Richmond to forgets him."

"They lights on downstairs now!" Henny said, ducking behind the hedge.

Peering around the boxwood, they saw the lamplight grow stronger as the occupants moved nearer the windows opening onto the porch. The shadows converged and moved toward the door. When the door opened, a group of dark, indistinct forms came out on the porch.

Henny easily recognized the stooped, bird-like shape of Emma, holding a basket, and the squat figure of Aunt Beck. The white hair and shrunken shape of the man holding the lantern could only belong to Uncle Lemiel.

The small woman wearing the bonnet embraced Uncle Lemiel, then moved toward Aunt Beck, who also drew her close and held her. Henny could discern nothing of the group's hurried, anxious whispers, but the exchange seemed highly emotional, and she was certain she heard a choked sob from one of the women.

"Who that?" Reuben asked.

"Aunt Beck and Uncle Lemiel and Emma. Everybody except Piney and she at the hen house."

The lantern light fell on the sweet features of the diminutive Angelica, as she moved to the open arms of Emma.

"And Angelica...in the bonnet...carrying something," Henny whispered as the woman in the bonnet embraced Emma and clung to her.

"And Miss Vinny! She the othern," Reuben said.

The other woman, wearing a white dressing gown and carrying a bundle in her arms, stood beside the blacks, just outside the circle of light provided by Uncle Lemiel's lantern. But even in the diminished light, it was obvious the woman was Lavinia Hawthorn. The dark hair drawn back from her uplifted face, the imposing height as she towered above her servants, the statuesque figure, held straight and erect like a queen before her subjects, made it unmistakably Lavinia Hawthorn.

Henny swallowed hard. Her mistress's formidable image intimidated the little girl, and second thoughts created doubts about approaching her.

"What they doin'?" she mumbled.

In answer, Angelica released Emma, slid the basket on her arm and, burying her head in her hands, turned and rushed down the steps. Henny was certain she heard a sob now, and the distinct sounds of weeping. In confirmation, Emma produced a handkerchief and dabbed her cheeks and Aunt Beck lifted her apron to her face.

Lavinia took the lantern from Uncle Lemiel and raised it before her. As if in the presence of a great personage, the servants parted before her, and, still carrying the bundle under her arm, she descended the steps. The servants closed the gap and stood huddled at the edge of the porch. Their mistress, looking dead ahead, proceeded across the yard with brisk, purposeful strides.

Angelica stopped to wave and throw kisses, then rushed to follow her mistress, who continued on with determined swiftness while the servants waved and wept and watched them depart.

As Lavinia and Angelica retreated, the lantern light grew fainter, and at Emma's gruff command, the servants went back into the house, which was once more engulfed in darkness.

Perplexed by what they had seen, Henny and Reuben exchanged questioning glances.

"Miss Lavinia must be sendin' Angelica off to Richmond now," said Henny.

"Let's go see."

Henny followed Reuben as he dashed to the end of the flower garden and through an opening in the fence. As they followed, they could see the light from the lantern as Lavinia and Angelica approached the stables.

"This way," Reuben whispered, and Henny followed him around the stable and through a small door at the back. "This lead to the loft. We'll watch from the feed way."

"I can't see."

"Get up this ladder. And hurry!"

Henny, with Reuben guiding her hand, felt the rung of a ladder and pulled herself up. When she reached the loft, she heard the crunch of straw under her feet. Reuben grabbed her hand and guided her toward an opening through which hay was passed to the stalls below.

Reuben sat down and peered below, but Henny, reluctant to assume a position that might soil her dress, remained standing. When they heard the creak of the door and saw the flicker of Lavinia's lamp, Reuben grabbed Henny's hand and pulled her down beside him. Afraid she would be heard, she controlled her desire to lash out at his roughness and remained quiet.

Below them, within the blurry edge of the lantern light, they could see Lavinia and Angelica moving about in urgent efficiency.

"And if you are stopped, show your papers immediately." The melodious voice of Lavinia Hawthorn, her southwestern Virginia accent absent of its serene authority and sharpened with uncharacteristic anxiety, reached their ears. "You did bring your papers?"

"Yes, ma'am."

Lavinia handed the bundle she carried to Angelica and went to a stall. In the flickering light, Henny caught glimpses of their faces: grim, tense, and fearful.

"Don't use the lantern until you are past the Morton woods and some distance from the spring behind the Presbyterian Church," Lavinia continued in low, urgent tones. "Romulus and I have ridden this path many times and he knows it well. We checked it yesterday and there are no low limbs, so it will be safe not to use the lantern. Be cautious going past the Clay's cow pasture because their overseer lives not far from the edge..."

As Lavinia hurriedly issued her instructions, she opened the door to a stall and led out a luxuriously groomed horse, his shiny mahogany coat gleaming like satin in the lamplight.

"Good morning, my baby," she cooed to the handsome gelding who emerged. "Is my precious Romulus ready for an early ride today?" She nuzzled the horse with her face and patted him lovingly while Angelica hurriedly unwrapped the bundle Lavinia had given her.

Reuben gave Henny a nudge as Angelica unfolded the package's contents: a man's coat, a shirt, a pair of trousers, and underclothes. Lavinia disappeared inside the tack room and returned with a bit and bridle.

"The blanket," Lavinia said, nodding toward a horse blanket, and Angelica put aside the men's clothes and threw the blanket across Romulus's back, while her mistress quickly fitted the bit in his mouth and the bridle over his head, her expert fingers racing to engage the nose guard and fasten the chin and head straps. Then Lavinia brought a saddle from the tack room and hoisted it onto the handsome animal's back as he pawed restlessly.

Henny's jaw dropped in surprise. Although her mistress was an expert in all matters concerning horses, she was shocked to see her lift a saddle. Such menial duties always were assigned to stable hands.

"I does that," Reuben whispered with surprise.

Henny strained to hear, but could make out nothing of the muffled, urgent words the women exchanged. But their anxiety and tension was obvious.

Suddenly the cry of a bird pierced the air. It was the sharp whistle of a bobwhite, from outside the stable but very near.

Lavinia and Angelica froze at the sound and exchanged relieved glances. At once, their faces lost some of their distress and Henny detected the beginning of a smile on Lavinia's face. Suddenly, the women sprang into action as Lavinia grabbed the lamp and Angelica snatched up the clothing. The bird cry was heard again, and Lavinia opened the stable door and raised the lantern.

Like an apparition, the giant figure of a man slipped through the door into the light.

"Gabriel!" Angelica cried out.

Henny and Reuben looked at each other in open-mouthed amazement, the tiny glow of the reflected lamplight shining like pinpoints in their widened eyes.

Almost six-and-a-half-feet tall, the huge black man started to embrace Angelica but stopped and looked down the length of his muscular physique. His clothes were soaking wet and clung to his body like a second skin, outlining the deep cut of his enormous chest muscles, the bulk of his arms and legs, and the width of his broad shoulders.

"Mornin', Miss Lavinia," he said in a deep, resonant bass voice and nodded his head respectfully toward Lavinia. Then, fixing his eyes adoringly on Angelica, he added shyly in a lower tone, "and Angelica."

"Good morning, Gabriel," Lavinia said, setting down the lantern and disappearing into the tack room. "We must hurry."

"Why you so late?" Angelica asked. "You supposed to be here before the morning bell. I've been at the window listening for you for hours."

"The creek up...with all this rain we havin'. I just about get washed off."

"You sure nobody see you?" Angelica asked.

"I fairly certain. Nobody but my mammy knows I goin'."

"Your mammy! You weren't supposed to tell anybody! Miss Lavinia be in bad trouble if they know she help us."

"Mammy don't know Miss Lavinia helpin' us, darlin'. I never speak Miss Lavinia's name. All Mammy know is we leavin'. I between twenty-five- and thirty-years-old, as best my mammy can recollect, and I couldn't just run off without sayin' goodbye when I might not never see her again long as I live."

"Shh," Lavinia admonished as she came out of the tack room with a saddle blanket.

"I come by the creek, just like you say, Miss Lavinia," Gabriel said. "I heads out the other way across the big pasture, got in the creek, and then backtracks all the way here."

"Splendid. Let's hope that will confuse them. They're sure to use the dogs and maybe they'll think you've run in the opposite direction. Dry with this."

She thrust the blanket toward him and directed him toward an empty stall. "In there. Quickly."

Taking the blanket, and with a quick, loving look at Angelica, Gabriel took the clothes and approached the stall.

"Put your old clothes in this. I'll dispose of them later." Lavinia handed him a gunny sack and he went in the stall and closed the door behind him.

"And Master Wroughton? You sure he—" Angelica hovered close to the closed door.

"Master Wroughton on another bender and not likely be stirrin' for a day or two. Mammy goin' to tell I down sick if they misses me right off."

Throughout the exchange below, Henny's shock rose to ever higher levels of incredulity. "They runnin' off!" she whispered in disbelief.

Lavinia and Angelica finished saddling Romulus, attached the basket and carpetbag to the saddle, and made sure the stirrups were at the correct level for Angelica's short legs. Through a crack in the floor, Henny watched the women lead the horse just outside the stable. She strained to hear what they said, but their voices were too low. Angelica hung her head and her shoulders shook as she wept quietly while Lavinia produced a handkerchief and dabbed her face. Then they embraced and held each other as Angelica rested her head on Lavinia's shoulder.

Finally Gabriel emerged from the stall wearing his new clothes and carrying the gunny sack with his old ones. The women broke apart and returned to the stable as Gabriel stood self-consciously for their inspection. Lavinia lifted the lamp as Angelica adjusted the collar of Gabriel's yellow-and-black checked coat, smoothed out the sleeves, and directed him to turn around before them.

"Very good," Lavinia ruled approvingly, taking the sack of wet clothes and holding the lamp closer to inspect a large V-shaped dart in the back of the coat, taken from a matching vest and expertly sewn in by Angelica with loving care to accommodate the man's wide shoulders.

The matching yellow-and-black checked trousers, let out to the maximum, were slightly shorter than the impeccably dressed Lionel Hawthorn would have worn, but this deficiency in perfect tailoring would have gone unnoticed by anyone accustomed to seeing house servants dressed in their master's made-over clothing. The arms of the jacket and trouser legs were too snug and short, but Gabriel's size would beg forgiveness for this minor imperfection.

"You think people think I a house servant, Miss Lavinia?" Gabriel asked.

"Indeed, they shall. But more than that, they will probably think you are a free man. Now you must be off. It will be sunrise soon."

"Oh, Miss Vinny!" cried Angelica, breaking into new sobs. She fell to her knees and clutching Lavinia, buried her face in the folds of her dressing gown. "How we ever thank you?"

"By living a good, happy life—and getting safely North," said Lavinia, raising Angelica to her feet. "By being free!"

Setting aside the lamp, the women embraced again. "I shall miss you so," Lavinia said. "And pray for you every day. You have been like a daughter to me."

Fighting back tears, they reluctantly broke apart and Lavinia waved them out of the stable.

"Quickly. We have no more time."

Lavinia held the reins as Angelica swung herself on the waiting horse.

"We mighty 'bliged, Miss Lavinia," Gabriel said.

"Take care of my Angelica, Gabriel."

"I do my best, ma'am. We always be thankful to you, ma'am."

Gabriel, surprisingly graceful for so large a man, smoothly hoisted himself onto the horse behind Angelica. Lavinia handed him the lantern and after one long, loving look at her mistress, Angelica nudged the horse into motion.

"Pray for us, Miss Lavinia," Angelica said, choking back tears as she galloped into the darkness.

With the lantern light gone, Henny and Reuben were in total darkness. They heard the stable door squeak closed and, when the sound of the departing horse faded into the distance, they sat for a long time in silence.

"You reckon they make it?" Reuben whispered at last. "All the way to up North?"

"The last one run off the Wroughton place never. The one they call Booker," Henny said, remembering the excitement a male slave's attempted escape had caused a week earlier. "Reckon old Wroughton nearly beat him to death."

"I knows Booker. Dogs sniff him out. He back chained up in one day. Wroughton people down at the fence line says Wroughton beat him mighty bad. Lay his back clean open and he down yet and can't do nothin' and ol' Wroughton say he goin' to sells him off if he ain't no better by plantin' time."

"Piney tellin' he beat so bad he goin' to die."

"Can't go by what Piney says. But the others tellin' my mammy they not think he goin' to heal up good a-tall his cuts so deep."

"Reckon he do that to Gabriel? And Angelica?"

"He can't do nothin' to Angelica. She ain't his. Reckon Big Gabriel get it good though."

For a long time they talked about the escape and the wickedness of Horace Wroughton and finally fell into silence. Henny nodded with fatigue and was about to drift off to sleep when the crow of a rooster prodded her fully awake.

"I got to go back," she said.

"I figure you get some sense. Old Emma scare you out?"

"No. I goin' to the side porch and waits for Miss Lavinia." She struggled to her feet and looked about for the ladder. "I wants to be Miss Vinny's maid."

"Piney been up there learnin' maid ways ever since it out they sendin' Angelica to Richmond. Why you think you can maid?"

"Get me down and I shows you."

Reuben led Henny to the ladder and helped her down from the loft. He located a flint box, lighted a lantern, and sat it near a bench where Henny, having inspected her dress and found no more serious damage than a few easily brushed-off straws, sat down.

"Piney been givin' out she takes over when Angelica gone," Reuben said.

Although Piney's ascendancy was unanticipated, Henny dismissed it. "Piney too sorry to be Miss Lavinia's maid. She can't remember to bring Emma eggs or nothin'. And I say she can't do this."

She jumped to her feet, pulled her dress out on each side of her like a fan unfolding, and dipped.

"I ain't never seen Piney do that. It called a curtsy. I say she ain't never even done it once. My mammy teach it to me. She a house servant to old Miss Hawthorn in Richmond and she teach her and all her house people to curtsy."

Reuben snickered. Jumping up and spinning around, he bent over and clapped his hands and threw back his head with howls of laughter.

Henny watched his performance in mute outrage. How dare he laugh at her when she had so carefully rehearsed her bow and intended to curtsy for Miss Lavinia the minute she was in her presence. Her confidence shaken, she wondered if her mistress would also ridicule her efforts. Reuben's insult continued as he mimicked her bow, bobbing up and down again and again in comic imitation.

"How you think pullin' your dress up and half squattin' going to get you in the big house?"

"You're just mad because I be Miss Lavinia's maid and your sweet thing Piney won't. I know you're sweet on her. She tells it to ever body."

Reuben's amusement vanished. "That a lie. I ain't sweet on nobody, much less that cornstalk, skinny bean pole. She so ugly it make me sick to look at her."

Henny grinned tauntingly. "Ain't what she says. And I know how she slips out eats from the big house for you. She bring you peach cobbler day 'fore yesterday. Aunt Beck bring me some, too, and tell me she seen her snitch it for you. Aunt Beck laughs about it, and I do, too. Ever body laughs about it."

"That don't mean I's sweet on her."

"Aunt Beck thinks you is. And I does too."

"I ain't sweet on nobody and you just get that in your nappy head right now."

Reuben's anger subsided into sullen resentment. "Next time she bring me cobbler, I throw it on the ground. I told her to stop tellin' everybody I her man."

"Man. Man?" Henny laughed. Imitating his performance earlier and delighted to pay him back, she spun around and clapped her hands and chortled with glee. "Man! She ain't claimin' you her man—she claimin' you her boy! You ain't no man."

"I more man than you think I is. And Master Lionel promises me someday I can take over for Uncle Lemiel and drive the carriage. But I ain't fool enough to think I be in the big house. Or ever goin' to be. Like some people I knows."

"You ain't big enough ner old enough to drive the carriage."

"I comin' up on fifteen and last three Sundays in a row Uncle Lemiel lets me drives the carriage to church and that 'bout two miles. And Miss Lavinia say I do mighty fine. Say she can't tell when it Uncle Lemiel or me at the reins. I reckon I be a right good carriage driver."

"And I reckon I be a good maid, too."

"You don't know nothing 'bout bein' a maid. You go up there squattin' with your curtsy and pullin' your dress up in

Miss Lavinia's face and actin' like you addled and she have you whipped good. You ain't goin' to be house people no more than one of these horses is."

"I is, too!" Henny said. "Next time you see me, I be all dressed up in maid clothes and doing my curtsy and come to tell you Miss Hawthorn want her horse saddled and brought 'round. You wait and see."

"You don't know nothin'. Bet you ends up in the fields in one week!"

With anger and hurt and new doubt welling up in her, Henny opened the stable door and ran out into the darkness with Reuben's voice ringing after her.

"Master Lionel comin' home dreckly and Mr. Mudley say he plowin' next week rain or shine. The plows and harnesses all ready and..."

Henny fled the sound of his voice. She didn't want to hear about plowing and planting or anything else to do with the fields. Her heart aching with despair, she ran back to the flower garden and dejectedly sat down on the bench.

She hated Reuben and wished she had given him a slap in the face. He was mean to send her hopes plummeting, but even in her anger, she knew that what she hated most was the truth he spoke, even as his words destroyed her dream like a rotten pumpkin being splattered against the ground. It was just as Reuben said, and Old Sheba's fortune warned—her destiny lay in the fields. And now she had learned the hateful Piney was likely to get the position she coveted.

The thought of the fields filled her with dread and she wished she could cry. But her misery was too great for tears. The hateful memory of when she was six-years-old and had been sentenced to a week's labor in the fields came back to her: the day in the wash house when Mrs. Mudley, the despised wife of the overseer, had slapped her for being too slow in bringing rinse water from the spring.

"I goin' fast as I can," Henny had responded in a tone Mrs. Mudley had felt was impudent. She had ordered the six-year-old child to the cornfield.

Henny could almost feel again the pain of her blistered hands after only one day of trying to maneuver the large, oversized hoe and after two more days, the agony of raw, bleeding fingers and peeling skin. She could see the toothless grin of Mrs. Mudley as she had inspected her injuries with satisfaction and, unmoved by her suffering, had demanded the full week be completed.

"You can wrop 'em with rags," Mrs. Mudley had said, savoring her power. "Hit'll larn you not to get uppity with me."

The memory of her humiliation and pain deepened Henny's sorrow and the tears finally came as she remembered how Old Sheba and Aunt Beck had soaked her injured hands in cold water and applied sheep tallow to her raw, bleeding fingers.

Remembering blistered hands and the long days of backbreaking work under the hot Virginia sun had for so long fueled Henny's ambition that seeing its futility tore at her heart and she hung her head and her narrow shoulders shook with sobs for her lost dream.

Reuben's taunting words, "Bet you ends up in the fields in a week!" echoed over and over in her head. And the high, screeching voice of Piney, smirking in triumph, joined in the litany.

But then she remembered something else. Another voice. She remembered the encouraging tones of her mistress, Miss Lavinia, only moments earlier, urging Angelica and Gabriel to have a good and happy life. And to be free!

To be free! The thought lifted Henny's spirits and she felt new hope as the consolation of possible freedom flowered in her consciousness with startling clarity. She had never considered freedom before, but now she did—and her mind reeled with the realization of what true liberation could mean.

Freedom! If she could not be Miss Lavinia's new maid she would seek freedom! She would run away! She would do what Angelica and Gabriel had done and escape the fields to a good and happy life of freedom in the North.

With her self-confidence restored, Henny quickly re-embraced her mission and boldly crept to the side porch as the first rays of the morning sun began to dispel the darkness and burn away the April mist.

On the porch, Henny noiselessly positioned a chair with a clear view of the door and eased herself into it, tucking her legs under her neatly arranged dress. Still shivering from the cold, she wished she had brought her mammy's faded, woolen shawl, or her own well-worn, woolen cloak. But she had rejected both as too shabby. She had decided that Miss Lavinia would not be able to see the cold she felt, but she would find a tattered shawl or cloak all too visible.

She practiced in her mind just what she would say to Mrs. Hawthorn. In spite of Reuben's ridicule, she decided she would curtsy just the same, impressing her mistress with her knowledge of the ways of house servants.

As she waited, she felt the fatigue of her early rising and the stress of constant, fearful vigilance. She yawned and settled more comfortably into her chair, relaxing her guard now that she felt safe from discovery by Emma. Her broad forehead lost the furrow of concern and as her anxiety faded, her face became sweetly composed and childlike.

At nine, Henny's features were as yet unfixed, a canvas of innocence on which nature had yet to paint its final picture. The lightness of her skin revealed white ancestry as well as black, and her face was a harmonious blend of both, with slightly pouting full lips and a firm jaw and high cheek bones. Her black, crinkly hair was neatly woven into a dozen short plaits, tied with tiny bows made from scraps of maroon velvet from one of Mrs. Hawthorn's cast-off dresses.

But Henny's most arresting feature was her large eyes, luminous and startlingly blue. Their jewel-like quality, indigo and of surprising intensity, almost always drew incredulous stares and caused eyebrows to raise in surprise. Henny was both proud and ashamed, puzzled and embarrassed when comments, kind and unkind, were made about this rare feature. She knew few black people had blue eyes and was uncertain if this was a blessing, a curse, or neither. She had often studied her features in the shard of mirror on the wall in her cabin, but the mystery, as deep and unfathomable as the blueness of her eyes themselves, remained unsolved.

But now, as the warmth of day came with the rising sun, heavy lids fluttered over the tired blueness of Henny's most striking feature. The strain of the morning began to slip away as she eased into the temptation to rest and at last surrendered to it.

She rested her head on her clasped hands and against her best intentions to remain awake, fell into a deep, peaceful sleep.

An hour later, she was still held fast in the serene slumber of a child when Lavinia Hawthorn, mistress of Hawthorn Hill Plantation, discovered her sleeping there.

Chapter Two

Lavinia Hawthorn twisted a tear-soaked handkerchief and paced the floor of her darkened bedroom. Haunted by doubt, the thirty-eight-year-old mistress of Hawthorn Hill Plantation battled the second thoughts that Angelica and Gabriel's escape had any chance of success.

She closed her troubled gray eyes and reviewed the plan, which the day before seemed as perfect as a fastidiously executed piece of embroidery, but now seemed ready to unravel with a dozen unanticipated pitfalls.

Trying to shake off the fear that she had sent her servant into the hands of slave patrols, she went to the fireplace and stirred the banked ashes, exposing the red-orange coals underneath. Trying to shut out the thoughts of Angelica's being captured, she put the gunny sack containing Gabriel's abandoned clothing on top of the coals. Impeded by the wetness from the creek, the bundle smoldered and stubbornly refused to burn. With added kindling and lamp oil, the clothing at last flared into final, blazing oblivion.

Moving from the warmth of the fire to the window, she looked out into the distance. The sun hovered just above the horizon and as the morning mist faded, the outlines of the tombstones gradually became distinct in the distant family graveyard.

Lavinia often stood at this window waiting for the sun to light the final resting places of her two dead sons and daughter. She felt nothing morbid in this daily vigil. It had become for her almost as if, had these children survived their childhood illnesses, she was saying good morning to them, or welcoming them, as she once had, when they bounded into her room upon awaking, to leap into her bed and burrow under the covers and snuggle close against the morning chill for stories, or reports of dreams, or plans for the childhood adventures of the day. Lavinia had borne five children—four sons and a daughter. Her daughter had died two years before of typhoid; her twin sons had not survived their fourth year. The two surviving sons were grown now; Randolph, twenty-one and a year married, was learning to manage another plantation owned by the family near Richmond. Eighteen-year-old Frederick had left a month before to read law prior to his studies in the fall at the College of William and Mary.

Now that her sons were away, Lavinia awoke each morning to a house of silence, absent of the sounds of children, or the shouts and banter of her early rising sons on their way to breakfast, noisily bounding down the stairs in heavily booted gallop, exchanging good natured insults as they raced for the hunt, to inspect the fields with their father, or off on their horses for some secret courtship or adventure to which she was not privy.

This morning the silence was even greater without the hum of Angelica's pleasant prattle as she laid out her mistress's wardrobe for the day and chattered on about her courtship with Gabriel, the activities of the plantation, or some item of county gossip heard in the quarters by way of the ubiquitous black grapevine, which linked the slave population and their masters in mysterious and inexplicable communication.

Angelica had been Lavinia's maid for ten years, since she came to her at the age of sixteen. Like many women and their servants, Lavinia and Angelica had become bound in a closeness difficult to define. The differences in racial and social levels was far too separate for familial bonds or friendship. They had not been friends, nor could their alliance be likened to kinship, yet trust, respect, and affection bound them closely even as it remained nebulous and undefined. The openness between them had led Angelica to reveal her romance with Gabriel and her desire to escape with him once their hope to be married was thwarted by Gabriel's owner, Horace Wroughton.

Lavinia tried to take comfort in the knowledge that every detail of the escape had been planned, foot by foot and minute by minute, from Hawthorn Hill to Richmond, where professionals in the Underground Railroad waited to guide the runaways to freedom outside Virginia. Still staring out the window, the tension tore at her, even as she prayed for Angelica's safe delivery and a release from her own anxiety and fear.

It was then that she noticed the figure of a thin, ghostlike little black girl, wearing a white dress, approach the house with great stealth and disappear under the shelter of the side porch roof directly below the window.

Lavinia recognized the little girl as one of her own people.

"Most likely one of Nancy and Clevis's," she said, thinking the child likely belonged to the plantation's most fruitful couple who had produced a dozen children. It was the little light-skinned black girl who always appeared in church wearing the same white dress and seemed so unlike most children in the quarters. The others, upon seeing their mistress approach on her daily horseback ride, always fled into the cabins or behind trees and fences and peeked at her from their hiding places, timid yet curious. Only this little girl, now covertly invading her yard and porch, had always stood her ground and made no move to hide herself, watching with fascination as her mistress rode by.

Lavinia hoped it was not fear but shyness that drove the children into hiding, or perhaps a wariness of the hooves of Mercury, her prized stallion, who thundered through the quarters as proud as if he led an invading army. But this child showed no fright, and Lavinia wondered what sparked the dauntlessness of her countenance as she stood unmoving, lost in the cloud of dust created by Mercury's hooves.

"She just an uppity piece of business, Miz Livy," Emma, an authority on every man, woman, and child on the plantation, had told Lavinia when questioned about the girl. "Got a sassy streak. In church, she show-off tryin' to sang louder than the other children. She just a blackbird tryin' to be a peacock."

"Another runaway," Lavinia said, prodding herself into action. "No doubt fleeing a switching for some mischief in the quarters."

The morning bell had sounded hours ago and she could delay facing the day no longer. Moving toward a wardrobe to select her clothing, she was almost moved to tears when she saw that Angelica, faithful to her to the end, had taken the time, even with the rush and pressure of the escape, to lay out her clothes. Her stockings and undergarments, the black velvet riding habit, bonnet and gloves, and her riding crop were neatly arranged on the chaise lounge. Even her boots had been dutifully polished and slouched in gleaming readiness. And fresh water and towels were ready at the washstand.

Touched by Angelica's final thoughtfulness, Lavinia felt the emptiness of her new solitude as she washed and dressed, for the first time in many years, alone and without her maid's assistance. Once dressed and her hair arranged—again she felt the painful absence of Angelica, who always put up her hair—Lavinia surveyed herself in her full-length dressing mirror.

Her superbly tailored riding habit emphasized the narrowness of her waist and the contours of her hips, and Lavinia was relieved to see she did not yet need the shaping created by a corset. No, she decided with satisfaction, as she rotated her body before her reflection and ran her long slender fingers down her waist and hips, she did not need stays or whale bone, and wouldn't for years.

At thirty-eight, regarded as middle-age and often the beginning of the last third of a woman's life in 1853, Lavinia's figure was still shapely, even after the birth of five children. Her jaw was still taut, her throat smooth and unlined, and her breasts were firm, full, and upright, having been spared the pull and tug of nursing babies, that duty having been assigned to carefully selected wet nurses. Her hair showed no sign of gray and remained the same dark brown of her youth; the only concession to her age was that she wore it up now. No longer hanging freely down her back or touching her shoulders, its lustrous thickness was arranged in a roll, and sometimes a plait, which encircled her head on either side of a central part.

Her skin was unlined, without freckles or splotches from the sun, and she had no need for the use of cosmetics, tools to which a few of her contemporaries had surrendered, although in secret and with firm denials. The healthy glow and pink of her cheeks was completely her own, unaided by carefully hidden pots of rouge and boxes of powder.

Taking a deep breath, Lavinia straightened her shoulders to go down and face her household. Then she thought of the little black girl she had seen earlier. Perhaps she could intervene on the child's behalf and prevent her from being switched, provided her misbehavior had not been too serious. At least she could stay the harsh penalties of Emma, who showed no mercy to children trespassing the yard and meted punishment far too severe for the crime.

Downstairs, she entered the library and crossed to the side porch door. With none of the servants about, she could resolve the little black girl's fate without Emma's interference. Looking out the panel of glass panes that lined each side of the door, Lavinia could see the little trespasser curled up asleep in a chair. She wondered what crime one with so innocent a face could have committed.

As she watched the sleeping child, her eyes fell to the lace dress she was wearing. As she examined the dress, she caught her breath and her eyes widened, transfixed. Then, as she further scrutinized the child's face, the thin arms, and knobby kneed legs twisted awkwardly in the chair as she slept, a strange pageant of variant emotions played across Lavinia's face.

Recognizing the lace dress as her dead daughter's, Lavinia felt a bittersweet sense of happiness at seeing the old garment, even as it renewed the memory of her loss and grief. Although dead for two years, her daughter was never far from her thoughts and her sorrow still returned with harsh and merciless swiftness at the slightest prodding.

She released her breath and, as her eyes moved from the child's broad forehead to her slightly parted, full lips, the little girl stirred. Then, as if jolted awake, she bolted upright in her chair and looked anxiously around her.

Rubbing her eyes with her fists and blinking away the last vestiges of sleepiness, she looked frantically about her, her eyes wide with apprehension.

The sight of the child's eyes brought an astonished gasp from Lavinia. There could be no doubt now: the broad forehead, the angle of the jaw, the blue of those eyes—especially the blue of those eyes. Lavinia was certain. She felt both a tingle of joy and a pang of distress at her discovery.

"She's one of his," she said in an amazed half-whisper. "She's one of Lionel's."

With startling clarity, harsh and undeniable, Lavinia Hawthorn realized she was seeing one of her husband's black children and discovering another of his innumerable infidelities.

Chapter Three

⊶═◉═⊷

Henny, as if yanked by a cord, sat bolt upright in the porch chair. Relieved her nap had not been interrupted by the rough clasp of Emma's hand, or the bark of her scolding voice, the little girl hugged herself for warmth and wondered how long she had been asleep.

The door opened and Lavinia emerged from the house. "Good morning," she said.

The leap of Henny's heart propelled her to her feet. Her mistress towered over her and, in spite of the gentle smile and soothing voice, intimidated the little girl into frozen silence. Then, as if prodded by an invisible hand, she executed her carefully rehearsed curtsy.

"Mornin', Miss Lavinia," she said, and she watched closely for her mistress's reaction. She was proud of her curtsy, performed with not the slightest wobble or unsteadiness.

Lavinia acknowledged the bow with a smile and nod of her head. "And what is your name?"

Henny drew herself to her full height. "I am Henrietta Valentine Hawthorn," she said. "But ever body call me Henny."

"Either way, you have a very pretty name," Lavinia said, and bending closer added, almost in a whisper, "Are you running away?"

"Oh, no, Miss Hawthorn," Henny said with a vigorous shake of her head. "I ain't runnin' off. I come to see you. I hears you sendin' that sinful Angelica to Richmond because she makin' baby for that trashy big fellow from the Wroughton place and I wants to be your new maid when she go. My mammy was a house girl some of the time and she teach me to curtsy..." Again Henny demonstrated her skill. "And how to say *ma'am* and *please* and *thank you*, and work hard and...I...I thought since you needin' a maid and since Angelica went and got in love with Gabriel who Old Emma say ain't nothin' but a piece of field-hand trash and done got a baby started and cause us Hawthorns so much shame and you so much trouble wantin' to get married and I be a good maid and won't never has no trashy babies and in love and want to marry no trash ner nobody and have to be sent off for sin and shame..."

Henny stopped her babbling. Her carefully rehearsed words had deserted her, replaced by a shrill, almost unintelligible, garble of words. She wanted to bite off her tongue and her face drooped in painful, frustrated humiliation. Ready to burst into tears for having ruined her opportunity, she waited for her mistress to dismiss her—or even demand she be whipped.

But Lavinia seemed not to have heard her rambling and was looking wistfully at her dress.

"You look so sweet in that dress," she said in a quiet voice. "You remind me of someone else..." Her thoughts seemed to be far away. Then she looked back at Henny, who hung her head and hugged her shoulders against the cold.

"There's a chill," her mistress said. "Come inside."

Confused, but grateful she had not been dismissed, Henny followed her mistress into the house.

"Wait here and I'll get you a wrap," Lavinia said, and she left the room.

Henny looked about her. She could not remember having been in the big house before except at Christmas, and then only in the front hall when all the people attended a brief religious service on Christmas Eve and gifts were distributed.

During that formal, once-a-year visit, Master Lionel and Miss Lavinia distributed newly cobbled shoes, blankets, and a new outfit of clothing to the men, and new dresses, slippers, quilts, colorful scarves, and trinkets to the women and children. Henny had last year received a home-made rag doll, a new dress, and a pair of sandals.

Servants with long years of servitude were sometimes given more elaborate presents: brass bracelets, small mirrors, and inexpensive jewelry. Emma and Aunt Beck and Old Sheba had once even been the recipients of gold earrings— signs of their rank and stature among the people. And Uncle Lemiel received a tall, black silk hat, which he wore on special occasions when he drove the carriage. In celebration of his fiftieth Christmas in service to the Hawthorn family, he had been rewarded with the highest token of esteem a master could bestow on a black man: a pocket watch on a chain.

But now Henny was in one of the formal rooms, not just the cavernous front hall. And she was in a room with smooth, plastered walls and ceiling, no rough, splintery boards anywhere. And even the boards she did see—the floors—were smooth and shiny as glass and covered in thick carpets that were larger than any quilt she had ever seen.

Other than in church, Henny had never seen rooms with ceilings so high, or furnishings as elaborate and unlike the crude table, chair, and bed of rough, unfinished pine in her own cabin. Some of the library tables and chairs even had legs that looked like animal's feet, an astonishing discovery to Henny, and a little frightening, suggesting the furniture had once been alive and might even be capable of movement now.

The child's eyes darted from object to object, each more awesome than the other: the ornately carved fireplace and mantle, above which hung what must have been the largest mirror in the world, the large curving settee, and more impressive than anything else, against one wall, between tall windows hung with heavy, brocade draperies, a whole cabinet of nothing but Bibles!

Henny had seen only one book in her life, the Bible, which Reverend Pooley read at church, and she assumed all books were Bibles. And here was a whole wall of them, in different sizes and colors and thicknesses. Henny knew her mistress was religious; Lavinia required all the people to attend church, and everyone had to be baptized. But her mistress's piety had never been so impressively demonstrated until she saw her numerous Bibles.

Henny had been baptized numerous times, although she had been told once was sufficient. Nevertheless, she enjoyed the attention the ritual brought and thought the experience a pious expression of her religion. When new candidates lined up on the creek bank for the rite, she often slipped into their number to receive the sacrament again and again— at least a dozen times so far.

"It one of the good things," Henny had said of the experience.

Lavinia returned with a blue knitted shawl and draped it around Henny's shoulders. "Sit here by the fire and warm yourself," she said as she placed kindling in the grate and with a poker stirred the embers into new life.

Henny thought the fine chairs in the library were likely only for white people, and choosing not to display disrespectful behavior, sank to the floor in front of the warming flames.

This the man's room, Henny thought, as she recalled how she and the other children in the quarters would sneak up to the big house and peek over the fence when their masters had a party and more people than she had fingers and toes gathered for elaborate suppers, dancing, card playing, and endless talk and laughter.

On these occasions, the lane and front yard of Hawthorn Hill would be choked with the guests' carriages, buggies, and horses. With Emma and the other servants too occupied attending the guests to monitor the yard, the children would slip up to the big house to share in the excitement. The little trespassers had made a game of following the guests as they proceeded from room to room in the house: the parlor when they first arrived, then the dining room, and finally, after supper, when the sexes separated, the men to the library for brandy and tobacco, the ladies to the parlor. Thus, the designation of the library as "the man's room"; the parlor, "the lady's room."

With Emma too busy to be a threat, Henny and the more adventurous children cautiously slipped right up to the windows for a closer look at the guests' progress from room to room.

"There Miss Vinny!" someone would say, spying their mistress charming the guest of honor, sometimes an important person such as a senator or once even a governor who happened to visit the county.

"And there Emma passin' 'round a big tray of glasses."

"Miss Vinny going to play the pi-anna! And Benjamin playin' the fiddle and Ance the banjo!"

"Master Lionel dancin' with one of them old Barksdale sisters!"

"Mr. Lewis done got tipsy agin and old Miss Lewis layin' him out!"

The children found each detail exciting, and it was an especially proud moment when Uncle Lemiel, at a signal from Lavinia, stood as straight and tall as his short stature allowed and announced imperiously, "Dinner is served." The children were awed that Uncle Lemiel exercised such power, that saying only these three words prompted the whites to leave their chairs and conversations and move as a unit toward the dining room. Masters doing what a slave told them!

It was also the signal for the children to run around the house to the dining room windows for another secret look at the stylish, mysterious whites, dressed in fine, rich clothing, as they sat down at the long mahogany table, extended to its maximum length by the addition of all its leaves, and enthusiastically devoured Aunt Beck's elaborate feasts.

Such events were the culmination of the entire plantation's effort for as much as a week, with even the field hands pressed into additional service as stable hands, kitchen workers, and maids. Major celebrations almost always brought overnight guests and the need for extra help to care for the children and assist with the extra cooking. The hum of the guests' conversation and laughter, blending with the music of fiddles and song, created a kind of muted, distant happiness, lighted by a hundred candles, flickering and elusive.

But as Henny watched these festivities, she had been made aware that the finery the guests wore and the elegance of the rooms in which they celebrated had been bought with the labor of her people by drudgery in the fields and through the suffering of slavery. She had learned this from Old Sheba and heard other blacks lament their exploitation as well. And the few adults from the quarters who also crept up to the house to observe their masters and guests watched with a grim lack of appreciation and found no joy in the celebrations they witnessed. Their faces were somber and bitter, their bondage felt more painfully than that of Henny and the children, who had yet to sense the full reality of servitude and captivity.

But Henny had not been without some awareness. The stoic hardness of her own people observing the whites had made the little girl aware of her own low estate—wearing shabby clothing, eating from a tin plate, living in a one-room cabin with dirt floors—while her masters wore linen, silk, and velvet and lived in fine houses where they were waited on at every turn by her people. She stood outside the luxury and splendor of the big house, separated by more than walls, and finally understood what she had heard from the older blacks.

After a time, the awe and pleasure of the luxury she witnessed in the sweetness of the honeysuckle-, rose-, and magnolia-scented air of hot summer nights was mixed with a sickly resentment of the whites' almost gloating extravagance. Soon the white spectacles made her ill, in much the same way that years before an over-indulgence in ripe papaws and honey had also made her sick.

And how these genteel, white rituals paled beside the more robust and lively black celebrations, when her people also danced, sang, and prepared feasts. Not with wispy candlelight in elaborate rooms, but to the light of towering bonfires and torches of pine knots in the great outdoors with the dome of a starry sky as a ceiling. And, with boisterous, unrestrained dancing and singing of tunes with real exuberance like "Blackberry Betty," and "Speckled Fox Run," and "Swing the Goose and Gander," so unlike the demure marching and skipping of the white folks' refined reels and waltzes.

Such differences early on alerted Henny to the chasm between her people and her masters. She was glad she was black and didn't have to curtsy to her own people or repress the Holy Ghost in church the way white people, who never shouted, did, or act grand, and put on airs, and always wear shoes, and deport themselves in an artificial manner that was restrictive to her free-spirited nature.

But now the rooms that had so often reverberated with music and laughter, and at the same time ignited both her awe and resentment, were silent and empty, with only Henny and Lavinia. There was only the sound of the crackling fire as mistress and slave appraised each other, Henny curious about the totally unfamiliar environment of the house and the woman whose domain it was, and Lavinia about the child whom she was certain had been fathered by her husband with a black slave.

Something of a bond was born in that intimate moment of unguarded, honest appraisal of one another. Lavinia smiled at Henny and the little girl's hopes were resurrected. Maybe her awkward petition hadn't offended Lavinia after all, and she could make her request again, this time with the carefully rehearsed words she had so painstakingly composed.

A rumble from Henny's stomach betrayed her hunger.

"Have you eaten today?" her mistress asked.

Before she could answer, the strident voice of Emma was heard. "Benjamin up here from the stables sayin' a horse missin', Miss Lavinia."

Henny looked frantically at Lavinia, who sprang to her feet. "Just tell him Angelica is riding him, Emma."

"That what I say, but he act like he mighty disbelievin'."

The old woman's eyes fell on Henny, cowering fearfully on the floor. "What you doin' up here? You get yourself back down that hill right this minute or I'll switch you 'till you can't stand up." Glaring at Henny, she drew back her cane as if to strike her.

"Henrietta is my guest, Emma," Lavinia said.

Emma shot her mistress a look of disbelief and lowered her cane. "Now, Miss Vinny, Master Lionel done give out strict orders that nobody from the quarters is to come nowhere near the house and yard and..." She rotated her head from side to side, her lantern jaw drawing circles in the air.

"I shall deal with Mr. Lionel, Emma," Lavinia said evenly.

Henny was about to burst with triumph. She wanted to shout and jump up and down the way she had seen old people do at church when under the Spirit. She knew Emma's being rebuffed meant trouble for her later, but for the moment, she felt safe from the wizened old woman, even as her heavy jaw seemed to project further from her face with the promise of later retribution.

"Henny will be joining me for breakfast, Emma," Lavinia said.

Emma stared in open-mouthed shock at the invitation. She narrowed her tiny eyes in an ominous glare at Henny before leaving the room.

"And where did you get your pretty dress?" Lavinia asked when Emma had gone.

"Aunt Beck give it to me. Emma sent down lots of things from the big house way back yonder and it was in with it and

I got it." She decided it would be wiser not to reveal that she had come to blows with Piney for the dress.

"It was once my little girl's dress, my Oralee's, before she died." Lavinia reached out and lovingly fingered one of Henny's sleeves. "It was one of her favorites. That and the blue silk. I almost put her away in it, but I chose the blue silk instead..." Her voice faded and a look of sadness came to her gray eyes.

"I sorry, Miz Hawthorn," Henny said, and she hoped her mistress would not cry. Instinctively, she reached out and touched Lavinia's hand, which still caressed the lace sleeve. Then, thinking such a gesture inappropriate, she quickly withdrew it. She had never touched a white person before.

Lavinia smiled as if moved by the little girl's expression of sympathy and took her hand. "Do you remember when the great sickness came to the plantation a few years ago?" Lavinia asked. "The typhoid epidemic?"

"Yes'um."

"That was when Oralee died."

Lavinia released Henny's hand and rose from her chair. She walked toward the window that faced the cemetery and looked out. For a time she was silent.

"I come down with it, too," Henny said. "And my mammy. She die with it."

Lavinia, shaken from her reverie, turned away from the window.

"I had no idea we had orphan children in the quarters," she said. "And your mother's death left you all alone? You have no other relatives?"

"No, ma'am. I just got me."

"Emma should have told me. I was ill too at the time, and I suppose I was so preoccupied with Oralee's illness and...death that...I suppose I thought too much of my own suffering and not enough of others."

"You done good, Miss Lavinia. Back then Aunt Beck say the typhoid might not kills all the people, but grief and mournin' for your little girl goin' to kill you and Master Lionel sure as certain. She say she never see nobody in her life grieve as bad as you and Master Lionel for that little dead youngin' of yorn. She say you go lose your mind for certain over that child if it don't stop soon and I reckon you done good and never did."

Lavinia smiled at Henny's candor.

"My mammy and Tina and Earl die, and them babies of Olaf and Ginger's, but nobody else does," Henny added, hoping that being reminded of survivors would be comforting to her mistress.

"Yes'um, Miss Vinny, I reckon the rest of us does real good and not die and just goes right on. I sure is glad you never die. And myself, too. And I sure glad I ain't got it now," she hurriedly added, lest being ill diminish her chances of becoming Lavinia's maid.

Lavinia continued to examine Henny's features. "You look so much like my Oralee. She had beautiful blue eyes, too—just like yours. How old are you?"

"'Bout nine, I reckon," Henny said.

"The dogwood is beginning to bloom," her mistress said looking out the window beyond which the white and pink blossomed trees could be seen. "Would you like to gather some and take it to Oralee's grave with me? I'm sure she'd like to see that dress again. She wore it to her last birthday party...she was twelve and we were in Richmond..." The warmth of happy remembrance colored Lavinia's face. "We had a party in Mother Hawthorn's back garden, with children and games and a pony..."

At once Henny was seized with a new concern. Visiting a cemetery! And in broad daylight where the dead could see the clothing she was wearing! To Henny, daylight offered no protection or comfort and a visit by day was as terrifying as one at midnight. All the superstition and legends she had heard from her people about ghosts and haunts and cemeteries came back to threaten her now.

Torn between her fear and her desire to please Lavinia, Henny burst into tears.

"What is it, my dear?" Lavinia asked.

Unwilling to reveal either her terror of visiting the graves or in refusing, the appearance of disobedience, Henny said, "I's—I's just sorry 'bout your little girl."

Lavinia, visibly moved, was at once on her knees in front of Henny and took her into her arms.

"How very, very sweet—and kind," she said and held the little girl close to her. "Oralee was very tender-hearted, too."

The soft velvet of Lavinia's dress felt soothing to Henny's cheek and she could smell the faint aroma of roses from her mistress's sachet.

"It has been so long since I've dried a little girl's tears," Lavinia said as she dabbed Henny's cheeks with her handkerchief. Then she rose and went to a tall mahogany secretary. Henny watched as her mistress opened the desk and from one of the several small drawers inside removed a small, velvet-covered box.

"This belonged to Oralee," she said, opening the box and removing a flat, heart-shaped pendant attached to a chain. She held it out for Henny to examine.

Henny was almost reluctant to touch the object. She had never seen a chain with such tiny links, and the golden heart, the size of a robin's egg, gleamed as it rotated in the light.

"I'd like you to have it," Lavinia said, opening the chain's clasp and placing the pendant around Henny's neck. "It was very precious to Oralee, so you must be very careful not to lose it. I wouldn't wear it every day, and be sure to keep it in a safe place."

Henny was so awed she was speechless and could only look back and forth between her mistress's smiling face and the gleaming treasure around her neck. "It was a gift to Oralee on her tenth birthday. It can be the same for you."

Henny's hunger prodded her stomach to roar into action once more. She wanted to die of embarrassment but was grateful that her mistress seemed not to notice and took her by the hand.

"Come. Let's see what we can find for breakfast."

Emma awaited them at the library door when they emerged.

"We be ready to serve soon as the biscuits bake, Miss Vinny," she said. She then turned her attention toward Henny. "And I'll wear you out if you gets so much as one drap of gravy on that table."

"You may remove the linen if you wish," Lavinia suggested.

"I done done it. Ain't no sense ruinin' a fresh-washed cloth for field people. But I ain't having that table top ruint neither."

"Do you remember this dress, Emma?" Lavinia said.

The old woman squinted her eyes and bent closer for a better look. Instantly her scowl changed into an expression of joy.

"Why, that's little Oralee's dress!" she cried, and she clasped her hands together, her anger replaced by the softness of happy recollection. Henny could never remember having seen Emma smile before, or any sign of tenderness in the old crone. "Oh, how that sweet child love that dress."

For a moment, Henny thought the old woman was going to cry, but her anger returned as fast as it had gone. "And how come you got it?"

"You send it to us. With a whole lot of other things."

Flustered by her collaboration in Henny's possession of the dress, Emma was speechless for a second, then quickly sputtered, "I was agin it, Miz Vinny. I done told Mr. Lionel them little dresses and things of little Oralee's was sacred. Me and Beck both. I said to leave 'em be, but he said you in such a shape mournin', he takin' you to Richmond and for me to gets 'em outta the house while you gone. I never want to, but he say I has to, and we 'bout had a row over it. I was agin it, Miz Vinny."

"I understand, Emma," Lavinia said, leading the way into the dining room.

Henny was so entranced by the splendors of the dining room she was unaware of Emma's hostility as she limped to the sideboard, opened a drawer, and produced a square of oilcloth and several linen napkins.

"And have you noticed Henrietta's pretty blue eyes, Emma?" Lavinia said in a voice almost musical in its smoothness and without a trace of malice. "I've never seen eyes as beautiful as Henny's before—or have I?" She smiled sweetly and waited for Emma's reaction.

The old woman's face seemed to darken a shade deeper than the ebony of her natural color. Her long, protruding jaw became even more fixed and her eyes narrowed within the folds of wrinkles around them as she searched Lavinia's face suspiciously.

"You may sit here, Henrietta," Lavinia said as she sat down at the head of the table and motioned for Henny to sit on her right.

"And I don't want none of the dishes broke, neither," Emma said. "These field people ain't used to things, Miss Lavinia. They breaks everything. You want me to get the tin plates or the pewter?" She spread the oilcloth in front of the unwelcome guest and unfolded the napkins on top as added protection.

"I'm sure the china will be safe, Emma," Lavinia said.

Henny found the dining room even more splendid than the library. She was so entranced by the many strange vessels of silver and porcelain that she was only half aware of Emma roughly tying a large napkin around her neck.

"And I don't want a mess on that precious baby's dress. You ain't fit to wear it no ways and—"

"Henrietta is my guest, Emma," Lavinia said firmly. But Henny was too distracted by the wonders she saw to notice Emma's harsh words. In the corner cupboard and behind the glass and mullioned doors of the giant china cupboard, even more treasures were displayed, and on an elaborately carved serving table the silver gleamed and reflected the other objects in the room in warped, distorted images.

Henny twisted in her seat and craned her thin neck to follow the stenciled images of flowers and vines wrapping themselves around the room at the ceiling's edge, and in the center of the room, hanging over the vast expanse of the gleaming, highly polished surface of the table, her eyes found the large brass chandelier with tiers of gracefully curving arms holding more candles than she had ever seen at one time in her life.

She was actually in the same room, and seated at the same table, that she had stood on tiptoe to spy on. Here she had seen Miss Lavinia preside serenely at one end of the table and Master Lionel stand at the other, holding aloft sparkling glasses you could see the contents through in tribute to important people like congressmen, senators, and judges. These were the politicians, and according to Old Sheba, they were all white devils because they made the laws that enslaved her people. They were even worse white devils than slave patrols, militia, sheriffs, and deputies who carried out the orders imposed by the politicians.

"Set up here!" Emma ordered, roughly seizing Henny's arm and draping a second napkin around her neck and spreading another in her lap.

When Emma left, Henny finally tore herself from her examination of the dining room and directed her attention toward her mistress, who was watching her with patient amusement.

"You may look at anything you wish, Henrietta."

"That ain't why I come to see you, ma'am," Henny said. Deciding she could no longer put off the purpose for her visit, she slipped out of her chair, made a deep curtsy, and fell to her knees before Lavinia.

"Miss Vinny," she said quietly, this time taking her time and remembering her prepared speech. "Would you let me be your maid now that Angelica's got herself bigged by that Gabriel feller from over at the Wroughton place? I knows it hurts your heart to have to sends her to Richmond to have that sinful baby, but I won't do no nastiness like she done and has no babies. I ain't got no mammy to love no more, and if you lets me be your maid, I waits on you good and won't love nobody else but just you and Jesus."

Henny felt her request this time was much more satisfactory than her earlier effort on the side porch. She was particularly proud of herself for not betraying that she knew Angelica was already gone, and since she had left so early that morning, was probably already in the North, safe, happy, and free at last, never to return to be Miss Lavinia's maid ever again.

"Don't know what Miss Vinny goin' to do next," Emma fumed to Aunt Beck in the kitchen. "It bad enough when she allow house people take up with field hands like she do Angelica and that Wroughton trash. Now she invitin' 'em right in the house to her table! Never happen while Miss Cornelia here. Miss Cornelia she never even know a field hand by the name."

"Shh," hissed Aunt Beck, warning her of Piney's presence at the other end of the kitchen where she kneaded biscuit dough.

"And not in the pantry or kitchen neither," Emma continued, "but right in the dinin' room! Ain't been a field hand set at that table in the history of this family."

Aunt Beck, waddling from egg basket to frying pan and coffee pot to serving tray, was reluctant to disparage her mistress. "Miss Vinny always been good to ever body. She don't see no wrong in it."

"And Master Lionel sometime eat in here with us," Uncle Lemiel said. "And little Henny can't help it. She just a child." The old gentleman, looking no bigger than a child himself, sat inconspicuously beside the fireplace chewing tobacco.

"It different when Master Lionel eats with us," Emma said. "We house people and I his mammy."

"Reckon he rather be in here with us than eating by hisself, anyhow," Aunt Beck said. "Him and Miss Livvy don't never eats together no more since that last row they had. We 'bout has to have company or somebody in the family visitin' to gets them at the same table."

Piney, rolling the dough to be cut into biscuits, suddenly straightened. "What row? I never knowed nothin' about Miss Vinny and Master Lionel havin' a row."

"You just mind you business," Emma stormed. "Master Hawthorn and Miss Vinny can have a row if they wants to."

"Miss Vinny eat with us all the time," Piney said.

"We is house people!" Emma said. "Miss Vinny got to eat with us to find out 'bout the people—who sick, and got a baby coming, and who need baptizin' and not workin', and crossin' the blanket—"

"What crossin' the blanket?" Piney asked.

Emma angrily slammed her cane on the table. She had brought Piney to the big house as a kitchen girl having found her snooping a useful source of gossip and information from the quarters. But she did not appreciate the same inquisitiveness when used to learn big house secrets.

"You mind your business or I'm sendin' you to the fields."

"I sorry, Aunt Emma," Piney mumbled, feigning humility as she returned to rolling the biscuit dough into a flat oval. "That ol' Henny comin' up here where she ain't supposed to sure do look awful bad to me," she said, and she began cutting biscuits from the dough.

"Nobody don't ax how it look to you," Emma said as she inspected the biscuits. "You done roll that dough too thick. Them biscuits be raw in the middle. Do 'em agin!"

"Then you say they too thin—"

"Do 'em agin, I says! And hurry up. Ham 'bout ready."

Piney, narrowing her slanting, slit-like eyes, fell into sullen silence and began gathering the circles of dough to be kneaded again. It had taken Piney years to scheme her way into the big house and she felt threatened by Henny's presence, especially now that she had her own sights set on

Angelica's position as soon as she was sent to Richmond. She was burning to know why her old enemy was Lavinia's breakfast guest.

"What she doing up here anyhow?" Piney asked, flouring her hands and reworking the unsatisfactory biscuits into a new ball of dough.

"That none of your business," Emma, equally curious, snapped.

"It got to be somethin' no good. She about the meanest girl I ever see. Stole a white dress off me once."

"She just ain't had no mammy in a long time, that's all," Aunt Beck said. "Little child like that with no mammy and let run wild bound to be troubled. I reckon her not being who she is, she be sold off by Master Lionel a long time ago. And he don't ax 'bout her no more."

"He ax me 'bout her," Emma said.

"Still don't seem right."

"Hush!" Emma cautioned with a meaningful glance toward Piney. "They some people don't got to know everything."

Occupied with the dough and rolling pen, Piney prattled on. "She got them right mean-looking blue eyes that just ain't right for black folks to has. I believe blue eyes in colored people is devil's eyes and—"

"Nobody care what you believe. You ain't the Bible," Emma said. The old woman placed previously warmed plates for eggs and ham on a large linen-covered tray. "You wantin' to be a maid to Miss Vinny so bad, you can just takes the tray in. I ain't able to serve this mornin'."

Piney's rolling pin froze. "I ain't able neither. I sick as a dog today. I—"

"You do it or else you cleans out the chicken house!"

"Ah, Aunt Emma, get Angelica to serve 'em. She do it. And where is she anyhow? I ain't seen her all mornin'."

"Ain't none of your business where Angelica is."

"I go upstairs and gets her. She ought to be down here helpin' us."

"Chicken house!" Emma shrieked, pointing toward the kitchen door, and Piney retreated into resentful silence.

"That dough too thin," Beck snapped, snatching the rolling pin from Piney. "I does it. You wash the flour off you and do what Emma tell you."

"Where is Angelica?" Piney wailed. "I sick enough to die and you—"

"Chicken house!" said Emma. "You going to clean out the chicken house anyhow. Teach you not to nose in where it none of your business."

Uncle Lemiel, long accustomed to the acrimony of the kitchen, only chewed his wad of honey-sweetened tobacco and occasionally spat into the fire, hearing little of the conflict around him but only the more pleasant hiss and sizzle of his expectorations as they danced and sputtered on the hot coals.

In the dining room, Lavinia, moved by the sincerity of Henny's innocent, awkward candor, searched for some temporizing answer that would not crush the little girl's hopes of becoming her maid.

"We will have to consult Master Hawthorn about that," she said.

Henny grinned happily at her mistress's response. She rose from her knees and took her place once more at the table.

"And it is not true that Angelica is expecting a baby," Lavinia said. "Angelica is a very good girl and would never even think of...of having a child...prior to marriage."

"Everybody sayin' that why you sendin' her to Richmond."

"But it isn't true. And you must do all you can to correct such a hurtful untruth. Angelica is being sent to Richmond so that her broken heart can heal and to visit her sister in Mr. Lionel's mother's household."

"Yes'am. I tells everybody I know Angelica ain't bigged a-tall."

"Perhaps you could just say 'isn't expecting a baby.'"

"Yes'um," Henny said, and she continued to fondle and look at the pendant around her neck as if to reassure herself that it was still there.

Lavinia's fascination with Henny more than matched the little girl's enthralled exploration of the dining room.

She is so like Oralee, Lavinia thought, *the bony elbows on the table, the way she cradled her chin in the ball of her hand, angling her head quizzically as she pondered some object.*

Her eyes still wandering busily about, Henny absently raised the gold heart to her lips and popped it into her mouth. How often Lavinia had seen Oralee do the same thing. Henny's every gesture seemed to duplicate those of Oralee at the same age. It was almost as if Lavinia could anticipate the little girl's next movement or gesture.

The blue eyes came to rest on a large, nearly life-sized portrait over the mantle. A friendly, aristocratic old gentleman, looking slightly uncomfortable, posed stiffly, although his eyes and mouth reflected warmth and humor and even a touch of mischief in spite of his formal, unnatural posture. His eyes were the same blue as Henny's.

"That's Master Hawthorn's father, Mr. Edmund."

Henny switched her attention to the opposite wall and the portrait of a woman Henny wondered where she had seen before. A pile of stiff, red curls towered above the wide brow of the woman's haughty, aristocratic face. Her chin was lifted proudly above her long, thin neck as she looked down from the frame with imperious, condescending disdain. Her head tilted to one side, Henny pursed her lips and wrinkled her nose, and with narrowed eyes, critically scrutinized the formidable figure.

"That's the master's mother, Miss Cornelia," Lavinia said. "You've seen both Miss Cornelia and Mr. Edmund before. They live in Richmond but visit us often. Do you remember their being here at Christmas?" Lavinia smiled to herself as she realized Henny was looking at her own grandparents, and how shocked they would be if they knew of her existence. But they could hardly deny it. Not if they observed her as Lavinia did, noting one similarity after another to Oralee, not just physically—the eyes, the wide brow, the entire composition of her features—but in the way she moved. Even the way she wrinkled her nose, pursed her lips, and tilted her head to one side as she inquired about the portraits, might have been Oralee herself, matching her every gesture and expression, as she asked why her grandfather was such good company and so much fun, and her grandmother was so formal and humorless and always reminding her to sit up straight or remove her elbows from the table.

"Who takes care of you, Henny?"

"Just me, I reckon." Henny removed the pendant from her mouth and pondered it as she spoke. "Last little bit anyways. When my mammy die, I stays with Old Sheba. But she mighty old and snores so bad, I just goes back to me and my mammy's cabin. It right next to Old Sheba's, anyhow."

"Alone?" Lavinia said. "Without a family? Oh, Henrietta, I should have been told."

"Nah. Weren't no need to tell nobody, Miss Lavinia."

Henny slipped the heart back down the neck of her dress. "Old Sheba and Aunt Beck all the time wantin' me to stay with them, but I'd rather stays in my own cabin."

"But aren't you afraid, all alone?"

"Nah. I puts the bar on the door when it get dark. Can't nothin' get me. Old Sheba live on one side of me and Nancy and Clevis on the othern. And Clevis and Uncle Lemiel sees I always got a good fire when it cold. And Aunt Beck all the time bringin' me things to eat. I eats with Nancy and Clevis and Old Sheba and just 'bout anywhere I wants since Mammy gone."

Lavinia's concern and guilt increased. She wondered if Henny's care by the servants had been arranged by Lionel or Emma. Since the maintenance and well-being of an orphaned nine-year-old would normally have been her responsibility, Lavinia suspected that Henny's paternity was the reason the little girl's presence had been concealed.

"Emma should have informed me," Lavinia said.

She remembered her own battle with typhoid during the epidemic, when Oralee died and Henny became an orphan. Lavinia had also contracted the disease and almost died herself. Her lengthy recovery and deep mourning at the death of her daughter would have made dealing with black orphans impossible.

At last a reluctant Piney emerged from the pantry carrying a large tray, the girl's outrage and humiliation at having to serve Henny distorting her features. Lavinia immediately sensed the coolness between the two girls as swift, hostile glances were exchanged and mouths formed half-smirks. Henny, as if sensing Piney's humiliation, brightened at the sudden reversal of their places in the slave hierarchy, and broke into a triumphant grin.

Exchanging smirk for grin, Piney sat the tray down on the table.

"Thank you, Piney. Do you want to say the blessing, Henrietta?" Lavinia placed her hands together prayerfully and waited for Henny to respond. "Do you know a blessing?"

"I reckon my mammy or Old Sheba teaches me one sometime or other but I forgets it. I usually just says, 'Thank you, Jesus', and plows right on in."

"That would be a very suitable blessing. I shall teach you another later. Would you say it now?"

Henny, imitating her mistress, pressed the palms of her hands together and bowed her head. With Lavinia's eyes closed, she turned sideways and stuck her tongue out at Piney. "Thank you, Jesus. Amen."

"Amen," said Lavinia.

Lavinia served Henny's plate and noticing her eyes searching the tray and table, inquired. "Was there anything else you would like, Henrietta?"

"You got any bee honey, Miss Vinny? I sure do like bee honey."

"But of course. Piney, would you bring us a pitcher of honey, please."

"Yes'um," Piney said weakly, and she left the room.

After a brief, contentious exchange from the pantry in which outrage and protest were muted with only partial success, Piney floated stiffly back into the dining room with a tray bearing a small pitcher of honey. Glaring at Henny, Piney set the pitcher down with a thud, as Henny tore open a biscuit.

"I think we have everything now, Piney. I'll ring if I need you," Lavinia said.

"Yes'am."

With a final dark glance at Henny, who regarded her with the scorn and haughtiness of a sovereign looking upon the lowest minion, a sulky, fuming Piney left the room.

"She can't sing worth nothin' at all," Henny told Lavinia in a confidential whisper as she looked expectantly at the servings of eggs and ham and biscuits. "They nobody wants to set next to her in church she throw them off so. And she ain't been baptized but three times. And I been way lots more than that."

Seizing the honey pitcher, Henny covered everything in her plate with the thick, golden liquid.

"Bee honey one of the good things," she said, and she began to eat.

Lavinia had never seen such a voracious appetite, even among field hands. The little girl's manners were appalling. Instead of cutting her ham, she took the entire slice in her hands and gnawed off a bite at a time, without the slightest hesitancy or self-consciousness. When she did use cutlery, it was only her spoon, heaped with bites so large she could barely get them into her mouth. Chewing noisily, food escaped her lips, although she held her head well over her plate and was careful not to let anything fall on her dress or the table.

Lavinia was so amazed at the little girl's capacity that she was concerned that the people were not being adequately fed. Perhaps Virgil Mudley, the overseer, whom she was reluctant to trust in any case, was withholding and selling provisions intended for the people, a not-unheard-of offense of dishonest overseers. Or perhaps the rations had simply been inadequately allotted.

"Do you have enough to eat, Henrietta?" she asked.

"Oh, yes'um, I got ever thing."

"Is anyone in the quarters ever hungry?"

"No, ma'am. Everybody got enough. If we runs out of anything, we just go to ol' Mudley—uh, Mr. Mudley, or Uncle Lemiel, and they gives it to us."

Lavinia was relieved and Henny smothered another biscuit with honey and quickly devoured it. As Lavinia watched, she tried to recall which of the women in the quarters had been Henny's mother. She reviewed the casualties of the typhoid epidemic, and knew at once.

Of course, she thought, taking into account her husband's taste. It would have to have been the pretty one. Yes, the beautiful one called Susannah, with the rich mahogany color who carried her body like an African queen, proud and aristocratic and strangely aloof from the other servants and even Lavinia. As mysterious as Africa itself, Susannah had brought to Hawthorn Hill a quiet dignity that at the same time fascinated and distanced her from the other blacks, some of whom labeled her uppity because she was a city black.

She had been brought from Richmond by Lionel as a possible nurse for Oralee. Lavinia remembered the exotic girl clearly now. She had seen her in the washhouse and smokehouse at hog-killing time, and sometimes in the kitchen assisting Aunt Beck and Emma. She had been like a shadow about the place, shy and deferential, her dark beauty and allure enhanced by a quiet grace and enigmatic evasiveness.

Lavinia acknowledged the beauty of her voluptuous rival and once again bowed to her husband's good taste in women. His unfaithfulness, which in the early years of her marriage had broken her heart, brought only a dull ache now, like the throb of an old injury suffered long ago. She could hardly be jealous of a dead woman. Susannah had been as much a victim of her husband's libertine behavior as Lavinia had been a victim of his deception. The girl had been a slave, at the mercy of her owner, and Lavinia knew not what pressures Lionel brought to obtain her acquiescence to adultery. Yet even as she felt little resentment toward Susannah, Lavinia sensed the sting of disappointment and hurt that echoed her original unhappiness when she first discovered she had married an incorrigible, unrelenting philanderer.

She had banned him from her bed the last three years, since another of his numerous affairs had come to her attention, the one with the Richmond seamstress on Fushee Street. The strikingly beautiful widow had sent a note to Lionel, which had been accidentally delivered to Lavinia. This liaison had been discovered within a month of her having taken him back—after a great show of repentance—following an even earlier indiscretion with another complying widow from Williamsburg. And before that, it had been a saloon girl, and prior to her, numerous prostitutes from Richmond brothels and other women "of low character," even including women from the stage.

Now she understood why Susannah had always avoided looking her in the eye, and why she had been quick to disappear from a room Lavinia entered. She also understood the servants' silence when Susannah's name was mentioned, and why they quickly busied themselves with useless tasks whenever Lavinia visited the kitchen, pantry, or wash house and Susannah had also been there. It was as if the household had conspired to keep Susannah out of sight and make her non-existent to Lavinia.

She was disappointed with Angelica, who must have known. But perhaps, like the other servants, her silence was an attempt to spare her the pain of the truth.

At last Henny, adequately fed, emitted an unselfconscious belch of satisfaction. "I never got nary a drop of nothin' on your table or my dress or anywhere else but inside me, Miss Lavinia," she said brightly, flashing a wide, self-satisfied grin.

"Are you sure you have had enough?"

"Yes'um. Believe I full as a tick."

"Then perhaps we could gather some dogwood for the graves. We'll visit Oralee's and your mammy's, too."

Henny's grin vanished instantly and her brow knitted in distress.

"Are you alright, my dear? Do you feel ill?"

"Yes'um, I think I is." Her voice had grown small and guarded.

"Would you like to lie down for a while?"

"I reckon it might help some. If it alright with you, I just go to my cabin now and rest a spell."

"Very well. I'll have Old Beck look in on you later."

Miraculously, Henny's pained expression disappeared and her illness seemed to vanish. She brightened and her happy, natural expression returned. Lavinia felt her forehead and detecting no fever decided Henny's discomfort was no more serious than the results of overeating. She rang the small service bell.

When Piney appeared, Henny's grin disappeared. With an expression of superiority, she lifted her chin and watched Piney gather the dishes with condescension that was identical to the hauteur of the senior Mrs. Hawthorn's portrait. Lavinia suppressed a smile as Henny sat upright as straight as a rod and patronized Piney with a disdainful nod of her head.

Blood will tell, Lavinia thought to herself. *Oh, how blood will tell.* A crown of corkscrew red curls, sixty more years, and lighter skin, and Henny's haughtiness would have been hard to differentiate from that of Cornelia Hawthorn's portrait on the wall above them.

"Did you ever get them eggs Emma was needing to make that custard for when Mr. Lionel come home?" Henny airily asked Piney as she reached for the last remaining dish.

Piney stopped cold as her slanted eyes widened and her jaw sagged in surprise. Then she seized the dish and slammed it noisily on the tray.

"Gently, Piney," Lavinia admonished. "We mustn't break the china."

"Yes'um," Piney said as she picked up the tray and started toward the door.

"Can't make no custard without eggs!" Henny sang out after her, as the mystified, enraged girl left the room.

Chapter Four

Henny had never been so happy. Her heart sang as she bounded down the side porch steps and turned to give Lavinia, watching from the window, a final deep curtsy. After her mistress nodded and withdrew, Henny skipped around the house.

She had reached the kitchen yard when she heard Piney's voice.

"There she is, Aunt Emma!"

Emma appeared as if from nowhere and hobbled toward Henny with fire in her eye and a switch in her hand.

"She act just awful at the table, Aunt Emma," Piney said. "She make a pig of herself and don't use no manners a-tall."

"You just stay where you is, you ugly little piece of business," Emma said. She grabbed Henny by the arm with one hand and with the other began to flail her with the switch. "You lower than dirt! I teach you to come up here wearin' that precious baby's dress and break Miss Vinny's heart all over again! And just when we gettin' her over her grief at losin' that child."

"She lower than dirt!" chimed in Piney from the covered passageway. "She done make Miss Vinny grieve all over again!"

Henny was stunned at the accusation and the fury of Emma's attack.

"I never done it!" she protested, mystified by the charge.

"After Miss Lavinia done 'bout lost her mind when that precious child die, and you comes up here in one of her little dresses. Remindin' her—"

"Give it to her good, Aunt Emma!" Piney said. "She make Miss Vinny grieve and near lose her mind!"

The old woman continued to flail Henny's legs, striking her with stinging, painful accuracy.

"Miss Vinny done near died herself over that child. Took most a year to get her over her grievin'!" Emma continued to beat the child.

"She make Miss Vinny nearly die!" Piney screeched.

Henny began to cry, less from the sting of the switch than the accusation that she might have hurt her mistress.

"That's the way, Aunt Emma!" cried out Piney, jumping up and down and clapping her hands to the rhythm of Emma's licks. The old woman soon tired and her blows slowed.

"Don't lighten up, Aunt Emma. And make her take off that dress she steals from me. That my dress anyhow!"

Emma's faltering blows stopped. Gasping for breath, she rested for a moment, still clutching Henny's arm, as much for support as to prevent her escape.

"Lay it on her, Aunt Emma," Piney said, clapping her hands.

Emma made two more weak attempts, faltered, and let her switching arm fall to her side.

"Dirt girl! Dirt girl!" Piney shrieked and, alarmed that the whipping might end, came down the porch steps. "Now, Aunt Emma, you ain't able to do that! Just give me that switch and I'll finish up on her. You ain't strong enuf—"

She reached for the switch but Emma struck Piney sharply on her thin, outstretched arm. She screamed and jumped back as Emma, gasping for breath, relaxed her hold on Henny.

Suddenly Piney emitted a scream and pointed at Henny. "She done stole Miss Vinny's blue shawl!"

"Where you get that blue shawl?" Emma asked.

"Miss Vinny gets it for me—" Henny tried to explain as Emma snatched the shawl from her shoulders and gave her another stinging swipe with the switch.

"Now you get back down this hill and I don't want you nowhere near this house again! I teach you to come up hear makin' Miss Vinny grieve and stealin' her blue shawl and—"

"She stealin' Miss Vinny's shawl! She stealin' Miss Vinny's shawl!" Piney screamed and jumped up and down in triumph.

Henny turned and fled with Emma's and Piney's voices ringing after her.

"I thrash you with the leather strop next time."

"Dirt girl! Dirt girl!"

Chapter Five

That afternoon, Lavinia went to the office in the rear of the house, which also served as her husband's bedroom since she had exiled him from her own three years earlier. She disliked the room and its masculine disorder, although she often worked there, recording accounts and inventories and attending other plantation business. Littered with kegs of whiskey—for the plantation's social and medical needs—and saddles, trunks, and old copies of *The Richmond Whig* and *The Richmond Enquirer*, the room smelled of leather, tobacco, dogs, and the slightly rancid odor of insufficiently cured pelts from Lionel's hunting.

Stepping around an impressive rack of still-unmounted deer antlers, which would join her husband's other trophies on the wall with his extensive collection of muskets, pistols, and rifles, Lavinia made her way to a massive oak desk.

Sitting at the desk, she removed a large, time-worn ledger, labeled in faded ink, "The People Book." Its pages ready to fall from its cloth-covered binding, the book had been in use by the Hawthorn family for nearly a hundred years. Since the time of Lionel's great-grandfather, the ledger contained the meticulously documented vital statistics of the slaves owned by the family for several generations. All purchases, sales, births, marriages, and deaths were recorded between the tattered, gray covers.

Lavinia opened the ledger and began turning the pages from the back toward the front, until she found the latest entry, the Christmas-day baby, born the previous December. In Lionel's flowing handwriting was written: *Born: healthy female—named Mary Starr Hawthorn—December 25, 1852—parents—Clevis and Nancy (Hawthorn). 12th surviving child.*

This had been the latest black child born at Hawthorn Hill, only five months before, to the plantation's most fecund couple, Clevis and Nancy, whom Lavinia had earlier mistakenly suspected were Henny's parents.

Continuing her search, she found the entry she was looking for: *Born: healthy female—named Henrietta Valentine—August 13, 1844—parent—Susannah.*

Quickly Lavinia searched the ledger for other listings, seeking out births, one after another, to confirm her observation that in only this child had Lionel failed to assign the newborn a last name—Hawthorn—or give a surname to the mother—also Hawthorn—as he had done in every other entry when the child and parent had been Hawthorn property. No mention of this child's paternity was recorded either.

"Coward," she said, and long dormant bitterness returned to her like a tight fist clutching her heart. "He doesn't even have the courage to give his child and the ignorant black woman he used to get her the dignity of a last name."

As she started to close the book, a loosened page, slipped to the floor. Retrieving it, she saw it contained the death records of the typhoid epidemic two years ago:

Died—Earl Hawthorn—aged 69—Typhoid Fever—August 8, 1851.

Died—Tina Hawthorn—wife of Earl Hawthorn—aged 66—Typhoid Fever—August 12, 1851.

Died—Eva Hawthorn—aged four years—Typhoid Fever—August 14, 1851

Died—Lou Hawthorn—aged one month, two days—August 15, 1851—Typhoid Fever—infant daughter of Olaf and Ginger Hawthorn.

Separated from the earlier entries by an inch of blank paper, and in a script notably less steady than the self-assured flair of Lionel's usual penmanship, was:

Died—Susannah—aged 32—Typhoid Fever—August 23, 1851.

Died—Lionel Hawthorn—four day old infant son of Susannah—Typhoid Fever—August 24, 1851.

For a long time, Lavinia looked at the page and reread the last two entries. She was suddenly overwhelmed by a great emptiness when she realized that Susannah had died three days following her own Oralee. And the little son Susannah had borne Lionel had died only a day after his mother.

As she continued to stare at the words, the letters seemed to change and come alive, moving and rising from the page like tiny black threads. Then she realized that drops of her tears had fallen on the page and were dissolving the ink into watery, moving smudges.

Her feelings were confused, one emotion struggling against another—anger, resentment, pity—and in spite of her disdain for her husband, a feeling of sympathy wove its way into her muddled thinking. Poor Lionel. In the space of only six days, he had lost his white daughter and black son.

In the past, he had sworn to her that his women, black or white, were mere casual indulgences and meant nothing to him. But surely he felt something at the death of his own child and that child's mother. How could he not have cared? He had actually given this child his name: Lionel. And Hawthorn. More than he had done for Henny at her birth.

She knew the depth of his grief for Oralee, and painfully remembered during the delirium of her own illness, their clinging to each other and weeping without restraint when their daughter breathed her last and their sense of loss even banished for a time the bitterness of their estrangement. The memory of his tortured face, all masculine stoicism abandoned to sorrow, would haunt her forever. As would the poignancy of his grief when she nearly died herself, and he had cradled her in his arms, begging her not to die too, and prayed to God that she be spared.

Nor could she forget the weeks after death had claimed their daughter, when his weeping had been private but revealed by red-rimmed eyes, their blue dulled by sorrow. Then, putting aside his own grief, he had made painfully desperate, futile attempts to bring her out of her own despair. He had certainly been unselfish then, and she knew she had not, indulging too long in her grief, tormenting herself and in doing so tormenting him.

She was about to put the journal away when she heard the yelping of hounds. Alarmed at the excited braying, she paused and listened. They could hardly be Hawthorn hounds. The day before she had instructed Horace Mudley to lockup Lionel's dogs to prevent their alerting the plantation of last night's escape.

"Slave patrols!" she said in a panic. "After Gabriel—"

But as the dogs got nearer and louder, they sounded unmistakably like the hounds of Hawthorn Hill. Lavinia knew the sound well, and sighed with relief when she recognized them as Lionel's. The red, scampering quartet's spirited yelping was distinctly their own, a combination of howl and bark impossible to belong to any other pack. No doubt Virgil Mudley had released them and the noisy commotion announced the arrival of company.

Company was rare in the isolated plantation country and Lavinia wondered who could be calling this morning. As she placed the loose page back in the ledger, she heard a familiar male voice booming through the closed door to the front hall.

"Now where's my mammy?" a rich baritone intoned.

It was Lionel.

Lavinia tensed at once. In an instant the deep, resonate tone of his voice was answered by a whoop and cackle from Emma as she rushed into the front hall to greet her master.

"Thar my baby!" the old woman cried joyfully, and although she could not see them, Lavinia knew, having observed the performance many times before, that she was rushing into Lionel's arms and he would sweep her up and twirl her around as one did a child.

"Now you set me down right this minute," she cried out. "You gonna breck these old rib-bones one of these days doing that!"

What a ridiculous performance, Lavinia thought. She knew Lionel indulged in such displays as much to annoy her as to please his mammy, since he knew she overheard them from the parlor or library. She listened with annoyance as the foolishness between child and mammy continued.

"You ain't too big for me to whip, young master," Emma threatened, and Lavinia knew the lines in his broad, tanned forehead had creased with feigned fear.

"Now, Mammy, how can you whip your baby when he brought you a present all the way from Richmond?"

Lavinia knew some families housing similar bonds of affection found these displays of devotion between master and mammy amusing and touching. Lavinia did not. To her, such demonstrations were childish and patronizing.

"You give me my present this minute. Then I whips you anyhow! I done give one whippin' today, reckon I can gives another."

"And I've got a secret to tell you, too," Lionel continued. "You can tell Aunt Beck and Uncle Lemiel but not Miss Lavinia. But I'm sure not going to tell you if you're threatening to whip me."

"You tell me this minute," Emma ordered, and there followed a moment of silence, during which Lavinia knew the secret was duly imparted, and then she heard Emma release a whoop of joy.

"Praise the Lord, Master—"

"Shh. Now go fix me some corn pone and I'll bring your present. I'm half starved."

"I fix it. And griddle cake, too. And I tells 'em." The old woman's happy chuckle faded away as she departed for the kitchen.

Lavinia quickly put the people ledger in the desk drawer. She could hear Lionel looking for her, opening the door to the parlor, then the library and dining room. She knew the office would be next.

Instinctively, her hands flew to her head in search of an out-of-place strand of hair as she quickly checked the security of the neat roll from her temples to the back of her neck. Adjusting her collar, she sat erect in her chair, and smoothed out her dress. Searching for something to occupy her, she reached for the supply book just beneath a rack of pistols hanging on the wall above the desk.

Lionel opened the door.

"Ah, Mrs. Hawthorn. I've been looking for you. Good morning." He came into the room and bent his tall broad-shouldered form forward in a grand, sweeping bow.

"Doing the accounts or selecting a weapon to use on me?" He gestured toward the rack of guns above the desk. He smiled widely, the dimples in his well-boned face deepening into pits, his full sensuous lips parting to reveal perfect teeth.

"If I had any intention of using a weapon on you, Mr. Hawthorn, I would have done it long ago."

"I have always been at your mercy, Mrs. Hawthorn. I still am."

Even though she despised herself for it, Lavinia felt her pulse quicken at the sight of him. He was an imposing figure, she could not deny. At forty-four, his good looks had only deepened with age, becoming more defined as the softness of youth had been replaced by a handsomeness more mature and solid. The tall, six-foot-three-inch frame showed few of the signs of aging. Immaculately attired by the best tailors in Richmond, his tan trousers and dark blue coat enhanced his muscled physique, and he betrayed no hint of the consequences of a lifetime of easy self-indulgence. No paunch, the aftermath of years of rich Virginia cooking, had yet altered the slim waist, and no loosening of his jaw into jowls softened the sharpness of his chin, nor the deep cleft within it. Only the deep furrows in his broad brow beneath the still-golden hair revealed his age. The startling indigo blue eyes remained as vividly arresting as in his youth, and just the shadow of the beginning of pouches beneath them betrayed the years of late nights of gaming, women, and bourbon.

His long legs, booted to the knees in the finest leather, moved his broad-shouldered form with the same grace Lavinia found so admirable in a good horse, and in friendlier times she had told him that with more intelligence he would have made a fine one. Although a gentleman planter and practicing lawyer, his powerful body was that of a man who spent his time outdoors, his brawny physique the result of a life spent not at a desk or lounging on the veranda, but in physical activity, riding and hunting and even laboring side by side with his slaves, plowing and clearing woodland and working his fields, these strenuous pursuits counteracting the effects of his periodic revelries.

With saddle bags tossed carelessly over one shoulder, Lavinia was forced to acknowledge that his still-riveting good looks held her as much today as they had since the day she had first laid eyes on him.

"You look so well, Mrs. Hawthorn. Dare I presume the bloom in your cheek reflects your pleasure in seeing me, or has your morning ride created the glow?"

At once suspicious and on guard, Lavinia wondered what lay beneath this cordial display of chivalry and charm. Gentlemanly affectation from Lionel usually masked cynicism and she was careful not to be quarry for his sarcasm.

"Neither, Mr. Hawthorn. I have as yet not ridden today."

He approached the desk and deposited the saddlebags on the floor. The necks of two wine bottles, wrapped in a protective cloth, projected from the open flaps.

Rising to his full height, he reached for her hand and lifted it to his lips, kissing it gently, all the while watching her closely. A lock of his thick blond hair, only slightly less golden than when she first met him, hung over his broad, sun-burned forehead. As his hand continued to hold hers, and his lips lingered above it, she forgot herself and almost reached out to sweep the wayward lock back from his brow. But wariness of his elaborate politeness kept the impulse in check.

"I am so glad to be home," he said in a lower voice, his tone sincere and intimate. He still held her hand and she searched his face for some hint that he was playing one of his games. Unsure of his intentions, she decided to maintain caution and ignore his courtliness.

"And it is time you were. There is so much work to be done, and many matters require your attention. Your presence has been needed here for some time."

"You flatter me with your needs, Mrs. Hawthorn."

"I speak of the plantation's needs, sir. Mr. Mudley informs me the people's meal supply is getting low and I have directed that twenty bushels of corn be milled. Plowing is to begin soon, but because of rain and Mudley's delay when the weather was suitable, we are behind." She knew her babbling was an attempt to conceal her nervousness, but prattled on lest he sense her vulnerability. "Ivan and Douglas still fight every day over the affections of that Daisy, who still will not choose between them. Several of the cabins have leaking roofs and—" She stopped short when she caught a look of self-reproach in his eyes.

"Ah, yes. I know."

He looked at her with an expression of sympathy, whether feigned or mocking she was uncertain. "And now that it is spring, the children must be wormed and I should make one more effort to buy Gabriel from Horace Wroughton for Angelica. And because our overseer becomes more useless day by day, my poor wife is beleaguered with so many responsibilities her life is no better than a slave's."

Lavinia resented his flippancy in dismissing her very real concerns and withdrew her hand. His true nature was surfacing and she rose to leave the room.

"Obviously, you cannot appreciate what I deal with here every day, and—"

Gently he caught her by the arm. "Please," he said. "Don't leave."

She stopped and allowed him to turn her toward him. Once again, their eyes engaged and his sincerity seemed to return. "I do understand how difficult it is to run the plantation alone when I am away. I appreciate your efforts and I would at least like to make a token effort in expressing my gratitude." Smiling, he reached for one of the bottles in the saddlebags and unwrapped it.

"A new shipment from France. Just in from Philadelphia. Its reputation is impeccable and—"

How like him, she thought. *I have for weeks assumed total responsibility for the entire plantation, go from morning until night working harder than any slave on the place, and he thinks pretty words and a bottle of wine can repay me.*

As if reading her thoughts, his hurt expression returned, and with it a yearning soulfulness.

"Lavinia," he said quietly. "I have wonderful news. I want to share it with you. I know you have been overburdened since I have tried to help Randy learn to manage the new farm. But he is our son. I thought you understood my absence and were willing to make the sacrifice for him. And Papa is getting old and I feel a duty to help him. In a year or so, maybe Frederick can come into the office and take on some of the work. These are our sons, Lavinia. We are forging a future for them."

How clever of him, Lavinia thought. *He brings our sons into his manipulations to make me feel guilty. His white children. I wonder what he feels for the future of his black ones.*

"You know I would do anything for the boys," she said. "And how is Randy?"

He smiled proudly at the mention of their oldest son. "He is well and sends his love, as does Sarah."

"Tell me everything. It has been so long."

"They are still very much the newlyweds. Even after almost a year." His smile deepened and his voice became a caress. "They almost remind me of us." He eyed her closely. Embarrassed at so intimate a memory and sensing the beginning of a blush, she avoided his gaze and looked away.

As if to spare her modesty, he quickly went on. "But I shall tell you everything later. And thank you for your understanding my neglect. And I appreciate your missing me." His grin provoked the return of her hostility. She did not find his deliberate misinterpretation of her words amusing.

"—of the plantation, I mean," he quickly added, as if sensing her irritation. "And now, if you will indulge me with the pleasure of your company at supper tonight, I will share with you the news I bring, and perhaps we can celebrate together something wonderful—"

Startled at his request—they never shared meals together unless some member of the family or company was present—Lavinia was at a loss for words. But in his invitation she saw opportunity. He was asking for a truce in their war, and, a momentary suspension of hostility between them could serve her objective in getting Henny some justice and her position in the household which she deserved. Indeed, she would use the temporary peace to petition the little black girl's case. Whatever the outcome, Lavinia was determined that Henny's fate would not be that of a field hand.

"Of course. I shall be happy to have supper with you, Mr. Hawthorn," she said. His eyes widened with surprise and his dimples deepened in a smile. He held her gaze for a long moment, then bent his head in another bow.

"Until this evening, Mrs. Hawthorn," he said, moving toward the door. "The servants will be so surprised that we are dining together. And now I shall join my mammy for gossip and corn pone and apple butter." With a final bow, he was gone, closing the door behind him.

How smug he is, she thought, and she wondered what lay beneath the surface of this sudden civility. Suspicious from past experience, Lavinia was wary of Lionel's every word and wondered why the sudden display of charm and friendliness when he usually returned her coldness with an equally polite frostiness of his own.

And what could this wonderful secret be? No doubt his clique of Richmond politicians had persuaded him to run for the Assembly or Congress. Various Virginia politicians had been after him for years to seek public office, offers he had always declined. Perhaps he had at last succumbed to the lure of politics.

He would be good at it, Lavinia thought. *With manipulation and chicanery the mainstays of politics and clay in his hands, he could hardly fail. He is adept at all the things politicians need, except a just political philosophy—and he's too much a Southerner for that.* But she decided she would hear him out and perhaps engage in a kind of politics herself.

He had always been more clever than she in the games they played. Using charm, wit, and keen insight into her hidden feelings, he could outmaneuver her into unwinnable positions. It angered her to be outmatched by him, and she could no longer dismiss even inconsequential defeats.

But tonight she would be more clever and play for higher stakes. She would put into the game a new pawn—Henny, his daughter. By now, she knew that she wanted the child. Black or white, bastard or not, slave or free, she realized that for the first time since Oralee's death, she had, through the little girl's presence that morning, experienced something close to the happiness that for so long she knew only as a memory. A bond had been formed with the child and she decided she must have her at all costs.

She knew Lionel would oppose the idea, but neither he nor anything else would stop her. She was at once filled with the excitement of challenging him and heartened by the advantage that he was as yet unaware of her campaign. He was an opposing force to be caught off-guard by the ambush of his own charm. She would turn his own weapons against him.

She had conquered him with these devices before; she could do it again. Just as she had tricked him into proposing to her years before when she had pretended to be enamored with a rival suitor she would actually have chosen spinsterhood to have avoided marrying. When he had learned he could lose her to someone else, he had immediately fallen to his knees and begged for her hand.

It would be the same with this child, Henny. He had fathered the child and as his wife that somehow made the little girl Lavinia's as well. She knew he would be quick to demolish such specious reasoning, but she would deal with that later. This child was half her beloved Oralee. One of his children died; one did not. Only their mothers' fates had been different. Had Lavinia and Henny died of typhoid, and Susannah and Oralee survived, would not Lionel have appointed Susannah as Oralee's mammy? Almost certainly he would have.

So why not the converse? Was it any less obvious and inevitable that she, surviving, should not bring up Henny? Discounting the stringent racial barriers, it seemed to Lavinia almost preordained.

"I shall raise her as my own," she said in a whisper to herself. "I shall take this child into my house and under the appearance of her being my maid, I shall raise her as my own daughter."

Euphoric with the excitement of her mission, Lavinia once more opened the bottom drawer of Lionel's desk and removed the People Book. Finding a pen and inkwell, she opened the ledger and found the page which listed Henrietta's birth:

Born–healthy female– named Henrietta Valentine–August 13, 1844–parent–Susannah.

Dipping her pen into the ink, she imitated the florid style of Lionel's liquid script, and added, beside the name Henrietta Valentine, the name *Hawthorn*, and beside the name Susannah also the name *Hawthorn*.

And below these entries, in her own handwriting and with no attempt to imitate her husband's:

Henrietta Valentine Hawthorn–Adopted by Lavinia Williamson Hawthorn–April 1853.

Chapter Six

When Henny returned to the quarters, she sought solace in the arms of Old Sheba, pouring out her anger and hurt as she displayed the stripes on her legs and laid her head in the shriveled old woman's lap.

"It over now," the old woman comforted, just as she had done to countless other children who had fallen under Emma's unfair punishments in the past. "It don't hurt no more. Old Sheba loves her baby—"

"Emma say I make Miss Vinny grieve! And steals her shawl!" Henny sobbed.

"I tries to tell you, but you not listen to Old Sheba," the old woman said, holding Henny close. "I done tell you, you get whipped if you go up there. Emma been with the white folks so long, she gettin' right much like 'em. Don't matter what Emma says or white folks neither. And ain't I told you 'nough times that white devils always out to give black folks misery? We just has to wait for Jesus to get real justice."

"But it wasn't white devils! It was Emma and Piney. They black devils!"

Old Sheba's passive expression vanished. Her eyes flashed with anger and she drew back her arm and slapped Henny soundly across the face. Henny sprang back, her hand flying to her stinging cheek.

"Don't you never calls black people devils!" Old Sheba said. "You brings your own self down when you does. Your blackness is your glory!"

Her ear ringing from the blow, Henny backed away from the old woman. "How many times I has to tell you that? Your blackness is your glory! It like the cross of Jesus you has to carry."

Henny didn't want to hear about blackness and how it was her glory, and how black people had to carry crosses and bear the suffering heaped on them by white people to pay for sin and to get to heaven. She tried once more to communicate her loss and raised the hem of her dress to again show the stripes on her legs, but old Sheba dismissed her wounds with a wave of her hand.

"Come here and I loves you a little..."

The old woman reached out and drew the sobbing little girl into her lap.

"You think gettin' a little switchin' sufferin'? You ain't never knowed real sufferin', child." She dropped her head and shook it back and forth with incomprehension. "I tells you 'bout real sufferin'." The old woman's deep-set eyes seemed to recede farther into the folds of leathery skin around them as memories long in her past returned.

Henny knew what was coming and wanted to flee. Old Sheba would begin the story of her own childhood suffering at the hands of white people, and Henny wanted comfort and sympathy only for herself. Henny had heard the story of Old Sheba's family's abduction and forced importation across the ocean from Africa many times.

As she grew older, Old Sheba often explored the past, making the people in the quarters ashamed when they complained of their own hardship. Henny knew from the faraway gaze in the old woman's eyes she was looking back eighty years to her own family's dreadful history.

"They done pack us in this big boat like grains of corn on a cob," she said. "Packed in tight so they be enough of us still alive after crossin' the big water to makes the white devils a profit. We been on the water so long it like it never end and that water go on forever. Sickness come and we hungry and some nearly lose they sense. Day after day after day, and never endin'. The closeness, and the water and sickness, and the rockin' just go on and on. Week after week. My Pappy get the fever and can't stand another day of it and loses his sense. He scream out he can't take no more and jumps over the side."

Old Sheba stared before her as if she was watching the scene as she told it, her eyes hard as flint as her mind reached back for the memory that would never release her, and even now haunted her dreams.

"My mammy get the sickness, too. When the white devils see she gots it and gettin' weaker, they say she gonna die anyhow and they ain't no use to feed her no longer. They say they goin' to throw her overboard, just like she already dead."

Old Sheba's voice dropped so low Henny could barely hear it, her words spoken as if only to herself, or to the dead spirits that seemed to swirl around her. This part of Old Sheba's story frightened Henny and her own sorrow paled beside the horror the old woman had suffered.

"I just a child, 'bout six, but I wraps my arms 'round my mammy and tries to hold her from them. She too weak to fight 'em, but I holds on to her long as I can. If they goin' to throw her over, I wants to go, too. But the white devils, they the strongest and beats me off, and snatch her 'way from me and no cryin' or beggin' I do make them wait till she dead—and they throwed her over."

Old Sheba fell silent and continued to stare into space, swaying slowly back and forth, as if in the rhythm of the listing boat that had been the scene of her loss.

"I tries to jump, too, after my mammy, but the white devils say since I ain't got it yet, and don't eat much, I sell for somethin'. And they chains me up."

Henny sniffed back the last of her tears and waited for Old Sheba to return from her reverie. After a moment, the old woman sagged in her chair as if exhausted from her memories. Then the familiar Old Sheba returned and she was herself again, her eyes snapping and angry, her tongue sharp and unforgiving.

"That the way white people is. They the devils! Devils pure through. Ain't no black folks mean like that."

Then, in exhaustion, the old woman closed her eyes and sank back in her chair, her anger and strength expended.

Henny knew Old Sheba's ordeal was far greater than her own and that it explained her opposition to Henny's desire for a house position.

"Don't know why you wants to be in the same house with white devils in the first place," she had said.

Old Sheba soon fell asleep. Henny spread a quilt over the old woman and tucked it around her shoulders. Wretched and uncomforted, she slipped back to her own cabin and fell on her bed to ponder her uncertain future and pray that Lavinia would overrule Emma's judgment and rescue her from the fields.

When Lionel left the house for the fields, Lavinia instructed Piney to have Reuben bring her horse for her morning ride. With Mercury thundering across the fields, down some isolated country road, or through some as yet unexplored woodland, Lavinia hoped to leave behind her the cares of the plantation, her unhappy marriage, and worries about the safety of Angelica. She would plan how to move Henny from the quarters to the big house, an objective she was certain Lionel would oppose.

"Mr. Lionel not like you ridin' by you self, Miss Vinny," Reuben said at the side porch when he brought Mercury from the stables.

"Mr. Hawthorn will never know, unless you tell him."

"I not tells, Miss Vinny. But you watch the bushes mighty careful. These dangerous times, folks say, and you never knows when another ol' Nat Turner goin' to turn up."

"Nat Turner was years ago, Reuben. But I shall be especially careful." A crazed Virginia slave named Nat Turner had staged a murderous rebellion years before in southern Virginia, only a little more than a hundred miles away.

Lavinia usually began her ride seated sidesaddle, as was proper for women of the day, and at a gait no faster than a leisurely, ladylike trot. Only when she was out of sight of any critical eyes from the house did she hike her skirts and straddle her steed in the more comfortable style of a man.

Today, however, she didn't care who saw her brazen disregard of propriety. She leaped astride Mercury the moment Reuben handed her the reins and sped away, catching in a glimpse over her shoulder the boy's startled expression at her unfamiliar mount. Laughing at his surprise, she immediately gave full reign to the powerful animal and thundered across the yard and down the lane where she guided him toward the open pasture. She welcomed the rhythm of Mercury's gallop in sympathetic cadence to the fevered thoughts racing through her mind.

Bounding at top speed with her skirt and petticoat billowing behind her made her feel alive, free, and unburdened. She loosened the strings on her bonnet and released the tight roll of hair that encircled her head and let it fall unrestrained to blow wild and free in the wind. She felt like a girl again in the mountains of southwestern Virginia where she had grown up. The vast acreage of Hawthorn Hill's meadows and woods provided ample privacy for Lavinia's rides of abandon and escape and she often lost any sense of time or distance as she rode for miles beyond the plantation's boundaries.

Later, she slowed Mercury to a pace she called her "thinking gait," a slow trot in which she found the calmness in which to pray and think through the problems of the day.

This morning the air was ripe with the smell of new growth, and the fresh green of the Virginia spring glistened all around her. The blossoms of dogwood and fruit trees in the orchards were beginning to burst forth in full brilliance and the energy of new life lifted Lavinia's spirits as she made plans for Henny's induction into her household. In the shaded, cooling darkness of a pine forest, she found the seclusion within which she could weigh her options and mold her strategy.

Beginning with table manners, she would train the little girl in proper comportment, introduce her to Christianity uncontaminated by black superstition, correct her grammar, and eventually teach her to read, just as she had taught her own children and Angelica, although in Virginia it was against the law to teach a slave to read. Her successful instruction of Angelica had proven the stupidity of those who said blacks were uneducable, and her violation of the law had given her supreme satisfaction. She would also teach

Henny to ride and love horses, just as she had taught her sons and Angelica.

In the dense woods just beyond Hawthorn Hill boundaries, she followed the twisting, narrow trail that paralleled the banks of a rocky creek. Brimming from the recent spring rains, the creek's splashing music joined the noisy chorus of birds in a song of spring, and the forest itself seemed to hum with the vitality of fresh growth. Every shade of green glimmered in the sprouting leaves, and the air was heavy with the smells of earth and new life, and every sound joined with the song in Lavinia's heart, which sang out with a message of bright beginnings.

For the first time since Oralee's death, Lavinia felt released from the intensity of persistent grief. With her estrangement from Lionel, the absence of her sons, and the loss of Oralee, Lavinia's life had become a void of isolation and sadness. Henny's presence would fill the emptiness that often seemed to overwhelm her like a great, heavy darkness. The mantle of loss, pain, and hopelessness seemed to miraculously lift from her shoulders as Henny's appearance in her life brought the dawn of restored meaning and purpose.

Lavinia would have someone to love again.

In her room later that day, Lavinia dressed for dinner with unusual care. The challenge of persuading Lionel to allow her to bring Henny to the big house infused the evening with an urgency that made every device at her disposal important. The selection of her wardrobe became a major decision. She must have something attractive, which at the same time did not betray her intention to use allure as a stratagem.

Looking through her armoire, she selected a black taffeta dress that flattered her figure and to which she had only recently added narrow bands of white lace at the collar and cuffs, a concession to the solid black mourning she had worn for the two years since Oralee's death.

Lavinia dampened her fingers with a light coating of glycerin and rose water and smoothed her hair, giving it a flattering sheen and the faint aroma of roses. Nervously, she searched through her jewelry box for appropriate earrings and perhaps a pin. Her grandmother's old cameo might go well with the dress's white trim, but perhaps the smaller garnet broach would be a better choice, and help anchor the lace dickey that cascaded from her throat and draped gracefully over her breasts. But which of her earrings should she wear?

Lavinia chided herself. *I'm like a silly school girl—foolishly unable to select a pair of earrings in which to receive a suitor.* Yet the enforced intimacy of dining with Lionel unnerved her, and her hands shook as she tried to choose between the gold and jade and pearl drop earrings.

In the past, Lionel had always been repentant, Lavinia forgiving, and reconciliation followed. But in time, the repentance produced neither forgiveness nor reconciliation— even after three years, longer than ever before.

Only the servants had heard the bitter quarrels from behind closed doors, and seen the reddened eyes of their mistress following these long, caustic exchanges. And helpless to interfere, only morose expressions expressed their sadness at the resentment and anger in their master's marriage.

Family and plantation business brought them together only for brief, quickly conducted exchanges. But tonight would be different. At other dinners, she could direct her attention and conversation to family or guests relieving her of all but the most obligatory conversation and acknowledgment of his presence. The charade of civility they so expertly presented to friends and family would be useless tonight.

Of course, she thought, trying to calm herself. *I'm anxious because I haven't had my nightly toddy.*

Troubled by marital discord and the death of Oralee, Lavinia suffered from insomnia, which was relieved by a bedtime drink of whisky. Although she did not approve of hard liquor, she justified her own nightly intake of two or three ounces of pure bourbon for medicinal reasons. Dr. Hunter had recommended moderate consumption of hot toddies as a mild sedative. After a time, Lavinia found neither sugar nor heat necessary, and every night indulged in the soothing medication of pure bourbon.

Finding the flask she hid in her washstand nearly empty, she decided she would have time to slip into the library and avail herself to Lionel's well-supplied liquor cabinet. Uncle Lemiel had not rung the evening bell and after selecting a broach and a pair of earrings with gold pendants, she tiptoed down the steps and into the library.

The library lamps had already been lighted and a fire crackled in the grate. Opening the rosewood liquor cabinet, she found that Uncle Lemiel, long familiar with his master's custom of bourbon before dinner, had already laid out the necessary ingredients: fresh mint from the spring, a bowl of sugar, and water. The old gentleman had even cooled the glasses with ice cut from the pond that winter and stored in the underground icehouse.

She took a glass and crystal decanter of the liquid and moved to the settee where she poured herself a generous quantity and placed the container on a marble-topped table beside her. Tonight she felt the need of more fortification than usual and filled the glass half full.

She sipped the bourbon, undiluted, just as she did each evening in the solitude of her bedroom. At first she had hated the taste of liquor, but in time she had come to enjoy the burning bite of the hot liquid as it stung her throat. As the comforting warmth spread through her body, she waited for her anxiety to subside, gazing into the half-consumed glass. She took another deep drink and sank back into the curve of the settee, closing her eyes as the bourbon-generated warmth suffused her body, bringing with it the serenity she sought.

The toll of the evening bell startled her to her feet. She hurried to the door and opened it to the sound of footsteps. Closing the door, she rushed for one final inspection of her appearance in the mirror above the fireplace. The bourbon had brought a pink glow to her cheeks but because she did not feel sufficiently calmed, she returned to her glass and hurriedly drained the last of its contents.

Drawing herself erect, she inhaled deeply and reminded herself to hold her breath lest it betray her secret indulgence. Then she remembered her glass, snatched it up, and rushed to the liquor cabinet to replace it as the door opened to reveal Lionel.

"May I prepare you a julep, Mr. Hawthorn?" she asked quickly, swirling toward him with the glass still in her hand, her voice almost too musical in its friendliness. If Lionel suspected that her invitation was to cover being caught red-handed, he seemed not to notice.

"Indeed, Mrs. Hawthorn," he said entering the room.

She was about to comply, when she realized the decanter was across the room on the marble-topped table where she had just served herself. Smoothly, she sailed to retrieve it, catching the glimpse of Lionel's faint smile. His insight made her furious, and immediately the self-protective barrier which governed communication with him returned.

It was enough that their meeting in the presence of others was marked by the formality and artificiality of a staged peaceful interchange between enemies. But even encounters when they were alone, although icily courteous, seemed to Lavinia to be secret battles, unacknowledged contests, masking some more significant negotiation concealed beneath their formal civility.

He had caught her drinking and she silently cursed herself for carelessly allowing her hypocrisy to be exposed, even as he chose to ignore it by his maddening adherence to gentlemanly behavior.

For years she had successfully hidden her drinking, allowing Uncle Lemiel's occasional secret imbibing to cover her theft of Lionel's bourbon.

"And will you join me, Mrs. Hawthorn?" he asked smoothly. His voice revealed nothing, but the twinkle of his blue eyes and knowing half-smile made her seethe.

Lavinia wondered if this uncouth offer was but a careless lapse reflecting the social conventions he employed when in the company of the common women with whom he consorted.

"Hard liquor for a lady, Mr. Hawthorn?" she said. "You surprise me."

"My apologies, Mrs. Hawthorn," he said with a contrite bow of his head, and added smoothly, "Force of habit."

Surprised at his admission, she handed him the decanter. "But indeed, I shall."

Startled by her response, his surprise pleased Lavinia, and her acceptance appeared to disarm his cynicism. She welcomed the calming of an additional drink, and it would explain her breath. After all, he had only seen the evidence after the fact, not the act of her actually drinking.

"Uncle Lemiel seems to have been at my bourbon again," he said, and Lavinia felt ashamed that by her silence she allowed to remain unchallenged his belief that the old servant alone consumed his liquor.

"I'd get a less expensive brand for him, but I'm afraid his tastes have grown far too refined for anything but the best."

Lavinia sheepishly dismissed her guilt with the knowledge that Uncle Lemiel, scapegoat for her though he was, would be neither corrected nor criticized by his master, who found the old gentleman's secret nipping amusing and harmless.

He had dressed formally for dinner in his black waistcoat and trousers, ruffled shirt, and polished black boots and—rare for him unless guests were present—a neatly tied cravat. She was glad she had matched him in the care he exhibited and had worn both a broach and the more ornate pendant earrings.

"You look lovely, Mrs. Hawthorn," he said as he prepared the drinks, hers with sugar and water and mint, his own undiluted and with only ice.

She nodded her acceptance of his compliment as he looked her up and down with appreciation.

"It will be such a pleasure to see you out of mourning. Do you not think that nearly two years is enough?"

"You know that I shall never stop mourning, Mr. Hawthorn."

"Nor shall I, madam. But perhaps there comes a time when one's sorrow need not be worn as a banner. I remember you wore colors so well—almost any color. There was none you could not make your own. Why not take a trip to Richmond and order some new dresses? I remember that violet and green striped silk was a particular favorite of mine—and the yellow frilly one, which fell around your lovely figure in tiers."

Lavinia laughed. How little he knew of fashion and what was appropriate for a woman her age. His taste reflected that of his paramours, the common women he found in saloons and touring stage companies. She remembered the fleeting glimpse she once caught of one of his mistresses, Mrs. Flyndell, at a ball in Richmond, and how inappropriate she had found the vulgar, girlish ball gown the woman, clearly in her late thirties, had worn.

"I am flattered you remember, Mr. Hawthorn, but those were the clothes of a young woman and most unsuitable for one as old as I. I'm afraid that at my age I shall not be able to get away with ruffles and pastels and—"

"What foolishness. Your age, indeed. I see women far older than you dressed in bright colors." Lavinia repressed the desire to say, "In a brothel?" She chose not to reopen the path to bitter quarrels like so many in the past. She knew that her own three years of celibacy had not been reciprocated by her husband, but marching into old battlefields would do her mission no good now.

He smiled at her with genuine warmth and placed the glass in her hand. She returned his smile and they looked at each other for a long time without speaking, openly appraising each other as they had not done in years, with no sign of hostility or defensiveness.

"And now, Mrs. Hawthorn," he said, "let us drink to the safe arrival and good health of our first grandchild."

At once, the walls that had separated them so long began to crumble as his secret news was at last revealed.

"Oh, Lionel!" She was unconscious that she had addressed him by his first name for the first time in three years. She was so happily surprised that her first impulse was to embrace him, but she remembered herself and retreated behind a more reserved facade. "What wonderful news. Tell me everything."

He directed her to the settee, where they sat down before the fire. "I have never seen an expectant father so proud," he said, his own pride as great as his son's. "He struts like a peacock and will accept no possibility that the baby will be anything but a boy. He tells everybody. And he has named and renamed the child a dozen times. We had many laughs in his attempts to find the masculine equivalent of Lavinia."

"I'm flattered—but I can wait for a granddaughter. And Sarah?"

"Scared to death, and terribly afraid Randy will be disappointed if it is a girl—which he won't, of course. She's quite puzzled by her husband's behavior and Randy constantly embarrasses her by mentioning it to everybody he meets. She spends the day going from one blush to another. She is so modest that she vows to even stop going to church if he doesn't stop treating her like an exhibit."

"Poor, sweet Sarah. He should be ashamed. Ever since childhood he has managed to tease her one way or the other."

"To Randolph and Sarah," he said.

Facing each other, they brought the rims of their glasses into brief contact.

"And our first grandchild."

As they drank their eyes again engaged. For a moment she suspended her hardness and looked deeply into them. The eyes with the same intense indigo, reflecting the library lamps and a light entirely their own. Once his eyes had beguiled her and even now threatened to bring her again under their spell. Sensing danger, she tore away from his gaze and looked into the fire.

"I must visit at once. Do you think I could go next week?"

"I have to return to Richmond tomorrow. Papa's law office and the tobacco factory are overwhelmed with work, and his health allows him to only work a few hours a day."

Lavinia's expression turned grave. "I do hope everything turns out well. That the baby will be...alright."

"You mean because Randy and Sarah are cousins? I've told you a dozen times that in good stock that has relatively little to do with progeny. I have several ancestors who were cousins, and your own grandmother was distantly related to your grandfather."

Lavinia and Lionel's son had married his first cousin, the daughter of Lionel's sister, over the muted concerns of Lavinia, who thought the closeness of blood portended weakened offspring.

"We can only hope and pray all will be well," she said. "To think, little Randy having a child of his own. And for so long it was doubtful he would survive his first year."

They drank in silence and looked into the fire as they remembered their first son's sickly early months of life, when his frailty seemed to warn of uncertain survival, until his second year when he began to thrive and eventually amazed them all, and by adulthood equaled his father in strength and stature and good health.

Warmed by the fire and alcohol, something of the old cordiality that had marked their relationship prior to separation returned. To her surprise, she found they were talking as they had long ago, easily and without guarded defenses and the wariness and coldness that had so long attended their conversation.

They talked of things unmentioned in years—old stories of their son's childhood, memories of family, friends, the plantation, and servants. They even laughed, and a stranger chancing upon them would have thought they were long-separated friends catching up on old times. Like an uncorked bottle turned upside down, the words and anecdotes rushed from them and by the time they had a second drink and Uncle Lemiel, formally attired in his butler's livery, appeared to announce supper, the night was fully upon them.

"Uncle Lemiel, have a toast with us," Lionel suggested, preparing the old man he regarded as a second father a generous drink.

"Don't know, Master Lionel." The old man shook his head doubtfully. "Beck mighty down on it."

"Aunt Beck doesn't have to know," Lionel said, and it was enough to entice the old man into sharing their celebration. And Lavinia to have another.

"But Mr. Hawthorn, I'll get tipsy," she protested, a delicate hand laid across her breast as if with temperate uncertainty. But she accepted the glass nevertheless, every bit as readily as Uncle Lemiel accepted his. The old man beamed to see his master and mistress on such good terms, so rare in the household in recent years.

"Randy insists that the baby be born here, Uncle Lemiel," Lionel continued. "With Aunt Beck and Mammy Emma and Old Sheba all telling Dr. Hunter just how to do it. He doesn't trust the doctors where he is, or any in Richmond."

"Beck and Emma and Sheba bring many a one, sir. Reckon they be right good at it by now. I remember when they bring you, Master. Beck still say you the loudest she ever bring—and Emma say you the prettiest. And Old Sheba buries the cord in the yard and tells your fortune and say you likely make a preacher—"

Before she could remember to censor herself, Lavinia laughed at the absurd prediction. To her relief, Lionel joined her.

"Don't laugh, Mrs. Hawthorn. I may take the cloth in my old age."

"I'm sure," she said with only the slightest touch of sarcasm. She wanted to add, "The only cloth you'll ever touch is a woman's skirts."

In the dining room, Emma and Piney served the elaborate meal created by Aunt Beck. All of Lavinia's favorite dishes were in evidence—candied yams, Virginia ham, corn pudding—as well as those of Lionel's—stuffed peppers, turnips, and the special carrot-pepper-and-onion concoction only Beck could create to his satisfaction.

As usual, when there was something to celebrate, the meal became a feast. To even sample small portions of everything—ham, chicken, beef, and half a dozen vegetables—would have filled a dinner plate two or three times.

Both Emma and Piney wore their formal black dresses, usually reserved for company, and fresh, stiffly starched aprons and ruffled caps, and Emma sported around her neck the red silk kerchief Lionel had brought her that morning.

After effusive compliments, Lavinia protested, "Emma, tell Aunt Beck I'll look like Agnes Thornton or old Judge Goode if I eat all this." She cited two friends whose obesity was known to them. "But it's a wonderful dinner. Someday we'll tell that grandchild what a wonderful meal we had to celebrate the news of his coming."

"Or hers," Lionel corrected. "Since Randy is so determined it will be a son, I think I shall put my odds on a girl. Ah, but I almost forgot the wine."

He sprang to his feet and went to the sideboard where, as he had instructed, the white wine cooled in ice and the red was maintained at room temperature. He opened the red and poured for himself and Lavinia.

"Oh, Lionel...I'm not sure—"

"Nonsense, my dear. This is a once-in-a-lifetime occasion. We must celebrate to the fullest. Isn't that right, Mammy?"

"This a special day, alright. Happiest I see this house in a long time."

Neither Lionel nor Lavinia missed Emma's insight and for a time they ate in silence as the old woman, watching every move they made, occasionally signaled Piney with a nod of her head or softly spoken order, "butter," or "rolls," to which Piney sprang into action and served.

The happiness at seeing her mistress and master so congenial was radiated in Emma's face as the old woman circled the table like a hawk, quickly filling any empty area of their plates.

"I plowed almost all of the field down by the swamp this afternoon, Mammy," Lionel said. "Clevis said he saw snakes down there, so I thought I'd just do it for him."

"About the only snake I knows is that Clevis for gettin' you to do his plowin' for him," Emma said. The old woman's movements revealed her feebleness as she limped around the table, steadying herself by occasionally holding to the back of an empty chair.

"Mammy, you should have gotten Angelica to help you," Lionel suggested. "And where is she? I haven't seen her since I got back."

Emma quickly looked at Lavinia, who returned her glance and coolly dabbed her mouth with her napkin.

"I sent Angelica over to the Barksdales earlier today. I heard in church that old Mrs. Barksdale had another stroke and with only Miss Maude and Miss Phoebe to take care of her, I thought the least we could do would be to lend a hand. The old ladies have had to nurse her day and night—"

"Pity neither of them ever married," Lionel said. As he reviewed the history of the spinster sisters' unmarried state, Emma and Lavinia exchanged faint smiles of relief. He suspected nothing, and perhaps would know nothing of Angelica's absence for days since he was returning to Richmond the next morning.

"Now, Mammy, we've got everything we need right here. You go on off to the kitchen and rest yourself. And you too, Piney. We'll just wait on ourselves and ring if we need anything."

When they were gone, Lionel's mood became somber and the lines in his brow deepened with concern. "I notice Mammy's getting more feeble by the day," he said.

"I've tried for months to persuade her to move from the attic to the first floor," Lavinia said. "But she refuses. She's giving Piney some of the duties but I'm afraid she's quite insulted when I suggest she ease up a bit."

"Mammy can't seem to realize she can still rule the roost from a rocking chair," Lionel said. "She's been in charge so long, how can any of us stop obeying her now?"

"My efforts to move her downstairs are stubbornly resisted. Perhaps she would do it for you."

"I'll mention it in the morning," he said, and the pleasant chatter resumed.

They both ate heartily and between them finished both bottles of wine. Although Lavinia's unsophisticated palate found the wine no better or worse than any other her husband had bought in the past, Lionel judged both vintages exceptional and worthy of the celebration. By the time she had consumed a second glass, she was quite intoxicated and aware her speech had thickened. Lionel revealed nothing, but she knew he noted her every slurred word.

The meal concluded with Lionel's favorite dessert—pound cake and boiled custard—and he insisted Aunt Beck, beaming with pride, be sent to the dining room for them to praise and thank personally for the superb dinner.

As they rose from the table and the servants began to clear the dishes, Lionel suggested brandy in the library. Lavinia agreed, and as they sat before the fire, Lavinia thought of a way to introduce her scheme.

"I think Angelica could easily assume more household responsibilities and give Emma a rest," she said. "And I'm sure I could easily find another girl as a maid—"

"Do you still insist on sending Angelica to Richmond?" he asked.

"Indeed. I am so tired of her tears and moping about over that Gabriel. I'm sending her next week. I've already purchased the train passes and instructed the station master that she would be traveling with Uncle Lemiel." She felt comfort at how easily these deceptive words flowed from her lips. Already the source of train passes had been explained, and she had only told the station master that "another servant" would accompany Angelica, with no specific designation or description of who that would be.

"She'll forget that Gabriel soon enough after a stay in Richmond," she said.

"One doesn't forget one's first love so easily, Mrs. Hawthorn. And what of 'absence makes the heart grow fonder'?"

"'Romantic hogwash.' Isn't that what you used to say?"

"And so I did. But perhaps only because you labeled me a cynic and I was trying to fit the mold you made for me.

Maybe I have become a romantic and shed my cynicism. Perhaps I even believe that, indeed, absence does make the heart grow fonder..."

He moved closer to her and took her hand, which she allowed him to hold. She suspected he was performing for her, but when his voice suddenly changed and became almost a whisper, she became confused.

"Perhaps I have found out that one cannot forget one's first love. Even after three years of separation."

His directness flustered her. She had not anticipated his taking this path and was unwilling to take it with him. Her composure shaken, she nevertheless tried to conceal the ripple of excitement his words stirred within her. "Are you making love to me, Mr. Hawthorn?"

"Indeed I am."

"Then I implore you to stop."

"But you are my wife, and it is within my rights as your husband to make love to you."

"But a husband can have only one wife, Mr. Hawthorn. Not two or three—" She stopped short. Their dialogue was veering dangerously near the precipice over which lurked the threat of a quarrel over old infidelities. A fight now would only jeopardize her bid for Henny. She covered his hand with her own and smiled at him, using his ardor for her own objective.

"Later, Mr. Hawthorn," she said softly with a hint of promise. "But at the moment, we are discussing Mammy and how we can coax her into retirement. With persuasion, I think she might allow Angelica to be eased into her position. But we must first deal with Angelica's affairs of the heart." She lowered her eyes modestly. "Others will have to wait."

Lionel chuckled. She did not know if he knew she was manipulating him, but with her mission back on course, she continued. "I think some distance between Angelica and Gabriel will eventually cool their ardor. The girl is so love sick I am afraid that to continue to have her here will...that she...they..."

Lionel threw back his head and laughed heartily.

"You're afraid they'll sleep together! How like my Lavinia to protect her maid's virginity and the purity of black and white alike far and wide."

He had always laughed at her Puritanism, but she did not care, as his attention had been successfully redirected.

"Against my best council, they still meet secretly down at the fence line. Piney spies on them and reports everything to Emma. There is...physical expression...in their affection—only embraces and kissing so far, but it is potentially dangerous."

Lionel continued to laugh and released her hand to slap his thigh heartily.

Lavinia, ignoring his laughter, continued, "I'm sure this is very amusing to you, but Angelica is of real concern to me."

"Forgive me," Lionel said, his laughter subsiding. "I suppose another offer to Wroughton would be useless."

"That dreadful man opposes us solely out of stubbornness. You've already offered him a fortune. He just doesn't want us to have him."

"He's a stubborn man alright, and a hard one." Lionel sipped his brandy and looked thoughtfully into his glass.

"I can take over for Emma until Angelica returns from Richmond, and get a new maid for myself."

"Piney?"

"No. I think she belongs in the kitchen. She's shifty and deceitful—and a tale-carrier. I have in mind a new girl to replace Angelica," she said cautiously.

"One of ours? Mother could always find someone in Richmond, or loan you her Ibby until you found someone to your liking."

"Oh, but I think I might have found one of our own people who would do. A little girl from the quarters—"

"The quarters?"

"Yes—"

"The quarters can hardly provide you with anyone suitable, even to train."

"Oh, but I think perhaps this girl might do. I can instruct her myself."

"Very well," Lionel said, as if to conclude the subject. But then he looked at her and narrowed his eyes. "Do I know this girl?"

"I'm—I'm not sure. Of course you must have seen her. She's about nine- or ten-years-old, rather tall for her age, thin." She tried to be casual, knowing he was watching her, and hoped her awkwardness was not apparent to him.

"And what is her name? Who does she belong to?" he asked easily, and she knew from the smoothness of his words that he knew, or suspected, who it was.

"She's called Henny—for Henrietta, I believe. She's quite sweet and intelligent and I'm sure she will be easily trained."

"Why this particular girl?"

"Oh, I—I don't know. I've observed her for some time, from a distance. In the wash house, and last fall, at hog-killing time. She seemed so industrious and helpful to Aunt Beck—"

Not to look at him would certainly appear evasive, and she turned to face him as his eyes stared into hers and seemed to ferret out all she was trying to conceal. He said nothing but continued to watch her until finally she knew she would have to break his gaze.

"Give her to me, Lionel," she said at length.

"You know her parentage?"

"I am unconcerned with her parentage."

"Perhaps it matters to me." His voice was cold and hollow.

"Oh?"

"Why not another girl? One of Clevis and Nancy's?"

"I considered their Martha," she lied, "but she's too much like that Piney—impudent and surly—and Nancy's other girls are too young. I'm sure you would agree with me that Henny is perfect. If you knew her—"

"I know the girl of whom you speak."

"You have seen her?"

"Many times."

"And?"

"And what?"

"And have you not seen her eyes?" She waited for him to answer but he looked at her blankly. She knew they were at an impasse and she pressed him again, a suggestion of urgency in her voice. "Have you not seen her eyes!"

His voice lost some of its coldness. "I have seen them."

Perhaps, thought Lavinia, *he too had noticed, and was remembering, Henny's startling resemblance to Oralee.*

"And?" Lavinia asked and waited.

His cold, defensiveness returned. "And what?"

"You must have seen how much she looks like Oralee!" she blurted. "Her eyes, the shape of her face—all so like Oralee." She looked at him imploringly. "And...and like you."

She had said it. Without judgment or censure, but she had said it. At last the truth was before them.

Lionel's face remained resolute for a long moment and then his features softened into weariness. Dogged resignation replaced some of his hardness. "What do you want, Lavinia?" he asked in a listless voice.

"The child. Henny. I want her."

Although he continued to look at her, it was if she were not there and he stared beyond her. She tried to read his face, but saw only despair. Unable to penetrate his inscrutable gaze, she bent close to him and lowered her voice to an imploring whisper.

"And have you not seen in her our sweet Oralee?"

His remoteness vanished and he snapped back in full anger. She saw outrage flash in his eyes as the lamplight flickered across his furrowed brow, and the contours of his cheeks and jaw tightened, making him appear sinister and cruel.

"And her skin? The nappy hair? Does that remind you of Oralee, too? Do you think it proper to compare our child to a...a...mulatto?"

"Do you know half the blacks in the South have white ancestry? Even your illustrious cousin, Mr. Jefferson, is said to—"

"That charge was the creation of political enemies and never proven!"

"Were there no red-headed, freckled-faced offspring romping the grounds of Monticello with which to compare the great man? Perhaps these attributes are not as striking as blue eyes—"

"Enough! You don't know what you're talking about."

"But she's yours!" she pleaded. "She's yours and she's just a little girl and it doesn't matter who she is. That can't be changed—"

"Is this some Christian maneuver you have devised to stir my conscience? Is it your intention to display 'my sin' before me so that you might further martyr and ennoble yourself?"

"No, no! I just want this child. I—need her."

"Well, you can't have her. She stays where she is."

"But she's yours!" she shouted. "She is your own child. Just as much as Oralee was yours." She would not have been surprised if he struck her, but she didn't care. Her anger flared at his callous disregard for his own blood. That he could allow his own child to grow up no better than a field hand infuriated her.

"Skin color and hair texture didn't matter when you slept with her mother, did it?" she said, a twisted half smile on her face. She waited for the full avalanche of his wrath to fall upon her. Instead, his temper faded. The change in his voice frightened her more than his anger, as he became unnaturally calm and earnest.

"You're such a fool, Lavinia. You're letting your jealousy and spite kill our marriage little by little. Now you've dug up an indiscretion that ended ten years ago and want to crucify me."

"No. No. I don't care about that! I don't care about your sleeping with her mother. It happened so long ago. It doesn't matter who her mother was, or her color...or... None of that can be changed. All I know is that when she came to see me this morning, she was wearing an old dress of Oralee's, and for one precious moment I had my child back again. When I was with her, I was...happy again and...and I was even glad she was yours...and..."

Against her will she began to cry. She hated herself for losing control. If only she hadn't drunk the liquor. Liquor always heightened her emotions and weakened her self-possession. Her temper, her feelings for him, her sorrow, all seemed to intensify beyond her capacity to rein them within her control. Her shoulders quaked as deep sobs poured from her, honest grief released at last without any attempt at restraint.

Instinctively, Lionel reached for her and drew her into his arms and held her close as she buried her head against his chest and wept for the loss of her long dead daughter and her long dead marriage.

"Oh, Vinny, Vinny," he whispered into her ear. "Why do you continue to shut me out when I love you so?"

He placed his hand under her chin and raised her face to his own. She saw in his eyes pain and longing. She tried to shut him out by closing her eyes and made an attempt to twist away from him, but he bent nearer and she felt his hungry lips on her mouth. Resisting at first, she struggled in his arms but he held her tightly to him. As his kiss deepened, she felt her resistance faltering as her mouth and arms and body yearned to respond to his embrace.

It was as if she was caught in a whirlpool—the liquor, the passion laid dormant and unexpressed for years once again surging to the surface, the desire for him she had vowed she would never surrender to again, seizing hold of her.

"I'm not one of your whores," she heard herself protest thickly.

"You're my wife!" he hissed, and he returned to the hungry exploration of her mouth.

"I'm not Fanny Shelton!" she cried, naming the Richmond seamstress, once his mistress.

"You're my wife!" he hissed.

"Or that Bessie...Bessie Reynolds," an attractive widow from Manchester with whom he dallied.

"You're my wife, and I love you."

Their breaths both came in rapid gulps, making it difficult to speak.

"Or that...that other one..."

"Can't remember their names? Neither can I. Or the dozens of others. But I remember yours. Lavinia. Lavinia, Lavinia—and I love you and want you."

"That...saloon girl...and...that vulgar Flagon woman—"

His large, strong hands urgently fumbled with her skirts as his breathing quickened.

She suddenly grew weak as her resistance further failed her. She felt faint and closed her eyes as she seemed to be drawn into a spinning, dark pool of blackness. Why had she ever allowed him to come near her? How could she have been such a fool to let herself be so manipulated by liquor and wine and brandy and feelings she thought she had long subjugated into oblivion? Why had she so foolishly abandoned wearing a corset? She heard herself laugh aloud as she thought of how useless the protection of that garment would be against him—or herself.

She felt his hands fumbling with the pins in her hair, the last bastion of her defenses. He lifted her up, his hands working fast and expertly, removing her combs and hair pins one by one. The neat roll of her hair fell free about her shoulders and he burrowed his face in its thickness and murmured her name over and over again.

Why was her voice mute? Why didn't she say no now? Why didn't she stop him? He would stop—he might stop—he would not take her against her will. Why didn't she cry out?

The only sounds were their desperate breathing, the murmur of his voice repeating her name over and over again, the rustle of taffeta falling away from her under the urgency of his quickly moving hands, and finally the unrestrained cry of a distant voice she recognized as her own as the three-year battle they had fought so passionately had at last been lost. And won.

Chapter Seven

When Lavinia awoke the next morning, she did not know where she was. A brilliant light blinded her when she tried to open her eyes, causing her to moan in pain at its searing brightness. Her head throbbed with each beat of her pulse, and as she struggled to an upright position, she was assaulted by a wave of nausea.

As the room seemed to spin around her, she shaded her eyes with her hand and realized that she was in Lionel's bed in the downstairs office-bedroom. Shocked to find herself totally naked, she reached for the tangled sheets and quilts piled carelessly on the floor beside the bed, but they were too far from the bed for her to grasp.

A gigantic moose head, mounted high on the wall across the room, looked down at her in astonished, wide-eyed condemnation, like some stern preacher from a pulpit.

Laboriously, with every muscle paining her, she managed to turn her body and extend her reach to clasp the corner of a sheet and pull it over her. Her gesture of modesty seemed to make no impression on the moose, whose shining glass eyes continued to glare at her with outraged, judgmental contempt. As she finally managed to sit up, the stench of tobacco, dogs, and rancid, uncured animal pelts increased her nausea. She fell back against the pillows, put her arm over her eyes, and drew her aching body into a ball.

She tried to shake off her mind-numbing stupor, but her eyes found difficulty focusing and her thoughts seemed as if in a fog. She wondered if she was still drunk, and was overwhelmed by guilt for her overindulgence the night before. Gradually, fragments of the night before began to filter into her consciousness. She gasped in horror as she remembered the sordid details. As if viewing the actions of a stranger, her own behavior became clear and her mouth fell open with shock as she recalled the animal passion that had led to her resistance crumbling into submission and her submission into acquiescence, leading to her ultimate active participation.

She emitted a little whimper of horror as she remembered where it had happened—in the library! And it had happened twice! And, to her abject humiliation, the second time on the floor! She covered her face with her hands and whimpered with shame.

"I have behaved like one of his whores," she said. In imagining the behavior of prostitutes, Lavinia assumed such women's sexual behavior was wild, gymnastic, and with animal-like abandon.

As she moaned in mortification, she vaguely recalled Lionel's carrying her to bed and cradling her in his arms most of the night, as she alternately sobbed and slept and drifted in the haze of alcohol and spent passion. All the while he had held her and stroked her hair and whispered comforting endearments in her ear.

She wondered where he was now. She hoped he had already left for Richmond, and wondered how she would ever face him again. She could picture his smiling, taunting face, gloating at his conquest and thinking that the events of the evening before once again opened her bedroom door to him. And for all the humiliation she had endured, it had been for nothing; Henny's fate was still unresolved. She covered her face with her hands as she realized Lionel had won the war and all the spoils as well.

She knew from the angle of the sun pouring through the window that it was mid-morning and the household, up for hours, were wondering at her absence. Slowly and with great effort, she slid her legs over the edge of the bed, modestly trying to conceal her nakedness with the sheet. Holding onto the bed post, she pulled herself to her feet. Overcome by dizziness, she quickly lay back until her equilibrium was restored. Then, looking about the room for her clothing, she saw her dress tossed carelessly over the unmounted rack of deer antlers. A single stocking hung from a bed post. But there was no sight of the rest of her clothes — her pantalets, petticoats, shoes, and the other stocking. She searched the bed clothes, shook her dress, and even got on her hands and knees and looked under the furniture without success.

She caught sight of her refection in Lionel's washstand mirror and gasped in shock at the hag who looked back at her, gaped-mouthed and wild-eyed, the face bloated and a decade older than her own. Her eyes were blood-shot, and her hair hung about her shoulders in unruly, twisted tangles. She turned away from her image with revulsion. Another wave of shame washed over her when she realized her missing clothing must still be in the library.

Horrified that the servants would find the incriminating garments, she quickly gathered up her dress and the stocking and, covering herself with the sheet, cracked the door to the hall.

Emma's voice, with its usual booming authority, reached her ears. "Don't you lay nary a hand on nothin' in that room."

Piney's snickering followed. "But Miss Vinny be wantin' her underdrawers and stocking and things," she said. "And her shoes and earrings and everything in there, all on the floor and ever where—"

Lavinia closed her eyes with dread. With Piney privy to the event, it would be common knowledge in the quarters by noon. And no doubt spread from there to the neighbors and become known all over the county in a week. Such was the speed and efficiency of the black grapevine that linked one plantation to another.

Uncle Lemiel's chuckle came next. "Reckon it be warm in there when she do get up. Done left a good load of kindlin'. You thinks I ought to get some hands to move Master Lionel's bedroom back upstairs, Em'?"

Lavinia's face burned at Emma's chuckle and Piney's giggling as they returned to the kitchen.

When they were gone, Lavinia drew the sheet around her and staggered to the library. Her missing stocking lay between the settee and the hearth, along with her shoes and petticoats. And halfway across the room, her pantalets were draped obscenely from a marble-topped table—a banner to her shame.

Feeling her face flush again, she snatched up the evidence of her debauchery and rushed out of the library, almost colliding with Lionel in the hall.

"Good morning, Mrs. Hawthorn," he said, beaming before her, fully dressed and revealing no sign of his overindulgence in their torrid night of drink and pleasure. How could he possibly look so fresh when she had only a moment before seen her own swollen, red-eyed image?

"I've just talked to Mammy. She's agreed to move downstairs."

Lavinia, feeling like a fool, could only stare at him. She shut her eyes and tried to banish the image she had of herself—barefooted, naked except for a sheet, clutching her shoes and clothes, her face bloated, her hair as wild and unkempt as a mule's tail.

Suddenly another voice, shrill and excited, drew her attention to the back of the hall as Piney ran in from the pantry screeching.

"Master Hawthorn! Master Hawthorn! They slave patrols out back!" she shrieked. "They a whole passel of Wroughton blacks done run off last night. Bingo and Jane and that big Gabriel what wants to marry Angelica! They done gone! Run clean off!"

Lavinia backed against the stair banister as if to hide herself, but Piney was too excited by her urgent message to notice her mistress.

"Slave patrols say they runs off for certain and wantin' to know if Angelica run too! They thinks that Gabriel and her has it made up to run together! Done it last night!" Piney shrieked.

Lavinia felt herself grow weak and sank to the steps as Piney's panicked yelling continued.

"I can't find Angelica nowhere! She done run—or ain't back from the Barksdales yet!"

With a gasp of shocked breath, Lavinia struggled to her feet and backed farther up the stairs, as if to escape the terrible news she was hearing.

Angelica and Gabriel's flight had already been discovered.

Chapter Eight

⊷⟾⟾⊷

Lavinia Hawthorn's awakening to physical passion after three years of celibacy disarmed the weapon she had used to punish Lionel for his numerous infidelities. By withholding her wifely favors, she believed she not only punished her husband, but raised her own sanctity above that of the sordid women who had abandoned all decency in the pursuit of lust and sin.

But now she felt she had behaved no better than the wanton women she had so harshly judged—and to whom she thought her own virtue superior. Lionel's adulteries had made her embrace all the more the narrow, sin-choked doctrine of her parents, which proclaimed desires of the flesh wrong and only tolerated by God as necessity for procreation within a deity-blessed marriage. Lavinia's attitude was not atypical of women in the nineteenth century and found its origins in her upbringing in her home in southwestern Virginia.

Her father, John Williamson, was born of a pioneer family that had migrated to the Cumberland Mountains in the company of Daniel Boone and other intrepid adventurers prior to the American Revolution. These pioneers paved the way for other settlers who peopled the area from the Carolinas and Virginia along with the more massive migration of Scotch-Irish settlers moving down the Shenandoah Valley of Virginia from Pennsylvania and Maryland where they established the first white settlements in the mountains of Virginia, Kentucky, Tennessee, and western Carolina.

Bringing with his pioneering spirit an Oliver-Cromwell piety and religious conservatism sometimes at variance with his less temperate neighbors, John Williamson's family religion mandated adherence to the strictest code of morality as laid down by the most narrow interpretation of the King James Bible. Only through his wife's more moderate Methodist-Episcopal religion was Lavinia's father's fanatical conservatism mollified. Yet the Williamson household remained strict and exacting with regard to religious doctrine. Being the only daughter in a household that would eventually include nine sons, Lavinia was all the more sheltered and carefully instructed in the proper attitude and conduct appropriate to young Christian women of the day.

But demure and quietly reflective Lavinia was not, in spite of her parents' good intentions. It would only be later in life that she would adopt the stringent religious teaching of her youth. When younger, a natural restlessness directed the spirited Lavinia toward less restrictive rules of conduct, and she learned early how to use her unfailing charm to manipulate her doting father into a permissiveness resulting in behavior he soon came not to see at all in his only daughter and only recognized in his sons.

By the time she was fifteen-years-old, Lavinia's free-spiritedness had become the despair of her mother, who saw her daughter too quickly abandon her early efforts in the instruction of ladylike behavior. Lavinia did not sit in a chair, she flopped into it; Lavinia did not gracefully float down the stairs, she galloped down them two at a time; Lavinia did not ride side-saddle like a lady, she rode astride. Receiving little support from her husband in her efforts to correct Lavinia's deficiencies, Rebecca Williamson watched helplessly as her daughter became too much like her brothers, too much like her horses, and too much like her mountain neighbors.

These independent, free-spirited individuals had for generations resisted restriction, religious, political, or any other, often to a degree beyond the most individualistic colonists. Those embracing the isolation of the rugged mountains sought an independence sometimes characterized as untamed, unruly, and undisciplined. They had not easily forgotten the old world restrictions and repressions they had so recently come to a new land to escape. The refined deportment of English parlors was not a priority in these mountain households. It was hardly a consideration at all, and Rebecca Williamson saw her fifteen-year-old daughter, Lavinia, drifting more into the direction of mountaineer laxness and nonconformity and becoming less the refined daughter of a genteel, third-generation English heritage that had been Rebecca's.

Born of a well-connected Virginia family from Hanover County, Rebecca Williamson's background was Tidewater Virginia. A demure, self-possessed woman of quiet strength and sweet-faced plainness, she had married John Williamson after he had fought in the War of 1812 and lingered in eastern Virginia after the war. But the tall, raw-boned fundamentalist's conservatism guided his actions and, disgusted with slavery and vowing to have nothing to do with it, he returned with his new bride to the relatively slave-free mountains of Washington County.

Armed with a land grant for six hundred acres rewarded for his war service, John Williamson was determined to be as successful with hired labor as he could with slaves, and dedicated his life to proving it. By the time his family had grown to nine sons and a daughter, his acreage had increased and he was, in both land and the new American currency—dollars—a rich man. He had, through hard work and careful management, proven his anti-slave philosophy and remained a firm abolitionist, echoing the ideology of William Lloyd Garrison, John Quincy Adams, and others who opposed slavery.

Although Rebecca Williamson was happy with John Williamson and her new life in the wild and remote reaches of southwestern Virginia, she grieved that her only daughter was becoming too much a daughter of the mountains. That her brusque and hearty sons had only the superficial fundamentals of refinement might be permissible, but such a deficiency in a daughter was a serious matter.

In 1830, when these observations and concerns were being made about the fifteen-year-old Lavinia, Washington County was still pioneer country and miles from the more refined Virginia that characterized the youth of her mother.

Just two or three decades after the last Indian raids, it was only now that the fields could be cultivated more than running distance from the protection of a fort, or that migrations of new homesteaders felt safe enough to risk permanent settlement in this savage but bountiful part of Virginia.

Adventurous souls, including Lavinia's Grandfather Williamson, opened the way for others to follow by challenging the Cherokee and Shawnee tribes who zealously protected the prized hunting grounds the white men invaded. But the toll had been heavy, and few of the early families settling in that part of Virginia did not have relatives who perished in Indian raids or from the ravages of disease and cruel winters and unrelenting labor in wresting out of the wilderness a civilized place to live.

With such struggles only a generation behind them, concerns for education, social amenities, and the proper instruction of young ladies in genteel refinements was not a high priority for most of the citizens of Washington County. That a man could write his name on a deed and know enough arithmetic to count his stock and measure his crops was deemed sufficient education by many. Women need not even have the burden of learning to sign their name. The mark of a crude X on a document would satisfy the legal requirements of any county clerk in Virginia and was deemed sufficient use of pen or quill for any female—or male.

But Rebecca Williamson disagreed and required more. Within the confines of her home, she painstakingly taught her sons to read and write. Because Lavinia was at hand during this mandatory schooling, she became literate as well, and equaled or exceeded the scholarly accomplishments of her brothers.

Her father, barely literate himself, indulged his wife's penchant, grudgingly proud of her desire to elevate his progeny, and offered no resistance to her instruction as long as the Bible remained the primary reading material and novels and other non-Biblical reading, unless it was an anti-slavery tract, were kept to a minimum.

The oldest of Rebecca Williamson's sons attended the College of William and Mary, others nearby Emory and Henry College, and with these successes behind her, the proper instruction of her only daughter as an acceptable wife and mother became Rebecca's major concern.

Shaped by the permissiveness of her early years, Lavinia rebelled too often against embracing those things necessary for the proper "finishing" of young females at the beginning of the nineteenth century. Cooking, sewing, gardening—any domestic art—she avoided in favor of her favorite pursuits: books and horses. She thought nothing of spending the entire day riding, and talked of little else but breeds and gear and equestrian skills. Her knowledge and ability was formidable, and she found herself a worthy consultant to the most experienced and clever horse traders. She was considered one of the best riders in the county, male or female, and more than one man had learned to create an excuse to avoid her challenge to race in the face of almost certain defeat and humiliation before his male contemporaries.

Only books could tear her away from the stables and her beloved mounts, and her father once proudly asserted she could shoe a horse with one hand and hold the book she was reading in the other. She had, indeed, been observed combining her passions when seen, book in hand, sauntering along on one of her favorite steeds.

While other girls relished gossip and giggling around the spinning wheel, loom, or churn, Lavinia found such activities resulted only in butter, homespun yarn, and unreliable speculation about local romances. Lavinia preferred a horseback ride or a good story between the covers of a book, not whispered rumors from the next farm.

That her daughter was adept at assisting at the foaling of a colt and mending bridles yet could not so much as make a pone of corn bread was a great concern to Rebecca, as was Lavinia's inappropriately riding a horse astride, and sometimes even wearing a pair of trousers, borrowed from one of her brothers, to do so.

Frustrated as to what to do, Rebecca had only to wait for the rebellious Lavinia herself, extending her restless, independent nature too far, to provide adequate reasons for a more critical appraisal of her development.

Her long-indulgent Grandmother Williamson noted it first. The tiny old lady, always dressed in black and never without a bonnet or cap to conceal the scars of having been scalped by marauding Indians and left for dead when she was a six-year-old child, said little but observed everything. As the barely five-foot matriarch sat quietly in her rocking chair, smoking her long-stemmed clay pipe, her sharp gray eyes missed nothing as she monitored her son, his wife, and her ever-increasing number of grandchildren.

A more objective observer of her granddaughter than anyone else in the family, the old lady finally spoke out—and when she spoke it was with irrefutable authority and there was no appeal from, or challenge to, her judgments.

"The girl," the old woman announced one evening after supper—she never referred to Lavinia by name, even though it was her own, but always "the girl"—"needs took down a notch or two."

After his mother's judgment, John Williamson became more sympathetic to his wife's concerns. When Lavinia herself provided reason for action, her father was fully prepared to prescribe stern measures. She was caught playing cards and smoking tobacco.

Devoted to her grandmother, so long her protection and refuge from any discipline, Lavinia defended the old lady's life-long habit of smoking a pipe. Regarded as socially unacceptable by Rebecca, the old woman nevertheless smoked with impunity, protected from more than muted criticism by her age and prominence in the Williamson dynasty. The use of tobacco—smoking, chewing, or dipping snuff—was just something many old ladies of the mountains did, with no regard to what more rigid codes of etiquette might mandate elsewhere in the Commonwealth.

So entrenched was Granny Williamson's smoking that most of her grandchildren learned to fill the old lady's clay pipe, an exacting art that required just the right amount of tobacco, packed to precisely the density the demanding old matriarch required. One draw from its long stem revealed whether the tobacco was packed too tightly or too loosely and failure either way, it was returned promptly to be done again.

"Pack ain't right," she would say, and she would thrust the pipe back for immediate correction.

Lavinia became an expert, meeting all of her granny's requirements, and in the process had learned to test her work by taking a trial puff or two. She came to enjoy the dizziness a single inhalation of the raw, unprocessed tobacco gave her and soon looked forward to the after-supper ritual her grandmother enjoyed daily.

When her father discovered her sharing a corncob pipe with her brothers in the stables while engaged in a game of loo, drastic measures ensued. When Lavinia revealed smoking was a daily indulgence and that she was a far better loo player than any of her brothers, her father took immediate action.

The loo cards were burned, her brothers whipped, and after consultation with Granny Williamson (resentful that her granddaughter should share smokes with anyone but her), it was decided that fifteen-year-old Lavinia would be sent to Miss Estelle Fraley's Academy for Young Ladies, in nearby Abingdon, Virginia.

Her protests unheeded by her father, and Granny Williamson having joined her parents in a solid front, it was useless for Lavinia to protest, and she finally agreed to a term at the school, drawn at least by the promise of a supply of books she had not read.

Rebecca hoped Miss Fraley's school could turn her daughter into a proper young lady prepared to take her place as a suitable wife and mother. The school offered courses in Latin, art, and music, and church attendance was mandatory. Further, there were no stables on the grounds.

Little did Lavinia know that her granny's old clay pipe would alter the course of her life forever.

As Rebecca Williamson found the solution to the problem of her daughter's unrestrained behavior in the mountains of Washington County, three hundred miles away in Richmond, Virginia, another concerned mother was wringing her hands and shedding bitter tears at the defiance of her daughter, Margaret Hawthorn, also fifteen years of age and in a state of open rebellion.

The tumult began one Sunday after services at St. Paul's, as the Hawthorns returned home in the family carriage. The pretty, round-faced Margaret surprised her family with a startling announcement.

"I have the most wonderful news," she said, her deep blue eyes sparkling with happiness and her red curls bouncing as the carriage jolted along toward the Hawthorn house on Clay Street.

"Tell us, dear," the aristocratic Mrs. Hawthorn said.

"I should only tell Papa, because he will be the one who has to give my hand."

"Oh," trilled Mrs. Hawthorn, her eyes dancing with expectation.

"A certain gentleman of my acquaintance has asked for my hand in marriage," Margaret said, smiling brightly. "And

I have accepted." Her plump, doll-like face glowed with the happiness of first love.

Her mother's expression, however, became a startling contrast. Cornelia Hawthorn's hauteur collapsed into stunned, fearful alarm. A gloved hand flew to her breast, and she turned in astonishment toward her husband.

"Whoever can this gentleman be? Is it Mr. Lee? Mr. Carter? The Byrd boy?" Cornelia asked.

"None of them," Margaret chimed happily, her dimples deepening with pleasure at the interest her unknown suitor's identity created.

"Then who? And how has this friendship progressed to such a...serious stage? I cannot have my own daughter being proposed to unless I am aware such a request is from a suitable gentleman with whom I am acquainted."

"Mr. Alexander Harvey is the gentleman."

"Harvey?" questioned her father, the patrician Edmund Hawthorn, his broad forehead furrowed as he scrutinized his daughter over spectacles resting on his fine aquiline nose. Accustomed to emotional arguments between his wife and daughter over the style of a bonnet, or color of a pair of silk slippers, he sensed Margaret's announcement portended even greater travail than the usual contests of wills between mother and daughter.

"Yes," trilled Margaret, fairly squirming with delight. "Alexander Morton Harvey! And he's a friend of Lionel's."

"Al?" shouted her nineteen-year-old brother, Lionel, sitting beside her. "That's great, Marg! That rascal never even gave me a hint."

"Oh, surely not he!" came the cold, pinched voice of a previously unheard-from passenger in the carriage. "Not that mousy little Harvey man." It was Ariadne Woodhull,

Lionel and Margaret's orphaned cousin and ward of the senior Hawthorns. The thin, seventeen-year-old girl drew her narrow lips into a smirk and her large, liquid black eyes widened with surprise.

"He is not mousy," Margaret said.

Her brother, Lionel, laughed and slapped his thigh. "I knew he was sweet on you, but I didn't think he was that serious," he said, grinning at his sister.

"Oh, Lionel, you can't mean you approve," Ariadne said, bending her boyish body forward and turning her long, thin neck to better see him.

Margaret, beaming, ignored her and gushed on. "He asked me day before yesterday. And I said yes, and he'll be coming this very afternoon to ask Papa. And you'll have to say yes, Papa, because I already have."

A thrilled Margaret searched the faces of her parents for a reflection of her own joy, but saw only bafflement in her father and stunned affront in her mother. Turning to her brother Lionel, she received a supportive nod, smile, and brief hug, but her parents and cousin continued to stare at her like a stranger.

"Why, he's practically common!" said Ariadne with disdain, her barely distinct chin dropping in disbelief.

"Who is Alexander Harvey?" her mother asked.

"The most ordinary man you can imagine, Aunt Cornelia," Ariadne said, drawing her narrow shoulders together in a shudder of distaste.

"You should be so lucky as to have a gentleman as fine as Mr. Harvey interested in you, Ariadne Woodhull," Margaret said, her long-lashed, blue eyes snapping with indignation. "I've had three times as many suitors as you've had—"

"And every one of them the most ordinary, common—"

"Now, girls," Edmond Hawthorn interrupted. "It's the Sabbath."

Margaret, her cheeks flushed with anger, gave Ariadne a threatening glare.

Ariadne pursed her thin lips with haughty disapproval and directed her gaze out the coach window.

"He's a friend of Lionel's," said Margaret. "And he's wonderful and I love him more than anything. Everybody thinks he's wonderful—" She gave Lionel a sharp nudge with her elbow.

"Oh, Alexander is a great fellow, Mother," Lionel said.

Margaret was annoyed at Lionel's slowness to attest to the virtues of her Mr. Harvey, especially after the trouble she had gone to prodding him to attend church for that very purpose, something he rarely did unless he was in pursuit of the company of some young lady of his liking who did. She nudged him again.

"Oh, yes indeed, Mother," Lionel stammered. "Alexander Harvey is one mighty fine fellow—"

Ariadne smirked with contempt and Mrs. Hawthorn emitted a feeble whimper and sank back in her seat.

"Now don't you dare faint," Margaret said. "It's too late anyway because I've already accepted and it would be dishonorable to go back on my word."

"Hush, baby," her father said gently. "Wait until we get home." He turned his attention toward his wife, helplessly patting her hand. "Now, Mrs. Hawthorn, this is just some misunderstanding—"

Ariadne's large, liquid black eyes glistening in satisfaction as the opposition to Harvey seemed to increase.

"It most certainly is not a misunderstanding," Margaret insisted.

"Shh," her father hissed. "Home," he called to the driver, and the carriage picked up speed.

"You should be ashamed of yourself," Ariadne said, jumping from her seat to sit beside Cornelia, whose free hand she snatched and placed in her own. "Now, Aunt Cornelia, once we have made Margaret see the unsuitability of this Mr. Harvey—"

At home, Cornelia took to her bed and wept quietly, comforted by hand-holding, smelling salts, and awkward attempts by her husband and son to calm her.

Ariadne berated Margaret with pleased coldness. "You're just awful to upset dear Aunt Cornelia like this—"

"Oh, hush."

Cornelia sobbed into Edmund's handkerchief and her hurt eyes glared at her daughter. Employing all the histrionics observed in melodramatic portrayals she had seen on the stage of Richmond's Granville Theater, she wailed, "How could you even think of such an alliance without consulting me?"

Her son and husband were completely taken in by her performances, but Margaret was not. "Mother, would you please stop this shameless display of theatrics?"

"You have broken all our hearts, Margaret," Ariadne said.

"This has nothing to do with you, Ariadne," Margaret said.

Cornelia ignored them both, expressing her discontent with even greater intensity. "And when did you even secure permission from me to see this Harvey person in such intimate confines that...that...betrothals could be considered?"

Margaret refused to answer and stomped to the window and looked out while Ariadne, her lips curled in a thin, self-satisfied smile, cooed soothing endearments to Cornelia. "Now, now, Aunt Cornelia, try not to cry."

Taking his cue from his father's imploring look, Lionel sprang into diplomatic action. "Now, Mama," he said. "Alex Harvey is a good fellow. I've known him a long time and—"

"I might have known you would have something to do with it. That's why you went to church today, wasn't it?"

"Why, no, Mama...I..."

"You never go to church. You don't belong in church!"

"Mama!" Margaret said, turning back from the window. "What an awful thing to say. Lionel needs church more than anybody I know!"

"We're talking about your shortcomings, sister, not mine."

"Worthless children, the both of you!"

"Now, Mrs. Hawthorn, let's try and remain calm—"

"Don't defend them," Cornelia ordered her husband.

"How can you be so disrespectful to your own mother, Margaret Hawthorn?" Ariadne said.

"To allow this stranger to associate with your only sister!" Cornelia said. "You, who should be her protector. It's a wonder you don't bring that awful Poe man into this house."

"Now, Mama, Edgar is a good fellow, too."

"Your opinions are hardly creditable. Nor are they wanted. The lowlifes you associate with are hardly acceptable members of the human race, much less as suitors for my only daughter. And to think you have allowed one of them to put foolish notions in the mind of your own sister!"

As the conflict intensified, the natural pallor of Ariadne's narrow face warmed to a pink glow of pleasure. Lionel looked miserably at his father as his mother broke into fresh tears.

"Now, Mrs. Hawthorn, stop this immediately," her husband ordered. His wife's sobs increased.

"Cornelia!" he thundered, his handsome jaw set firmly, the wide brow above his indigo blue eyes distorted with irritation. Jolted by his sternness, his wife's sobs instantly subsided into muted sniffs.

"Now, who is this man, son?"

"Alexander Harvey. He's a good chap I met at the university."

"Never heard of the Harveys," said Cornelia. "I cannot believe you would consider marrying someone we are not related to!"

"The Harveys are mighty fine people, Mother. They have a plantation about thirty miles from Granddaddy Hawthorn's place—"

"His family has property?" Cornelia's interest stopped her tears.

"Yes, Mama. I think the Harveys are very well-off. And—"

"And he's thinking of entering the seminary," Margaret said. "He wants to be a minister."

"A minister?"

"Yes, Mother. He's discussed it with Bishop Price, who thinks he would make an excellent candidate for the clergy."

"Bishop Price?" The mention of this respectable name lessened Cornelia's concern even more and, dry-eyed, she signaled for assistance in being raised in the bed.

"But the ministry. As noble as that calling may be... without funds...you would be practically...poor!"

Margaret angrily whirled from the window. "Mother! I'd be ashamed. You just want to marry me off for money!"

"You spend enough of it! It would take six months of a clergyman's earnings to buy just one of your dresses—"

"I'd wear rags and be happy as Reverend Harvey's wife!"

"But why would anyone of a religious nature be friends with Lionel?" Cornelia asked.

"Why, Mother, that hurts my feelings."

"I've asked myself the same thing, Mama. And it just shows you what a good Christian Alexander is."

"Margaret!"

"But who is he?"

"I just told you, Mother—"

"No. No." She waved her hands and bounced impatiently in the bed with frustration. "I mean, who is he? What's his father's name? And who was his mother?"

"She means his family," Margaret said wearily.

"Rather ordinary people, I should think," Ariadne said. "No one we would want in our family."

At last everyone understood, and Lionel searched his brain for some mention his friend might have made of a family name which might placate Cornelia's concern for Margaret's suitor's blood line.

Cornelia Oralee Hawthorn had been born a Randolph. In the hierarchy of Virginia aristocracy, there was no name above, and few even on the same level, as that of Randolph. Selecting marriageable men and women was sometimes a dilemma for the Randolph family, whose kinship to several Virginia governors, Chief Justice John Marshall, and Thomas Jefferson, made appropriate matches difficult to find.

Cornelia Oralee Hawthorn's ambition for a brilliant marriage for her only daughter had been second only to that for one for her only son. Since the day they had been born, she had dedicated her life to that end, spending most of her own scant inheritance and that of her husband's earnings in the process. Only the best families visited Edmund and Cornelia Hawthorn's parlor, only those of the most illustrious pedigree dined at their table.

Being a Randolph by birth, no one suspected that she, already at the top of the list of First Families of Virginia, used her influence as an F.F.V. as assiduously as the most brazen social climber. How could she attempt to climb in society when she was already there? She did—for her daughter and son. And, she thought, she had succeeded.

She had watched her daughter, Margaret, mature into a true beauty, unaffected and charming, as popular and sought-after as any belle in Richmond. Margaret's success in selecting any eligible bachelor in Virginia was all but assured, and just such an alliance was inevitable, Cornelia was positive.

The proud mother remembered her own great compromise in selecting Edmund Hawthorn as a husband. At the time, her own mother had counseled her against the young lawyer. But Cornelia, at the age of twenty-two (past twenty-one was considered by many the official boundary of perpetual spinsterhood), saw in Edmund a chance to escape the loneliness of being an old maid, the tyranny of her mother, and the genteel poverty that awaited them both when the meager inheritance from her father was exhausted.

She was also, though reluctant to admit it, smitten by the courtly blue-eyed Edmund Hawthorn from Hawthorn Hill Plantation. Besides, the Hawthorns were perfectly respectable, enjoyed more prosperity than her own struggling family, and Edmund's grandmother had been a Branch with connections to the Cocke family, two honorable names in the history of the colonization of the James River.

Still, years later, when it came to her own daughter's betrothal, the bias of her own mother came to the surface in

Cornelia, who sought to justify her years of entertaining only Carters, Harrisons, Lees, Byrds, and others in the lengthy accumulation of aristocratic Virginia families she hoped would provide a marriageable son and daughter for her own offspring.

And now, an attempt had been made to thwart her carefully planned campaign by a young man she knew nothing about: Alexander Harvey.

While his wife remained opposed to the match, Edmund Hawthorn was more sanguine. Edmund even found wisdom in his popular daughter's rejection of the suits of certain of the half dozen or so serious suitors who petitioned him for Margaret's hand. Even at the age of fifteen, it was not considered too young for a young lady to be "promised," or "to have an understanding," and swains were making their offers early.

Margaret had found the rotund, red-faced Theophilus Cary unattractive, and even Cornelia would not have wished the simian-like Throckmorton on her daughter, illustrious blood line or not. Jeremy Custis, regardless of his impressive pedigree, who showed few signs of good breeding in appearance or behavior, was deemed unsuitable by the Hawthorns. Likewise the dim-witted Lee who pressed his case, the bad-smelling Robertson, and the intemperate Harrison were all eliminated.

Those acceptable to her parents were rejected by Margaret herself: "I don't like his sister," or "He can't sing a note," or "He didn't say one word about my new bonnet and yet he expects me to marry him." The myriad rejections were in reality offered because Margaret had already found her heart's desire in Alexander Harvey, and no one else could take his place.

All Cornelia's tears and tirades and threats failed. The offers of a trip abroad, new dresses, a new piano, a carriage with rig all her own, were also rejected.

"I wouldn't trade my Alex for the biggest, finest, most wonderful piano in the world," she defiantly told her mother. "And if you want to have that fancy garden wedding you've been planning for me since I was born, it will have to be with Alex as the groom or not at all!"

"But, precious, wouldn't you like to spend the summer in Charleston?"

"Unless I marry Alexander Harvey, I shall remain an old maid. Or I shall elope with Mr. Harvey, move to New York or some other awful place in the North, and you shall never see me again."

And neither could Alexander Harvey be dissuaded nor bought off by attempts masterminded by Cornelia and executed by anyone of any influence she could induce to divert his interest away from Margaret.

The young man showed real character in turning down all offers Edmund Hawthorn extended, from a position in his law office to cash offers to take a trip abroad. Edmund even came to respect the young man's sincerity and devotion to his daughter and was ashamed that he had allowed himself to be wheedled by his wife's plans to thwart what he came to believe was a very good match indeed. Young Harvey was also ambitious and had been first in his class at the University of Virginia, even though his late calling to the ministry was stronger than that to the practice of law, for which he had been educated.

Steering a course Cornelia had launched toward almost certain disaster and unhappiness for all concerned, the more reasonable and less emotional Edmund had proposed a compromise: The marriage of his daughter Margaret to Harvey could take place, but only after waiting a year to prove that their feelings toward each other remained unchanged.

Alexander agreed and agreed to persuade Margaret to agree.

Cornelia, her red curls shaking, her pink cheeks even more flushed than normally, firmly denounced the plan. (It was rumored that she used subtle applications of rouge and face powder, and whispered that she was prematurely gray and because the red of her hair often varied in hue, that she hennaed it.)

"How could she ever be trusted to wait a year? Hasn't she already demonstrated her deceit in her courtship with this Harvey?"

"I have received Margaret's solemn word that if you will protest no more, she will wait a year," her husband explained since all negotiations had been handled by him because Margaret stopped talking to her mother altogether. "Mr. Harvey has also agreed."

"And you believe them?" Cornelia said incredulously.

"I do not believe Margaret. But I do believe Mr. Harvey. I think the young man is honorable and will keep his word. Further, I think he might be an admirable choice for our headstrong daughter."

Her husband's wavering in his opposition, and with little alternative but to accept, Cornelia agreed to the terms of the postponement but only if the couple was willing to be separated with no possibility of their seeing each other secretly.

A school in the North would be an ideal place to send Margaret for a year, Cornelia believed, providing enough time for a headstrong, romantic fifteen-year-old girl to get over her infatuation with Mr. Harvey. Edmund Hawthorn would have no part of sending his daughter to a Yankee school, so a search was made for a suitable institution in the South.

Those in Richmond, Petersburg, and Lynchburg, were too close, Cornelia decided, and other sites too far away. She was not so old and unwise as to have forgotten the puissance of young love and took no chance on the agreement being broken.

A small girl's school in far off Abingdon, Virginia, came to her attention and after several letters and a consultation with knowledgeable authorities familiar with the institution, Miss Estelle Fraley's Academy for Young Ladies was selected as a school for Margaret. With an excellent reputation for the instruction of art and music, Miss Fraley's was within the boundaries of Virginia yet three hundred miles away and seemed an ideal choice.

Sure of their undying love, Margaret and Alexander agreed to the year's separation, provided they could see each other, properly chaperoned, during Christmas.

Cornelia had won the battle and sighed with relief when her daughter and husband boarded the coach that would take them from Richmond to Abingdon. She had rescued her misguided daughter, reconciled with her, and her own family's preeminent blood line was secure. For the moment.

The tears and hugs and kisses Cornelia and Margaret exchanged at that bittersweet parting, and promises of a spectacular wedding to whomever Margaret chose in a year, reaffirmed in mother and daughter a new determination: Cornelia to see that Margaret, once an acceptable young man had been selected, would have the most brilliant wedding in Richmond's history; Margaret, to see that Alexander Harvey was the man at her side at that wedding.

Chapter Nine

Lavinia Williamson had never been so miserable. After a single week at Miss Estelle Fraley's Academy for Young Ladies—the only time she had ever been separated from her family—homesickness struck the fifteen-year-old like a debilitating disease. Although the school was only thirty miles away from her home, her misery grew with each passing day.

By the third week, Lavinia wished she could just die and everyone would be sorry they sent her there in the first place. Even escape in new books only briefly freed her from her affliction. Nevertheless, she refused to petition her parents for rescue and face her brothers' inevitable taunts that she did not have the gumption to stick it out.

She also hoped the lovesick Will Reynolds, a neighbor's son who was smitten with her, might forget her and relieve her of the obligation of sometime accepting him in marriage, a union approved and encouraged by her parents. A pleasant young man of excellent character, the twenty-year-old Reynolds even shared with Lavinia a love of horses—the only thing they had to talk about during the interminable Sunday afternoons when he came calling and she was obligated to sit with him in the parlor or on the porch awkwardly trying to make suitable conversation. But he reminded Lavinia of a sad-eyed hound and his soulful glances and sighs pushed her to the edge of the politeness that concealed her boredom and lack of interest.

Lavinia's homesickness at Miss Fraley's School had become almost unbearable when she made the acquaintance of an equally unhappy student with whom she shared a class in Latin and art. Margaret Hawthorn, a young lady from far-off Richmond, was homesick, too, but her yearning was for but a single person, her sweetheart, Mr. Alexander Harvey, about whom she talked incessantly and who became for Lavinia and the other girls an image of perfect manhood.

The two unhappy girls were soon sharing their dilemma and finding comfort in one another's company. Lavinia also began to appreciate the good humor in Margaret Hawthorn that often surfaced and made both girls laugh in spite of their unhappiness. They were fascinated and amused by each other's strange Virginia accents, neither realizing she had an accent to begin with.

Lavinia's mountaineer drawl, with its flat i's ("I'm tired" sounding like "I'm tarred"), made Margaret hysterical. Likewise, Lavinia was amused by Margaret's Tidewater speech, even as it reminded her of a more pronounced version of her mother's Hanover County accent.

Both skilled mimics, the girls entertained their classmates with satirical imitations of their teachers, and harmless imitations evolved into mischievous pranks. Reprimands and threats of punishment did little to curtail the girls and inspired them to devise a plan that would solve their problem.

"If we did something really, really bad we might get expelled!" Margaret suggested one day when she and Lavinia had been required to "sit in" after class for hiding their teacher's textbook.

"What a wonderful idea!" Lavinia agreed, and plans were devised to that end. They first tried tardiness, then complete absence from class. This was only rewarded by the punishment of additional work. Giggling and inattention in class were likewise rewarded with the revocation of privileges the girls had come to enjoy.

"Well, we know we can't kill anybody, or steal anything, or burn the school down, but there must be something a little less bad we could do to get us out of here," Lavinia proposed.

Little did they know the faculty, weary of the girls' endless mischief, was searching for precisely the same kind of offense.

It was soon forthcoming.

Only two weeks after the girls' most recent attempt to have themselves asked to leave, by appearing in class wearing a thick coating of rice powder and rouge on their faces, an incident occurred at Miss Fraley's that brought the situation to an abrupt conclusion.

The problem solved, Miss Fraley immediately dispatched letters to each of the girls' parents. Two letters for Edmund and Cornelia Hawthorn arrived on the same day. Cornelia, recognizing Margaret's childish scrawl, on one of them, opened it at once:

Dear Mama and Papa,

The most awful thing has happened and it is not my fault. Yesterday in Art Class, Miss O'Donald, our teacher, wanted us to paint a rose and that started it all. She was simply awful and made this big scene. She put a picture of roses up in front of the class and our assignment was to paint them. Roses are very hard to paint. Especially with water paints which run all over the paper.

A Daisy or Violet or Black eyed Susan is easy to paint but Roses are relly hard. No one in class does very well on Roses except my friend Lavinia. I think I told you about Lavinia in my earlier letters. She is the one that talks so slow and funny. She is my best friend and the best art student at school and paints roses really well they look so real and good and she was just being helpful and painted my roses for me and Miss O'Donald threw a fit and insulted us both by saying we cheated!

I had tried to paint the roses myself two or three times and Miss O'Donald kept making me do them over and over about three times before I got Livvy to do them for me.

This is so awful and we are innocent but what is so bad is old Miss Fraley took Miss O'Donald's side against us and they had a meeting with some of the other teachers who don't like us either and we are being asked not to return for the next term. We are not being expelled, just asked not to come back. I feel so awful and have just cried my eyes out. You must not breathe a word of this to Mr. Harvey or let Lionel know or he will laugh and think it a big joke and tell Mr. Harvey.

Miss Fraley says she is writing you a letter but I want you to read this letter first because this school has insulted our whole family.

I don't think these teachers come from very good families.

I want to come as soon as possible from this awful place. May I go home with Lavinia now ?? Instead of waiting for the session to end in two weeks. She lives in Williamsville and is so upset she needs me to explain to her Mama and Papa just how awful we were treated at Miss Fraleys. I just hope her parents are as loving and understanding and fair minded as mine are.

*Please send permission to Miss Fraley for me to go home
with Lavinia when her father comes to get her when he gets
a letter from Miss Fraley too.*

*I love and miss you so much and am so thankful I have
such wonderful Parents.*

Your loving daughter,
Margaret

Please don't tell Lionel a word of why I'll be coming home.

M.

The second letter, written by Miss Fraley, read:

Dear Mr. Hawthorn,

*After careful consideration by the faculty, we at the Estelle
Fraley Seminary For Young Ladies regret to inform you that
we will be unable to accommodate your daughter, Margaret,
as a student after the current term.*

*We have carefully evaluated Margaret's progress here
and feel that it is wanting. This lacking extends as well to
her attitude toward her studies and her general reluctance
to cooperate in the proper advancement of her education.*

*We request that arrangements for Margaret's removal
be facilitated on or before June 1, 1830, unless you accede
to her wishes that she be allowed to leave our care and
supervision in the company of her friend, Miss Lavinia
Williamson, who also will not be returning to our school,
and who will be escorted to her home in Williamsville,
Virginia, by her father, Mr. John Williamson, a gentlemen
of good character known to us, and in whose good care we
would have no reservation in entrusting Margaret.*

Please advise us if these plans meet with your approval.

The return of all tuition and fees for Margaret's second session is being facilitated and will be sent to you forthwith.

> *Very truly yours,*
> *Estelle Hendricks Fraley*
> *Headmistress*

The Williamsons' weekly mail also contained a letter from Miss Fraley, almost identical in content to that of the Hawthorns'. There was also word from Lavinia:

Dear Ma and Pa,

Well, they've asked me to leave this hateful place and I'm glad. I'd rather look at a hound-dog face like Will Reynolds the rest of my life than stay here one more day. Pa, you can come and get me tomorrow, they are so anxious to see us leave. US means my friend, Margaret Hawthorn, from Richmond, who also got the boot and wants to visit us and you will love her as much as I do she is so much fun. She wants to stay with us a few weeks since her family might take on a lot and think she had disgraced them because they are the kind of people who worry about things like that a lot. Thank goodness we don't. Remind the boys not to be so crude and country when Margaret visits and to use good table manners as she is a real city lady and would be shocked if she knew my brothers acted like hogs at the trough at the table. That goes for you too, Pa.

Come as quick as you can but wait a day or two because Old Lady Fraley won't let Margaret come with us until she has permission from Maggie's parents to come with me.

Give my awful bros. and sweet Granny kisses from me.

> *Love,*
> *Livvy*

PS: Oh yes, the reason they are throwing me and Margaret out is I painted a Rose or two for her in Art Class. Isn't that silly? The Art teacher, Miss O'Donald, is a Roman Catholic and I don't think she likes us because Margaret and I are good Christian Protestants.

Love again.
Me

The Hawthorns did not violate Margaret's request to tell Mr. Harvey, but they did tell their son Lionel, who was dispatched immediately to bring his errant sister home to Richmond from a place in the far-off wilds of Western Virginia he had never heard of, Williamsville, where she was visiting Lavinia Williamson, known only as "a friend."

The friend, Lionel learned, had also been asked to leave Miss Fraley's, and was described by Margaret in letters as being much prettier than their cousin, the cold and haughty Ariadne. Margaret further reported that not only was Lavinia prettier than Ariadne, she was an accomplished horsewoman and could outride him any day of the week.

Having an eye for beauty and confident of his riding skills, Lionel looked forward to the challenge.

Prior to his assignment to fetch his sister home, Lionel had worked diligently on behalf of his friend Alexander Harvey's suit for Margaret's hand. Lionel found his mother's preoccupation with pedigree and harsh underrating of Alexander unjust and preferred to judge people more for themselves than who their great-grandfather had been. He was grateful that his father, not born of so lofty a pedigree as Cornelia, had passed on to him a standard of judgment reflecting more democratic values.

The news his sister would soon return to Richmond meant that his friend Alexander Harvey's boat was once again afloat and his ambition to wed Margaret would be revived and strengthened with new stratagems.

Although the circumstances of his sister's expulsion were unclear, Lionel slapped his thighs with glee and threw back his head and laughed uproariously when he heard of it. That his own endless episodes of impropriety found a comparable incident in his sister's behavior gave him amused satisfaction.

"Well, at least I didn't get shipped from the university!" he had rejoiced when told of Margaret's misfortune.

His mother, weeping with shame, was aghast at Lionel's lack of concern. "How can you possibly find this amusing?" she asked. "That university has ruined you! Why, I doubt even that Mr. Harvey will marry her now."

"Don't be ridiculous, Mama," Lionel said. "That Miss What's-Her-Name's School is so far away no one ever heard of it. I wager not a soul in Richmond will know a thing about it. I bet Alex would get a kick out of it though."

"He is not to be told!" Cornelia ordered. "This is not to go outside the family."

"But Alex is almost family," Lionel reminded his mother. "Only eight or nine months and the agreed year will be up."

"Indeed, Margaret has already disgraced us all," said Ariadne with poorly concealed pleasure. "How can you support this unsuitable marriage that will only further embarrass the family?"

Cornelia sank back into her pillows. With Margaret returning home she was right back where she started in her mission to stall and prevent the marriage.

Lionel and Alex Harvey were great friends, having often spent time at various gentlemen's clubs and even less respectable haunts in Richmond, prior to Alexander's sudden religious vocation. Lionel had even been one of the agents aiding and abetting the romance of his sister with Alex, often covering for them when they met to gaze longingly in each other's eyes while Lionel, as unofficial chaperone, loitered nearby.

Lionel's campaign on behalf of his friend Alex had begun as soon as the sweethearts had been separated, and whether she would admit it or not, Cornelia had developed a kind of wary tolerance for the young man.

At first, she vowed never to allow Harvey into her house, but gently reminded that she was being unfair, and even unmannerly, she had relented. In a gesture of noblesse oblige, she agreed to allow Mr. Harvey to join the family at supper.

"He is here as your guest, young man," Cornelia told her son, "not as Margaret's suitor."

Lionel began to carefully guide his friend in winning Cornelia's approval.

"Now, in dealing with Mother," Lionel said, "always agree with her, whether you do or not. Margaret is the only one in the family to cross her, but Papa and I have learned the easy way is to agree with her and then do what you want anyway. The servants handle her the same way. The country servants, the ones at Hawthorn Hill, like Mammy Emma and Lemiel and Beck, are best at it. The Richmond servants haven't learned that as well as the rest of us."

Lionel, finding himself embroiled in one potential scandal after another—escapades of gambling, intemperance, or involvement with women of dubious character—had more reason to master the art of manipulating Cornelia than any member of the family. So frequent were his misadventures that he had become an expert, using the precise blend of charm and flattery necessary to obtain his ends.

More than once, Cornelia had come to his aid, unknown to his father, who was less subject to his manipulations, by paying a gambling debt, convinced by her son the cards had been stacked against him. And he convinced his mother that the scandalous reports of a jealous husband out for his hide was simply the result of an innocent misunderstanding—his good manners in paying a lady a compliment, or his entering her boudoir in a gentlemanly attempt to return a glove she had dropped earlier. And it was just gossip that he had been involved in a barroom brawl at the Bird and Owl Tavern; that black eye he sported was the result of a fall when his horse stumbled in a pothole on Main Street.

He did his best to pass on his skills to his friend Alex. "Now just remember, Mama is as vain as a peacock and does everything she can to look younger. Just say something about not believing she could be the parent of offspring as old as Margaret and she'll be eating out of your hand. And if she rambles on about the family genealogy, try to hide your boredom and appear interested."

The balding, mustached Alex Harvey pursed his lips and squinted through thick-lens glasses, pondering his assignment. Although Margaret found her beau the most handsome man she had ever seen, in reality he was unremarkable in appearance, paunchy and short, his virtues more apparent in character—a personable disposition and total devotion to Margaret—than in physical good looks.

"Now, what did you find out about your family history?"

"Well, Mother says her grandmother was a Ligon and Papa's mother was a Woodson," Alex reported, and mentioned two other families who were ancestors.

"Great! Ligon and Woodson are good, I think. But just don't say anything about those other two."

Lionel fully approved of Alex Harvey as a husband for Margaret, and even confided to his friend that he was too good for his spoiled, willful sister. Lionel owed much to Alex. More than once the level-headed Alex had rescued the more impetuous Lionel from a fist fight or drunken brawl and once even the challenge of a duel.

But both young men, at twenty-one years of age, were different in character and demeanor. Alex was quiet, even-tempered, self-possessed, and thoughtful; Lionel was extroverted, choleric, immature, and undisciplined. Indulged by his doting mother and Emma, Lionel saw life as one great adventure of pleasure and self-indulgence. With good looks, charm, and family connections, his devil-may-care disregard for convention was forgiven, overlooked, or concealed by a cadre of well-placed friends. Laughter filled his throat as easily as a breath and he was never known to frown, unless he was losing heavily at cards, which was often, or a belle he had pursued had rejected him, which was seldom.

His good humor rarely left him, and on the occasions when his dreaded temper and belligerence did erupt, it was likely the result of too much to drink. He charmed everyone who met him, used flattery freely, and made every woman he met from twelve to ninety believe she was the most captivating creature he had ever seen. He genuinely liked people and his popularity rescued him more than once from many of the consequences of his own self-indulgence. Gambling debts would be deferred, a minor scandal would be silenced, a jealous husband appeased.

No stranger to the fleshpots of Richmond and the more unsavory gaming houses, Lionel cut a swath through all levels of Richmond society. He could be seen dancing with a senator's daughter at a ball at the governor's mansion one night, and the next he might be found in the arms of a newly arrived French prostitute. He spent money freely, a great concern to his father, who still paid most of his bills. The practice of law, a profession he had half-heartedly selected and endured the study of for two years at the University of Virginia, he had yet to embrace with much more seriousness than to show up once or twice a week in his father's law office to spin tales or occasionally draw up a will or write a deed.

He took more interest in the family's investment in a tobacco factory. The tobacco business, both as a planter at Hawthorn Hills and manufacturer of the processed leaf in the factory in Richmond, contributed ever increasing profits for the Hawthorn family. The factory provided Lionel an endless supply of female workers, slave and free, black and white.

His mother had for years tried to match Lionel with a suitable wife. But her son was unwilling to surrender the freedom of bachelorhood. He was "a catch" in every sense of the word. With a good family, good looks, and a promising career, he could have picked a bride from a dozen daughters of the finest families in Virginia.

To please his mother, and in an attempt to indicate to his father that he would soon settle down, Lionel "kept company," in a more or less official capacity, with the plain Ariadne Woodhull, his orphaned cousin. Ariadne, cold and aloof, looked upon the world through large, liquid black eyes, waiting patiently for Lionel to finally relent and make her his bride.

That an official announcement of their intention to marry would soon be forthcoming was fully expected by

Cornelia and Edmund, but as yet, Lionel had demurred. The Hawthorns hope was that the collected, serious Ariadne would be the perfect antidote to Lionel's wildness, and they believed that their marriage would provide a stabilizing effect on the irresponsibility and recklessness of their son.

His introduction to Lavinia Williamson, however, upset his desire to remain single forever. One look at her and he was ready to extend his involvement with the female sex from dalliances no longer than one to six weeks to a lifetime commitment.

The first time he entered the Williamson house, Lavinia brushed aside the required pleasantries called for by the rules of polite conversation and said, "Margaret says you claim to have the fastest horse in Richmond. I hope it's not that broken-down old nag you rode in on."

Aghast at such an insult to his prized roan mare, one of the finest examples of horseflesh in the entire Commonwealth, Lionel launched into a spirited defense of his mount.

Lavinia, hearing his stammered excuses, threw her head back and laughed. Then, fixing him with the loveliest smile he had ever seen, her voice lost its challenge and became soft and musical. "I'm only teasing, Mr. Hawthorn. I could tell at fifty paces your filly is one of the best. I'd like to look her over if you will allow me." She stepped toward him and extended her hand. "Welcome to our home. I hope you will have an enjoyable visit."

Lionel was instantly besotted with love. Never before had he been so affected by a smile so enchanting, a voice so bewitching, a woman in every way so disturbingly challenging in her charm and beauty. A master in the art of courtship, he faltered in her presence like a tongue-tied adolescent beginner. He was speechless before the girl's statuesque beauty. The large gray eyes, bordered with long black lashes, were alive with wit and mischief. Her lovely oval face, framed by dark brown hair, her figure, her skin, her humor and intelligence, surpassed any woman he had ever seen before. Only a moment in the presence of Lavinia, and the thin, demure coldness of his cousin Ariadne Woodhull and all the other women who had ever captured his interest faded into oblivion.

Lavinia's country directness, so unlike the more reserved demeanor of Ariadne and other Richmond belles, disarmed and challenged him as he had never been by a female before. He had met his match and she didn't mind showing him her mettle. The tried and true techniques of courtship Lionel had used so often with success in the past seemed totally inadequate with this girl. Lavinia laughed at the fancy words that brought giggles, blushes, and coy peeks from behind timidly raised fans in Richmond parlors.

When he had first met her, she had rendered him tongue-tied and he stared at her mutely until he felt like an idiot.

"Miss Williamson," he finally managed, somehow recovering a trace of his aplomb. "My sister said you were the prettiest girl west of the James River, but she has not done you justice." He bent in his most courtly bow and kissed her hand, hoping she would not laugh.

Now it was Lavinia's turn to be disarmed. None of the young men in Washington County were the hand-kissing type, and she was charmed by the gesture, even though she thought it affected and probably insincere. Kissing hands was completely contrary to the shuffling, hat-holding efforts of Will Reynold's awkward attempts at gentlemanly courtship.

"Margaret was very kind to give a favorable report of my appearance, but perhaps she is not the best judge. I understand she does not really have an artist's eye—"

Lionel caught her meaning and laughed. "Only when painting roses, I am told."

"Margaret is like a sister I never had. I don't know how I shall ever allow you to take her away from me back to Richmond. And just to turn her over to that Alexander Harvey."

After a week's stay, the Williamson family, already under the spell of Margaret's charm, was completely in Hawthorn hands with Lionel having finished the conquest his sister had begun.

Even the stern, watchful John Williamson liked the young man. Alerted to Williamson's staunch anti-slavery position, Margaret had cautioned Lionel to avoid the subject. As ridiculous as it seemed to both girls, Lavinia's father actually predicted his area of the newly founded United States would someday vote to secede as a separate nation free of slavery and the evils it nurtured. And sometimes his zeal actually advocated that the issue would bring the opposing factions to war. Her father's extremist views embarrassed Lavinia, as well as bored her, but Lionel always listened politely and thoughtfully as if the elder Williamson's words offered profound insight and convincing analysis.

Unable to lure Lionel into serious debate about the evils of slavery and the necessity of its abolition, Williamson and the young man found common ground in their love of hunting, horses, and agriculture. Instead of the pros and cons of slavery, their spirited but less dangerous arguments concerned the merits of various firearms, skills in marksmanship, and breeds of horseflesh. These lively exchanges diffused more serious debates and at the same time a passionate exchange on which of two horses was the faster provided pleasant sparring but allowed the friendship to remain intact when the matter was decided and the race was over.

In the company of one or more of Lavinia's brothers, and Lavinia herself if she could persuade them to allow her to tag along, Lionel and her father rode the woods and fields, fished and hunted, and Lionel came to appreciate the vast, fecund hunting ground that was the sparsely populated Blue Ridge Mountains. Proving himself skilled with a gun and adept astride a horse, Lionel found Lavinia's brothers to be willing hunting and riding companions, who suspended their natural mountain skepticism and suspicion of the eastern Virginian. No dandy he, the young man from Richmond was welcomed as an equal.

Lionel's visit with the Williamsons was idyllic. While dancing, alcohol, and card games were forbidden in the Williamson household, these deficiencies were more than compensated for by unrivaled hunting and fishing opportunities, an impressive supply of blooded horses in the Williamson stables, and most of all, by the presence of the hauntingly beautiful Lavinia Williamson, who continued to enthrall him and with whom he fell deeper in love every day.

Lionel even shocked Margaret by regularly attending church with the Williamsons—even evening services during the week. Margaret knew her brother's piety was pure hypocrisy, but it served to further ingratiate himself with the Williamsons, who knew nothing of his sullied reputation in faraway Richmond.

The only flaw in Lionel's happy world was the existence of a gentleman named Will Reynolds who Margaret explained had been keeping company with Lavinia on properly chaperoned Sunday afternoons for almost a year.

"Her pa would be glad if she married him. He's going to inherit a thousand acres and the Reynolds are abolitionist, too. But Lavinia says she doesn't want to marry anybody just yet."

Given some hope by this report, Lionel delayed his return to Richmond.

"I will not postpone getting home to Alexander another day," Margaret said. "I'm leaving next week if I have to walk."

"But we've only been here three weeks," Lionel had protested. "The Williamsons will think we have no manners at all if we go so soon. It would be rude."

Lavinia joined in the campaign, "Oh, Margaret, you know you can't leave before September. Ma and Pa would be so hurt—and so would I."

Lionel added, "And it's going to take another month at least for Mama to get over your disgracing the family by getting shipped—"

Against the united front of her brother and the entire Williamson family, Margaret reluctantly agreed to extend her visit a week more. Grateful for the additional time he would have in Lavinia's company, Lionel was nevertheless uncertain how he stood with her—a rare situation for him with regard to females.

Before, Lionel had always known how women felt about him. Whether a respectable virgin or a saloon slattern, he could read the disguised or deliberate messages they sent him. But with Lavinia, he had no clue and he could not be sure if her fondness was simply the same fondness she had for one of her brothers. She was like a skilled card player he could not read and he was left to stew in uncertainty.

Unknown to him, Lavinia was going through the same dilemma. A week before Lionel and Margaret's scheduled departure for Richmond, Lavinia was desperate.

A conversation with Granny Williamson, the only one to whom she confided her confusion, gave her needed insight. "Granny, Will Reynolds wants me to marry him."

"Good boy, Will," the old woman said, taking a draw from her pipe.

"But...but what if I...what if I like somebody else better?"

The old woman put aside her pipe, bent close to Lavinia, and whispered, "I'd heap ruther git under the kivers with that Richmond feller than that Will Reynolds you're thinkin' of choosin'."

"Granny!" Lavinia exclaimed in shock.

"He's yorn if you want him," Granny advised her. "I can tell. He's just like a big ripe papaw hangin' low on a tree just waitin' to fall right in yer lap."

The next Sunday, after evening church services, Lavinia and Lionel lagged behind the rest of the family, who rode or walked on home ahead of them. Margaret and Lionel were to leave the next day.

As Lavinia and Lionel strolled in the churchyard, pondering their approaching separation with sad, private thoughts, an uncharacteristic silence fell between them. There was no easy banter, teasing, flirtatious jousting. They had reached the edge of the churchyard and the brick horse-stile where riders mounted and dismounted for services when Lavinia realized the rest of the congregation had all departed and she was alone with Lionel. She had never been alone with a male before, without an adult no farther than a room away, unless it was one of her brothers or her father. Suggesting they return home immediately, Lionel insisted she sit with him for a moment on the steps of the horse-stile.

"After all, Lavinia...I mean, Miss Williamson, it is my last evening here..."

To her delight, Lavinia detected a suggestion of sadness in his voice.

"I shall miss Margaret so when you leave, Mr. Hawthorn."

"But you must visit us soon, Miss Williamson. Perhaps in a month or two. Certainly for Marg's wedding to Alex next spring."

"Oh, I suppose I shall be already married myself by then," she said shyly, casting her eyes demurely to her neatly folded hands in her lap.

"You—married?"

"Why, yes. I thought you knew. I have been keeping company with Will Reynolds from the next farm."

Seizing her hand, Lionel instantly fell to his knees. Imploring her to reconsider her choice, he begged her to give him a chance to earn her affection.

Startled by his sudden ardor, Lavinia was almost disappointed that her objective had been so easily won. She demurred at first, which only increased Lionel's insistence.

Affecting the most modest demeanor she could summons to hide her desire to shout with joy, she at last relented and accepted his proposal—provided her father would grant his permission, and if she could receive an honorable release from Will Reynolds, even though she had promised him nothing and a more serious culmination to their keeping company on Sundays had only been implied.

John Williamson's opposition had been perfunctory and quickly routed by the united front of his determined daughter, sons, wife, and mother. The fact that his daughter was marrying into a family of slave-holders was abhorrent to him, but he acknowledged other merits in the match and could not bear to see his daughter's happiness spoiled. Besides, the young man seemed almost indifferent about being the son of a slave-holder and might, with the influence of his wife, see the error of his family's ways. And, Mr. Williamson admitted, he was a church-goer and seemed unfamiliar with liquor and cards and other vices.

A hurried exchange of letters between Lionel and his parents brought predictable results. His father wrote him that his mother had taken to her bed and was inconsolable, and if Lionel would delay the marriage until he could visit the Williamsons and meet his son's intended bride, he was sure he could placate his mother into accepting Lionel's choice.

Ariadne Woodhull, although denying it, was also showing unintended signs of regret. Red-rimmed eyes, long periods of isolation in her room, the contours of her thin face rigid with stoic, controlled hardness, Lionel's cousin was suddenly stricken with mysterious episodes of ill health, which required numerous visits by physicians. Further, the normally reserved girl developed a harsh change in personality, abandoning her self-contained timidity by suddenly becoming strident and abrupt, even rude and caustic, her new belligerence especially directed toward her servants and expressed with a savage intensity the placid, almost mousy girl had never shown before.

In a tear-stained letter from his mother, Cornelia remonstrated her son for deliberately breaking Ariadne's heart, rated his conduct despicable, and insisted he had an implied obligation to his cousin that was as binding as a formal announcement of their engagement, whether words to that effect had been spoken or not.

It is what your family has always expected and assumed would transpire, and to abandon this poor orphan girl is so dishonorable a deed, I am unable to find words to characterize it, she wrote. *You have always been determined to break your mother's heart, I know. Your choosing that university over the College of William and Mary, your association with that dreadful Mr. Poe and others of low character, your frequenting one saloon and gambling hall after another with the most disreputable of people has shattered my nerves. Don't for a minute think the efforts to shield me from your escapades have always been successful–*

Cornelia's letter was followed by an even more impassioned entreaty from Ariadne herself. Although careful not to plead her own case to be Lionel's bride, she would have her entreaty appear as concern for Cornelia, frantically imploring Lionel not to "break your mother's heart with this reckless betrothal."

"It's her own heart she's worrying about," Margaret sniffed, still smarting from Ariadne's unkind remarks about her Alexander Harvey. "Ariadne never thinks of anyone but herself. It's her own cause she's pleading; she doesn't give a hoot what Mother thinks."

In a lengthy response to Cornelia, labored over many hours by Lionel and Margaret, Lionel reminded his mother that Lavinia's father owned nearly six thousand acres of the finest land in Virginia and that Mr. Williamson had mentioned something like fifteen hundred acres of it would probably be Lavinia's inheritance. "And, although it is vulgar to mention such things, the Williamsons have a lot of money, too—wealth not only in land and horses and cattle but in good American dollars from the sale of hemp and wheat and tobacco." And although Mr. Williamson's ancestors were vague and unimpressive, Mrs. Williamson's pedigree boasted a clearly provable kinship to Dolly Madison.

Lionel's father, Edmund Hawthorn, visited and was delighted to return to Richmond and verify as true all the glowing reports from Lionel and Margaret on the Williamsons and Lavinia. The elder Hawthorn had even strengthened Lionel's case by predicting to John Williamson that when enough free states were added to the Union, slavery would be abolished and the South would have to adapt to a new economic system free of human bondage.

Cornelia surrendered to the united front of her family and consoled herself with the comfort of her daughter-in-law's dowry of wealth and acreage her husband had described as "a garden of Eden."

They were married within the week and Lavinia traveled to Richmond with her new husband to meet her new family, and to say goodbye to the Eden her father-in-law described to his wife, who was unable to attend the wedding because Ariadne Woodhull, upon learning that her cousin Lionel's betrothal was inevitable, had suddenly been stricken with a malady described by Cornelia in the vaguest of terms as a "nervous disorder."

And regardless of what you hear when you return home, Cornelia had written Lionel and Margaret, her writing suddenly increasing in size, the pen strokes pressed so hard the script was thicker and darker than any other words in the letter, *Ariadne's illness was an accidental overdose of her new medications—opiates and bromides for the nerves. She simply misunderstood the instructions.*

"Hmm," Margaret said, reading her mother's letter. "Mother has spent nearly three pages going on about how Ariadne 'accidentally' nearly died from taking too much medicine. What was that line, 'Me thinks she doth protest too much,' in that awful play we had to study at school?"

"*Hamlet*," said Lavinia, guilt-ridden at having been the reason for Ariadne's hysterical reaction. "And all because of me."

"Mother's made it obvious; it was no accident at all. Ariadne has deliberately tried to kill herself."

Chapter Ten

Lavinia, clutching the sheet and clothing retrieved from the library, rushed up the steps as Piney's shrill voice chased her up the stairs.

"Slave patrols here! They lookin' for Angelica! That big Gabriel from the Wroughton place done run off yesterday. Charles Hicks here, and them patrols of his'n, and—"

Lavinia heard Lionel's footsteps retreat toward the back of the house as Piney followed him, excitedly babbling the information again.

"They wantin' to talk to Angelica and she at the Barksdales! A whole bunch of 'em! And they sayin' they more run off from the Wroughton's—Bingo and Jane and they little baby—"

Upstairs, Lavinia stumbled toward the back hall window.

Gabriel's escape already discovered! And the patrols at the doorstep!

Peeping out the window, she saw Charles Hicks and four other men on horseback at the kitchen yard fence. Armed with holstered pistols and rifles hoisted and ready at their sides, the disreputable-looking group appeared no better than the pack of emaciated bloodhounds who yelped and scampered about them in undisciplined, aimless confusion.

Clearly not of the gentleman class, Hicks and his companions were rough and unwashed men with shifty eyes and suspicious, unknown histories. Lavinia noted the inferior quality of their horses and gear. The patrols attracted the people and they could be seen slowly approaching the house to huddle about in tight, protective groups as they watched with fearful curiosity, wondering if the patrol's presence involved the escape or capture of someone they knew.

Defensive and scowling, Hicks and his men watched the curious, approaching slaves with sharpened, unfriendly wariness, their hands inching closer to their pistols. Like natural enemies, the slaves and slave hunters appraised each other from behind masks of hostile silence.

One of Hicks's men, wearing a long black moustache, suddenly sat erect in his saddle and quickly hoisted the rifle at his horse's flank to upright readiness. As a unit, the cautiously approaching blacks froze.

Hicks, the coiled black snake whip he was never without at his side, dismounted and with short, thick legs walked toward the fence when he saw Lionel approaching from the house. A dark, swarthy man in his thirties, Hicks looked with hooded eyes from beneath thick eyebrows and spoke through a wooly black beard which covered most of his face and extended down his barrel-shaped chest. His beard concealed his features except the beady eyes and his flat, spreading nose. He reached across the fence and shook Lionel's extended hand as one of the patrolmen gruffly ordered the yelping hounds into silence.

Noted for his tenacity and success in apprehending runaways, Hicks generated fear among the slaves, even as he stirred their curiosity. As his identity spread through the cluster of blacks, children sought the safety of their mother's skirts, or peeked from behind trees and outbuildings, even more intimidated than the adults by the ready rifles and hostile warning in the threatening glares of Hicks's companions.

Lavinia eased open the window and strained to hear what Hicks and Lionel were saying. But they were too far away to hear. Hicks pointed toward the Wroughton place as he spoke and nodded as Lionel responded to his questions. What were they saying? How had they discovered Gabriel's absence so soon? Hicks, said to have come to Virginia from New Jersey, had become a particularly militant and dedicated hunter of runaway slaves. He had even gone as far as Boston to return wanted fugitives, sometimes even if the monetary reward was exceeded by the expense of the capture.

Prior to 1850, a slave who successfully fled slavery and reached a free state was safe from apprehension and return to bondage. But the Fugitive Slave Act of 1850 made it legal for escaped slaves to be apprehended, even in free states, and returned to their owners. The new law created a profitable enterprise for both bounty hunters in the North and South, and men like Charles Hicks sought to return, for often generous rewards, the vulnerable runaways, now without legal protection against recapture.

But it was the challenge of the chase that fired Hicks's passion, even more than the lucrative financial rewards. His dislike for blacks fed his determination never to allow a runaway to avoid capture and triumph over his determined pursuit. To elude him very long was an insult to his sense of racial and intellectual superiority, and his failures were far more galling than his successes were satisfying.

Emma, having no fear of anything or anybody, had by now hobbled from the house and crossed the yard to her master's side like a furious hen protecting her chicks.

"She at the Barksdales nursin' the sick," the old woman said defiantly to Hicks, so loud even Lavinia could hear her. "Miss Hawthorn sent her over there yesterday mornin'."

Hicks seemed to place little credence in Emma's statement, but when Lionel confirmed the information, Emma retreated back to the house. Hicks and Lionel talked at length, during which time Lavinia's anxiety grew until she wanted to scream. Finally, seemingly satisfied with the interview, Hicks nodded and the men shook hands again. With his companions giving the blacks a final glare of contempt, Hicks remounted his horse and the group galloped away, followed by the yelping hounds.

In her room, Lavinia discarded her clothing in a wardrobe, threw on a dressing gown, and quickly twisted her hair under control in a bun, which she stabbed into place with a comb. Climbing into bed, she pulled the covers up to her chin, like a child hiding from some imagined fear.

But Lavinia's fear was no childhood fantasy. It was something very real. Beneath the thud of her headache, she was seized with panic. Would they question her? Would she, the mistress of Hawthorn Hill Plantation, be subjected to the indignity of interrogation by the likes of trash like Charles Hicks? And what would she say? Had the patrols connected her with Gabriel's disappearance? What would she do when the patrols discovered Angelica had never even arrived at the Barksdales?

The sound of Lionel's footsteps on the stairs made Lavinia feel like a cornered fugitive herself. How would she ever elude his penetrating insight? When he knocked on the door, she turned away and pretended to be asleep. After a pause, she heard the door open and footsteps, soft and tentative, approach the bed. She felt the down-filled tick give as he gently sat down beside her and caressed her cheek.

He bent over her and whispered in her ear, "Livvy? Is my sweet Livvy awake?" His lips brushed her cheek.

There was no escape. She would have to face him now and she pretended to be aroused from sleep. She turned to find his blue eyes looking at her adoringly.

"Good morning." He slid closer and wrapped his arms around her, lifting her from her pillow toward him. Steadying her hand, she brushed aside the wayward lock of hair that fell over his eyes.

"I...I don't feel very well..."

"My poor baby." Holding her, he gently pressed her head against his shoulder and patted her back as if comforting a child. "It's all my fault. I was just so caught up in the joy of our celebration, and the joy of you, that I allowed you to drink too much."

In spite of her anxiety, his strong arms gave her comfort. She was frightened and wished she could blurt out the truth of her crime and be soothed by his comforting words. But that was impossible; she feared Lionel even more than the patrols. Even as she wanted his protection, she knew revealing her participation would only unleash his rage at her complicity and stupidity.

She even felt guilty herself. A slave owner's wife assisting in the escape of her husband's property. It was like theft.

"What was Piney talking about? Slave patrols and—" she mumbled against his chest.

"Wroughton's man, Gabriel, the one we tried to buy for Angelica, has run off. And another of his hands with his wife and baby. Mrs. Wroughton found out this morning and notified Hicks. She told them about Gabriel's involvement with our Angelica and they wanted to know where she was, if perhaps they ran off together–Mrs. Wroughton's theory. I told them Angelica was at the Barksdales."

"Oh," was all Lavinia could manage, but her spirits lifted when there was no trace of suspicion in his voice.

"Don't be troubled by it, my love." He gathered her into his arms and held her close.

Relieved that her worst fears for Angelica and Gabriel were not yet realized, Lavinia at last allowed herself to breathe easier.

"Are you still going to Richmond today?"

"I regret I must. I'm leaving now."

He kissed her on the forehead and eased her back on her pillow. "I'll have Piney bring your breakfast up here."

She managed to give him a weak smile. At least he was leaving and would be gone before learning that Angelica also had fled.

He kissed her again and rose. "We're not as old as we thought, my darling," he said as he approached the door. "Last night was like a second honeymoon." He turned and smiled at her lovingly. "I'll have Uncle Lemiel get some of the hands to move my bed back upstairs. With your permission, of course."

She only looked at him, and then quickly averted her eyes. The matter of Henny's being brought from the quarters still had not been resolved. Getting him to Richmond seemed to take precedence over anything else, so she said nothing, even as she hated herself for her cowardice in giving her own protection priority over Henny's well-being. But the matter was far from closed, even if she had to banish him from her bed again.

"I love you," he said, and with one final lingering look, he was gone, closing the door behind him.

The fool, Lavinia thought. *He thinks because I forgot myself last night, all is forgiven.* She was furious that he presumed he had erased his sins so easily, just as he had done so many times in the past. But at least he was gone. In his absence, she would have ample time to prepare herself and the house servants for any questions the authorities might have.

She watched from her window and as soon as she saw Lionel ride down the lane toward the main road, she dressed and went downstairs.

The moment she was in the kitchen, Piney began to excitedly recount the arrival of the slave patrols.

"They four of them, Miss Vinny. That old bearded one, that Mr. Hicks, he at the head of 'em. He had that big black snake whip he beats people with and everything. He tells me to fetch Mr. Lionel and wantin' to know if any of us run."

Lavinia tried to steady her shaking hand and took the cup of coffee Aunt Beck brought her while Piney babbled on. "They say that Hicks man got sich a sense for ketchin' run-a-ways, they ain't no bloodhound in this world that can match him. They say he don't even need to use hounds. They say he just hold his own nose up and can tell which way they runnin' bettern any dog they is. They say they three others run off from ol' Wroughton's place besides that big Gabriel. They say one of the field hands and his wife and baby, that Bingo and Jane, done run off, too. They say—"

They say, they say, they say— Lavinia thought Piney's litany would drive her mad. The plot she had designed seemed to have trapped her like a fly in a web. She had to get out of the house and think how to untangle herself .

"Prepare me a basket to take to old Mrs. Barksdale. I'm riding over there this morning," Lavinia said. "Piney, go upstairs and make my bed."

Alone with Emma, Aunt Beck, and Uncle Lemiel, Lavinia once again reviewed the story they would tell should they be interrogated.

"And be careful of Piney. She eavesdrops. And this family that ran from the Wroughton's—the man, wife, and baby. Do they have any connection to Gabriel?"

"Don't reckon so," said Uncle Lemiel, "Wroughton threatenin' to sells Bingo away from Jane and the baby." He shook his head sadly. "They not get far, don't 'speck—on foot and with a baby not more than a month old."

"Field people," Emma said with a contemptuous snort.

With a basket containing ham, a jar of apple butter, and pound cake, Lavinia left for the Barksdales immediately. Hoping to reach her neighbors before Charles Hicks and the patrols, she took a shortcut through the woods that brought her to the rear of the Barksdale house.

The Barksdales, Miss Maude and Miss Phoebe, were Lavinia's nearest neighbors, except for Horace Wroughton, and their big, rambling house was isolated far from the main road almost two miles from Hawthorn Hill.

In their seventies, the spinsters were the last of their family to live on the plantation, their two brothers having pursued careers in the ministry and law in Philadelphia. Miss Maude and Miss Phoebe were free spirits, and their company had for years been a welcome respite from the isolation and loneliness Lavinia often felt in the country. Lavinia sometimes went weeks without seeing another soul except the Mudley overseers and her servants and field hands. Her neighbors' goodness and humor were always a welcome restorative for her sometimes sagging spirits, and their lively conversation and sharp minds stimulated Lavinia on every subject from religion to politics to the books they shared.

Unlike most of the women Lavinia knew, the Barksdales were staunch individualists, their thinking often at variance with prevailing social and political views. But they were proud Virginians and grieved at the Commonwealth's ever-deepening sympathy and alliance with the militancy of the pro-slavery states farther South. Increasingly, Virginia's southern neighbors talked of secession and rattled sabers with threats and hopes for war to settle the slave question.

The abolition of slavery was an obsessive dream of the Barksdale sisters, and they could talk and debate politics as well as any man. Well read and religious, they were noted for their uncompromising abolitionist sentiments. Any man expressing such heretical views would probably have been driven out of the county, or, so passionate were feelings on the subject, called out to defend his honor in a duel. But being elderly spinsters without a vote, their unpopular opinions were tolerated and they were regarded as harmless eccentrics. Female intellect, without voting power and the voice of any legitimate platform, was considered unimportant, unthreatening, and had no impact in the Virginia of 1853.

"Oh, we're just squeaking wheels," Miss Phoebe said. "Squeaking wheels attached to no wagon and moving nothing."

Twenty years before, their father had freed his slaves. Not content to simply live on the adequate inheritance he had provided for his daughters, Miss Phoebe and Miss Maude had elected to continue running their plantation as before, except with paid tenants—not slave labor—as a gesture of open defiance against the system of slave labor that surrounded them. Theirs was an economic enterprise very much like Lavinia's own father's in southwestern Virginia.

"We'll show you we can do just as well paying free people to work as you ungodly slave owners can working the poor souls you have in bondage!" Miss Maude had challenged Lionel.

"Thank God you aren't in the legislature, Miss Maude," he had countered. "You'd bankrupt us all."

"But you'll bankrupt yourselves!" she had argued. "Sooner or later, slavery has to fall under its own weight."

"Now, Miss Maude, that's dangerous talk. Didn't you know the legislature passed a law against openly opposing our system?"

"'Our system,' poppycock!" she had countered. "Don't try to pretty up a dirty business with fancy names. And I'll say what I please. Don't they teach the Constitution at Mr. Jefferson's school? When I read it, it mentioned free speech."

Lionel and his father, Edmund, had listened for years to the sisters' anti-slavery arguments. But in the end, the old ladies' opinions were like a wren's breath in a gale. With no vote they could do nothing but harmlessly rant on.

The Barksdale and Hawthorn families had been neighbors for generations, and the good will between them remained unchanged even as political and philosophical differences in the two families had diverged. The Barksdales couldn't change the Hawthorns and the Hawthorns couldn't change the Barksdales, but they remained friends nevertheless, just as the staunchly abolitionist sisters did with other slave-owning families in the county.

"What joy!" trilled Miss Phoebe, clasping her hands and rushing out on the back porch to greet Lavinia as she dismounted. A spirited old lady of seventy, Miss Phoebe moved with the restless energy of a woman half her years. Tiny and girlish, Miss Phoebe's fluttering, bird-like nature belied a more serious demeanor with her keen mind concealed by a stream of giddy, inconsequential chatter and the appearance of scatterbrained frivolity.

"Thank God it's you. We've been invaded by an army of slave patrols and deputies all morning. Seems some of the Wroughton people have fled. They've sent everything but the militia to look us over."

"They've been to our place, too. That's one reason I came the back way."

"They were asking about your Angelica. Wanted to know if she was here. Said something about your—"

"I'm afraid she'd fled."

"Just hitch Mercury up here at the porch. The people are all in the fields today and we don't have a soul working the stables."

After exchanging embraces and kisses, Miss Phoebe linked arms with Lavinia and ushered her into the kitchen. Always in high spirits, Miss Phoebe's presence was an immediate antidote to Lavinia's anxiety and gloom.

"Now rest yourself and tell me about the Wroughton runaways while I fix us some cider and my field workers some dinner," she said over her spectacles, her periwinkle-blue eyes alive with humor and pleasure. The energetic old lady busily resumed preparing food for her field hands, laughing merrily as she floated as smoothly as if on wheels from steaming pot to cupboard to oven. Tiny and with the energy of a child, Miss Phoebe seemed to have no bones, and her arms and hands were constantly in motion, gesturing and emphasizing every word she spoke.

Lavinia placed her basket on the kitchen table. "Maybe Mother Barksdale will be able to eat some of Aunt Beck's pound cake."

"How splendid!" Miss Phoebe exclaimed as she examined the basket's contents and clasped her hands delightedly. "If she won't, I shall. And ham and apple butter—"

Said by Lionel's father to have been the belle of the county in her youth, Miss Phoebe still retained her girlish charm and had never changed the hairstyle of dozens of thin, corkscrew curls, now quite gray, which circled her head and swung to and fro, bouncing up and down like springs with every animated gesture she made. It was said that old Judge Winston Finch had remained a bachelor because Miss Phoebe had refused him her hand, and that Theophilus Baker had been forced to make a painful compromise in marrying the dowdy Lena Fields following a similar rejection by Phoebe's sister, the then comely Miss Maude.

Although the old ladies were old maids, it was clearly by choice, and everyone knew it. Theirs was not spinsterhood born of lack of opportunity. Lavinia marveled at how different their lives were compared to her own unmarried aunts, Puss and Lyla, little rabbit-like women who lurked in the shadows of other relatives' charity and obligatory goodwill.

Although Miss Maude and Miss Phoebe had been reared in the protected and genteel manner befitting their class, and educated in the finest schools in the North and South, the sisters embraced menial work with as much enthusiasm as they might a piano sonata or discussion of poetry. Totally unprepared for any but the most refined occupations— painting china, crocheting, or music—when their father freed his slaves and most of them left the county, they literally took up the reins themselves with the help of only two black families who chose to remain in their service as paid tenants.

Cooking, chopping wood, even plowing the fields when they were younger, were all duties they performed, relishing in the physical activity required in running a large plantation almost single-handed.

"There is no honor save through honorable work," was Miss Phoebe's credo, and she often said, "Let others yield to the idleness of the devil, but not I."

Lavinia and Miss Phoebe were soon joined by Miss Maude from upstairs. "It's a comfort to see you, Lavinia, darlin'," said the stout old lady, the eye-catching figure of her youth only a memory. She embraced Lavinia and sat down heavily at the kitchen table, her round, heavily jowled face etched with care. A startling contrast to her more buoyant younger sister, Miss Maude, seventy-five, was tall and full bodied, her steel-gray hair drawn into a tight shapeless lump on top of her head. Lumbering and shapeless, the elder Barksdale sister projected a more serious, sometimes even harsh and imperious, demeanor, which nevertheless concealed a generous, tender heart. Glaring with the hooded eyes of an eagle, and brusque and uncompromising in her candor, Miss Maude suffered fools poorly and her tongue had been known to sting with the sharpness of an adder.

"And how is Mother Barksdale?" Lavinia inquired.

"Finally drifted off to sleep, poor dear," Miss Maude said gravely. "I've sent for Dr. Hunter again." Her eagle-like eyes cast Miss Phoebe a quick glance. "Poor Mama turns ninety-five in a month, and I'm afraid she won't last long."

The old lady's eyes glistened with tears and she brought a handkerchief to her nose. Lavinia placed a comforting hand on her arm. She felt guilty in using her good friends as a diversion in the escape of Angelica, but had no choice but to appear as shocked as the Barksdales at her flight.

"Why that ungrateful girl!" fumed Miss Maude. "I suppose it was for that...that...what's-his-name of Wroughton's!"

"Yes. Gabriel."

"For love, no doubt," said Miss Phoebe with a snort and disgusted shake of her head that set her corkscrew curls swinging. "I would never have thought your Angelica such a fool."

"Everybody's a fool when they're in love, Phoebe," Miss Maude said. "Well, be that as it may, one should never allow romance to compromise one's loyalty. They're bound to be caught. Why that Gabriel must be nearly six-and-a-half-feet tall. He's too big to hide and he'll be recognized anywhere."

"And what Wroughton won't offer to get him back. Why, how much did he pay to recover that poor boy who ran off last week? And nearly beat to death when he got him back—"

"Six hundred dollars, I heard. And he could have replaced him for half that amount," Miss Phoebe said.

"Oh, he wanted him back to serve as an example to his people. When they brought him back—Booker was his name—that brute Wroughton beat him unmercifully. Our tenants heard Wroughton opened his back to the spine, and the man may not even live."

"He should be prosecuted. And it must not have been much of an example if that Gabriel and three of his other people took flight yesterday."

"Why, Lavinia, dear. Are you unwell? You've grown so pale—"

"Oh, no...I'm...I'm just appalled by such cruelty..."

Seeking other, less painful topics, Lavinia told the sisters of her expected grandchild and for a short time the heavy cloud of slavery and human suffering was banished from the Barksdale kitchen.

A series of sharp thumps from the ceiling—old Mrs. Barksdale's cane rapping on the floor above—brought smiles of recognition, and Miss Phoebe wiped her hands on her apron and raised a restraining gesture to Miss Maude.

"My turn, sister," she said, heading toward the door. "That's Mama, awake again. Even though she's bedfast, she can raise the dead with that cane." Miss Phoebe laughed merrily and sailed out of the room, calling after her, "She'll want to see you, dear. I'll rap when I get her prettied up and you just come on up."

No sooner had she left the room and Miss Maude had again picked up the subject of Horace Wroughton's brutality than the sound of a baby crying floated into the room. Although there was no mistaking the sound, Miss Maude chose to ignore it and continued her tirade.

"That Wroughton treats his blacks the way they do in Alabama or Mississippi—not like Virginians. A Virginian would be more civilized." She twisted her mouth and nose into a smirk. "He's supposed to be from Carolina. Or is it Georgia? Certainly not Virginia."

The baby's cries, which came from the cellar, continued. Miss Maude, seemingly oblivious to the noise, babbled on, her voice rising as if attempting to drown out the sound of the baby. Lavinia stared in bewilderment at the old lady, who looked away and avoided her scrutiny.

Shifting uncomfortably in her seat as the cries continued, Miss Maude's agitation increased until she finally stopped talking, slammed her hands on the table, and pushed herself to her feet. "We'll go and see Mama now," she said, and turned toward the door.

"But that baby!" Lavinia said. "There's a baby crying in the cellar—"

"I don't hear it... I...I..." Miss Maude sputtered, and fixed Lavinia with her eagle eyes as if she could, through the sheer intensity of her glare, force the sound to stop or Lavinia to stop hearing it. Finally, unable to ignore the cries, which had risen to the level of a wail, Miss Maude's frustration mounted until she blurted out in exasperation, "Alright. I've had a baby and hidden it in the cellar!"

Lavinia stared at the seventy-five-year-old woman's stricken, serious face for a second, let out a whoop, and collapsed on the kitchen table in helpless laughter. The eruption of mirth was so sudden, even the normally staid Miss Maude's stony seriousness was broken.

When Miss Phoebe entered the room, Miss Maude quickly added, "No. It's not mine. It's Phoebe's!"

This brought a new torrent of merriment from Lavinia, who slapped the table and shook with laughter. She could not remember when she had found anything so hilarious. Lavinia's eruption was like a floodgate opened, releasing not only her laughter but the long pent-up tension of her burdens as well.

Miss Maude, as if she, too, had been relieved of great stress, joined in the laughter, while Miss Phoebe looked from one to the other, her mystification only making them worse. When at last Miss Maude and Lavinia recovered their composure, tears streamed down Lavinia's face.

Miss Phoebe, still bewildered, looked with alarm at her sister, as the baby's cries continued with even greater intensity.

"That sick cat...There's a sick cat in the cellar—" Miss Phoebe said, managing a weak smile and titter, but it failed to conceal her alarm at the betraying cry. Then the old lady's uncomfortable, totally unconvincing attempt to fabricate indifference with a weak, forced giggle fell silent.

"It's not a sick cat!" Lavinia struggled to repress her laughter. "It's your...your...baby!"

The laughter began again and Miss Phoebe managed a weak, helpless smile.

As the wailing from the cellar continued, Miss Phoebe's face grew serious and she looked meaningfully at Miss Maude. "I'll go down," she said quietly, and she went to a cupboard and removed a bottle. "Maybe a drop or two more of turpentine, until Dr. Hunter gets here. Take Lavinia to see Mama."

Suddenly the picture cleared and Lavinia knew her friends' secret.

"They're here, aren't they," she said, more a statement than a question. "Those runaways from the Wroughton's. That's the baby in the cellar."

For a long time the women seemed to be frozen, suspended in the heart of a moment in which time stands still and fate and destiny suddenly veer in an unexpected direction.

Miss Maude, her face taut, sat down heavily in her chair.

"Yes," she said simply and she looked at Lavinia, waiting for her reaction.

Sensing her friends' predicament, Lavinia broke into a smile. "It's alright!" she said.

The spinsters said nothing but continued to stare at her.

"I'm glad! I understand! I would have done the same thing!"

The Barksdale sisters sighed with relief, and looking at Lavinia with gratitude, reached across the table to grasp her hand.

"Thank God," said Miss Phoebe. "You won't turn us in to the slave patrols?"

"Of course not. Don't be ridiculous."

"Harboring fugitives is a serious crime, you know," Miss Maude added.

"Well, it's no crime to me."

"The baby's very ill," Miss Maude said. "It coughs and wheezes and may have lung fever. I'm afraid we old maids know less about sick children than the poor mother. Do you think turpentine would be helpful?"

"Yes. And do you have any Cherry Bark Syrup?"

"We do. And whiskey."

"Bring all three and we'll see what we can do."

With Miss Phoebe leading the way, the three women went out the kitchen door. At one end of the back porch, a staircase led down to the dark, musty cellar.

Miss Phoebe led the way. "After the patrols visited us a second time this morning, we were afraid they would come back and search the house so we've hidden them in the cellar," she said.

"We sent for Dr. Hunter," Miss Maude said. "We didn't know what else to do. The child is so ill. This morning one of our tenants was milking and heard the baby crying and found the three of them hiding in the barn. I was going to tell Dr. Hunter the baby belongs to one of our tenants. He'd never know the difference."

Once in the cellar, Miss Maude fired a lantern to reveal the fugitive family huddled in the shadows in a far corner.

"It's just us," she said. "And we've brought a friend who can help the baby."

As Lavinia's eyes adjusted to the darkness, the lantern light fell on a black man and woman, cowering like frightened children. In their twenties, the couple clung to each other and crouched on the floor, holding between them a tiny, whimpering infant.

"Lavinia, this is Bingo and Jane—and the baby is Samuel. This is our neighbor, Mrs. Hawthorn," Miss Maude said.

"May I see Samuel?" Lavinia asked gently, and Miss Phoebe held the lantern as the terrified mother looked questioningly at her husband.

"You mustn't be afraid," Lavinia said gently, but fear still shown in the blacks' eyes as they huddled closer to each other. "I'm only here to help."

The baby's cries had subsided into sickly whimpers, but a deep, raspy cough and one touch of the dry, hot forehead told Lavinia the child was gravely ill.

"It's too damp and cold down here. Can we take the child upstairs?"

Miss Maude nodded and Lavinia turned toward the door. The woman held the child protectively to her breast and looked desperately at her husband.

"It's alright. No one will see us," Lavinia said. "The baby is very ill and we must take him upstairs where he will be warm—"

"You can come, too," said Miss Maude, waving them toward the door. "But be ready to rush back down here if the patrols return."

Bingo uncertainly nodded to his wife and she handed the child to Lavinia.

"Now don't be frightened. You'll be safe here," Lavinia said, moved by the couple's fear and helplessness. She looked at the Barksdales, who smiled with pride and gratitude that she had joined their enterprise.

"Thank God you're with us," Miss Maude said. She motioned for Bingo and Jane to follow them and turned down the lamp.

Once upstairs in a bedroom, Lavinia lay the baby on the bed and examined him carefully. He was only two months old and small for his age. She had Miss Phoebe hang the small, dirty quilt in which the infant was wrapped near the fire to warm and rubbed a small amount of turpentine on the child's chest.

"Do you have milk?" she asked the mother.

"Yes, ma'am." Her reply was almost inaudible.

"How long has the child been ill?"

"Just since last night, ma'am," Bingo said. "We leave out real early this mornin'. We come right far in the creek—" His voice fell off in uncertainty.

"You must tell me everything. It's very important."

"It pretty cold this mornin' and foggy and the creek up and mighty cold. But he not get wet. I holds him up the whole time, but we never had much to wrop him in—"

"Perhaps it is just a chest cold, but he does have a fever." Lavinia turned to the sisters. "Do you have any ice?"

"Why, no. We haven't filled the ice house in years."

"Then send one of your people over and get some from Uncle Lemiel. Tell them it's for your mama."

Miss Phoebe flew into action and left the room. In a moment she was back, her face pale and her eyes shining with fear.

"The slave patrols! That Hicks man and his men! They're riding up the lane right now."

No sooner were the words out of her mouth than the baby started to cry, soft little protests of discomfort at first, which grew suddenly into a wail.

Jane flew to Bingo with a cry of alarm and the two looked in helpless desperation from Miss Phoebe to Miss Maude.

Lavinia raced to the window and looked out as the baby's cry became an ear-piercing bellow. She saw Charles Hicks and the same four men she had seen that morning at Hawthorn Hill reining their horses to a stop just outside the yard fence.

Hicks dismounted, entered the yard, and approached the front porch.

"Hicks," gasped Miss Phoebe. "Whether he sees the baby or not, he'll hear his cries, even from the porch."

Seizing the child, Lavinia rushed out of the room as the mother's wail rose with that of the baby's and Bingo began to pray aloud, "Oh, Lordy, Lordy—"

"I'll take the baby to Hawthorn Hill," Lavinia said, racing down the hall to the kitchen. "When Dr. Hunter comes, send him to me. I'll say the child is one of ours. Just stall Hicks and his men until I can get a head start."

In the kitchen, Lavinia snatched the tablecloth off the table and quickly wrapped the baby in it. Grabbing the basket she had brought, she dumped the contents on the table and put the baby inside.

Miss Maude crammed the bottle of turpentine and cherry syrup in the basket and opened the back door. With a quick nod and grim conspiratorial smile, Lavinia was out the door and in seconds astride her horse.

Holding the reins with one hand and the basket with the other, she gave Mercury a sharp jab with her heels and he leapt toward the concealment of a thick growth of trees that lay behind the house. As she entered the woods beyond, Lavinia glanced over her shoulder to catch a glimpse of Bingo and Jane as they hurriedly disappeared down the porch stairs to the cellar.

Thank God she had come the back way and Mercury had not been tethered at the front of the house. Galloping at full speed, she was a good mile into the woods before she reined Mercury to a stop. Seeing no horsemen in pursuit and hearing no sound of hooves or hounds, she peered into the basket.

Lifting the tablecloth, she thought the silent, unmoving child was dead, but was relieved when she heard the infant's faint, raspy breathing and saw the tiny chest and stomach heave in its struggle to take in air. Amazingly, the baby was fast asleep. She sighed with relief and patted Mercury fondly.

"Your gait has rocked the baby asleep, Mercury," she said.

Covering the child again, she nudged Mercury into a trot and directed him out of the woods toward a pasture that bordered the main road and would shorten the journey home. It was imperative that she get the sick baby to Old Sheba and the warmth of a fire at once.

When the Barksdales sent Dr. Hunter, she would pass the child off as the latest born to Nancy and Clevis. Dr. Hunter would never know the difference. He had never seen Nancy's real child, the little girl born on Christmas day, who would be replaced at her mother's breast by little Samuel.

Midway across the field, the baby awoke and began to whimper again. Holding the reins and trying at the same time to comfort him with her voice and gentle pats and strokes was unsuccessful. A full-throated cry arose and Lavinia slowed Mercury to a canter, pulled back the tablecloth and cooed soothingly to the distressed infant. When she reached the edge of the pasture and the gate to the main road, she dismounted and led Mercury through it and gave the child her full attention. Taking him out of the basket, she laid him against her shoulder and watching the road for anyone approaching, gently patted him until his cries once more subsided. Quieted at last, she returned the child to the basket and covered him with the tablecloth. Holding the basket away from her and taking care that her movements did not disturb him, she remounted.

With no one approaching, Lavinia returned to the main road, holding Mercury to his slowest gait. To further keep the baby as motionless as possible, she positioned the basket in front of her, extending her arms through its handle to hold the reins.

She had traveled no more than five hundred yards when she heard the approach of horses behind her. Glancing over her shoulder, Lavinia's heart was seized with a spasm as sharp as if a knife had been driven through it.

Lionel Hawthorn was galloping toward her.

To Lavinia's horror, she recognized the riders accompanying him—Tom Hudspeth, the county sheriff, and Charles Hicks and the slave patrols.

Her chest tightened and it was only the realization that if she fainted she would drop the baby that kept her from losing consciousness. The baby emitted a fitful gurgle, a tiny cough, and a whimper Lavinia prayed was not the beginning of a wail. Lionel raised his hat and waved it in recognition.

Her dread increased when she saw that tethered to Lionel's horse was another familiar animal: Romulus, the horse Angelica and Gabriel had ridden on the morning of their escape.

Chapter Eleven

Lavinia had no time to maneuver her horse into the woods, conceal the baby, or ride away. Lionel had already seen her. He approached in a gallop with the sheriff and patrols right behind him. There was only time to fight off another attack of fainting and try and conceal the baby by quickly pulling a corner of the tablecloth over his face and arms.

"God, help me," she said, part prayer, part expression of panic. How had they found Romulus? Had Angelica been caught? Did the sheriff and Lionel know of her involvement? And what would he think when he discovered that at that very moment she carried the child of another runaway?

She glanced frantically at the basket. The baby was quieter, but his little hands and feet were busy, their movements clearly visible as the tablecloth rippled above his flailing arms and kicking legs.

"Lavinia!" Lionel rode up beside her. The sheriff and Hicks followed a few paces behind. Lavinia tried to make the basket as inconspicuous as possible by lowering it to her side.

"You're back," she said lamely with an unsteady smile. "And with Romulus...and Sheriff Hudspeth..."

"Good afternoon, Mrs. Hawthorn," the sheriff said, removing his hat. Lavinia's voice seemed suddenly paralyzed and she could only give him a nod while ignoring Hicks and his men.

"Mr. Hicks and his men have just come from the Barksdales," Lionel said, as yet taking no notice of the basket. As he leaned toward her to kiss her on the cheek, his expression grew grave with concern. "My dear, you look so gaunt and white."

Afraid to move or make any sound that might rouse the baby, Lavinia stared back at him in speechless confusion, her sickly smile making her face ache.

"Ah, you know..." he said gently, as if understanding her pallor and stunned expression. "You know that Angelica has fled?"

She nodded stupidly. "Yes. I'm just returning from the Barksdales. They said Angelica never even—"

"I know. Sheriff Hudspeth told me. He was bringing Romulus home when I ran into him on the road. He explained what he thinks has happened. Gabriel also ran and I'm afraid they used the train passes you purchased for Uncle Lemiel to take her to Richmond."

Lavinia felt the basket jiggle in her hand. Lowering her head to avoid Lionel's gaze, she stole a glance in its direction. Like a breeze stirring calm water, the basket's cloth cover fairly rippled with movement. *Oh, God, don't let him see it*, she prayed, and her throat tightened with anxiety.

Lionel looked straight ahead and shook his head thoughtfully. "I'm really disappointed in Angelica. We did everything we could to help her."

"Has...has she been caught?" Lavinia's voice was so tight she could hardly speak. "Or the man—Gabriel?"

"Not unless they've been apprehended in Richmond. Brazen as all get out. Just boarded the train and—" His eyes suddenly caught sight of the basket and widened at the sight of the moving tablecloth. "What the devil is that?"

"Kittens," Lavinia blurted, not quite sure where her response came from. Then she remembered Miss Phoebe's futile effort to attribute the baby's cries to a sick cat. Seizing the idea, she gushed on, "The Barksdales' mother cat died. With no time for anything but caring for their mother, I told them I'd take them—"

A faint gurgle reached her ears. Then a tiny cough. *Oh, God, please don't let the baby cry out,* she prayed.

Lionel's concern deepened the crease of his brow. "Oh, my darling. You look absolutely stricken. I know how betrayed you must feel. I'm surprised at Angelica, too."

"Yes!" she responded almost too quickly. "Please, Lionel. Just go on home. I'm terribly upset and need to be alone for a while." Turning to the sheriff, she added, "I do hope you will forgive me...and understand..."

"Of course, Mrs. Hawthorn," the sheriff said.

"Mrs. Hawthorn and the girl were quite close," Lionel said.

"I can understand your loss, Mrs. Hawthorn."

"We'll go on, then," Lionel said. "Do you want me to take the cats for you?" He extended his hand to take the basket.

"No, I'll do it. Just—" Another little sound emanated from the basket, the prelude, Lavinia feared, to a full throated cry. If only he would go on!

"If you're sure you'll be alright."

She nodded quickly, as another un-catlike gurgle came from the basket. She was ready to scream with anxiety.

Lionel, still looking at her with concern, gave her a tender, sympathetic smile and caressed her cheek with his hand.

"I'll take the horse on in, Tom," he said, reigning his horse toward the center of the road. "Thanks for bringing him back."

The sheriff nodded, and as Lionel dropped back to secure Romulus's reins to his own mount, the sheriff pulled alongside Lavinia. "I will not trouble you now, Mrs. Hawthorn, but perhaps when you have recovered from your shock, you could answer some questions?"

Another gurgle came from the basket.

"Yes...yes," she said in a voice unnaturally loud to mask the sound of the baby's increasing agitation.

"I am sorry for your loss, ma'am, and good day to you."

The sheriff nodded, replaced his hat, and joined by Hicks and the patrols, followed Lionel, who had Romulus in tow.

Lavinia, aching with tension, watched as they rode away. When they were out of hearing range, but still visible in the distance, the baby broke into a bellow of full-throated cries.

Lavinia held her breath and watched until the riders were out of sight, relieved that the retreating horses did not suddenly stop and turn around. Then, daring to breathe again, she drew back the cloth that covered the baby.

"Go ahead and scream, you little monster," she said. "You've nearly given me heart failure. And if you live, I'll make you pay for it later. And you are going to live, you little dragon. You've put me through too much for me to let you die on me now."

Released from her uneasiness, Lavinia laughed wildly with relief. That she had stood within feet of her husband, the sheriff, and Hicks's slave patrols while holding a runaway slave in her very hands pushed her into momentary hysteria. Saying a prayer of thanksgiving for her deliverance, she gave Lionel and the sheriff time to get well ahead of her before continuing to Hawthorn Hill on a path through the woods away from the main road.

The baby alternated between feeble whimpering and raspy coughing, and by the time she reached the back road that ran through the quarters, he had fallen asleep again. Fortunately, only Reuben was in attendance at the stables.

"Master Lionel just come back, Miss Lavinia. He done gone to the house. And he brings back Romulus."

No sound betrayed the contents of the basket as Lavinia dismounted and handed the reins to Reuben. "Go to the big house and have Aunt Beck meet me in Old Sheba's cabin. And then brush down Mercury."

Inside Old Sheba's cabin and away from the slaves, curious as to their mistress's presence in the quarters, Lavinia revealed the contents of the basket.

The old woman narrowed her eyes suspiciously. "Where you get this baby?"

"I found it in the woods," Lavinia said, knowing the old woman probably knew the child's origin before she even asked. "It may have been abandoned by those two slaves who fled the Wroughton place. His name is Samuel and Dr. Hunter will be here soon. It is absolutely essential that no one, not even Dr. Hunter, know it is not one of our own people. He's very ill."

"It tell you its name?" Old Sheba asked. "Right keen youngin' can talk 'fore it much older than a month." Her eyes bored into Lavinia, who avoided her gaze by looking about the room at the bundles of roots, stems, dried flowers, and leaves suspended by strings from the ceiling and along the walls. Everything from corn, tobacco, sweet potatoes, long strands of dried beans, and a dozen other plants less identifiable lined the walls, some used in Old Sheba's medical potions. Around the fireplace and on the narrow mantle, gourds, jars, pouches and bottles held leaves, bark, animal fat, and other ingredients found in her remedies. The smell of the various herbs was slightly floral, yet mixed with an aroma similar to Lionel's office, earthy and pungent. But the dominant odor was the unpleasant smells of asafetida and jimson weed.

When she finally looked at Old Sheba, the old woman's disbelief was so apparent, Lavinia abandoned any attempt to hide the baby's origins.

"You know Wroughton would give the baby no care," Lavinia said. "He sells children as fast as they grow up, and he can get something for them. He'd probably let this little one die to be rid of it. With the parents gone, the baby has a better chance here with us—unless it becomes known where he came from."

Glancing out the cabin's single window, Lavinia saw Aunt Beck waddling down the hill and giving Old Sheba no chance to respond, she left the cabin to tell her about the child.

"You makin' youself more trouble with this, Miss Vinny," Aunt Beck said.

"But the patrols were right outside," said Lavinia. "They would have heard the baby's cries." It seemed preposterous to Lavinia that trying to save a sick baby was illegal. "Just try and save the little fellow. No one will know."

"Don't you fret none about me and Lemiel. We's too old for 'em to do nothin' 'cept wait for us to die. It you I be worryin' about. You just diggin' yourself in deeper and deeper."

In the cabin, Old Sheba had already wrapped the baby in a blanket, laid him in a quilt-lined kindling box, and placed him near the fire. His little chest rose and fell like a bellows as he gasped for air.

Aunt Beck shook her head as she examined the baby and mumbled, "Um, um, um," either in uncertainty for the baby's survival or the recklessness of his rescue.

Lavinia was grateful that she could at least trust Aunt Beck, Emma, and Uncle Lemiel. She was less certain about Old Sheba, who continued to watch her with disturbing suspicion. Old Sheba's dislike for white people was thinly veiled, and as she grew older and her advanced age made her less likely to be rebuked, she was freer in her candor and hostility. Aunt Beck and Emma would coerce Sheba into some degree of loyalty, but even as they did, Lavinia regretted she was making them a party to illegal activities not of their own doing.

"Will he live?" Lavinia asked as the old woman lifted the baby and tapped him gently on the back.

"Shh," she ordered, and she pressed her ear to the little boy's heaving chest. "He got lung fever," she said. "They some can throw it off, but most not."

Old Sheba placed the baby back in the wood box. "Lungs ain't full of water yet and I'll know by mornin'. If the fever break."

She went to the mantle where she found a jar of salve which she rubbed into the baby's chest. "Maybe this draw out the pizen. I'll send Piney to the ice house. If we cools down this baby's head it help."

"I'll get it. I don't think Piney should know anything about it."

Old Sheba, her gaze less hostile and suspicious, looked at Lavinia. "How 'bout you new maid, that Henny, fetchin' it?" she asked, eyeing Lavinia coolly as she handed her a dented copper kettle.

Lavinia, mystified that the mysterious black grapevine already knew of Henny's petition, took the kettle and left the cabin. When she returned from the ice house with a shard of ice, Old Sheba wrapped it in a rag and applied it to the baby's brow.

Watching the two women minister to the child, Lavinia said, "We'll keep him here. Dr. Hunter is coming. He is to be told the baby belongs to Nancy. And Mr. Lionel, if he finds out the baby is here before he goes to Richmond. I met him on the road. He knows Angelica has fled and thinks the baby is a litter of kittens."

"Won't be no trouble deceivin' Dr. Hunter," Old Sheba said. "But Mr. Lionel know right off this child ain't four months old. This one barely one. And I reckon he know a boy's pecker from a girl's parts."

"Keep the baby covered as much as possible," said Lavinia, ignoring the old woman's vulgarity and salacious grin. "He can't know we've made a switch. He..."

Old Sheba narrowed her eyes and shook her head doubtfully before she spoke. "This a bad web you weavin'. Likely ketch you self in it. It worry enough when you helps your own people to run, but when you helpin' them that belongs to the wicked, like Horace Wroughton, it can bring big trouble to you."

Lavinia paled. "What do you mean, 'help my own people to run'?" she asked. She stiffened indignantly. But Old Sheba's withering appraisal of her feigned innocence destroyed her denial and exposed her as a liar.

"They ain't nothin' been boilin' long as that idee you and Angelica been cookin' that don't get to me sooner or later. But I ain't to be tellin' it. No more than Beck and Emma and Lemiel and any of the others what knows."

"Thank you, Sheba," Lavinia said. She knew it would be useless to deny her involvement and she was too weary to try.

With the baby in Aunt Beck and Old Sheba's care, Lavinia returned to the big house to await the arrival of Doctor Hunter.

Having slipped up the back stairs to avoid Lionel, she had changed from riding attire into an afternoon dress when barking hounds announced a visitor.

Dr. Hunter, she thought, and she raced to the window. Instead of the familiar old buggy listing up the drive, her pulse quickened when she saw a single horseman, Sheriff Hudspeth.

She slipped into the upper hall and heard Lionel's voice.

"Come in, Sheriff. Uncle Lemiel, take Sheriff Hudspeth's hat and bring us some coffee in the library. Or something a little stronger, Tom?"

"Thank you, Lionel. I'll just keep my hat. I'm pressed for time. And just coffee, thank you. I'd like to speak with Mrs. Hawthorn, if I may. I know she's upset and I hope I'm not coming too soon."

Knowing she would be interrogated sooner or later, Lavinia took a deep breath and started down the stairs, smiling pleasantly as if she were a belle ascending into a roomful of suitors.

"Sheriff Hudspeth, how kind of you to return our horse. My apologies for my behavior this morning. I was so upset, having just learned of my servant's flight." She was surprised at the calmness of her voice and how well she concealed her anxiety.

"A pleasure to see you, Mrs. Hawthorn," the sheriff said with a slight bow. Sheriff Hudspeth was a large, graceful man with a black, flowing moustache that extended below his chin. Serious in demeanor and soft-spoken, he seemed embarrassed and uncertain. Although not of the planter class, he was nevertheless considered a gentleman and was a hunting companion of Lionel's.

"I hope you feel well enough to answer a few questions now," he said.

"I shall cooperate in any way I can."

In the library, Uncle Lemiel served coffee and Lionel and the sheriff briefly discussed the winter's hunting season while Lavinia tried to calm herself.

"As you know, Mrs. Hawthorn, your girl and the Wroughton slave left by train for Richmond. Because they were unaccompanied by whites, they rode in the baggage car. The station master thought they were house servants. I believe you had spoken to him earlier."

"Yes, I had. I believe my husband has explained why I felt Angelica should be sent to Richmond for a time. It was to avoid just such a situation that seems to have actually occurred—an elopement." Lavinia looked modestly at the floor.

With Lionel watching her and the sheriff nodding his head respectfully as he tugged at his moustache, Lavinia prattled on about Angelica. "When I think of all we had done to try and buy that man from Mr. Wroughton so they could marry. I feel so betrayed." She lowered her head and pressed her clasped hands against her mouth, as if trying to hold back tears.

"I understand, ma'am," the sheriff said, shifting uncomfortably in his chair and looking at the carpet. Holding his hat before him by the brim, he began to slowly rotate it around and around like a wheel.

Wondering if she was overplaying, Lavinia stole a glance at Lionel, but he only leaned casually against the mantle, his arms folded as he watched her evenly. A smile played at the corners of his mouth. When he crossed the room to hand her his handkerchief, he looked as if he knew something she did not—or something she did—which disturbed her even more.

"And...and where did you find our horse?" she asked the sheriff.

"At Baker's Blacksmith Shop. Adjacent to the train station. She told Baker the horse would be picked up later."

"We often leave our horses with Mr. Baker when traveling by train. He stables them for us until we return."

"Your husband said you had given the girl permission to leave the plantation?" The sheriff continued to rotate the hat in his hands.

"Yes. I did not know until today that she had fled, although I had heard that the Wroughton slave had this morning. The patrols were here. I had no idea this was a joint enterprise, a collaboration."

"I'm afraid that it was—is." The hat in his hand stopped rotating like the wheel of a wagon suddenly brought to a halt.

"That wretched, thankless girl."

"If we could go back to the beginning, Mrs. Hawthorn. When and why you allowed the girl to leave the property on a horse."

"Oh, yes," Lavinia said, refusing to look directly at Lionel but conscious of his intense surveillance. The hat in the sheriff's hand slowly began to rotate again.

"Well, you see our neighbor, Mrs. Emerson Barksdale," Lavinia continued. "I'm sure you know Mrs. Barksdale—quite elderly and ill for over a year."

"Yes, ma'am. I know the Barksdales."

"Well, Dr. Hunter's wife told me at church that she had had another stroke. I was feeling like a terrible neighbor for not having visited the poor old dear in several weeks. And only rarely this winter. The weather was so terrible, and that cold snap in March..."

"Yes, ma'am." The hat rotated faster in the sheriff's hands.

What a gentleman Sheriff Hudspeth is, Lavinia thought. *He's bored to madness with these petty details, but he's too polite to do anything but listen.*

"Beck, our cook," she went on, "Beck cut this particularly good ham last week and I decided I would make some sour dough bread and send it over...with a jar of apple butter..."

Lionel shifted with impatience; the sheriff spun his hat faster in his hands.

"Since I had so many duties to do here... Mr. Hawthorn has been away for some time..."

"You sent your girl, Angelica, instead?"

"Why, yes. And with instructions that she was to assist the Barksdale ladies in caring for their mother if she was needed. I'm sure you know the Barksdales have only those two black families on their place now. And Angelica is so good with sick people. I've loaned her before to nurse the sick. That is why I thought nothing of it when she didn't return last evening."

"And you purchased the train passes for her?"

"Yes, last week. I wanted the station master to know why she would not be accompanied by a white person and explained that I was sending her with Uncle Lemiel. I suppose they thought the Wroughton slave was who I meant."

"The man was described by the ticket agent as well-dressed. Assumed he was a house servant. Do you know where he might have gotten his clothes?"

"I am sure I have no idea."

Without looking at him, she was aware Lionel shifted from one foot to another.

"Mrs. Wroughton assures me he had no access to anything but the usual field-hand garments at her place. And nothing from Mr. Wroughton's wardrobe is missing."

"How very strange," Lavinia said.

"And they both had papers," the sheriff said, looking at her.

"I always see to it that my servants have travel papers when venturing off the plantation. Even on short journeys to the neighbors. And I had already written her permission papers to travel to Richmond next week... Oh! Do you suppose she used them?"

Lavinia jumped to her feet and rushed to the desk, where she opened a drawer and shuffled through the contents. The sheriff rose from his chair.

"They're gone!" Lavinia gasped. "That wretched girl. No doubt she stole them!" Further searching the drawer, she added, "As well as the passes!"

Hudspeth nodded. "Obviously. Everything seemed in order at the train. But that would not explain the man's papers. Could your girl read and write, Mrs. Hawthorn?"

"Oh, I assure you she could not. I am aware of the law against teaching blacks to read, Sheriff Hudspeth."

"Mrs. Wroughton assures me the man was also illiterate. Someone, however, prepared permission papers for him to use."

"But whomever could it be?" Lavinia said with great indignation and returned to her chair. She stole a quick glance at Lionel, who pursed his lips and furrowed his brow with mock mystification.

The sheriff sat down. Looking thoughtfully at the carpet, he continued turning his hat in his hand, its rotation halting and uncertain. At last he thanked Lavinia and Lionel for their help and bid them good afternoon.

As Sheriff Hudspeth was seeing himself out, he turned with a final question.

"Have you missed any clothes, Lionel? The man was wearing a black-and-yellow-checked outfit. Coat with matching trousers. The ticket agent remembered his great size and could tell the clothes had been altered for him."

"Never wore a black-and-yellow-checked outfit, Sheriff. I don't like yellow—or checks either."

Lavinia was shocked at his answer and felt his eyes boring into her. She remembered only too well the circumstances leading to Lionel's possession of the outfit and knew he remembered it, too. Ten years earlier, his mother had hired the Richmond tailor both he and his father used to run up a suit for Lionel's father. Pleased with the results, she had ordered another in exactly the same woolen fabric for her son. Lionel had hated it on sight and refused to wear it even once for his mother, leaving it to hang unworn in his wardrobe for a decade—until it had been altered for Gabriel by Angelica.

Lavinia knew he remembered the suit because it had been a source of amusement between them for years. "I will not dress like a stage comic for either Mother or you," he had insisted when Lavinia had teasingly urged him to wear it, perhaps only for a single evening at supper when his mother was in attendance. But to the sheriff, he had denied possession of the garment.

After the sheriff had ridden out of sight, Lavinia and Lionel returned to the library. Like a guilty child unsure of how much was known of her culpability, Lavinia sat stiffly awaiting Lionel's judgment, her hands nervously employed with her embroidery hoop and hook.

Lionel slowly walked to the end of the room and for a long time looked out the window, his hands thrust deep in his trouser pockets. Then he turned and looked at her.

"Angelica can't read?" he asked, angling his head quizzically. Lavinia hesitated, uncertain why the state of Angelica's literacy and not the whereabouts of the yellow-and-black-checked suit was relevant enough to begin his inquiry.

"Of course she can't."

"Then why, for the last ten years, have I heard the slam of a book being shut every time I have entered a room where Angelica was? And why, when caught unaware, the frantic scramble to conceal some volume behind a cushion or in the folds of her skirts?"

"Picture books. Looking at pictures."

"Then why the secrecy?"

"Perhaps she did not want to appear in idleness."

"They were not picture books, Lavinia."

"She...she may have picked it up...when I taught the boys and Oralee. She was often around...and she's very quick witted. That's how I learned to read, when Mother taught my brothers."

"But, dear wife, you made it abundantly clear to the sheriff that you knew it was illegal to teach a black to read—and that Angelica had not been taught. As mournful as your performance was, unequaled in anything I have seen since the latest melodrama graced the Roxy stage in Richmond, I am puzzled at your unseemly defense of Angelica."

"I am convinced Angelica was coerced into this by that man, Gabriel."

"Yet you removed the possibility that she might have forged his papers."

"I have no idea what you are talking about."

"Oh, Lavinia, don't take me for a fool. Your hand is in this somewhere."

"My hand in it? Are you saying I am...was...a collaborator?"

"Now what could ever stir such suspicions in my heart?" His voice was petulantly mocking.

"You insult me, Mr. Hawthorn." Putting aside her embroidery, she rose to her feet indignantly, as if to conclude the conversation.

"Act two," Lionel said wearily. "The heroine continues her outraged martyrdom."

"I will not listen to one more word of these preposterous allegations. And stop comparing me to a vulgar stage actress." Tossing her head and lifting her skirts, she started for the door.

"I have as yet made no accusations, Mrs. Hawthorn," he said. "Even though I know damn well you are an abolitionist at heart. You're just like your father and always have been."

Lavinia turned and glared at him. "How dare you insult me by such an accusation."

Lionel threw back his head and laughed.

"The abolitionist slave-owner's wife. Not that rare a breed, I can assure you. You women may be the death of slavery yet. The Christian conscience of Southern women is a potent, unrecognized force. And conscience in women is far stronger than in men. Papa always said old Colonel Barksdale freed his blacks because of pressure from the female Barksdales. And even now Maude and Phoebe rant like yelping hounds about slavery. Your numbers increase every day. Only you lack the courage to back your convictions. Those like the

Barksdales do not. Thank God you can't vote. You've helped your Angelica and I know it. I wouldn't be surprised if you planned it, paid for it, wrote the papers for it, and even gave Gabriel that ugly suit of clothes Mother had made for me."

Lavinia stopped at the door and whirled around. Her eyes gleamed with a spark of triumph. "But you denied to the sheriff having clothes of that description. Perhaps you have been the mastermind behind this. Perhaps—"

Lionel laughed again, "I said 'I never wore' those clothes, not that I didn't own them."

Lavinia felt trapped, like hunted prey treed and toyed with before the kill. She seethed that he knew of her guilt and that he had branded her a coward for concealing it. She was ashamed her cowardice had spurned her to hide a position she considered honest and principled, and that she had lied about it.

"I was only protecting you, my dear," he continued. "Besides, no one can connect me with those clothes. I never wore them."

"Angelica was mine. Your mother gave her to me."

"You are misinformed, dear wife. Allow me, a practicing attorney and well-versed in the subject, to enlighten you on the law. My mother may have thought that she 'owned' Angelica when she gave her to you, but the legalities of ownership in the Commonwealth of Virginia say otherwise. The law allows no married woman to own anything. Everything is her husband's. Angelica belonged to my father and when she was given to you, she was, in fact, given to me because, as your husband, I own all your property. Actually, since she was never mother's property in the first place, she still belongs to Papa."

Lavinia stood in mute confusion.

Lionel smiled. "Interesting point of law, isn't it? The only women who can own any property of any kind in Virginia are widows, spinsters, and female orphans. A married woman can own nothing. It all belongs to her husband."

"I don't believe it. You're just like every lawyer of the name. You twist things around and make things up. Your entire profession is that way. That's the most unfair thing—"

Lionel shrugged. "Perhaps. But fair or not, it is the law."

"But the Barksdales—"

"Spinsters. Let either marry and their property automatically becomes that of their spouse. But we are afield of what I want to tell you."

Taking her arm, he directed her to the settee, where they sat down. Holding her hands in his, his mood became serious and his blue eyes pinned her with a gravity that frightened her.

"Whatever the law says regarding the ownership of Angelica is irrelevant to me. Law or no law, I give you complete control of her. I really don't want to know what you have to do with her escape—and I shall not have you arrested for absconding with my property."

He smiled at her, then grew serious again. "The legalities that concern me are not what you have done with my property—in this case, Angelica. But if you have in any way aided and abetted in the crime of Gabriel's escape, I am most gravely concerned. He is the property of Horace Wroughton, and I cannot believe that Wroughton or the courts would observe the same restraint as I."

Rebuked and suddenly less defiant in her denials, Lavinia felt the chill of real fear at the prospects of charges brought against her by Wroughton. She had thought of this before, but hearing it from Lionel made the threat more real.

"As your husband and attorney, I must remind you, innocent though you are, severe consequences could befall all of us should you even entertain the thoughts of becoming a slave runner."

"Us all?" she asked weakly.

"Let me tell you about the amended Fugitive Slave Act. But you have heard of the Fugitive Slave Act of 1796?"

"Of course I have, you fool."

"And the amended act? Of 1850?"

"Yes..." she said, with less certainty. Although she had heard of it, she knew little of what it said and dreaded to know the specifics.

"You are aware of the serious repercussions contained therein for its violation?"

"I am not a magistrate...but I know...there are fines."

"More than fines, my dear. Helping slaves escape has become far too serious a crime for mere monetary consequences and jail terms. Slaves are expensive and constitute a significant portion of Virginia's wealth. Because the loss from those escaping has become so great, and increases every year, our lawmakers have made the penalty more severe."

He waited, observing her closely.

"So?" she said, confused as to the importance of some revisions in an old law. "This can have nothing to do with me."

"Let us hope," he said. "The economic burden of losses by slave owners from blacks fleeing north has caused our esteemed politicians to view legislation less in terms of human suffering and justice but in dollars and cents. Congress decided the old law be made more threatening, and in January of 1850, the penalty for aiding and assisting in the escape of slaves is bankruptcy. They take everything. One is left destitute."

Lavinia withered at the thought. "Everything?"

"Every asset in the possession of the guilty. Money, land, slaves, home, everything."

His gaze held her like chains as the full impact of what could happen to them burgeoned into fierce realization.

Finally his smile returned. "I have every confidence that my beloved wife would never allow her romantic nature in matchmaking cost her everything her husband had through bankruptcy."

"How absurd," she stammered. "You insult me with this kind of talk."

"My apologies. Let us speak of it no more." He rose and started for the door, where he stopped and turned back to her. "I'll continue on my way to Richmond now. Do I get a goodbye kiss?"

She approached him cautiously, grateful that his full wrath had not descended upon her. He kissed her deeply. She felt he shared her sadness in parting, and when he got to the door he turned back toward her. Suddenly, his regretful look was replaced by a broad grin.

"Thank you for getting rid of that hideous yellow-and-black-checked suit, he said. "I always hated it."

From the front porch, she watched him ride away as the seriousness of what she had done, and the possible consequences, struck her with full gravity.

What a fool I've been, she thought. But then she remembered Bingo and Jane, huddled in fear, in the Barksdales' cellar. How could she regret rescuing the sick baby? What else could she have done? Allow a black child to die because of some foolish, unjust law? Could any

Christian, abolitionist or not, Southerner or not, do any differently?

Lionel had called her an abolitionist and she knew that she was an abolitionist, if only one of conscience. He had also called her a coward. And that was also true. Before today, her beliefs had no more conviction than weak words at teas, quilting parties, and religious society meetings—safe, polite protests that were little more than self-righteous platitudes. But in the last two days, she had expressed her opposition with more than Biblical quotations. She had acted with deeds that smote the face of slavery itself. And she was both frightened and elated by her defiance.

She couldn't wait to tell the Barksdale sisters. Suddenly their radicalism didn't seem foolish at all, even when they spoke of such far-fetched realities as women voting and holding office, suggestions that only brought a wary exchange of glances and laughter from most men—and women—in 1853.

While it was true that as Mrs. Lionel Hawthorn she could not own property, or vote, or serve on a jury, or in any way affect change in unjust laws, she was not powerless. The law could not control her conscience and she had the option of disobedience—the only weapon to fight the injustices evil laws sanctioned. Disobedience could free her from impotently enduring a system she found repugnant. She was surprised that her conscience was not even faintly troubled by the prospect of breaking the law—only of getting caught.

Her mind was like a beehive; one thought after another raced and chased another as the possibilities of her new commitment overwhelmed her. But she had no time for that now. She sprang into action at the sound of the hounds and ran to the window as she heard the crunch of wheels on the graveled drive and saw Dr. Hunter's buggy roll to a stop. She was relieved Lionel had already left.

She had criminal activities to attend to: the treatment of a sick black infant, little Samuel, in Old Sheba's cabin.

Chapter Twelve

A week later, in Richmond, Virginia, on the second floor of a boot-maker's shop on Twelfth Street, six blocks from the Capitol Building on Capitol Square, a group of slaves and former slaves gathered at eight o'clock on an April evening in 1853. The occasion was the marriage of Angelica Hawthorn and Gabriel—last name unknown, or as yet unchosen (but definitely not Wroughton, as Gabriel's owner's name had been vehemently rejected as a possibility).

The couple had arrived under the cover of darkness only minutes before and waited for Angelica's sister, Ibby, and brother-in-law, Alonso, servants in the household of Edmund and Cornelia Hawthorn. The wedding was to be performed by Reverend Robert Thurman, a respected free-black leader of the black community in Richmond, publicly esteemed as a spell-binding preacher of the Gospel and covertly an important member of the Underground Railroad.

Having arrived in Richmond by rail five days earlier, Angelica and Gabriel had been sent on their way from the train station with no more than a cursory examination of their travel papers, written by Lavinia and explaining their "owners," origin, and destination. From the depot, they walked to a previously designated meeting place where Angelica's sister, Ibby, and her husband, Alonso, met them and guided them to a "friendly house," as safe houses along the Underground Railroad were known, to await a "conductor" who would further guide their flight to freedom.

The couple had first found refuge in the home of Reverend and Mrs. Thurman, but because Reverend Thurman was spied upon by authorities suspicious of his possible link to the Underground Railroad, it was decided that it would be safer if Gabriel and Angelica were housed elsewhere. During the week they had been in Richmond, they had been shuttled between two other safe houses prior to being taken by Reverend Thurman to the boot-maker's building to be married and await transport out of Virginia.

"Now everything will be alright, child," Mrs. Thurman said in an attempt to calm Angelica, who anxiously peeked around the edge of a tightly shuttered window draped in black cloth to block out nearby buildings and the street below.

"It's those notices in the newspapers that worry me," said Angelica, turning from the window. "Yesterday, Mr. Wroughton offered a thousand dollars for Gabriel's return— and today he upped it to two. It's in both the *Richmond Tribune* and *Richmond Whig*."

Worry creased Angelica's forehead as she adjusted the lapel of Gabriel's coat. "And the notices even describe the yellow-and-black-checked coat and trousers you're wearing, and how tall you are and—"

"Well, that increase to two thousand dollars hasn't done a bit of good, has it, young lady?" said Reverend Thurman, peering over the spectacles that rode low on his short, flat nose. "Looks to me like that owner of yours is wasting his money, son."

"And Ibby is bringin' me some new clothes, Angie," Gabriel said. "She's been sewing every free minute she got to make over one of Alonso's suits for me."

"And what a good hand she is with a needle," said Mrs. Thurman. "Why, that dress you wearin' makes you about the prettiest bride I ever lay my eyes on."

Angelica tried to smile and acknowledged the compliment, lowering her head and shifting uncomfortably in the once-elegant blue taffeta dress.

"Thank you, ma'am. This one of Miss Margaret's old dresses she gave to Ibby. She done cut it down to fit me right good, I reckon."

"Got to cut 'em down for you; cut 'em up for me, look like," Gabriel said, standing proudly beside the tiny, almost boyish form of his bride.

Outside the room, the sound of feet rushing up the stairs brought panic to the faces of the wedding party. Reverend Thurman responded to a timid knock by cautiously opening the door. A collective sigh of relief welcomed Ibby and Alonso into the room.

"Thank the Lord," said Mrs. Thurman. "We thought the patrols—"

"Nary a one in sight," said Alonso, a tall, thin man with neatly trimmed sideburns halfway down his face. Dressed in the formal livery he wore as the Hawthorns' butler and coachman, he smiled and set two large baskets on a table. "It right easy to slips by them in the alleys. They mostly patrols the main streets."

"And we just has to come a little ways," said Ibby, his thirty-five-year-old wife, an older version of Angelica, with the same sweet features and large, dark eyes. "And most of the police knows us, and that we Hawthorn people and all the time rushin' 'bout makin' trips for this and that." Ibby also wore the attire of a house servant, a long black dress, white apron, and white linen cloth wrapped around her head.

Ibby handed Gabriel a package wrapped in brown paper. "Here my weddin' gift, brother: an almost new suit of clothes."

"Mighty grateful, Ibby," Gabriel said, taking the bundle.

"Open it!" Ibby ordered and Gabriel tore into the package. "Sure do hope it fits. I use just 'bout all a second pair of 'Lonso's britches in lettin' out the coat and waist of them trousers. It the same color and matches up right good, though."

"Look mighty fine," Gabriel said holding up the coat. "Think maybe I puts 'em on now for the weddin'?"

"Do!" said Angelica, and she pushed him toward a door to a back room where he disappeared with the clothes.

"And I love my dress, sister," said Angelica, giving Ibby a hug.

"Let me see," said Ibby. She lifted Angelica's arms to better examine her work. "That dress make you sure look mighty pretty. I done get right good guessin' a fit with my sewin'. It one of Miss Margaret's old ones and I cuts it 'bout half down to fit you. Since she has that last baby, she can't wear none of her old dresses. Reverend Harvey say she big as Jonas's whale."

Starting at every horse whinny and noise from the traffic outside, the tension in the room was as sharp as a knife. Even Ibby's attempts at levity did little to lessen the anxiety. She went to the baskets brought by Alonso and began to remove the contents.

"Done filled up a day mighty tight with all this sewin', and bakin' a cake, and gettin' Miss Cornelia all prettied up for Miss Ariadne's birthday party this evenin'. Reckon it goin' to be a mighty fancy shindig, the way they talkin'. Ain't had no time to catch my breath, hardly."

"We had to wait 'till Miss Cornelia and Mr. Edmund and Mr. Lionel leaves out for the party 'fore we could slip off," said Alonso. "With them all over there, they not miss us."

"I skeered I'd have to go over to Miss Ariadne's myself and helps serve like I usually do when she gives one of her fancy dos. I has to fix Miss Cornelia's hair, what got me out of it. She sends word to Miss Ariadne I not be able to help at her party, that I has to help her. She done colored up this mornin' and got so much henna on it, it look like she stick her head in a bucket of hog's blood. She try some kind of new color and been most of the day tryin' to wash that red out. We use vinegar and lye soap and just about everything and it still take three washins and make ever body late. Mr. Edmund see me carrying down that red rinse water and say, 'Did you kill her?' like it blood, and say he goin' to, and it be real blood if she don't hurry! He so mad he threaten to go off to Miss Ariadne's without her."

Polite laughter greeted Ibby's story, and she looked toward Alonso as if he should try to dispel the anxiety in the room.

"Now you all don't let it slip me when it nine and half o'clock," said Alonso. "I has to be at Miss Ariadne's house 'bout then to drives Mr. Edmund and Mr. Lionel and Miss Cornelia home after the party,"

"Why, we goin' to has us a real fine weddin', sure enough," said Ibby, who turned to Alonso. "Did you bring the cider?"

"Done got it right here," he said. "And glasses, too."

"Now, Angelica, you quit frettin'," said Ibby. "It you weddin' day, little sister!"

"And tomorrow evenin' Mr. Scott goin' to slip you out of Richmond to Fredericksburg," said Alonso. "And from there the next conductor goin' to take you all the way to Pennsylvania. Why, you be free people in just three or four more days."

Reverend Thurman lifted Angelica's chin and fixed her with his kind eyes. "It all goin' to be fine, little lady. Good Lord watchin' over us."

Angelica returned his smile, and struggled to quell her fear, even as she realized everyone in the room was in danger. If discovered, all of them faced serious charges: she and Gabriel as fugitives, the others for harboring and assisting them. Further, it was a violation of the law for more than four blacks to congregate for any reason in the evening, even for religious services, unless a white person was present. No white was present that evening.

When Gabriel appeared in his new clothes, Ibby's tailoring was judged to be perfect, and Gabriel was showered with lavish praise.

Three sharp raps on the door and once more the group seemed to turn into statues. Reverend Thurman raised his hand in a signal to remain calm and then opened the door. His tense shoulders relaxed when he opened the door to reveal a black man with a hat pulled low over his head.

"Praise the Lord!" he said, "It's Ezekiel. Come in, come in! This is Ezekiel Scott, who owns the boot shop downstairs."

"We can trust him," said Mrs. Thurman and her voice fell to a whisper. "He often lets us use this room as a safe house."

Ezekiel Scott, already known to Ibby and Alonso, entered and nodded to Gabriel and Angelica.

"You mighty good to take all these chances for us, Mr. Scott," said Gabriel.

"That's why I'm here," Scott said. His voice was serious and his grave expression suggested he did not bring good news.

"Our conductor out of Richmond has been arrested, along with our contact in Fredericksburg. Bounty hunters again. It was during the last run. We're going to have to delay your transfer—"

"But how long?"

"Don't rightly know..." His voice was evasive and he looked at the floor.

"What will we do? Where will we go?"

"You'll be safe here for a time. In a few days, I'm goin' to move you to another safe house down by the river."

"But when can we leave Richmond?"

"Can't rightly answer. They been right many arrests lately. We're not sure, but we think one of our own conductors may be a spy. And they so many bounty hunters lately. For the time bein' most of the conductors bein' mighty cautious; they think it best to just lay low and waits awhile."

"The Slave Recovery Act," Reverend Thurman said sadly. "It's turned every other white in Virginia—and quite a few blacks—into slave hunters."

Angelica slumped against Gabriel in despair.

"Now don't be troubled, child," Mrs. Thurman said. "We are in the Lord's hands."

"Ain't goin' to stop this weddin' anyhow," said Ibby. "Ain't baked this cake for nothin'."

"And we sure don't want this good, sweet cider to go to waste," said Alonso.

Renewing her earlier promise to remain hopeful, Angelica concealed her disappointment with a smile.

Gabriel invited Scott to remain for the wedding, and the ceremony was performed with the solemn ritual prescribed by Reverend Thurman. Saluting their love and the courage they had shown in their escape earlier, the group watched the radiant bride glow with happiness in the flickering candlelight as she and Gabriel quietly repeated the words that would join them as man and wife. Even under the constant threat of discovery and arrest, a sense of protection and peace descended on the group during the brief ceremony.

In a nod toward tradition—one not entirely approved by more enlightened blacks, and not at all by Reverend Thurman, who felt the practice smacked of paganism—the couple "jumped the broom," hopping backwards a step over the handle of a broom placed on the floor. The ritual was observed by many blacks in the South as essential in the rites of marriage, often performed with no more official or religious formality than that determined by the couple's masters, who sometimes performed the ceremony.

When Reverend Thurman pronounced them married, the couple embraced and shyly kissed, their faces aglow with joy, and for the moment oblivious to the dangers that threatened them beyond the small sequestered room.

"Oh, how I wish Miss Vinny were here," Angelica said. "I must get her word that we are safe. And that we are at last married."

"Ever thing goin' to be alright, Angie," Gabriel said. He lifted her chin and she bravely smiled into his broad, open face.

"You've been so kind and taken so many risks to protect us. But the longer we're here, the greater the danger we are to everyone who help us—"

"Now, now—don't you give that a thought. We've been doing this for a long time." Reverend Thurman smiled over his spectacles. "You'd be surprised at how good we've gotten at our tricks. Just like foxes, and mighty hard to catch."

Outside in the street, a horse could be heard approaching at full gallop and everyone froze. When the sound of the hooves raced past them and faded into the even cadence of the slower paced traffic, the group relaxed and Ibby produced a small cake. Alonso, who had observed such rituals in his capacity as butler in the Hawthorn household, filled the glasses with cider and offered a toast.

"To the bride and groom and their freedom. God protect them and all of us in the name of Jesus."

"Amen. Praise His holy name," said Reverend Thurman, and they drank the cider and ate small pieces of the cake.

Six blocks away from the secret wedding party, in the dining room of the elegant mansion of Miss Adriane Woodhull on Marshall Street, another group of guests raised their glasses in celebration of Ariadne's fortieth birthday, although the exact number was discreetly unmentioned in the festivities.

The hostess modestly accepted the compliments of her guardian, the patrician, eighty-year-old Edmund Hawthorn, who stood and lifted his glass in a toast to her accomplishments. The silver-haired old gentleman extolled Ariadne's merits in elaborate terms, and caught up in his own eloquence and the excellence of the wine at dinner—and bourbon before—departed from his prepared remarks into an extemporaneous tribute of her virtues on his own, to the consternation of his wife, Cornelia, who attempted to squelch his oration with a glare and unobtrusive, under-the-table pokes of her foot.

His wife's attempts to end his long-winded tribute failed, however, when even her long legs could not reach across the wide table, and she was forced to content herself with frenziedly batting her fan and hope that he would eventually catch the signal of her squelching glare.

Around the glittering, candle-lit table, its length extended by the addition of eight leaves, an assembly of family and friends numbering two dozen lifted their glasses in consensus with the old gentleman's flowery accolade. The guests, many of them elderly and satiated by another of Ariadne's bounteous feasts and several glasses of excellent wine, lingered over a dessert of berries and caramelized fruit.

The champagne for the toast had been provided by Ariadne's cousin and son of the speaker, Lionel Hawthorn, who had arrived in Richmond earlier from Hawthorn Hill Plantation. The dinner had been served by Ariadne's excellent staff under the supervision of Madison, her imposing, formally dressed black butler who had moved with silent dignity from guest to guest distributing the crystal glasses of champagne from a silver tray and now stood in unobtrusive, watchful attention in the shadows outside the long splash of candlelight that flooded the table.

The tall, distinguished Madison had come to Ariadne's household from the West Indies, where he had previously been in service to a wealthy French family. When the fortunes of the family collapsed, Madison had been sold and sent to Virginia, where Ariadne purchased him. Aristocratic, well-educated, fluent in French, and knowledgeable of French cuisine, Madison had become the envy of prominent hostesses all over Richmond. He managed Ariadne's household in every capacity with impeccable efficiency and because of his excellent taste and flawless guidance, her entertainments were elegant. Because of Madison, invitations to any social event at Ariadne Woodhull's were coveted throughout the city.

As Edmund continued, the honoree sat impassively, her large, liquid black eyes cast downward in a tableau of genteel humility. Dressed in black silk, in startling contrast to her milk-white skin, she sat expressionless, her thin lips a straight line, humorless and cold, with no hint of the perfunctory smile she would eventually command to reward her uncle's toast.

Her elder cousin and surrogate mother, Cornelia Oralee Randolph Hawthorn, sat at her left, her too-red mountain of tight curls piled high on her head (and still shining with dampness from Ibby's last washing). With her cheeks subtly rouged and powdered to mask the passage of seventy-odd years, and aided by the candlelight from the towering candelabra, dappling the length of the table, the aristocratic Mrs. Hawthorn's deception was a success, and even Ariadne's paleness and spinsterish plainness took on an uncharacteristic warmth.

Cornelia's fan still fluttered desperately, but her husband took no notice and continued, now in praise of Ariadne's accomplishments at the pianoforte, "like a goddess, providing dulcet tones, as her graceful fingers bring to mortal ears heavenly chords rivaling the harps of angels..."

Beside the queenly Cornelia, her son, Lionel, lolled in good-natured boredom, his indigo blue eyes sparkling with amusement, the familiar wayward lock of golden hair falling over his forehead as the corners of his sensuous lips suppressed a smile at his father's flowery declarations.

As the old man continued, pleased with his eloquence, Ariadne's eyes slid from the blue-veined, folded hands in her lap toward her distant cousin Lionel. There her gaze lingered, her inner longing and regret for a moment painfully revealed, before she quickly recovered, and catching the sharp eye of her cousin, Margaret, Lionel's sister, seated farther down the table, directed her attention once again to her lap.

Beside Margaret sat the pompous Judge Addison Povall, who had spent most of the evening ranting about the arrogance of northern politicians, and now ogled Jennie, one of the six maids assisting Madison in serving. The unusually dark black woman, her skin coal black and shiny in the candlelight, seemed to transfix the old man, and throughout the meal his little pig eyes gleamed with thoughts and fantasies known only to himself as they followed her hungrily from buffet to table as she served the guests.

The balding, cherubic Reverend Alexander Harvey sat on the other side of Margaret, who squirmed in private consternation, fuming in frustration at having been seated beside the offensive Judge Povall, still smacking his lips and throwing sly little grins at Jennie. Judge Povall had long ago earned Margaret's enmity by his pomposity, bad breath, and uncontrolled flatulence, and tonight he had surpassed himself in all three, boring her for the entire dinner with complaints that *The Richmond Whig* had refused to publish his latest diatribe against blacks in which he suggested capital punishment for such crimes as theft. Margaret had expressed her intense dislike for the repulsive, pig-eyed old man to Ariadne many times, and she was certain her cousin had seated the old lecher beside her for her own spiteful amusement.

Other guests at Ariadne's table included a prominent retired newspaper editor, the banker who had skillfully invested Ariadne's vast holdings into even greater wealth, a former senator, and a dozen more of Richmond's most distinguished citizens, numbering among them a former governor well in his dotage and even now nodding, awake only because of the constant sharp prodding of his wife's elbow.

The rest of the party were related by blood or other obligation to Ariadne and were included solely as a buffer against the criticism their omission would have occasioned. Uncle Cuthbert and Aunt Priscilla and Cousin Gertrude were there solely by the necessity their kinship to Ariadne mandated.

Although the guest list was a model of propriety and respectability, Ariadne included no close personal friends because she had none. At least none that would have comfortably blended with the elite group in her dining room that evening. Ariadne had always been too aloof for close attachments, and her contacts could more accurately be termed acquaintances or formal associations, always distant and empty of any real warmth and intimacy.

Ariadne's quick, longing glance at Lionel, like a child snatching a forbidden bon-bon, and her quick recovery into modestly staring into her lap, had been observed by Margaret, who also observed her brother, as he exchanged frequent glances with the one stranger among the group, Mrs. Bithia Clevinger.

Mrs. Clevinger was from New York, the wife of a business associate of Lionel's who was an important customer of his tobacco factory. Because Mr. Clevinger was in Washington on business, Ariadne had graciously agreed to include Mrs. Clevinger as a guest at Lionel's request.

Because Margaret had known all the other guests at the table for years, Mrs. Clevinger, the stranger, became the focus of her scrutiny. Seated only a few seats away, Margaret studied the lady from New York carefully, one of the few Yankees she had ever met, and found her beautiful and charming, although she decided her dress was too low-cut and with too many ruffles for a woman in her mid-thirties. Margaret also thought Mrs. Clevinger wore too much jewelry, laughed too readily, and spoke in a voice too loud. But there was genuine warmth in her excesses and it was easy to see why she was a success at the party. She had a glittering smile and large, lively green eyes and was excellent in dealing with the boring conversation of Uncle Cuthbert, seated on her right, and the fatuous babbling of Aunt Priscilla on her left.

Her only other deficiencies seemed to be the impression that she was too anxious to be liked, and her blonde hair, elaborately styled, was interwoven with too many pearls, as if she had haphazardly twisted a strand of them throughout her tresses, the effect theatrical and overdone like that of a stage-girl. And she spoke with a glaring, harsh Northern accent, which Margaret's southern ears found grating and unattractive. Clearly not a daughter of the South, Bithia Clevinger's excesses could all be explained by her being a Yankee. And a New York Yankee at that, whom Margaret had been told was the worst kind, even more offensive than those from New England.

Margaret was certain Mrs. Clevinger had been responding all evening to Lionel's glances and fleeting, private smiles with as much interest as they were offered. They were clearly flirting, although Margaret suspected she was the only one to catch it—unless Ariadne's stolen glances at Lionel had detected it.

Margaret gave her husband, Alexander, a nudge and when he inclined his balding head toward her, she glanced toward Mrs. Clevinger and whispered, "Brother," just as Mrs.

Clevinger threw Lionel a quick, secret smile, and producing a handkerchief, extended her smooth swan-like neck and dabbed herself just above her bosom which protruded in well-rounded firmness above her low-cut gown.

Oh, yes, Margaret thought, *he's set his sights on another one.* And, as indicated by Mrs. Clevinger's covert responses, succeeded. Poor Lavinia. At least she was at Hawthorn Hill and Margaret hoped that perhaps this, like countless other of Lionel's dalliances, would be over and done with before she found out about it.

At last Edmund Hawthorn's toast was completed and when the guests had drunk, Ariadne rose to polite applause. Standing before them, the exquisite design of her expensive black silk dress only further emphasized her shapeless, boyish figure, revealing almost no sign of breasts. Ariadne spent a fortune on clothes, her fashions made to her specific reed-thin measurements in Paris or Philadelphia, yet they only made more apparent the straight boniness of her figure, just as her black hair, drawn severely back in a small chignon at the nape of her neck, emphasized the skeletal plainness of her face.

Giving the assembly a stiff nod, she thanked them in her even, cold voice, as devoid of warmth as her large liquid eyes were of light and happiness.

"Such a tragedy," people often said when speaking of Ariadne. "Orphaned at so early an age." Ariadne's parents had been killed in a fire which destroyed the plantation house on one of her family's holdings in Prince Edward County. The six-year-old Ariadne, rescued by a servant, had become one of the wealthiest orphans in the Commonwealth. Edmund Hawthorn became her guardian and she was reared principally by Cornelia in the Hawthorn household in Richmond and at Hawthorn Hill, although her other well-meaning and solicitous cousins, Aunt Priscilla and Uncle Cuthbert, shared in her care.

"Poor Ariadne," people said, "first she lost her parents, and then she lost Lionel to Lavinia." And she was frequently cited as an example of enormous wealth being no guarantee of happiness since the loss of her parents and spinsterhood had in no way been prevented by her being one of the richest women of Virginia.

The disappointment at not becoming Lionel's wife was no less acute to Ariadne than to her sympathetic family and friends, although she made every effort to conceal it. Lionel's own mother had, from the day her son married, often said to family and close friends, whispering confidentially in the gravest of tones from behind a momentarily stilled fan or gloved hand, "The day Lionel married Lavinia, a light went out in Ariadne forever," because she thought the phrase particularly original and poetic, and at the same time expressed the truth of the situation.

When Richmond finally met the charming and beautiful wife Lionel had selected in place of Ariadne, they realized that by any measure of beauty and charm, there was no contest. Ariadne's coldness, her plain, narrow-shouldered thinness were no match for the unaffected warmth and physical beauty of Lavinia. Only in her enormous wealth did Ariadne surpass her rival, but even in that she seemed to find little happiness and through the years—from the gnawing disappointment at having lost Lionel Hawthorn, it was conjectured—her heart had hardened and by her fortieth year, bitterness had permanently etched the corners of her thin lips.

She was, nevertheless, an impeccable hostess and her expertise as such, along with her prestigious bloodline and wealth, made an invitation to her celebrations a coveted entry to the finest food, drink, and society in Richmond. With Madison's flawless guidance and Ariadne's unlimited resources, she entertained in the grand style and reveled in her position as a social maven. Like many with little excitement in their own lives, she relished in the gossip and scandal of others and collected it with zeal. But while rumor, slander, and dishonor were her stock and trade, it was collected and disseminated in the most circumspect and discrete manner—as was her association with the seamier element of Richmond society.

These less refined, unconventional, and sometimes scandalous acquaintances—poets, actors, and artists—she would entertain at another time when she provided a more informal, even rowdy atmosphere, and the house was devoid of these genteel personages.

Of the guests currently at her table, only Lionel attended these less staid functions, occasionally as his cousin's escort, more often in pursuit of some compliant female too unsavory for the more respectable gatherings in Richmond's better homes. For one so unapproachable and personally isolated, Ariadne's social contacts, though shallow and perfunctory, had a remarkable range. Other than Lionel, those with a more unsavory reputation who attended Ariadne's less respectable gatherings were unknown to the first, except by reputation and, with the exception of one or two, would not even have been received in the parlors of those in Ariadne's company now.

Her less reputable friends were known only through whispers and gossip, and occasional headlines in the *Richmond Tribune* or *Richmond Whig*, where reports of duels, saloon brawls, legal actions, and other disreputable conduct were reported and devoured by the scandal-hungry. Only when their wealth necessitated business contacts—or their legal troubles required the services of their law firms—did the less desirable visitors at Ariadne's house come in contact with those she entertained now.

Adulterers may have met at her parties, the challenge to a duel may have been issued over a card game played at her gaming table, an embezzlement scheme may have been hatched in a whispered conspiracy in her garden, but Ariadne herself remained untouched by the unsavory events themselves.

Finally, the meal concluded and the guests waited for Ariadne to signal the procession to the parlor and drawing room where the sexes separated, and each group would sit in satiated languor for more conversation. The ladies would be served cordials and the gentlemen would be provided with cigars and stronger drink.

Judge Povall, however, was so swept up by his abusive tirade against Richmond's free blacks that he did not notice when Ariadne rose at the head of the table.

"The free ones should all be sent back to Africa! Anyone who frees them should be required to provide them with passage back to where they came from!" Povall said, oblivious to the presence of the servants and the embarrassment of the guests.

"Why, you ate every bite of that delicious dinner Ariadne's servants prepared this evening," said an irritated Aunt Priscilla, ready to challenge the ranting old man's extremist views.

"Indeed," said Margaret, "I wonder where any of us would be without our people."

"Now, Margaret, let's not start that war everyone talks about," sputtered Cornelia, giving Lionel a nudge to divert the conversation to less controversial subjects.

Lionel diplomatically moved into less troubled waters by announcing the impending birth of his first grandchild, which provided the grateful guests the opportunity to offer profuse congratulations and another toast to the grandparents, Lionel, Margaret, and Alexander, and the great-grandparents, Cornelia and Edmund.

"Shall we retire to the parlor and library for coffee?" Ariadne said.

As the guests got to their feet, Uncle Cuthbert clumsily reintroduced the subject of slavery by referring to a notice he had seen in that day's *Richmond Enquirer* offering a reward for the capture and return of Gabriel.

"Isn't that the man you've tried to buy from Wroughton for years?" Uncle Cuthbert asked.

"It is. And I'm afraid he took Lavinia's maid with him."

Ariadne was immediately at Lionel's side. She took his arm and together they led the guests out of the dining room.

"Lavinia's Angelica has fled Hawthorn Hill?" she asked. Her large, liquid eyes glistened with the pleasure of new intrigue and the source of a possible fresh scandal. She clung to every word as Lionel related the details of the escape and at once came to the conclusion that Lavinia had to be an accessory to the plan.

"You mean the girl and her suitor actually left with travel papers, on one of Lavinia's horses, and boarded the train for Richmond? But where did they get the money for the train?" Ariadne asked.

"Lavinia had bought tickets earlier. She was planning to send the girl to Mother, accompanied by Uncle Lemiel."

"She had fallen in love with a Wroughton black," whispered Cornelia confidentially as if the matter was a family scandal. "And stole those train passes from Lavinia!"

The old woman's whispers became indignant as she took Edmund's arm and followed Ariadne and Lionel into the hall. "And to think, I practically reared that girl myself. She's my Ibby's sister, you know. And was brought up here in Richmond after we moved from Hawthorn Hill."

"But how will she pay to get out of Virginia?" Ariadne asked with a knowing smile. "Certainly not from a Wroughton slave. They're barely ever fed, I hear."

"Oh, all blacks hoard money," said Cornelia. "And she's picked up a coin or two on birthdays and at Christmas."

Lionel said, "Mammy Emma has been hoarding her Christmas and birthday dollars for fifty years—probably quite wealthy, if the truth were known."

"I suspect quite a few of these escapes are done with outside help," Uncle Cuthbert's voice came from farther behind the procession. "They're too well-planned and executed to have been done without assistance."

"Indeed. And more and more of them every day," Ariadne said darkly. "It seems the newspapers contain nothing but notices of escapes."

"It's these damn Northern abolitionists and religious fanatics," Judge Povall stormed, and, noting the presence of ladies, quickly added, "Oh, I beg your pardon, ladies," before plunging on. "This Underground Railroad is getting more brazen every day. Stirred up and financed by Northern interests determined to destroy our way of life. Why, if Congress doesn't—"

Sensing the conversation was drifting toward the heated subject of slavery, states' rights, and secession, which so divided Virginians, Margaret interrupted to prevent some inadvertent, but almost inevitable, remark about "damn Yankees," which might offend Mrs. Clevinger.

"You gentlemen solve the problems of the world," Margaret said. "We ladies want to talk of more important things. Did you know that Mr. Foster has written a new song? I have the music and it's much prettier than 'Old Folks at Home.'"

"My dear Ariadne," a musical voice rang out as the group reached the front hall. It was Mrs. Clevinger. "You have been so kind to include me in your beautiful celebration, but I wonder if you would forgive me if I requested Lionel return me to my hotel. I have a very early train to Washington tomorrow to join my husband."

Margaret noticed the familiar use of her brother's first name. Addressing him as "Mr. Hawthorn" would have been more appropriate. But perhaps such familiarity was acceptable in the North.

"But of course," Ariadne said, giving Lionel a sly smile.

"I shall be delighted, Mrs. Clevinger," Lionel said, bowing slightly as Margaret, throwing him a cold glare, sailed past him.

"Madison, have my carriage sent around," Ariadne ordered.

While Mrs. Clevinger waited for her wrap and said good night to the guests, Margaret cornered Lionel and hissed, "You should be ashamed. And after you told me you and Lavinia made up."

"And so we have, little sister," he said in a whisper. "I am simply being courteous and accommodating to the wife of a good customer. Alonso is coming to pick up Mama and Papa."

"You mean you aren't coming back?" his sister asked.

"Nosy little sister—you're becoming just like Ariadne."

Within moments, the carriage appeared at the front of the house.

"Good night, pretty little sister," said Lionel, as if amused by Margaret's suspicion and repressed indignation. "Just tell Alonso not to wait for me. I may be later than I expected."

Lionel returned Margaret's scornful glare with a wink and mysterious smile as he ushered the voluptuous lady from New York out the door.

Once seated in the parlor, the ladies were served small glasses of blackberry cordial and discussed Mrs. Clevinger at length before moving on to the merits and faults of Harriet Beecher Stowe's *Uncle Tom's Cabin*, dismissing the book as a radical Northern slander against Christian slave owners.

"That may be the way Kentucky slave owners treat their people, but Virginians certainly don't," Cornelia decreed indignantly, dismissing the book with a toss of her head and wave of her hand.

Bored with the ladies' detailed comments on Mrs. Clevinger's attire and literary discussions, Ariadne returned to a subject which interested her more.

"How sad for Lavinia to have lost Angelica. Of course, she's always been something of a country girl, reared in those wild mountains in western Virginia, she must feel quite alone now with the boys both gone—and now even her maid."

"Yes, and still mourning little Oralee," said Cornelia, shaking her head sadly. "She still wears only black, you know. And runs Hawthorn Hill almost alone since Lionel is so often in Richmond managing the tobacco factory."

"And does it so well, I'm sure," cooed Ariadne. "But she always was something of a farm girl, wasn't she? A hill person? And her family didn't represent—well, I'm sure they're good country people."

"Actually, her father owned a great deal of land in Washington County," said Margaret testily.

"Indeed." Ariadne's thin lips formed an arch smile. "Lionel says she is a much better farmer than he. I suppose hill people have a talent for the rustic arts. I understand their women plow and work the fields much as our blacks do."

Margaret bristled at Lavinia being termed "farm girl" and "hill people." Ariadne took every opportunity to criticize and disparage Lavinia, both in private and in the presence of the family. Although Margaret understood the origin of Ariadne's animosity, many did not, attributing her caustic remarks to snobbery and sarcasm.

"Are her people still abolitionists?" Ariadne asked, as if amused by the possibility. "I remember some of her brothers' peculiar ideas about slavery when they visited Hawthorn Hill. Rather crude people, I remember, quite unaccustomed to refinement and very much mountaineers. And their wives!" Her dry, mirthless laugh failed to soften the unkindness of her words. "They dress no better than house servants—weave and spin their own cloth, I'm sure. And had the most terrible skin, dark and freckled from the sun, like tenant hands. From working their fields, no doubt. They claim moral grounds for not owning slaves, but I suspect the lack of funds to buy them is the true reason."

"I think Lavinia's family is quite sincere in their objection to slavery, Ariadne," Margaret said. "And they are delightful, wonderful people."

"Well, we would expect that from a Harvey, wouldn't we," Ariadne said, adding a sprinkling of salt in her sugary tones.

Cornelia, observing Margaret stiffen and her blue eyes snap, quickly expounded on Lavinia's kinship with Dolly Madison, defending her pedigree with extravagant claims of eminent connections.

"And Alexander's message last Sunday was so inspiring, Margaret," said Aunt Priscilla, also sensitive to Ariadne's bad manners.

"Indeed," said Cornelia. "About God and Nature. It made me long for Hawthorn Hill where everything must be budding now. The crocus, hyacinths—"

Margaret beamed at the praise for her husband.

"Why so happy, cousin?" Ariadne asked Margaret. "You ate hardly anything at dinner tonight."

"If you had to sit beside old Judge Povall, you'd eat even less," Margaret said. "And you know why. I've told you enough not to put me near him and the last three dinners I've been seated right next to him."

"But he is so fond of you," Ariadne purred as Cornelia continued to extol the glories of the dogwood and crocus and the sweet smelling hyacinths of Hawthorn Hill.

When the guests had departed, Ariadne's house returned to the usual oppressiveness the gaiety of her party had only temporarily dispelled. Ariadne reflected on the news of the escapees at Hawthorn Hill and Wroughton Plantations. Lavinia's closeness to Angelica could only mean the enterprise had been a collaborative effort. Delighted with the possibility, she was pleased to feel her long dormant jealousy and dislike of Lavinia renewed, like a fire reignited from beneath dormant, banked ashes.

If what she suspected was correct, she would have even more satisfaction than she derived from the anonymous letter she wrote to Lavinia that evening reporting the rumors that Lionel was having an affair with Mrs. Clevinger. Now she had Lavinia's own improprieties in slave running to report to the authorities. What a triumph it would be to covertly engineer the arrest of Lavinia for her crimes. What glorious satisfaction she would derive from not only seeing Lavinia disgraced, but possibly imprisoned.

Sitting before the fire in her bedroom, Ariadne convened a meeting of her household staff, as was her custom following her major entertainments. With her cook, serving girls, parlor maids, and Madison gathered around her, she reviewed the evening.

"The evening went very well. I did find the wine less than remarkable, except for Lionel's champagne, of course."

Listening silently, the servants stood in a tableau of humility, their dread of rebuke concealed behind lowered heads and hands meekly folded in front of them.

"In the future, I shall expect the butter to be firm, but not hard as a rock." A harsh glance at the cook induced a mumbled, "Yes, ma'am."

"And Jennie, you were far too slow in your service. Twice I noticed Judge Povall was forced to signal you to fill his wine glass. No guest should have to indicate the need for service at my table, and I do not want to see it in the future."

"Yes, ma'am," a low voice responded.

Dismissed, the staff, relieved that no further criticism befell them, scurried from the room, except Madison, who approached his mistress with a pen and several bank drafts.

"If I may trouble you to sign these drafts, Madam," he said.

"What now?" Ariadne said, snatching the pen and scribbling her name on half a dozen pieces of paper.

"The household expenses, ma'am. And the dressmaker, and for the repair of the coach, and..."

"Oh, alright. Now, go." She shoved the signed documents back to him. "And Madison, send a note around to Judge Povall. Invite him to tea next Tuesday. And make sure

Jennie serves—or at least assists you in serving." A thin smile enveloped her words. "Judge Povall seems so fond of Jennie."

When she was alone, Ariadne stared into the fire until it faded into a struggling glow. But her own thoughts still flared, seething with intrigue as she searched for a plan to ensnare Lavinia and expose her role in Angelica's flight.

When she at last decided to retire, she summoned her maid, Ogletha, to prepare her for bed and mix her nightly draft of Tincture of Opium and bromides with water, which she drank in a single gulp.

Having for years suffered her mistress's abusiveness, the thirty-five-year-old Ogletha's dignified beauty was etched with the signs of stress from unhappy servitude under Ariadne's harsh domination. Lines of anxiety creased her serenely composed features, and her graceful movements were marked by a tentativeness born of fear her mistress's temper could at any moment turn upon her. Slapped, kicked, struck with any object at hand, even jabbed with pins or stabbed with scissors, Ogletha and the rest of Ariadne's servants were in constant dread of one of her unprovoked attacks.

Ariadne's brutal treatment of servants earned her one of the highest runaway rates of any household in Richmond. When recovered, the runaways were promptly sold, but not before being beaten by hired thugs engaged for that purpose and carefully directed and observed by Ariadne.

Tonight, Ogletha found Ariadne in an uncharacteristically buoyant mood. Basking in the glow of yet another social triumph, and the narcotic high from the opium and bromides, she seemed almost pleasant as she related the details of the evening.

"I am in possession of some very interesting information," Ariadne said, patting the back of her neck, a signal for

Ogletha to help her out of her dress. As the long row of buttons down her back were unfastened, Ariadne watched Ogletha's reaction in her dressing mirror as she related Angelica's escape.

"Little Angie ran away?" said Ogletha, pretending surprise. The news of Angelica's arrival in Richmond had spread quickly among the Hawthorn and Woodhull servants days before. "Angie that is Ibby's little sister?"

"One and the same," Ariadne said as she slipped out of her dress and kicked it out of her way, all the while watching Ogletha's reaction carefully. "And I would not be surprised if Lavinia has not masterminded the entire scheme."

Ogletha's large black eyes sparkled with satisfaction beneath thick, long lashes, even as her fine-boned features remained composed and betrayed nothing of her inner pleasure in Angelica's escape. Because Ariadne was adverse to being touched, even by her maid, Ogletha made no move to assist her mistress as she freed the chignon at the nape of her neck and began brushing her hair. She picked up her mistress's dress and hung it in an armoire.

Ariadne slammed her hair brush on the table. "That mousy Angelica would never have had the courage to run without Lavinia's prodding her. And so elaborate an escape had to have been her planning. I know it. They were too close. Even Aunt Cornelia says Lavinia allowed that girl too much familiarity. Hill Girl never had servants before she married Lionel. She's always allowed the Hawthorn Hill blacks to become far too uppity for menials."

Ogletha remained expressionless as Ariadne's eyes narrowed and she prepared another dose of Tincture of Opium and bromides.

"But why would Miss Lavinia—?"

"Because our dear Vinny of the Valley is a romantic. To women like her, romance is everything. She buries herself in books—poetry and such foolishness. She was even in league with Margaret when she married that inferior little preacher who doesn't have two coins to rub together." She sniffed contemptuously. "Preaching sermons. And embarrassing the family by trying to convert these impudent free blacks that are taking over Richmond. I do believe he spends more time preaching to blacks than he does whites."

"Couldn't Miss Lavinia just ask Mr. Lionel to free Angelica?"

"Maybe. But the problem was the man, Angelica's lover. His trashy owner, Wroughton, wouldn't sell. Angelica is probably in the city right now."

"But it was over a week ago. They're probably North by now—"

Ariadne swirled around. "And how do you know it was over a week ago? Do you know where they are?"

"No, ma'am—"

"I did not say when the escape took place. How else could you know it has been a week? You know something, don't you?"

"No, ma'am. But you said Mr. Lionel brought the news of the escape. He come back from Hawthorn Hill near a week ago—"

"But how did you know that?" Ariadne said "How is it Mr. Lionel's arrivals and departures are known to you?"

"Ibby told me. At church."

Ariadne's suspicion, not completely erased, faded and she turned back to her dressing table.

"You're probably lying. You all lie. You probably know where she is right now. But whether you know or not,

Aunt Cornelia's Ibby will know since she and Angelica are sisters." In the dressing table mirror, Ariadne's eyes locked on Ogletha, sending her both a challenge and a demand. "You find out. Or see that Jennie does. She is a cousin to Angelica and Ibby. Ask her their whereabouts."

Ogletha tensed, dreading her mistress's assignment.

"How much do you know about this Underground Railroad we hear so much about?"

"Not much. I hear runaways try to avoid Richmond—the patrols are so active here."

"But you have sources. You're part of that secret black world, remember. Don't pretend you can't find out everything I need to know. Nothing escapes black eyes and ears. Ask about. Find out who might be a contact for this Underground Railroad around Hawthorn Hill." She laughed her dry, mirthless laugh, and her eyes hardened. "What would Lionel think if he found out his precious wife was involved?"

By the time she was ready for bed, Ariadne said, "Aunt Cornelia always visits Hawthorn Hill in the spring. Since dear cousin Lavinia has no maid at the moment, how thoughtful it would be if I loaned you to her for a time."

Ogletha straightened as alarm distorted her strained, faded beauty, and Ariadne continued, "Nothing can happen at Hawthorn Hill that escapes Emma. She will know. You are to find out all about it. And Uncle Lemiel and Aunt Beck probably know, too. You have a number of sources. Pursue them all."

Taking no notice of Ogletha's dread and discomfort, Ariadne continued while her servant stood with ever increasing anxiety even as the main reason for her concern had not been mentioned. But Ariadne's next words confirmed

Ogletha's fears and clarified the primary reason for her false generosity in offering Ogletha's services to Lavinia.

"We may be fortunate enough for you to be delivered to Cousin Lavinia by Mister Lionel himself." Ariadne's voice cooed with suggestive promise.

Ariadne's large eyes slid in Ogletha's direction at the mention of Lionel. Ogletha's features were tight with ill-concealed discomfort.

"Perhaps you and he can catch up on old times. Before Cousin Lavinia made those unkind accusations and you were banished from Aunt Cornelia's house to mine. Why not take the opportunity to renew your earlier...friendship? Mister Lionel was not blind to your charms once...and you still have your shapely hips and breasts and prettiness. Perhaps he will appreciate you once again."

Ariadne smiled lasciviously, her face alive with lewd implications, as if she enjoyed the black woman's anxiety.

Behind Ogletha's troubled eyes, anguish and doubt roiled as she thought of once again being accessible to Lionel Hawthorn. It had been the ancient dalliance with Lionel almost fifteen years earlier that had brought Ogletha into Ariadne Woodhull's household in the first place, subjecting her to the domination of a woman she knew had regarded Lavinia Hawthorn for over twenty years with unrelenting hatred.

"I'm a Christian now, Miss Ariadne," Ogletha managed, her voice tight and dry. "I done turned to the Lord—"

"Your religious conversion is of no interest to me," Ariadne said, her leering smile vanishing, the lightness of her earlier tone replaced by her more characteristic harshness. "I am only interested in settling an old score with Mrs. Hawthorn. But why not? Why not try and seduce him. He did you."

Ogletha lowered her head. Only her faith could make Ogletha defy her mistress. "That would be a sin, Miss Ariadne. I cannot—"

"You fool, you don't actually have to bed him. Just make Lavinia think you will—or have. Keep your foolish Christian standards, but make her suspicious, uncomfortable, insecure. If Lavinia thinks he has betrayed her, it will be enough. In matters of romance, illusion is as good as truth."

Ogletha was silent, her head lowered in stinging humiliation as her mistress's laughter washed over her.

Finally, Ariadne's malevolence reached into the past. She lowered her voice and spoke only to herself, her speech slurred by the opium and bromides.

"I will bring her down yet," she said. "One way or the other, I will grind my heel in the face of that mountain tramp who usurped my rightful place in this family. And Hill Girl herself has provided me with just the opportunity I need."

Ariadne's thin, ugly laugh made Ogletha's blood chill. Noting her servant's expression, Ariadne fixed her with a look of contempt, the pupils of her eyes dilated by the opium.

"What fools you black people are. You're trapped by your own blackness, by your own foolish devotion to religion, and your own stupid subservience. Why do you think you ended up in my service? Because the charming Miss Lavinia banished you, that's why. I took you as a favor to Lionel, to prevent Aunt Cornelia and Uncle Edmund from learning of your affair with him."

She is only happy when she is plotting evil, thought Ogletha. Noting her mistress's dilated pupils, she waited for the opium to lull her into the sleep, which would finally free Ogletha from her presence.

"It so long ago, Miss Ariadne—"

"You fool. You should hate his hill girl as much as I, you stupid Christian." Ariadne's eyelids grew heavy as the narcotic haze engulfed her and lulled her into a stupor, the glint in her watery eyes fading as she nodded and chuckled to herself.

Ogletha stood helplessly, praying for the sedative to complete its work. She would have cried if she could, but after years of suffering Ariadne's abuse, her sadness had curdled into an ache too tight and hard for weeping, and there was nothing left except to endure day by day the despair and weariness that lay just beyond the tears she could no longer shed.

Chapter Thirteen

In the Hawthorn Hill slave quarters, the battle for little Samuel's life raged on as the child's condition worsened, then seemed to improve as the frail little boy struggled to live. When Dr. Hunter first visited Old Sheba's cabin, he predicted the infant would be dead within a day.

"Too small, too weak, and not enough lung capacity," he said, his prognosis based on fifty years of experience.

Old Sheba was vague and made no predictions. But she, too, had seen innumerable life-and-death struggles. Her contempt for the learned doctor and his science was as poorly concealed as his for her and her superstition. The old woman's consultation with the phases of the moon and the mysterious potions and brews on her mantel were anathema to Dr. Hunter, but in this case it mattered little that the old woman gave the child the liquid from a maceration of elderberry bark and poke salad roots boiled with sugar. Even the onion wrapped in brown paper she hung over the makeshift crib would do no harm—or good.

"Can't you at least keep that damn asafetida and stinkweed somewhere else?" the doctor complained, sniffing the foul-smelling plants Old Sheba had hanging in her cabin. "The stench will kill him if the fever doesn't!"

More to annoy the old physician for doubting her powers than for therapeutic value, Old Sheba often rattled a gourd filled with beans over the baby and chanted half-remembered African phrases from her childhood. This only increased Dr. Hunter's contentiousness, but as far as he was concerned, when the baby died, science would be vindicated and Sheba's witchcraft proved a failure.

Lavinia became obsessed with the child's recovery. Little Samuel had become a symbol of her life's new direction, and she ordered the entire plantation to pray that he would not die. Seldom leaving Old Sheba's cabin, she hovered over the child as if it were her own and the sheer force of her will could banish his sickness.

Henny was assigned to assist Old Sheba in the baby's care. Aunt Beck told her that Lavinia had repudiated Piney's and Emma's accusation that she had stolen her shawl, and in Sheba's cabin she was greeted warmly and promised attention later. Although she was not designated Lavinia's maid, she was encouraged when Lavinia told her, "I have cancelled the overseer's order that you be assigned to the fields, Henny. You are to continue assisting Old Sheba in caring for little Samuel."

Nancy, still nursing her own six-month-old daughter, Mary Star, shared her bountiful supply of milk with little Samuel, and Old Sheba grudgingly followed Dr. Hunter's instructions (but refused to relinquish her own remedies) and applied cupping glasses, small glass tumblers heated and placed open-ended to the child's chest, to "draw out the poison" and stimulate circulation. Hunter watched with professional outrage as Old Sheba insisted that the baby's ears be filled with warm milk expressed from Nancy's breasts.

"That milk is supposed to go in the baby's belly, not his ears!" the old man shouted, but Old Sheba paid him no heed and responded by picking up her gourds and rattling them defiantly over the baby—and Dr. Hunter, too.

Henny glowed with pride when Lavinia praised her assistance in helping with Samuel, mitigating her sense of Lavinia's neglect since the baby had come to dominate her mistress's attention.

On the third day under Old Sheba's and Henny's care, the baby's chest seemed to heave with less desperation, the hot, dry fever broke, and the little boy, drenched in perspiration, finally seemed to strengthen and rally.

"He suckin' stronger," Nancy announced on the fourth day, and by the fifth, Dr. Hunter gave the little boy a better than fifty-fifty chance of survival.

Old Sheba shook her head. "He be all dead, or all alive—one or the other. Ain't no such thing as being both." When Dr. Hunter finally confirmed the little boy would survive, Old Sheba glowed like a lantern and chanted and danced and rattled her gourds over patient and physician with triumphant vindication. "Hit my salve and potions does it," she said.

Lavinia visited Bingo and Jane every day to report on the baby. Soon she began to fear she was being watched. Rustling in the underbrush and the sound of retreating horses betrayed unknown presences. Although she took different routes, she detected other signs—the prints of horses' hooves, a man ducking behind a tree, the whinny and blow of a horse concealed in a thicket—all evidence that it would be unsafe to return the baby or risk an attempt for Bingo and Jane to visit Samuel.

At first frightened for herself, in time Lavinia grew more concerned for the Barksdales, who seemed the target of the surveillance.

"Nothing to worry about, dear," Miss Maude said, dismissing Lavinia's concern. "They've been watching us for ages—and our tenants as well."

"Why, the other day I was visiting Papa's grave and almost came face to face with one of them," Miss Phoebe said. "He was hiding behind a tombstone. I recognized him at once as one of Charles Hicks's men. I simply waved at him and sang out, 'Good morning,' and asked him if everybody was still there. He fled like a deer." She laughed and set her corkscrew curls bouncing with a dismissive toss of her head.

But Miss Maude's hooded eyes narrowed with concern. "The only thing we worry about is the safety of our free blacks. Even though they have been freed and have permission to remain as our tenants, that Hicks and his patrols would not be above snatching them and selling them back into slavery. We've warned them not to stray too far from the place."

"But wouldn't that be illegal?" Lavinia asked.

"Indeed, it would. But, my dear, when thieves are in charge of enforcing the law, what good is the law?"

"Foxes in chicken houses."

"Precisely. And we make sure our free blacks' poll taxes are paid—that's the law now, too, you know. They're supposed to be free but are taxed!"

The day Lavinia brought the news that little Samuel would live, Jane wept tears of gratitude and fell on her knees at the good news.

"How we ever thanks you ladies?" Bingo said.

"Why, you already have!" Miss Phoebe said. "Jane's practically taken over Mama's care and Bingo is our sentry. Warns us when he sees that Hicks and his patrols snooping around."

In the parlor, Lavinia noticed a grimness in the old ladies as Miss Phoebe settled in her rocking chair and took up her knitting and Miss Maude closed the door.

"You're our dearest friend, Lavinia," Miss Maude said, seating herself. "And we've decided to share something with you."

"Since you know we're harboring Bingo and Jane, we might as well tell you everything," Miss Phoebe said. She began rocking slowly in her chair and confessed they were a link in the Underground Railroad.

Lavinia caught her breath at the words: Underground Railroad! A term anathema to slave-owners. The old ladies might as well have confessed to being devil worshipers.

"We're a 'station' or 'safe-house,'" said Maude. "We hide runaway folk who come to us from down the line, keep them a few days, and send them on."

"We've been doing it for years," said Phoebe. "Since we freed our own slaves. Only occasionally at first, but when the conductors learned about us—"

"Conductors?"

"Conductors in the Underground Railroad," Miss Phoebe said. "They bring us runaways from Georgia and the Carolinas and even farther south. And of course surrounding Virginia counties."

"But the dangers—" Lavinia asked.

"True. And we were frightened at first."

"Well, at least your underground is only symbolic," Lavinia said. "I used the actual railroad for my activities." She watched as Miss Phoebe's rocking came to a halt and the sister's incomprehension change to shocked disbelief.

"You mean you...assisted Angelica?"

Lavinia nodded.

"Oh, sister," trilled Miss Phoebe, "we're not the only outlaws in the county after all! There's one right next door!" She smiled and began rocking again.

Miss Maude was more somber. "But Lavinia, does Lionel know? This is far more serious an offense for you than for us. We're elderly spinsters, old ladies. Just what can they do? Put us in jail? Hang us?"

"Lionel does not know. But suspects. But I don't care."

"But you must care, dear," Miss Maude said. "It's very dangerous."

"But how else can we attempt to right such a wrong?"

"Indeed," said Miss Phoebe, increasing the rhythm of her rocking. "If you only knew the suffering slaves have to bear. Not just being in bondage, but the whippings and cruelty and every kind of abuse."

She slowed her rocking, bent closer, and whispered, "Have you noticed Bingo's ear?"

Lavinia had noticed the notch cut out of Bingo's right ear and nodded.

"The work of Horace Wroughton. He clipped it with a tobacco knife one day in the fields when Bingo got behind on his row. Would have cut it off except that would have diminished his market value. Docile slaves are unmarked; disobedient ones wear scars."

"Bingo tells us Wroughton has a kind of dungeon in his cellar. A 'breaking room,' he calls it. To punish and crush the will of those he finds disobedient."

"Wroughton's a drunkard, you know," Miss Maude said. "Bingo and Jane tell us that's when he commits most of his atrocities. He gets liquored up and not even his wife can restrain him."

As Lavinia listened to the stories of Wroughton's brutality, her blood chilled. She was further stunned when she learned of the mistreatment of slaves by some of her own neighbors, people she knew and respected and counted among her friends. Even deacons in some of the Christian churches were guilty of neglect and providing living conditions that were appalling by Hawthorn Hill standards.

"You mean Agnes Thornton allowed Mr. Thornton to break up a family?"

"Indeed, she did. Wept and begged him not to do it, poor thing, but what can a wife do? He sold the mother to one buyer, the husband to another, and the two children to two other buyers."

"And they even quote the Bible to justify slavery!" Miss Phoebe snorted.

Lavinia sagged in her chair as one abuse after another was revealed. She had always thought such crimes were committed by slave owners farther south, never by people she knew.

"I really don't think Lionel would ever try to do something like that. He hasn't, has he? I mean, he would never let me know—"

"Oh, no, dear," Miss Phoebe said. "Hawthorns never broke up families, and seldom sold their blacks, except a willing one who wanted to marry a black of another owner."

"Lionel complains about the imbalance in our people," Lavinia said. "Too many old ones and too many young ones and not enough between to do the real work." Lavinia had often heard Lionel say his only protection against bankruptcy was that the old ones finally died off, and the young ones eventually grew up and could finally earn their keep.

"Well, thank God for a few decent owners. And at least he doesn't resort to the hypocrisy of some owners, who free their people once their years of productivity are over. Oh, yes. They wait until they can labor no more and turn them out as free blacks to try and make it on their own. They make a great show of being benevolent masters rewarding their servant's long years of service. The poor things have nowhere to go and no way of making a living and—"

"Or," whispered Miss Phoebe as if she might be overheard by the great man himself, "do what George Washington did. Specified in his will that his slaves be freed after his death. Easy enough to do that when you've worked the life out of them yourself and in death don't need them anymore."

"Indeed, it seems there are those who can have their cake and eat it too," Miss Maude said. "The father of our country being one."

At the same time Lavinia embraced her new commitment, she feared Lionel. She drew hope from his decency toward his blacks and the memory of what followed his single episode of violence toward a slave, Silas, who had been caught stealing years before. Lavinia had begged him not to use the whip but choose some other punishment, but Lionel had refused. Silas had stolen a ham to trade for liquor and had been caught red-handed. Insisting he had to make an example of Silas, Lionel had turned aside her opposition, forged his will, and vowed to give Silas ten lashes so the people would know stealing would not be tolerated at Hawthorn Hill.

But in the end, he could not do it. After assembling the entire slave population to witness the punishment, he had administered but a single slash across Silas's back, and unable to continue, thrown aside the leather strap and stalked back to the house, miserable at the one lash he had administered and the nine others he could not.

Lavinia had found him an hour later in the office, holding his head in his hands, not even looking up to see who it was who came into the room. But even not seeing her, he knew it was she. Suspending their estrangement for the moment, she had put her hand on his shoulder and said nothing in judgment of his crime—for the one lash he had administered or the nine others he could not—and allowed him to hold her and bury his face into her skirts like a grieving child.

Whether he had wept for his act of cruelty, or his failure to complete it, or the insane world which seemed to demand such inhumanity, she did not know. But she had never loved him as much as that moment when he had let her see his regret, knowing that he would never allow another to witness such a moment—parent, mistress, friend, or child. Only she. She had been moved to see a man weep, spurred by the depth of his compassion, even as she knew he also wept because he thought he was weak to have it.

When at last he had released her, she had gone to his desk and poured him a tumbler of bourbon. He had drunk it in a single gulp, and a second one, and she had his supper brought to the office and they had stayed there together the rest of the day as he got drunker and drunker and finally unburdened himself in cruel, intoxicated examination of the world in which they found themselves.

He had been the first since his grandfather to cut into the flesh of a slave. He had never struck his own sons, his thundering voice enough to enforce his will. His barroom brawls had been of a different character and in no way the same as using a leather strap to open the flesh of a man tied, kneeling, and defenseless.

As he had drunkenly poured it all out, he had questioned why he hadn't whipped Silas as he had done when they were boys, with his fists. Silas had beaten him enough in these boyhood skirmishes, when momentarily the companionship of youth had suspended the boundaries between black and white, master and slave, and an argument over who had caught the biggest fish could be resolved in no other way. They had fished together, and swum together, and bated and collected the catch of traps together. They had, in boyhood, been friends, as if unconscious of the other's color or hierarchy—and might even have expected, once boyhood was behind them, that these differences would never even matter.

But in time they had mattered, and Silas had held out his arms with not a quiver of resistance to be bound to the whipping post and fallen to his knees as his shirt was stripped from his back.

"He did not even look at me," Lionel had said, staring into the liquor that had brought his conscience to his tongue. "Nor I at him. And he took it because of who he was—and who I was."

Lavinia had said nothing as he had babbled drunkenly of the old, gone forever boyhood friendship, mournful for the loss of it, and the ugly failure and impossibility to continue it when adulthood made the differences between black and white, and master and slave, visible and palatable as it never had been in the spring and summer of youth.

The next week, Lionel had granted manumission papers to Silas and his wife and two children and given him five hundred dollars and passage to Ohio. Lavinia never knew if they exchanged farewells and never asked. Many in the quarters believed the family had been sold because of the theft and Lionel did nothing to disabuse them of that impression.

Lavinia hoped that Lionel's freeing Silas had freed his conscience as well, but she never knew. She never asked and Lionel never spoke of the beating or of Silas ever again.

Chapter Fourteen

Lionel returned from Richmond a week later. Lavinia's exchanges with him were formal and awkward but without the old hostility.

"Oh, I almost forgot. Ibby sent the bonnet she said you left the last time you were in Richmond," he said, removing a package from his saddle bags.

Lavinia's heart leaped. When Lionel left for the fields, she raced to her room and quickly examined the bonnet, previously chosen as a method of concealing word from Angelica. In the brim's edge, she located a loose string which, when pulled free, opened a hidden pocket containing a piece of paper. Holding the paper in her trembling hands, she read:

Dear Miss V.

We are safely arrived & wed. Our happiness is complete, except travel beyond R. is blocked as conductors at next stop in Fred'burg arrested. Hiding in boot maker's shop. Sister Ibby wonderful to us and they move us around as it is very dangerous in R. More when I can write & sister Ibby can get word to you. Pray for us. Love. A. and G.

At supper, Lavinia told Lionel the latest county gossip and plantation news. "Mr. Mudley has been sober and diligent," she reported. "Plowing is complete and we are back on schedule. I think we're past any frosts and can begin planting now."

Lionel related the family news and detailed Ariadne's birthday dinner with humorous impressions of Uncle Cuthbert and reported his mother's hair was now only slightly less red than a cardinal's feathers. Lavinia listened appreciatively while wondering how she might once again propose Henny as her maid. She also burned to know, but was afraid to ask, if he had found out anything about Angelica's escape. Tonight would be her last opportunity, as the tobacco factory required that he return to Richmond the next day.

Throughout dinner, he looked at her with a shy version of his usual sensual smile, and his blue eyes twinkled with mischief. Lavinia avoided his flirtatious gaze by reading letters from her son and daughter-in-law reporting their joy at impending parenthood.

During dessert, Lionel reported on his investigation of Angelica's escape. "The Richmond people doubt she will be recovered."

Lavinia breathed a sigh of relief, but it was short-lived when he added. "But if they are still in Richmond, they may be caught. Recent arrests have slowed the flow of the Underground Railroad out of the city. I also spoke with Sheriff Hudspeth on the way back. He's concerned about the Barksdales."

"Phoebe and Maude?" Lavinia held her breath and waited.

"He suspects either they or the free blacks on their plantation may be a link in slave escapes. For years, runaways have been traced to their property where they lose the trail.

Patrols say they detect ether or chloroform and kerosene, which destroys the dogs' ability to follow a scent beyond their fences."

"The Barksdales? Slave running?" said Lavinia. "That's preposterous."

"Well, they're abolitionists, and don't seem to care who knows it. And those free blacks would have no qualms about helping escapees."

"But they would hardly break the law—"

An awkward silence followed during which they both seemed to only play with their food. "The sheriff was also puzzled because we have posted no reward for the recovery of Angelica when Wroughton is offering exorbitant amounts for his man."

"We should offer nothing. I don't want her back. Her betrayal was unforgivable."

"The sheriff says you're often at the Barksdales." His tone seemed too casual and Lavinia knew he was suspicious.

"To assist in the care of their mother," Lavinia said, too quickly. "I have been all over the house and assure you there are no runaways there. Are you accusing me of—"

"I am accusing you of nothing, Mrs. Hawthorn. But your defensiveness accuses you."

"Lawyer talk. Always twisting people's words, distorting their meaning. I have helped the Barksdales because they are short-handed and with Angelica gone, I could not send her. Which reminds me. I should like to move Henny up from the quarters. I can use her now more than ever."

"I have plans for her. In a year or so, I will send her to Mother in Richmond to be trained for a suitable position there."

"I can train her here."

"I'm afraid you have allowed your attachment for her to grow beyond mistress and servant. It would not be in the best interest of you or the child."

"And why not?"

"The child—"

"'The child, the child.' Your child!" She spat at him. "Can you not at least acknowledge—"

"We will not speak of that."

"It would seem to have some relevance."

"Not to me." His voice was cold and he looked at her evenly.

Lavinia was aghast at his insensitivity. Her temper ignited, she rose from the table.

"You got what you wanted the last time you were home," she said. "Now give me this child."

Lionel's features turned sinister. Placing his napkin beside his plate, he appraised her carefully. The adversarial turn of the meal seemed to quell his appetite and he rose to his feet.

"Was our reunion but a trade-off? Your favors for the child?"

His remark made her feel cheap, as if he likened her to the prostitutes he paid. She felt her face color with anger and embarrassment. "I shall not discuss this further." Anxious to escape the scrutiny of his blue eyes, she turned and left the room.

Upstairs, she retired immediately to her room, where she went to bed, but only after locking her bedroom door and consuming her nightly tumbler of bourbon.

The next morning, she watched from her window as Lionel left on horseback. He had not said goodbye. Emma's shrewd reading of everything in the household and accusing look told Lavinia she knew the shadow of a row had once again fallen on her marriage.

"Old Sheba up here this mornin'," Emma said. "She say they slips over here from the Wroughton place in the night wantin' her to come 'tend that Booker what Wroughton beat so bad last week. She go and say he mighty bad and they nothin' she can do. He needin' Dr. Hunter but Wroughton won't fetch him. She wantin' to see if maybe you can gets him."

Lavinia reported the Wroughton slave's condition to the Barksdales, who passed it on to Dr. Hunter when he visited their mother. Later that day, the doctor called on little Samuel and related his exchange with Wroughton.

"Didn't charge him a dime," he reported to Lavinia after giving Samuel a good report. "He never calls me unless it's a sick horse or cow. Too stingy. He thinks more of his stock than his blacks. I've told him he'd have fewer runaways and get more work out of his people if he treated them better."

Dr. Hunter shook his head doubtfully and pursed his lips with concern. "Don't think that man he beat is going to make it. Blood poisoning has set in."

"And he can get away with that? If the man dies, he'll face no charges?"

"Afraid not. It's his property and he can do with him what he wants." Dr. Hunter, grunting from the effort, hoisted himself into the seat of his buggy.

"I told him, better to lose them by running off than by killing them. And he lost his best man, Gabriel. Why, I've won a tidy sum of money at foot races and wrestling bouts on that man. And Wroughton's won many a dollar on him, too."

With a flick of the reins he was off. "Keep the baby warm and he'll heal himself. And tell that old witch the milk goes in his belly, not his ears!"

The next afternoon, Lavinia was surprised to see Horace Wroughton riding up the lane to the house. Wroughton never called upon his neighbors, and his appearance disturbed Lavinia, fearing he had some news of Gabriel and Angelica.

"Good afternoon, Mr. Wroughton." Lavinia greeted him on the front porch. Although she disliked him, she was determined to be polite. He reined his horse beside the porch but made no move to dismount, watching her with unfriendly coppery-colored eyes beneath bushy red-orange brows.

"My husband is away, but won't you come in?"

"Ain't got the time." His raspy voice came from barely moving lips, revealing wide-apart, stubby teeth, his mouth surrounded by a tobacco-streaked beard the same red-orange as his eyebrows. A gnarled, pointy nose veered to one side above his scraggly moustache.

Horace Wroughton was not regarded as a gentleman, and it was no surprise to Lavinia that he did not have the good manners to remove his hat or even tip it, courtesies the lowest class of white, or even a field hand, would have known to observe.

"Reckon you ain't seen no stray blacks around here lately, have you?"

"No, Mr. Wroughton, our losses remain the same."

Although a planter, he was looked down on by even the lowest classes. Based on the criteria of acreage, number of slaves, and wealth, he qualified as a planter, yet socially he was regarded more in the class of poor whites, those who struggled to survive on small farms dotted about the county. Indeed, he was not even granted admittance into the rank of "good country people," which included honorable landowners of modest holdings with few or no slaves, but who were respected and valued as neighbors by those of the gentleman planter class because of their decency and integrity.

What gained one entry into either of these two classifications was based on standards that went beyond vast acreage, number of slaves, and wealth. Wroughton's inferior blood line was not held against him but regarded as an accidental circumstance that could be forgiven any man if he proved himself worthy enough through good character and respectable conduct. It was his behavior after he came to the county that had earned his neighbors' scorn.

Unknown before he arrived, Wroughton had appeared mysteriously from nowhere fifteen years earlier with a deed to the old Moseley plantation. He had purchased the valuable twenty-five hundred acres from heirs to the property who had moved out of Virginia years before.

Lionel Hawthorn and other planters had coveted the land since the original owner died, but none had had the opportunity to even bid on it. Wroughton arrived one day with nothing more than a rickety wagon filled with broken-down furniture, a hostile-faced, square-jawed wife sitting beside him, and a crisp, newly-recorded deed to twenty-five hundred acres of the finest land in the county.

"And not only does he arrive with title to the property, but it's laid fallow for ten years, rested under scrub grass, saplings, and overgrowth, and had renewed its strength," Lionel had fumed. "It's like getting rich, virgin soil to cultivate for the first time, before being leached by years of tobacco."

The two wagonloads of slaves came later, the plantation's original blacks having been sold years earlier. A distinctly different kind of black than those of the county, these slaves, frightened, hard-eyed, and with a difficult-to-understand dialect, had accents that spoke of origins in the deep South. Sapped of life by drudgery long before they set foot in Virginia, the scars on their backs and defeat in their eyes told the story of their woeful past.

The local Virginia planters shook their heads piously and bemoaned the reality they had heard characterized slave treatment in other areas of the South.

There was nothing illegal or irregular about the transfer of the property to Wroughton; it was simply a land sale like any other.

Wroughton had first tried too hard to become one of his neighbors, and his aggressive bid for inclusion had been deemed offensive. Early on, he had been distrusted and labeled "forward." His attempts at unctuous flattery also failed to gain him entry into the closed, long-established ranks of the leading planters. His failure to realize that it could take generations to prove to these class-conscious Virginians his worthiness frustrated Wroughton, and his anger turned to dislike and he soon came to hate the people he had once aspired to join.

Although they exhibited no hostility toward him and were gracious in their isolation from him, he resented more than outright insults the always polite and insufferable condescension of their subtle rebuff. Overnight he became just the opposite of the presumptuous, proud interloper he was when he first arrived in the county, and later the subservient, grinning supplicant he had affected with even less success. He became surly and alienated his neighbors through unfriendliness and contentiousness. He abandoned his efforts to ingratiate himself and made every effort to offend the other planters. His vast acreage bordered nearly a dozen land owners and within ten years, he had made enemies of them all.

A break in a neighbor's fence had resulted in a threatened lawsuit because a cow had wandered onto his property. He had shot prized hunting dogs for no greater violation of his stringent trespass ban than following the scent of a rabbit onto his land. Fishing a stream within the boundaries of his domain resulted in charges of theft and threats of violence.

"I come to tell you I ain't lettin' my blacks come to that Sunday School you set up," Wroughton said to Lavinia. "And to let you and them Barksdale women know I'll deal with any sickness that comes to my blacks without them nosin' in and sendin' doctors that ain't wanted."

"But Mr. Wroughton," Lavinia said, "I don't understand. The Sunday School is so beneficial to our people."

"Just makes 'em tale-carriers. And they get radical idees. Churchin' just makes 'em want to set up rebellions and be free."

"I can assure you, Mr. Wroughton, that the church services are only religious and are in no way political."

"Oh, they got their ways of gettin' abolitionist idees in. They dress it up with preacher talk and Bible verses, but hit's the same thing."

The only reason Wroughton had permitted his blacks to join the slaves from other plantations for Sunday services in the first place was because they were followed by footraces and competitions of strength, which were won by Gabriel more often than any other participant. Although frowned upon by various members of the church, wagers were covertly made on the contests and Wroughton had collected substantial amounts on Gabriel's victories. There was also a free meal served after the morning services, contributed by the blacks' owners—except Wroughton, who was spared the expense of feeding his people a meal on Sundays.

"I do hope you will reconsider your decision about the church services, Mr. Wroughton. It is our responsibility to see that our people are instructed in Christian—"

"Don't reckon Christianizin' 'em do no good. They got the mark of Cain, the Bible says."

"Are you a religious man, Mr. Wroughton?" Lavinia asked.

"My old woman is. Brought up on the Bible. She says hits in the Scripture that Cain kilt his bother and God marked him and throwed him out of the Garden of Eden. That was the beginnin' of the blacks—"

"Perhaps Cain didn't want to remain in Eden and be a slave," Lavinia said. "Perhaps he and his people chose to leave Eden—"

Wroughton only snorted impatiently. "Reckon that's why yore girl took out?"

"I think it is apparent why our blacks fled, Mr. Wroughton," Lavinia said.

Wroughton narrowed his eyes and watched her closely, while with slow deliberation he removed a plug of tobacco from his pocket and bit off a chew.

"You mean you ain't had no letter from them?"

Lavinia was stunned by his question and the contempt in his voice.

"I figure with your girl writin' them travel papers to get to Richmond, she mighta wrote to you by now."

"Angelica was illiterate, Mr. Wroughton."

"Somebody wrote them papers. Don't reckon they writ themselves." His challenging disdain incited her anger but she resisted showing it.

"Well...perhaps your man wrote them? What was his name? Gabriel?"

"Gabriel. The same it's always been. The same it was when you was wantin' me to let him marry up with your gal. The same it was when your man and half the planters in this county wanted to buy him off me."

Lavinia ignored Wroughton's rudeness. He removed his hat, revealing a mottled, bald dome, fringed at ear level with the same yellow-red hair as his beard. The gesture was not out of respect for Lavinia's presence, but to wipe his brow with his sleeve.

"Mighty strange thing to me when a slave's given a horse and basket of eats to run away on." He watched Lavinia's reaction carefully from above his gnarled, veering nose.

"I assure you, sir, the horse was provided for Angelica to take the food to an ailing neighbor."

"You mean them Barksdale women ain't got enough to eat? I knowed they freed their blacks but I never knowed they was goin' hungry 'cause of it." An ugly grin revealed his wide-spaced, nubby teeth. "Mighty quar the wench had travel papers writ all proper and money to get train passes. Went right out of this county in fine style, if you ax me. Nary black of mine's got money to buy a train pass."

"I have no idea how the funds for the train were procured. We have on occasion rewarded our people with small amounts of money in the past. Perhaps Angelica saved it, or found other sources—"

"Did she buy a fine suit of man's clothes, too? Train people say he dressed like he a high-up house black. My blacks ain't got fancy outfits to run off in."

"Nor do our people, Mr. Wroughton." For the first time she suspended her attempts at civility. "None of this would have happened if you had allowed Angelica and Gabriel to marry."

"I don't let my blacks marry off the place."

"Indeed. And now we both suffer losses as a consequence of your refusal."

Wroughton's horse lurched forward a step and he quickly reined him into control. "How come you never reported your girl gone? Reckon if my old woman hadn't got curious it woulda been another day 'for we knowed they run. Mighty good fortune for them havin' near a day's head start before they was missed."

"I have already answered these questions for the sheriff. Perhaps if you consulted him he can explain the delay."

"Hit don't matter. The sheriff done told me. But I'll get my black back. I been to Richmond and got some specialists at work on it. Might cost me, but they'll get him."

"Specialists?"

"Specialists. Slave trackers. Not like Charles Hicks and these we got local. These is experts, the specialists. They'll go North to get 'em and bring 'em back. They'd get your girl back, too, if you really want her."

"You would have to discuss such matters with my husband."

Wroughton leaned forward so close to her Lavinia thought he might topple from his saddle. His eyes bore into her, his mirthless smile fixed as he spoke.

"Hit took yore little fancy house maid gal to get him hot to travel. Used them black, wall-eyed love looks and moonlight down at the fence line to get his juices stirred up. Done used fleshy enticements to get the damn fool to risk his life for a little piece of honey-hole."

Lavinia gasped and recoiled. "How dare you speak in such a manner in my presence! My husband—"

"I dare it!" Wroughton bellowed. His ferocity unsettled Lavinia and his horse stirred restlessly as he straightened to full belligerent erectness in the saddle. His face twisted into a snarl as he spat, sending a stream of tobacco juice splattering on the porch only inches from Lavinia's feet.

Lavinia took another step back and felt her face flush. She wished she were a man and could physically attack him. If she had a gun she would shoot him.

"You stupid fool," Lavinia said icily. "Don't you realize I could have you shot for what you have done? One mention of this to my husband—the best shot in the county—and he would call you out and put a bullet clean through you. And half the county urging him on and glad he did it. Now you get off this place or I'll have you driven off."

Horace Wroughton's eyes flickered with momentary doubt and then, giving Lavinia a final look of contempt, he pulled his horse back from the porch. "You and them blabby Barksdale sisters can just keep yer mouths shut to Dr. Hunter about who needs doctorin' at my place." He then turned his horse and galloped down the lane toward the main road.

Still shaken, Lavinia leaned against a porch support and watched him until he was out of sight.

She knew if she told Lionel of the encounter, he would call Wroughton out and shoot him within a day. But she could not tell Lionel; it would only direct more attention to the accusations against her, all of them true. At the same time, when Lionel made no move to avenge the offending charges, Wroughton would know she had not reported his insult, her silence confirming her guilt.

But what could she do? Who could help her? She felt such inner turmoil, she needed a drink of bourbon to calm her. But whatever complications Horace Wroughton might have added to her problems, Lavinia knew the consolation of liquor was only momentary and she would have to face her difficulties alone.

Chapter Fifteen

⋆⇒◯⇐⋆

In Richmond, a new wave of gossip spread among Margaret's friends concerning Lionel and Bithia Clevinger, the wife of his Yankee business associate.

"Gossip. Gossip," Margaret said in repeated attempts to squelch the story. "Lionel says Mr. Clevinger is one of his best customers and buys tons of chewing tobacco from our factory. Mother has even had Mrs. Clevinger to supper."

The rumors persisted, however, and Margaret, already concerned with suspicions of infidelity by Alexander Harvey, paid Lionel an unannounced visit at the tobacco factory.

Lionel quickly reassured Margaret, "Why, Maggie, that's ridiculous. Alexander is the most virtuous man I know."

"But these mysterious meetings at night," Margaret said, weeping against his shoulder. "He's out all hours and won't tell me where he is, except to claim he's visiting a sick parishioner, or helping sober up a drunken deacon, or comforting the widow and children of a deceased church member."

"Which, indeed, he is," Lionel said. "Now stop imagining something that is not even remotely possible. Believe me, I'd know. I've been a scandal so often in Richmond, I know everyone else who is. And your Al is not one of them."

Reassured, Margaret dried her tears and felt guilty at having suspected her beloved Alexander. "And this talk about you and Bithia Clevinger—" she said.

"Mrs. Clevinger? Merely a business associate's wife. And he's making us quite rich."

"But you have been seen riding with her in an open carriage right down Main Street in the middle of the day."

"Once. On a complimentary factory tour, my dear—"

"And back to her hotel, The Bird and Owl, by way of Broad Street!"

"My God, don't tell me you gossips have a street plan of my movements!"

"Well, one can't help but see you when you flaunt her in the busiest, most traveled streets in Richmond."

Lionel laughed. "Oh, so I should travel with Mrs. Clevinger by the back streets and alleys?"

"Well...there would be less talk."

"But there would be only more talk, Marg. Like I was hiding something."

"But you could use a closed carriage. She draws such attention to herself with those outrageous clothes she wears."

Lionel laughed louder and slapped his thigh.

"I'm told she wears red and big feathered hats and it isn't even full spring."

"Ah, but more subdued colors would make her less visible and less notorious? And in a closed coach totally invisible." He laughed again.

Margaret failed to appreciate his humor. "Livvy is bound to hear it. And Mother. Ariadne will see to it if no one else does."

"Mother knows Mrs. Clevinger and the profitable association I have with her husband and I shall inform

Lavinia of your concern. Mother will believe anything I say and Lavinia will understand, too."

Meanwhile, in the kitchen of Ariadne Woodhull's Clay Street mansion, Jennie pleaded with Madison to be relieved of serving tea to Ariadne and her guest, Judge Povall.

"Can't you just tell Miss Ariadne I sick and gets me out of it, Madison?" she said. "I serve every time this week and makes up for it if you do."

"I'm sorry, Jennie," said Madison, "I shall be right outside the door and you have nothing to fear. Just do it and it will be over before you know it."

"But she been threatenin' to sell me if I don't find out where Angelica hidin'."

"It's just a threat, Jennie. And I will see to it that you are not sold. Put on a fresh apron."

The fifteen-year-old black woman, the blackest servant of the household, with thick lips and wide, flared nostrils, left the kitchen with dread even as Madison tried to reassure her.

"You serve well, Jennie. And you will do well today," Madison said as he accompanied Jennie to the parlor. Giving the frightened girl a final nod of encouragement, Madison knocked on the door.

"I shall be right outside," he whispered as Ariadne's voice bid her enter.

Ariadne stood before a large pier mirror between the windows overlooking Marshall Street. Her thin, boyish figure attired in green silk, Ariadne surveyed Jennie's reflection for a time before turning from the mirror.

"Ah, Jennie," she said. "I've noticed your improvement for some time—very prompt and unobtrusive, just as a serving girl should be."

"Thank you, Miss Ariadne," Jennie said, relieved she had not fallen under a storm of abusive criticism.

"Have you found out anything about Angelica?"

"No, ma'am."

"But you did hear Mr. Lionel discuss the escape at dinner the evening of my birthday?"

"I...I don't remember, ma'am," Jennie said. Jennie had missed nothing, but servants were to remain oblivious to anything heard at their master's tables.

"You're lying, of course," Ariadne said, "but you are correct in pretending to know nothing. You know Angelica, of course?"

"Yes, ma'am. She a cousin to me."

"Ah, yes. I remember." Ariadne turned back to the pier mirror and stroked her thin, long neck. "When my grandfather died, your family was divided between mine and Aunt Cornelia's. I inherited you and...and another one, your sister. Aunt Cornelia inherited the other branch of your family, your cousins, Angelica and her sister Ibby. What happened to your sister?"

"She died, ma'am."

"Ah, yes. So many people do. And even being related to Angelica and Ibby, you have not found out Angelica's whereabouts?"

"No, ma'am."

"But you have seen Ibby."

"Only at church, ma'am."

"At church. Religion means so much to you people, doesn't it? How nice for you. Keeps you happy and humble and helps us, too. By quelling the rebellious among you. Or does it inflame the rebellious? I suspect it does both."

Ariadne, as if in deep thought, strolled around the room before she spoke. "You disappoint me, Jennie. I told you to find out about Angelica days ago and you have not. Perhaps I shall give you another chance. I want you to have a nice visit with Ibby."

"I doubt Ibby will know—"

Ariadne's lightness vanished and her voice became harsh and angry. "Of course Ibby will know, you black fool! Angelica is her sister. And don't come back here pretending you could not find out. And to sharpen your ears and memory, know I have been observing you lately. You seem more interested in that boy who delivers firewood than in performing your duties. Don't think I don't know everything that goes on in this house. And don't think I haven't seen you with the wood boy on the back porch and loitering with him in the back garden."

Jennie shifted uneasily and lowered her eyes.

"You malinger. You're a sneak, and just because your service has improved doesn't mean I don't know you make a great show of being busy when you are not. You blacks seem so confident you cannot or will not be replaced. Well, don't feel so comfortable." Ariadne smiled and her large eyes flashed with guile. "I've a buyer interested in you at the moment and he's made me a very good offer."

Jennie shuddered at the thought of the dreaded slave market.

Swirling away from her but still watching her in the mirror, Ariadne brightened at the girl's visible fear.

"But perhaps your performance will improve. Perhaps I shall not have to sell you to Judge Povall after all."

"Judge Povall?" The words of alarm were out of her mouth before Jennie could think.

The seventy-year-old widower, who had made Margaret's evening so unpleasant at Ariadne's birthday dinner, was the dread of every dark-skinned black woman in Richmond. Jennie had noticed the repulsive old man watching her whenever he dined at Ariadne's. He always smacked his lips, arched his brows, and threw her leering grins, which she had pretended not to notice.

Ariadne continued, "Judge Povall has often spoken favorably of you. Singled you out from Esta and Velvet and the other serving girls. He seems anxious to own you."

Being owned by Judge Povall filled Jennie with terror. She swallowed hard and beads of moisture broke out on her brow. It was because of the darkness of her skin, she knew. Povall had a predilection for only the darkest of blacks and Jennie was of the deepest ebony.

"But Miss Ariadne," Jennie protested, her voice shaking. "They awful talk about Mr. Judge Povall—the way he treats the women that works for him—"

"Talk?"

"Yes, ma'am. The girl he got now, Bella...she tell awful things. And the one before, she run off. And the one before her, she...they find her...she hangs herself." Jennie was almost ready to cry.

"You insolent wench! How dare you slander that fine, well-bred old gentleman!"

Outraged, Ariadne swirled toward the girl and slapped her hard across the face. "Judge Addison Povall is a distinguished legal mind from a very fine Virginia family. These rumors are nothing but attempts by blacks to smear a great legal mind who will not bend the law to allow treasonous attempts at emancipation."

Jennie lowered her head and began to cry. She tried not to think of the horror stories that had raced from servant to servant throughout Richmond for years about black women in servitude to the perverted old man. It was said he called the women he used for his sport "blackberries," and it was only boredom with his victims—or their death—that released them from his cruel preference for strange, unconventional sexual practices.

"Stop your sniveling," Ariadne demanded. "Find out Angelica's whereabouts and I'll cancel my arrangement with Judge Povall. And find out just what part Lavinia has had in this."

Later, while waiting for Judge Povall, Ariadne busied herself by signing various bank drafts laid before her by Madison.

"Do I do nothing but sign away my money? How many more?" she asked.

"Only a few, ma'am," said Madison, pushing four more neatly stacked pages before her on a writing board. "For the carriage and—"

"I thought that had been paid!"

"The repairs, yes. This is for the new horsehair upholstery."

"Oh, alright." Ariadne quickly scribbled her signature on the remaining drafts. "Ah, there's Judge Povall now!" she said, brightening at the sound of the door chimes. "Remember, Jennie is to serve," she reminded Madison, and shoving the signing board away, she rose to greet her guest.

"Judge Povall," Ariadne said, extending her hand as Madison ushered the old man into the parlor.

"My dear Ariadne," Judge Povall said, waddling toward her. He grinned widely to display the protruding row of oversized rectangles that made up his ivory false teeth. Thinking his dental prosthesis quite handsome, the old man seldom relaxed his smile, giving him an expression of perpetual, grinning stupidity. Above his garish dental work, a bulbous, purple-veined nose and little pig eyes settled in the middle of his face, which he lowered over Ariadne's extended hand as he made a deep, sweeping bow.

Judge Povall thought himself quite courtly and struggled to pull his lips over his too-large teeth and plant the brush of a kiss on Ariadne's hand.

"It is such a pleasure to be here," he said.

"Do sit, and I'll have Jennie serve the tea," Ariadne said, arching an eyebrow meaningfully as she rang the service bell. Judge Povall's eyes sparkled with anticipation. Easing his egg-shaped body, resting on short, match-thin legs, into a chair, his grin widened as Jennie entered the room followed by Madison, who carried the silver tea service and cups and saucers.

"That will be all, Madison," Ariadne said. "Jennie can pour." Her eyes slid toward Judge Povall, enthralled with the girl, his protruding dentures all the more evident as he grinned with delight.

"Is she a spirited girl?" the old man asked Ariadne when Madison had left. A breathy little chuckle followed his question as he squirmed in his seat while his fat fingers fidgeted in his lap.

"Quite spirited," Ariadne said.

"Such dark skin—so very black. Did you buy her?"

"Oh, no. She was part of my inheritance from my grandfather."

"Very black, don't you think?" The little pig eyes gleamed. "And sixteen?"

"Fifteen," Ariadne said, "and generally a well-behaved girl. She even sings and dances, you know."

Povall squirmed with delight to learn of Jennie's talents. His grin widened.

"Do your little song and dance, Jennie," Ariadne said. "The one about the molasses cake. I heard you and Esta singing it when you were cleaning the dining room one day."

"I...I've forgotten..."

"Oh, come, come, girl. Enough of this shyness," Ariadne said with impatience. "You see Judge Povall? There is a streak of disobedience in the girl."

"It's in all of them. But the dark ones are more obedient, I think."

"Do you really think so?"

"Oh, yes. I seldom have to discipline the very black ones in my household. Only the threat—"

"I must remember that. I have a man who does the whippings for me. He's a gunsmith on Clay Street. I used him to stripe a sassy stable boy last week."

"I do my own," said Judge Povall proudly. "They're less likely to forget when their master does it. I'd be delighted to assist you, should you need me—and I never break the skin."

"Oh, but I should not want to impose—"

"Pshaw! No imposition at all. Just send her over. I find my leather suspenders as effective as the strap or whip most use."

"How fascinating."

"Any good leather belt or thin strap. That'll bring them to obedience quick enough. Or dipping a finger in boiling water is effective, too."

"Then I must send you my stable boy. He's so...uppity. And this kitchen girl, Esta, is arrogant, too."

Ariadne smiled at Jennie meaningfully. "Do you think you can sing now, Jennie?"

The old man grinned and exchanged knowing glances with Ariadne as Jennie's quivering voice sang: "I'm just a little molasses cake, all sticky and sweet deep inside. And if you takes a bite of me—"

Povall's little pig eyes bulged and his grin widened over the large, ivory dentures. He popped a tea-cake into his mouth and chewed vigorously as Jennie sang, her face paralyzed with humiliation. "You know why I Mammy's pride—"

Ariadne watched the old man's appetite for the girl grow. He shifted in his seat, making quick little guarded touches to his crotch as Jennie's tight, uncertain voice struggled to bring some semblance of melody to the words she half-sang in a faltering voice.

"Louder, Jennie, and dance!" Ariadne instructed. "Show Judge Povall how well you dance!"

"Oh, yes. Do dance," the old man chuckled, nodding enthusiastically.

Swaying side to side, Jennie awkwardly turned and lifted her arms as the unsteady words continued, "I just a little molasses cake, as good as good can be. And if you takes a bite of me, you surely goin' to see how sweet I is, how juicy, too. How sticky good all through and through."

"Louder, Jennie!" Ariadne directed sternly. "Dance faster!"

"Yes, faster. Faster," Judge Povall prodded. He squirmed and rocked back and forth in his chair as his face darkened from pink to red.

Ariadne watched the two in fascination, as if enjoying Jennie's agonized humiliation and Judge Povall's consuming enchantment as his pointed tongue stretched beyond his ivory dentures to moisten his lips.

Tears streamed down Jennie's face as she struggled to continue. But she could go on no longer and dissolved into sobs, standing with her shoulders shaking, her head lowered and her arms lifted at her side in an awkward tableau of her dance.

Ariadne was enraged. "You stupid fool. If you can do no better than cry when all you are asked to do is sing, get out!" After Jennie fled the room, Ariadne said, "I am so sorry, Judge Povall. But as you can see...her disobedience..."

"Indeed," said the old man, pouting like a child.

"I shall have her appropriately punished, of course."

"That's exactly what she needs," Povall agreed, and quickly brightened with enthusiastic anticipation. "And remember, I am always at your service—and still anxious to purchase her."

Ariadne now moved to her second objective, prying into the secrets known by Judge Povall regarding various crimes and investigations in the city.

"The blacks grow more insolent and rebellious every day," she said.

"Indeed, they do. I do not see why the Legislature doesn't—"

Primed with lust and racist outrage, Povall was ripe for in depth questioning by Ariadne who, by mid-afternoon, had pried lose nearly everything of the covert investigations, surveillance, and informants connected with the secret investigation of the Richmond Underground Railroad—even what anti-slavery groups in the city had been secretly infiltrated and were being watched. His position in the judicial system had earned Povall contacts that provided him with detailed, confidential information, which Ariadne artfully pried from the old man, having suffered numerous runaways herself.

"How absolutely fascinating!" Ariadne said with feigned awe.

"Ah, but we are on our guard!" Povall trumpeted proudly. "Our vigilance is never relaxed and our secret sources are always ahead of them."

Ariadne's pretense of enthralled interest flattered the old man, and the more she responded with admiring surprise at the slave patrol's cleverness, the more Povall outdid himself in revealing their secrets and extolling their successes.

"Why, tomorrow evening we are scheduling raids on several safe houses in the city," he confided. "A boot maker's shop on Thirteenth Street is to be a major target."

"Boot maker? Thirteenth Street?" asked Ariadne. "Why, I know that shop. His wife has covered slippers with fabric for me."

"He's a free black, you know," said Povall with distaste. "And long been suspected of harboring fugitives. But tomorrow night we'll nab him—and any runaways he's holding, too!"

When Povall had gone, Ariadne sent for Ogletha and her Tincture of Opium and bromides.

"But Miss Ariadne, it not time," Ogletha said. "Dr. Rudd says you takin' too much again and—"

"Since when does a black tell me what to do? Get my medicine at once! And send in Jennie."

Ogletha did as she was told and Ariadne drank the opium and bromides.

When Jennie appeared, her composure seemingly restored, the black girl expected to fall under Ariadne's wrath for her performance before Povall, but her mistress had been lulled to calmness by the narcotics she had just consumed.

"In spite of your emotional behavior before Judge Povall this afternoon, he still wants to buy you. Just find out what I want to know and I'll delay the sale."

"Yes, ma'am," Jennie responded in a small voice, grateful for the reprieve.

"And you are not to mention this to anyone else."

"Yes, ma'am."

"Not Madison, not Ogletha, not Esta. And none of those kitchen wenches. Or the stable blacks. Is that clear?"

"Yes, ma'am," Jennie said, and waited to be dismissed.

Instead of sending her away, however, Ariadne's harshness fell away, and a sparkle of interest and curiosity flashed in her large shining eyes. She sat down and snuggled into the comfortable curve of a velvet-covered settee and the softness of the silk pillows about her. Removing her slippers, her voice once again assumed dulcet, soothing tones. "Now, dry your tears, Jennie, and come closer. Sit down here on the floor beside the settee, and talk to me."

Narrowing her eyes, she snuggled further into the softness of her cushions and her voice became a caress.

"Now tell me, Jennie. What have you heard about Judge Povall and the girls he calls his blackberries? Just what is it he likes to do—?"

Chapter Sixteen

After planting, Lavinia received word that the Richmond Hawthorns and Harveys would be making their traditional late spring visit to Hawthorn Hill. The household shifted into busy preparation for their appearance.

As usual, Cornelia steadfastly refused to travel by train. "You can risk your life if you want, but not mine or my grandchildren's," she said to Margaret.

"But Mother, the train would be so much faster," Margaret said.

"Those trains are too dangerous," Cornelia said, shaking her head so vigorously the mountain of tight, hennaed curls piled on top of her head tittered precariously. "Those things go over fifteen miles an hour!"

The debate was settled by Cornelia arranging her journey to Hawthorn Hill by closed carriage, and Margaret and the four youngest of her nine children traveling by train, leaving the remaining five with their father in Richmond. Although the Hawthorn Hill household looked forward to Margaret's visit, they dreaded her accompanying brood, which never numbered less than four or five. It seemed as soon as one child left home or was away at school, Margaret and Alexander replaced it with the birth of another. The children were spoiled, high-spirited, and undisciplined, and a trial to

Lavinia, even though she loved them and they responded to her gentle admonitions far more readily than they did their mother's.

Putting aside her dread of the younger Harveys, Lavinia was waiting at the station when the train chugged noisily to a stop. A wide bonnet appeared at a window and a plump hand waved a handkerchief.

In seconds, a chubby figure with red curls appeared at the door of the coach. Holding the hands of her five- and six-year-old sons, and followed by her maid, Molly, holding the latest Harvey baby, Margaret joined the children in squeals of delight when they saw Lavinia.

Lavinia noticed Margaret was stouter than at Christmas, but at least she didn't look pregnant, although it was more difficult to tell since she grew more portly with each addition to her family. But the blue eyes sparkled with the same girlish sense of fun, and the doll-like mouth, smiling sweetly, created dimples even deeper in the increased chubbiness of her face with its flawless peaches-and-cream skin.

After happy greetings and hugs and kisses were exchanged, Lavinia herded the group to the carriage.

"You scamps have grown too big for the coach!" Lavinia teased the children as they squeezed inside. "I'll have to send Uncle Lemiel with a tobacco wagon next year."

There was much to catch up on, and as the coach headed for Hawthorn Hill, the two women chatted non-stop, often overlapping their sentences, and as always since they were in school together, the friendship resumed as if they had been apart only a day.

The topic of greatest interest was the impending birth of their grandchild, the child of Lavinia's son, Randolph, and Margaret's daughter, Sarah.

"Imagine a child descended from both of us," Margaret said, and they both laughingly predicted the most unsavory attributes and future for the child.

"Well, it will probably be an outlaw," Margaret said, then suddenly grew serious and clasped Lavinia's hand. "Lionel told me...things were better between you. He's so happy."

Lavinia nodded and tried to push aside the uncertainty created by an anonymous letter she had received from Richmond that said only, "Lionel Hawthorn and Mrs. Clevinger are often seen together these days."

"What about Mrs. Clevinger?" Lavinia asked.

Margaret's color drained and her mouth fell open. "How—" she began.

"The usual unknown informant notified me of Mrs. Clevinger."

"Ariadne!" Margaret said. For years she and Lavinia had suspected that the anonymous letters revealing Lionel's indiscretions were sent by Ariadne.

"Gossip, Lavinia," Margaret said, rushing to defend Lionel. "Mrs. Clevinger is an important customer's wife. We've all entertained her, even Mother." Her defense was vigorous and convincing, but Lavinia saw a subtle doubt in Margaret's blue eyes.

As the carriage proceeded toward Hawthorn Hill, the afternoon slipped into early evening. The shadows lengthened and the forest fell into darkness and mystery.

"To smell the woods and hear birds singing again!" said Margaret. "Richmond is so awful. It grows and changes all the time. Only the country seems unchanged. I do wish Alexander would accept a congregation in a small country church somewhere. Why, Richmond has nearly thirty-five thousand people now! Everybody all squeezed together. Our garden is no bigger than an onion patch. I really think cities should be against the law."

As Margaret looked out the window, she heard the new deepness in Reuben's voice as, instructed by Uncle Lemiel, he ordered the horses to a slower gait for a rough patch of road.

"Reuben's grown so tall," Margaret said. "I suppose things do change. And Uncle Lemiel seems more feeble. I suppose it really isn't just the city that changes, but the country, too."

"It does indeed," Lavinia said, thinking of the recent changes in her own life: her assistance in Angelica's and Gabriel's flight, her reconciliation with Lionel, and her discovery of Henny. And her new commitment to the abolitionist movement. How would Margaret react to the news that she had become a criminal?

Lavinia knew caution was wise, and secrecy guaranteed safety, so she told her nothing of little Samuel's rescue. Not through lack of trust, but Margaret sometimes allowed things to slip unintentionally.

It was dusk when the coach crested the final hill that brought them to Hawthorn Hill. Every window in the house was aglow and welcoming.

"Home!" Margaret cried, and sticking her head out the window, urged Uncle Lemiel to drive faster. "Faster, Uncle Lemiel!"

"I's drivin', Miss Margaret," Reuben called out. "I done drove ever speck of the way from the station."

"He's very proud," Lavinia whispered. "Do brag."

"I knew all the time, Reuben. And next to Uncle Lemiel, you're the best driver I ever saw! I want Uncle Lemiel to give you permission to go faster."

"Little bit faster, son," Uncle Lemiel said.

The gait increased and the lights of the old wooden house drew nearer. The front yard was dappled by light from a dozen lanterns as blacks from the quarters, whom Lavinia had given permission to welcome Margaret, gathered, including the children who anticipated the hard candy the visiting Hawthorns always brought them from Richmond.

When the carriage finally came to a halt, a round of greetings were exchanged with Emma and Aunt Beck as Reuben and Uncle Lemiel unloaded the luggage. Greetings exchanged, and the hard candy snatched by anxious little hands, the family finally went into the house.

"You all get outta my yard and down that hill!" Emma ordered, shooing the children back to the quarters. With jaws bulging with pieces of candy, they fled as Emma's usual threat brought instant obedience. "Git on now! I'll have you whipped and sold off."

It was well into the evening before the excitement of Margaret and her children's arrival exhausted itself. With dinner finally served, the noisy children were finally silenced by Emma, who ordered them to bed. Even though Molly, the children's nurse, had accompanied them, Emma would surrender no area of authority at Hawthorn Hill to some upstart Richmond maid and refused to allow anyone to tuck the children in but herself.

"Just like I done Miss Margaret and Mr. Lionel when they little," she said. When Margaret and Lavinia were at last alone, they sat by the fire in the library and talked until after the clock on the front hall landing struck one.

Lavinia defended Alexander Harvey against Margaret's nagging suspicion that he was seeing another woman and Margaret was once again mollified. She expressed her guilt at having suspected her husband and turned her attention once more to Lavinia's inept knitting. An expert in the craft, and Lavinia a clumsy amateur, they soon despaired at the hopeless jumble of knots and missed stitches.

"Oh, don't let me forget to give you your muff," Margaret said, picking free a knot in the blanket. "The one you left at Thanksgiving. Ibby sent it."

Anxious to examine the muff for another smuggled message, Lavinia pleaded fatigue and early rising as an excuse for bed.

When she was alone, Lavinia turned up the flame on the lamp beside her bed and sat down to examine the muff. Thrusting her hand inside, she explored the satin lining with her fingers. She quickly located a small, almost undetectable seam expertly tacked with a single, loosely sewn thread. Tracing its origin, she tugged at the thread and it slipped free, revealing a pocket in the lining which contained a tightly folded piece of paper.

Lavinia removed the paper and recognized the neat, perfectly formed letters of Angelica's handwriting. Her pulse increased as her eyes raced down the page.

Dear Miss L., the message said. *Our hiding place in the boot maker's shop was raided by patrols. We were warned by Ibby's Alonso, told about it by an eavesdropping servant at Miss Ariadnes. We missed capture by seconds, but thank God we were not caught. We fled by a second story window at back. Gabriel jumped easily, but in the darkness, I broke my ankle. With no place to go, Alonso took us to Miss Cornelia and Mr. Edmund's where we are hiding in the cellar and are safe. G. will flee in day or two with a whiskey merchant passing through to Charlot'ville to Penn. They will not take me because of my broken ankle. I will follow*

when ankle healed. Pray for us. We are safe but frightened.
Love, A & G

Lavinia read the letter a second and third time, trying to glean more information than the message revealed. Now she had new concerns. It would take weeks for a broken ankle to heal—and how long could she escape detection in Mr. Edmund and Miss Cornelia's house? It was as if fate had thrown the evidence of her crime in Lionel's lap.

"I'll have to go to Richmond," Lavinia said to herself. "I'll have to get her out of Virginia myself somehow."

Chapter Seventeen

The next morning Margaret was awake at the morning bell and anxious to visit the quarters. During breakfast, she questioned Emma and Piney about the people. Because Emma's feebleness limited her forays to the quarters, Piney's embellished reports seemed to be more current than Emma's, to the old woman's annoyance.

"And tell me about Daisy, Mammy," Margaret asked. "At Christmas, she still hadn't made a choice between Douglas and Ivan—"

"They still fightin' over her, I reckon," Emma said. "Durin' plowin' they got into it when she bring water to the field for one and not the othern."

"I seen Daisy holdin' hands with Douglas one day, and she kiss Ivan the next," Piney volunteered.

"When you see this?" Emma thundered, furious at no longer being the ultimate authority on all activities at Hawthorn Hill. "Be no kissin' on this place."

Margaret was also told of the latest Horace Wroughton brutality when the slave Booker's failed escape was punished by a beating so severe his death was eminent.

"Old Sheba slips over there last night and say he ain't goin' to live," Piney reported. "Say his back look like raw meat and all festered and pus runnin'—"

"Hush," ordered Emma. "Miss Margaret eatin' her breakfast."

Having heard the county news from Lavinia and the servants, Margaret wanted the same stories as reported in the quarters—often more accurate and scandalous than the demure, sometimes censored versions of the whites. The black grapevine, carrying tales from quarters to quarters, was more dramatic, and the white version of a drunken argument, as told in shocked whispers in Lavinia's parlor, became a brawl with bloody noses, quotable oaths, insults, and threats of duels when told in the quarters.

Like most whites reared on isolated plantations such as Hawthorn Hill, Margaret had grown up with black people and with no white companions within miles, she had often played with slaves as a child. Cornelia objected, but the gregarious, headstrong Margaret managed to evade her mother's and Emma's watchful eyes and could be found in the quarters with her friends, Nancy, Katie, and Paulina, sharing her dolls and playing tag and hide-and-seek as readily as she could be found in the more genteel little-white-girl socials arranged by Cornelia and various governesses employed for Margaret's and Ariadne's proper education.

Only Ariadne acceded to Cornelia's mandated segregation, and she often sulkily took her tea alone. But like an earlier-day Piney, she was only too ready to report Margaret's errant behavior.

"You're going to end up talking like them, thinking like them, behaving like them," Cornelia had fumed. Consequently, Margaret's every violation of Cornelia's strict code of proper behavior for refined young ladies was duly blamed on her daughter's association with her slave playmates. "Why can't you be a proper little lady like cousin Ariadne?"

Cornelia's lament had been frequent and interminable: "It is entirely improper for white children to be too closely in contact with field people. You are not to visit the quarters again. You are losing all perspective on the differences between whites and blacks, masters and slaves, mistress and servant. That would be intolerable and lead to all kinds of trouble. This fraternization is to stop. It is as bad for the blacks as it is for you, distorting the proper perception of who they are and their position. It will only lead the blacks to become impudent and uppity."

Ignoring this, Margaret had slipped away from lessons with stuffy tutors and boring teas with Ariadne at every chance to enjoy the company of her friends in the cabins. While Ariadne, a model of proper decorum in Cornelia's eyes, never sought such company and acquired a fanatical aversion to blacks, Margaret found the intrigues, romances, and imbroglios of the people of Hawthorn Hill as interesting as that of the whites in the county.

"Oh, and how is the Christmas baby, little Mary Star?" Margaret asked.

The birth of a daughter to her life-long friend Nancy the previous Christmas had been a major event at Hawthorn Hill, both at the big house and the quarters. With all the Hawthorns in residence, when news reached the big house on Christmas Eve that Nancy was in labor, wagers as to the newborn's sex were made and everyone had suggestions for an appropriate name. All agreed the child must be born on Christmas day, and Nancy was practically ordered not to deliver the child before midnight. There had been much suspense as the hours of her labor seemed about to culminate in a Christmas Eve birth, and an even greater celebration in both the quarters and big house when the child was born two hours after the clock on the landing struck twelve.

The baby, in good health and weighing almost nine pounds, had been a Christmas baby after all. After much discussion and a good-natured, lengthy debate, the baby girl was named Mary Star, to the disappointment of Lionel, who opted for Virginia, and Alexander Harvey, who had hoped Christ's stepfather, Joseph—whom he felt was neglected liturgically—might be honored and the child named Josephine. Ariadne, disgusted with the family's interest in the birth of a black, had voted for Herodotus to the shock of more Christian sensibilities.

Anxious to visit the quarters and see Mary Star's growth and progress, Margaret went unannounced to see Nancy only to be told she could be found in Old Sheba's cabin. Margaret was shocked when she saw the baby at Nancy's breast. The child was no larger than an infant of one or two months, and Mary Star should have been twice that size.

"But Nancy, can this be Mary Star?" Margaret asked, alarmed.

"Reckon it is," Nancy mumbled and hung her head. Another child, much larger and healthier, cooed happily from a hammock near the fireplace and half a dozen more of Nancy's children romped around the hearth.

"But is she ill?" Margaret quickly counted the months between December and May and knew that something was wrong if this was a five-month-old child.

"It been sick, but I reckon it going to be alright now." Nancy looked anxiously at Old Sheba.

"Does Miss Lavinia know?" Margaret asked. "She said everyone was well in the quarters."

Nancy avoided Margaret's eyes.

"Let me see her," Margaret said, and she reached for the child. "I've had nine babies myself—almost as many as you—and know this child is not developing properly." She took the infant and began to remove the blanket. "Does she eat well? Do you have enough milk?"

"Yes'um."

Nancy's voice had grown almost inaudible now, and she bit her lip as Margaret's examination continued. As her hands felt the tiny ribs and swollen stomach, the blanket fell open to reveal the child was male.

"Why, this isn't Mary Star. It's a boy!" She looked first at Nancy, who began to cry, then at Old Sheba, who returned her searching gaze with a defiant evenness that revealed nothing.

"Whose baby is this?" Margaret demanded. "And where is Mary Star?" One glance at the well-developed baby in the hammock answered her question, and Margaret returned the male child to Nancy.

"Has one of the unmarried girls had a baby?" Margaret said in an excited whisper. "Are you hiding it from Miss Lavinia? Who is it? I won't tell."

"No, Miss Margaret, it ain't that."

Margaret was disappointed. "Then where did it come from?"

Nancy looked pleadingly at Old Sheba who, after a weary sigh, said, "That baby Nancy nursin' ain't hers. It belong to them two that run from the Wroughton place three weeks ago. I gatherin' roots in the woods and finds it."

Noticing Henny lurking in a corner with wide eyes and mouth agape, Old Sheba ordered her to Nancy's cabin to watch the children there. When she was gone, Margaret continued, "But we must get a doctor—"

"Done got one. Dr. Hunter been here. Miss Vinny fetches him."

"Lavinia knows? Did she find the baby?"

"Done tole you. I finds it when I gatherin' roots for my medicals."

"I don't believe you."

Old Sheba's defiant, even-eyed silence , neither denial nor confirmation, told Margaret her suspicion was correct.

"Besides," Margaret lied, "Miss Lavinia already told me she found it."

Margaret eyed Old Sheba with triumph and her bluff succeeded. The old woman's expression lost its resolve and she sat down in her rocker. "Miss Vinny says she found it in the woods. But she never. Word done slip out from the Barksdale tenants saying the Barksdale ladies is hiding Bingo and Jane. And Miss Vinny hidin' this baby. It mighty bad off when I first gets it. But I reckon it goin' to live it out after all."

As the revelations poured out, Nancy broke into quiet weeping. "I just doin' what Miss Vinny say do, Miss Margaret. I has milk and 'bout to wean Mary Star shortly when she bring that baby and say I has to feed it. If you tells Mr. Lionel, he beat us all to death, and Miss Vinny be in bad shape, too—"

"Oh, hush crying," Margaret snapped. "Of course I won't tell Mr. Lionel. And he wouldn't beat anyone to death if I did."

She covered her eyes with her hands and sighed heavily. Sitting down on a bench, she thought of the consequences of what she had learned. "She's got us all involved now. Harboring runaways!" Horace Wroughton would be livid. And the Barksdales were involved! And some disgruntled black in the know could expose them all—and what black wasn't disgruntled under the weight of slavery? They were all like an injured bird awaiting the pounce of a cat.

Margaret finally rose. "Continue to care for the baby," she said, and she returned to the big house to await Lavinia's return from the Barksdales.

Before supper, Margaret wasted no time seeking answers to the questions that had been boiling in her head since her discovery in the quarters that morning. Lavinia, embroidering a pillow cover, lifted her eyes from her sewing and sighed with relief. "Thank God it was you and not Lionel who discovered it. It's true. I wanted to tell you earlier, but I was afraid you'd let it slip."

"I most certainly will not," said Margaret indignantly. She listened as Lavinia told her everything.

"Miss Maude and Miss Phoebe!" said Margaret in astonishment. Caught up by the intrigue and excitement of Lavinia's story, Margaret's blue eyes grew wider and she was soon bouncing in her chair like an excited child. "What adventure! It's like a story by Mr. Poe! How deliciously wicked! I mean in a good, Christian kind of way."

Lavinia looked at Margaret with alarm. "Oh, but Margaret, it is a very dangerous path I'm on. And not an episode in a novel. We deal with real dangers and it would be disastrous if our participation were discovered."

"That's what makes it so exciting. The danger! It's thrilling!"

Lavinia sighed and resumed her needlework. "I envy your seeing only adventure and excitement, but I was brought up an abolitionist—and then married Lionel—" The anguish on her face told Margaret of her conflict. "I think there is a chance Lionel and I can be happy again. Yet I feel like I am betraying him."

Margaret could not dismiss the thought that Lionel was probably in the arms of Bithia Clevinger at that very moment, but she said nothing, even as she had been Lavinia's lone confidant during Lionel's past indiscretions.

"An abolitionist married to a slave owner," said Lavinia. "How can it ever be reconciled?"

Margaret had no answer.

"And what makes it worse," Lavinia said, grateful for someone other than the Barksdales to whom she could unburden herself, "I want to do more! I want to help them all! I feel it is something very right. Yet the only way I can is in a manner the law judges as criminal. It's more than just freeing a slave I know and love. It's all of them. Right now it's the poor Wroughton people. Oh, Margaret, they are so mistreated. The Barksdale sisters have opened my eyes to so much. The wrong of it, our unjust defense of it."

"You sound just like Alexander," said Margaret. "He even alludes to the sin of it in his sermons, which will do us no good, I am afraid. Already some of the deacons remarked he sounded like he was preaching in a Yankee church."

"But surely more people share our view than we know about."

"Oh, I'm sure they do. Alexander says if people of our class don't lead the way, the issue will never be resolved."

"But an end must be put to it. And I'm afraid, Margaret. I'm afraid I'll go too far. So far I'll really get in trouble and disgrace myself and Lionel and our sons and the whole family." She put her sewing aside and looked straight into Margaret's eyes. "And I won't care."

Later at supper, Margaret met Henny when she assisted Piney in removing the dishes from the dining room table.

"My apprentice maid," said Lavinia. "And doesn't she have lovely eyes?"

"Indeed she does," said Margaret, shifting her gaze. Margaret had observed Henny in past visits to the quarters but said nothing of her suspicions regarding her parentage, just as she had withheld from Lavinia the rumors of her brother's affairs with black women who worked at the tobacco factory. After Henny had executed her most accomplished curtsy and left, an awkward silence engulfed the room and Margaret fidgeted nervously. The child was so obviously a Hawthorn it was embarrassing, and she wondered if Lavinia noticed her similarity to Oralee.

"You know who she is?" Lavinia asked.

Margaret made an elaborate display of feigned ignorance.

"She's your niece. The child of your dear brother, Lionel," Lavinia said.

"No!"

"Do you think those blue eyes just fell out of the sky? Her mother was Susannah, who died in the same epidemic that took Oralee. Do you remember her?"

"Yes...the beauty...the mysterious one we called the Queen of Africa. She was a house girl at Mother's. Lionel brought her up from the tobacco factory, I remember. Unmarried and expecting a baby..."

Lavinia nodded. "Henny, Lionel's child. I only found out recently. That's why he brought her here—to keep your mother from finding out. And he used the excuse of getting Emma additional help to hide the real reason."

"And Lionel knows you know?" Margaret's blue eyes grew even bigger.

"Yes. And I want to raise her as my own."

Margaret's eyes brimmed with tears. "Oh, Lavinia. You've always been so much smarter than I. And thought so much deeper about things than I have. I'm just fortunate to have Alexander and our babies and really don't care about anything else—or understand anything else. But you scare me a little."

"I scare myself, too," Lavinia said.

Margaret had no answers for Lavinia's dilemma. But just as Lavinia was at first alarmed by Margaret's careless, flippant disregard for the dangers of slave running, now Margaret felt the same fear for Lavinia's full commitment to a course that could only lead to the unfortunate ends she had herself already predicted.

"Oh, Vinny," said Margaret. "Why is everything such a trouble?"

Chapter Eighteen

A week later, Lavinia received a letter from her mother that her father had suffered a stroke. She immediately made plans to visit him—and take Bingo, Jane, and little Samuel with her.

"It's far too dangerous, dear," Miss Phoebe said when told of her plan.

"Less dangerous than your continuing to keep them here," Lavinia said. "The patrols suspect you, practically camp on your front porch, and they harass your tenants. You're bound to be caught sooner or later."

"The risk is too great," said Miss Maude.

"But my family has assisted runaway slaves before. We often found them hiding in our barns. We fed and housed them and assisted them on to Ohio through Kentucky. Washington County borders Kentucky. I have brothers living there only a few day's journey away. Dedicated abolitionists, they love helping runaways. I think they've always been a little ashamed that I married a slave-owner. This is my chance to redeem myself. My brothers will see Bingo and Jane on to Ohio."

The Barksdales were still doubtful, but Lavinia argued away each concern the sisters presented. Finally, she detected a wavering in the old ladies' opposition, and at last elicited a reluctant "maybe."

"And northwestern Virginia borders Ohio, making it unnecessary to go through Kentucky at all. And most mountain people oppose slavery. While many Virginians want to secede from the union to preserve slavery, where I come from, Virginians actually talk about secession from Virginia to establish another state altogether—a slave-free Virginia."

When Bingo and Jane welcomed the chance, the matter was settled. The next morning the couple was hiding at a designated spot by the road where they were reunited with their little son in Lavinia's coach. Seeing Samuel returned to good health, Jane wept and Bingo beamed with pride. Just as Lavinia had predicted, Bingo fit nicely under the seat, and with Jane's skirts flared and a leather bag placed beside her feet, her husband was completely concealed.

With Uncle Lemiel and Reuben at the reins, by evening the coach was out of the county and halfway through another. Stables along the way provided fresh horses, exchanged for the exhausted ones, just as Lavinia had done in previous journeys to and from Washington County.

Bingo became adept at quickly concealing himself in his hiding place when Uncle Lemiel signaled with a rap on the coach roof the approach of riders or other vehicles. Reuben volunteered to drive the horses well into the night. A full moon blessed their efforts and by midnight, only consideration for the exhausted horses prompted Lavinia to stop at an inn she had visited in the past. Jane, posing as Lavinia's maid, slept on a pallet beside her bed; Uncle Lemiel and Reuben were bedded down in the stables, and Bingo concealed himself in the coach.

The next morning, they were off again with Reuben proudly commanding the horses with Uncle Lemiel by his side. Bingo, who had often driven farm wagons on the Wroughton plantation, soon became adept at handling the coach as well, and there was no shortage of available drivers. Lavinia, to Uncle Lemiel's shocked protests at such unladylike behavior, even took her turn at the reins and with every mile they left behind them, the group felt more and more confident the plan would succeed. Lavinia heaped well-deserved praise on Reuben's driving skills and was surprised to know that the young man had known the identity of Bingo and Jane from the moment they were first picked up.

"I knowed right off, Miss Lavinia. All the Hawthorn people knows all the Wroughton people."

"Then you must promise never to tell—not even any of our people at Hawthorn Hill, and especially not Mr. Lionel."

"Oh, I not tell. Just like I never told nobody 'bout you helping Gabriel and Angelica the mornin' they runs off."

Lavinia almost dropped the reins. "How did you know?" she asked.

"Me and Henny seen you. We hidin' and watched it all."

Lavinia was too stunned to speak. *They know everything,* she thought to herself. *I'll never understand how, but they know everything.*

"And I not tell Miss Cornelia you been drivin' the coach, neither," Reuben said. "That be about the worst thing, I reckon—you actin' like you ain't no lady at all and ridin' outside and crackin' the whip, and Miss Cornelia findin' it out."

"Far worse than exposure to the slave patrols, Reuben," Lavinia said.

The first two days of the journey, they were not stopped even once and the chances that they would grew less and less as they proceeded westward. Traveling by coach was in itself protection against suspicion, the luxury of such transportation indicating travelers of prosperity who would be unlikely to transport runaways.

Passing through Bedford County, a militia group riding patrol stopped them. Lavinia quickly took little Samuel into her arms and hurriedly unbuttoned the front of her dress. When an officer stuck his head into the coach, Lavinia indignantly shielded the child and intoned in outraged modesty, "I am nursing my child, sir!"

The embarrassed officer immediately apologized, tipped his hat, and ordered the coach to proceed without further interruption. The performance was immediately selected as the quickest and most efficient way of getting rid of inquisitive patrols and militia.

"These foolish Virginia gentlemen," said Lavinia. "They'd wave Nat Turner on through rather than embarrass a lady."

Pressing westward, the roads became more undulating as they entered hill country. Past Lynchburg, the Cumberland Mountains of the Appalachian range soared before them. The sight of the majestic blue crests sent a surge of happiness through Lavinia as she thought of being home again. She welcomed the embrace of the mountains and felt the danger of the journey recede as she neared the security of her childhood home.

Less traveled, the more curving, poorly banked, and often deeply rutted roads provided an excellent terrain for Uncle Lemiel to train Reuben. Soon the boy was almost as adept as his mentor in negotiating the twists and pits of the roadbed and escaping the trapping soil at the road's edges. After a few days, it was more often Reuben shouting orders to the horses, and Lavinia smiled to herself as she realized the proud old gentleman was surrendering his position as carriage master of Hawthorn Hill to his young apprentice.

As Reuben's control of the horses became more sure, and a particular stretch of road was less challenging, Lavinia persuaded the fatigued Uncle Lemiel to ride more comfortably inside the coach, which he reluctantly did, although much of the time with his head out the window shouting instructions to his pupil.

During the long days of the journey, Bingo and Jane told stories of their life as Wroughton slaves and what had prompted them to make their escape.

"He done say he goin' to sell Jane when she has the baby. He say she can't do no work with a baby, but she show him how she tie little Samuel on her back and work just as good with him as without. She even try to feed that child tied to her, and hoe and carry brush and churn and do all the other work she got at the same time. But he say he sells her as a wet nurse while she still fresh. He say he hear a family lookin' for one in the next county. That why we decides to run. He going to sell me 'cause he say I sorry and—" Bingo looked at his wife and child and hung his head. "Don't want to lives without my Jane and little Sam."

"Don't talk about it. You're free now. You can forget these painful memories," Lavinia said, although she wondered how anyone could ever forget such experiences.

But they seemed to want to tell her, as if recounting it unburdened them of the suffering they had known in servitude to Wroughton.

"Sometime he feeds the people in a trough," said Jane, lowering her head. "Miz Wroughton...or me or Naomi, puts the fatback...what little they is of it...and a few beans or 'taters or maybe a possum or rabbit or something we ketch ourselves...in a big kettle and cooks it. Then she pour it in a wood trough Master Wroughton got and the people has to get on they knees and eats from it like hogs. He don't give no spoons. Lots of us got gourds we use but he seem to like to watch us eat with nothin'. He stand at the gate to the slave yard and laugh and say, 'Lap it up, hogs.' He laugh like it make him feel mighty fine to see us eat like that."

"But we never does it," Bingo said defiantly, his face lifted proudly, his eyes ablaze with indignation. "Me and Jane and right many of the others won't get down like a hog for him. Reckon we starves 'fore we do. We just stands back and waits till ol' Wroughton get tired of laughin' and goes on off. Then we gets our wood bowls and spoons and gourds and eats like people do. We ain't never let him turn us into no animal."

"Reckon we'd a starved for sure if we never had our own patches," Jane said, referring to the small plots of ground behind the cabins were they grew a few potatoes and other vegetables. "We grows what we can, workin' it by the moonlight since he works us in the fields till it so dark we has to use lanterns to see to hoe. And at night, we slips to the orchards for apples and pears when they on, but he don't want us gettin' nothing but what falls on the ground, and them he mostly wants gathered for the hogs."

"And he got this lock-up room in the cellar of his house he locks us in," Bingo said. "Ain't got no winders or any way out and dark as a cave, day and night. He put me in there two days when he finds out Jane with a baby."

They also told Lavinia about the merciless beating Wroughton had given Booker when he had been caught attempting to escape. "He cut up the worst I ever saw," Bingo said, "and he made us all watch him do it. Lord come to Booker, I reckon, 'cause he pass out and just hang there 'fore long. Old Wroughton just keep on whippin' him after he done gone out. It like he tryin' to beat him back awake. Reckon he'd done even worse than that to us if you and Miss Maude and Miss Phoebe not help us."

"It's alright, now," Lavinia said with quiet sadness. "We'll soon be at my father's house and my brothers will help you get to freedom in Ohio."

"What we goin' to call ourselves in Ohio, Miss Lavinia?" Bingo asked. "Since we owned by Wroughton, we just called Bingo and Jane. Ain't even got no last name like white folks, unless it Wroughton, and we sure don't want that."

"Perhaps you can choose your own last name when you're in Ohio. It doesn't have to be Wroughton."

"I guess I'll just have to study on it," Bingo said, and he drifted into thoughtful silence.

As she pondered the abuses they revealed and remembered the stories of similar treatment of blacks told by the Barksdale sisters, Lavinia realized Bingo and Jane faced a profusion of difficulties in making the transition from slavery to freedom. Just choosing a surname and new identity would be but one. Other, more difficult hurdles they did not even anticipate were sure to follow.

She hoped the funds she and the Barksdale sisters had pooled would lessen some of the difficulties in tiding them over until they found employment. Hearing of Bingo and Jane's suffering made Lavinia reaffirm her commitment and dismiss her concern of the dangers.

While Wroughton's abuses may have been extreme and not typical of all slave owners, Lavinia's conscience stung her at the thought that she, as the wife of a slave owner, was as culpable as Horace Wroughton. The violation extended beyond the individual cruelty visited by some owners on their people. It was the system itself, just as her Pa had preached since she was a child. Now she understood. Slavery was the ground in which flourished the seeds of cruelty, debasement, ignorance, and every manner of evil she could name.

As the coach made its way deeper into hill country, the mountains rose like a welcoming wall of protection.

Bingo, who had never seen land except the gentle undulations of the Tidewater and Piedmont, marveled at the grandeur of the terrain.

"Ain't never seen no land rise up as steep at this, Miss Hawthorn," he said, observing fields planted high on the side of steep hills. "Must be mighty hard to plow goin' straight up like that."

"It's plowed crossways, Bingo," Lavinia explained. "And that's why our valleys are so fertile, collecting the richest soil in Virginia brought by the runoff."

Lavinia was awed by the magnificent blue peaks, too. Mr. Jefferson had been correct when he dubbed the wondrous Virginia mountains "an Eden." It was an Eden, and as she looked at Bingo, Jane, and Samuel, she realized that slavery was the serpent in that Eden and should be driven out.

The night before reaching home, they stayed in Abingdon, only a day's journey from Williamsville. It was the town in which she had met Margaret when they had been sent to school there. Lavinia was grateful that none of her family was waiting for her at the inn they knew she would visit en route. It was a good sign that her father was still alive, otherwise one of her brothers would have met her with the news prior to her arrival home.

The next day, they left Abingdon before sunrise and by late afternoon approached the last mile before reaching home. Lavinia held her breath as she saw the steeple of

Johnson Springs Church loom over the pines as the carriage lurched up the rutted road.

Uncle Lemiel insisted that it should be he who was at the reins when the carriage arrived at the house, and Lavinia, sitting beside him, stood up and stretched to catch a glimpse of the graveyard beside the church. When at last it came into view, she released a long sigh of relief. There was no freshly dug grave or pile of hand-picked wildflowers to mark it in the Williamson family plot. Her father was still alive.

At the crest of the hill, she could see the twinkling lights of the Williamson house. She had made it to safety. Home! Her spirits soared with pride and she suddenly wanted to cry with happiness.

She had completed her first run of runaway slaves and opened a new link in the Underground Railroad.

Chapter Nineteen

Ariadne, breakfasting in bed, angrily crushed the *Richmond Whig* into a ball as Jennie and Ogletha shifted uneasily under the barrage of their mistress's anger.

"The fools! The patrols actually had them located in the boot maker's shop and missed them by minutes! They even found the yellow-and-black suit the man was wearing!"

Snatching up the *Richmond Enquirer*, she read another account of the raid on Ezekiel Scott's Bootmaker Shop. "The imbeciles didn't even arrest the boot maker and believed he did not know the second floor had been occupied by fugitives." Wroughton's notices offering higher rewards were on the same page.

Tossing the paper aside, she gestured toward her breakfast tray. "Take this away," she ordered Jennie. "And have Madison ready my carriage."

In an hour, Ariadne's coach arrived at the cobbler's shop on Thirteenth Street. She understood immediately why no charges had been brought against the boot maker, Ezekiel Scott. His shop was a popular establishment in Richmond and the excellent workmanship of the owner had earned the free black the right to remain in Richmond long after he had bought his freedom. His expertise was so valued that his absence from the Commonwealth would mean a great number of Virginia's most prominent citizens would be shod with less comfort and satisfaction than Scott's work guaranteed. Even the boots Lionel favored were fashioned by this expert artisan, as well as a great number of Richmond's gentry, who, contemplating the loss of the soft, sturdy leather work in which their feet so comfortably reposed, could easily dismiss any serious effort to have him punished or exiled from Virginia for unproven charges.

Dismissing the impropriety of a woman of her class entering a cobbler's shop unescorted, or at least accompanied by her maid, Ariadne flouted convention, entered, and demanded to see the proprietor. In a moment, a respectful, quiet-spoken black man wearing a leather apron appeared from the workroom.

When she identified herself, Ezekiel Scott knew immediately who she was.

"I will come directly to the point...Mr. Scott," Ariadne said. She had never addressed a black by the respectful title *Mister* before. The word lodged in her throat like gall.

"Recently the second story of your building protected two runaways," she said, lowering her voice. "One of them, Angelica, was the maid of my dear cousin, Mrs. Lionel Hawthorn, who assisted them in their escape."

Ezekiel Scott's face remained fixed in its expression of respectful humility.

Ariadne, her voice as smooth as flowing honey, brought a gloved hand to her mouth. Glancing around, she spoke in a confidential whisper, "You see...my dear cousin and I are sympathetic to...liberation. Although secretly, of course, for reasons I am sure you must understand. From time to time we have aided and assisted financially those of your race fleeing—"

"Beggin' your pardon, Miss Woodhull, ma'am, but I don't know nothin' about no runaways."

"But, Mr. Scott, I am afraid you don't understand." Ariadne bent closer to the black man and lowered her voice even more. "I am, along with my dear cousin, Mrs. Hawthorn, in total sympathy with the escape. Together we plotted that our charges arrive in Richmond by train, with papers we had...created." She waited for Scott's expression to soften into belief and trust, but it remained unchanged.

"You must believe me, Mr. Scott. Certainly you can understand that it is necessary that my activities be kept as much a secret as yours. Should my participation in the movement become known, I would lose everything."

She watched Scott closely as the unblinking, unyielding look in his eyes at last seemed to vacillate. "We must trust each other, Mr. Scott. To succeed, it will take both black and white in a joint effort...to...to...secure total abolition."

"I do not know how I can help you, ma'am," Scott said cautiously.

"Tell me where they are. Mrs. Hawthorn is depending upon me to deliver additional funds to see Angelica to the North. We have learned that it may be necessary to pay certain people a bribe."

Scott broke her intense gaze and shook his head. She could detect his uncertainty, the first sign of a crack in his granite facade.

"Can it possibly be that you would block your own people's efforts, Mr. Scott? How will you feel when you learn that you have, by your silence, prevented the funds that would have ensured their safe transfer from reaching them in time? Please know I am not insensitive to the dangers of your operation. And the expense." She opened her bag and removed four pieces of paper. "I have prepared some financial support for the cause, Mr. Scott, all made out to you—one for immediate negotiation, three others post-dated for next month and the months after, so as to divert suspicion any single contribution for so large a sum might generate at my bank. We can always say this money was for your excellent services, or the poor among your people. But of course, it will be used by you for the cause—"

Scott's eyes widened when he saw the extravagant amounts made out to him and signed by Ariadne.

Ariadne won the battle for Scott's trust and he finally spoke. "I will make inquiries, Miss Woodhull. And notify you if I learn of the couple's whereabouts—"

Although she hoped the money she gave Ezekiel Scott would produce valuable information later on, she was angered when Scott had reported nothing after four days. Jennie also claimed failure in her efforts to pry information from Ibby.

Ariadne's wrath held the household in suspended terror, her temper erupting at the slightest provocation. Servants from the stables to the kitchen were in a state of nervous dread that their mistress would follow through on threats of beatings, being sent to one of her several plantations as field hands, or outright sale.

Receiving the greatest share of Ariadne's abuse, Jennie was certain her fate lay at the whipping post, slave market, or clutches of Judge Povall.

"But Ibby swears she don't know where Angelica hidin', Miss Ariadne," Jennie sobbed.

Ariadne's raging voice echoed throughout the house, traveling from her room down the back stairs, where Ogletha beckoned to Madison at the pantry door.

"I think it's happening again," she said in a low tone, her resigned weariness sharpened, her eyes shining with foreboding and alarm.

They moved from the pantry into the back hall as Ariadne's tirade against Jennie reverberated down the stairwell.

"She's already in a state—and getting worse."

"It's been a long time," said Madison. "Wait until you're sure. It may play out and not go as far—"

"Madison!" Ariadne's bellow from the upper hall made Ogletha start. "Madison!"

Madison took a quick step back from the bottom of the steps to avoid being seen as Ariadne looked over the banister of the stairwell. "Ogletha, send Madison up at once. And then get up here yourself."

She drew back from the railing and the violent slam of her bedroom door echoed through the house.

Ogletha looked at Madison helplessly and trudged up the steps, passing Jennie, who fled past them.

"She havin' another one of her spells," the weeping girl said in retreat.

Ariadne's explosions of temper, referred to as "nervous spells" by the family and servants and "pre-melancholic mania" by Dr. Rudd, were violent episodes of rage and hysteria followed by periods of dark, silent withdrawal.

For all of her appearance of modesty, shyness, and self-possession, underneath Ariadne's demure facade there lurked a restlessness of disturbing complexity and unpredictability. Since childhood, she had expressed this imbalance of temperament through tantrums of staggering intensity. In her youth, such demonstrations could be discounted, soothed, and forgiven by the solicitous Cornelia and indulgent nurses, mammies, and governesses. Now, in adulthood, her rages were played out in private, the results visited upon her helpless, suffering servants.

After years of experience, Ogletha could read the subtle signs of an approaching mild incidence of temper, a more intense tantrum, or the full storm of an episode requiring Dr. Rudd and the administration of sedatives. Unpredictable and irregular as to frequency and severity, they could occur at any time and with little warning since it took so little to ignite her fury.

In her mistress's room, Ogletha found Ariadne had returned to bed and was ranting about Jennie's failure to incriminate Lavinia and leaping erratically from one subject to another, a certain sign of trouble.

"I want Madison to deliver this letter to Judge Povall immediately. I'm selling Jennie."

"He's still in the stables, ma'am. I left word in the kitchen for him to come up," Ogletha lied, hoping she might delay Jennie's fate.

"I must find out where those blacks are hiding. When they're arrested, the patrols will make them talk. They can beat it out of them—and Judge Povall has told me other methods to loosen their tongues. When I expose her, we'll see how well Mrs. Lionel Hawthorn fares."

"Have you selected which dress you will wear today, Miss Ariadne? I think the weather would be nice for a drive if you'd like—"

"I would not like."

Ariadne leaped from the bed and paced the room like a caged animal. Flinging aside a satin dress held up for her inspection by Ogletha, she went to her dressing table and sat down. "I shall spend the day in my room. I am not well."

"Perhaps a visit with Miss Cornelia and Mr. Lionel before he returns to Hawthorn Hill—"

Ariadne spun toward Ogletha in fury. "And have all of Richmond think I'm chasing Lionel? My carriage always seen at Aunt Cornelia's when it is known he is in Richmond? You fool!"

Ogletha regretted mentioning Lionel and wished she could recall her words. But it was too late; the floodgates of Ariadne's wrath had been opened.

"You know very well that all of Richmond expected that Lionel and I would be married," she said darkly to no one as she sat and stared at her reflection in the dressing table mirror, her long-fingered, blue-veined hands knotted in a fist..

Ogletha stood mutely, her face tense, dreading the onslaught she saw smoldering under the cold, contained anger of Ariadne's voice. "Aunt Cornelia expected it—and Uncle Edmund. And Aunt Priss and Uncle Cuthbert. Even stupid Cousin Gertrude. All our relatives and friends. But then that hill girl ruined everything!" Her large eyes glistened with hatred. "It was that idiotic Margaret's fault. If she hadn't fallen for that dreary little preacher and had to be sent away, Lionel would never have had to get her from that school and met the hill girl. That was the beginning of my exclusion. From Lionel and even stupid Margaret's wedding. I should have been her maid of honor when she married that preacher, but no, she chose Hill Girl, even when Aunt Cornelia protested her choice."

She clenched the lace spread on her dressing table as if it were Lavinia's throat. "And Lionel married her!" she shrieked. She snatched the cloth from the table, spilling the contents of bottles of fragrances, powders, and containers of jewelry. Ignoring the damage, she sprang to her feet and began to pace the floor again, rubbing her hands together, her long, thin fingers working in nervous agitation.

"And then he brought her here!" She spat out each word in disgust. "To Richmond! Into his own home and those of our family and friends! To flaunt his success and display his mountain prize." Her features twisted into bitter resentment at the memory of her rejection, humiliation, and the beginning of her life-long bitterness and self-imposed spinsterhood.

"And all the parties and dinners and entertainments that should have been mine were given for Margaret and that preacher—and Lionel and his hill girl! And I had to sit there and endure them, suffer the humiliation of knowing what everyone was thinking: that I had been replaced, usurped, supplanted by a piece of mountain trash. And having to smile and pretend I didn't see their glances of pity and amusement and even gloating. Goddamn them all."

Ogletha made a sudden intake of breath at hearing the Lord's name taken in vain.

Ariadne stopped her pacing and gripped the back of her dressing table chair. "Oh, I know what people said. 'Poor Ariadne.' 'Isn't it sad about Ariadne.' And I could say nothing but sit in silence and watch Hill Girl take my rightful husband and my rightful place in this family and—" The thought brought her fury to the boiling point and she flung aside the chair and began her pacing again, waving her arms in extravagant gestures.

"All the dresses I had bought and had made and could never wear. My trousseau rotting in trunks in the attic."

"But you could have married, Miss Ariadne," ventured Ogletha, bending down to clean up the spilled powder, overturned perfume bottles, and jewelry box.

"Ah, yes. I could have married!" she said with an ugly, mirthless laugh. "But to whom? The second-raters? The trash? Those after my money? Do you think I would even consider taking the cast-offs of others? Those Margaret—who settled for so little with that insipid little preacher—would not have?" She shook her head with bitter remembrance of her other suitors and her anger seemed to suddenly melt away as she drifted into a still, suspended reverie. Ogletha held her breath, hoping the explosion she feared might be defused.

Ariadne's wild and flashing temper suddenly lost its fire. As her eyes became vacant, her voice dropped to an almost inaudible whisper.

"Lionel. Only he would do. Only he could be the one. He was the only one it ever could ever have been. No one else. Only he..."

She fell quiet for a long moment and, as if the ferment within her troubled spirit had suddenly passed, she wearily returned to her bed like a sleepwalker and crawled beneath the bedclothes, pulling the cover up to her chin.

Ogletha, daring not to move, prayed that the dazed, unearthly silence signaled the end of the storm and a full-fledged episode had been avoided. But suddenly Ariadne's cutting voice, seized by anger again, rose and renewed its frenzy as she bolted upright in bed.

"But it didn't last, did it?" Her eyes flashed and her voice surged with triumph as she hurled the question at Ogletha. She laughed hysterically with the strange, bitter laughter, devoid of all joy, that so frightened Ogletha.

"The perfect love didn't last more than two years, did it? The hill girl didn't bring him endless rapture, did she?" She glared at Ogletha. "Did she? Answer me! Did she?"

"No, ma'am."

"And who was it? Who? Whom did he turn to for his passion?"

"The seamstress, ma'am. Mrs. Price."

"Yes. Her own seamstress! He was sleeping with her the first year! And who else?"

"I...I don't know, ma'am."

"Mrs. Flagon, you fool. And probably Harriet Stafford and Aquila Howard, sluts the both of them. And God only knows how many wenches he found at the tobacco factory. And that widow from Manchester. And then? Do you know who was next?"

Ogletha lowered her head. "No, ma'am."

"But of course you do, my dear. Of course you do. Think hard."

Ogletha lowered her head sensing Ariadne's large, glaring eyes boring in on her.

"Why, it was you, my child. You. Obviously he had run through the harlots at the local whorehouses and the factory wenches, and he chose you. Have you forgotten?"

Ogletha pressed her chin against her chest as the old shame washed over her. Ariadne continued, "Mr. Lionel chose to find his wenches closer to home—in the home. You were available, white enough to pass, young and pretty and shapely. And why not? How convenient for him." Her unhappy laughter trailed into silence as she scooted deeper under the bed covers and pulled the lace-trimmed sheets up to her chin.

"But Hill Girl found out, didn't she? Tell me how—and when—and where."

Ogletha shifted uncomfortably. Ogletha hated it when Ariadne forced her to remember and relive the humiliation of her affair with Lionel.

"I said tell me how, and when, and where!"

"She came in the room—"

"Louder, girl. I will not be mumbled to."

"She came into the room—"

"Who came into a room? What room?"

"Miss Lavinia. In the—library."

"What library? At Hawthorn Hill or Aunt Cornelia's?"

"At Miss Cornelia's, ma'am."

"What were you doing in the library?"

"I was dusting and sweeping up the ashes from the hearth."

"And what happened?"

"Mr. Lionel came in...to get a book..."

"What book? Which door? From the hall or parlor?"

"I...I can't remember..."

"You fool. If you remember his coming in the room, why can't you remember what door he entered?"

"I...I don't know."

"And what did he do?" Ariadne stared above her into the tent-like canopy over her bed. "Well? I said, what did he do?"

"He...he put his arms around me."

"In what manner? Did he grab you? Or embrace you slowly, gently, like a caress? Did he embrace you face to face or approach you from behind?"

"Gently, I believe... I was facing him..."

"And did he kiss you? Did he press his lips to yours? His body, too? Was that pressed against you?" Her mistress's eyes glistened as, hungry for details, she waited for the specifics she had forced Ogletha to reveal so many times before.

"He was about to...to kiss me, only...only Miss Lavinia came in."

"Miss Lavinia! Valley Vinny caught you!" A cruel laugh came from deep in her throat. "The kiss was interrupted? He did not complete his kiss? Only his embrace?"

"Yes, ma'am."

"Now, now tell me slowly what happened next. What did she do, say... Everything!"

Again Ogletha related how Lavinia had at first stared in stunned silence at her husband as he held her and then, her face crumbling with hurt, she had silently left the room.

"And she said nothing?" Ariadne asked. "She simply saw you in Lionel's arms and left the room?"

"Yes, ma'am."

"Was she angry? Hurt? Did she cry?" Ariadne's pleasure was complete now. It was as if Lavinia's discovery of Lionel's indiscretion had been her personal revenge. "And what happened later? Did you hear them arguing? Did Aunt Cornelia or Uncle Edmund hear?"

"Miss Cornelia and Mr. Edmund were in the country, ma'am. There was an argument upstairs, but I was downstairs."

"And you didn't eavesdrop? You little fool! A servant who doesn't eavesdrop! I don't believe it for a minute. You all eavesdrop and you know it. But what happened next?"

"I was sent here to you, ma'am. The next day."

Ariadne broke into full-throated laughter. She suddenly sat bolt upright in bed, allowing the coverlet to fall from her chin. "Yes. Yes, I remember. Hill Girl refused to have the little serpent who spoiled her Garden of Eden in the house and Lionel sent you to me! And I kept you. Do you know why I kept you, little serpent?" Ariadne twisted herself toward Ogletha and almost hanging over the edge of the bed watched her closely.

"No, ma'am."

"Because you invaded sacred ground and desecrated it! You sullied the sanctity of perfect little Hill Girl's marriage."

Ariadne lay back against the pillows and again pulled the bed clothes up to her neck, like some perverse child requesting a bedtime story.

"Now. Tell me about the first time. Before Lavinia caught you. Tell me how the perfect union failed to last." Her voice became a whisper, deadly calm but intense and venomous, like the soft hiss of a snake. "Tell me how you entered their idyllic Garden of Eden and brought it crashing to an end."

Ogletha, hating the ordeal, wearily complied. She hung her head and, still holding the breakfast tray before her, said, "I...I've come to know the Lord, Miss Ariadne. I been baptized and repented my sins. I don't like to remember—"

"Nonsense! You black fools and your religion. I want to hear about it. Think of it as a kind of confession."

Reluctantly and with great shame, Ogletha once again related the circumstances that had led to the two or three sexual encounters she had with Lionel over fifteen years earlier.

"Well, go on!" Ariadne prodded. "You've told it before, don't feign shyness or modesty now."

"It was after Master Randy was born. Miss Lavinia had lost another child—it come too early—"

"Born early and dead. Dead. Dead. Dead. Go on."

"When Miss Lavinia with a baby again...she was afraid to...to..."

"She was afraid to sleep with him!" Ariadne laughed and her voice rose in shrill amazement. "She thought sleeping with him had brought the baby too soon and made it die! The nasty thing they did to make their babies made them die, too! Sin, sin, sin! Just the way your religion teaches! 'The wages of sin is death.'"

Again Ariadne's mirthless, chilling laughter rose as Ogletha shuddered at the blasphemous rendering of Scripture. "But continue. Tell me what Mr. Lionel did for his pleasure when Hill Girl refused him."

Tears of shame coursed down Ogletha's face as she continued, still holding the breakfast tray in front of her.

"He...he come to me—"

"Ah! Paradise lost! The Garden of Eden fouled by sin!" Ariadne burrowed under the bedclothes, squirming like a child. Then she became very still and grew earnest, almost grave, her voice strangely calm, her eyes sparkling with anticipation. "Tell me what you did."

Once again, a shamed Ogletha related the specifics of her encounters with Lionel, answering one question after another as Ariadne, oblivious to the black woman's humiliation, pressed for every detail. Her face was transformed into ecstasy, her large eyes glassy and limpid with a kind of hypnotic, depraved rapture. How often the encounters occurred. In what rooms. The hour of day, the state of undress, the whereabouts of Lavinia and the servants and the senior Hawthorns. No detail was too small or insignificant to be recalled with elaborate elucidation. Even the weather—whether it was raining or the sun was shining—if it ever happened on Sunday, and if so, before or after church—nothing was too inconsequential for Ariadne to know.

Ogletha's recounting could never vary, either in content or minor detail from earlier versions, lest Ariadne's rage erupt at the inconsistency. Every lewd and salacious detail had to be repeated, with as much foulness as possible, the very vulgarity seeming to excite Ariadne's wrath and pleasure at the same time. Each specific was often embellished by

Ariadne herself with filthy, nasty particulars as she added the most obscene details of her own imagining to the narrative, making it repellant and perverse.

"And in the end," Ariadne said in a voice eerily controlled, her eyes closed as if visualizing the scene. "At the culmination, when his pleasure was at its peak, what did he say? What did he do?"

"He...he...cried out. He...cried out...Miss Lavinia's name," Ogletha said, wretched with humiliation. "He said, 'Lavinia, Lavinia!'"

This was always the worst part, and it propelled Ariadne's hysteria to full force. At once, her fury erupted and she bounded from the bed, bellowing like a crazed animal, "He could not even commit adultery without thinking of her!"

Ariadne pressed the sides of her head with her fists as if she could squeeze the name and image of her rival from her brain. "Lavinia! Lavinia! He could not even be unfaithful to her without her being in his mind!"

It was as if her long, slender fingers became claws as she ripped the lace trimming from her bed covering and pillow cases. With surprising speed and unexpected strength, Ariadne's wrath reached its pinnacle and she began to overturn chairs and tables in an attempt to demolish the room.

Ogletha, prepared by experience, quickly looked about her for any lamps or candles that might be burning. Seeing nothing which could cause a fire, she ran from the room into the upper hall.

"Madison!" she called down the stairwell.

A small chair hurled by Ariadne crashed through a window, and she attacked the velvet-covered crown cupola over her bed, pulling down the draping velvet from the bed posts and the canopy from its frame.

Madison, alerted by the sound of the window smashing, bounded up the stairs two steps at a time. As he entered the room, he barely avoided being hit by a water pitcher hurled across the room. Ariadne was attacking the draperies now, ripping them down from the windows, all the while screeching like an animal.

Madison grabbed her from behind and holding her thrashing body tried to restrain her. Pinning her arms against her sides, he struggled to still her rampage as she raged and cursed and twisted.

"Get your hands off me you filthy—" she shrieked.

But his size and strength outmatched even the passion of her outrage, and he at last subdued her. She sagged in defeat, whimpering hysterically, then sputtered into silence as she drifted into the dark, sullen melancholy that marked the second stage of her malady.

Ogletha once witnessed these episodes with exasperated puzzlement but now calmly watched as one would observe a far-off storm eventually pall and dissipate and finally disappear altogether.

She pushed aside the crumpled frame of the canopy and its cope and Madison carried Ariadne to the bed and laid her on it.

"My medicine," she said vacantly. "I need my tincture."

She lay rigidly and stared at the ceiling while Madison prepared a mixture of Tincture of Opium and powder of sodium and potassium bromide. Ogletha rushed down the steps where the other servants, attracted by the commotion, huddled at the foot of the stairs.

"Go back to your business," Ogletha said to them. "And someone fetch Dr. Rudd."

Within the hour, Dr. Rudd arrived.

"She's using too much morphia," he said to Ogletha and Madison in the hall outside Ariadne's room as he prepared to leave. "It's addicting, you know."

"But Dr. Rudd, sir," Ogletha said, "her tincture the only thing that bring her peace."

"Try and keep her dosage at a minimum. And give it as infrequently as possible. I've told you that before."

Plans were made for Ariadne to be taken to Hot Springs, Virginia, the next day to "take the waters." Taking the waters had proven beneficial to Ariadne in the past and had become the standard therapy when her melancholia required more intensive treatment than the administration of Dr. Rudd's bromides. A visit to the stylish health spa, enjoyed by many affluent Virginians, also provided an excuse for Ariadne's absence that would not be attributed to anything more than a lady of leisure seeking the restorative measures of healing waters after a long winter in the city.

Cornelia, notified by the servants of the recent episode, visited her ailing cousin later that evening. The shutters had been closed to hide the broken window, the draperies re-hung, and Ariadne's bedroom had again been made presentable.

Still sedated and unresponsive, Ariadne stared with glassy eyes at the restored canopy above her bed while Cornelia, sitting at her side, held her hand and wept quietly into her handkerchief, remembering the tragic loss of her ward's parents.

"Now, precious, you'll be just fine and as well as can be once you've taken the waters. Why, you might even miss the heat of summer in Richmond—you know how miserable it is. The waters have always been helpful before. Why, I may escape the heat in July and join you, if you're still there. Can you speak to Aunt Cornelia, precious?"

Ariadne continued to stare with dead, unseeing eyes. Cornelia suppressed a fresh sob by pressing her handkerchief to her lips and looked beseechingly toward Dr. Rudd.

When Ariadne finally fell asleep, arrangements were made for her trip to Hot Springs and Cornelia went home.

"Poor Ariadne," she said to Edmund when reporting the incident at dinner. "You know, Mr. Hawthorn, when Lionel married Lavinia, a light went out in Ariadne forever."

Chapter Twenty

The wails from the quarters floated into the second-floor bedroom where Horace Wroughton sat on the edge of his bed. He had been drinking corn liquor all afternoon and was already drunk. Ignoring the mournful cries, he licked his thumb and peeled off a series of bank notes, which he neatly stacked in one of the carefully arranged rows spread across the quilt. Outside, the anguished cries of the slaves rose and fell in a mournful litany along with the flickering bonfire they had built to honor the dead.

"Damn blacks," Wroughton said, continuing to count his money.

Just back from Richmond, Wroughton added the money made from the sale of a sixteen-year-old slave to his growing treasure. When the young man had suffered a seizure in the fields, Wroughton, ignorant of epilepsy and afraid the disorder would lessen his effectiveness as a laborer or spread to the other blacks, had sold him at a handsome profit. Wroughton grinned smugly to himself, proud that he had managed to pass off the slave as a laborer in perfect health and the boy had gone on the block in Richmond with no hint of the epilepsy that would have diminished his price.

As the mournful cries from the quarters continued, Wroughton cursed the blacks again and placed the money in a metal box on the bed. Trusting no bank, Wroughton kept his growing fortune in his house. He regularly counted the box's contents, deriving satisfaction that he would neither have to endure the condescension of bankers, nor suffer the loss of his money through their dishonesty or theft. Nor could they sneer that his assets were secondary to the more wealthy planters.

Wroughton moved an oil lamp closer to the edge of the washstand beside the bed. Emptying a sack of gold coins in the center of the bed, he looked at his gleaming treasure reflecting the glow of the lamplight and the bonfire outside. For a long time, he watched the glistening fifty- and one-hundred-dollar gold pieces seeming almost to move as they caught the light and reflected the flash and flicker of the flames. He ran his fingers through the sparkling coins, caressing their coolness, and lifted a handful, which he let rain through his fingers onto a mound on the bed. The tinkling of the coins pleased him and he did it again and again, scooping them up and listening to the agreeable, almost musical, clatter as they fell back into the pile.

"You eatin' or not?" a harsh female voice called from the downstairs hall. "I ain't waitin' all night. And see if you can't git them blacks to hush up."

"I'm comin'," Wroughton said, and he began gathering up the coins. Once he had put his hoard back into the metal box, he forced the loudly squeaking lid closed. The whining scream of the box's hinges made Wroughton smile as he placed the box on the floor, where he pushed it under the bed with his foot. The cry of those hinges was so loud the screech could be heard several rooms away and had more than once alerted him of his wife's pilfering the box when she thought he was asleep or out of the house.

His wife called again, and he picked up the bottle of corn liquor and started downstairs.

"You deaf? I said I'm comin'."

In the kitchen, the cries from the quarters were even louder than upstairs. The bonfire around which the blacks gathered for their grief-stricken requiem was just outside the backyard fence. Through the window, the kitchen walls became a flickering battle of light and shadow.

Wroughton stared with distaste at the tin plate of beans and cornbread his wife wordlessly slammed down on the table before him.

"Damn blacks," Wroughton said. He slammed the bottle of corn liquor on the table and picked up a spoon.

"They been hollerin' and moanin' like that since sundown," his wife said.

"Can't you fix nothin' but beans and bread?" Horace asked. He watched the hulk-like block of a woman with sloping shoulders and broad hips shuffle across the kitchen on thick, post-like legs with bulging ankles, her bare feet making soft little slaps on the floor. Her unusually small head topped her torso, and her small, pinched face was framed by course, gray-streaked hair falling in tangles down her back. She wore a dingy, loose-fitting dress and a stained apron with untied ties trailing behind her.

"I said, can't you fix nothin' but beans and corn pone?" Wroughton said again, his voice louder and rising above the moans of grief outside. His wife remained silent, her face hard and cold as stone. Outside, the moans rose and fell, sometimes almost subsiding into silence, then beginning again in a crescendo of renewed mourning.

"I'll put a stop to that," Horace said, his copper-colored eyes snapping with anger. "That bellern ain't gonna bring him back to life."

He ate a spoonful of beans and, scowling with disgust, took another drink. "That black wench, Jane, could do bettern this."

His wife spun around. In the flickering light, her eyes shone with anger and her weathered, tired features were contorted with hatred.

"Then why don't you jest git black-gal to fix you somethin'?" she said. "Hit ain't like I got nobody to hep me none since she run off."

From the quarters, a sole, mournful female voice rose above the rest. "Lordy, Lordy," it implored, and other voices rose to echo the lament.

"I'll git her back. And Bingo, too."

His wife snorted with disgust. "I heared that before. Like you goin' to git Gabriel back." Her expression of loathing turned into a smirk, gloating and sarcastic. "You ain't though, have you? And if you did, would you beat him to death, too?"

Horace gritted his nubby, wide-spaced teeth. "I never beat him to death."

"What's that screechin' from the cabins then?" she taunted. "Them blacks whoopin' and hollerin' 'cause Booker done healed up? Last time I seen him, he was dead as a rock."

She brushed a strand of gray-black hair out of her face, thrust out her abdomen, and placed her hands on her hips. An ugly, malicious grin lifted the corners of her mouth as she lurched forward and said, "And...you...kilt...him!"

"That's a goddamn lie . I never kilt him." His face, already flushed from the alcohol, darkened into a deeper red, his copper-colored eyes hardened into a deeper bronze.

"You kilt him!" she spat out again, and then turned away.

"I said that's a goddam lie. I never kilt him. He died o' blood pizen," Horace thundered. "Ole Doc Hunter said so hisself. Hit blood pizen what kilt him."

"You beat him to death; I don't keer what you say—nor Hunter neither."

"You got to teach 'em a lesson."

"You never taught nobody nothin'. Hit never stopped Gabriel, did it? Hit never stopped Bingo and Jane, did it? You done had more run-offs than anybody in the county." The fire outside flickered on her expression of contempt.

"I'll git 'em back. The money I'm offerin' will git Gabriel back."

"Ain't done it yet, has it?"

She laughed contemptuously, her question a taunt and a challenge. "Looks to me like you're wastin' good money takin' out them notices in the Richmond and Lynchburg papers offerin' hundreds of dollars."

"I'm thinkin' of raisin' it. You make it high enough and their own people will sell 'em out."

"Well, now, ain't you the smart one. Buying your blacks twict." She sniffed.

He washed another spoonful of beans down with liquor and suddenly jumped to his feet. Seizing a rifle leaning beside the door, he staggered outside to the back porch.

"Hush that damn-fool ragin'!" he bellowed in the direction of the quarters.

When there was no lessening in the wails, he raised his rifle and fired into the night sky. The report brought startled screams from the women and the sound of rushing, fleeing feet.

"I said hush it up!" Horace yelled into the now silent night. "And put that fire out and go to bed. You're goin' to ketch somethin' a fire. And they's work to do tomorrow."

He fired the rifle again and returned to the kitchen. He sat down and took another bite of beans. "These beans done got cold. Needs to be het up."

"Heat 'em yourself," his wife said. "I'm tired of bein' treated no better'n a sorry, low-down black. Since Jane run I have to do it all."

"I said I'll get her back!" He banged his fist on the table.

"Well, 'till you do, you'll eat what's put out fer you and hush up 'bout it. I can't do ever thang on the place. Cut the kindlin', and milk, and warsh, and cook, and all of it. I ought to have some hep."

"Can't spare 'em. Gotta use 'em in the fields. I'm shorthanded as it is and in the mornin' I got to use a man to bury that damn Booker. I ourt to just let him rot on the ground."

"If you didn't sell off the youngins as fast as they growed up, I'd use one of them. What you tryin' to raise here anyhow, tobaccy or blacks?"

"That damn boy was takin' fits. Can't do no work jerkin' around on the ground. And liable to give it to the others. And little 'uns ain't no 'count. They don't earn they way till they're up nine or ten—even when you put 'em out at six or so. And I done made nigh on to eight hundred dollars this year sellin' 'em."

"If you had any sense you'd know it'd be cheaper to grow your own blacks from little 'ens rather than have to buy 'em already growed. You ain't goin' have no blacks a-tall if they keep runnin' off."

"They's others had runaways this year. Hawthorn's done had one to run."

"Why, I thought you done had that figured out a made-up piece of business by ol' lady Hawthorn, herself?"

"Reckon it was," Horace conceded and took another drink.

"Can't figure why yore set on that idee. Don't make no sense to me helpin' yore own blacks run off."

Wroughton stared into his plate. "That Hawthorn woman's in it, alright. Them Hawthorns treats their blacks like they prize horses. They act like them house wenches and that old man that drives the carriage was as good as white people."

"You done spent enough on wanteds in the papers to a bought another'n."

"Not like Gabriel. He was the prize slave in the county. That gal of hern wern't no loss to 'em. They'll jist bring in another'n from Richmond."

"You coulda got me one in Richmond."

"Reckon you wantin' me to fetch you a high-toned Richmond black to take over for Jane. Reckon next you goin' to be wantin' a fancy lady's maid and to go to them fancy quiltin' bees they has."

His sarcasm ignited his wife's anger anew as she swung toward him. "You shet yore mouth!" she snarled. "I'm sick of workin' like a dirty black. I'm done with hit. I'm going to Carolina tomorrow and you can fix your beans and pone yerself!"

She snatched off her apron and threw it on the floor and stomped out of the kitchen, her voice ringing after her. "I'll be leavin' in the mornin'. And I might come back and I might not. I ain't havin' you turn me into a black. Been treated like one long enough."

"I'll be glad to git shet of you!" Horace yelled after her, his voice rising as he heard the stairs strain and squeak under the weight of her steps. "You ain't no count no more. Can't cook nor even keep the house no better'n a pig sty."

"If they was somethin' besides a pig to live in it with, I might!" she yelled back, followed by the slam of a door upstairs.

Hours later, near midnight, Wroughton, having consumed most of the bottle of corn liquor, lurched up the stairs and stood outside the door to their bedroom. He listened for a long time but heard nothing. Then he tapped on the door—a tentative, almost gentle knock.

"What do you want?" her voice rang out, blunt and harsh, each word as full of anger as earlier in the kitchen. He knew he had not waited long enough for her temper to cool, but pressed on, his words slurred by alcohol.

"Air you still goin' in the mornin'?" His voice was almost gentle.

"I am."

He tried to charm her now, his words caressing and seductive. "Ain't safe a good lookin' woman travelin' that distance by herself."

"I got a pistol. I got it right here with me now if I need it."

"You takin' the buggy? You take the buggy if you want to."

"I was plannin' to. I ain't goin' to ride a horse all that way."

"Reckon you be gone quite a spell then." His tone was still soft and coaxing.

"As long as needs be."

"You ain't been to see your people in a spell—"

"That's where I'm goin'."

"Then I thought I'd come on in with you since it be a right long spell 'till you're back." He put his hand on the doorknob and turned it. It was locked.

"I reckon not. I ain't no use to you. You said it yourself. You said you'd be glad to be shet of me."

"Sometimes a man don't mean everythang he says when he's heated."

"But sometimes he does."

He inclined his head toward the door and waited but could hear no sound of her approaching to admit him.

"You still too put-out to let me in? Just for a little while—"

"You was the one said it. You said I can't cook. You said I can't keep your pig sty clean. Reckon I can't do the other you want neither."

"I got a real wantin' fer you tonight. Be a long time till you're back—"

"If I even bother to come back. Now go on to bed. I'm tarred."

Silence followed and even his half-hearted apologies brought no response from the cold, closed door. "Maybe it was just the liquor talkin'. Me and you been together right long. I ain't tole you in a long time, but I still got a feelin' for you," he said, but was answered only with silence.

He finally released the doorknob and skulked to a room across the hall, his bitterness deepening, his pride bruised because he had asked for admittance in the first place and even confessed his longing for her.

For a long time, he sat on the edge of the bed and stared into the darkness. He did not even light a lamp but sat in the strangely agreeable midnight blackness reflecting on his hunger, unsatisfied by the beans and corn pone, and that for the aging, fat, familiar body he had grown used to after so many years.

But another gnawing, in more than his belly and loins, tormented him from the darkness: the nagging defeat in what he had lost in Gabriel and Bingo and Jane and even the dead Booker, whom he regretted not selling a year ago.

Brooding as he had done every day since the escape, Wroughton replayed in his mind the loss of Gabriel, always with Lavinia the principal instigator, attributing to her the scheme from beginning to end.

"She's put them up to it," he mumbled to himself. "They might have thought it up, but she's the one that put a fire under it. They would have just rutted at the fence line and stayed where they was without her eggin' 'em on." Now he even blamed her for Bingo's and Jane's flight. He decided it was all of one sheet—Gabriel and Lavinia's maid, Bingo and Jane, and maybe even Booker—all planned and encouraged by Lavinia.

Now that Booker was dead, Wroughton wished he had questioned him about that. Over and over, he mulled it, like picking the scab of a sore, and always he came to the conclusion that Lavinia was responsible for all his losses. And he hated her for it.

He hated them all. Mainly the Hawthorns, who were the nearest to him, and mainly her—Lavinia—of the Hawthorns, but he hated all the other planters in the county, too. He sensed their superiority, their noblesse oblige. He knew he could never be one of them, even owning property that had once belonged to one of them.

For only one thing during the years he had lived among them had he received any respect. In only one had he drawn any attention beyond the haughty nod of a head at the courthouse when he paid his taxes or voted, or received a perfunctory greeting at the tobacco market when he sold his crops. Only in his ownership of the slave Gabriel did he generate the interest, and even envy, of his fellow planters. Although it galled him at first that a black slave was his only entree to their company at competitions held in the county, he soon came to regard his possession of Gabriel as a source of pride. He knew they all coveted him, and they all made money when they wagered on his abilities in wrestling, running, and contests of strength. He had never known defeat. They all wanted him for their own—to display, to possess, to wager on as one would a blooded stallion.

He loved bating them when they made their extravagant offers to buy Gabriel, toying with them, pretending to consider their ever more generous offers, then dashing their hopes by refusing. It was exhilarating to turn them down, the delicious exercise of the only power he had. Saying "no" to them rewarded his hatred of them, gave him a measure of control and even, through retaining possession of the champion they coveted, elevated him above them.

But now his prize was gone, taken away from him by that damned Hawthorn woman.

The next morning when he awoke, still in the clothes he had worn the night before, he knew that she was gone. The morning light made the house's dusty, gray drabness seem all the more empty. He listened to the heavy, oppressive stillness for a long time before moving or making any sound.

Finally he called for her.

"Delphe!"

He listened as if waiting for his voice to reverberate from room to empty room seeking her out.

"Delphe, I say!"

There was no response.

"You gone yet?"

The stillness of the house, empty of her hymn singing, or verbal abuse toward Jane, or the rattle of her activity in the kitchen, answered his question.

Suddenly seized by alarm, Wroughton jumped from the bed and stumbled into the upper hall. He found the door to their room unlocked and ajar. His eyes wide and wild, he lurched into the room and fell on his knees beside the unmade bed. Bending his head to see beneath it, he extended his arms and reached for the metal box, which he pulled toward him.

Sitting on the floor beside the box, he fumbled to open it, his breathing hard and fast as the squeak of its hinged lid finally responded to his nervous fingers and screeched open. He tried to recall if the betraying creak of the lid's hinges had penetrated the alcoholic haze of his sleep, but he could not remember.

Bending close to the open box, he quickly counted the stacks of bills and removed the sack of gold coins, which he dumped on the floor and counted piece by piece. Once finished, he determined that his wife could have taken only two or three hundred dollars—certainly no more—since he had counted it only the night before. Relieved as he was to find his treasure nearly intact, he was still left alone and sat on the floor for a long time reflecting on his predicament, clutching his money box protectively in his arms like a baby.

"Hawthorns," he muttered to himself with disgust. "It's all them goddamn Hawthorns' fault."

Chapter Twenty-One

Lavinia found her father much improved since the original dire report she had received by mail. His stroke had been mild, its effects disappearing within days, and other than slightly slurred speech, he had returned to normal. Granny, ninety-five, was bedfast and nearly blind, but still keen of mind and dominated the household as always. Her father's illness had brought six of Lavinia's nine brothers to the old home place, and for three weeks, Lavinia enjoyed her family, seeing her nieces and nephews, many for the first time.

Bringing Bingo, Jane, and the baby to freedom received the family's enthusiastic endorsement. Within a week, the runaway blacks were spirited out of Virginia into Kentucky by one of Lavinia's brothers.

She received letters from Margaret and Cornelia detailing the county news and Ariadne's latest emotional episode. Lionel wrote to tell her he was back at Hawthorn Hill and to extend her visit with her family as long as she wished. "And why didn't you tell me our Christmas baby had been so ill? I heard it from a field hand, but she's thriving now and looked no worse for her ordeal."

A week before she returned home, Lavinia received word that Bingo's family arrived safely in Ohio and Bingo had found work in a stable. The run had been a success.

"And they have changed their names to Bingo, Jane, and Samuel Hawthorn Barksdale," her brother wrote on behalf of Bingo.

In celebration of the first success of the new branch of the Underground Railroad, the family began planning future runs. Her younger brother Richard, and his wife, Ellie, were particularly enthusiastic and anxious to join Lavinia's efforts.

She persuaded Ellie and Richard to return to Hawthorn Hill with her to help Uncle Lemiel and Reuben with the driving and plan future projects in running slaves on the new route in the Underground Railroad.

After seemingly endless days, the coach finally topped the last rise to reveal Hawthorn Hill before them.

"Miss Cornelia is here, Uncle Lemiel," she said, noticing the senior Hawthorn's coach. "And she's brought the rest of Margaret's brood."

"There goes the peace and quiet of summer," said Uncle Lemiel who, to conserve his strength, had been persuaded to surrender the reins to Richard.

When the coach turned into the lane to the house, Lavinia saw the familiar figures, alerted by the hounds, began to appear on the front porch—the stooped Emma, bending heavily on her cane; the little round ball that was Aunt Beck, wearing a fresh apron and head rag; the taller round ball that was Margaret, holding the youngest of her children; the towering but slightly stooped Mr. Edmund; and the tall, queenly Cornelia, fan aflutter and her hair freshly colored and baked by curling irons into tight, stiff curls.

Around them clustered a half-dozen of Margaret's children and Piney and Henny. Lavinia's heart warmed when she saw Henny, obviously no longer exiled from the house by Emma, probably on orders from Margaret, who had promised to advance the girl's mission and shield her from Emma's hostility.

"Oh, dear," said Lavinia. "With the rest of Margaret's brood, we'll have to sleep in the trees."

"Mother Hawthorn, how will I ever thank you for keeping house and home together while I've been gone?" Lavinia greeted her mother-in-law.

"Bless you, daughter," the flattered old lady responded. In the years since her marriage to Lionel—and Alexander Harvey's to Margaret—the old lady had come to appreciate and love her children's spouses, and being the true aristocrat that she was, long ago acknowledged the error in her initial disapproval of them. Very early, she had realized that both Lavinia and Alexander were more than worthy of her son and daughter and wholeheartedly accepted them for their goodness and beneficial influences on her willful, puzzling children.

She gave Reverend Harvey full credit for bringing some semblance of serenity to Margaret's willful obstinacy, and felt Lavinia was worthy of canonization for taming the beast in Lionel.

"And how is your father?" the old lady said, releasing Lavinia.

"Much better. And he continues to improve every day. The doctor—"

"My dear, how many times do I have to tell you? A lady never sticks her head out the window of a coach. Nor does she allow her arm to rest over the edge of an open carriage—or ever allow her elbows to rise above her bosom at any time. Only the most ordinary—"

"But Mother Hawthorn, that was my sister-in-law, Ellie."

Cornelia, flustered, was presented to Richard and Ellie, whom she had not seen in years.

Ellie, pink with embarrassment, had only a second to throw Lavinia a dark glare when her discomfort was further increased by one of Margaret's younger children who blurted, "Why, you talk funny!"

"Oh, we'll never escape ridicule for our southwestern Virginia accents," said Lavinia, and laughed as Ellie's cheeks reddened even more as the children requested that she repeat certain words such as "ice" and "nice" and "twice" to better appreciate—and laugh at—her flat *i*'s.

"Children!" Margaret scolded. "Ellie, I am so sorry."

When greetings had been exchanged, Emma ordered the children into the yard.

"I've brought everyone gifts," Lavinia said, seeing the young ones' peeved faces. "I have knitted stockings and scarves and crocheted dickeys and put borders on every handkerchief I could find. And I stopped in Lynchburg for gifts for particularly well-behaved children."

"That's nobody here!" Cornelia said.

Margaret's children disagreed and raised a clamor for their gifts.

"But where is my husband?" Lavinia asked, in the parlor over coffee and cake.

"Called back to Richmond," said Cornelia. "Some need at the tobacco factory."

"He was so disappointed he could not be here," Margaret said. "But he promises to be back within the week."

"Oh, that hateful factory makes me feel like a widow."

"Oh, but dear, it's made us quite rich," said Cornelia in a whisper, as if the family's affluence was somehow shameful.

Then the old lady began a lachrymose history of Ariadne's most recent "nervous episode."

"Oh, but I have wonderful news. When Ariadne notified me she was returning to Richmond from Hot Springs, I suggested she stop here on the way. She will arrive any day. My dear, when Lionel married you, a light went out in Ariadne forever."

"Well, it flares up again whenever she throws one of her fits," Margaret said.

"Margaret! How unkind," said Cornelia.

When they were finally alone, Margaret gave Lavinia a letter.

"Read it quick," Margaret said. "It may have news of Angelica."

Margaret had intercepted the mail before Lionel saw it.

"Thank you for watching the mail for me," Lavinia said, tearing into the letter.

"I felt just like a spy in a Poe story!" gushed Margaret. "Pilfering the mail before anyone else could see it!"

The letter was from Philadelphia, the address written in a labored, unfamiliar handwriting. Puzzled that the writing was not in Angelica's neat script, Lavinia read:

Dear Mrs. Hawthorn,

I am a friend of Gabrile who has asked me to rite you for him.

I am from Virginny also freed by my master and come north like Gabrile did. We works in a blacksmith shop together where he told me of his wife Angeleca. Gabrile is lucky to get work as the white folks get the work first. Most of the time the Irish. You are to get word to A. that he lives on Strother Street and work at John Wyeths Blaksmith

Shoppe. Be careful for agents are everwhere and even the marshals grabs our people free or not and sells them back into slavery. He would writ befour but never nowed who could rite to trust. He thanks you for your help.

A friend of Gabrile

"Thank God, Gabriel has made it to Philadelphia. But where is Angelica?" she said to Margaret, her fears renewed. "Is Ibby still hiding her in Richmond? She can't travel with a broken ankle. We'll have to get word to her where to find Gabriel."

"But how? We can't just write her at Papa's. How can we get a message to her the way she got one to you?"

"Lionel wants me to stop wearing weeds. I could send some patterns to Ibby by Lionel—he'd never look inside to see what a dress pattern looked like—and it could contain a letter to Angelica. Ibby could get it to her."

Margaret bounced up and down in her seat like a child. "How thrilling! Lionel will be an unknown party to our scheme! It is like a spy story!"

"I see Henny has been allowed in the house."

"I told Emma I needed her to help with the younger children, which is true. She's very quick and anxious to please and Mother loves instructing her."

The next morning, Lavinia rode to the Barksdales'. As she turned off the main road onto the lane that led to the Barksdale house, she met a wagon loaded with a family of blacks. The wagon was piled high with furniture and other possessions and half a dozen children crowded in among the mound of chairs, tables, bedsteads, and household goods.

When the driver tipped his hat, Lavinia recognized him as one of the Barksdale tenants. He reined the wagon to a halt.

"Corbin? It is you, isn't it?"

"Yes, ma'am, it me."

"And Mercy?"

"Yes, ma'am," the woman sitting beside him responded.

Lavinia looked questioningly at the sad-eyed couple and the haunted, frightened expressions of their six children, ranging in age from infancy to late teens, perched on mattresses squeezed in with the humble furniture.

"You look like you're moving."

"Yes'um, I reckon we is," Corbin said, avoiding her eyes.

"But...but why?" Lavinia wondered if the law requiring free blacks to leave Virginia was being enforced.

"Reckon we just figure maybe it time we mosey on," Corbin said, looking at the reins in his hands.

Reluctant to embarrass Corbin, if indeed his departure had been ordered by the authorities, Lavinia only expressed her regret to see him go.

"Sure goin' to miss bein' here, Miss Lavinia. Me and Mercy been here all our lives and all our children born here."

"Then why are you going?" Lavinia said, abandoning her restraint. "And what will Miss Phoebe and Miss Maude do without you?"

Corbin looked at Lavinia with troubled, suffering eyes. "Just think it be best, ma'am. Just don't want no trouble for nobody or my family. And Miss Phoebe and Miss Maude still got Wilkins and his family. I reckon they be right much help to them."

Lavinia regretted her inquisitiveness and, seeing the unspoken pain in Corbin's face, wished she had not pried. "But where will you go?"

"Miss Maude and Miss Phoebe got it all fixed for us to go to Pennsylvania. They thinkin' it the best we go, too. Got proper papers signed right here in my pocket. We goin' to Mr. Thomas Barksdale, the Misses' brother, in Philadelphia. But we mighty worried 'bout Miss Maude and Miss Phoebe with them patrols always snoopin' 'round like they knows somethin'."

After wishing the black family good fortune, Lavinia watched the wagon and its forlorn passengers continue down the lane and turn onto the main road.

Greeting her effusively, Miss Phoebe led her upstairs to old Mrs. Barksdale's bedroom.

"I am so glad to hear your father is better," Miss Phoebe said. "Cornelia and Margaret have kept us informed through your letters. They have been so faithful and visited us often. Look who's come, sister."

Miss Maude, usually the least demonstrative and more controlled of the sisters, wept copiously upon seeing Lavinia. "Oh, dear, we have missed you so. And indeed Cornelia and Margaret have given us much sustenance. They have both volunteered to relieve us in sitting with Mama, but..."

Dabbing her eyes, she led Lavinia to the old woman's bed where she lay unmoving except for her almost imperceptible breathing, a tiny, shrunken mummy as pale as fresh dough with wisps of white hair.

"I brought all of you gifts," Lavinia whispered, patting the old lady's hand and presenting the sisters with handkerchiefs with lace borders and a ruffled cap, similarly decorated, which they placed on their mother's nearly bald head, adjusting her wisps of corn-silk white hair with loving care.

"We were so concerned you wouldn't be back...in time..." Miss Phoebe said into her handkerchief. "Dr. Hunter says she may go at any moment. We've sent word to our brothers that the end is near and expect them any day."

Although Lavinia's letters had already informed them of Bingo and Jane's successful delivery to Ohio, they delighted in the details Lavinia provided. Sitting at the opposite end of the room while their mother slept, they listened as Lavinia talked quietly of her success.

"Praise God," Miss Phoebe said as she clasped her hands, her springy curls bouncing with delight.

"We were stopped three times," Lavinia continued, "and I pretended to be nursing the baby and the patrols were quite embarrassed when they interrupted me. We passed other riders who looked like they might have been patrols or militia but they simply nodded and waved us on."

"Well, dear, runaway slaves hardly make their getaway in fine coaches such as yours," Miss Maude said. "And in the company of a white female."

"But one mustn't get overconfident," cautioned Miss Phoebe. "We understand the militia and patrols meet more often these days, convinced there will eventually be war with the North—and preparing for it. The next time there may be legions of patrols."

"My brother Richard and his wife, Ellie, are anxious to help us."

"Wonderful," Miss Phoebe said, "and the route from your home in Washington County through Kentucky to Ohio sounds ideal. All those mountains to hide in. I don't see how anyone who really wanted to hide could ever be found."

Lavinia said, "I'm told people running from the law or debtors or enemies can disappear into the mountains of Virginia and Kentucky and not be seen or heard of for years—even generations."

"The Richmond bottleneck is no better, I fear," said Miss Maude. "This is a concern as we expect another run any day. We heard from down the line only last week—well, not directly; our free black tenants heard."

"Is there anything I can do to help?"

"Well, you might try to bail us out of jail if we're caught," Miss Phoebe said. "And try and get some ether or chloroform from Dr. Hunter. Tell him you have some sick cats you need to put to sleep. He's suspicious of our never-ending requests. And it's very expensive and hard to get, you know. But more effective than that awful concoction of skunk juice and stinkweed the blacks use to confuse the dogs."

"I'll do it the next time he calls, and with Mrs. Hawthorn there, I'm sure he'll get a call soon. You know how hypo she is. But with Richmond blocked—"

"They are to be picked up here and taken North through Nelson County and up the Shenandoah Valley. A new route."

"I passed Corbin and his family as I rode in," Lavinia said. "They're very worried about you."

With a toss of her curls, Miss Phoebe dismissed Lavinia's concern.

"Now don't you fret about us, Lavinia dear," Miss Maude said.

Miss Phoebe struggled to smile. "Yes, we have had tears today, and not just for Mama. Corbin and his family have been with us so many years—since Papa freed them."

"The Sheriff and the patrols finally got to him," Miss Maude explained. "You know how they've been spying on us for ages. They made so many visits and veiled threats to Corbin, the poor man was scared to death. He was afraid that because he had remained in our employ long after the year of his freedom—nearly twenty years ago—he would be placed in slavery again, or forced to leave."

"Hicks and the patrols even implied they had evidence they did not—that he was a part of the Underground Railroad. He knew they could accuse him of anything and, true or not, his word as a black would be worthless against that of a white. We decided it would be better if he left and urged him to go."

Miss Maude shook her head. "Oh, an enslaved black has enough trouble, but they hate and fear a free one even more. They'll probably try the same tactics to scare our other tenants, too."

"Freedom for blacks is entirely different than freedom for whites," said Miss Phoebe.

"You've got yourselves to worry about, too," said Lavinia. "You're as suspected as your tenants."

Tears welled up in Miss Phoebe's eyes and she looked at Miss Maude. "I think we should tell you now, dear. This may be our last run."

Lavinia looked at them questioningly, waiting for them to explain. Miss Phoebe continued.

"When Mama goes—" She paused and wept quietly a moment. "When Mama goes, our brothers want us to come to Philadelphia or Baltimore and live with them. They say we're too old to run the plantation anymore. And it's true."

"Oh, Miss Phoebe." Lavinia fumbled for her handkerchief.

"Our brothers arrive soon and can find positions for our other black tenants in Philadelphia."

There was a little child-like whimper from the bed, which brought the sisters to their feet. It was nothing more than another involuntary murmur, and they returned to their chairs.

"How foolish to be mourning her going, at ninety-eight, when she hasn't known who we are or spoken in weeks," said Miss Maude. "Seventy and seventy-five is a little old to be behaving like orphans."

"I don't think it's too old at all," Lavinia said. "One never stops loving one's mother."

But Lavinia knew they would be mourning more than the loss of their mother. They would be mourning the loss of their plantation, their home in Virginia, and the independence of living according to their own terms.

Back at Hawthorn Hill, Lavinia selected a dress for dinner and went to Cornelia's room for assistance in fastening a long row of buttons up the back.

"But my dear, I have to do my hair!" Cornelia said with astonishment, curling irons poised in a furious attack at curls fallen limp since their last application of henna. "If only I had brought Ibby. Why not see if that little new girl from the quarters is free? Little Henny. She's a sweet little thing. Anxious to learn and quite subservient. Margaret has already suggested you train her as a replacement for Angelica, and I think she would be far superior to that uppity Piney."

"What an excellent idea!" Lavinia said. "What would I do without your good counsel? Now, why didn't I think of that? You have such good ideas."

"Thank you, dear," Cornelia beamed.

Lavinia, euphoric at how easily Henny's acceptance had been won—even suggested—found the child in the kitchen, where she buttoned her dress.

"Thank you, Henny. Mother Hawthorn and Miss Margaret suggested I train you as my new maid," Lavinia said loudly, so even Emma at the other end of the kitchen could hear. Emma's sour-faced disappointment was only exceeded by Piney's, who glared at Henny's triumphant grin with loathing.

"Ain't no room for her here," said Emma. "Miss Margaret's children got—"

"Oh, we'll wait until later to move Henny in permanently," Lavinia said. "For the time being, she will remain in the quarters and help Old Sheba—but she will also assist Miss Cornelia and me from time to time."

Henny's position was made even more secure a few evenings later when she and Lavinia met Mr. Edmund coming down the stairs to supper. An elderly, white-haired version of Lionel, the old gentleman, his features mellowed and sweetened by age, gave Henny a warm smile, which made him look younger and more like his portrait in the dining room.

"Ah, Miss Blue Eyes," he said to the little girl. He approached Henny and gently lifted her chin in his hand for a longer, more critical appraisal, rotating her head back and forth. Plunging his hand deep into his pocket, he gave her a paper-wrapped piece of hard candy. Lavinia missed none of the irony in having seen the old gentleman perform the same gesture with his acknowledged grandchildren.

"Thank you, sir," Henny said, and she gave him one of her deepest curtsies.

Mr. Edmund dismissed her with a pat on the head and directed Lavinia into the drawing room, where he prepared himself a drink of bourbon.

"No need to mention this to Mrs. Hawthorn," he said, holding up his glass and giving Lavinia a wink. "I can trust you and Margaret not to reveal my indulgence to Mrs. Hawthorn. And fortunately, Ariadne has not arrived yet. She's a tattle."

He sat down and sipped his drink and discussed with Lavinia the business details of Hawthorn Hill since she had been away.

Her father-in-law had enormous respect for Lavinia's expertise in managing the plantation. He could rely on the accuracy of her estimates, figures, and balances far more than he could from the overseer, Virgil Mudley. She took good care of the people and had as good a business head as any man he knew. She could even keep the slothful overseer, Mudley, to the task.

"I wish the overseers on my other properties were as effective and successful as you, my dear," he said.

"Thank you, sir."

The old gentleman sipped his drink in silence for a time and said, "Your new house girl—the one Margaret says you want to apprentice as a maid—"

"Yes?"

The old gentleman watched her closely. "Does she belong to Lionel? Or is she one of the boys'?"

Shocked into silence, Lavinia could only stare at the old gentleman. He had posed the question as nonchalantly as he might have an inquiry of her estimates on the yield of a new wheat field, or the results of a recent county horse race. It was a full minute before she spoke.

"She's Lionel's," she said at last, her tone matching her father-in-law's informality, as if calmly stating her estimate of the yield or who had won such a race. "She's nine-years-old, almost ten. Randy was eleven-years-old when she was born, and Frederick was just nine."

"Ah, yes." Mr. Edmund smiled and nodded. "The grandchildren always seem so much older to me than they are. I should have known she couldn't belong to them. Lionel named her Henrietta, after my mother, who died when he was a boy. Lionel was very fond of her." He paused in deep thought for a moment before proceeding.

"Does Lionel know you know her paternity?"

"Yes."

He reached out and patted Lavinia gently on the hand. "You're a remarkable woman, Lavinia. Quite a treasure in this family. I hope you know how you are appreciated."

"Thank you, sir."

"We must do well by the child. I can spot a Hawthorn almost anywhere. There were a few blue-eyed, light-skinned blacks on the place when I was a boy," he said. "Not mine, mind you. My father's. But Papa freed them and they went North. I've lost touch with them through the years, but I should imagine that by now we have an extensive branch of the family up North. I think of them often."

He lowered his voice and bent closer to Lavinia. "I have two half-brothers—if they are still alive—living in New England and passing as white. Haven't heard from them in nearly forty years." He smiled sweetly and reflected on his Northern relatives silently for a moment. "No need to discuss this with Mrs. Hawthorn, of course," he cautioned. "She hardly believes such reproduction is possible—like breeding horses and cows." He chuckled.

"And I'm not sure it would be beneficial if Mrs. Harvey knew either," he added, creasing his brow thoughtfully. "But certainly Lionel needs no excuse to increase the population except through you, my dear." The mention of Lionel brought a look of disappointment and annoyance to the old man's face.

"Your husband loves you very much, you know," Edmund said. "He has suffered during your separation. And is happy now that he has won your trust again." He smiled kindly and the warmth in his eyes returned.

"I have wanted to bring the child into the house as my maid since I...I...found out about her," said Lavinia and she added cautiously, "should there be no objection from anyone in the family."

"Excellent idea. And Mrs. Hawthorn is taken with her, I think. We must do right by our own. You're very understanding, my dear. Many wives object strenuously to such children—make their lives intolerable and even demand they be sold. I'm sure there were a few objections at her conception—I think any now are a little late. Continue as you see fit."

Without waiting for Lavinia to respond, he plunged back into a discussion of the plantation, her estimates of the tobacco yield as compared to last year, the health and well-being of the people, and how blessed they were that so far there had not been the first sign of the dreaded blue mold.

Lavinia was dismayed at the casualness with which the old gentleman acknowledged his black relatives. With Mr. Edmund approving Henny's being brought to the house, and Cornelia's and Margaret's earlier endorsement, Lionel would be all but powerless against so united a family stand. She marveled at how simple it had been—without her direct request but through the suggestion of the heads of the family. As she answered the old gentleman's questions about clearing certain woodlands for more tobacco acreage, she noticed his blue eyes begin to flutter with fatigue.

Soon the silvery-haired head tilted against the wing of his chair and he nodded off to sleep, his easy, rhythmic breathing punctuated by an almost musical snort and sniff.

He even snores like a gentleman, Lavinia thought as she studied his face, saluting his tolerance and wisdom, before removing his drinking glass, still in his hand, and slipping quietly out of the room to delay supper a little so that his nap would not be interrupted.

When Lionel returned to Hawthorn Hill, Lavinia waited for his opposition to Henny's presence in the house. After seeing the little girl in the kitchen and providing maid service to Lavinia and his mother and sister, he sensed a conspiracy was afoot, revealed by Margaret's too lavish praise of the child's abilities and Cornelia's commendation of Lavinia for having judged her house-worthy.

"Such a polite child," Cornelia said at supper one evening. "Always curtsies and is humble and unobtrusive. I suggested to Lavinia she train her—"

"And one has only to tell her once how to do something and she remembers it," added Margaret.

"And a sweet disposition, too!" Mr. Edmund said with a quick glance at Lavinia.

Lavinia remained silent, but sent Lionel a sly smile down the table, which he acknowledged with a smile of his own, a raised glass, and nod of his head.

I've won, thought Lavinia. *Henny's foot is in the door. Before the year is out, I will have her living in this house.*

After supper, Lionel confronted her in the front hall as she was going upstairs. "Congratulations, Mrs. Hawthorn," he said. "It seems you have allies in your quest and you know I cannot fight the whole family." He bowed to her and started toward the back of the house just as Uncle Lemiel came out of the dining room.

Lavinia called to him, "Uncle Lemiel, tomorrow send for two strong field workers. I want Mr. Lionel's bed, dresser, and press moved back to his room upstairs."

Lionel stopped and turned.

"If...that meets with your approval, Mr. Hawthorn?" she said.

"Indeed, Mrs. Hawthorn, you honor me," Lionel said. He bowed deeply as she swept past him and started up the stairs. His eyes followed her to the top step, where she turned and looked down at him.

"You need not wait for the furniture, Mr. Hawthorn," she said, and turning, proceeded to her room. "You may move in tonight."

Chapter Twenty-Two

When Lionel left the next morning for Richmond, the household happily noticed the lingering whispers, hand-holding, and long embrace he and Lavinia exchanged as they said their goodbyes.

Watching from the parlor window, Uncle Lemiel whispered, "They jest like two sweethearts not wantin' to say good night."

"And she done has me to search out her old dress patterns for him to take to Richmond to has new dresses made up," said Emma.

"And at breakfast he say he ain't gonna 'low none of them dresses be black or has so much as a black button on 'em," Aunt Beck added.

Henny understood nothing of the exchange about her mistress's wardrobe, but later that day in Lavinia's room, she noticed her mistress was in a particularly happy mood as she explained the differences in silk, satin, taffeta, and brocade and told her the original bright colors her dresses had been before they had been dyed black.

That day, Cornelia received a letter from Ariadne that she had recovered from her latest nervous attack and would return to Richmond by way of Hawthorn Hill.

"And I was hoping they would keep her at Hot Springs all summer, so we wouldn't have to put up with her here," Margaret said.

"Margaret, how unkind," said Lavinia facetiously. "I am always overjoyed to see Cousin Ariadne."

"Don't act so noble with me. You'd be as happy as I if she didn't even come this summer."

For years, the residents of Hawthorn Hill had dreaded and endured Ariadne's twice yearly visits: Lavinia, her veiled insults, the servants, her harsh, abusive orders. Although the household made every effort to ensure Ariadne's comfort, their efforts were rewarded with withering disdain and stinging ingratitude. Her large, liquid eyes watched black and white alike with condescending disapproval and judgmental arrogance.

"Well, at least I'll be going home next week. Reverend Harvey says he can't stand it another day without me," Margaret said with a modest smile. "You'll just have to suffer her alone."

"Well, at least Mama and Papa will be here," said Lavinia.

"And Mother will baby her," said Margaret. "I've watched Ariadne's childish fits since she was six-years-old, and I say a good spanking when she was young would have done more good than calling in doctors to treat her. And calling her childish temper tantrums 'melancholia' and 'hysteria' and all these fancy names they use trying to make pure meanness a medical problem."

"Well, there were those Woodhull cousins of hers," Lavinia said. "That Uncle Philemon and..."

"Oh, he went completely mad. Had to be locked away," Margaret said.

"And how ashamed and secretive Mother Hawthorn was about Ariadne's episodes," Lavinia said. "So afraid people would think it came from her side of the family."

"Mother only made her worse by spoiling her and letting her have her way. It was always, 'Let Ariadne have the doll, Margaret,' and 'Let Ariadne wear your new bonnet if she wants to, Margaret,' and to me later, 'You're so sweet to understand about poor Ariadne, Margaret. She doesn't have a Mama and Papa like you, so we must make sacrifices.' And when we were older and I had more beaux than she, she became worse."

Margaret shook her head at the memory of growing up with Ariadne and her cousin's troubled, self-indulgent childhood.

"I used to get so tired of her selfishness. I remember when we were about seven, Mammy Emma gave us an old torn lace curtain and we decided to play bride and use the curtain as a veil and come down the stairs and she threw a tantrum if she couldn't be the bride every time!"

"And still ended up an old maid," said Lavinia.

"Pity the poor man who might have married her."

"She's always seemed so unhappy. Ever since I first met her, it was as if she bore some unexpressed grief. No doubt because of the horrible way her parents died—in the fire. She was only six."

"Being a tragic orphan hardly justifies her behavior thirty-five years later," Margaret said. "And the old servants who cared for her when she was an infant said she was as mean and hateful before the fire as she is now. And I can remember Emma saying how strange it was that at her parents' funeral, Ariadne shed not a tear. And Mother, being unable to comprehend such stoicism, kept shoving a handkerchief toward her, almost as if she was telling her she should cry. Or go through the motions at least, so people wouldn't talk, not just stand at the graveside with those big pop-eyes as dry as egg shells staring at nothing."

"Well, it wasn't my fault Lionel didn't marry her. I had never even met her when he married me. Maybe Ariadne could have civilized him. I certainly failed."

"Oh, but Livvy, you didn't. He went an entire year without being called out, or getting into a single barroom brawl, or—"

"A whole year!" Lavinia laughed. "But I haven't given up yet."

The fleeting image of Bithia Clevinger flashed in Margaret's mind but she quickly dismissed it. "'The day Lionel married you, Lavinia,'" Margaret imitated her mother, "'a light in Ariadne went out forever.'"

They both laughed as the old saw was once again appropriately applied.

"Everyone talks about Ariadne's wealth," Margaret said. "I wonder just how much money she does have. Papa hasn't handled her finances in years."

"Nor has Lionel. She grew highly incensed when he suggested she contribute something to a black charity and removed him as her financial advisor. And since she's convinced there's going to be a war over slavery, she puts half her money in Richmond banks and half in Boston so whichever side wins, she'll have funds."

"She has so much wealth, she'll never exhaust it. No matter how fast she spends it, it just builds up again. She owns so much property—the plantations in Henrico and Hanover and Goochland and the big one, Fleur de l'Eau, down the James River."

"She probably doesn't even know what she's worth."

"Well, it's like the Bible or Shakespeare or somebody said, 'Money can't buy you happiness,'" Margaret said. "It certainly hasn't for Ariadne."

The news of Ariadne's arrival at Hawthorn Hill was greeted by black and white alike with the same dread and weariness as always. Margaret's children immediately raised a howl of displeasure.

"Does Ariadne really have to come while we're here?" seven-year-old Lionel asked.

"That's 'Aunt Ariadne,'" corrected his grandmother.

"Will we have to eat at a separate table in the pantry?" little Cornelia Randolph wanted to know.

Ariadne's aversion to Margaret's children necessitated new rules when she was in residence, reinforced by Cornelia's insistence that they were justified because of Ariadne's "nervous condition."

"Now, your Aunt Ariadne has been ill. Although you are to make no mention of it," Cornelia said, considering any illness of a *nervous* nature something of a disgrace and too close to mental illness, which she considered shameful and almost dishonorable. "Because of her delicate nerves, we must do all we can to accommodate her ill health. She dislikes noise and you children are the noisiest in the world. She also wants nothing to do with the kittens, baby chickens, and lizards you adopt every summer, so don't bring them around her. You can just as easily play your games in the front pasture as well as you can in the front yard where Aunt Ariadne is disturbed by the noise."

Cornelia also put the servants on notice, beginning with the kitchen. "Miss Ariadne will require breakfast served in bed each day at ten o'clock. Under no circumstances is Miss Ariadne to be served eggs prepared in any fashion, liver, sauerkraut, squash, turnips, parsnips, or collard greens. I know these are all favorites of the rest of the family, but none are to be served during Miss Ariadne's visit."

"You think the Holy Ghost comin', " Emma said.

"It more like the plagues of Egypt," said Aunt Beck under her breath.

Ariadne, her health much improved but with no apparent change in her disposition, arrived within the week. Because Margaret and Cornelia both voiced approval of Lavinia's apprentice, Henny, it was suggested that Ogletha, who accompanied her mistress, be sent on to Richmond.

"But I shall need her myself," Ariadne protested.

"There's simply no room with my children and Mama and Papa here," said Margaret. "And we have Piney and Henny to assist you."

Ogletha was sent on to Richmond to prepare for Ariadne's arrival there in two weeks.

"And you can return with me!" Cornelia said joyfully. "Edmund takes the train, but I won't, and you'll be perfect company for me in the carriage!"

Learning that Margaret's children were in residence, Ariadne shortened her stay. "I will be staying only a few days," she announced at the supper table the day she arrived. "I just brought enough of my medication to last that long."

"Oh, we had hoped you could stay longer," Lavinia purred, daring not to glance toward the relieved black and white faces in the dining room. "Perhaps Dr. Hunter can—"

"That old fool? I would as soon trust that old witch in the quarters with her rattling gourds and herbs as him."

Lavinia stiffened to hear Dr. Hunter and Old Sheba demeaned.

"I cannot believe you are still wearing black, Cousin," Ariadne said with the trace of a sneer, as she regarded Lavinia critically. "How long has it been?"

"Only two years," said Lavinia.

"More than long enough."

"Lavinia is going to Richmond for an entire new wardrobe," Margaret said. "She's already sent patterns for Ibby and the dressmaker."

"I'm delighted to hear it. I suppose mountain people prefer drabness to match their lives of isolation, but you need color, Cousin. Isn't it true you people of the hills still actually weave your own cloth—homespun, I think you call it? Or do you still wear the skins of animals? How unfortunate your background provided so little. Certain influential people are trying to persuade Lionel to seek public office. Your rustic origins must be held in check—not only in your attire, but your speech and demeanor. We should hope that as his wife, you would wish to represent him in the best light and not, by lack of style, taste, and background, encumber his efforts."

"Really, Ariadne," Margaret fired across the table, her eyes snapping. "Lavinia's taste and style have never been questioned. Lavinia has always had enough natural beauty not to have to hire Paris and half of Europe to dress her to get attention. She has the best figure of anyone in the family and wears black crepe with more style than you wear all those vulgar, outrageously expensive get-ups you have made up in Philadelphia and Paris."

"Margaret!" Cornelia gasped. "We all know Lavinia has beauty, poise, and style quite adequate for Lionel without either of you girls being rude."

"Oh, but Margaret, dear, you misinterpret my humble efforts to only be of help," Ariadne said, her eyes flashing with delight at the conflict. Directing her arrows at Margaret, she said, "And I was going to suggest your own growing stoutness calls for more subdued colors. And stripes, I understand, often give the illusion of a slimness to heftier females—but only vertically. In circling a girth such as yours horizontally, they make the figure appear...bovine."

"Poor old Mrs. Barksdale," Cornelia almost shouted, her eyes making a panicked search of the table for assistance in changing the subject. "Probably won't last a month."

Margaret's face deepened from pink to red and her snapping blue eyes promised the beginning of all-out war.

"And poor Phoebe and Maude are grieving already," Lavinia quickly interjected, restraining Margaret's wrath with a gentle hand on her arm.

"We must pay a call, perhaps this week," said Cornelia. "This custard is delicious!"

Civility was saved, and the meal resumed quietly, but Margaret's eyes still snapped and Ariadne's thin lips maintained a sly, self-satisfied smile.

But more than inciting discord, Ariadne's main purpose in visiting Hawthorn Hill was to glean information implicating Lavinia in Angelica's escape. With Emma, Beck, and Uncle Lemiel providing nothing helpful, and the new house girl, Henny, seldom seen and more often in the quarters taking care of the field hands' children, Ariadne discovered the best source of information on the plantation was Piney.

Piney was fascinated by Ariadne, her grand manner, and elaborate wardrobe. In an effort to impress her, she reported everything.

"Douglas and Ivan back to fightin' just as bad as ever over Daisy," Piney announced when she brought Ariadne a pitcher of water and a glass to prepare her nightly medication. "They talkin' it in the quarters last night, sayin' Ivan after me agin, but I wouldn't have him. And now they say he back sniffin' round Daisy—"

"How absolutely fascinating," Ariadne responded sarcastically, withholding an impulse to slap the girl for the impertinence of speaking before being bidden. "And what makes you think I find the slightest interest in the romances and brawls of Hawthorn Hill field hands?"

"Miss Margaret sure do. She all the time wantin' to know when they fit. And who Daisy gonna marry. And Mr. Lionel and Mr. Edmund got big bets a goin' on which one Daisy ends up with."

While Ariadne's own servants cowered in silence and the rest of the Hawthorn Hill blacks were less forthcoming with household gossip, Piney, new to service to Ariadne and so far unscathed by her abuse, thought she was being helpful and interesting and to Ariadne's disdain prattled on about everything.

But Ariadne soon realized that in this slant-eyed girl, as thin as the newels on her four poster bed, was a cornucopia of knowledge about everything that went on at Hawthorn Hill from the fields to the master's bedroom.

When Piney arrived with her breakfast tray at precisely ten o'clock the next day, Ariadne decided to test the depth of Piney's knowledge.

"I notice Mr. Lionel has moved his bedroom furniture back upstairs. Didn't he reside on the first floor when I was last here?"

"Yes'um. Miss Lavinia done has his things moved back. She gets two big fellers from the field and move his bed and press and all his things 'cept his desk up. Miss Lavinia—she there the day they come and she have to send for another field hand to help move that big press. She keep tellin' 'em, 'Don't you scar my banister movin' that press,' and they gets it up the stairs just fine."

"So Mr. Lionel sleeps upstairs again?"

"Yes'am. But he don't never sleep in his own room no more. Emma been makin' me make the beds since way back yonder, and I ain't had to make Mr. Lionel's a single time since he moves up here. He just piles in with Miss Lavinia all the time now."

Ariadne stopped eating and laid her fork on her plate. Piney continued. "When Mr. Lionel here and sleepin' in Miss Lavinia's room, that bed the worst to make up of any in the house. When he ain't here and Miss Lavinia by herself, it hard to tell that bed even been slept in—barely a wrinkle in it. All I has to do is just run my hand over it and smoothes it out a little. But when Mr. Lionel here that bed all to pieces. Cover tore up something awful and so bad I just has to start all over it such a mess."

Ariadne narrowed her eyes and her face darkened. She asked that her tray be removed.

"Ain't you goin' to eat no more than that?"

"How dare you question what I do!"

"But Aunt Beck be wonderin' what wrong with her breakfast she take so much pains with."

"Hold your tongue! I've got a headache. Now take it away and bring me my medicine."

Piney removed the tray and brought Ariadne her bromides and Tincture of Opium from the washstand.

"Now tell me more about Miss Lavinia and Mr. Lionel."

The dark scowl on Ariadne's face deepened as Piney continued.

"Well, I mighty glad he sleep in Miss Lavinia's bed. Save me havin' to make his. But I has to make two trips to bring 'em breakfast when they eats in bed—one for her and one for him. Emma and Aunt Beck all time laughin' and goin' on 'bout how glad they is they sleepin' in the same bed agin, and not even get out to come down and eat sometimes."

"Emma and Beck's delight is hardly of interest to me," said Ariadne. "But tell me, did Miss Lavinia miss Angelica terribly when she ran away?"

"I reckon she did, but she never show it much."

"Oh, and why not?"

"Well, Miss Lavinia had Mr. Lionel tryin' to buy Gabriel for her a mighty long time. They sayin' in the quarters that Miss Lavinia fix it up so Angelica can slip off when he run."

Ariadne, her eyes glistening with anticipation, sat up so fast in the bed she almost spilled the Tincture of Opium and water mixture she sipped.

"Do...do you think she did?" Ariadne tried to subdue her excitement. At last it seemed she might have found the mother lode. This unaware, stick-thin girl could possibly provide her with the information for a smile that she had failed to get in Richmond after futilely spending hundreds of dollars.

"Don't know for certain, but I know she helps Bingo and Jane."

"Bingo and Jane?"

"Them other two that run off from the Wroughton place—" Piney seemed suddenly to have second thoughts about talking so freely.

"Oh, but you can tell me," Ariadne coaxed, sensing the girl's self-imposed silence. "I'm family—and I'm sure that other little girl lurking around here, Henny, would tell me."

Piney frowned at the thought of being outdone by Henny and told everything as Ariadne's features radiated her pleasure and satisfaction with every new revelation.

"Well, when Miss Lavinia got back from visitin' her people when her Pa took sick, I heared Uncle Lemiel tell

Emma and Aunt Beck he nearly scared to death they get caught goin' all the way across Virginia with 'scapees."

"You're sure? You're absolutely sure of this?" Ariadne prodded, her eyes glistening with satisfaction.

"I heared it alright. They don't never say nothin' around me when they know I there, but sometimes I sets in the kitchen by the sideboard behind Aunt Beck's big churn and they forget I there and says lots of things."

"How very clever of you, Piney," Ariadne said. "You must sit behind the big churn often. My headache has suddenly completely disappeared. If you would be so kind as to bring back my tray, I think I shall have some breakfast after all."

A few days later, Cornelia, Lavinia, Margaret, and Ellie decided to visit the Barksdale sisters and other nearby neighbors. Ariadne, already bored with a week of country people and visits to one family after another only to hear the same gossip and same discussion of the same topics she had heard in the household visited the day before, pleaded a headache and sent her regrets.

With the house empty, even of Emma and Piney, who were at the wash house, Margaret's children were with no more adult supervision than their ineffectual nurse, Molly. Ordered to play in the front pasture, the children nevertheless migrated into the front yard, where they noisily romped right below Ariadne's window.

Molly was powerless against them and resigned to accepting that she was outnumbered and that her authority would go largely ignored. She concentrated only on keeping the toddlers out of harm's way.

Ariadne loathed children, particularly Margaret's. She had insisted that Cornelia ban them from the dining room altogether, but Lavinia had overruled her and they had been isolated at one end of the room at a separate table where Emma's stern supervision elicited a modicum of civility and order.

"Little animals," Ariadne fumed as the squeals of their youthful frolicking continued, even after repeated shouts and threats out the window. Finally, with the din of their cavorting undiminished, she rose to banish them to the pasture herself, especially since the yelping of Lionel's hounds had joined the squeals and laughter.

Once on the front porch, however, she saw that the hounds barked independently of the children's play and raced to meet Lionel, who was riding down the lane.

Racing inside, Ariadne dashed upstairs for her sewing basket and quickly returned to the parlor. By the time Lionel returned from the stables, she was seated demurely, her skirts neatly flared around her with her crochet needle working feverishly.

"Just when I thought all my women folk had deserted me," Lionel said, discovering her alone in the house.

"They're visiting the neighbors, Cousin," Ariadne said.

She put aside the crochet needle and rose as he bent and kissed her on the cheek. "You look so well, Ariadne," he said. "I am so glad you are home. So, the busy bees are collecting pollen?"

"Bees? Pollen?"

"Mother, Lavinia, and Margaret. Those three will have collected gossip this afternoon like a bee collects pollen."

"Oh, Lionel, you're absolutely terrible." Ariadne always drifted into her girlish mode with Lionel, especially when she was alone with him. As she grew older, such posturing only made her seem more spinsterish, but Lionel responded with a playful, brotherly repartee.

He eased his large frame into a chair and laid a bundle wrapped in brown paper and tied with string on the table beside him. "Remind me to give this to Lavinia. It's new fabric samples from her dressmaker in Richmond. Ibby got them for me to bring."

Ariadne's eyes fell hungrily on the package, certain it contained a message from Angelica. How satisfying it would be to tear open the package and expose Lavinia to Lionel at that very moment. But caution restrained her.

Lionel continued, "I think I have finally talked Vinny out of wearing nothing but black after the past two years."

"I am so glad." Ariadne's voice was as smooth as silk. "I was suggesting the same thing only the other evening. Lavinia has such a lovely figure."

"Margaret has tried to talk her out of weeds for a year. Even Mother, a stickler for proprieties, agrees a year is sufficient for crepe. Help her select something and I'll have it run up for her in Richmond."

"It will be a pleasure. I've always felt Lavinia needed guidance in selecting her wardrobe, even before she went into mourning. I do hope she will not be offended if I try and direct her away from...from improper, rather ordinary choices lacking in refinement and good judgment."

Lionel ignored the criticism of Lavinia's taste.

"Select three or four. Or more. She deserves a reward. I've been so busy with the tobacco factory in Richmond, she's had to run Hawthorn Hill almost entirely alone."

"What a splendid idea," Ariadne said, as calmly as she could. Although she tried to listen to Lionel's report on the success of the factory, in which she was also an investor, her eyes kept moving to the brown paper package.

"Three hundred thousand dollars! In just over three years? And a quarter of that is mine?" she said in response to Lionel's report of the factory's profitability, but her real enthusiasm was for the brown package. She had to get to it before Lavinia returned. With enough time, she could open it, find any communication from Angelica, replace it, and wrap it exactly as it arrived. As she plotted how to get the package, Lionel continued to report on the success of their joint investment.

"Oh...I'm sorry, Cousin," Ariadne said, jolted back from her reverie of intrigue. "Such success and so quickly... I'm speechless."

"I'm boring you. I forget women find business details uninteresting. And I'm sure Mother would say money was an improper subject to discuss with a lady."

"Not at all, Cousin."

Lionel rose. "You're just indulging me. But if you will excuse me, I am here for only two days before I must get back to the factory. I'd best use my time well and look over the accounts and try to see if my shiftless overseer is sober."

"I understand completely. Don't let me keep you," Ariadne said as Lionel bowed and left the room. And left the package. She listened as his feet retreated toward the back of the house and went in the office.

She snatched up the package and was in the hall almost ready to take the first step up the stairs when he emerged from the office and saw her. His eyes fell to the brown paper bundle in her hand.

"You said not to let you forget to give this to Lavinia. I thought I would just put this in her room," Ariadne said.

"Thank you," he responded, and he turned back to his office.

Upstairs, Ariadne left her door partly opened so she could hear any approaching footsteps on the stairs. She raced to her bed, carefully untied the string around the brown package, and folded back the paper to reveal the contents. A dozen squares of cloth in various fabrics—velvet, silk, satin, brocade, taffeta—in numerous colors—purple, deep blue, green, burgundy, as well as stripes and checks—revealed nothing hidden between them. On top, a small brocade bag with a drawstring contained samples of buttons made of brass, ivory, and cloth-covered wood. Opening it, Ariadne's fingers explored the inside but felt nothing except the smooth satin lining. Puzzled at finding no letter, she examined the swaths again, before crushing the brocade bag angrily in her hand. It was then that she heard the crumple of paper. Turning the bag inside out and dumping the buttons on the bed, she saw the satin lining was tacked loosely to its brocade cover by a single string.

She rushed to her dresser, found a pair of scissors, and clipped the string. The silk lining separated from the velvet cover and she removed a tightly folded piece of paper. Her eyes raced down the page:

Dear Miss V.

Got news of G. in patterns. Thank Jesus he safe. Still in R. same place safe and protected good. Need more money cause of danger they say — to pay for safe delivery to North. Ankle better but got to wait till I can walk on it. Love u, pray for me. And G. Love, A.

Ariadne read the letter twice before she refolded it, put it in the bag, and carefully resewed the lining in place with the single thread. Then she put the button samples into the bag and placed it with the swatches of cloth exactly as she had found them. Rising to place the package in Lavinia's room, she stopped abruptly when she saw Henny watching her from the hall just outside her open door.

"Them green and yeller ones heap the prettiest, didn't you think, Miss Ariadne?" Henny said.

Ariadne gasped and stared at the girl who had seen everything.

Henny, head swathed in a head rag, carried a pail of water and cleaning rags over her shoulder.

"You little wench!" screamed Ariadne. "Where did you come from? Why are you spying on me?"

Henny's face fell in hurt and disappointment. "I just comes to clean, Miss Ariadne," she said. "Like Mammy Emma done tole me to."

"Eavesdropper! Spy! You should be switched for this! Have you been in my room?" Ariadne rushed to her dressing table and quickly lifted the lid to her jewelry box. Suddenly her hand stilled and she looked back at the cowering little girl. For the first time, Ariadne gave the new little black in the house more than a quick dismissive glance. With ever-increasing shock and disgust, she examined the little girl's features with more exacting scrutiny. Henny's blue eyes glistened with tears of fright, hurt, and uncertainty. But it was the color, not fear, that incited Ariadne's astonishment. She had never noticed the blue or its intensity before.

"My God," Ariadne said. "She's—" Instantly, Ariadne perceived in Henny the same bloodline as had Lavinia and Mr. Edmund. The thought of Lionel having a black child increased her revulsion for the little girl.

"Get out!" she bellowed, and when Henny fled her presence, Ariadne's head swirled with the implications of being caught snooping in Lavinia's package and discovering Lionel had fathered a black child. Lionel's blood mixed with a black meant that her blood was mixed with a black. The thought revolted her and she wanted to smash the child out of existence. Her hatred at the sight of those blue eyes created a knot in her stomach and she fell back on her bed limp with outrage and humiliation. She felt disgust that in this child, her blood flowed with that of black slaves. Her blood, the noblest of Virginia, blood which could be traced to the kings of England, France, Germany, a dozen Magna Carta barons, William the Conqueror, and Charlemagne—mixed with that of a dirty black.

To calm herself, Ariadne took a strong dose of Tincture of Opium and bromides. But even opiates could not still the disgrace she felt in knowing this half-breed child could expose her snooping in Lavinia's package. Somehow it was as incriminating as being caught reading Lavinia's mail. And the girl would surely reveal it. Ariadne wanted to prove Lavinia's guilt, but indirectly, with her participation in the exposure never known. Perhaps she could bribe the girl into silence. A few coins or a trinket might ensure her silence. But how could she be sure? How could she ever rest knowing this child knew? Ariadne knew she must create a plan that would eliminate Henny as a source of exposing her as a snoop and further eliminate her as a reminder that her aristocratic blood had been contaminated.

Unlike Ariadne's meticulous method in opening the brown paper package from Ibby, Lavinia ripped into it with savage disregard for the covering. Alone with Margaret, she examined and discarded swatch after swatch and then examined the drawstring bag of buttons.

"Just like the muff," said Lavinia. "It's in the lining."

Having read the letter, Lavinia passed it to Margaret.

"Oh, dear," said Margaret. "She's still in Richmond. And it's been almost three months. Well, at least Gabriel is safely North. And he was the major difficulty."

"But she needs money. Obviously, someone is willing to risk getting her out, but they want more for the greater risk."

"I shall see Ibby the first thing when I get to Richmond and let you know."

"Lavinia, dear," a smooth voice called from the hall. Margaret and Lavinia swapped weary glances.

"Yes, Ariadne, I'm in here," said Lavinia, quickly stuffing the letter under a pillow just as the door opened and Ariadne appeared.

"Lionel had a package for you. Oh, I see you've found it. Now if we can only find something suitable for you." Approaching the bed, she saw a sample of yellow silk. "Ah, this is interesting. Mrs. Clevinger had a frock made of this. She looked so fetching in it at Mary Willis's party earlier in the spring, didn't you think, Margaret?"

Chapter Twenty-Three

On a bright summer afternoon two weeks later, the crunch of gravel in the lane signaled the first carriage to arrive at Lavinia's sewing circle.

"Oh, no!" said Margaret, watching from the parlor window. "Mrs. Hunter has brought her mother. We'll have to shout ourselves hoarse."

"Maybe she brought her ear trumpet," Lavinia said as Reuben assisted a stooped old lady dressed in black in her descent from the coach.

"Her ear trumpet doesn't help at all. We'll still have to shout."

"And listen to the medical details of every case Dr. Hunter has had for a year."

"That's sometimes interesting," Margaret said.

"Now remember, girls," Lavinia reminded Henny and Piney, "take the ladies' wraps and help them carry things in."

The girls stood in excited readiness in fresh dresses with stiffly starched white aprons and lacy caps. It was Henny's first official social function as a house servant and she fidgeted with excitement, determined to perform her duties well.

"This one of the good things," she said to herself as she stood on tiptoe to check her appearance in the front hall mirror, adjusting her collar and her lace cap while ignoring Piney's self-assured smirks.

"I done helps with the sewin' circle 'bout a hundred times and you ain't even onct," Piney boasted.

"Piney, you may assist Emma in serving refreshments," Lavinia said before Henny could lash out at her more experienced rival. "Emma serves beautifully, and you would do well to observe her skills."

"I don't need neither one of them gawkin' while I serves the ladies," Emma said. "They just be in the way."

By mid-afternoon, Lavinia's parlor was crowded with more than a dozen ladies from nearby plantations and farms, busily occupied with their tasks under the soft hum of murmured conversation. The women sat in chairs from the dining room arranged in a large oval around a rectangular wooden frame on which was stretched the broadcloth backing for a quilt. On the surface of the backing, the mosaic of the quilt's design was laid out.

At the other end of the room, the half-dozen black women brought by their mistresses sat in a little huddle sewing the squares of cloth together in lengths for borders, or at random for larger areas for the quilt's center. The quilts were usually of a simple checkerboard layout, but when there was a sufficient supply of color and fabric of an interesting or distinctive combination, the squares were arranged with greater care for design and an eye for the geometry of the pattern.

"I cannot believe you are having black servants sit in the parlor with your white guests," Ariadne had said earlier in the day.

"We've been doing it this way for years, Ariadne," Lavinia said.

"Well, I suppose you'll be having them to other social occasions next," she said. "Does Aunt Cornelia know?"

"Mother had no objections," said Margaret with tired patience. "It was never a matter for debate until you brought it up. It is just perfectly natural."

Lavinia added, "After all, aren't we with our maids in the most intimate of situations when they assist us in dressing and for fittings?"

"It is most inappropriate. I would not be surprised to find them dining with the family the next time I visit Hawthorn Hill," she sniffed. "They grow bolder by the day. They'll want to live in the governor's mansion next!"

"She thinks she's Queen Victoria," Margaret whispered to Lavinia. "She's much too above us all to lower herself to sewing a quilt that might end up on a black's bed. She'll have a headache, wait and see."

Lavinia also expected Ariadne's regrets and was surprised to see her enter the parlor with her embroidery hoop and sewing basket sometime after the other guests had arrived. Giving the whites her usual cool, formal greetings, she regarded the little huddle of black participants at the far end of the room with contempt as they rose respectfully when she entered. She then seated herself among the whites, but only after she had directed Piney to place her chair with its back squarely toward the black women.

Those not actively engaged in making the quilt busied themselves with crochet or knitting, including Ariadne, who worked tiny stitches into a floral design for a pillow cover.

Henny and Piney, separating squares of cloth according to material and color, sat on the floor on either side of Lavinia's chair. Henny felt proud, and wished Old Sheba and her friends in the quarters could see her now, being a real maid.

She had never been in the company of so many white people before and was fascinated by the women whom she had only seen at a distance or heard about in gossip in the quarters.

Here at last was the formidable Mrs. Penelope Clay, whom Henny had heard beat her slaves with her cane for disobedience or slowness, and the wealthy Mrs. Florence Epsom, whose husband owned more blacks that anyone in the county. Beside her sat old Mrs. Minerva Branch, Mrs. Hunter's mother, too disabled by arthritic hands to participate in the sewing, but missing little of what was said as she directed her large, brass ear trumpet from speaker to speaker and croaked, "What's that? What did you say?" at every unheard comment.

Following the curt directions of Mrs. Quinton Bondurant, two black servants stretched the backing on the quilting frame as dainty Miss Mittie Pugh and the elephantine Mrs. Agnes Thornton pondered the intricacies of a challenging new quilt pattern brought by Mrs. Thaddeus Richardson, wife of the Methodist minister.

Henny was soon to learn that at least as important as sewing and quilting and other arts of needle and hoop was the exchange of county news and gossip. The din of conversation grew as the ladies, caught up on the latest, unleashed the store that they brought and filled up again on what they had not yet heard. Henny had already heard some of the stories before in the quarters in different, sometimes more scandalous versions.

Everyone was delighted to see Cornelia and Margaret, who brought news of Richmond and, along with Lavinia, glowed with pride when they announced that Lavinia and Margaret were soon to be blessed with a grandchild.

Ariadne drew her thin lips into a bored straight line as she endured another retelling of the stale, unwelcome news of another loathsome baby in the family.

But she was soon rewarded with a subject more to her liking and the veil of boredom lifted as her eyes glistened and fastened on Lavinia. The rash of runaway slaves in the county was discussed and Angelica's disappearance.

"Is it true she stole your silver?" the tiny Mrs. Polly Wheeler asked in her small, childlike voice.

"Oh, no, nothing was missing," said Lavinia. "But I am so embarrassed, and hurt by Angelica's disloyalty. A Hawthorn Hill servant running away."

Ariadne's crochet needle slowed as she scrutinized Lavinia closely and weighed her words, knowing her concern was only a performance.

Lavinia continued, "While anyone can understand why Horace Wroughton's blacks would run—they're mistreated. But a Hawthorn black? Why, it's a reflection on our family."

"Everyone knows the Hawthorns are good to their people, dear," Mrs. Agnes Thornton defended, her large breasts heaving with indignation that anyone would think otherwise.

"Not your fault at all," the chinless Mrs. Tyler Thacker said. "It was her romance with that Wroughton slave."

"Is it true she was with child?" Mrs. Wheeler asked, lowering her voice.

"What was that? Who had a child?" Mrs. Minerva Branch croaked, bending forward in her chair and swinging her ear trumpet toward Mrs. Wheeler.

"She wanted to know if Angelica was expecting a baby," said Mrs. Hunter to her mother.

"Was she? Whose baby?" Mrs. Branch's eyes grew wide and the stooped old lady swung her brass ear trumped in a wide arc around the room in pursuit of the information.

"No," Lavinia said, shaking her head so the old woman could see the answer, if not hear it. "Angelica was a very virtuous girl. She was never alone with the man. Only courted him in church and across the fence in the fields."

Ariadne emitted a sniff of disgust, Mrs. Wheeler looked disappointed, and crestfallen expressions appeared on other faces. But there was a chorus of agreement that Lavinia's treatment of blacks was exemplary.

"Who was the father? Did she have the baby?" Mrs. Minerva Branch shouted and Mrs. Hunter for the second time defended Angelica's purity.

Ariadne cast her gaze at Margaret, who, ignoring her stitching, scrutinized the ladies for a sign of their suspicion, her blue eyes falling on each one for a quick analysis before passing on to the next until they locked with Ariadne's and, reading her unconcealed skepticism, quickly returned to her sewing. Ariadne smiled to herself and wondered if Margaret was also a part of the escape plot.

"If anything, you Hawthorns are too good to your blacks," said Mrs. Angus Lewis, ignoring the cold silence from the cluster of blacks at the end of the room.

"Why, my Thaddeus says I treat our people better than my own family," Mrs. Agnes Thornton said, her huge bosom swelling with pride. "It's just a few Virginians that abuse their blacks—like that Horace Wroughton. If every slave owner was as benevolent as Virginians, the North would hush their mouth about slavery and stop making such an issue of it. It's the abuses in Georgia, Alabama, and Mississippi that have the Yankees in a snit."

The ladies agreed. The stories of beatings, lynching, and separation of families at auctions were dismissed as exceptions by these Christian souls, and they applied the soothing balm of their own blacks' good treatment to mollify any sting of conscience by knowing such incidences would never happen on their plantations.

The recent death of Booker, Horace Wroughton's slave, was agreed to be an aberration of Virginia's treatment of slaves and not to be considered typical.

"Wroughton is from North Carolina, I hear," Mrs. Thornton said.

Oblivious to the black servants at the other end of the room, whose earlier quiet mumbles went unheard beneath the din of the white women's full-voiced gossiping, Mrs. Bascom Taylor continued, her beaded earbobs swinging like large clock pendulums. "Oh, we have our lazy ones that have to be prodded, but Mr. Taylor only has to threaten to use the lash and they hop to it quick enough."

The black women bent lower over their sewing.

Lavinia and Margaret exchanged glances and stiff smiles as the self-righteous defense of slavery continued. "Thaddeus says the North is jealous of us because we have cheap labor."

"And they'd be treated no better in the North," Mrs. William Davis said. "They're a gentle people, childlike and docile, until the Yankee agitators get them stirred up."

"They'll turn on us sooner or later," Ariadne's voice rang out. "In spite of their friends who abide their crimes." She threw Lavinia a quick, accusing glance. "You don't know what it's like in Richmond. Free blacks are taking over. They almost outnumber the white population and plot and scheme all the time. Someday they'll revolt and kill us all."

Even the insensitive Mrs. Taylor seemed uncomfortable with Ariadne's outburst as the ladies exchanged ill-at-ease glances and looked apologetically at the servants.

"They're hardly more than animals, you know. Fifty years ago, they revolted in Haiti—killed I don't know how many. And that Nat Turner—"

"Ariadne!" Lavinia's voice rang out and she inclined her head toward the black women at the end of the room.

"Now, don't excite yourself, dear," Cornelia said, and Lavinia quickly brought up a question about a long-standing family feud of interest in the county.

"Has anyone heard the latest in the Woodson squabble?" she said a bit too merrily.

Grateful for the change of subject, several ladies spoke at once.

"Still raging."

"I hear Ed Woodson was talked out of calling out his own brother!"

"Adela is grief stricken. Hasn't spoken to Celestine in over a year."

"Oh, I got the complete story from Adela only two days ago," Cornelia said. "She said the heirs cannot agree on how to divide the property. None of them are speaking to each other and the courts will probably have to decide."

"If only old Mr. Woodson had left a will—"

"But he did!"

"Adela swears Ed burned it!"

The Woodson controversy was a grateful leap from the troubled waters of slavery and Ariadne's outburst and the buzz of gossip began again with grateful enthusiasm.

"What's that? What did she say?"

The black women were relieved, too, and silently resumed their sewing.

As the conversation once again began on various subjects discussed by smaller groups, Henny strained to catch snatches of each. She wasn't interested in the Woodson feud—didn't know them or what it was about, found the exchange of a recipe to preserve peaches boring, and couldn't understand an intense exchange involving Lavinia, Margaret, and Mrs. Theophilus Richardson concerning the publication of *The Pro-Slavery Argument*, a collection of essays.

She finally isolated and concentrated on a whispered exchange between Mrs. Percy Sowell and Miss Arrissa Wyatt, seated nearby, about breech birth. She particularly enjoyed the gynecological details of the discussion. When the ladies described a baby born with its umbilical cord nearly strangling it, Henny wanted to tell them about the calf born with three legs Old Sheba had told her about, or the baby born with three nipples that died, but decided not to.

Finally, Lavinia rose and, signaling Emma, excused herself to assist in serving the refreshments. Cornelia and Piney joined her.

"And old Mrs. Barksdale—no better, I suppose?" said Mrs. John Price.

"Much worse," intoned Mrs. Hunter, sitting upright in her chair, her pince-nez resting on her hawk-like nose. Mrs. Hunter was the group's official source of information about the health of the county.

"What? What did she say?" old Mrs. Branch said, waving her telescoping brass ear trumpet, which she had extended to its maximum length, in search of the speaker.

Although Dr. Hunter had told his wife repeatedly not to discuss the private information he passed on to her about his patients, she enjoyed the special importance of being privy to such details, and often violated his rule.

"Dr. Hunter told Maude and Phoebe her heart was failing fast and they'd better send for their brothers," Mrs. Hunter continued, adjusting her pince-nez. "Said it was only a matter of days." Then she bent forward and added in a lower tone, "And the poor old thing has locked bowel now."

"What was that?" Mrs. Branch called out, leaning so far forward in her chair that she almost hit Mrs. Thaddeus Richardson in the head with her ear trumpet as she swung it wildly about her. "Who's got locked bowel?"

"Old Mrs. Barksdale," her neighbor enlightened Mrs. Branch, trying to be sufficiently loud for the old lady to hear, yet not too loud considering the nature of the information. Mrs. Branch grunted and resumed a more secure seat in her chair.

There were sympathetic murmurs of regret and concern for Mrs. Barksdale's condition followed by a contemplative silence.

"They ought to call in Aunt Beck or Old Sheba," a little voice announced.

The clicking of knitting needles ceased as the ladies turned their attention toward Henny, who remained on the floor beside Lavinia's empty chair.

"Old Sheba be a lot better than Dr. Hunter or anybody else at curin' locked bowel," the little girl said. "She say once you get the plug moved it all comes out."

Mrs. Hunter could be heard to faintly gasp as her pince-nez slipped the length of her hawk-like nose and fell to her breast, caught by a ribbon around her neck. All eyes, black and white, fell on the little girl on the floor, who, pleased to be helpful, continued, "Last year they was looking for that tenant hand over on the Bailey place to die with locked bowel. He mighty old and Dr. Hunter give him ever thing he had to open him up, but it never worked worth nothin' a-tall."

"What's that? What did she say?"

Henny raised her voice to accommodate Mrs. Branch's handicap, and since all the ladies seemed transfixed with interest, she got to her feet so they all might more easily see as well as hear her. "They finally gets Old Sheba to come and she give him calomel and croton oil and Old Sheba tell Aunt Beck it weren't no time a-tall till that old man broke loose and mess the bed! She tell Aunt Beck he mess the bed so many times they had to change his linens over and over again. He fill the chamber pot full three times, and them two girls of his done spent half the night runnin' up and down the stairs emptyin' his pot he so backed up. It done been nigh on ten days!"

"What was that?" Mrs. Branch called out, more from disbelief than deafness.

"He fills the slop jar three times! Been blocked-up for ten whole days!" Henny fairly yelled toward the old lady.

"Henny!" Lavinia's voice suddenly interrupted as she stood at the parlor door beside a paralyzed, horror-stricken Emma, Cornelia, and Piney, who carried trays of pound cake and boiled custard. "That is enough information from you. Perhaps you can be more helpful in the kitchen."

"Yes'um," Henny said as she put aside the quilt squares. Her stunned audience stared at her as she executed her most accomplished curtsy and floated proudly toward the door. She could not understand why Emma stood staring with wild-eyed disbelief, her jaw hanging loose.

Later, when the guests had departed after completing six quilts and scheduling another meeting at Mrs. Thaddeus

Richardson's in a month, Emma and Piney recounted Henny's performance to Aunt Beck and Uncle Lemiel.

Uncle Lemiel chuckled to himself and Aunt Beck shook her head in disbelief. Henny could not understand Emma's rage and Piney's euphoric satisfaction.

"You done finished in this house, little sister," Emma said.

"Finished!" said Piney.

"Don't see what I done. I think I right much help to Miss Lavinia. I stacks my quilt pieces just like Miss Vinny say—all the red velvets together, all the red cottons together, all the blue—"

Piney whooped with laughter and even Emma added a chuckle at Henny's ignorance. They were certain her candid medical suggestions would guarantee her expulsion from the house and that she would be in the fields the next morning.

"Get another hoe ready!" Piney pretended to call toward the quarters. "Be another new field hand tomorrow!"

Emma joined Piney's hand-clapping laughter until it was squelched by Aunt Beck. "You's ought to be ashamed. Poor little child. Bad enough she maybe has to go, and you two makin' it worse." She handed Piney a tray and ordered her to take it to the dining room.

At supper, Ariadne suggested a thorough beating. "Put a few scars on her back, and put her in the fields. That will teach her her place," she suggested. "I'd sell her if she were mine."

Cornelia advocated a less severe punishment but wavered as to appropriate action.

"It was her first service with guests," Lavinia said. "I should have been more thorough in my instructions. She has been told by now in the kitchen, I am sure. And no real harm was done."

"I thought it was quite amusing," said Margaret, whose enjoyment of the episode was quickly squelched by glares from Cornelia and Ariadne.

Given another chance, Henny remained as an apprentice in the big house. But only after she had been carefully instructed that in the presence of white people, servants only spoke when spoken to, and that certain subjects were never discussed at all—including Mrs. Barksdale's malady and its cure.

But Emma's disappointment that Henny had not been banished to the fields brought the little girl even greater hardships. Assigned to Emma for instruction, that unfriendly mentor made no effort to conceal her loathing and imposed the most severe standards on the little girl. Her apprenticeship was difficult and painful. Henny could never satisfy Emma's impossible expectations and the old woman did everything she could to impede and belittle her progress.

A quick and willing apprentice, Henny was quite successful in most challenges, but this only provoked Emma's animosity even more than the girl's occasional lapses.

"You think you mighty smart, don't you?" Emma scoffed when Henny performed some task particularly well, such as setting the table perfectly and remembering exactly the correct positions for placing the cutlery, china, and crystal after a single demonstration. "You'll come off your high horse in time. Miss Lavinia won't tolerate no uppity blacks. You won't last long."

Hurt and her confidence eroded by Emma's impossible standards, Henny's insecurities grew and she was often in tears by the end of the day. Her misery was compounded because she dared not reveal to Lavinia Emma's cruelty lest such an action further increase the old woman's ill will.

Henny's one comfort, other than her mistress's quiet encouragement and occasional words of praise, was the kindness and friendship she found from Aunt Beck and Uncle Lemiel. Having crossed swords with Emma many times themselves, they understood Henny's suffering and encouraged and comforted her.

Piney was also a major hindrance to Henny and erected stumbling blocks whenever she could, quickly reporting any failing she might observe to Emma or Lavinia. When she saw nothing to tattle about, she invented something.

"Henny suppose to polish Miss Lavinia's candelabrums, but never did. They look just awful," she would report to Emma, or "Here your things from the wash house, Miss Lavinia. Emma told Henny to do it but she so triflin', I reckon I has to do her work and mine, too."

While Henny did little to defend herself against her two adversaries, she was unaware of a third, Ariadne, who waited with a final weapon to destroy her.

Lavinia was not blind to the efforts of Emma and Piney to thwart Henny's progress. She often surreptitiously evened the score. Because hours at the churn rated as one of the most hated duties in the kitchen, Lavinia, in planning the day's labor, would smoothly suggest, "Piney, the butter was so good last time. I think your churning is the best I've ever seen. I want you to do it again today." Then, giving Henny a secret smile, she would leave the kitchen and a befuddled Piney, proud that her churning was rated superior to Henny's, was also disgruntled that she had to do the unpleasant chore more than anyone else.

Old Mrs. Barksdale died a few days later and on the day of her funeral, Ariadne pleaded a headache to avoid attending. With all the Hawthorns in attendance, she waited only an hour after the family departed for the rites to call Emma to her room.

"Emma," she said. "I'm missing some jewelry. I've searched my room thoroughly and can't find my ruby earrings, a pin, a ring, and two clips. I saw Henny looking through my jewelry box only this morning."

Chapter Twenty-Four

Henny's brow creased with confusion when Emma accused her of stealing Ariadne's jewelry. Only after a stiff, cold-faced Ariadne stood glaring at her with hard, accusing eyes and repeated the charges did the little girl's face fall into disbelieving shock.

Henny's denials only brought Ariadne's lips into an even firmer tight line. Now Henny understood Old Sheba's branding white people as "devils," and for the first time in her life, she felt the full wickedness of one person toward another. The little girl stared in disbelief and terror at the ease with which Ariadne's cold lies poured out to doom her.

"I caught her examining pieces in my jewelry box only this morning," Ariadne said. "She was holding up the missing earrings to her own ears."

A personal search of Henny's person by Emma produced nothing, but an examination of the pocket of Henny's apron hanging behind the door in the pantry revealed the missing articles. Speechless when confronted by the evidence, Henny was switched by Emma and banished from the house.

"You just wait 'till Miss Lavinia and Mr. Lionel hear this!" Emma said.

"And tellin' lies on Miss Ariadne, too," added Piney, overjoyed at the incident. "Denyin' goin' through her jewelry box when she seen you."

Banished from the big house by Emma, the heartbroken Henny fled to the quarters. She wanted Old Sheba's comfort but realized the old woman would say she had warned her that her attempts to be a maid would come to no good end.

She went to her own cabin and waited until the hounds announced the return of the coach from Mrs. Barksdale's funeral. Henny was gripped by shame. What would Miss Lavinia and Miss Cornelia and Miss Margaret think when they heard of her disgrace? And what would Mr. Lionel do?

When he heard of her crime, he would whip her and possibly sell her to Horace Wroughton. She knew she was worthless—being a thief even further diminished her value—and Mr. Lionel would sell her cheaply just to get rid of her. Trouble blacks—those lazy, surly, violent, sick, or in any way undesirable—were gotten rid of by quickly selling them at a low price. Horace Wroughton, noted for his miserliness, would be able to buy her for nearly nothing. Fear now joined shame in the little girl's confused thoughts and she wanted to die.

Not even the treasured gold heart and chain Miss Lavinia had given her could bring her any consolation. Holding it before her, she fell on her bed in a torrent of tears, certain it would be taken from her.

Henny knew that nothing happening at the big house remained unknown in the quarters very long. A teacup broken at breakfast and the details—who did it, whether it was the handle or bowl, and what consequences befell the clumsy hands responsible—were known in the cabins by sundown.

And so it was, when Piney visited the quarters that evening after supper.

Henny, hiding in her cabin, could hear Piney's voice outside as she joined Nancy, Katie, and Paulina on the porch next door.

"Well, I has just about worked myself to death this day," Piney said.

Henny drew close to the window and listened.

"This mornin' Miss Lavinia wanted her work basket and I had to fetch it for her. It slip her where she puts it, and I had to look all over that house to find it for her. She fixin' a loose button on her dress for ol' Miz Barksdale's buryin'. They all gone biggest part of the day, and I had to just about run the house all by myself."

Since she had connived her way into the big house by currying favor with Emma through snooping and spying, Piney was regarded with scorn in the quarters. Feeling superior to the field people from whom she came, Piney would have them believe her life as a house servant required no more than polishing silver or searching for a missing sewing basket. She took every opportunity to gloat about her easy life, but made no mention of the floors Emma made her scrub, the slop jars she had to empty and scour, or the back-breaking struggle to move the heavy furniture when cleaning.

Although Henny could not see the women, she knew they were exchanging covert glances of contempt and rolling their eyes as Piney continued to lie and exalt herself.

"Aunt Emma say she think I 'bout the best worker she ever see and say she goin' to see I be Miss Lavinia's maid since Angelica runs off."

"Thought Henny was learnin' for that," said Nancy.

"You mean you ain't heared?"

"Heared what?"

"You mean you ain't heared what she done this mornin'?"

"Not yet, we ain't."

Piney's voice rose to the level of a shriek. "Why, me and Emma and Miss Ariadne ketch her stealin'!"

Henny closed her eyes tightly and lay her head against the door in shame.

"Henny? Stealin'?" Mumbles of surprise passed among the women.

"Sho was! Reckon she slips in Miss Ariadne's room and done took nigh ever piece of fine jewels she got. But me and Emma and Aunt Beck find where she hides it and gets it back. It in the pocket of one of her aprons!"

"Henny?" Katie asked. "She carry off the dinin' room table and beds and everything?" The women laughed.

"Well, I reckon she would have if she could," Piney said. "She load herself up jest about all of Miss Ariadne's fine gold and diamonds and things. And her fancy ruby earbobs."

Henny put her hands over her ears and shut out Piney's voice.

"That ain't like Henny," Paulina said.

"She just mean, I reckon. It them blue eyes of hers that make her that way. Nobody but white people and devils supposed to have blue eyes. She done been stealin' all her life though. She stole one of Miss Vinny's blue shawls onct and lied out of it. And a white lace dress off me, too, but I never said nothin' 'bout it."

"What else she steal?"

"Well, I reckon me and Emma keeps her from gettin' the rest of the things she wantin'. But she 'bout get the most of Miss Ariadne's jewels."

Henny heard steps on the porch approaching her cabin. She shrank behind the door as Paulina rapped and called out, "Henny! You in there?" Paulina pushed the door open, but finding the room dark and seemingly empty, closed it.

"She ain't in there," Paulina said, and she joined the others as Piney continued.

Henny listened until she could bear it no longer. She knew Piney would not stop here but spread her lies in every cabin in the quarters. She was about to reveal her presence and tear into Piney when stopped by Katie's next question. "Miss Vinny know about this?"

"Reckon Miss Ariadne or Emma tells her. And Mr. Lionel, too. They been at ol' Miss Barksdale's buryin' all day. Mr. Lionel be mighty mad when he find out, I reckon. You know what he done to Silas when he steals them hams."

The mention of Silas caused Henny to stop and she felt herself grow cold as her anger became chilling fear. A memory none of the people wanted to remember came back to Henny with startling clarity.

Years before, Mr. Lionel had summoned all the people to the whipping post located where the road passing through the quarters joined the path leading to the big house. Henny hadn't even known the ancient, weather-worn oak post was anything other than a hitching post, even though it was equipped with a large metal ring and chain. Then she saw Silas, a field worker, stripped to the waist, his arms wrapped around it and tied with a rope.

She remembered her puzzlement as the slaves, silent and fearful, gathered, and Mr. Lionel, carrying a leather strap, approached the quivering man and addressed the transfixed, frightened huddle of blacks.

As he removed his coat and rolled up his sleeves, her master had looked into the glistening eyes of the hard, black faces around him, and explained that the culprit who had for some time been stealing hams from the smokehouse had at last been discovered.

"There is one thing I will not tolerate on this place. And that is a thief!" Lionel had said, his voice cold and threatening. There was none of the familiar goodwill in his tone. "No one has the need to steal because your needs will be supplied." Henny felt a wave of dread as she recalled his words, words that now seemed to be directed at her and her own particular crime. "Silas has stolen hams to trade for whiskey, and for this he is being punished."

Then, Henny remembered, Lionel had suddenly swung around and given Silas one hard, flesh-cutting stripe across the shoulders. The sharp crack of the strap on flesh even now seemed to echo in her ears. She could still hear the cry of Silas's pain and see the stricken black faces gasp in shock as they recoiled.

Then, Lionel had abruptly flung the whip to the ground and taken long strides to the big house, looking straight ahead and avoiding the searching, wounded eyes of the slaves who had never seen violence or cruelty from their master before.

"I sure do feel mighty bad for Henny," Piney said, with false piety, jarring Henny back from her reverie. "Reckon it not right that Mr. Lionel give her another whippin' after Emma done stripe her good. But I reckon he will just the same." Piney's voice was almost musical with poorly concealed satisfaction.

Henny could stand no more and fled to the other end of her cabin as Piney continued, "I done beg Emma not to whip her but she do it anyhow."

Shame washed over Henny that Nancy, Katie, and Paulina knew of the accusations against her and the news would eventually spread throughout the quarters. With nothing but humiliation, a beating, and possibly being sold awaiting her, her despair reached new depths, her chest tight with fear and hopelessness.

"Henny!"

She was spared more of Piney's slander when she heard her name called and saw Aunt Beck lurching from side to side as she waddled down the hill with a basket on her arm.

"Emma needin' you," she said gruffly to Piney. "You get on back to the house. And where Henny?"

"Reckon she hidin' out—or run off," Piney said.

"Yo, Henny!" Aunt Beck called again.

Unable to face her, Henny scrambled up the ladder to the low loft beneath the roof. The door groaned as Aunt Beck opened it.

"You hidin' from me?"

Peering through a crack, Henny watched as the old woman found a broom behind the door and, lifting the handle, rapped it against the ceiling.

"You up there? If you is, you better come down. Ain't got no time to fool with you."

Henny remained still and Aunt Beck banged the ceiling again.

"If you up there, I come and get you." Henny felt no fear from this threat; Aunt Beck was too fat to climb ladders, and even if she tried, the thin rungs were barely adequate to support Henny's weight and stood no chance accommodating Aunt Beck's stoutness.

"What you mean trying to walk off with Miss Ariadne's earbobs? You ain't even had you ears pierced. And where you gonna wear fine jewels?"

Fresh tears stung Henny's eyes as she realized that now even Aunt Beck believed her guilty.

When she got no response, the old woman grunted, set down the basket, and left the cabin.

Moments later, she heard Old Sheba. "She be back," she said, cackling with a lack of concern. "That belly git empty and she be back to fills it."

She remained hiding in the loft the rest of the evening, during which she could hear Katie, Nancy, Clevis, and Reuben calling her name. Even Old Sheba called for her, threatening another switching if she didn't appear.

Only Reuben had ventured to look for her in the loft, climbing the ladder to wave a lantern, which revealed nothing but an old corn-husk tick, underneath which Henny's thin, flattened form was undetectable.

"Better come on out right now," Piney had shrieked as she paraded up and down the quarters. "Mr. Lionel layup extra licks for you if you don't. And Miss Vinny wantin' to see you right now!"

That Lavinia wanted her could only mean she had been told. Lavinia's belief in her guilt pained Henny more than anything else. But how could her mistress not believe her guilty with only her word against Ariadne's, a white woman, and the evidence in her apron pocket?

Henny felt trapped. As the evening darkness grew deeper and silence fell on the quarters, she decided she had but one choice. She would have to run away. When she climbed down from the loft, her foot struck Aunt Beck's basket on the dirt floor and she ate a small piece of cornbread and ham, reserving the rest to take with her when she fled at first light.

Of her few possessions, she decided what she would take with her. Besides the treasured lace dress, she had only two others. As soon as she outgrew an outfit, it was passed on to a younger slave, or too well worn for this, found use as scrap cloth for a quilt. She would wear the older, more frayed brown dress to wade the creek and the blue one for later. She would also take her cloak, her mammy's old shawl and bonnet, and all the scraps of ribbons Aunt Beck had given her for her plaits. She would leave her blanket and single pillow for Old Sheba. She would wear her only pair of shoes. She packed her woolen stockings, her three pairs of underdrawers, and sandals in a gunny sack used for gathering fire wood.

To prevent Piney from making a claim for her lace dress, Henny decided to leave it on the side porch where Miss Lavinia would find it. Knowing its origin, her mistress would protect it and keep it out of Piney's hands.

The golden heart, she decided, had been a gift and would remain safely around her neck for as long as she lived. She would never give it up.

When she had placed her belongings in the gunny sack, she crawled into bed and pulled the patch-work quilt around her neck. As she had done so many times in the past, she lay in the darkness while her fingers explored the various fabrics which made up the squares of the quilt. Once again, she found the rare, single patch of silk, soothing and cool, and the soft, pliant velvet one. These squares were Henny's favorites. The touch of the velvet under her fingers reminded her of Miss Lavinia's riding habit. Henny had often caressed these two patches of material as she waited for sleep, and dreamed of having an entire garment made from fine cloth like these.

But now, knowing that clothing like this would never be hers, nor would she ever know the ease and luxury of being a house servant, she touched the golden heart around her neck, hoping the memory of the moment it had been given to her would lessen her sense of loss. But the treasure seemed cold and hard and brought her no comfort. It only reminded her that her goal was gone forever, receding farther and farther away as she finally drifted into the restlessness of unhappy sleep.

Chapter Twenty-Five

Grover Steele stewed impatiently behind the counter at Steele Mercantile Store. He was anxious to close the store to keep an assignation with Mattie Rose Mudley, the fifteen-year-old daughter of Virgil Mudley, the overseer of Hawthorn Hill Plantation. The pudgy, buck-toothed, nineteen-year-old boy furrowed his brow when he saw the two loafing sharecroppers still lounging on the store's porch in stuporous idleness as the sun hovered lower on the horizon.

Instructed by his father to remain open until six o'clock, Grover waited for the last two idlers' hunger to finally rouse them into prodding on home. Stretching themselves like two long-lounging cats, the sharecroppers finally wound down the day's gossip and talk of farming and politics and drifted on home to face their grumbling wives who waited to serve supper.

Now Grover knew his father would be none the wiser if he left early. With two twists of licorice candy tucked in his red flannel shirt, he locked the door and headed for the road behind the store that led to Hawthorn Hill.

In thirty minutes, he was in the loft of a field barn where he and Mattie Rose had been meeting secretly for over a year.

The pudgy boy's receding chin fell and scowling lips covered his protruding teeth in a frown when he realized

Mattie Rose was not nestled expectantly in the special nook they had culled out of the loose hay.

Uttering an oath, Grover reached into his pocket and produced a plug of tobacco, bit off a chew, and lay back to wait. He hoped Mattie remembered to bring a quilt. The horse blanket they had been using was rough and after a session with Mattie, his knees, elbows, and back were scratched and chafed.

Darkness came and Grover's impatience grew. From a door in the loft, lights in the windows of the Hawthorn big house were visible a half mile away. The faint toll of the evening bell could be heard and the squeak of the ladder under the weight of the large, fleshy girl announced Mattie Rose had arrived, first revealing her pear-shaped head with its thin wisps of oily, dun-colored hair.

"Where you been?" Grover said. "I been waitin' for you an hour."

"They watchin' me, darlin'," Mattie Rose cooed as she entered the loft. She grinned rapturously at him, her large, close-together eyes giving her a look of perpetual, confused amazement. "I done come as soon as I can. Looky, I brung a blanket for us."

Mattie Rose, giggling, crawled across the hay and spread the blanket. In the deep shadows, Grover attempted to encircle her substantial girth with his arms.

"Doncha want to kiss me?" She tittered again and brushed her thin, oily straight hair out of her face.

"I reckon."

They fumbled in the darkness, lips seeking lips, until Mattie Rose pushed him away.

"Oh!" she said, twisting her face with distaste and wiping her mouth with the back of her hand. "You been chewing tobaccy agin. I done told you I wasn't givin' you no kisses if you been chewin' tobaccy."

"Just hush and lay down."

"Ain't gonna do it. I'm right mad at you anyhow. Ourt not to come."

"What you mad about now? I ain't done nothin'."

"You wantin' to kiss me with tobaccy mouth...Never brang me nothin'..."

"Did so. Brought you this horehound candy you cut sich a shine over."

"Give it to me."

"Ain't going to 'till you lay down."

"You give me that candy and I'll kiss you even with tobaccy. And then I tell you what me and Ma plannin'."

Snatching the candy, Mattie Rose plopped it into her mouth and lay down beside Grover.

"Ma says they caught that little old blue-eyed youngin' Miss Lavinia teachin' to be her maid stealin' today. Me and Ma got it made up to ax Miss Hawthorn if I can be her maid. That blue-eyed one hidin' out or run off after they caught her. Miss Lavinia has 'em all lookin' fer her and they can't find her."

Grover eased his hand around her waist and drew her to him.

"Now you quit it." Mattie squirmed and made a halfhearted slap at his hands. "I'm gettin' tired of you grabbin' at me the very first thang! We don't never talk ner nothin'."

"Ain't no need of talkin'. You know what we like."

"You just hush. You talkin' about what you like. You think you can bring a little old piece of horehound candy and get anything you want." Her lower lip protruded in a hurt pout and her voice fell to a muted whine. "And what about that pretty red calico cloth you been promisin' me? I just needs enough to make me a dress."

"I done told you that red calico ain't been cut on yet. If I bring it now, I'll have to cut it myself and Pa knows we ain't sold none. If I wait till he's sold some, it'll already be cut and he won't be able to tell if I snitch some then."

Sullen silence followed, then the rustle of reaching arms and twisting bodies, and Mattie said, "And you never say nothin' about us gettin' married no more."

"Why you got to start on that agin? That's all you ever talk about."

"'Cause you been promisin' me for a year, that's why."

"I told you I was waiting for Pa to give me part of the store. He won't give me nothin' if I get married right off. He's waitin' till I'm twenty-one—just two year from now. Then he'll give me part of the store and a house to live in."

"I ain't livin' in that house down from the store you tole me about."

"See? Here I just about has Pa talked into fixin' up that house and you—"

"I done told you a dozen times I ain't livin' in a house that black people has lived in. Be like livin' in slave cabins."

"Why, Mattie, ain't no blacks lived in that house for years."

"Don't matter. They was blacks that used to live there."

They lay in the darkness in silence for a while but soon Grover heard quiet sobs coming from beside him.

"What you cryin' about?"

"Sometime I think you don't really love me."

"I done told you I loved you about a hundred times. Why I have to keep saying it agin and agin?"

"A girl just likes to hear it ever now and then. Sometime you act like you don't want to marry me at all. Sometime I think you just claim you love me so you can have your way with me."

"That ain't so. And what about you and Freel Shankrall?"

"Never seen Freel but twict. Don't like him near as much as you."

"Well, don't I bring you candy? And that silk ribbon for your hair? My Pa kill me if he knowed all the stuff I slip out of the store for you."

"Well, when we going to git married?" Her tears were angry now, her voice strident with frustration. "Ma and Pa both told me they'd make the X for me. You been promisin' and promisin' to marry me for near a year. I done begged you to go to the courthouse with me last month. And last Christmas woulda been a good time, too. I think we ought to get married next month or I ain't going to see you no more."

The threat of being denied Mattie Rose's favors alarmed Grover almost as much as the thoughts of marrying her.

"Now, Mattie, honey...darlin'..."

Mattie jerked away from his embrace but Grover moved closer and eased his arms around her. After momentary, perfunctory resistance she rested her head on his chest and whimpered softly.

"You reckon we could get married before the summer's over? Ma and Pa done caught me gone three or four times and threatenin' to kill me if they find I with a man. If we could git married, they couldn't do nothin'."

Grover stroked her limpid, oily hair and made further promises of marriage and a house that had only been occupied by white people. Presented with the second piece of candy, Mattie Rose was forthcoming with her affection and Grover felt that his efforts had been adequately repaid.

After a second, less satisfactory coupling an hour later, he was still determined he would never marry Mattie Rose Mudley, but he hoped she would not realize that for at least the rest of the summer—and perhaps a little into the fall before cold weather set in again.

The next morning, Grover awoke to find Mattie Rose asleep beside him, her dun-colored hair falling in thin wisps over her pear-shaped face. Sometimes she slipped away during the night, or before sunrise the next morning, but this time the plump, submissive girl was still there, lying on the blanket breathing quietly, her mouth ajar, her body sprawled provocatively beside him.

Unsure of the hour and expected to open the store that morning, Grover wondered if he had time to awaken Mattie Rose for another encounter. With her ever-increasing talk of marriage, he hesitated. As her close-set eyes began to flutter awake and she brushed aside the strands of her hair, his eyes fell to her prone form with her small, almost indistinct breasts and her milk-white legs and arms askew like a tossed-aside rag doll. Grover's desire was stirred anew. It wouldn't take that long if it weren't for all the promising and pledging and pacifying she made necessary before.

Propping himself up on one elbow, Grover tried to see if the sun had risen or if this was just predawn light intensified by the whiteness of the mist. As he heard Mattie Rose yawn, he felt her chubby hand reach for him.

But he ignored the gentle tug she gave him, distracted by the sight of something outside the open loft door. In the distance, something was moving in the fog that hovered over the twisting creek.

Barely discernable in the mist, he saw a small figure wading the shallow edge of the water. As the figure advanced, he saw it was a little black girl cautiously maneuvering her way through the water.

"Mornin' darlin'," Mattie Rose's sleepy voice greeted him.

Grover grunted and continued to watch the black girl's progress up the creek. She held her shoes and a gunny sack above her head as she wobbled unsteadily, her balance challenged by the slippery stones of the creek bottom.

"What you lookin' at?" Mattie Rose said, rubbing her eyes.

"Down there, in the creek. That little ol' black girl."

"Whut?" Awake now, Mattie Rose sat upright and draped one arm over Grover's shoulder. "Well, if that ain't the dumbest thing I ever seen. Out wadin' the creek as cold as it is. She ain't got no sense at all."

"She runnin' off, you fool. Must be bloodhounds after her."

"I don't hear no hounds. And how you know she runnin'?"

"'Cause she took to water—tryin' to lose her scent."

Suddenly, the little girl lost her footing and fell backward into the creek. Mattie Rose let out a whoop of laughter and pointed to the child, submerged up to her chest and struggling to hold the shoes and sack she carried above her head.

"Looky! She done got all wet!" Mattie said, laughing with delight.

The little girl, still managing to hold the shoes and bag above the water, regained her footing and continued up the creek, where she cautiously waded ashore just below a corn crib down the hill from the barn.

"I know who that is!" Mattie Rose cried. "Hit's that little old blue-eyed 'un I told you about—the one they catch stealin'.'"

Grover's brow knitted in thought as he watched Henny scurry from the creek bank to the corn crib.

"Reckon the Hawthorns pay much to get her back?"

"Reckon not and her stealin' off 'em."

"But they's others that might. Down South."

Reluctant to confide in Mattie Rose the details of his family's occasional involvement in the illegal slave trade, Grover said no more. Grover and his brothers had more than once discovered runaway slaves and sold them to the Stratchey brothers, slave traders who passed through the area looking for such deals and asked no questions as to the slave's origins. The Stratcheys promptly transported them out of Virginia for sale farther south.

Stolen horses, slaves, a barrel of whiskey snatched by some dishonest overseer from his master's cellar, even a pack of good hunting dogs were the Stratchey brothers' stock and trade, and the legalities of their possession mattered not as long as they were miles away before the property was missed. The contraband was mixed with the occasional legitimate purchase of property, human and otherwise, and the Stratchey brothers operated freely, passing through states from Virginia to Alabama.

Grover watched Henny approach the corn crib and circle it until she found the door and disappeared inside.

"Tell you what, Matt," he said, getting to his feet. "I'm gonna lock that black piece in the corn crib. Bet I can get a pretty penny for her next time the Stratchey brothers comes through."

"Maybe you can get enough for us to get married on," Mattie Rose said, but Grover made her no answer.

Three nights later, Grover and Mattie Rose once again met in the barn loft. It had been the first time since they had seen Henny's fall in the creek and her retreat to the corn crib.

The urgency of their three-day separation brought them into almost immediate copulation and when their passion was exhausted, they lay sprawled side-by-side on the blanket-covered straw. Grover, proud of his business acumen in the sale of Henny, told Mattie about his cleverness.

"That uppity old black woman that runs the Hawthorn house come to the store buyin' stuff."

"That must been that hateful ol' Emma. I hate her. Treats me no bettern a black in the wash house when I helps Mommy."

"She was wantin' embroidery thread for ol' Miz Hawthorn and vanilla flavorin' and I axed her if they ever caught them Hawthorn runaways. She said they never and when I ax her if they was offerin' a reward, she said they wasn't, that neither one was worth two grains of corn. I ax her why ol' Miz Hawthorn takin' on so 'cause that little one gone and actin' like she want her back so bad and the old woman say it 'cause she a thief and they wantin' to teach her a lesson."

"And you had done sole her off!" Mattie Rose said with admiration.

"Yep," Grover said with pride. "The Stratchey brothers will see she's on the block in Carolina or Georgia inside a week or so."

Although Grover was proud of his transaction, he did not mention the gold pendant in his pocket, which he assumed Henny had stolen, and told Mattie he had only gotten thirteen dollars for her when it was actually twenty. He would wait until a peddler came through to try and sell

the pendant, or go to Lynchburg or Richmond where he was
sure he could get a better price.

"I fetched her from the corn crib when the Stratchey
brothers come through and told her they was going to
Canada. She was right ready to go and when she seen them
other blacks in the Stratcheys' wagon, she jumped right in."

Grover laughed at Henny's gullibility and his cleverness
in so easily securing her trust. "She never noticed they was
two in chains, I reckon. Just climbed right on in like she
bound for Canada for sure. Guess she be mighty surprised
when she find out the Canada she going to gonna really be
Georgia or Alabama!" Grover whooped with laughter and
slapped his thighs.

Mattie Rose made a playful swat at Grover and giggled.

"You right awful, Grover Steele," she said, grinning at his
cleverness.

Grover neglected to tell Mattie Rose of Henny's stricken
face when the wagon pulled away from the store. He made
no mention of the girl's outstretched hand and pleading
cries for the return of her heart-shaped pendant he had
forcibly taken and the resulting struggle to keep her from
leaping from the wagon once she realized it would not be
returned. His laughter faded as he remembered the look of
the agonized black face, her large blue eyes pleading in grief
and heartbreak, and the sound of her cries as the wagon
lurched down the road, the desperate child restrained by
one of the shackled slaves from attempting to jump from the
wagon and retrieve her treasure.

"Hell, she stole the damn thing," Grover told himself,
and the image of the outstretched hand and watery blue eyes
vanished from his conscience, just as the retreating wagon
had, never to be recalled again.

"And you got thirteen dollars for her. Why, we ken git married on that!"

Grover shifted uncomfortably on the blanket. "Not before Pa gives me the store. And he ain't doing that till I turn twenty-one."

Mattie Rose rolled away from him and her voice became small and childlike. There was a long, sullen silence before she finally spoke. "I...I ain't had my...my issue this month."

"You ain't had whut?"

"My woman-time..."

She turned back toward him, her lip extended in a pout, her close-together eyes stealing shy, embarrassed glances at his reaction.

Grover stared back at her blankly. Then the dawn of unpleasant realization crept into his consciousness and his features froze in quiet terror.

"What I ain't had means we got a baby started!" Mattie Rose blurted.

Grover was too stunned to speak.

"You can put your eyes back in your head now. Ain't that surprised, are you? We ain't been in this barn loft churnin' butter all last year, has we?"

"You...you bigged?"

Matilda Rose nodded, watching him through the strands of dun-colored hair hanging over her face.

Grover's jaw fell slack and he blinked his eyes rapidly, the weight of his dilemma lodging like a chunk of ice in his chest.

"I for certain now. Done missed twict. I ain't never been late with it a single time since I started." She lowered her head, as if ashamed to be speaking of such things. "Me and my sister, Zena, always starts and finishes the very same days and this time I never—but I never told her. Same way last month. Me and Zena been noticin' we alike in timin' since we thirteen. Never missed it by so much as a day 'till these two times."

Mattie Rose snuggled close against him and laid her head against his shoulder and spoke in a small voice. "Well, ain't you happy? We has to get married now. I mean with us got a baby started and all."

"Not yet, we ain't."

"Well, I reckon we does!" Mattie Rose sat upright. Her voice grew strong with conviction. "I ain't havin' people talk 'bout me got a baby and not married. Like Macy Shankrall. I'm tellin' Ma and Pa this very night. They both beat the devil out of me in a baby-way and not married. I ain't tellin' 'bout the baby, but I'm tellin' them we gettin' married next week! So there."

"How you know it ain't Freel Shankrall's?"

Mattie Rose pounded him on the shoulder with her fist. "'Cause I never done it with Freel Shankrall but twict way back six months ago. It couldn't be hisn."

"How I know it never got lodged-up and just now took root? Don't see why we got to do it next week, no how. Looks like we ought to wait—"

"I ain't waitin' no longer than a week and I'm tellin' Ma and Pa tonight." Mattie Rose began to cry and her weeping soon became noisy sobs. "You just tryin' to git out of it, I know. You goin' to try and leave me with a baby and not marry me and then nobody want me but somebody like Freel Shankrall and I ain't havin' it. You marryin' me whether you wants to or not. Pa'll make sure of that. Reckon you no better than Burl Walters when he got my sister, Zelda, in the family way. Pa threatened to shoot him unless he done the right thing. And the Hawthorns ain't going to like the way you done me neither. Miz Hawthorn don't even allow blacks on the place to have babies if they ain't married up right."

"I was jest thinkin' we ought to be engaged for a while. Like proper folks do. Not just run off all of a sudden and get married. Maybe even has the weddin' at the church and not at the courthouse or preacher's parlor."

Matilda Rose shook her head violently.

"Don't want no 'gagement. What we been doin' in this barn loft for near a year 'gagement enough." She struggled to her feet and, still sobbing, slipped on her dress and headed toward the loft ladder. "I'm tellin Ma and Pa right now."

"Wait!" Grover said. Panicked and desperate, his thoughts raced to find a reason to halt her action. "What if I done got you something to prove our engagement? Something to stand for it? A special engagement present I been layin' off to give you?"

Mattie Rose, her pudgy face still petulant and hurt, stopped and turned around. Still suspicious but interested, she brushed aside the hair caught in the moisture of tears on her cheeks. "What you talkin' about?"

"Got it right here in my pocket."

"You think an ol' piece of horehound candy—"

"Ain't that. Somethin' I been savin' for you. I bought it off a peddler."

"You got me a rang?" Her eyes brightened at the prospect.

Grover reluctantly removed the pendant from his pocket and dangled it like bait in front of Mattie Rose, who eyed the talisman suspiciously.

"See? That a lot better than a rang."

Mattie Rose's suspicion softened. Grover placed the chain around her neck and she glowed with happiness. Her close-together eyes glistened and her lips curled into a vacuous, rapturous grin.

"Reckon it wouldn't hurt none to wait just one more week," she said.

Chapter Twenty-Six

⊷⇒⇐⊷

A shadow of sadness fell over Hawthorn Hill as Henny's absence extended day after day. Soon hope that she was hiding because of humiliation, or fear of punishment and sale, could no longer explain her absence. That a nine-year-old child could flee alone on foot, eluding hounds and slave patrols, added to the mystery and anxiety. After a second week, deep despair descended on the plantation as black and white alike grieved at the little girl's disappearance.

Lavinia was in a state of near hysteria and ordered every inch of the plantation, including the swamp, be searched again and again. The efforts of Margaret, Edmund, and Cornelia—and even Lionel—did little to alleviate Lavinia's sense of loss and suspicion that Henny was the victim of a great wrong.

No one believed Henny was a thief, the opinion angrily expressed by the blacks out of earshot of the whites and bolstered by their long dislike of Ariadne. Privately, the whites agreed with the blacks.

"It's a scheme of Piney's or You-Know-Who," said Margaret.

"Margaret! You know Emma would never do such a thing!" said Cornelia, and added in a lower, less certain voice, "nor would Ariadne."

– 409 –

Only Emma and Piney asserted Henny's guilt, and Ariadne, pleading headaches, remained sequestered in her room and chose not to discuss the matter.

Even Lionel seemed disturbed by Henny's disappearance and explored with the sheriff the possibility that the child might have been abducted, as sometimes happened when a slave, on the run or hiding, was snatched and sold in another area. It was rumored that Charles Hicks was involved in such trading when the reward for a runaway was less than could be realized through selling the slave at a distant market.

Lavinia's exorbitant financial rewards for Henny's recovery eliminated that possibility, however, and Hicks and his men diligently searched for her locally and even in surrounding counties. Yet the little girl's crime and disappearance remained a disturbing, frustrating mystery.

One afternoon shortly after Henny vanished, two little sheepish Harveys appeared in the parlor where Lavinia and Margaret were listening to Cornelia's latest collection of gossip from a visit that morning at Mrs. Hunter's.

"We got something to tell," said nine-year-old "Little" Lionel in a quiet voice.

"Then tell us, dear," his grandmother said.

"Well...the day you all went to that old lady's funeral." The boy looked at the floor as his sister, "Little" Lavinia, shuffled uncomfortably at his side.

"Go on, dear," Cornelia persisted.

"Well, Mammy Emma told us to stay outside and Ariadne...Aunt Ariadne said so, too."

"Yes?"

"Well, we was playing hide-and-seek and since everybody else was hiding in the yard me and Lavinia decided to hide inside. We was just going to be there for a minute."

"I'd been 'it' nearly all morning and was tired of it," said eight-year-old Little Lavinia. "The best hiding places is in the house, and...and we slipped in the pantry and hid beside Mammy Emma's pie chest."

"And Ariadne—Aunt Ariadne—came in and put things in Henny's apron pocket that was hanging behind the pantry door. She didn't see us but we saw her and stayed hid and looked to see what she put in there when she left."

"It was earbobs and rings and things," said Little Lavinia. "And then she claimed Henny stole them. But we knowed better."

"Knew better, dear," corrected Cornelia in a strange voice as she looked helplessly at Margaret and Lavinia. "But why didn't you tell us earlier?"

"We was afraid Ariadne would whip us. Or Mammy Emma because we was in the house when we wasn't supposed to be." Little Lionel hung his head.

Lavinia embraced both children and kissed them. "Thank you, darlings, you have done the right thing by coming forward."

"I am so proud of my girl and boy," said Margaret, also giving her children a hug and kiss. "And you will not be punished because you told the truth."

"Kiss Granny, too," said Cornelia, unable to hold back her tears. "It was very brave and honorable of you to come forward in Henny's defense."

When the children returned to their play, the three women sat silently and contemplated Ariadne's deed.

At last, Lavinia's anger found a voice. "How utterly evil. To incriminate a child." She shook her head in bewilderment and blinked back her tears.

"Let's say no more about it," Cornelia said. "Ariadne returns to Richmond next week and she need not know we are on to her."

"But I wonder why?" Margaret asked. "Why?"

"Yes," said Lavinia. "Why?"

Cornelia, sobbing without restraint now, dabbed at her eyes with her handkerchief and said, "Lavinia, dear, the day Ariadne lost Lionel, a light—"

Chapter Twenty-Seven

Henny's disappearance and the injustice done to her continued to haunt Lavinia, as did her concern for Angelica's fate in Richmond. No news arrived to clarify either black's fate. The search for Henny was continued by Charles Hicks.

A visit from Lavinia's youngest son, Frederick, from Williamsburg, where he was to enter the College of William and Mary in the fall, provided her with a pleasant distraction but failed to alleviate her gnawing anxiety and sorrow. Frederick's enthusiasm for the study of law was so great, however, that she felt deprived of her son's company.

"I suppose I'll have to go to law school to have more than five minutes with my baby," Lavinia lamented. "All he wants to do is retry old cases with Lionel and his grandfather."

"Well, after all, dear, his cousin was Chief Justice John Marshall," Cornelia said. "We are related on my side of the family. It's in the boy's blood."

"Well, it's not in Lionel's blood," Lavinia said. "He's first a farmer and second a lawyer. He'd rather draw up the plans for a slave cabin than a will."

In the early, happy years of their marriage, Lavinia had often taken a hamper of food to share a picnic with him to find him in the fields, rubbing the satin-like surface of a tobacco leaf against his cheek in appreciation of the good yield and quality of the crop. Knowing that he felt embarrassed and guilty in preferring work in the fields to that of the more prestigious profession for which he had been educated, she had told him she was much happier married to a farmer than a lawyer.

"It was my destiny to be married to a farmer in the first place," she had told him. "Either to you or Will Reynolds, and I'm mighty glad it was you."

With Frederick at home, he could combine the two—work in the fields or repair a broken wagon axle—and at the same time discuss law with his son, who accompanied him every day on his duties.

Inevitably the subject of slavery came up and Lavinia was pleased to hear her son voice his doubts about the institution and its legal and moral implications.

Maybe my abolitionism has been passed on, Lavinia thought, proud of her son's thoughtful evaluation of slavery.

Lionel countered with the standard rhetoric that had sustained slavery for thousands of years in the world and two hundred fifty years in America.

"But Papa, what about the Omnibus Bill, the Compromise of 1850—" Frederick said at dinner one evening.

"Enough, the both of you," commanded Cornelia, who had listened to nothing but legal discussions and debates between her husband, son, and grandson for four successive evenings. "Isn't it enough that you practice law every day in Richmond? Must you practice it at the dinner table, too?"

"Oh, Granny, we're just having a discussion of—"

"I don't care. It's not interesting," Cornelia said. "Why, I don't imagine you even know your kinship with Justice

Marshall! His mother was a Keith, and her mother a Randolph, and—"

A lengthy monologue on the Randolph genealogy followed until one of her bored grandchildren, seated at the children's table set up at the far end of the dining room, said, "Granny, tell us about that cousin of ours that had a baby and hid it in a stump in the woods and—"

"Why, Lionel Harvey, where did you ever hear such a thing?" Cornelia gasped, and she threw her son an accusing glare.

"Uncle Lionel told us about it."

"And Uncle Lionel should be ashamed of himself. And at any rate, there shall be no discussion of it. It happened fifty years ago. And it's not true."

Grunts of disappointment came from the children's table and Cornelia changed the subject. "Tell us about this young lady you've been seeing in Fredericksburg," she said to Frederick.

His cheeks turning red, Frederick told them about Miss Frances Robertson, with whom he was developing a serious attachment.

To the family's relief, Cornelia knew of the young lady's family, found them to be of suitable lineage, and gave her blessing to her grandson's continued courtship.

"Now, Granny, I'm not sure Frances feels the same way about me as I do her."

"She probably won't have you," Lionel teased as he served himself a slice of ham.

"There's no young lady that wouldn't have my Freddie," said Lavinia. "She's probably head over heels in love. But she will let you know in the most clever and unsuspected way when she wants. You see, son, you men think you are so smart, but it is we women who control all stages of courtship. Right on up to the altar."

"Indeed we do," said Margaret. "I know I did." She threw her mother a little look of triumph, remembering the long ago conflict over Alexander Harvey.

"Do you agree, Papa? Is it all controlled by the female?" Lionel asked.

"I'm afraid in the case of your mother and sister it was," Mr. Edmund said.

"Well, I wish Frances would give me a hint," said Frederick. "I haven't been forward, but I've been attentive and always a perfect gentleman and she... Well, Frances is so shy she just blushes and sighs all the time."

The Hawthorns laughed and only Ariadne seemed to find no humor or interest in the young man's dilemma. Since Henny's innocence had been established, Lavinia's coldness toward Ariadne had been undisguised, and Margaret was outright hostile to her cousin. Lavinia told the blacks in the house and quarters of Henny's innocence, calling it only "a mistake" at Cornelia's insistence. Cornelia had also insisted that direct confrontation with Ariadne be avoided, if only to protect the grandchildren who had exposed her.

"My dear," said Cornelia, swept up by the discussion on the art of courtship, "I used to blush constantly around your grandfather. And he proposed right away!"

"Mrs. Hawthorn, you have no shame," Mr. Edmund chided. "And your devices were a complete waste. I was yours without them."

Cornelia beamed at her husband's flattery. "You're such a gentleman, Mr. Hawthorn. But you know as well as I that girls in my day were never as forward and crass in courtship as young ladies of today. Why, I don't believe either of you girls could ever blush at will."

"I could, but never needed to," said Lavinia.

"I always did," said Margaret.

"Why, you inherited that from me!" trilled Cornelia. "It's a Randolph trait, you know."

"A good fake faint is good, I hear," added Lavinia.

"Oh, I found it essential," bubbled Cornelia. "A faint will get you anything you want and—" Remembering she was accused by her family of still using the device, she bit her lip and elaborated no further.

"Mrs. Hawthorn," Lionel said to Lavinia, rescuing his mother from further exposure. "You make me look like a simpleton. Surely I wasn't that easy."

"I think it took six words."

"What were they, dear?" Cornelia leaned toward her.

"'I suppose I'll marry Will Reynolds.'"

Lionel laughed and Lavinia felt the happiness of a genuine blush.

"So many belles were after my boy," Cornelia said proudly. "Pined away. Why, he broke more hearts—"

Then, as if everyone remembered her presence at the same time, all eyes turned toward the one person who had said nothing during the conversation: Ariadne. She sat, not eating and as still as a statue. Stiffly erect, like a dark malevolent presence, she seemed unaware they were looking at her, her mouth drawn in a cruel straight line, her eyes fixed on Lavinia with withering disgust.

"It is no surprise to me that common women of your class and background would use less than honest tricks to accomplish your deceitful aims," she said. "Mountain people are known for their disregard of principle and decency, aren't they? Secretive, backward, undermining, like—" Her voice was cold and even, little more than a whisper. It was as if she were speaking only to herself, her words only a thought, but the menace with which she spoke as passionate as a shout, chillingly intense and vicious.

"Well, not all blushes work," said Margaret sarcastically. "You used to turn red as a beet. Brought bulls charging from the fields—but no husband!"

At the children's table, little faces were open-mouthed and wide-eyed, and the main table was likewise speechless, forks and glasses frozen in hands as if turned into stone.

Ariadne ignored Margaret and directed her intense, vicious words at Lavinia. "And why should you blush? I hear shotguns spur more marriages than civilized behavior in the backwoods where you come from. Did you tell him you had a baby in you, too?" Ariadne said, her voice rising.

There was a simultaneous shocked intake of breath. "Was that also a part of your plot to get him? With your inferior family, what else could one expect?"

Even the seldom nonplussed Lionel seemed taken aback, and Margaret's fork slipped from her fingers and clattered to her plate.

"I will thank you to know, Ariadne Woodhull," Lavinia said, her face ashen, "that when you insult me it matters little, considering your jealousy, and spite, and small-mindedness. But when you insult my family—"

"Now, ladies," Mr. Edmund sputtered to no avail. "Let us remember—"

"You go too far, Ariadne," Margaret interrupted.

"And what do you know?" Ariadne directed her ire toward Margaret. "You married beneath you when you took that fat little preacher. Did you—"

Margaret's voice joined Lavinia's in insulted outrage, like two threatened animals defending their young.

"Enough, enough!" Mr. Edmund said sternly, and Cornelia emitted a hysterical little shriek, desperately looking from face to face as if seeking rescue.

"You know the Harveys represented no family—"

"How dare you talk about my Alexander's family! The Harveys were governors of North Carolina!"

"Oh!" Cornelia cried. She seized the small brass bell beside Lavinia. Rattling it frantically, she whimpered helplessly in an attempt to break the hold of the three women's scalding exchange.

"I can think of no member of my family who would have the dishonor to besmirch the reputation of a child by falsely accusing her of theft, " Lavinia said.

"Or make her servants hate her and run away more than any household in Richmond," Margaret added.

All three women bent over the table and vented their long suppressed invective, now beyond restrain, and shouted angrily, overlapping each other with insult and fury.

"It's not my fault you couldn't find a husband," Lavinia's voice rang out. "You had nearly a lifetime to get Lionel—fifteen or twenty years. I had three weeks. It's not my fault you couldn't snare him."

"Snare me?" Lionel blurted. "Was I no more than a fox in a hunt?"

"More like a rabbit, as I recall," Lavinia said, her anger so intense she was surprised its sharpness extended to her retort to Lionel.

"You're a wicked, hateful old maid! Just jealous be—" Margaret said, suddenly cut off by a hysterical scream from Cornelia.

"Stop! Stop! I won't have this!" The old lady looked desperately at Mr. Edmund and gave Lionel a sharp kick under the table. "Mr. Hawthorn, order them to stop!"

"Civility, girls, let's maintain civility," the old gentleman stammered, rapping his knuckles on the table.

"I could have married," Ariadne said.

Lavinia lifted her head in triumph. "But not Lionel Hawthorn! Not after he met me!" she said, gloating. "And you didn't marry, did you? From what I hear only the impoverished knocked on your door."

"I could have!"

"Someone after your money?" Lavinia asked. "A meal ticket?"

"Oh, you should have seen some of her callers, Lavinia!" Margaret said, laughing. "Ancient old things...and ugly...and repulsive... Old Judge Povall even!"

"No white trash field hands? Why, I bet Mr. Mudley was available at the time! If only you had known!"

"Or one of the Shankrall boys!" Margaret suggested with glee.

"Now, girls," Mr. Edmund had become quite pale. "You exceed all—"

"Margaret! Lavinia! Ariadne!" Cornelia's protests had become wails.

"I could have married! Alfred Byrd or Lucius Claibourn," Ariadne insisted.

Margaret shrieked with derisive laughter. "Alfred Byrd! Why, you were eighteen and he over fifty when he called on you! Ended up a drunkard. And Lucius Claibourn, the ugliest man in ten counties. And landless! Penniless good-for-nothings, all. Only after one of your daddy's plantations."

"It could hardly have been for your charm or good manners," Lavinia added. "For all your highborn airs, your behavior is worse than any field hand I've ever seen. Every black in this county has more refinement that you."

"How dare you compare me with filthy blacks!"

"Mammy is present, Ariadne," Lionel said sternly. "You have said enough."

The battle had waged beyond his appreciation of a good cat fight, which he had enjoyed in barrooms and brothels for years when fought in the most violent and vulgar extremes. To see one now, among women more refined, was amusing for the variance of the participants, who, ladies or not, abandoned decorum as readily as the less respectable of their sex and vented spleens with equal ferocity. But he would tolerate no ill words or insults to his Mammy.

"Dessert! Emma! Dessert!" Cornelia shrieked, waving her napkin like a flag of surrender with one hand and ringing the calling bell with the other. "Edmund! Make them stop!"

When Margaret made a move to rise, Lionel quickly restrained her and rapped his knuckles on the table.

"Ladies! Please!" he said. "Remember the children." He nodded toward the children's table, where six little faces were transfixed by the conflict, mouths agape and eyes bulging with delight, astonishment, and even a little fear.

"Children, perhaps you should sit at the adult table and we'll put your mother and aunts Ariadne and Lavinia at your table," Mr. Edmund suggested.

"An excellent suggestion, Papa," Lionel said. "Put perhaps at the Shankralls' would be even more suitable—the Shankralls' barn!"

Their uncle's suggestion brought uncertain giggles from the children.

"Dessert! Cake! Pie! Anything!" Cornelia weakly cried again, sinking back in her chair and sobbing into her napkin.

"I fetch it, Miss Cornelia," Emma said, rushing to the sideboard where she began scooping servings of cobbler into dessert dishes.

With the acrimonious exchange smoldering beneath a thin veneer of silence, the three combatants sat down. Challenging glares between Margaret and Lavinia and Ariadne subsided into guarded, defensive stares. Only the sound of Cornelia's weeping and Emma's scraping the servings of the cobbler into dishes interrupted the silence.

Finally, Lionel, recovering his diplomatic mien, presented a soothing smile and said, "Mammy, I believe this is the best apple cobbler I ever put in my mouth."

"I think so too, Lionel," Mr. Edmund said.

A forced, awkward discussion of Aunt Beck's cooking skills between Lionel and Edmund failed to restore genuine harmony at the table and the dining room was quickly vacated.

Ariadne, leaving her dessert untouched, announced that she would be leaving Hawthorn Hill for Richmond the next day and retired to her room.

"Wasn't that good?" Little Lionel whispered to his sister, Little Lavinia, as they left the dining room.

"Better than some ol' baby in a stump," his sister replied.

When the men decided to play cards in the library, Margaret and Lavinia joined Cornelia in the parlor, where the matriarch of the family still wept.

"I cannot stand such discord in the family," Cornelia sobbed.

"Well, she started it," said Margaret. "She insulted Lavinia, her family, and my Alexander, too. And those grandchildren you love so much."

"But to comment on her unmarried state was cruel."

"Not as cruel as what she did to Henny," said Lavinia.

Even Cornelia, who attempted to palliate any unpleasantness, had no defense for the injustice done to Henny. "Oh, but dear, poor Ariadne has lost so much. First her mama and papa in that awful fire. I tried so hard to be a mother to her."

"And you were, Mrs. Hawthorn," said Lavinia, taking Cornelia's hand. "No one could have been a more devoted mother than you."

"You're so sweet to say so," Cornelia said, managing a weak smile. "You know, Lavinia, when Lionel married you, a light went out in Ariadne forever."

Part Two

Chapter Twenty-Eight

For days the Stratchey brothers' wagon lumbered along the rutted, uneven roads. Henny ached from the constant jolting of the rickety vehicle as it lurched and rocked behind the two broken-down horses driven by the Stratcheys.

Harsh, cruel men, the taller, gaunt Stratchey was the leader. A snarling, sallow-faced man in his forties, he gave orders to his younger brother and hurled threats and invective at the blacks huddled in the wagon. He had an ax-blade nose, sunken cheeks, and dirty, gray-streaked hair. His mismatched eyes frightened Henny; one, non-seeing and dead, saw nothing from behind a half-closed, slanting lid, while the other bulged with wide-eyed intensity as if to compensate for the unseeing one. He sometimes wore a patch over his bad eye, but more often he did not, making his appearance frightening to Henny and the two younger children also in the wagon.

His younger brother, in his twenties and sprouting a sparse, rust-colored beard streaked with tobacco juice, had the same menacing countenance. Cruel, shifty eyes darted from one passenger to another beneath the brim of a hat pulled low over his forehead. To evenly return either man's gaze ignited an attack of verbal abuse: "And what air you lookin' at?" followed by curses and foul names. Henny was particularly shocked when the men took God's name in vain.

As the wagon rattled on, the sun sank low in the sky. Henny ached for pone bread, mush, or a yam the men allowed the passengers at the single meal they received each day. Her throat hurt when she swallowed and the cough she had developed after falling in the chilling creek the morning she ran away was worse.

"Hush that damn hackin'," the slant-eyed Stratchey ordered, and she tried to suppress the cough as much as she could. She felt hot and weak and longed to sleep but was kept awake by the lurching wagon and the maddening screech of a warped wheel every time it rotated.

The other passengers were black also, consisting of two men in their twenties, chained at the ankles and wrists; a woman with a baby; and an elderly man who looked even older than Uncle Lemiel. Completing the group were two little girls, six- and seven-years-old, who sat isolated from the others, huddled together in periodic, fearful whimpering. The frightened little girls had become a target of sport for the older Stratchey, who took pleasure in climbing into the back of the wagon and suddenly lunging toward the girls, pressing his face close to theirs with his head turned to expose the frightening dead eye and drooping lid. When they cried out and drew back, he laughed with sadistic satisfaction.

Henny wondered why her companions seemed so morose since Grover Steele had said they were bound for freedom in Canada. The two chained men were brothers named Jefferson and Washington, called Jeff and Wash. Jeff and Wash often stared at Henny threateningly and made her feel uneasy. The iron bands on their wrists and ankles were attached to chains bolted to the sides of the wagon.

When the two chained men weren't watching Henny, they watched the Stratchey brothers. They sat in the rear of the wagon behind the sacks of potatoes and corn. The only slaves chained, the Stratcheys watched Jeff and Wash more closely than any of the others.

Henny soon learned why Wash and Jeff watched her so carefully, and why they took such care not to allow their chains to rattle or touch the floor with any noise. Partially concealed by the potatoes and corn, they labored feverishly to disconnect their bonds from the side of the wagon by silently twisting the metal rings anchoring the chains. At the faintest rattle or clink, the Stratcheys instantly sprung to their feet with their rifle poised in readiness. The fettered men quickly abandoned twisting the chain and shifted to make it appear the rattle came from their natural movements in changing to another position or in lying down.

Henny could see the metal mounting that anchored the chain being worked free as the twisting motion gradually eroded and enlarged the hole in the wood through which bolts secured the chain. Now she understood the black men's threatening glares were a warning not to betray their efforts. At night, the men remained fettered, permitted only to get out to relieve themselves on the side of the road at no greater distance than the tether of the chains permitted.

While one Stratchey drove the wagon, the other acted as guard, a rifle laid across his lap. The older man guarded them now and seemed as weary as the passengers, the lid of his good eye sagging almost as low as his unseeing one. Finally, he ordered his brother to pull to the side of the road.

"Everybody out!" he ordered.

The slaves, listless and bone-weary, began to stir, prodded by the white men's curses, threats, and jabs of the rifle.

"Hurry up, you black dog," the older Stratchey said to the old man who grunted in the struggle to move his stiffened joints over the side of the wagon and find footing on the hub of a wheel. The younger Stratchey gave him a hard push with the barrel of his rifle.

The woman with the baby was ordered to prepare the mush and distribute the cornbread and single sweet potato or turnip provided for the meal. Henny held her baby as she prepared the meager supper over a campfire for which the old man and little girls had gathered twigs and leaves.

Even the tasteless food, especially the sweet potato, seemed good to Henny, who had eaten nothing that day except the single dry crust of cornbread thrown to her that morning by the younger Stratchey. Forbidden to speak, the blacks ate in silence while the white men watched them from the seat of the wagon. When they had eaten, the men ordered the woman with the baby to take the tin plates to a creek beside the road and wash them.

"And be quick about it or I'll bust this damn youngin's head open," the younger Stratchey brother said as the woman handed the baby to Henny. "And wash our plates separate from yorn, and don't be gittin' ourn mixed up with you burr-heads'."

When one of the chained men, slowed by the manacles, had not eaten fast enough, the younger white struck him across the shoulders with the stock of his rifle.

During the days the wagon prodded down the meandering road, Henny's fellow travelers spoke little, and then only in guarded whispers. Any attempt to talk was silenced by the white men, who were mostly silent themselves. Their only sounds were an occasional muted exchange, periodic spitting of tobacco juice, and impatient oaths at the two ancient horses.

"White trash," Henny mumbled to herself, "and the worse I ever see."

The setting sun was only a smudge of light now, blocked by dark, storm-threatening clouds. As the wagon lurched on, the sound of distant thunder and a sudden whipping wind brought rain. At the first drops, the older Stratchey pulled off the road beside a deserted barn.

"Don't get no ideas of runnin'," the man with the drooping eye said, tying the horses' bridles to a tree. "We'll be watchin' and just soon put a hole in any one of your nappy heads as a rabbit's." Both men got down from the wagon and took shelter in the weathered, sagging barn with a roof of warped, upturned wooden shingles. Inside, they watched the blacks who scampered to the center of the wagon and sought shelter under a large scrap of canvas as the rain began to fall with full force.

Huddled under the canvas, his whispers covered by the sound of the rain, the elderly black man asked Henny, "What your name, child?" He had white, crinkly hair, just like Uncle Lemiel, and a short, sparse beard. His black face was deeply lined, and his eyes were kind in spite of their sadness.

Henny felt none of the suspicion and wariness of him that she did the two men in shackles who had eyed her with such coldness and hostility. "I's Henny."

"I's William. Folks mostly call me Uncle Will," the old man said with a soft, gentle voice. "This is Stella and her little baby, Hannah. And over yonder is Jeff and Wash—they chained up. We all come from Albemarle County. We gets sold when the overseer say I too old for workin' and Stella and her baby don't pay they way neither."

Ashamed because her presence was because she had been accused of stealing, Henny said, "I from Hawthorn Hill Plantation."

Uncle Will continued, "They gets rid of Jeff and Wash 'cause they done tried to run two or three times and our master tired of havin' to pay to has them caught and brought back."

"Hush up under there, you burr-heads!" the voice of the older white man rang out from the barn.

The group was silent until the rain again increased and once more provided the cover to speak.

"How old are you, child?" Uncle Will asked.

"I nine. Pretty close to ten, I reckon."

"Why, you right good-sized for nine. How come they sells you?"

Henny lowered her head and said softly, "Reckon they just don't need me no more—just like you."

Uncle Will nodded with an understanding grunt.

"Who them little girls?" Henny asked, nodding toward the two children, still huddled together.

"Ain't got they names yet," Uncle Will said, shaking his head sadly. "They so grieved and scared they won't say nothin'. They sold away from they mammy and pappy before we come through Lynchburg, though. I heard one of the traders say they part of an estate they dividin'. Somebody died and the children never wants them, so they sells them and divides the money."

Henny didn't know what an estate was and didn't ask. She was too confused by the circumstances which had brought her, bound for Canada, to share the same wagon with Uncle Will and these people. She was running away; the others had been sold.

Then she realized that she too had been sold, just as the others, and the harsh reality settled in her chest like an icy, heavy stone.

"We...we ain't headin' for Canada, are we," she said, more statement than question as a sick, empty feeling greater than the hunger she felt for food, settled in her stomach.

"Lawd, no, child," Uncle Will said. "We done in Carolina. In a few more days, we be in Georgia or South Carolina. Them Stratcheys ain't said, but I 'low we be sold or traded in Savannah or maybe Charleston."

Henny hung her head and tears flowed down her cheeks. She did not want the others to see her cry and hoped the darkness of the approaching night and the canvas covering would conceal her tears. Anger and disappointment overwhelmed her as she realized Grover Steele had lied to her from the beginning and she had believed him. She should have known as much when he forced her to give up the golden heart Lavinia had given her. Old Sheba had spoken the truth: white people were devils and they could never be trusted.

Henny hated white people—all of them. Even Miss Lavinia was probably mean inside, just like Mrs. Mudley and Horace Wroughton and Miss Ariadne and the other white people who pretended to be kind and good but were wicked.

"Wolves in sheep's clothing," Old Sheba had said, and said God put that in the Bible as a warning for black people.

"Now, child, don't fret youself," Uncle Will said. "You is young and pretty. You get a real good buyer—somebody that be good to you."

The old man gently brushed away Henny's tears with his fingers, but his kindness brought her no comfort. She was beyond consolation. Now she wished she had stayed at

Hawthorn Hill and endured Mr. Lionel's flogging. It would be over now and she would still be at home. And even if he sold her to Wroughton, she could slip over after dark to see Old Sheba and Aunt Beck and all her other Hawthorn Hill friends. Homesickness and her yearning for Old Sheba and Aunt Beck tore at her heart.

The word *Georgia* had brought Henny new fear and dread of a place fabled for its harshness and cruelty toward blacks. Old Sheba had known blacks, including some of the Wroughton slaves, from Georgia. They had passed on stories of the abuses black people suffered at the hands of Georgia slave owners. Just as Henny had come to believe that white people were evil, she believed Georgians were among the worst of all, outdone by only those from Alabama and Mississippi and Louisiana.

"Now don't be sad, child," Uncle Will said. "That little lip of yours just about to drag the ground. You be alright. You young. You not be like me." The old man chuckled to himself. "I done dumped my hopper and no use to nobody. Doubt they be nobody bid for me. I too old." His voice trailed off and his face took on the look of weariness of his lifetime of hard labor.

While the downpour lasted, Wash and Jeff worked feverishly to loosen the chains that shackled them to the side of the wagon. At last, the repetitive, twisting motion succeeded in enlarging the hole until the bolt slipped free. Quickly replaced, the bolt appeared as secure as before and its removal was undetectable.

When the men, wearing hard, proud smiles, showed the others their success, Stella said, "You goin' to get us killed for sure. What you think you do when you get that other chain loose? They still locked on you, ain't they?" She held her baby close to her protectively. "You think you do youself or any of us any good with locks still on you legs and arms?" The men did not answer. They turned their attention to the chain on the other side of the wagon, tugging and twisting to enlarge the other hole.

When the rain soon stopped, the Stratchey brothers emerged from the barn, mounted the wagon, and once again the weary travelers lurched down the road.

Two days later, they were deeper into Carolina when they stopped for the night. The white men pulled the wagon off the road into a pasture, where they unhitched the horses and tethered them to a fence to graze.

The younger of the Stratcheys distributed supper of a single yam to each of the blacks. Even unwashed, with the dirt brushed off with her hands, the raw sweet potato tasted good to Henny, who had not eaten since the morning's mush breakfast. She would like to have had a second potato, but was afraid to ask.

The two white men also ate—bread, cheese, and ham they stored under the seat of the wagon for their own use. They also passed a jug of whiskey between them after eating. Then they held a brief, whispered conference during which they grinned and watched the group in careful appraisal. While the younger man stood guard, the one with the slanted eye motioned for Stella to get out of the wagon. When she did not immediately respond, he snarled, "Get out, I say!"

Still uncertain, she looked fearfully at the other blacks and held her baby close to her breast. The man removed a section of canvas from the wagon.

"I said get out, burr-head!" he said. "Leave your youngin' with her."

Stella, her face crumbling, handed her child to Henny and climbed to the ground. The man tossed the canvas over his shoulder and motioned Stella to follow him into the woods across the road. His brother chuckled to himself and remained in the wagon with the rifle across his knees.

After a time, the older man stepped from the edge of the woods and whistled for his brother, still sitting on the wagon. The man got down from the wagon and when he met the other man, he passed him the gun and disappeared into the woods just as his brother had earlier. Stella's baby began to cry and Henny tried to quiet it by rocking it in her arms but with no success.

The man guarding them snarled. "Git that baby quiet!" he said.

Henny rocked the baby faster, but it seemed to increase the child's wailing. The older Stratchey continued to glare at Henny. Suddenly, his good eye lost some of its hardness as it fell from her face and scanned her body right down to her legs and feet.

"Hey, Clem," he shouted toward the woods. "Hurry it up 'fore I have to shoot the wench's damn burr-head youngin'. This squallin' drivin' me loco."

After a while, the man and Stella returned. The man threw the canvas in the back and Uncle Will reached out to assist the woman into the wagon. Her face was expressionless and she stared emptily ahead. Henny caught the hopelessness and bitterness in Stella's flint-hard eyes before she turned away from the others and began to sob quietly. The other blacks watched her with deadened, suffering faces. In the driver's seat, the Stratchey brothers whispered and laughed.

Suddenly, Henny understood what had happened to Stella. The younger Stratchey brother turned in his seat and leered at Henny, "Might break you in a little later, little burr-head. You look like you 'bout ripe enough."

His laughter and that of his brother brought Henny a shudder of sickness. What had happened to Stella could happen to her, too. Then the driver flicked the reins and the wagon lurched forward. The maddening screech of the ungreased axle marked each revolution of the wheels as they took her farther and farther away from Hawthorn Hill and her now hopeless quest for freedom.

Chapter Twenty-Nine

To pacify a saddened Cornelia – who refused to return to Richmond until cordiality was restored between them – Lavinia and Margaret affected a facade of peaceful co-existence with Ariadne. Marked with icy glares, little communication, and veiled insults which passed over Cornelia's head, the women's truce was transparently false but at least satisfied Cornelia, who would tolerate no hostility as had been played out at supper only a few days before.

"My precious husband's latest letter says he simply cannot stand it without me another day," Margaret boasted. "Isn't it wonderful having a husband, Lavinia?" Margaret gave Ariadne a gloating glance. "I must return tomorrow."

The day Margaret arrived in Richmond, she wrote Lavinia, using code words they had previously agreed upon. "Juliet" (code for Angelica) "is still in Richmond! She wants to join her Romeo in P., but it will take at least six weeks for her injury to heal, which is essential because further travels are partially on foot. Ibby is hiding her in Mama and Papa's cellar! Isn't that exciting? Right in our own house, right under Mama and Papa's nose! Ibby thinks she can do this without detection until Juliet's ankle is completely healed. I have written to Romeo's friend in P. of the situation and told him to be patient."

That day, Lavinia visited the Barksdale sisters and expressed her concern that Angelica would be forced to hide indefinitely in her in-laws' house and the continuation of her flight would involve walking.

Miss Phoebe suddenly sat erect in her rocker. "I know exactly what to do!" the old lady said, her corkscrew curls swinging. "When our brothers returned to Baltimore after Mama's funeral, they wanted to take us with them. We wouldn't go because of planting, and our poor tenants being watched and harassed every day." Watching Miss Maude and Lavinia as she developed her plan, she concluded with a flourish, "We'll go now! And we'll take Angelica with us."

"Splendid idea, Phoebe," Miss Maude said with a clap of her hands. "We could pick her up in Richmond and continue right on by train! Whether her ankle is completely healed or not, she'll ride all the way and pose as our maid!"

"Oh, but the risk," Lavinia said, but she was intrigued by the idea.

"Nonsense! What risk is it for two old ladies to be traveling with a maid?"

"Indeed!" agreed Miss Maude. "And we owe you, dear. You got our Bingo and Jane and the baby out of Virginia. We'll get your Angelica out!"

The old ladies squelched Lavinia's doubts and protests exactly as Lavinia had done theirs when they initially opposed her transporting Bingo and Jane to freedom. She finally agreed. "I'll start forging Angelica's papers at once."

"We'll go in a month!" said Miss Phoebe. "That will be time enough to advise our brother."

"And I'll go with you as far as Richmond," said Lavinia. "I have the perfect excuse—fittings for new dresses, which will be ready by then."

With Margaret no longer at Hawthorn Hill, and Lavinia's seeming indifference to Ariadne interpreted by Cornelia as a restoration of peace, the old lady agreed to Ariadne's adamant demand that she return to Richmond at once.

To quickly alert Angelica, Lavinia concealed a message to Angelica of the Barksdales' plan in a package of additional dress patterns to be delivered to Ibby.

Once again, her conscience stabbed her as she thought of Lionel and yet another betrayal of his trust. But it was too late now, and she knew she had gone too far in her betrayal to turn back.

Confined with Cornelia during the long coach ride from Hawthorn Hill to Richmond, Ariadne's nerves were worn to shreds by the old lady's endless discourse on genealogy, her grandchildren, and whispered scandals she had told a dozen times before. Finally, exhausted from her efforts, and rocked by the rhythm of the coach, Cornelia fell asleep and Ariadne stealthily removed the dress patterns from her valise and read the message from Lavinia to Angelica:

Stay where you are. Barksdale sisters and I will be in Rich.
in a month and they will take you by train North with your
posing as their maid. Love, L.

The message returned to the package of dress patterns, and Cornelia still ignorant of its presence, Ariadne pondered the information thoroughly. Its incompleteness left her confused. There had been no indication of where Angelica was now, but she knew she was still in Richmond and could still be caught.

The Hawthorn Hill household released a collective sigh of relief when Ariadne had finally left for Richmond. The absence of her hostility and perniciousness brought peace to the remaining summer days. When Randy left to pursue the hand and heart of his Williamsburg sweetheart, and Mr. Edmund returned to his business and social obligations in Richmond, Lavinia and Lionel were alone at last.

The couple felt a return of the happiness of the early years of their marriage, but after only a week, Lionel was called back to Richmond by responsibilities at the tobacco factory and his law practice.

The morning he left, he and Lavinia embraced on the front porch and held each other for a long time, each reluctant to release the other. Reuben, who had brought Lionel's horse to the front of the house, sneaked glances at his master and mistress, never having seen such expressions of affection between them before.

Lavinia loved the strength and tightness of her husband's arms around her. She wanted to melt into his embrace, and her eyes misted at the thought of his departure. "If only you didn't have to go."

"How happy I am that we are like we used to be," he said.

"What a fool I was to cost us so much time together by my jealousy. Can you forgive me?"

"There is nothing you could do that I would not forgive, my love," Lionel said. "Never forget that."

"Nothing?" She remembered her crimes in assisting runaway slaves.

"Nothing."

They kissed deeply until a whinny from Hercules reminded her that Reuben was present. Her sense of decorum returned and she broke their kiss.

"This is most improper behavior — kissing out in the open and in front of the servants," she said in a whisper. "Come back to me soon, my darling."

Brushing back the lock of hair falling over his forehead, she formed the silent words, "I love you."

When they reluctantly broke apart, she watched him mount his horse and gallop away, turning when he reached the main road to wave at her.

When he was out of sight, she sent Reuben to the stables for Mercury. As she galloped across the pasture, as if trying to run from the heartache she felt in being separated from him, his words, "There is nothing you could do that I would not forgive," echoed in her heart.

But the words carried the promise of forgiveness for misdeeds she knew he had never considered. She hoped she would never have to compel him to honor his pledge. He might forgive her assisting his own runaway slaves, but not those of other owners.

As she pushed Mercury to ever-increasing speed, her hair fell free, trailing unrestrained behind her, released from her sunbonnet, held around her neck by its strings and flapping in the wind. But she knew that no matter how fast she rode, the impossible dilemma that she sought to outrun would always be before her. She could not outrun it, escape it, or hide from it. It held her as surely as slavery held the blacks she wanted to free. Slavery was her bondage, too. Just as it was for every slave-owner.

Chapter Thirty

After traveling deep in Carolina, Henny's sickness worsened. For two days, she lay in a stupor, her fever and cough having grown worse as she drifted in and out of delirium, calling for Aunt Beck or Old Sheba and once even for Lavinia. Uncle Will held the little girl in his arms and tried to cool her fevered brow with cold water from a spring or creek when they filled the water jugs.

Stella feared the sickness would be spread to her own child, and Uncle Will begged the Stratcheys to get a doctor.

"We're used to burr-heads makin' out sick," the older Stratchey said. "Ain't nothin' but a little hack-cough. Hit'll pass." The men ignored further pleas from the old man and showered him with violent threats and abusive names.

Finally, when her incessant coughing got on the men's nerves, they conferred and allowed her a small quantity of whiskey. This brought no cure and they decided that while she might pretend to cough and toss and turn in feigned delirium, she could not so easily fabricate a fever.

"She won't bring nothin' sick," the slant-eyed Stratchey said.

"Never paid that Steele boy but twenty," said his brother. "Might git what we got in her back at least."

"Not if'n she sick we can't. Can't give a sick black away."

"What if she gives it to the rest and they all come down? Lose the whole bunch. I say we ditch her."

The older man considered the suggestion, but demurred. "If she was found and nursed back well, it might make trouble for us."

"We can make sure she ain't found."

"Give her another snort of whiskey and we'll see how she is by mornin'."

By morning, Henny had improved. She ate well and the Stratcheys, hopeful their investment might not be lost, gave her an extra portion of mush.

As the journey continued, the wagon seemed to meet fewer and fewer travelers. Earlier, they had passed various riders, singly and in groups, as well as wagons and even an occasional coach or carriage, but now the roads seemed less traveled, and more isolated and deserted.

One late afternoon as the sun sank lower in the west, they encountered a group of six men on horseback, a slave patrol known to the Stratcheys who pulled the wagon to a halt. The Stratchey brothers told the men their destination and the poor luck they had in the quality of blacks this trip to Virginia had produced.

"Just about the worse lot I ever had to contend with. But they was worser ones we wouldn't give two coppers fer."

The leader and spokesman for the slave patrol looked into the back of the wagon. "Got a good kitchen wench?" he asked. "John Wheatley's woman's just had another baby and lookin' for a kitchen wench. The Wheatleys live about a mile on up the road yonder."

After a few more exchanges, the horsemen moved on and the wagon once more groaned into motion. They soon reached a dilapidated, weather-worn farmhouse and stopped.

The older Stratchey placed the black eye patch over his slanting, dead eye, got out of the wagon, and walked across the grassless front yard and knocked on the front door.

A tall, emaciated white male in his forties came out on the sagging front porch. After a brief exchange with Stratchey, the pale, shirtless man looked toward the wagon and called inside for his wife, who came to the door. She wore a loose-fitting, faded dress and dirty apron and held a baby in her arms.

"Must be the woman looking for a kitchen girl," Stella whispered. The slaves watched as the older Stratchey pointed and nodded toward the wagon.

Mrs. Wheatley, a fat, red-faced woman with a double chin and thin blond hair drawn in a knot on top of her head, waddled to the edge of the porch. Six of her pale-eyed, towheaded children appeared on the porch around her.

Watching from the wagon, Henny judged the Wheatleys as not very high quality people as white folk went—more in the category of the Mudleys and Shankralls—the kind of whites blacks, especially house servants, regarded as inferior.

White trash for sure, Henny thought to herself, echoing Aunt Beck and Uncle Lemiel in discussions of the Shankralls and lesser whites they knew.

Finally, Mrs. Wheatley handed the child in her arms to one of her older children and followed her husband and Stratchey to the wagon.

"All the women out," demanded Stratchey. "And be quick about it."

Henny reluctantly climbed over the side of the wagon. Stella handed her the baby and followed. When Henny returned the child to Stella, they both stood before the Wheatleys, who looked them up and down critically.

"You little 'uns, too," ordered Stratchey. "And hurry up."

The two little girls, assisted by Uncle Will, alighted, and holding each other's hands, huddled between Stella and Henny.

Mrs. Wheatley put her hands on her hips and continued her inspection while her husband rubbed his unshaven chin thoughtfully. Neither revealed any opinion of the appraisal, their faces remaining sullen and secretive.

"The Jones's down the road got one to hep them and we was thinkin' maybe we'd git one, too," Mrs. Wheatley said.

Stratchey seized Stella by the arm and pulled her out of the line. "This one got her own baby and be good with youngin's and a right big hep to you."

"Don't need no more little ones," Mrs. Wheatley said. "What I need is one to help me with mine—not to take keer of her own." She dismissed Stella with a sneer and hands on her hips, she began a slow stroll around Henny, looking her up and down. Henny was embarrassed and looked at the ground.

"That one be mighty good hep," the one-eyed Stratchey said, angling his head to fix Henny with a warning glare. "The feller that sold her to me said she was trainin' to be a house black."

"Ain't none of 'em sick, er they?" Mr. Wheatley asked. "Neighbor of us bought one last year in Atlanta that come down with lung fever and died not morn a week after he got him."

"All my blacks healthy. Don't buy no other kind and keeps 'um fed good. Can't get no price for the sick ones."

Suddenly, Mrs. Wheatley stopped circling Henny and stood directly in front of her. "Raise up yore head," she ordered.

Henny lifted her chin and the woman's fat jaw dropped with an intake of breath. "A mixed-blood!" Mrs. Wheatley said and pointed a fat finger at Henny. "Pa, looky here. Look at them eyes. You ever see one before?"

Mr. Wheatley approached and Mrs. Wheatley laughed as both of them peered into Henny's eyes. "Won't be wantin' no part-white, part-black."

"I swan—a blue-eyed black!" Mr. Wheatley said with amazement, bending closer and squinting to better see Henny's eyes. "Her hair got right much kink, but I reckon you can see it in her color. She's lighter than most."

"They the best kind for work, they say," Stratchey said, shifting uneasily. "Solid black won't work near as hard as one with a little white blood in 'em. Like addin' a little cream to dark gravy—makes it better."

"Ain't what I hear," Mrs. Wheatley said. "White blood just makes 'em sorry. And uppity, too, from what folks say."

Henny could not grasp the significance of what she was hearing, but she could feel a strange numbness creep over her. At the same time her cheeks grew hot and her mind whirled at their words.

These people were accusing her of having white blood.

"I ain't got white blood!" Henny heard herself say. She had never talked so forcefully to white people before; the vehemence of her tone surprised her.

"You hush yore mouth!" Stratchey bellowed, taking a threatening step toward her and raising his arm as if to strike her.

"See what I mean?" Mrs. Wheatley said and laughed. "She's uppity all right. Probably down right impudent. You can see it in them blue eyes. You git them blue eyes from yore white mammy? Or yore white daddy give 'em to you?"

She laughed loudly and waddled over to inspect the two little cowering girls.

"What about one of these little 'uns?" Mrs. Wheatley asked. "How much you ax fer one of them?"

"They be good. They young and ain't old enough to get uppity yet."

"Reckon they so little they be right much cheaper than them other two," Mr. Wheatley said, and the bargaining over the little girls' value, singly and as a pair, began.

But Henny heard none of it. She was so shocked and confused by what she had just heard, the voices of the Wheatleys and Stratcheys, now joined by the wails of the two little girls, became a blur, as if heard from a great distance. Her throat seemed to shut off and stop her breathing. Her knees weakened as her mind whirled at the horrible revelation.

White blood. She had white blood!

The words echoed over and over in her brain—*white blood, white blood*. It was the same as hearing she was a devil. Devil's blood! And that fat, ugly, unwashed farm woman, Mrs. Wheatley, who had never seen her before in her life, had known it with one look. With a single glance, this hateful, white devil who didn't have any background or family had seen it and revealed it, and the repulsive Stratchey man had not contradicted her and even agreed with her.

They had seen it in her blue eyes—blue eyes which only white people, except for herself—had. The eyes she had once almost been proud of because they made her unusual had exposed the disgrace of her mixed parentage. White blood and blue eyes. Now she hated them. She wished she could take a knife and drain all the white blood out of her, or pluck out her eyes so no one would ever see them again. Or put blackberry juice or walnut-husk stain in them and make them black. They had revealed the shame to her black race and now she understood why her eyes were so rare and peculiar, and why her skin was lighter than most blacks.

She held out her arm and compared its blackness to Stella's much darker hue. With horror she realized that her color was closer to that of the dark, swarthy Stratchey brothers than Stella, one of her own kind. Suddenly she felt herself falling to the ground, then being lifted up and placed in the wagon by Uncle Will. She felt herself spinning, and the voices speaking over her were as an echo from the bottom of a deep well.

"She's fainted."

"Burr-heads don't faint. No more than a mule can faint. Never heared of no mule faintin', did you?"

"She sick? These blacks got some kinda sickness?"

"We ain't interested in buyin' no sick blacks. Git the youngins back, Ma. Don't want them ketchin' nothin'."

"Nah, she just puttin' on. She ain't sick. Does this all the time when she think we're gonna sell her. I'll make her cheap."

After a whispered, secret conference and much private mulling, the Wheatleys came to a decision as Henny whimpered in Uncle Will's arms.

"Reckon we might be thinkin' to take one of these little ones," Mr. Wheatley finally said. "Don't want but one though—if you ain't axin' too much."

"Shore hate to break-up a set."

"Got no use fer but one."

"That second one be so cheap it be like gettin' two fer one. Just a little more..."

"They ain't too big, but I reckon one can keer for a baby and just one of 'em more in our price range."

"Was figuring on sellin' them as a set. They sisters and just six- and seven-year-old."

As Henny lay in the wagon, the sound of the negotiating voices faded in and out. Then she heard the screaming. The two little girls began to bellow as one of them was wrested from the other and sold to the Wheatleys.

The Stratcheys and Wheatleys laughed at the ineffectual efforts of the children as they fought their separation, neither a match in strength for even the tall, thin Mr. Wheatley, who easily restrained his new purchase.

"Hate to have to whup you the first thang," Mrs. Wheatley warned her resistant charge. She waddled to a nearby tree and broke off a branch, which she stripped of leaves and shook threateningly at the child.

The little girl continued to scream and struggle and Mrs. Wheatley swatted her about the legs with the switch. "Hush up, you!"

The other little girl was thrown into the wagon where Uncle Will, cradling Henny with one arm, tried to console the unsold child and shield her from the younger Stratchey brother, who stood over her, and with each attempt she made to leap from the wagon, roughly pushed her back with his foot.

By now, three of the Wheatley children had been drawn to the commotion and they all broke off branches of the tree and began to flail the little girl.

"Hush up, Mommy say," one of the Wheatley children said as the Wheatleys laughed. All three of the children beat the little girl with the switches.

"Mommy say quit it."

"We'll larn you!" Stripes appeared on the little girl's calves and small rivulets of blood ran down her legs.

"Now, you youngins, don't hit too hard. Just enough to let her know—"

Finally, a merciful blackness removed Henny from consciousness. She awoke sometime later to the familiar cry of the squeaking wagon wheel and the exhausted whimper of the little unsold sister. Sitting up, Henny saw that all of the original passengers were present except the little girl who had been sold. Her sister, huddled beside Uncle Will, buried her face in the old man's chest.

From behind the concealment of the sacks of potatoes and corn, the two young black men worked in fervent silence to free the second chain from its anchoring to the side of the wagon. The Stratcheys were distracted from their vigilant surveillance of the blacks by an animated discussion of their recent sale.

For a moment, Henny forgot the revelation of her white blood and then suddenly it came back to her with all the shame and revulsion as when she first heard it. Now she understood why some of the people at Hawthorn Hill seemed to resent her own mammy. There was no question that Susannah was black; Henny could remember her mother's rich, brown skin and the blackness of her eyes and hair. It was her father, whoever he was, who had made her unclean with his white blood, and Henny was sure it was against her mother's will. She had been the victim of some white devil just as Stella had been a victim of the Stratchey brothers. Maybe that was why her mammy always seemed so unhappy and withdrawn and seemed to prefer being alone or with just Henny rather than gossiping and laughing with the other women.

She had heard too often the black women in the quarters speak of the way white men debased black women who had no choice but to endure it.

Henny knew about the three great sins—the World, the Flesh, and the Devil—from Old Sheba. And it was in the Bible, too. She was a child of the second great sin, the Flesh. The sin of the World was almost exclusively a white sin—greed, theft, and wanting the riches and fine things of the world like fancy clothes, carriages, gold, and big houses the way white planters like the Hawthorns did.

The sin of Flesh was when women laid down to make babies with men who weren't their husbands. She was born of the second sin, the Flesh sin, even though she knew her mammy was innocent and had been forced into it by some white devil man who wasn't innocent because, like the first sin, he was committing the third sin—the Devil sin, another sin which was also almost exclusively the province of white people. Just as Old Sheba said, murder, cruelty, slavery, and all the other sins were mostly white people's sins because they yielded to the Devil.

As she brooded her circumstances, Henny was jolted into the present by the loud clank of the chains. Suddenly pulled free from the side of the wagon by Wash and Jeff, the bolt holding the chain to its mooring had been jerked free and flew across the wagon, where it slammed to the floor with a jarring clang.

Instantly, the one-eyed Stratchey swung around in his seat and seized the rifle at his side. Henny, seeing the freed bolt and chain on the floor, jumped to her feet, leapt, and snatched it up.

"Hold up there, burr-head!" Stratchey ordered, and Henny froze. With her back to him, she clutched the bolt and chain tightly to her chest. Trying to take in the two black men, Henny and the rest of the passengers with his one good eye, Stratchey's head bobbed about searching for the source of the sound. The two black men, wide-eyed with alarm, didn't move.

"What you doin', girl?" Stratchey asked.

Henny fell to her knees, her back still to her captor, and slid the bolt and chain toward the side of the wagon from which it had been wrested free.

"I just gettin' me another yam," she said. Her action blocked from Stratchey's view by a potato sack, Henny sank down and deftly shoved the chain out of sight with her foot and removed a sweet potato from the sack. "I done tripped over these men's chains," she said, holding up the yam.

Stratchey laughed and lowered his gun. "Got caught, didn't you? You put that 'tater back right now and set down. You done had morn yore share today."

Henny returned the potato to the sack and returned to her usual place.

"Gonna have to whup you fer stealin' when we stop," he said.

Henny looked at the two black men and saw a small smile of appreciation slowly warm the hardness of their faces. She was proud of herself and thought that even if she did have white blood, she was still black in her heart and nothing could change that—white blood, blue eyes, nothing.

Later, when the wagon had stopped for the night, one of the black men carefully lifted the freed chain Henny had prevented the Stratcheys from discovering and looped it in a circle. Then he glanced at the Stratchey brothers and drew the loop of chain into an ever-smaller circle, as if tightening it into a noose.

"Both chains free now," the black man whispered. "Tonight we kills 'em and makes a run for it. Been plannin' it that way all along."

The other man confirmed his brother's words with a nod. "We kills 'em before that if they tries to whup you like he threat. We not let 'em lay a hand on you, little friend."

Chapter Thirty-One

Once she was home, Ariadne was enraged that during her absence Jennie claimed to have found out nothing of Angelica's whereabouts. "You incompetent fool! I've found out more miles away in the country than you have right here in the city where the wench is hiding!"

Noting in the *Richmond Whig* that Horace Wroughton had increased the rewards for Gabriel's capture, Ariadne went to her desk and began writing.

"The fool thinks he's still in Virginia," Ariadne said to herself, and she quickly went to her desk where she scribbled an anonymous message to Horace Wroughton revealing Gabriel was actually in Philadelphia. When Madison appeared, she handed him the sealed envelope.

"Have this posted today," she said.

"Yes, ma'am," Madison said with a slight bow. "And if I could trouble you to sign these drafts, ma'am." He placed nearly a dozen pieces of paper before her.

"What is it this time? Is that all I ever do? Sign all my money away?"

"While you were away, Miss Ariadne, we have incurred numerous expenses. Your physicians...and medicine, ma'am."

Noting the great number of pages before her, she questioned, "And?"

"For the roof, ma'am. There was a rather bad leak while you were away. Rafters in the attic had to be replaced. The materials were quite expensive."

"And what else?" she said, scribbling her signature on the paper.

"The broken window, ma'am."

Remembering her tirade and the window she broke, she said nothing, and with a stroke of her pen, dismissed all memory of the incident.

"And the household expenses. And the repair for the carriage, ma'am."

"But I thought I paid for the carriage the last time."

"No, ma'am. That was for the new upholstery only."

"Oh, alright," she snapped, and she signed the other drafts without even looking at them.

Dismissing Madison, she once more returned to her writing. "I have a message for Judge Povall," she said.

Jennie held her breath, fearing her fate lay in the words her mistress wrote.

Seeing Jennie's fear, Ariadne's eyes glowed with pleasure. "As interested as Judge Povall is in buying you, I have other uses for you at the moment. This is an invitation for the honorable judge to join me for tea tomorrow." She thrust the envelope into Jennie's hand.

Jennie swallowed with relief as her mistress turned back to her desk, reached for her pen and another sheet of paper, and began to write again.

"When you have returned with Judge Povall's acceptance, you are to deliver another message. I'm inviting Aunt Cornelia to supper a week from Saturday. And mark my calendar that in a month, the Barksdale sisters will be in Richmond and I must hold a dinner for them."

She thrust the invitation toward Jennie and then snatched it back. "But it would be rude not to invite cousin Lionel, wouldn't it? He is in town, I believe." She added his name to the envelope and her eyes narrowed. "And perhaps Bithia—Mrs. Clevinger—will be available," she said with cunning smoothness. "I'm sure she will since Mr. Clevinger is away on business again."

She quickly penned another invitation and gave it to Jennie. "You are to deliver this to Mrs. Clevinger at the Bird and Owl Hotel. And wait for an answer. And make sure you take your papers with you."

"Yes, ma'am."

"And if you don't want a beating, you'll find out where Angelica is."

The next day, the pot-bellied, seventy-year-old Judge Povall gorged himself on more than a dozen sweet cakes and eyed Jennie with lustful appraisal.

"That will be all, Jennie. I shall ring if I need you," Ariadne said. "And perhaps you might again sing your little molasses cake song for Judge Povall."

"Oh, yes, yes," Judge Povall said, his hungry little pig eyes devouring Jennie as his tongue slid over his protruding ivory dentures.

When Jennie had left the room, he bent toward Ariadne and whispered, "You said in your letter you had business to discuss. Have you decided to sell?" His eyes glistened over a bulbous nose riddled with tiny purple veins, and his thick eyebrows bounced up and down like the tails of two racing foxes.

"Oh, Judge Povall," Ariadne said coyly. "I'm so reluctant to part with little Jennie. I wonder if she might not need additional training."

"But she does well for a beginner already. And sings so well," he said, chuckling and grinning stupidly.

"But Judge Povall, another situation brings me such distress I am afraid I have no one but you to whom I can confide."

Flattered by her confidence, Judge Povall was immediately solicitous.

"Whatever can it be, my dear?"

"Well, as you know, Uncle Edmund and cousin Lionel are my attorneys, and I would normally seek their counsel."

"Yes?"

"But my present dilemma—"

"Yes?"

"It is of such a delicate nature...and...and concerns the family."

"Yes. Yes." Smacking and licking his lips, Judge Povall's eyes widened and Ariadne thought if he leaned over any farther, the weight of his protruding belly would topple him onto the tea table.

"It concerns the runaway slaves at Hawthorn Hill. A servant there told me Lionel's wife had assisted in the escape, and when I questioned Lavinia she confessed to me it was true."

"No! You mean the lovely Lavinia?" Judge Povall sat erect as his lips stretched to cover his large false teeth and he blinked rapidly with disbelief.

"I'm afraid so. I'm so ashamed. Now you know why it would be impossible for me to turn to either Uncle Edmund or Lionel, neither of whom know." Taking a cue from Cornelia's arsenal of devices, Ariadne dabbed her cheeks with a handkerchief as if blotting tears.

"Of course. I'm stunned! Lionel's lovely wife!"

"Her parents are abolitionists, you know."

"No! And Lavinia such a lovely person. And she's been in your home!"

"True. But she's from a rather inferior family, I'm afraid."

"One would never know! She's always seemed so refined and genteel."

"Aunt Cornelia and I have done our best to...to elevate her. But she comes from rather coarse mountain people who own not a single slave. But the poor dear can't help her background. And I think she rues her error and I have a plan that I hope may save the family from disgrace and prevent her crimes from being known."

"How noble of you. However can I be of assistance?"

"If this Gabriel were apprehended and returned to his owner—anonymously—and the girl returned to Hawthorn Hill, perhaps Uncle Edmund and Aunt Cornelia and Lionel might be spared the shame..."

"Indeed, you are so thoughtful." Judge Povall pondered the matter, his eyes blinking rapidly. "Lionel's lovely wife! But how can I help?"

"By passing on the male slave's location in Philadelphia to the authorities. Discretely, of course. I have it written here." She handed the judge a piece of paper.

Giving her a conspiratorial nod, Judge Povall slipped the paper into his vest pocket.

"Consider it done, my dear. And with total confidentiality. But the female slave? How do you propose to get her back?"

"She is still in Richmond. I have learned she plans to disguise herself as a ladies' maid and leave Virginia by train! In league with those eccentric old Barksdale sisters who live near Hawthorn Hill. I'm shocked to say I suspect Lavinia may have deceived those sweet, innocent old things into believing she is a free black. They are quite elderly and trusting and Lavinia–" Ariadne turned away, as if revealing Lavinia's scheming character was too painful to continue.

"She must be apprehended at all costs! The slave, I mean."

"Indeed," said Ariadne, her prey having been snared. "When I think of how the scandal of Lavinia's behavior would break Aunt Cornelia's and Uncle Edmund's hearts. Uncle Edmund is distantly related to the Barksdales."

"Have no fear, dear Ariadne. We will avert such a tragedy."

Her true self surfacing, Ariadne continued in a harsher tone, "It has come to a pretty pass when an escaped black slave can be delivered to freedom on a train like a queen by upper-class people who should know better. But of course, she arrived in Richmond on a train, didn't she? Why not all the way?" She laughed at the irony and for a time, she and Judge Povall discussed the outrage of free blacks and the fools who liberated them and the treason of the abolitionist movement.

"The slave has become the master and the master has become the slave," Ariadne said bitterly. "Is there any progress in bringing to an end this dreadful Underground Railroad?"

Judge Povall brightened and passed on the latest he had learned from the police and slave patrols. "Of course, I have your pledge of complete secrecy–"

"Totally."

The little pig eyes gleamed as the fat old man bent closer to tell of the authorities' successful planting of a spy among a group of slave-runners in Manchester across the river from Richmond. Swelling with self-importance, he delighted in sharing information with Ariadne, who relished being privy to the confidential information as much as she did interesting gossip.

"A trap is being laid for certain slave-runners in Surry County and—"

Ariadne laughed appreciatively as the repulsive old man related the planned ambush of a group of runaways expected to arrive from the South in a few days.

"And another, more important raid is in the planning stages for a shipment of freight bound by train out of Richmond on the Richmond, Fredericksburg, and Potomac Railroad. Oh, it's been planned for months and isn't scheduled to be carried off for two weeks. But we know! And the patrols plan to stop the train and arrest them all!"

"How exciting," Ariadne enthused to the old man's delight as he chuckled and grinned widely.

She rang for Jennie, and when the anxiety-ridden girl appeared, her mistress requested she bring an additional supply of sweet cakes and to perform for Judge Povall.

"Oh, indeed, indeed," the grinning old man said, his tongue flicking the contours of his lips.

"I think that in a week or so our Jennie will be adequately trained to take a position in your household, Judge Povall," Ariadne said.

"Then you have decided to sell?"

"Perhaps I have. It all depends upon how well Jennie performs."

Povall grinned with such delight that Ariadne thought his ridiculous ivory false teeth would pop out of his mouth, as he squirmed and fidgeted in his chair and made quick, unconscious caresses of his crotch.

Chapter Thirty-Two

Since Henny had prevented the Stratchey brothers from discovering that Wash and Jeff had freed their chains, the two men's hostility toward the little girl vanished. Instead of threatening glares, the brothers now smiled and winked and briefly pulled the chain's bolts free of the holes in the side of the wagon, proudly sharing with her their success in freeing them from their mooring. This flaunting of their freedom was like an offer of trust and friendship, which Henny was somehow reluctant to accept.

Thrown in a quandary of anxiety and fear, Henny wondered what to do. She wanted to tell Uncle Will, but even an attempt to slide closer to him in the wagon was met with an angry rebuke from the Stratcheys.

"You stay put, burr-head," he roared. "I know you got your eyes on that 'tater sack. Sneak anothern and I'll lay more to the stripes you're gonna git."

But even as she was prevented from consulting Uncle Will, she knew she was not going to betray Wash and Jeff. Maybe they wouldn't kill the Stratchey brothers after all. Maybe, if they did break free, they would simply chain the men to a tree and make a run for it, or steal the wagon and take all the blacks.

Just before sunset, the wagon pulled off the road into an open field and the group began to prepare for the evening meal. Uncle Will unhitched the horses and the hungry animals searched for the occasional patch of grass to graze.

As usual, the men made Stella leave the baby with Henny while she went into the nearby woods and gathered firewood. She soon returned with twigs and dead leaves, started a fire, and begin cooking supper. All but the two chained men were allowed out of the wagon, and Uncle Will and Henny gathered more wood.

Although she was hungry, the Stratcheys had not forgotten her attempt to sneak an extra yam. "No 'tater fer you, burr-head," the elder Stratchey said, and he allowed Henny only the parched corn and grits Stella had cooked over the camp fire. "And I ain't forgot that lickin' yore due. Goin' to stripe you good first thang in the mornin'."

He went to a tree and broke off a thick branch, which he stripped of leaves and whipped back and forth in Henny's face.

Later, when the Stratcheys were not watching, one of the chained men slid his potato toward Henny, but she refused it, afraid his generosity would be seen.

When it was dark and the fire had dwindled to a few glowing embers, the Stratcheys lighted a lantern and ordered the blacks to bed down. They hung the lantern on a low limb of a tree not far from the wagon in a position that gave them a good view from which to watch their prisoners during the night. Henny crawled into a corner of the wagon and lay down beside the little girl, now without her sister. Stella and her baby were in the other corner; the two chained men were in the back of the wagon.

Uncle Will covered the children and Stella with the canvas and with creaking bones, curled up using a sack of potatoes as a pillow. As so many nights before, Henny could hear the old man whispering his prayers. Henny always joined him and tonight prayed for the little girl sold to the white family and for added protection against whatever consequences some rash action by Jeff and Wash might bring from the Stratcheys.

The older Stratchey brother took the first watch, sitting on the ground and leaning against the trunk of the hickory tree. His rifle lay ready across his lap. His brother slept not far away, wrapped in a blanket and curled up in a ball.

Henny prayed for sleep, hoping not to see what she feared might happen during the night. But she was unable to take her eyes off the Stratcheys in the small circle of lantern light and the two chained brothers in the darkness of the wagon, her eyes moving restlessly from one to the other as her heart hammered in her ears.

The moonlight made the trees glow as if they had been whitewashed, and a soft breeze made the leaves seem like a thousand tongues whispering ominous warnings. Strange birds Henny had never heard before cried out in the darkness as if in pain or fright while a bull frog droned soulfully in the distance. The little girl shuddered and drew the canvas cover up to her neck in dreaded anticipation of horrors she could only imagine.

Every sound and movement in the night seemed heightened and even the last few pops and snaps of the dying fire seemed like gunshots—or the crack of a whip. Finally, an eerie silence, as frightening as the foreboding sounds of the crying birds, settled on the night. Henny felt the tension in her body slip away. Against her will, she felt herself drifting into sleep. Her prayers to sleep were now replaced by a desperate struggle to stay awake. But she could not.

Sometime later, she was awakened by the soft clink of a chain. Although no louder than a fork touching a tin plate, it might have been the clang of the morning bell at Hawthorn Hill so quickly was she jolted awake. She sat up and in the startling bright moonlight saw one of the bound men cautiously pick up the chain attached to the bolt he had worked loose that afternoon. Taking great care to prevent it from striking the floor or sides of the wagon, it was now swinging free. He was naked from the waist up, his back and shoulders heavily scarred from past beatings, new wounds layered over the scars of old ones. Henny watched as he lifted the chains attached to the irons around his ankles and wrapped them with his shirt to smother the sound of their rattle as he slid inch by inch across the wagon floor. To silence the shackles, he wrapped them carefully around his arms, gripping the free ends in his fists.

The other man, also shirtless and scarred, was already out of the wagon, holding his chains carefully away from him so they made no sound and swung silently in the air.

Henny looked frantically for the Stratcheys. The lantern had been extinguished but in the moonlight, she could see the tree under which they reclined. The younger Stratchey lay on the ground and the other was still sprawled against the tree, his head slumped to one side. The sleeping men were close enough to the wagon for Henny to hear the faint rumble of the older Stratchey's snoring.

She held her breath as the man inched cautiously toward the back of the wagon and eased himself to the ground, holding the shirt-wrapped manacles aloft as he went.

Nodding to his brother, he moved away from the wagon and disappeared into the darkness.

Henny felt her throat grow dry and her heart beat like a rabbit's as she clenched her eyes shut and waited. Finally, unable to resist, her lids sprang open and she searched the darkness for the men.

For an interminable time she could see nothing. Then she heard a startled cry from one of the Stratcheys, an oath from the other, and the sounds of a struggle as chains rattled, strange choking noises came from the white men, and the contest of a life and death battle was fought in the darkness beneath the tree.

Uncle Will and Stella, awakened by the commotion, sat up. Confused, they searched the darkness for the battle they could only hear—the chains, the grunts and groans, and strange gurgling sounds, growing more furious and intense, then suddenly weaker and weaker.

Standing up, Henny could see the struggle—the toss and flail of legs kicking the ground and arms lashing while the black men, behind and over their victims, tightened and held the chains around the two Stratcheys' necks.

"Oh, Lord," Uncle Will said. "They done it."

Suddenly, Stella put aside her baby and jumped to her feet. Henny caught a glimpse of her face in the moonlight as her eyes grew wide and her features changed from surprise to pleasure. Her mouth formed a twisted smile as she cried out, "Kill them! Kill them!" her voice wild and unnatural.

Suddenly, she jumped over the side of the wagon and ran toward the struggle, where she threw her body over one of the Stratchey's flailing legs, holding them down with her weight, until they grew less forceful in their resistance. When their kicking subsided to no more than weak, ineffectual jerks, she knelt down by the barely struggling men and dug her fingers into the ground. Then she smeared the dirt in the Stratchey's faces, while her laughter, wild and guttural, came in gasps like desperate breathing as she pressed and ground the soil in their faces with the palms and ball of her hand.

"Dirt, dirt," she cried out, and finally, when the objects of her assault lay still and the two blacks had loosened their hold on the chains around the men's necks, she stopped rubbing the dirt in the prone men's faces and spat upon them.

Jeff and Wash tried to push Stella aside and began searching the pockets of their victims. Jeff finally found a key and matches. They lighted the lantern hanging from the tree above the dead men and unlocked the chains on their ankles and wrists. The swinging lantern's moving illumination seemed to animate the faces of the dead, open-eyed brothers, revealing with each sway their swollen faces, gaping mouths, and extended tongues.

No sooner had they discarded the chains than Stella seized them from the ground and began flaying the lifeless bodies. Over and over, she struck at them, making strange animal sounds of rage and satisfaction with each blow.

Uncle Will, by now out of the wagon, approached her with a restraining hand. "That enough, child," he said. "They dead now. You can't make 'em no deader than they already is."

The chains slipped from her hands and she broke into deep-throated sobs. Uncle Will put a comforting arm around her quaking shoulders and led her away. Henny shut her eyes tightly to block out the scene.

"They kill us for sure now," Uncle Will said as Stella whimpered against his shoulder.

"They got to catch us first, old man," Jeff said. "And they ain't even lookin' yet."

Wash was already dragging one of the bodies toward the wagon. As they neared, Henny opened her eyes and recoiling in fear, jumped to the ground.

"Help us hitch up the wagon so we can hide it in the woods," one of the men directed Uncle Will. "We got to bury 'em so nobody finds them."

"I'll help you," Stella said.

"You can take this youngin'." He nodded toward the little girl who was still asleep. "And Uncle Will, too. If you're caught, tell them you been stole and the slavers that done it set you out and run off when they hear the law after them. We goin' to bury the Stratcheys, hide the wagon, and head out to Ohio." He pointed to the sky. "We follow the North Star. We only moves at night and we'd take you with us but you'd slow us down."

"I want to go with you," Stella said.

The man shook his head. "You be safer without us. They kills us if they find out what we done. Not so likely kills you, a woman with a baby. Or the old man, unless you with us. We goin' to take this one 'cause they won't kill her, neither." He nodded toward Henny, who recoiled with horror. "Get in the wagon, girl."

Afraid to disobey him, Henny climbed into the wagon. To her horror, the men carried the corpses of the Stratcheys to the wagon and tossed them in the back. Henny felt herself go rigid with fear. She wanted to scream but she could only stare at the bodies, their arms and legs grotesquely angled and twisted, as if deformed in their attachment to their torsos. Dead people! Her greatest terror—and two of them and in the same wagon with her!

The younger of the dead men's faces was turned away from her, but the one with the slanted eyelid lay with his head lolled to one side, the angled eye half open as if staring straight at her. Henny squeezed her eyes shut against his gaze and buried her face in her hands. She was so frightened she could not breathe, and her throat tightened, choking off the scream she so wanted to release.

"Maybe you better leave the little girl with us," Uncle Will said. "We can take care of her."

"She done hep us. Maybe even save our life today. We take care of her."

The Stratcheys had nearly three hundred dollars on them and the men gave Stella and Uncle Will fifty dollars each. They gave Stella twenty more for the little girl, whom she promised to take care of. They also divided the sweet potatoes and meager food supply, including the better quality items the Stratcheys had reserved for themselves and stored under the driver's seat, taking for themselves only a few turnips, potatoes, and crusts of cornbread. They also left them a lantern and the canvas to sleep on, and then hitched the horses to the wagon and turned it toward the woods.

"Goodbye, Henny," Uncle Will said, and Henny forced herself to open her eyes and look past the dead Stratcheys as the wagon lurched away toward the concealment of the forest. Henny watched Uncle Will, the little girl, Stella, and her baby recede into the distance until they were finally swallowed by the darkness as the wagon penetrated deeper into the woods.

With one of the men holding a lantern to light the way, the other led the horses deep into the woods until the wheels became mired in a bog near a creek.

Cursing their bad luck, the men finally abandoned their efforts to free the wagon. Henny again closed her eyes when they hoisted the Stratcheys over their shoulders and carried them a short distance from the wagon where, with only the dim lantern light to illuminate their gruesome labor, they dug shallow graves with the blunt ends of sticks and two boards they had pried from the wagon floor. The work was slow and difficult, but they finally dug graves sufficient to conceal the bodies and put them in the ground.

After tossing the chains that had bound them on top of the corpses, they covered them with dirt and found a rotted fallen tree, which they attached to the horses and pulled on top of the shallow graves. To further conceal their work they added brush and dead branches and a few stones. Even Henny was pressed into service by gathering dried leaves and twigs to scatter over the graves.

Then the men unhitched the horses and Henny felt herself being lifted by Jeff and placed on one of the horses behind Wash.

"Put your arms around me and hang on," Wash said, and they rode off into the last remaining hours of the night, trying to guide the horses, unused to riders and without a saddle, and only the bit and bridle and portion of the long reins used in pulling the wagon.

For hours the two horses meandered through the brush-choked woods, their progress slowed by darkness, unfamiliar terrain, and their riders' uncertain guidance. But the black men persisted, winding aimlessly while trying to keep their direction northward by constantly scanning the starry sky, almost completely blocked by the thick trees overhead.

Henny's arms ached from hours of holding onto Wash's waist but she was glad to put as much distance between her and the dead Stratcheys as possible. But without Uncle Will and Stella, she felt alone and abandoned.

Finally, they came to a lane, too rough and grown up with weeds to be a main road and likely a farm trail used for access to a field or pasture. After following it for some time, they came to a barn used to store fodder and hay. The men tethered the horses in the woods and the three hid in the barn.

"We'll sleep during the day and travel at night," Wash said as they arranged the hay and fodder to conceal Henny and themselves and lay down. Soon Henny could hear the deep, exhausted breathing of their sleep. She wanted to join them but could not. Even though drained from the long day and emotional turmoil, she remained wide awake.

Somehow the little girl sensed she was in more danger now, in the company of two murderers, than she had been when a prisoner of the Stratcheys. At least with the Stratcheys, she had only them as a concern; now she had sheriffs and militia and slave patrols to fear. She remembered Old Sheba's saying, "You done swap the scratch for the itch."

The thought of Old Sheba brought her a longing for the old woman—and Aunt Beck and Uncle Lemiel and all her friends at Hawthorn Hill. Her heart ached for the comforting sight of their friendly faces and the warm embrace of their touch. Even Emma and Piney would be welcome company compared to what she endured now.

If only she had listened to Old Sheba who had probably seen all of her horrible future. Henny blamed herself. It was her white blood that had prodded her desire for more than a life of field work—and her uppity impudence to be a lady's maid. And it had brought her to this.

Yes, Old Sheba had been right: white devils would never permit blacks to be anything but drudges. They would keep blacks under their heel forever. They were doomed by their blackness to always be subject to the will of whites.

And there was nothing she, or any black, could do about it.

Chapter Thirty-Three

On the Monday morning of her wedding, Mattie Rose arrived at Steele Mercantile before sunrise and waited on the porch for Grover. Having two days before stolen a five-dollar gold piece from her parents and given it to Grover to purchase the marriage license, she had slipped away unseen by her family before the morning bell rang at Hawthorn Hill.

"Now you just be waitin' for me on the porch at the store about eight o'clock Monday mornin'," Grover had said. "We'll go to the courthouse for the license papers first thing. I know a preacher that'll get us hitched and we'll be on the road for Tennessee by ten o'clock."

Dressed in her finest white cotton dress with narrow borders of lace at the neck and wrists, Mattie Rose had packed the rest of her clothing in a carpet bag. A white ribbon held her dun-colored hair away from her face and trailed down her back. She had even made a detour through a cow pasture on the way and picked some daisies and wildflowers for a bridal bouquet. She held the bouquet and carpet bag in one hand and in the other clutched a paper written and witnessed by Lavinia granting her permission to marry Grover, duly marked with an X by Mr. Mudley.

When a horseman approached, she saw it was not Grover but his father, Abner Steele. Acknowledging Mattie

Rose with no more than a curious glance over his spectacles, he rode behind the store to the stables. Moments later, she heard the click of the store door and went inside.

"Help you, young lady?" Steele asked, peering over his steel-rimmed glasses as he leaned forward on the counter.

"I'm waitin' for Grover," she said.

Steele looked at her quizzically. His brow creased in surprise.

"Why, Grover's not here."

Mattie Rose looked around the store and the wonders it held, especially the shelf on which a half dozen bolts of cloth were displayed, including the red calico she had admired and had asked Grover to get her so many times. She was disturbed when she saw the jagged edge of the red calico hanging from the edge of the bolt, clearly cut and haggled by scissors. Disappointed at first, she quickly brightened when she thought the jagged edge was likely Grover's doing and he had cut some of the red calico to present to her as a gift—a wedding gift.

"I said, Grover's not here."

"Reckon I'll just wait for him then."

"Be a mighty long wait if you do."

"He'll be here before the sun's high. He told me so."

"You talkin' about my boy, Grover Steele, little lady?"

"Yes, sir. Me and him's gettin' married today."

For a long time, Steele did not speak and only looked at Mattie as the lines of surprise deepened in his forehead. For a time, he did not say anything and walked from behind the counter to a bucket containing dried corncobs, where he selected a few and went to the Franklin stove in the center of the store and started a fire, aided by lamp oil that he poured on the flickering blaze.

"Why, I guess you ain't heard the latest," he said, adding a few more corncobs and lamp oil. He looked over his glasses at the girl and inserted his thumbs in his suspenders. "Grover got married yesterday. He and Mary White got married at the Presbyterian Church yesterday afternoon."

Mattie Rose stood motionless as the blood drained from her face. The room was silent except for the crackle and faint roar from the stove as the fire established itself and rose in intensity.

"He and Mary White been going to church and spending Sunday afternoons together every week for nigh on a year now. They been promised for the last six months."

Steele chuckled and rubbed his chin with his hand. "Thought I had him talked out of gettin' hitched for a year or so—even promised to take him in as a partner in the store if he waited, but I reckon they was so keen on gettin' hitched. Grover paid the county clerk four dollars—two dollars extra—to open up the courthouse on Saturday when they're normally closed to get the license. They done left out for Tennessee right after the weddin' yesterday."

Mattie Rose, still motionless, was as white as her dress now, her limpid, close-together eyes shining with a new, unfamiliar wildness, like those of a fox in a trap.

"Now, what business you got with Grover?" Steele asked.

When he recounted it later, rubbing his chin in the astonishment that came back with each retelling of the incident, Abner Steele said the girl seemed to change from mute, death-like stillness to raging, uncontrolled fury in a matter of seconds. He told how, even though a fairly good-sized girl for fifteen, she seemed to take on the strength of a man twice as big and had lifted a fifty-pound barrel of salt crackers, from which not more than a dozen pounds had been sold, and hurled it across the store like it was no more than a five-pound bag of meal.

The barrel had struck and knocked over the Franklin stove which, containing the newly made fire, spilled the smoldering contents of its belly on the oil-treated floor. The ashes, soot, and smoke discharged from the stove's collapsed stovepipe had blinded Abner for a moment, long enough for the fire to find life from lamp oil spilled from an overturned can, which may have been upset by the collapsing stovepipe or further fury from Mattie Rose's rampage, Abner could not say for certain which.

Abner said he thought he could have contained the flame, but her attack had taken on additional fury and she started knocking anything her hands and arms could reach off the shelves, going behind the counter and throwing everything she touched, including lamp oil, which ignited immediately and spread the flames.

Abner said she seemed particularly anxious to get to the shelf holding the piece goods and bolts of cloth, which she threw into the fire, by now raging beyond control. To beat it all, he said, the girl was laughing as if she had lost her mind and crumpled up a piece of paper she carried and threw that in the fire, too. Steele said she had actually reached into the fire for the bolts of cloth and selecting one, a bolt of red calico, unrolled it in long swatches that she threw back into the flames, knowing it would burn better and faster unfurled than in the tightly wound bundle in which it came. The piece goods went up fast enough, Abner said, and bottles of liniment started exploding, and then the coal oil caught, and finally the whole store was engulfed in flames.

The girl picked up the carpet bag she carried and turned, grabbed a handful of horehound candy, and walked out as the fire spread and Abner tried to quell it but finally had to save himself and get out too, helpless to do anything but watch the building and everything in it turn into a wall of flame and black smoke and finally, in no time at all, crumble into charred, smoking rubble.

Abner went to Sheriff Hudspeth at once, only to find Mattie Rose had already been to Hawthorn Hill and reported to Lavinia the story of Henny's kidnapping. Lavinia promptly took her to Sheriff Hudspeth at the courthouse.

Mattie Rose was more than happy to cooperate with the sheriff and Charles Hicks, who sat in on the questioning, along with Lavinia and Mattie Rose's father.

Sitting stiffly before her examiners, Mattie Rose stared straight ahead with eyes narrowed and her face grim.

"Grover Steele—he was all the time aggravatin' me to court him," she said. "I never wanted nothin' to do with him—never like him a bit, but he come sniffin' 'round all the time. All the time pesterin' me. I done told him I was fixin' to tell Pa if he didn't stop it. But he never. One time I was tryin' to do my work—I was gatherin' aggs for Ma and lookin' fer a new hen's nest down by the field barn 'bove the creek, and he come down there tryin' to hang 'round me and said he just seen one of them Hawthorn blacks fall in the creek and ax me whichin it was.

"I thought maybe he'd just go on off and leave me alone if I did, so I went with him and watched that little old blue-eyed one they call Henny go in the corn crib. I knowed who she was 'cause she helps Ma in the wash house some of the time. Grover said he's goin' to lock her up and get a reward for her. I done told him she wasn't even off Hawthorn land yet and hadn't run off at all—just hidin' to keep from gettin' a whippin' for stealin', I was thinkin'. But Grover say he was goin' to snatch her anyway and sell her to them Stratchey brothers."

By altering only the truth concerning her romance, Mattie Rose happily incriminated Grover.

"I done told him over and over not to do it," Mattie claimed.

Less forthcoming, however, was information on Mattie Rose's role in the arson of Steele Mercantile.

"I was in there that mornin' fixin' to buy me a stick or two of horehound candy and that stove he got caught fire. I run out and went to the house. Never had nothin' to do with it." Although Mattie Rose's story seemed to have minor variations when concerning her relationship with Grover, her revelations concerning Henny never varied and the sheriff concluded her account, at least in that matter, was truthful.

It was determined that Henny, who had not left Hawthorn property when abducted by Grover, was not a runaway at all but hiding to avoid punishment. Grover Steele had imprisoned her in the corn crib for three days and forcibly sold her to the Stratchey brothers, who took her out of the county, and now, most likely, the Commonwealth of Virginia.

"I was goin' to tell it, but that Grover threatened to beat me if I did," Mattie Rose claimed. "But he done it. Got thirteen dollars fer her."

Mattie related the precise time schedule and other circumstances of the abduction, including the source of the pendant taken from the little girl, which was substantiated by Lavinia.

"He was all the time pesterin' me to marry him," she said. "Wouldn't marry him for nothin' a-tall. He married that Mary White, anyhow."

Mattie Rose's information provided evidence sufficient to bring charges against Grover for the theft of a slave. Further, she implicated Grover in other thefts of other slaves he had bragged to her about, some far more valuable than Henny.

Subsequent investigations determined that Grover and his new bride had not remained in Tennessee, as they had previously planned, but had moved on, indicating to his Tennessee relatives that he thought Missouri or Texas or perhaps even California might provide a more promising future.

"Hoping to get some California gold before it's all gone," his father said.

When Lionel returned to Hawthorn Hill, Lavinia insisted he intervene with the authorities on Mattie Rose's behalf because her information solved the mystery of Henny's disappearance. As Mattie Rose Mudley's attorney, Lionel was able to negotiate an arrangement between Abner Steele and Mr. Mudley, in which it was agreed that Lionel would bring no charges against Grover Steele for theft and kidnapping of the slave, Henny, as long as no charges of arson or suits for damages resulting from same were brought against Mattie Rose Mudley, a minor, or her father, Virgil Mudley.

Within a few days of the disposition of the case, Mattie Rose was quietly married to Freel Shankrall, an eighteen-year-old boy she had kept company with occasionally a year earlier. The Shankralls were sharecroppers who had lived on various farms and plantations throughout the county. Mattie Rose and her new husband settled not more than two miles away from Hawthorn Hill on a plantation owned by the Barksdale sisters, where they had been hired to replace free black tenant hands who had recently moved north.

Mattie Rose had agreed with the arrangements, but was irked when she learned she would have to live in a house that black tenants had once occupied.

Lavinia's heart was lifted by the hope that Henny might be found before she was sold in the deep South. Or, should the agents hired by Lionel to search for her be too late, such a sale would be nullified because she had been stolen property.

"If necessary, I will buy her back for you," Lionel promised Lavinia.

"Why not hire Charles Hicks again to search for her?" Lavinia suggested, but Sheriff Hudspeth revealed Hicks had been hired by Horace Wroughton, alerted by an anonymous letter from Richmond, to go to Philadelphia to apprehend Gabriel, whom he was informed was employed by a blacksmith shop there.

Upon learning this, Lavinia immediately sent a warning of Hicks's intentions to Gabriel's contact in Philadelphia.. The Slave Recovery Act made the return of Gabriel to slavery not only possible, but legal. She warned him to go into hiding or move elsewhere and told Angelica of the situation in a letter to Margaret.

Lavinia's letter crossed one from Margaret in which she warned that Ibby had received word by way of Jennie that Ariadne had learned of Lavinia's participation in Angelica's escape and the plan to send her north with the Barksdale sisters.

"Little Jennie eavesdropped when Ariadne had Judge Povall to tea and heard it all," Margaret reported. "Jennie reports everything she can to Ibby, but is endangering herself doing so. It is all so scary—and at first I thought it was just exciting. All Ariadne does is tell people how dull the country is. Why, I can't imagine what Richmond could provide that would equal all this country excitement," Margaret wrote. "Arson, kidnapping, pregnant girls forced to elope, stolen slaves—nothing in the city could be half as interesting."

There was further excitement of a less serious nature to report in Lavinia's next letter to Margaret when Daisy abandoned Ivan and decided she wanted to marry Douglas, who promptly dropped Piney as a prospective bride. Naturally, the two young men fought over the matter and Piney was thrown into paroxysms of grief at losing Douglas.

"You gots to make Douglas marry me, Miss Vinny," Piney had demanded in a flood of tears. "He done promised he would, and Daisy steals him off me. Only reason she sing in the choir at church so she can make eyes at him durin' service. It ain't right what she done."

Chapter Thirty-Four

⋖═◉═⋗

The Stratchey brothers' wagon was discovered by a hunter a day after it became mired in the bog. Suspicious that a wagon in good condition containing horse feed and gear would be abandoned, the hunter notified the local sheriff.

"Looks like the wagon them two brothers that trades slaves brings through here from Virginia three or four times a year," a deputy said.

The sheriff's bloodhounds quickly picked up a scent, but almost at once, the dogs fell into confusion, straining to go two separate directions.

"We'll put the hounds on two leads," the sheriff said.

The first group led the deputies to the fresh graves of the Stratchey brothers. When the manacles and shackles were discovered with the bodies, a more extensive search was begun and within hours, the hounds' increasing speed indicated a scent whose source became stronger the farther they went.

In the meantime, the second pack of hounds located Stella, Uncle Will, and the little girl only four miles away, cowering inside an empty Methodist church.

Questioned at length, Stella and Uncle Will claimed to have been abandoned the day before by two men who had abducted them from their owners. "They think our owners set out after us," Uncle Will said. "They fearful they go to jail for stealin' us and just rides off and leaves us."

When the sheriff told them the bodies of the Stratcheys had been found with the abandoned wagon, the slaves' reaction created suspicion.

"Don't think you're too old to whip, old man," the sheriff said. "Or string up by the neck, neither. We don't coddle blacks here the way they do in Virginny."

"I tellin' the truth, sir."

The sheriff knew the slave traders would hardly have bothered stealing an old man of minimum value for resale, or a woman still nursing a baby, and another child. The Stratcheys never passed through with less than six or eight slaves, often an inferior lot to be sure, but usually including at least one or two able-bodied field workers. The value of the blacks on this trip would not be profitable enough to merit a trip from Virginia. It seemed unlikely that an old man and a woman could overcome and murder two strong men and bury them. And to lift the fallen tree covering the quickly dug graves would be beyond the strength of a feeble old man and small-framed woman, even working together.

"We know you had help killin' those men," the sheriff said. "The killers took the horses and left you, didn't they? And where did you get the money we found on you?"

Threatened with hanging, Stella fell to her knees and revealed everything.

"Sir, I swear to Jesus we never kill nobody. They two men with us that done the killin'. We was asleep when they done it." Henny was unmentioned.

Stella and Uncle Will were lashed for initially withholding the truth and threatened with death by hanging if any inconsistencies in their story came to light.

The bloodhounds following the second trail became confused when the horses Jeff and Wash rode took to water a mile from the graves. The dogs could not pick up the scent on the other side of the creek and valuable time was lost before the patrols found tracks in the soft earth where the horses had emerged a short distance upstream. The hounds picked up the scent again, and following the hoof prints and trail of broken branches in the undergrowth, the deputies quickly closed in on the fleeing slaves.

On the second day, the horses, exhausted and hungry, could be pushed no farther and Jeff and Wash stopped to rest. Unaware they were being pursued, the men thought it might be days before their offense was discovered.

As the horses grazed and the men ate corn pone and potatoes, a weary Henny leaned against a tree and watched her rescuers guardedly.

"We gettin' into farm country," Jeff said. "I seen houses back yonder. Look like black folks outside."

"They quarters, I can tell."

A rail fence separated the dense woods that concealed them from a pasture in which they would be clearly visible. Leaving Henny to watch the horses, Wash and Jeff followed the fence in both directions, and failing to find a gate, they returned and decided to wait until nightfall to proceed. "Too open in the daylight," Wash said. They sat on the ground to rest beneath a large, spreading red oak.

"We'll make a hole in that fence tomorrow," Jeff said.

Henny suddenly set bolt upright and listened.

"Hound dogs," she said.

Jeff and Wash cocked their heads.

"I don't hear nothin'."

They listened again and now hearing the bark and howl, all three jumped to their feet. Jeff and Wash rushed for the horses.

"The fence," shouted Wash. "It just blocks us in if we follows it."

"We better go on the run."

The men, seizing only the Stratcheys' pistols and rifle, rushed toward the fence and with little effort were quickly across. Henny's attempt, however, was less successful.

"Wait for me," she called. Wash continued running but Jeff turned back and bounded back over the fence. Henny rushed toward him with her arms outstretched, expecting to be hoisted over the rails.

"They too close, little one," Jeff said, quickly seizing her and lifting her above his head. "They not stretch your neck, but they would us—and you slow us down." He took a step closer to the large, spreading oak tree.

"Get up this tree and climb up as high as you can. They not see you there and pass right on by."

Henny reached above her for a branch of the tree and as Jeff pushed her, she hoisted herself higher and secured a foothold, holding on unsteadily to a higher limb. Jeff bounded across the fence again and followed Wash, already well ahead of him in his dash across the field.

When Henny looked down, she could see neither of her rescuers, only hear the fading sound of their mad dash across the pasture in a direction opposite the sound of the approaching hounds.

She climbed higher in the tree, taking care lest she fall. Driven by fear, she climbed so high the branches grew so small she was afraid they would not support her weight.

Then she looked down, but saw nothing below her but the dense foliage of the tree.

As the hounds drew nearer, the yelping grew louder. Numbed with fear, Henny saw through a break in the leaves the approaching deputies and slave patrol. Six men on horses followed two on foot, who were pulled along by the leashes of a pack of six red hounds, sniffing the ground and yelping.

As they neared the tree, Henny prayed they would go on past, and thanked God she knew of no hounds, no matter how skilled at tracking, that could climb trees. To her distress, the dogs seemed to yelp even louder at the trunk of the tree. Although she could not see them, she heard the men shouting to each other above the din of the barking.

"There's the horses."

"They been here, alright. These horses still wet from the ride."

"They left a sack of 'taters."

"Here's the horses' tracks."

"Let's get on after them. Must be on foot now."

"The dogs is wantin' to go 'cross the fence."

"Rip down them damn rails."

Henny could hear the rails of the fence being torn away. The dogs scampered through the opening and away from the tree instead of remaining under it as she had seen them do when they treed a raccoon or possum.

"They got a fresh scent now, and it's still hot. We'll git 'em dreckly."

The group moved on and Henny laid her head against the trunk of the tree, her breath in gulps, relieved that she was safe at least for the moment. The safety of Jeff and Wash troubled her, and she prayed for their safe deliverance. The sounds of pounding hooves and braying hounds gradually faded until there was no sound of them at all.

Relieved that she had not been discovered, Henny remained high in the branches of the tree for a long time. So overcome by fatigue she feared she would fall asleep and fall, she slowly descended to the ground.

At the foot of the tree, she found the sack of potatoes and ate her fill, trying to decide what to do. Her body ached, and racked with fatigue, she curled up and quickly fell asleep. When she awoke hours later, the day had slipped away and long shadows had fallen across the forest floor. Other than the Stratcheys' horses, still tied to the fence, she was alone.

The sinking sun was only a weak, cloud-streaked smear above the horizon. The fading light transformed the forest into a world completely different from the one she had gone to sleep in earlier. She was now surrounded by strange sounds and the murky shadows of nightfall seemed to bring more than darkness—ominous presences she could neither see nor hear. She was frightened and wondered what had happened to Jeff and Wash, and if these woods were the home of wild animals.

She tried to pray, but it was almost as if Jesus was back in Virginia and even He didn't know she was far away and hiding under a tree somewhere in Carolina, alone and frightened and with nowhere to turn. The sounds of crickets, tree frogs, and roosting birds seemed to taunt her. She tried to calm herself with the thought that at least these sounds were familiar and non-threatening, but the darkness seemed to harbor other presences. Cries of creatures she had never heard before reached her ears: the barking of a fox, the shuddering, liquid wail of an unfamiliar night bird. Nearby flapping wings of a frightened fowl taking flight with a terrifying scream ripped through the more comforting, familiar sounds of night, and a distant owl screeched a warning of doom.

But suddenly, the clamor of the forest night was joined by a sound even more frightening and threatening—the yelping of hounds. Listening for only a moment, Henny could tell they were coming closer. Frantic, she saw the barking came from the same place where earlier the hounds and horsemen had pursued Wash and Jeff into the woods across the open pasture. Several lights flickered through the distant foliage and seemed to float in the air by themselves as they emerged from the dark woods. Henny saw they were lanterns held aloft by some of the men on horseback. Leading them, the dogs emerged from the woods and the dim shadowy outlines of the men following seemed suspended in the air like hazy, indistinct specters.

Seized with terror, Henny jumped to her feet. *They're coming back for me,* she thought, and she quickly tried to return to her hiding place in the tree. She raised her arms to reach the branches of the red oak in which she had taken refuge earlier, but they were too high. She looked frantically about her, trying to decide which way to flee. As the men and hounds drew nearer, she saw that one of the spreading branches dipped within her grasp where the ground sloped upward to form a small mound. She ran up the incline and pulled the branch toward her. Barely supporting her weight, the limb strained as Henny clambered onto it and reached for a higher branch. Holding on to the limb above, she inched toward the trunk of the tree as the men, whose number had increased to more than a dozen, came closer. Henny clung to the tree's thick trunk, afraid any attempt to climb higher would be seen or heard by the men who came through the opening in the rail fence. They were directly below her.

She could hear them speak and two voices rose above the others, angry and threatening.

"I done said I never aimed to do it," the voice of a young man said.

"You damn fool, you ought not fire unless you know what you're aimin' at," another voice responded.

"Now, boys, y'all calm down," a more mature voice said.

"But he kilt the best hound dog I got... Wasn't no sense in shootin'..."

"I done told you it wuz an accident, dammit! I thought it wuz one of them damn blacks in the brush. Never knowed hit was yore dog."

"That ain't no reason, you damn nit-wit."

The sound of a scuffle erupted and the two young men exchanged blows before the other men pulled them apart.

"Now, break it up, boys. Remember you're brothers!"

"Ain't no brother of mine. What kind of brother shoots his own brother's best hound?"

"Told you hit wuz an accident!" his brother said, and Henny saw for the first time that Wash and Jeff were in the group, silent and with wet, dark-stained wounds on their heads and faces.

"It's your damn fault," one of the arguing brothers said, and he raised his rifle and struck one of the black men across the shoulder with the barrel, knocking him to the ground. Wash and Jeff's faces were so beaten and bloody, Henny could not distinguish one from the other as their arms were tied behind them.

With the brother's anger vented in his attack on the black man, the last of the group of men passed through the opening in the fence and stood in a circle around Jeff and Wash. With the cluster of lanterns brought nearer, Henny escaped the brighter light by carefully stepping up to a higher branch.

"Better put that fence back," one of the men said.

"Make them blacks do it," another suggested.

"Have to untie them. We'll do it."

Henny clung to the tree so tightly the bark almost cut into the flesh of her arms and face. She wished she could climb higher, but she feared any movement she made would be detected by the men only a few feet directly below her. Cautiously, she felt a branch just beyond the one on which she stood and eased herself around the tree's thick trunk. She waited for the men to order her down from the tree, but their attention was on Jeff and Wash.

"You goddamned, black son of a bitch," one of the men said. "We'll just see how long that damn black neck will stretch."

"Let's do it here."

"Save the county a trial."

"Trial? Who has a trial for a goddamned—"

"Now, boys, let's not do somethin' we might regret."

"Regret, hell. They ain't nothin' but two sorry—"

The abusive language continued and Henny watched as the men dismounted and threw Jeff and Wash to the ground. Afraid to move, she watched in horror as the black men struggled to rise and their captors kicked them to the ground again. Doubled up with pain, their hands tied behind them, they could only twist and turn in futile attempts to avoid their captors' blows.

"Hadn't been for you, my best dog be alive—"

The yelping hounds were ordered into silence by their masters and, as if grateful for the opportunity to rest, curled up on the ground, their tongues lolling out the sides of their mouths as they panted for breath. Henny heard the crack of a whip and the cry of a man's voice.

"How about this one?" another male voice said.

"Yeah. Git me that rope."

Henny could hear something striking the leaves below her as the men attempted to toss a rope over one of the limbs. They were looking right up the trunk of the tree. They would surely see her. Her blood chilled as she realized they were going to hang Jeff and Wash.

"Now, boys, we ought to wait for the sheriff."

"Don't seem to be no sense in waitin' for the sheriff," another man said. He successfully looped the rope over the tree limb only a foot or two below the branch on which Henny stood.

"This ain't the law, boys. This ain't right."

"Wasn't right them killin' them white men neither, Boyd."

"Mighty good of you to let us use your tree, Mr. Hampton."

"Glad to do it," an older man said. "Want you to leave 'em hangin' for a day or two so my own blacks can see 'em. Some of 'em gettin' bold lately and I think they ought'a know what can happen to 'em."

Henny felt a wave of nausea when she saw Jeff and Wash doubled up on the ground below her as one of the men continued to kick them. The glow of two or three lanterns flickered through the leaves below, lessening the darkness. The cries and moans of the two black men mingled with the abusive words and occasional crack of a whip. She prayed that the splatter of light from their lanterns would not penetrate the darkness and thick oak foliage and expose her.

After a time, the men below tired of their sport, and as Henny watched she could see one last struggle as the doomed men thrashed and kicked and attempted one final, desperate effort to escape the noose. Wash, who had managed to stand, was kicking at his tormentors. Then a shot rang out. Nearby birds emitted shrieks of alarm and the noisy flapping of wings accompanied their flight. Wash fell to the ground with an agonized cry. Suddenly the sounds of the night—frogs, birds, crickets—all stopped, instantly leaving the woods in a chilling, deathlike silence.

"Get the other one," said one of the men restraining Jeff. "Git him in the knee. That'll bring him down."

A second shot brought a scream of pain from Jeff and he too fell to the ground. Even with her view partially obscured by the leaves, Henny could see the legs of both men's britches darken with the flow of blood.

"Now try to run, you damn—" a deeper voice snarled, calling him more abusive names as Jeff doubled up in pain.

After a second rope had been thrown across a branch adjacent to the first, the nooses of each were put over the men's heads and around their necks.

"Now, boys—"

"Hush up, Boyd. If you don't want to stay, git on to the house."

"It just ain't the law! Ain't right no way you look at it!"

"Then git on out of here! Go on."

"I'll go with you, Boyd," another man said, and the two men, joined by three others, mounted their horses and left.

"You outta think some more about this, boys. Might come to your conscience someday," one of the men said as they rode away.

Although she wanted to turn away, Henny watched in horror as the free ends of the two ropes were tied to the pommels of two saddles.

"Alright, let 'um swing."

As the nooses slipped over the black men's heads tightened around their necks, one of them—their swollen, bloodied faces and the darkness made Henny unsure which—looked directly above him and for an instant locked eyes with Henny. Then his eyes widened and she thought she saw the faint beginning of a smile come to his split lips as he gave her a wink before quickly lowering his head.

"What you grinnin' at, you black dog?" an angry voice said.

Henny almost cried out in her anguish and heartbreak but bit her lip so hard she could taste her own blood as she repressed her sorrow.

The crack of a whip, as loud as a pistol shot, rang out as the horses were slapped across their flanks and they lunged forward. The nooses tightened around the men's necks and another flick of the whip and the horses moved forward, lifting the two men from the ground.

Below Henny, Jeff and Wash kicked helplessly and she could hear the creak of the ropes straining with the men's weight and rubbing against the branch which held them. Henny could feel the shaking of the limb on which she stood as it moved with the final, useless struggle of the men. Holding tightly to the tree trunk, she inched around it until her foot touched another limb. Moving onto it, she raised her hand above her and flailed it around in the darkness until it struck a higher branch, which she grasped. She slowly moved away from the horror below her until she found a place to sink down where the limb divided into arm-like extensions.

Even though she tried not to look, she could still see the grotesque dance of the black men's legs as they flailed helplessly above the ground. Uncomfortable, awkward laughter came from some of the men, and harsh, abusive curses from the others. Henny was overwhelmed as a spasm of emptiness and sorrow ran through her and settled in her stomach.

Heartsick, the little girl choked back a sob and a wave of nausea forced her to throw up the potatoes she had eaten earlier. Fearing the vomit would betray her presence when seen falling from the tree, she caught as much of it as she could in her hands, and raised her dress to catch what spilled beyond her grasp.

"Dance, you black son of a bitch," a man said and laughed, but now he seemed alone in his mirth. His laughter was followed only by silence except the whine of the taut ropes as the bodies swung and the thrashing legs finally fell still.

For a long time, the men said nothing. Nor was there any sound at all. Henny wanted to scream at the deathly silence. Where were the frogs, the crickets, the night birds? And the barking dogs? Even the night breeze seemed to have retreated into silence, the rustle of the trees stilled to nothingness. Why were the men standing so still, like scarecrows, lifeless and saying nothing, as if they too were dead? How could they be so transfixed by two dead men swinging at the end of ropes? She would almost rather hear their violence and oaths and brutal cursing than the horrible, empty silence.

Finally, she heard the shuffle of feet and the men, still holding the ropes taut so the bodies would not touch the ground, untied the ropes from the saddle horns and secured them around the trunks of nearby trees. Henny shut her eyes against the sight directly below her of the still and unresisting bodies of Jeff and Wash as they continued to swing and turn slowly around and around.

"They're dead."

A bottle of whiskey was passed among the men and they briefly discussed what to do with the Stratcheys' horses.

"Ain't much more than plugs, the both of them."

"Might have a plowin' or two left in 'em, though."

They agreed to take the animals with them, as well as the rifle and pistols, and the mob began to disperse and move away. The brothers who had fought earlier over the shooting of the hound broke into a new argument, but it was quickly squelched.

"Now, boys, remember you're brothers," a man said, and the quarrel was reduced to muted grumbles as the group departed.

"Finished here..."

Just when Henny thought they were gone, a shot rang out some distance from the tree and one of the bodies below her suddenly began to spin at the end of the rope.

"Good shot," Henny heard one of the men say in the distance as she watched in renewed horror as the stilled body was reanimated and rotated again under the impact of yet another shot.

Distant laughter followed and a contest began as the men made wagers as to who was the superior marksman. A dozen more shots were fired at the hanged men, one of which tore through the foliage only a foot from Henny's head, another just below her feet.

Shot after shot followed as various marksmen took turns and tested their skills. Henny sobbed deeply as the noise filled her ears and the bodies below her spun and jerked under the impact of the barrage of bullets. With the superiority of various weapons and marksmanship demonstrated, a winner was declared, and the men rode off into the night.

Henny remained in the tree long after the men had gone, alone with the two swinging, bullet-riddled corpses. Then the horror of seeing first the Stratchey brothers murdered one night, and now Jeff and Wash, overwhelmed her and her sobs deepened. With no fear of being heard now, she allowed herself the luxury of deep, full-throated grief as she slumped weakly against the branches of the tree.

Finally, when she could cry no longer, she tried to think of what to do. All alone and without anyone to help her, she didn't know where she could go or even where she was. She longed for the bony embrace of Old Sheba and the comforting words of Aunt Beck and now would even have welcomed a tongue-lashing from Emma.

Gradually, as the darkness grew deeper and their home was returned to them, the frogs and crickets could be heard once more asserting their possession of the forest. The occasional cry of a bird returning to its nest filled the air and even the wind, as if earlier banished, came back to stir the trees, as if fanned into motion by the wings of a giant bird flying over the woods.

Strangely comforted by the sounds and knowing there was other life around her, Henny climbed down from the tree, feeling her way in the almost total darkness. As she dropped to the ground, she averted her eyes from the bodies of Wash and Jeff and dashed into the woods.

Putting as much distance between her and the corpses as possible, she finally slumped beneath a tree in exhaustion. Her whole body ached from the last two days, especially her arms, from holding on to Wash as she rode behind him on the horse and the hours clinging to tree branches. Now she let them fall beside her in relief that she could rest them.

Then she remembered the potatoes. She would need them the next day, when the sourness of her nausea would be gone. She would return for them tomorrow, before anyone found the bodies. She wouldn't have to look at the dead men; she would just snatch up the bag and run. But run where? The question seemed to chase itself around in circles in her head as fatigue finally overwhelmed her and she fell into a death-like sleep on the ground beneath the tree.

When she awoke the next morning, Henny's arms ached even more than the night before. The sour smell of her vomit on her dress brought back the memory of the hangings. The sun was up and she realized she must retrieve the bag of potatoes and flee lest the white devils who had hanged Jeff and Wash return and do the same to her. She wondered what had happened to Stella and Uncle Will. She wept anew at the thought of poor Stella and kind old Uncle Will being subjected to the cruelty she had seen befall Jeff and Wash. She wondered if white devils would hang Stella's baby and the little girl.

Looking around her, she rose from the ground and tried to retrace her steps to the tree. When she finally found it, she averted her eyes from the two bodies hanging there and looked for the bag of potatoes.

Picking up the sack and keeping her back to the corpses, she noticed she was not alone. Standing in front of her some distance from the tree were three children. Two little boys, five- or six-years-old, and a little girl, a year older, stood motionless before the two dead men. For a long time none of them moved, their mouths open, their eyes wide as they stood transfixed by the horrible sight in front of them.

They're black, thought Henny with relief. *My own people. I'll be safe with them. Thank God they aren't white devils.* But no sooner had she felt the security of being with her own kind than the little girl looked down from the gruesome sight, locked eyes with Henny, and turned to run away. The little boys followed and the three sped toward the woods beyond the meadow.

"Wait!" Henny called out, but they ignored her and raced on.

Holding the sack of potatoes, Henny ran after them, following until they disappeared into the woods across the meadow. When they saw she was in pursuit they ran faster, but Henny's long legs easily kept up with them until they reached a cluster of slave cabins, not unlike the quarters of Hawthorn Hill. Henny almost felt at home as she followed the children to a cabin in the middle of the settlement and remembered passing near these same quarters the day before.

A woman stood at the door and the children ran toward her and disappeared into the house while the youngest huddled behind her, clinging to her skirts. Henny rushed up to her and trying not to cry at the rejection of the children, pleaded for protection from the slave patrols.

"They white devils after me," Henny said to the woman. "They done hanged up Jeff and Wash and do the same to me!" She hoped the woman did not notice her blue eyes and think she was too much a white devil to offer protection.

To her relief, the woman waved her inside and when she had entered, closed the door behind her. The woman and children listened as Henny babbled out her story of abduction, murder, and hanging.

"We wait for my Walter to come," the woman said. "He know what to do." Then, noting the odor of Henny's clothes and her soiled dress, the woman asked for her clothing and washed it while Henny washed herself for the first time in days and hovered beneath a quilt while her dress dried before the fireplace.

When the woman's husband came home, there was an anxious, whispered conversation out of Henny's hearing, during which the man shook his head and the couple looked toward Henny with fearful, uneasy expressions.

"You can stay the night...but I got to get you off the place early in the mornin'," the man said. "My woman...she take you to the main road and shows you which way to go. And we feeds you good, too."

Before daylight the next morning, Henny was shaken awake by the woman. She quickly dressed in her clean dress, dried by the fire during the night, and was given a bowl of grits and a small sliver of fatback. The man and the children were still asleep. When she had eaten, the woman whispered to Henny that it was time for them to go. As they quietly left the cabin, Henny set down the sack of potatoes she had brought with her on the floor beside the door.

"This for helpin' me," she said.

The woman declined her offer, but Henny insisted. "It for helpin' me," she repeated, extending the sack and the woman reluctantly took it.

The woman nodded and led Henny from the quarters into the woods. It was so dark Henny was guided more by the sound of the woman's progress through the dense undergrowth than the sight of her, but after an hour they came to a break in the thick trees.

Pointing down a road, the woman said, "I has to leave you now, little one. But you just follow this road and it lead you to the Cath'lics. They help you. This road leads clear to

Savannah and it be best if you went through the woods and just keep the road in sight. Watch for snakes and don't go in no swamps. You jest stay close to the main road and you come to it. The sisters lives in a big brick house with a rock Jesus in front of it. You knows who Jesus is?"

"Yes'um," said Henny. "I been baptized lots of time and—"

"You know what He look like?"

"Yes 'um, I seen him in Aunt Beck's Bible. He got a beard and—"

"You just come to one of Him made out of rock, and you be there. It be daylight by the time you gets there and you won't have no trouble seein' Him. And if you ketched, don't let on it me what helped you."

Henny couldn't imagine a Jesus made out of rock. Before she could question her benefactor further, the woman turned, and with the words, "Keep off the road but close enough to see where it go to," disappeared back into the forest.

Henny did as she was told and followed the road within concealment of the woods. The traffic was heavy the farther she went—horses, buggies, coaches, every kind of vehicle Henny had ever seen—and more and more of them as she continued on down the road. She finally came to a large brick and stone building that resembled a church, in front of which stood the statue she sought.

A stone statue of Jesus stood before her, looking just like the etching of Jesus she had seen in Aunt Beck's Bible, His arms outstretched as if in welcome. *Why, Jesus is here after all*, Henny thought. He must have heard and answered her prayer the night when she was in the tree.

The strange church-like building was surrounded by an iron fence, the entrance of which was through a locked gate. Even as thin as she was, Henny could not force herself between the bars. Finally, she sat down and leaned against one of the gate's stone piers to wait for some sign of life within.

Within only minutes, she turned to see a face peering at her through the gate. Two large blue eyes looked at her from a face framed by a strange, black-and-white head covering.

A true white Carolina devil, Henny thought as she looked back into the face. Maybe blue eyes, even her own, were devil eyes the way Piney had said they were. The eyes continued to watch her, then drew back, and Henny could see they belonged to a woman dressed entirely in black, except for the white framing her face and an unusually wide white collar extending from her chin to her breast. Almost at once, she was joined by two other women dressed exactly the same way who looked at her with the same curiosity as the first one.

White devils, Henny thought as she drew back, and pressed herself against the stone piers. *Devils for certain.*

The bizarre clothing made it obvious, and Henny shut her eyes tightly to block out the sight of them, wondering if she was in worse company with these white devils than when she had been with the Stratchey brothers—or even the slave patrols.

"Can we help you, me darlin'?" the oldest of the women asked in a dialect Henny had never heard before. The peculiar manner of speaking was further proof they were devils.

"Woman up the road said for me to come here," Henny said, wondering if she had made a mistake by telling them and shouldn't just flee the place now.

"Another one," the older woman said with a sigh. She unlatched the gate and pushed it open. "Come in, my child," she said, and Henny reluctantly entered. The gates had already closed behind her when she remembered something in the Bible—or one of Old Sheba's sermons—about "the gates of Hell." But it was too late now. The gates were closed and she was trapped.

"Are ye runnin' away?" one of the younger women asked in the same strange brogue Henny had never heard before. "Are ye runnin' away?" the woman asked again. "You can tell us. We be ye friends and mean ye no harm."

In spite of the strange manner of speaking, the woman's voice was comforting and kind. Henny nodded and the woman placed a gentle hand on her shoulder and led her into the building.

"I am Sister Mary Raymond," she said, "and this is Sister Mary Lawrence and Sister Mary John and Sister Mary Theresa. Don't try to remember our names just yet. In time, you will come to learn them. We are the Sisters of St. Joseph, a new order in your country. We come from across the sea from a place called Ireland."

They goin' to keep me forever, Henny thought, and she prayed to Jesus to be delivered from these new and unfamiliar devils and yet another evil.

Chapter Thirty-Five

Jennie, having gotten the information by eavesdropping, immediately warned Ibby. "Miss Ariadne know the Barksdale sisters gonna take Angelica to Philadelphia by train."

Ibby informed Margaret, who immediately wrote to Lavinia. Thus alerted, the plan was abandoned and the old ladies quickly devised another strategy.

"An army of patrols and slave catchers can watch every train," Miss Phoebe told Lavinia. "They won't find us. We'll travel by coach, days earlier."

Miss Maude continued, "We will bypass Richmond altogether, pick up Angelica outside the city, and proceed directly on to Philadelphia. It will take longer, but it will be three or four days before anyone misses us."

"I do hate that we have to deceive Cornelia, who expects us in three weeks. We promised we would visit en route, but we will have to make our trip a week before," said Maude. "Once we're with our brothers, we'll write to her that we saw the wisdom of her fear of train travel and went by coach."

"She will be so proud that at last someone listened to her," said Lavinia.

As planned, Lavinia arrived in Richmond in her own coach two weeks later. The Barksdales departed at the same

time and bypassed Richmond to stay at an inn ten miles out
of the city to await Lavinia and Angelica.

"Come in, come in!" said Cornelia, embracing Lavinia
and waving her inside the big brick house on Clay Street.
"You're exhausted I know, but there's time for a rest before
supper. Lionel will be late as the factory always keeps him
until the last minute."

Anxious to see Angelica, Lavinia feared her message
to remain in Richmond had not arrived in time, but Ibby
appeared to direct the transfer of her luggage from the coach
and gave her a secret smile and glanced toward the floor with
a reassuring nod, indicating Angelica was still in the cellar.

"If I may borrow your Ibby to help me unpack, Mother
Hawthorn," Lavinia said. "With Angelica and little Henny
both gone—"

"But of course, my dear," Cornelia said tenderly. "Your
new dresses are lovely. I particularly adore the rose organza.
Why not wear it tonight for Lionel?"

Although tired from the long coach ride, Lavinia was
directed to the parlor for a visit with Mr. Edmund before
she was allowed to retire to rest and dress for supper. Mr.
Edmund knew from experience to give his wife full reign
to chatter before he could plunge into the facts and figures
relating to the business of Hawthorn Hill. Waiting with
practiced patience, the old gentleman sat in his leather,
wing-backed chair until his wife at last concluded her
discussion of the state of her health, Lavinia's new frocks,
and a detailed update on all the current gossip, much of it
involving Richmond people Lavinia did not even know.

"And how thrilled I am that Phoebe and Maude will be
visiting in just two weeks!" Cornelia said, rising from her
chair. "But I can see my husband wants to talk of crops and

yields. Don't get up, dear," she said to the old gentleman as he struggled to rise.

"Get your talking on all that done now, because I won't listen to business and tobacco-factory talk at supper. That's all I hear every night from you and Lionel. If it keeps up, I'll be chewing tobacco myself! Lavinia, did you know the cherry-flavored plugs sell far better in the North than the South, which favors sassafras and licorice? Isn't that correct, Mr. Hawthorn?"

"Indeed it is, Mrs. Hawthorn. What a pleasure to know you have taken note of Lionel's and my discussions of the market. You'll end up a business woman yet."

"And winning spitting contests as well, I'm sure. But get all that talked out while I check on supper. And when Lionel comes, I don't want any of that silly war talk, either. Why, the ladies in my sewing circle even discuss it. And at the Garden Club such talk is so unseemly, as if it were an appropriate subject for ladies—or remotely possible. Silliest thing I've ever heard." Leaving the room, she said, "Imagine, civilized Americans fighting each other! Such nonsense."

After a brief report on the people and crops of Hawthorn Hill, the discussion was concluded and Lavinia rose to leave the room. At the door, she said, "Oh, yes, the new field has been plowed and planted and will add to our yield. It's lain fallow for years and should have restored itself."

"Will this require new hands?" Mr. Edmund asked.

"We already have them. Clevis and Nancy have two sons, thirteen and fourteen, who are old enough for the fields now." The words were no sooner out of her mouth than her conscience was stung by the irony and hypocrisy of her covertly assisting blacks in escapes at the same time assigning others to slave labor.

She had no time to dwell on it, however, as Ibby was waiting for her in the hall outside the parlor, signaling for her to follow her down the cellar stairs. At the foot of the stairs, Ibby rapped on a door with a pre-arranged knock. The door opened on a darkened, musty room and as Ibby fired a lamp, Angelica emerged.

The women embraced with happy tears and related the latest in their perilous adventure.

"I watch for Miss Cornelia," Ibby said, moving to the cellar stairs. "Last week I ketch her comin' down here to fetch a can of pickles. I tells her I seen a big rat and she let out a whoop and turns 'round mighty fast. Don't think she ever set foot down here again."

"How is your ankle?" Lavinia asked.

"Just about all well. It still a little sore, but healed up right good, I think."

"You know the change in plans?"

Angelica's face clouded with concern. "Yes'am, I knows. And about Mr. Wroughton sendin' Charles Hicks to hunt Gabriel. Oh, but something wrong, Miss Vinny. Little Jennie been tellin' me and Ibby things. She say—" Her words faltered and she lowered her head.

"Go on. What is it?"

"Well, I knows black folks ain't supposed to say nothin' 'bout white people...and Miss Ariadne family and all."

"Oh, for heaven's sake, Angelica. Tell me," Lavinia said.

"Jennie say Miss Ariadne know all about how me and Gabriel runs off. She even know you in on it. Jennie eavesdrops on her and Judge Povall talkin' it. Miss Ariadne even know 'bout the Barksdale ladies goin' to take me North on the train. And she want to make you trouble, and Jennie to find out where I hidin'."

"Miss Ariadne and I had words at Hawthorn Hill," Lavinia said. "She's read the note I sent in the dress patterns. But we have changed our plan—"

Ibby reappeared as heavy footsteps could be heard on the floor above. She extinguished her lamp and whispered, "That Mr. Lionel. He back from the factory. We gots to go up."

"I'll slip back tomorrow. You'll be leaving in two days, and not on the train," Lavinia whispered, and she followed Ibby up the stairs. She went to her room, where Ibby helped her hurriedly put on her new rose dress. It fit her perfectly and after two years of black mourning, it helped restore her youthful radiance, aided by a subtle application of rouge swiped from Cornelia for her by Ibby.

Lionel found her moments later and they rushed into each other's arms. Lavinia was startled to detect the odor of whiskey on his breath when she kissed him, and an even more disturbing aroma—the distinct fragrance of a woman's perfume, sweet, floral, and vaguely of lilac. It was definitely not the bay rum he sometimes used after shaving, or leather, or tobacco, the familiar smells she associated with him.

She said nothing about the perfume, but asked him if he had had a drink.

"I stopped for a quick one at the Swan," he said with a wink. "You know how Mama is when she sees me drink anything but wine."

She was disappointed that he would delay seeing her after being separated for so long by making a detour to a tavern, especially since he could have imbibed in his room or drawing room or in the kitchen out of sight of his abstemious mother. But she was so pleased to be reunited with him she pursued the matter no further. Perhaps the scent was from the factory and the flavors used in manufacturing chewing tobacco. But lilac-flavored chewing tobacco? Her mind reeled that he might have just left a woman knowing she was waiting for him.

The suspicion dogged her during supper, even as he praised her new dress in lavish terms and showered her with compliments. "You look ten or fifteen years younger, my sweet," he said, beaming. He was also happy to report that he had engaged agents in Georgia and the Carolinas to look for Henny.

"These are reliable men and I think there is a good chance we can get her back."

"Oh, I do hope the child is found soon," Cornelia said. "It's so embarrassing having runaways in the family. First your Angelica, and now that little one. What did you call her?"

"Henrietta—called 'Henny' for short, I believe," said Mr. Edmund with a wink at Lavinia and glance at Lionel, whose expression remained impassive as he took another drink of wine and looked into his glass.

"Henny didn't run," Lavinia reminded Cornelia. "She was abducted."

"Ah, yes. Ariadne has had so many runaways," said Cornelia. "I've had to speak to her about it. She's so severe with them that people talk, and it's a disgrace when people think you mistreat your servants."

After two days, Lavinia left Richmond, pleading the necessity of visiting her son and daughter-in-law before returning to Hawthorn Hill duties. Easing herself from the still-sleeping Lionel's embrace, she slipped down to the cellar before even the servants were awake. Angelica was already in the coach house and had with her another, unexpected passenger.

"This little Jennie, Miss Lavinia," said Angelica. "She a cousin to me and done warn us 'bout Miss Ariadne and what she know. Miss Ariadne goin' to sell her to Judge Povall."

"Take me with you, Miss Lavinia," Jennie pleaded. "I rather die than goes to ol' Povall. He nasty with his girls. He—"

"Of course you can go," Lavinia said. "Your warnings have saved us from discovery and great trouble. We are greatly in your debt. You came to our aid; we will be happy to come to yours."

With Angelica and Jennie concealed under the seats of the carriage behind a large carpet bag and the flare of her skirts, Lavinia was well on her way out of Richmond before even the servants were awake.

Later that day, they arrived at the inn previously agreed upon as a meeting place with the Barksdale sisters and found they had arrived three days before. Everything was perfectly on schedule, and the old ladies welcomed the addition of Jennie.

"Why, sister Maude can't have a maid unless I have one, too," said Miss Phoebe, feigning indignation with a toss of her head, which set her corkscrew curls swinging.

"Well, I'm certainly not sharing my maid," said Miss Maude, taking up the game. "You'll have to get your own."

"Why, I'll take Jennie!" her sister said. She smiled over her spectacles at the puzzled black girl, so unused to kindness and lightheartedness from even a pretend white mistress.

"And Lavinia, dear," Miss Maude said. "We've decided to use our sister-in-law, Louise, as an excuse to Cornelia and Edmund for not stopping by on the way. And for leaving a week earlier than we expected."

"Brother Matthew wrote us last week she was much worse—heart dropsy, you know. She wasn't even able to come when we lost Mama," said Miss Maude.

"Isn't that wonderful?"

"Phoebe! Be ashamed of yourself. Poor Louise—"

"Oh, I don't mean her heart dropsy is wonderful, you old fool. I mean it's wonderful her condition can provide us with an excuse for rushing on past Richmond without stopping. Cornelia already knows why Louise wasn't at Mama's funeral and that will fit right in with our story."

"I think it's a splendid idea," Lavinia said. "And I prepared travel papers for Angelica last night and Jennie this morning."

"Oh, what good liars and forgers we are!" said Miss Phoebe.

"If necessary, we'll show the police our brother's letter as evidence that we're rushing to our dear sister-in-law's deathbed."

"We're very good actresses, you know," said Miss Phoebe, her eyes twinkling with excitement. "And can cry especially well, can't we, Maudie? They'll believe us."

Chapter Thirty-Six

At Hawthorn Hill, Lavinia waited in anxiety for nearly two weeks before she finally received a letter from the Barksdales.

"We made the trip in record time!" Miss Phoebe wrote. "Our brothers were quite taken aback that we brought our new maids with us. Sweet little things, they are, and we adore them. One will be reunited with her husband in another city soon, as we sent her on once we learned his whereabouts. Our sister-in-law, Louise, wants the one we call Jennie to stay with her, as her health has not improved, and she remains quite ill. Isn't that wonderful? I mean that Jennie can be of help to her, not that her health continues to decline."

Margaret had written a few days before of Ariadne's rage at Jennie's disappearance, adding to her long list of runaways. "Mother said she was in such a state, she thought she was going to have another of her temper tantrums. But Dr. Rudd got her calmed down before it became a full-blown fit. I don't know if she had anything to do with it or not, but for some reason the slave patrols questioned Ibby and Alonso about Jennie. I actually believe Ibby and Alonso would have been arrested or taken in for further questioning, but Mother was so outraged and insulted that anyone would think her faithful Ibby could be involved in illegal activities, she ordered the patrol officer out of the house!"

Cornelia herself treated the matter at length in her letter to Lavinia.

"Why, I told that hateful, common constable that Ibby was my property and she belonged to me and he would not remove her from my house any more than I would allow him to remove any of my other possessions. Since when can the police seize a private citizen's property? Will they want to carry off our furniture, silver, and jewelry next? I was so outraged, I decided to see Governor Wise about the matter.

"Mr. Hawthorn told me not to, but I showed him a thing or two, and did it anyway. I notified the governor of the intrusion at once and he and Mrs. Wise invited me to the governor's mansion for tea the following Sunday. Mrs. Wise shared my anger and Governor Wise said he would look into it. I will not have my Ibby bullied. Mr. Hawthorn was aghast and has fumed and grumbled for two days and I don't know why Lionel found the matter so amusing but he laughed and laughed and said I should be turned loose on the Yankees next. I told him I'd be glad to."

She also expressed great disappointment that Miss Maude and Miss Phoebe had not stopped to visit en route to Philadelphia but "had been called to their sister-in-law, Louise's, deathbed a week before." In another letter she reported that "Louise has made a miraculous recovery" and wouldn't die after all.

"And," continued Cornelia's long missive, "poor Ariadne has had another attack of her nervous condition. Even more severe than the earlier ones. I don't know why, but when I told her the Barksdale sisters were visiting, she planned one of her lavish dinner parties in their honor for the evening before their scheduled departure for Philadelphia by train, and she went all to pieces when I told her they had been in Philadelphia for nearly a week because of Louise. The news brought on the whole horrible episode and I didn't even know she was that fond of the Barksdales. I explained that you're not visiting her when you were in town (she did not even know you had been here, dear!) was because duties at Hawthorn Hill called you home. She seemed upset about that, too. And on top of everything else, her Jennie has run away! Poor Ariadne. Do you think it would be helpful if you send Piney to her now that Jennie has run away?"

By July, Lavinia confirmed the suspicion that she was pregnant. Her reconciliation with Lionel was secure and the prospects of motherhood brought her great joy. Only Henny's absence and the mystery of her whereabouts made her happiness incomplete. For the rest of the summer, Lavinia waited in vain for word of Henny.

Lionel reluctantly passed on to her his hired agent's report of the Stratchey brothers' murder and the fate of the men who killed them. This only increased Lavinia's fears, even as the agents located Uncle William and Stella, who had been sold and traced to benevolent masters in Georgia. They reported Henny alive and well when taken by the two black men who had killed the Stratcheys, but her whereabouts were still unknown and Lionel instructed the search be continued.

Lionel was delighted to be a father again. When the news was announced, the family practice of wagering on the sex of the child became a major contest, as did the suggestions for names for the newborn.

In August, Lavinia received a letter from Angelica. She was in Boston. The letter was sent to unknown sources in

Richmond, passed on to Ibby, and then to Margaret, who smuggled it to Lavinia in the stiffened brim of a sunbonnet she sent to Hawthorn Hill by Lionel.

The letter read:

Dear Miss Livvy,

Gabriel and I both have work now in Boston and are making every attempt to adjust to our new home. Gabriel is so grateful to be free from Mr. W.'s cruelty, I shed tears at his happiness. Although I do not speak my heart to him, I find that our freedom is not the paradise I had hoped it might be. We are still in danger of being captured and returned to slavery and the newspapers even publish warnings to escaped slaves to be watchful for bounty hunters who seek us out for reward money.

In spite of his skills as a smith, Gabriel is paid very little and whites who do far less are paid twice as much. We brought our blackness with us when we came North and even though free, we are regarded here much the same as we are in the South. We are considered less good than white folks and must take the unwanted jobs. I am now working as a maid for a white family to add money to our earnings. I wanted to tutor the children in this family but they hired a white man. In all honesty, my bondage under you was easier than my freedom here. But since my husband's life is happier and we are together, I say nothing.

Yesterday, my mistress told me to keep in my place when I helped her daughter with a spelling lesson. We may leave Boston for Canada, where we hear we will be safe at least from recapture.

I miss you so much and wish I could see you. I am sorry I have complained so much. You will probably think I am ungrateful for the great danger you placed yourself in by...

Lavinia wrote to Angelica, sending the letter to Margaret to mail from Richmond. She enclosed some money and tried to offer encouragement that her situation and those of her race would improve once the northern people understood that blacks were as capable as whites if given the opportunity. Yet even as she wrote the words, Lavinia found them empty and meaningless. If attitudes in the South had changed so little in over two hundred years of living with blacks, could it be very different in the North where the citizens sometimes found the presence of blacks a new experience?

As the pregnancies of Lavinia and her daughter-in-law, Sarah, progressed, they conducted a playful contest, which, surprisingly, Lavinia seemed to be winning. By October, only a week before Sarah's confinement, Lavinia, who was expected to deliver in January, exceeded her daughter-in-law's girth by several inches, and the movement within her, experienced only when she had been pregnant with twins before, caused Lavinia to suspect she carried two babies.

Dr. Hunter confirmed it, and new wagers and suggestions for names were put forth to include the third Hawthorn baby, although with some hesitation as Margaret and Cornelia were locked in a passionate battle as to the name of Sarah and Randy's child, Margaret insisting that if the child was a female it be named after her, the grandmother; Cornelia demanding it be named after her, the great-grandmother. Since Lavinia was expecting two babies of her own, she was to have no voice in the matter of Sarah's child's name.

In November, Sarah and Randy became the parents of a healthy son, Lionel Alexander Edmund Hawthorn, weighing nine pounds and bearing the bluest eyes of any Hawthorn yet, it was decided by doting parents, grandparents, and great-grandparents. That the child was male and named after both grandfathers and great-grandfather ended the squabble between Margaret and Cornelia, and Cornelia immediately turned her eye toward Lavinia and began her campaign for the name Cornelia at Hawthorn Hill.

Lavinia, experiencing a difficult confinement and wracked with nausea and every other imaginable discomfort of pregnancy, was unable to attend the birth of her grandchild, but each detail was reported. Lionel offered, as irrefutable proof, his grandson's perfect health and beauty buried forever the myth that first cousins could not produce perfectly normal children.

Lavinia's own confinement began in February when her daughters, Margaret Alexandria Hawthorn and Cornelia Rebecca Hawthorn, each weighing over seven pounds, were delivered by Emma and Old Sheba with Dr. Hunter's tolerated presence. Named for Margaret and Alexander Harvey and their grandmothers Hawthorn and Williamson, the twins were healthy and beautiful and Cornelia, rewarded and victorious in her campaign, announced her every goal in life was accomplished and she could go to her grave a totally satisfied woman.

Because Sarah's delivery came earlier than expected, Emma and Old Sheba had been denied its supervision, but being at Hawthorn Hill they attended every detail of Lavinia's, only surrendering the tying of the umbilicus to Dr. Hunter, who grumbled sarcastically that he was fortunate the old black women even allowed him in the room. Old Sheba buried the placenta of each child and predicted glowing futures for both little girls.

"One goin' to marries a preacher and the othern goin' to preach the gospel herself," the oracle of Hawthorn Hill predicted. "And they both goin' to has nine babies a piece and two husbands a piece."

By the spring of 1855, the babies were thriving, and when Randy and Sarah came to Hawthorn Hill, the families watched for hours comparing little Margaret, dubbed Maggie, in spite of Margaret's protests; little Cornelia, dubbed Corny, to Cornelia's horror; and little Edmund as they demonstrated their brilliance and superiority to all other babies ever born in the world before.

But peace at Hawthorn Hill was short-lived when Piney soon became locked in conflict with Ivan and Daisy, who had decided a week before her wedding that she didn't want to marry Douglas but Ivan instead. Naturally, the young men fought, and had to be assigned to different fields. Piney was furious and shrieked and wept bitterly. Not only had Ivan deserted her for Daisy, but Douglas told her he was no longer interested in her either.

Chapter Thirty-Seven

When Horace Wroughton's wife had not returned by the end of the year, nor answered three letters he had laboriously composed to suggest, order, and finally beg her to come back, he received word from her people that she had died of lung fever a month earlier. It was then that he brought a woman, Naomi, from the fields to act as his cook and housekeeper.

In time, his longing for a woman stirred him to pursue her as a mistress and move her into the house. Naomi's shapely form had grown increasingly pleasing to him as the memory of his wife's stocky body became an ever-receding memory. It had been easy enough, even before his wife left him, to satisfy a momentary urge for the pleasure of a woman by ordering a female from the fields or quarters for quick, unresisting compliance against a tree, or in a barn, or on the ground in the nearby woods. But there remained an unfulfilled emptiness in such easy gratification.

Since he had not immediately sought her services for any purpose other than as a cook and housekeeper, Naomi's features had lost the guarded, fearful expression of her first days in house service, and she had relaxed and become complacent and even occasionally surly in her relationship with him.

"Kitchen cold when I got up this mornin'," he said to her one evening at supper. "Fire done gone plum out."

"Can't do it all," Naomi said. "It banked good when I left last evenin'."

"Watch your lip, wench," he said. "You ain't the missus here. You ain't nothin' but a low-down, good-for-nothin' black and can be got rid of any time."

As usual, such threats brought an instant return to subservience and the appearance of any further rebelliousness was quickly squelched. He could read in her eyes her hatred for him and her forced submission gave him a feeling of power and pleasure.

Already drunk, he watched her steadily as he consumed more whiskey and requested another serving of corn bread. When she brought it and returned to the other side of the kitchen, Wroughton watched the undulations of her buttocks beneath her thin dress.

"More bacon," he said in a slurred voice. She returned to serve him, again revealing the shapely contours of her body as she walked back across the room. Wroughton chuckled to himself as she bent down and put sticks of kindling into the fireplace.

"More cabbage!" he said, and she made a third trip to the table.

"You could have told me all at onct and saved me two trips," she grumbled as she spooned the soggy vegetable on his plate.

His coppery-colored eyes narrowed while he watched her above his long, veering nose. "Who you think you are to be saved anything?" He slammed his glass on the table. "You watch your high and mighty ways with me. You think you're a Hawthorn black or somethin'?"

Naomi retreated into silence.

"I said, you think you're a biggity Hawthorn black?"

"No, sir."

Wroughton chuckled to himself and grinned. Angling his head to one side in a perverse attempt to radiate charm, his voice became low and gentle as he held up his glass. "Want a little drink?" he coaxed smoothly.

"No, sir."

"Thought blacks liked a drink onct in a while."

Naomi was silent. He refilled his glass again and his voice softened.

"How you like to move up here with me?"

Naomi said nothing and cast her eyes downward.

Wroughton continued, "Be mighty nice to have floor under your feet instead of dirt, wouldn't it? And a real tick with goose feathers at night 'stead of corn husks? And good thick quilts—"

Naomi remained silent.

"Old woman left two or three dresses you can have."

The silence continued and Wroughton's flirtatious voice turned hard. "You listening to me? You hear what I'm sayin'?"

"Yes, sir. I hears you." She began peeling a bowl of potatoes.

"Wouldn't you like them things?"

"I reckon I be just fine in the cabins."

"But your man's dead and I done made you a house black. House blacks lives in their master's houses, in the cellars and attics. I'm offerin' you a regular room right here in the house."

"I reckon I be alright where I is." She continued to peel the potatoes.

"Then I'm tellin' you to move up here. I can't be fetchin' you from the quarters every time I need the fire built or something."

Wroughton snorted in contempt, then again resumed a softer manner, his voice becoming low and caressing.

"What if I told you I had a feelin' for you?"

Naomi only looked at the floor.

"What if I told you I liked you more than any black on the place and was willin' to set you up right good here in the house with me? You be higher up than any slave on the place. It be right much like you was over them. Like my missus was over you and Jane and them."

"Don't need to be over nobody, sir," Naomi said.

"Don't want to be over nobody? Ever body over somebody. Even you blacks. Ain't you over your youngins?"

Naomi nodded.

"I put you over all other blacks on the place. A black don't git a chance like that ever day. To be brought up to the master's house and treated near as good as a white woman. I'd treat you mighty good. Might even get you a kitchen wench to help you. You'd be over her—she'd have to do ever thing you said."

"I beholden' to you, Master, but I'll just stay where I been."

Wroughton was insulted and outraged at her rebuff. "Then maybe that girl of yorn, that Dell. Ain't that her name? Dell? Maybe she could move up here with me. She ripe by now, ain't she?"

A thin coat of perspiration broke out on Naomi's forehead at Wroughton's mention of her daughter. A quiet intake of breath signaled her fear.

"She ain't but twelve. She not able to cook or do nothin'. She not be no help to you." She tried to keep her words calm, but her voice was tense as fear and dread tightened her throat.

"I reckon you could teach her. She be thirteen sooner or later. I reckon you could teach her like that wench Jane taught you."

"She just a child, Master Wroughton. It not right to bring her up here." She turned to face him, her face pleading, frightened and anguished. "She just a child yet...just twelve..."

"That's old enough. They droppin' babies by that age."

Naomi felt her apron tear as she gripped it. "Oh, please, Master Wroughton," she pleaded. "Not my Dell. She too little. It just ain't right."

"You think I let a black wench like you tell me what right or not right in my own house?"

Naomi was at once on her knees before him. "I begs you, Master Wroughton, leave my child be. I do anything you want, but leave my Dell be."

Wroughton looked down at her, his eyes falling from the pain and misery in her eyes to her heaving breasts.

"You be my woman?"

Naomi paused, desperate for a way out yet unable to find one.

"I treat you nice...real nice," Wroughton said.

"Yes, sir," Naomi said at last, choking on the words.

"Git up then."

Naomi was sobbing by now and remained on her knees.

"I said, git up!"

Naomi struggled to her feet and stood before him, her head lowered. Wroughton rose unsteadily from the table and stood facing her.

"Didn't I tell you I got a feelin' for you? Won't be like makin' 'um lay down with me in the fields. Not you. I'll bring you to the house. We'll have nice goose-feathered ticks to do it on."

He extended his hand and reached down the front of her dress. His voice lost its anger but not its icy intensity. Wroughton's hand encircled one of her breasts. He began to squeeze, increasing the pressure until Naomi, hunched forward, her elbows pressed tightly to her sides, whimpered in pain. "Please, Master Wroughton—"

"Gabriel done give Hicks and the men I harred to fetch him back the slip in Philadelphia. But he'll get word to that Hawthorn woman and her blacks where he gits to. I want to know where. You right thick with 'em, ain't you?"

"I knows a few, sir."

Wroughton released her breast and removed his hand from her dress, confident that he had implanted fear enough to ensure her obedience. Not only had he secured himself a live-in woman, he was likely to learn Gabriel's whereabouts.

Then Wroughton would get him back and once more he would be the envy of the county and the other planters would know who he was and that he was the slave-owner among them who possessed the finest black in the county.

Once again Horace Wroughton would be somebody.

Chapter Thirty-Eight

When Lavinia's brother Richard and his wife, Ellie, visited in late summer a year later in 1858, Lavinia decided to return with them for a visit with her parents. Granny, now ninety-seven, was failing, and with Margaret's family and the senior Hawthorns at Hawthorn Hill, Lavinia could visit her people and return before winter.

On a cold September morning, the day before she was scheduled to leave, Old Sheba struggled to the big house to speak with Lavinia. Gasping for breath from her climb up the hill, Lavinia motioned the old woman inside the kitchen.

"Why didn't you send for me, Sheba?" Lavinia asked. "I would have come to the quarters."

"Walls got ears down there. Needs to talk private." Taking the old woman to the office, Lavinia brought her a warming cup of coffee. "You can talk freely here," she said.

The black, leathery face with its prominent cheekbones looked like a skeleton, grim and exhausted, as the old woman caught her breath and sipped the coffee before speaking.

"You still leavin' to visit your people tomorrow?" Old Sheba asked.

"Yes, early tomorrow morning."

"Naomi, one of the Wroughton people, sneaks over to see me last night," she said in a raspy whisper.

"Catch your breath, Sheba. And take your time."

Ignoring her, Sheba continued, the urgency of her message precluding any consideration for her own well-being. "Naomi got a girl, Dell. She just thirteen and Wroughton wantin' to make her his bed-wench—"

Lavinia, bending over the table to hear, sat erect, her face somber with shock and outrage.

"He been usin' Naomi for most a year now. Now he tired of her and wantin' this child to bed with. Been talkin' it a long time and Naomi think he mean it. She wantin' to run but scared to. Wroughton say he kill any what tries it. He make good on his word and kills Booker, so she got a good right to fear, I reckon. But she rather die than has her child spiled."

Lavinia needed to hear no more and immediately sprang into action. "Get word to Naomi to bring her child and come here tonight at midnight. Have her come by the creek, when everyone has gone to sleep."

Old Sheba cupped her hand over her ear to hear, as Lavinia continued, "Tell her to enter the creek on Wroughton property and come by water all the way to our quarters as far as the foot bridge."

Old Sheba nodded and her eyes beamed with gratitude. "You be a mighty big blessin' to Naomi and little Dell," she said, and she struggled to her feet. "I sends word over there tonight."

Steadying her, she assisted Old Sheba down the kitchen steps and accompanied her back to the quarters.

"And have Reuben lock up the hounds so they won't alert the plantation of the Wroughton people's arrival."

"I do it. And then they something else I wants to tell you." The old woman stopped and leaned heavily on her cane. "They something you ought to know if you could come see me in the cabins when you gets back from your people."

"Why not now?"

"Be better after we gets Naomi and Dell out safe. You come sees me and I tells you."

Lavinia agreed with Old Sheba's request and as soon as she returned to the big house, she watched from the second floor as a small group of blacks converged on the old woman's cabin. Soon a fleet-footed field hand emerged and ran in the direction of the Wroughton Plantation.

Having confirmed that her message had been delivered, midnight found Lavinia waiting by the creek at the foot bridge. She had slipped down the back steps, out of the house, and to the stables for Mercury and led him past the quarters, unobserved and unheard. As instructed, Reuben had isolated the hounds in a barn, where they slept and made no disturbance.

Soon Lavinia heard the sounds of Naomi and Dell approaching in the water and waved a lamp to signal them farther down the creek.

"Did anyone see you?"

"No, ma'am," Naomi answered, a little breathless from wading the water up to her waist. The thirteen-year-old, Dell shyly huddled at her mother's side. "Mr. Wroughton done drunk agin and passed out like usual. He never sees us."

"Just stay in the water and follow me down the bank."

With Lavinia on the shore guiding them with the lamp, the two slaves continued to wade down the creek. When Lavinia reached Mercury, tethered and waiting not far from the bank, she unhitched and mounted him and guided him into the water. She then pulled Naomi and Dell up behind her and continued down the creek a short distance where she reined the horse toward dry land. She extinguished the lamp and returned to the stables, where she provided Naomi and Dell with towels and dry clothes, and concealed them in the carriage that would be driven at sunrise by Richard on the journey to Washington County.

After Lavinia, the twins, Ellie, and Richard left Hawthorn Hill with Naomi and Dell concealed under the seats, a heavy rain began, providing a logical explanation for the absence of a detectable scent when the patrols made an attempt to track Naomi and Dell with hounds.

The run to Washington County with Naomi and Dell went without a single complication. Exhilarated with the successful mission, when she returned to Hawthorn Hill, she was delighted to see Lionel's horse in the front pasture.

Margaret rushed out of the house to greet her. When no one else appeared, Lavinia immediately asked about Lionel.

"He's in the fields. He'll hear the hounds and be here directly. How are they all?"

"Granny is hanging on and everyone else is well." In the parlor, Lavinia gave a brief rundown on her family. "But where is everyone?"

"Mama's at a quilting and Alexander had to get back to his congregation. But before you rest, or unpack, or do anything, there is something that requires your attention immediately!"

Pulling Lavinia by the hand, Margaret cracked the door to the front hall and peeked out. Then she motioned Lavinia into the hall, returned to the parlor, and closed the door after her.

The hall seemed empty at first, but then Lavinia saw a retiring little creature lurking alone in the shadows beneath the stairs.

Dressed in a dress of white Alençon lace which cascaded about her bony frame in tiers, she recognized the little blue-eyed figure at once.

"Henny!"

She rushed toward her, stopping when the little figure took a step back. Sensing her insecurity and shyness—this was hardly the bold little girl who had approached her on the side porch almost five years before—Lavinia smiled and waited. Joy and relief filled her heart and tears streamed down her face.

Henny seemed thinner, but had grown taller. Her face was more mature, but still held the familiar look of the child whose absence Lavinia had mourned for almost five years. Taking another step backward, she bit her lip as she watched Lavinia cautiously. Finally, she took a tentative step forward, moving out of the shadows. She watched her mistress with apprehension for a long time before she spoke, her large blue eyes glistening.

"Miss Vinny—" She faltered, and Lavinia nodded her encouragement to continue.

"Miss Vinny, I never steals Miss Ariadne's earbobs and things," she said.

Chapter Thirty-Nine

At supper that evening, the family competed to tell
Lavinia the details of Henny's rescue. The excitement of
her return only a week earlier still held the family enthralled
and she heard the story from everyone at least two times.

Cornelia said, "Well, she's very vague about what
happened to her after that wretched Steele boy stole her...
and those brothers... What was their name, son?"

"The Stratchey brothers, Mother."

"Yes, the Stratcheys. Anyway, she ended up in a convent
of Roman Catholic nuns! They must have been kind to her...
and have taught her impeccable manners. One would never
believe for an instant she was from the fields. Anyway, after
several years, little Henrietta—isn't it the nicest coincidence
she was named after Mr. Hawthorn's mother?"

Lavinia cast a quick glance at both Lionel and Mr.
Edmund.

"Little Henrietta began to trust them and finally told
them where she came from. Poor child... She had seen those
brothers murdered, witnessed horrors we can only imagine,
and it took the nuns years to get her to confide in them."

"But she had never forgotten us," said Margaret. "She
knew she was a Virginian and a Hawthorn and even the
county we live in."

"You tell the rest, son," said Cornelia.

"When the sisters learned she had been stolen—and that we were benevolent masters—they wrote to me. I responded and when Henny expressed a desire to come home, I went to get her."

"She actually wrote the letter herself!" said Margaret. "The nuns had taught her to read and she said she was innocent of stealing and that Ariadne made that up because Henny—Henrietta—caught her reading your mail. A secret message hidden in dress patterns or something. Imagine reading someone else's mail!"

Lavinia shot Margaret a glance, and Margaret quickly followed with, "It was that secret letter you wrote Ibby about getting Mother a special bonnet as a surprise for her birthday. Ibby and I laughed about it for days, because I got the bonnet and Lionel delivered the secret message and didn't even know."

"I remember that lovely bonnet so well. I still wear it."

"And the nuns taught her to read and everything," Margaret continued, privy to Lavinia's covert efforts in that area prior to Henny's disappearance.

"Indeed, she is a remarkable little girl," said Cornelia. "You might have had reservations, Lavinia, but I was absolutely right. She is fully capable of being a ladies' maid. I think you should move her to the big house at once."

"I must write the nuns of my gratitude," said Lavinia as Lionel lifted his wine glass and toasted Lavinia's victory.

"I never believed that child stole Ariadne's jewelry," said Cornelia in a whisper. Lavinia was sure she saw a twinkle of mischief in Cornelia's eyes when she added, "I know Ariadne rejected my offer to loan Piney to her before, but since she's had another maid run away, I think I shall send her anyway."

Lavinia knew her mother-in-law knew of Ariadne's aversion to Piney, but revealed not a sign that she detected the older woman's subtle revenge. "What a splendid idea, Mother Hawthorn. What would any of us do without your wisdom and thoughtfulness?"

The next day, Lavinia remembered her promise to visit Old Sheba when she returned from her trip to Williamsville and visited the quarters. She found the old woman behind her cabin stripping dead leaves from a tall plant in the small garden where she grew the ingredients she dried, ground, steeped, and boiled when making her mysterious medical concoctions.

"Beck sent some soup, Sheba," Lavinia said.

The old woman nodded and gathered up her apron, in which she had placed the long, serrated brown leaves. "I be thankin' her. And you fer hepin' Naomi and little Dell. Mighty bad see a young child lak that—"

"It won't happen, Sheba. They'll be safe at my brother's for the time being, and will be in Ohio within a month."

Lavinia followed the old woman into her cabin with its strange herbal smells. Dodging the numerous bundles of plants that hung by strings from the ceiling, Sheba went to a table and dumped the contents of her apron onto it. Then, taking a few of the dry leaves and crumbling them between her fingers, she took a corncob pipe and filled the bowl, adding a pinch of dried tobacco flakes. After carefully tamping the mixture in the bowl, she lit it with a taper from the fireplace. Sitting in her rocking chair, the old woman took a puff from her pipe.

"The people," she said. She was silent for a long moment, during which she puffed on the pipe again, holding the smoke in her lungs for a long time before she exhaled. Her brow furrowed and her eyes blinked in deep concentration while she carefully organized her thoughts.

"The people...our people...the ones on Hawthorn Hill... has knowed a long time you been heppin' runaways." The deep-set eyes in the skeletal face watched Lavinia closely, almost accusingly, as she inhaled deeply from the pipe, which smelled like burning rope.

"I hardly expect it would be a secret after this many years," Lavinia said.

The old woman held the smoke in her lungs a long time before she released it and spoke. "You heps right many, I reckon," she said.

After a long pause, she spoke again. "But the people here. They right many of them that wants to be free, too. They don't know why you keeps them slaves and helps other people's slaves gets away."

The old woman's words hit Lavinia like a lightning bolt. Her own blacks wanted to be free? She was stunned by the suggestion. Other than Angelica's desire to be with Gabriel, it never occurred to her that her own people were unhappy or desired liberation. Even Angelica would have been happy to have remained at Hawthorn Hill if she had been allowed to marry Gabriel.

"You...you mean the people at Hawthorn Hill feel mistreated?"

"Ain't that," Old Sheba said with an irritated jerk of he head. "Hawthorn's better'n most masters, I reckon." This tepid commendation was followed by another long inhalation from her pipe before she continued. "The people here cares right much for you. We got enough to eat and clothes and ain't worked to death like some. But we still property and ain't free."

Old Sheba turned her attention from the pipe and looked at Lavinia.

"The people worries 'bout they children. What happen when you and Mr. Lionel gone? We still be owned by your children. What happen to us later? Not me, I too old to do nothin' but die. Us old ones ain't worried 'bout ourselves. Our real Master gives us justice." She nodded her head as if to make it clear to Lavinia that she and Lionel were only her masters here on earth. "But the young ones...they the ones wantin' something besides the fields and..." The old woman stopped.

Her pipe had gone out and she put it aside. Reaching in the pocket of her apron, she got a wedge of tobacco, bit off a portion, and began to chew it. "Reckon it alright if I chews?"

"I'd rather you chewed than smoked that vile-smelling pipe," Lavinia said. Old Sheba chuckled to herself, bit off a corner of the block of tobacco, and moving her mouth vigorously, worked it into a suitable consistency for chewing.

Lavinia was still numbed by Old Sheba's suggestion that Hawthorn blacks wanted freedom, even as they were better treated than any blacks in the county. She was almost insulted—angered that the Christian effort with which she had cared for her blacks went so unappreciated.

How many times had she worked late into the night to help nurse their sick and dying? Even to the point of bringing their diseases into her own house to strike and kill her own, as had typhoid when it had begun in the quarters and finally took her precious Oralee from her. How many hours a day, for twenty-five years, had she sewed and assisted them in making clothes and quilts? And seen to it that leaking roofs were repaired, cabins adequately daubed to keep out the cold, and that certain slaves be excused from labor because of injuries and sickness? Even when the overseer, Virgil Mudley, said they were malingering in all likelihood, but sometimes were given the benefit of the doubt anyway?

How many times had she settled injustices Mudley would have settled with the lash, intervening to prevent further suffering? How many infractions of discipline and proper conduct had she overlooked—petty crimes she had covered up—injustices she had rectified?

"Freedom," she said at last, her voice pinched with resentment. "What do any of them know about freedom? Where would they go? What would they do? Who would nurse their ills, feed them, clothe them, baptize them and bring them to the knowledge of Christ and salvation and moral conduct? And even teach some to read?"

Her thoughts spun with resentment and anger at the people's ingratitude, at the years of her labor on their behalf.

"Didn't I get your cabin floored, Sheba? Didn't I make Mr. Lionel have wooden floors installed in most of the cabins?"

"He done a few. He done mine and Beck's and another one or two. Most of them still hard earth, though. But freedom more than a wooden floor. Or a full belly. Freedom better'n all of it. Not havin' it worser than all of it."

Suddenly, Lavinia felt Old Sheba's malice with all of its intensity as the withered lips hurled charges and accusations at her she had never heard before. It was as if a floodgate had been opened and the old woman was infused with new youth as the intensity of her feelings erupted without fear of the consequences.

"I always say the goodness in you done buried with whiteness too deep to come out. Like whitewash on a privy. Emma say you no white devil like the rest, but she know you white just the same. She always take up for you and Master Lionel, but say you can't see no difference twixt a barn and a chicken coop. Reckon she right. You do the easy good but turns your back on the hard. You let on you so good and Christian but don't know nothin' 'bout what it mean. You a hypocrite, pure and simple—lovin' the people with one breath and keepin' 'em slaves the next."

As a white woman, an automatic resentment at a black speaking with such impudence aroused Lavinia's anger. No black had ever spoken to her in such a manner—not even Emma in all her unbridled candor.

"You almost got to be black to be a real Christian," Old Sheba continued, the intensity of her diatribe undiminished. "You got to suffer like Jesus. But you ain't made for real sufferin' or sacrifice like a true Christian. You can't see the speck in your own eye for the beam. You right much a rabbit tryin' to be a hound, but can't be neither. You all talk, but ain't got no real grit in your craw. Just like all the other white devils in this world."

She looked away and spat into the fire.

Lavinia was so surprised by Old Sheba's harshness that her indignation subsided into stunned dismay. How dare she! The arrogance of this ignorant, impudent... She could only stare at the old woman in silence. She knew from Emma that Old Sheba called white people like Horace Wroughton "devils," but had no idea she was held in so low regard as well.

"I have helped only those seeking escape from cruel masters, Sheba," she said defensively. "I can recall no incidence when my family has dealt with any of the people at Hawthorn Hill unjustly or with cruelty. I can recall of no one going hungry or cold or being overworked or who had an illness that went untreated—"

Old Sheba, chewing her tobacco vigorously, frowned as Lavinia went on, shaking her head as if in pity at her ignorance. "Done told you that ain't it!" the old woman said, her voice still sharp and hostile. "They wants freedom cause they know it ain't right not to has it. They knows they has it onct 'fore white devils got 'em. Why else you think they wantin' it? To be like white people?" She laughed with disgust and Lavinia felt her face grow hot to be laughed at by this impudent old woman. She actually looked at her like she was ignorant herself! Or stupid! A black, condescending to her, laughing at her, scorning her! Lavinia was outraged and humiliated, her pride injured all the more because Old Sheba sensed it, understood it, and continued to regard her as if she were a fool.

The wise old eyes gleamed above the sharp cheekbones as they scrutinized Lavinia closely for a long moment. "Our people thinkin' it a wrongful thing to enslave people. They been believin' you thinks that way, too." Old Sheba looked away from Lavinia and again spat into the fire. "But I reckon they wrong."

As she continued to avoid looking at Lavinia, the old woman's anger seem to fade into weariness and disappointment as she gazed sadly into the fire.

"Well, they can't go," Lavinia said. "How on earth would we raise a crop with no blacks?" Her words faltered, brought to a halt by the realization of what her blacks at Hawthorn Hill had done for her in exchange for her efforts on their behalf.

That's the way they feel! she thought, meaning the other slave owners. *I'm just like the other slave owners after all, spouting their arguments and defenses and—*

As if reading her mind, Old Sheba aimed another stream of tobacco into the fire, where it sizzled and sputtered as if expressing the anger and bitterness which showed in the old woman's hard, narrowed eyes.

Suddenly, Lavinia remembered the larger issue. Shame filled her as she acknowledged her own hypocrisy in denouncing slavery while at the same time defending her own ownership of slaves. No wonder Sheba thought her a fool.

"I'm sounding just like Mr. Jefferson and Mr. Washington," she said aloud, more to herself than Old Sheba. "And all the others the Barksdale sisters call hypocrites."

Stunned with what she should have thought of from the very beginning—even as far back as when she assisted in the escape of Angelica and Gabriel years ago—Lavinia experienced a revelation: the harsh awareness that freedom might be as precious to her own slaves as any other human being held in bondage.

Of course the others would want freedom. Of course they would wonder at their mistress's assistance of total strangers in their flight while ignoring their own quest for the same liberty.

She was at once ashamed and chastised that her new awareness had to be made known to her by one of her own people, by an old, ignorant black woman. No—by an old, very wise black woman.

"Oh, Sheba, I've been such a fool," she said, reaching for the old woman's hand. She sat down heavily in a chair opposite Sheba and tried to bring order to her whirling thoughts. "Of course, being mistreated isn't the only reason to want freedom. Or the hard labor and all the other terrible things slavery imposes."

She stopped, her mind flooded with a hundred reasons, some of them the slaves didn't even realize themselves. The forced ignorance caused by the laws forbidding blacks to be taught to read isolated them from any real perception of the meaning of freedom. They endured what they were not even aware they did not have to endure because they had never known anything else and were forbidden to learn anything else. Their unresisting acceptance of bondage was not unlike the acceptance by a million white women of the denial of certain rights: the right to vote, serve on a jury, or even own property unless they were widows or orphans or spinsters.

Hadn't the Barksdale sisters pointed out to her that as far as property rights were concerned, a married woman was no better than a slave? And as far as the right to vote, a woman of any station had no more freedom than a black. Indeed, if she felt these deprivations of so-called "freedom," how much worse must it be for blacks, male or female, who were forbidden to learn to read and write?

"I must think, Sheba," she said, her mind reeling. "But I shall be back to see you tomorrow. Say nothing to anyone of our conversation."

She released the old woman's hand and returned to the big house, her mind a storm of conflict and uncertainty. She had not used liquor to induce sleep for years, yet she was tempted to tonight. But she resisted the impulse. There was too much to think through, too many details to consider, too many consequences to contemplate. She needed only clear-headed sobriety to muddle through it all.

Sleep was impossible and the lamps in her room burned late into the night. For hours, she considered the challenge that taunted her. Sitting before the window in her room, she pondered her new awakening, waiting for the first light of morning that would bring into view the misty cemetery where her dead sons and daughter rested.

By the time the sun first edged above the horizon, she was committed. She rose from her chair and walked toward the window.

"I'll do it. I don't know how, but I'll do it. And if I have to, I'll lead them to Ohio myself. I'm going to free them all."

Chapter Forty

Henny's return to Hawthorn Hill was the cause of the greatest celebration since the birth of the twins and Margaret and Lavinia's grandchild. The little girl was slow to return to her usual self, however, and chose to spend most of her time alone in her cabin. A shadow of melancholy seemed to have descended on the child, which Lavinia could neither penetrate nor eliminate.

When gently questioned about her ordeal, Henny's brow creased with distress and her blue eyes hardened at the painful memories of her ordeal, even as Lavinia made every effort to show her joy in having her back and reassured her that at no time was she ever suspected of theft by anyone except Emma, Piney, and Ariadne.

"And Ariadne seldom visits Hawthorn Hill anymore. And only briefly when she does. And Piney is leaving with Miss Cornelia to be Ariadne's maid when she returns to Richmond in a week."

One day, Lavinia and Henny visited the Hawthorn graveyard. Lavinia hadn't been to Oralee's grave since before visiting her family and the last of the summer flowers was fast disappearing. A few roses lingered and with ivy and magnolia leaves, a suitable bouquet was fashioned.

"Used to be scared of cemeteries, Miss Lavinia," Henny said. "But I ain't no more. Don't seem to matter now."

"You may tell me about your kidnapping, if you wish," Lavinia said casually as she divided the flowers and placed them on the graves.

"They never hurt me none. But they mighty mean to Jeff and Wash."

In a sketchy summary, Henny told of the Stratchey brothers' murder and the hanging of Jeff and Wash. Far from complete, her narrative nevertheless shocked Lavinia, whose heart ached that a child could have witnessed such horrors.

"If it is too painful to remember, you don't have to tell me," Lavinia said.

The little girl hastily concluded her odyssey with her arrival at the Convent of the Sisters of St. Joseph.

"I never think much of them at first, them nun-people. They was all women." Henny shook her head in mystification. "And Miss Vinny, they wear the funniest dresses you ever saw. And the bonnets they wear not pretty at all but look like great big boxes and cover they whole head but they faces that peeped out. And they all got the same name, Mary, with somethin' else."

"Goodness," said Lavinia, suppressing a smile.

"Did you ever see one, Miss Vinny?"

"I think maybe I have, once or twice in Richmond. And there were quite a few in Philadelphia and New Orleans when Mr. Lionel and I visited there."

"They funny lookin' things, alright, but I believe they mighty good. Don't do much work but sings and prays all day long. I don't care what folks say about white people in Georgia. Them nun-women was good to me as you can be. But they teached me to read right where you left off. I decides they right good. I tells them I Mr. Lionel's and they writ him and I got to ride the train and everything. Piney ain't never rid no train and mad as a hornet I has. And Mr. Lionel never whip me, or fuss, or nothin', and say he always know I never steal."

"I must write the Sisters of my gratitude."

"You tells them I mighty gratified, too."

"You may write them yourself. And we will continue your reading lessons. Just as I taught Oralee and Angelica. Would you like that?"

"Yes'um," Henny replied, but she wasn't sure how reading and writing would be of much benefit to her.

"We will have to keep your lessons a secret, even from Mr. Lionel."

"I not tell nobody. Mr. Lionel or Piney either one. She be the one to tells it ever where."

"But she will be gone soon. When Miss Cornelia takes her to Richmond."

Henny smiled a soft, unsteady smile. Her ambition had been realized. She was going to be Miss Lavinia's maid after all. But even as she felt relief and happiness at her accomplishment, her mind went back to Stella and Uncle Will and the slaves she had seen in the quarters in South Carolina. Somehow, achieving her goal was no longer enough. She chided herself for her lack of gratitude, but then realized, even in her unsophisticated, uneducated, fourteen-year-old mind, that even though she had moved from the fields to the big house, advanced from field worker to house servant, she was still a slave, and being a slave, no matter how lofty that slave's position might be was still that: a slave.

Chapter Forty-One

In Richmond, Ariadne became weary of Piney's endless chatter after only two weeks. When she sniggered and emitted a stream of giggles at Judge Povall's repeated flatulence while serving tea one afternoon, and laughed aloud when his ivory false teeth slipped out of his mouth and, caught by his tongue, dangled from his lip until he could set aside his teacup and push them back into place, Ariadne was outraged.

She had Piney whipped and immediately returned to Lavinia when Cornelia and Margaret escaped the summer heat of Richmond in 1858 for a visit to Hawthorn Hill. It was hoped that Lionel would join them but the thriving tobacco factory and his father's law office kept him in the city.

Although Emma made no protests when the family honored her own birthday, or that of Uncle Lemiel and Aunt Beck, she adamantly opposed any celebration of Henny's. But Cornelia, Margaret, and Lavinia overruled her.

Henny would be fourteen-years-old and, unable to stand the suspense, had already persuaded Lavinia to allow her to peek inside the mysterious box containing her birthday present, which had arrived a few weeks earlier. It was a dress of Alençon lace, exactly like the one she had worn the day she first approached Lavinia to become Angelica's replacement.

Lavinia had noticed Henny still wore the old, tattered one and had especially ordered a new one.

The years since Henny first appeared on her side porch had brought the girl to the early stages of womanhood. Sweet-tempered and Lavinia's constant companion, she had responded well to her education. Her remarkable reading skills, grammar, and etiquette made Margaret despair when compared to her own children's accomplishments. Cornelia's praise for the little girl never stopped. "She has much better manners and social graces than cousin Gertrude's grandchildren," she said, "and they are Randolphs!"

Margaret and Lavinia exchanged wry glances.

Although she had been allowed only a peek at her gift before, on the actual day of her birthday she had risen early. With Lavinia still in bed, she tore into the package and tried on the dress. Thrilled, she hugged Lavinia and dashed to the full-length dressing mirror to twirl about and curtsy and hold out the skirt in unabashed vanity and pride.

"You look absolutely beautiful," Lavinia said, remembering the large, loosely fitting, earlier version of the dress hanging from Henny's thin shoulders the morning she had found her asleep on the side porch.

As Henny experimented with various positions of the bow at her waist—in front, at the back, to one side—they heard the sound of horses' hooves galloping up the lane to the house.

"He's come!" Lavinia cried, thinking Lionel had managed to get away from factory duties and had arrived after all.

Jumping out of bed, she rushed to the window. Even in the early morning light, she recognized the rider as Randy. The hounds soon started yelping and Lavinia, afraid her son's unexpected appearance brought bad news, rushed downstairs in her dressing gown and out on the porch as he rode to a stop and quickly dismounted.

One look at his face, drawn with worry and fatigue, told her she was correct.

"Is it Grandpapa?" she asked, fearing old Mr. Hawthorn had met with some malady.

"No, Mama," he said, looking away.

"The baby? Little Alexander? Sarah?"

He tossed the reins of his horse across the hitching post beside the front steps and gave his mother a quick kiss on the cheek, still avoiding her gaze.

"What's wrong?" Lavinia said urgently, clutching his arm as he rushed past her into the house, where he met Margaret and Cornelia in the front hall.

"Oh, what a surprise!" trilled Cornelia, missing the look of distress etched in the young man's features and throwing her arms around her grandson.

But Margaret caught the anguish in her nephew's expression. "Is it one of the babies? Are the babies alright?" she asked.

By now Cornelia also saw the distress in her grandson's eyes. "Mr. Hawthorn? Is it Edmund?"

"Everything—everybody's alright," Randy said, almost with irritation, gesturing with his hands for them all to calm down.

"Oh." Cornelia's hands flew to her mouth and she searched for a handkerchief. Although his words gave them some relief, the women knew that something was terribly wrong.

"Come into the parlor," Lavinia directed her son, Margaret, and Cornelia, still in dressing gowns. They followed her into the room, where she lighted lamps and pulled back the draperies to dispel the early morning darkness.

"Has war broken out?" Cornelia asked. "A slave insurrection?"

"No! No!" Randy said impatiently, his words instantly followed by a look of guilt and apology at having spoken so sharply to his grandmother.

The young man's tired eyes and rumpled appearance told Lavinia he had been riding for hours.

"You've ridden all night, haven't you?" Lavinia asked.

"Now, just be calm and I'll tell you," he said, his brow knotted with distress as he carefully organized his thoughts. "Everyone is alright. Just sit down."

The women obeyed, never taking their eyes from the young man as he paced in front of the mantle and finally spoke. "He's alright. He was not seriously injured, but... well...Papa's been shot."

Lavinia's heart seemed to stop and she grew deathly pale. Cornelia emitted a little cry and burst into tears, and Margaret gasped.

Randy continued to pace back and forth, his words tumbling out to quickly reassure them, while the women, bending forward on the edge of their seats, listened with indrawn breaths.

"He's not hurt seriously. Just his arm, his shoulder. He's fine. Just fine." He stopped abruptly, as if he had only now come to the difficult part of his story.

"Well, go on. Tell us," Lavinia finally said.

"What else? Is there something else?" Margaret asked.

"Well," Randy hung his head and looked embarrassed. Finally, he looked his mother directly in the eye and said, "Well, you'll hear it anyway. And it might as well be from me. It was night before last. I rode all day and night so you would hear it from me first."

"Sit down. You're exhausted. I'll–" Lavinia checked her concern and waited.

"Papa was at the Bird and Owl Hotel. That's where it happened. He...he was in a...a woman's room. A Mrs. Clevinger's..."

Cornelia emitted a little cry of shock and mortification. Lavinia sat erect and unmoving, her features taut and unreadable. Margaret, seated beside her and at once comprehending the entire episode, automatically put a comforting hand on Lavinia's arm.

"Well–" He looked uncertainly at Cornelia, who quietly sobbed in her handkerchief.

"Go on, son," Lavinia said, her voice calm. "We must know sooner or later."

"The terrible thing about it...or part of it. It's in the papers..."

"Oh!" Cornelia wailed, turning away from the others against the curved back of her chair. "A scandal!"

"Well, Papa was in this Clevinger woman's room and her husband came in and shot him." Randy blurted it out, as if to get the painful business over quickly.

At last unburdened, the distressed young man once again tried to comfort and reassure his family. "But only in the arm. He's not hurt and is at home with Grandpapa and he's going to be alright."

Lavinia looked sadly into her lap as Margaret continued to pat her arm.

"Oh, Mama, I'm so sorry," Randy said to Lavinia.

Lavinia patted the empty seat on the other side of her on the settee. Her son sat down and took her in his arms and she rested her head against his shoulder.

Cornelia's sobs continued quietly as the others sat in strained silence for a moment until Lavinia straightened and nodded for her son to attend his grandmother. He rushed to the old lady's side and knelt beside her chair. Cornelia leaned on him, her shoulders shaking with sobs, as he helplessly patted her hand.

"Now, Granny, don't you worry about a thing," Randy said. "Papa is just fine. Dr. Rudd came and said the bullet didn't strike a bone and he got it out and said all he had to do was wear a sling for a few weeks until it healed up and there would be no permanent damage at all."

Cornelia straightened and looked through her tears at her grandson. She took his face into her hands and gazed at him lovingly.

"You're so sweet to comfort Granny," she said, and she looked at Margaret and Lavinia. "Isn't he sweet? Isn't he the sweetest boy?"

"Of course he is, Mother Hawthorn," Lavinia said. "But we must get ready to go to Richmond."

"And the Clevingers—what about them?" Margaret asked, her voice grim.

"Well, Mr. Clevinger fled after he shot Papa. The papers said Mrs. Clevinger left the city as well. They didn't say where, but everybody thinks they probably went back to New York, where they came from."

"Of course, I daresay no charges were placed against Mr. Clevinger," Lavinia said coldly. "He being the wronged party."

"It's because Papa was thinking about going into politics," said Randy. "Granddaddy says the newspapers would have ignored the whole thing except politics in Virginia is so dirty."

"Indeed," said Cornelia. "Why, the newspapers even printed scandalous charges of Mr. Jefferson's improprieties with a black woman when—"

"Yankees!" said Margaret bitterly, and Cornelia broke into fresh sobs.

"To think I welcomed that woman into my house," she said.

Tears coursed down Margaret's cheeks. "I should have told you," she said. "But you and Lionel have been so happy. There has been talk about that Clevinger woman and Lionel for...for some time. I...I suppose I hoped it was only gossip."

"I never heard this gossip," Cornelia said indignantly. "Perhaps it isn't true...some mistake...a rumor..."

"Bullets are not rumors, Mother Hawthorn," said Lavinia. "And gossip is seldom only rumor when it involves Lionel." She remembered she had never before discussed either Lionel's alleged or real infidelities in the presence of her children or mother-in-law. "We must leave for Richmond at once. We have to present a united family front until this is past. We can be thankful that Mr. Hawthorn is not dead or seriously hurt. I suppose the papers detailed the...event?"

Randy nodded. "I mean, they mentioned Papa's name and Mrs. Clevinger's and Mr. Clevinger's and said Papa was in her room after midnight—"

"Oh." The lateness of the hour brought another moan from Cornelia.

"—and reported that Mr. Clevinger had not been expected to return from New York for several more days. But when he did...and entered his wife's bedroom..." Cornelia's sobs became quiet wails of grief. Randy shook his head with embarrassment and disappointment, and he looked at the floor.

Lavinia rose from her chair. "Since Mr. Hawthorn is not in immediate danger of death, I think we can wait until tomorrow to depart. Now Randy, you come with me. You must have something to eat and rest from your all-night ride."

Piney had eavesdropped at the parlor door during Randy's report and reported it to the servants in the kitchen.

"He nearly die, Mr. Randy say, but he alright now, I reckon. Bullet went clean through his arm. But I don't reckon they has to take it off. Just yet, anyhow. Like they did that man that got shot huntin' way back when. But he nearly kilt for certain."

Early the next morning, the sad group, consisting of Lavinia, Cornelia, and Margaret, left for Richmond. Randy was left in charge of Hawthorn Hill until Lavinia returned.

The trip to Richmond was mostly without conversation, with only Cornelia's sniffing and copious weeping breaking the silence.

"Oh, for heaven's sake, Mama," Margaret finally said. "Lionel's not dead. And you've cried enough."

"Lionel's problems all began at that university," Cornelia said. "I knew he should have gone to the College of William and Mary, like his father, but he wouldn't listen."

"I hardly think we can blame the University of Virginia for Lionel's being caught with a woman by her jealous husband, Mother Hawthorn," Lavinia said.

"But it was at that university that he learned drinking and those card games—and all manner of unseemly behavior."

"I'll have you know my husband attended the university," said Margaret, "and he's perfect!"

Silence embraced them again, but undercurrents too powerful to be ignored swirled. Finally, Margaret could restrain herself no longer and began lashing out at Bithia Clevinger.

"I said that Clevinger woman was common the first time I saw her, at a dinner party for Ariadne's fortieth birthday, five or six years ago. She...she was just too familiar and had her eyes on Lionel from that very night on. I could see it. I could have predicted she would go after him. I've seen her set her traps other places, too. Not just at your house, Mama, but all over Richmond at other homes—hinting for rides back to her hotel afterward. Of course with Lavinia miles away at Hawthorn Hill and Lionel in Richmond, he became the logical choice. Although she set her bonnet for any other man with money and good looks. And I dare say the rumors of her other gentleman callers are true, too."

"She's trapped the poor boy," agreed Cornelia, adding weakly, "I thought she was ordinary, too. I always knew. She never had me fooled for a minute the way she did other people."

"Her clothes—I used to expect her to be found dead smothered by ruffles, she wore so many. Or strangled by the vulgar jewelry and all those ostrich feathers she wore. Sometimes she appeared at balls looking like a giant bird she wore so many. And that stinking perfume she must have soaked herself in by the washtub full—"

"That smelled like lilacs," said Lavinia, remembering her long ago suspicions.

"Why, how did you know?"

Lavinia closed her eyes and waved her hand in a gesture to dismiss the subject as Cornelia suggested, "Oh, let's just not talk about it anymore."

When they arrived in Richmond, Cornelia rushed into the house the instant the carriage pulled up to the Hawthorns' front door. The house was shrouded in darkness, the hour long past Mr. Edmund's bedtime and of the servants, and only Alonso was still awake.

Lavinia sat for a long moment in the carriage, dreading the confrontation to come.

"Are you sure you won't come in?" she asked Margaret, who had decided to wait until the next day to see her brother.

"I'll just go on home. You can go home with me, if you wish. Or come over later if you don't want to spend the night under the same roof with him. Just have Alonso bring you. Or send Ibby or one of the others and I'll send Alex for you. I feel like I'm deserting you, but—"

"It's alright. I understand." She patted Margaret on the hand and got out of the coach.

Inside, Cornelia immediately rushed upstairs to Lionel's room. Before Lavinia was halfway up the steps, she dashed out into the hall. "It was all a mistake!" she gushed with a wavering smile struggling to assert itself. "Just as I suspected. I told you it was! Lionel had only escorted Mrs. Clevinger to her room at the Bird and Owl after a dinner party at Ariadne's, as any gentleman would. The Clevingers are very good customers, as you know. There was something about accidentally entering the wrong room—all a mistake—" Cornelia's voice faltered, her smile crumbled, as even her mother's love could not induce her acceptance of the story Lionel had told her. Bringing her handkerchief to her face, she gave Lavinia a single pained look of regret and rushed into her room.

For a long time, Lavinia stood outside Lionel's room, dreading to confront him. Even though he could have been killed, hurt, anger, and a sense of betrayal pushed aside her sympathy and hardened in her breast like a stone. Finally, taking a deep breath, she knocked on the door.

"Come in," his deep, familiar voice called. Then, before her hand could reach the knob, the door opened and Lionel stood before her.

For an instant their eyes met. His expression told her immediately that he dreaded the confrontation as much as she.

She was so overcome with rage that before she could restrain herself she drew back her hand and slapped his face with all the force she could muster. The blow cracked in the air like a shot and her hand stung from her effort. Her eyes flashing with rage, she pushed past him and entered the room.

He closed the door behind her. When she turned, her face dark with anger and hurt, she saw the red imprint of her hand on his cheek and that his right arm was in a sling.

Instantly, she felt a pang of regret. She suddenly wanted to take him into her arms, to comfort him for his wound and the blow she had given him, and to brush back the inevitable lock of blond hair that hung over the brow of his lowered head. But her anger and disappointment could not be dismissed so easily, fired as it was by anger at herself for her unbidden feelings of sympathy.

It was as it had been all the other times. She hated him; she loved him. She wanted to make him suffer yet when she did, she felt more guilt than satisfaction.

He raised his head and looked at her, his blue eyes so full of pain and helplessness she could not bear to look at them. She turned away as he approached her, almost as if he wanted her to strike him again. But she had no desire for violence and already regretted hitting him the first time. She felt so defeated and empty, even her anger could not sustain itself and she simply closed her eyes and hung her head as he approached her from behind.

He put his good hand on her shoulder as if to turn her toward him, but she stiffened under his touch and remained with her back to him. She heard him grunt under his breath as he freed his injured arm from the sling and placed his other hand on her other shoulder. Then he turned her around and as she turned, he took her face into his hands and tilted it upward toward him.

She could not avoid his gaze now and returned it with a steady stare of cold disgust. Even as she read hurt and regret in the deep blue of his pleading scrutiny, and her heart ached to comfort him, she was determined to show no mercy and remain unmoved.

"I know you have heard this before...many times," he began, his voice even and calm and almost without emotion.

"Yes, I have," she said. "The regrets, the apologies, the pleas for forgiveness." Her face twisted into an ugly expression of scalding sarcasm.

"You must give me a chance."

"I am afraid I have given you too many chances. I have heard it before."

"But...but what about us?"

"I am sure Mrs. Clevinger can provide you with anything that you need—although I hear she and her husband have left town."

"Bithia Clevinger means nothing to me."

"You took a bullet for her, didn't you? But of course, that sacrifice was unintentional, wasn't it?"

Out of the corner of her eye she caught sight of the *Richmond Whig* on his bed. Breaking free of his grasp, she snatched it up. On the front page the headlines read

Prominent Richmond Businessman Shot. She quickly read the first few paragraphs and tossed it in the floor with disgust. "Of course she means nothing to you. You've made scandalous headlines with her. You've embarrassed your family. Pulled all of us down to the level of a cheap, Yankee hussy. In all probability, you've destroyed your political prospects. Why not tell the *Richmond Whig* 'Bithia Clevinger means nothing to me'?"

She realized she was shouting, but she didn't care and released her pent-up fury with full force, denouncing him, berating him, calling him names and vowing that he was never to come near her again. He was worthless and beneath contempt. His morals were those of a cretin. She hated him and never wanted to see him again.

"Tomorrow, I shall return to Hawthorn Hill and begin legal actions to secure a divorce. As disgraceful as that will be, it can hardly equal your disgrace."

Lionel lowered his head and let her rave on.

"I shall take as much of your property as the law will allow. Since the grounds for my action have been clearly described in the newspapers, I am sure I shall have no difficulty winning the case. Then I shall take our daughters, whom you will never see again, and return to my parents in Washington County."

She finally checked her rage, embarrassed that she allowed herself to reveal to such a degree her hurt. Other quarrels may have penetrated the walls to reach the ears of the servants of Hawthorn Hill, but never those of Cornelia and Edmund. She knew her anger placed her at the edge of hysteria and she was beginning to sound like a shrew, raving and without propriety—like Ariadne when she launched one of her unrestrained tirades against blacks.

Recovering her composure, she sank wearily into a chair and covered her eyes with her hand. Her tirade was useless and would accomplish nothing. They never had in the past. Her anger spent, she suddenly felt tired, depleted of either energy or the desire to fight. Surrendering to despair, her sagging spirits sank into hopelessness.

Lionel stepped behind her and in a gesture of comfort, placed the hand of his injured arm on her shoulder. In a weary gesture to remove it, she placed her hand on his, but instead of pushing it away, she allowed it to remain. The rough firmness of his hand's weight was strangely comforting, even as it came from he who had brought her so much discomfort. But she was determined she would not let the warmth of that hand spread to her heart.

She rose and when he again tried to turn her toward him, she looked away. But she caught the sight of blood staining his shirt.

"You're bleeding."

He looked down and slipped his arm back into the sling that hung limply around his neck. The red stain widened.

"Was this not bandaged?"

"Yes. Dr. Rudd dressed it. The bandage feels like it's slipped off."

"Do you have any more?"

"Yes. It is to be cleaned and dressed every day. I can do it."

"You can't do it with one hand. Take off your shirt." Their voices were low, emotionless, weary. She moved the room's single lighted lamp to his bedside table as he removed his shirt and she sat beside him on the bed.

She put a fresh dressing on his wound, speaking calmly as he watched her.

"Was the wound probed?"

"Yes."

"Did he get it all?"

"It was whole."

The bleeding stopped, and she finished dressing the wound and tied the bandage both over his shoulder and around his arm.

"I don't think it will bleed anymore if you won't move it. Keep your arm in the sling."

When she had finished, she looked around helplessly as if she didn't know what to do next.

"We can get past this, you know," he said, his blue eyes watching her closely.

What did she see in his eyes this time? His eyes had always spoken to her with a clarity and directness more powerful than words. "I'm hurt. I'm sorry. Please take me back." Yes, but she had seen it before and heard it before and even now she was tempted by his repentance. Once she derived pleasure in refusing to forgive him and seeing the same hurt in him at her rejection that he had caused her by his infidelity. His suffering had been satisfying even as it had been painful. But now, his misery brought none of the old pleasing revenge. He had at last knocked dead something within her, as he might cudgel to death with a single well-placed blow an animal caught in a trap.

"I love you," he said at last, his eyes searching for the reaction it did not receive.

"I love you, too," she said wearily. "And I believe you. She meant nothing to you, none of them meant anything to you. You love only me."

"Then?" She saw hope and relief flare in his eyes like a new fire.

"Loving you is just too hard," she said. "I think I want to love you from a distance. I'm going home."

Slowly, she rose and started for the door.

"Lavinia," he said, but she did not stop. "Please come back."

She was across the room now and as he said, "I beg you," she opened the door and left the room, closing it softly behind her. She went to the guest room, where she stayed the night.

Early the next morning before any in the household except the servants arose, Lavinia wrote a loving message to be delivered by Ibby to Cornelia and Edmund. Then she left Richmond for Hawthorn Hill.

Chapter Forty-Two

Two months passed during which Lavinia exchanged no word with Lionel. But a barrage of letters arrived at Hawthorn Hill from Cornelia and Margaret. In her replies, Lavinia made no mention of her husband, limiting her response to reports of Hawthorn Hill's activities and news of the twins. She made no move to proceed with her threat of divorce, but completely ignored Lionel in her letters, even as Cornelia and Margaret reported on his exemplary behavior and recovery from the gunshot wound.

"Lionel works so hard," Cornelia reported, "and is exhausted by the end of the day. He is in bed by nine o'clock every night and off to the factory or Papa's law office early the next morning."

In other words, thought Lavinia, *he was not in whorehouses or hotels with the likes of Mrs. Clevinger, but home with Mama like a good little boy.*

Ariadne was quick to extend her sympathy to Lavinia by writing, "My dear cousin, how you have suffered, I know. What pain this dishonor must bring to you and I know that you find comfort in knowing your dear mountain family are so far removed they will probably hear nothing of the notoriety Lionel's escapades with yet another female has brought. Those who can read will no doubt be reluctant to pass it on to those who cannot. Perhaps you made an unwise choice in a husband."

The scandal had produced an uproar in Richmond and was the favorite topic of gossip for weeks. Both Margaret and Cornelia agreed that the only appropriate response the family could make to the disgrace was temporary withdrawal from society and isolation behind closed doors and tightly drawn drapes, neither attending social functions nor receiving any but family members and the closest of friends. The unfortunate episode was to be dealt with much as a recent death in the family: with decorous isolation and suspension of all social activities. Even the appearance at church was to be discontinued for a brief time. Later, when attendance was once again resumed, there was little contact with fellow parishioners before and after the services, and the family arrived and left the family box unobtrusively by a side entrance.

Ariadne seemed oblivious to these social amenities and created further embarrassment for the family by scheduling a gala ball immediately after the scandal was front page news. The invitations went out two days after Lionel was shot and the event was to take place three weeks later. Ariadne's timing only set wagging , once more , tongues that were just beginning to still.

Margaret, her letter dripping with outrage, wrote to Lavinia immediately of the family's distress and the elite of Richmond's shock that a member of the family would entertain, even on the smallest scale, with the ignominy of Lionel's shooting still fresh on everyone's lips.

"Ariadne practically stopped the presses at the *Richmond Whig* with her rush order to print the invitations," Margaret wrote. "And her servants told Ibby she was inviting nearly one hundred guests."

Aunt Priscilla was induced by Cornelia and Margaret to call on Ariadne and implore that she cancel the event. "That you would entertain so lavishly in the wake of such notoriety is a scandal in itself," Aunt Priscilla said, but Ariadne excused herself by claiming too many arrangements had been made to call it off.

"It will look as if we don't care that Lionel has disgraced us," Aunt Priscilla insisted. "Cornelia is distraught and taken to her bed. By being hostess to this frolic, you disregard proprieties as if nothing had happened."

"But Aunt Priscilla, my invitations have already gone out—and it would be a far more serious violation of protocol to cancel now that I have received so many acceptances. Besides, we should simply ignore the talk, rise above it by letting people know how little we care what they think."

"But it's irresponsible. Lionel and those Clevingers have done enough to sully our name—this ball of yours will simply look like you are celebrating it!"

Aunt Priscilla reported to Margaret and Cornelia, "She even refused to restrain the ball's elaborateness. I think she enjoys the upheaval. Flaunting her disregard for our feelings, claiming this will be the social event of the year!"

"Well, I've heard of engagement parties and anniversary parties but never a separation party, and that is exactly what Ariadne is doing: celebrating Lionel's and Lavinia's estrangement!" said Margaret.

"I cannot believe she would abandon such a sterling opportunity to demonstrate proper behavior at such a time," Cornelia said.

"Imagine not caring what people thought or said about you!" Aunt Priscilla said with astonishment.

Margaret forwarded the details of Ariadne's flagrant disregard for the family's mortification in her next letter to Lavinia. Although invited to the ball, none of the Hawthorns or the Harveys attended. Cornelia had insisted that to prevent further talk, Aunt Priscilla and Uncle Cuthbert should attend, lest the guests read into the absence of all the family an estrangement from Ariadne.

"Aunt Priscilla didn't want to go, and I agreed with her," Margaret wrote to Lavinia, "but Mama insisted, so she did. And stayed less than an hour."

Aunt Pricilla reported that, "Ariadne had never been so gay and spent the evening talking of nothing but Lionel's and Lavinia's separation, telling everyone that it would likely end in divorce. And she pretended to regret it."

Margaret wrote to Lavinia, "I shall do all I can to counter this story with denials and insist you will be reconciled very soon."

Aunt Priscilla also wrote to Lavinia, her usually fluid and artistic writing so charged with anger and outrage her words seemed to have been slashed across the page. "Although she affected regret, she fairly glowed with satisfaction. I was so disgusted, I pleaded a headache and left at once. Ariadne is a mean-spirited and wicked woman, my dear. Never believe her false sympathy for your troubles."

Margaret was pleased to pass on the condemnation of several of the other guests who were aghast at Ariadne's brazen delight in Lionel's misfortune and added, "I am trying to convince Mother that we should never accept Ariadne's invitations again, nor receive her here. Aunt Priscilla isn't. And neither are the Carters or Pages or Flemings..."

Ariadne's tactlessness and insensitivity offended many friends of the Hawthorns who considered her disloyalty to her family inexcusable. Certain dinner parties, which would have automatically seen Ariadne in attendance, found her conspicuously absent. Invitation lists all over Richmond were revised and various teas found her uninvited. Margaret rejoiced when Ariadne was not asked to Mae Bolling's annual garden party, the first social function that Cornelia and Edmund attended with an unobtrusive exit after the briefest appearance.

Margaret was delighted to write to Lavinia: "Ogletha told Ibby that she watched the mail every day for weeks, and when no invitation had arrived by the day before Mae's party, Ariadne left town for Fleur de l'Eau, her plantation on the James River! Tried to make people think she was invited but couldn't because of prior commitments. Needless to say, I have done everything I can to let people know she was not invited because Mae told me herself she wasn't."

Margaret's letter continued, "It's a good thing her father left her all those plantations to hide out in because that's what she does when she wants to save face."

Lavinia could not suppress her satisfaction in Ariadne's unsuccessful celebration of spite. She began to look forward to the gossip in Richmond, even as it concerned her own marital dilemma. Nevertheless, she continued her silence and steadfastly withheld any comments about Lionel.

Margaret, Cornelia, and Aunt Priscilla all kept her up to date, and from these and other sources, she received the most detailed description of the events. Privy to unassailable sources, the hostesses themselves, and their servants, the information came fast and thick.

Margaret reluctantly reported, "Mama's servants have the longest tongues in Richmond. Everything said in the privacy of our home goes directly by way of our blacks to

Ariadne. She even found out that you had Lionel's clothes
sent to Richmond from Hawthorn Hill. And laughed about
it to Rebecca Byrd, who told Aunt Priscilla when she had tea
with her the next day."

A year passed, and although Lavinia received innumerable
pleas to join the family in Richmond for Christmas and other
occasions, she declined and remained at Hawthorn Hill with
the twins. She even received a letter from Mr. Edmund, his
shaky script beseeching her to come for the holidays, but she
claimed the plantation made too many demands of her time
for her to accept. Cornelia and Margaret made their usual
spring and summer visits, but Lavinia made it clear she did
not wish to discuss Lionel or hear of his achievements at the
factory.

"But Lavinia, dear, Lionel says we are practically
millionaires!" Cornelia whispered from behind her fan,
as if making such enormous sums was somehow less than
honorable, but nevertheless, the achievement restored
Lionel to a position worthy of his wronged-wife's forgiveness.

Lavinia, unimpressed by her husband's wealth,
continued to support herself and her slaves solely on the
profits made at Hawthorn Hill. Even when a Lynchburg
bank advised her of generous deposits made by Lionel to
Hawthorn Hill accounts, and Lionel's intention that she
use the funds for whatever purpose she chose, she refused
to include it in her own financial records and used only
the income that passed through her hands. She resented
the implication that she might need funding outside the
income she was able to earn on her own. She was fully
capable, after twenty-five years of experience, of managing
every aspect of the plantation alone, and did so successfully
and with profits every year.

Lionel himself made a few brief visits to Hawthorn Hill. His presence, however, brought with it the resumption of the icy non-communication that had accompanied earlier separations. Their paths seldom crossed, and he spent most of his time visiting Emma, pampering his little daughters, or conferring with Mr. Mudley. Isolated in his office, where his bed and furniture had been returned, or away from the house in the fields, Lionel scrupulously observed the re-established rules of his and Lavinia's earlier conflicts.

Emma's health began to decline rapidly. She suffered a stroke and Lavinia notified the family that Dr. Hunter believed the end was near. She reported Emma's wish to see Lionel, the first time she had mentioned his name in a year's correspondence.

Emma remained in her old room on the third floor, even during the hottest days of summer when the attic was like an oven and while her sitters begged her to move downstairs where it would be cooler.

One evening, as Emma grew weaker, Henny was sitting with her, counting the minutes until it would be Piney's time to take over. The attic was unusually hot for September and Henny dabbed her forehead with a damp cloth.

Henny thought Emma was sleeping peacefully but suddenly the old woman's long-fingered, bony hand reached out and seized Henny by the arm.

"Set down close to me," she said, her voice raspy. "I wants to talk to you." She looked at Henny with rheumy eyes, all hostility gone now, but with a directness and urgency Henny found unfamiliar and disquieting. For a long time, she returned the old woman's gaze, noting the gaunt features of her face and the leathery skin stretched tightly over her skull. Emma continued to weakly grip her hand, pulling her toward her, her eyes glistening in the lamplight. There was something intense and strangely pleading in the old woman's gaze.

Henny moved from her chair and sat down on the edge of the bed as Emma continued to hold her fast. "Yes, Emma?" Henny said.

"I ain't been good to you," Emma said at last. "I done treat you bad all these years." She looked away from Henny for a moment as if in deep, troubled thought. Then she looked at her again.

"I never like you much all these years 'cause—" Her voice drifted away and once again she seemed to search her thoughts. "When Miss Lavinia first come into the family, she and Mr. Lionel happy. He calm down like Miss Cornelia and me pray he do. He quit the wenches and the gamblin' and fightin' and all them he do when he young and feisty."

She paused, again in deep thought, remembering the past. Then she suddenly snapped back and nailed Henny with a narrow, piercing gaze.

"You know he your daddy?"

Henny drew back at the comment. Even though she had conceded his paternity years ago, she had tried to block it from her mind, just as she had her shame in having mixed blood. Emma was the first person who had ever directly mentioned the possibility to her face before. "I say, you know he your daddy?"

"That's where I get my devil's blood, isn't it? You and Old Sheba always said white people were devils."

"I done re-study that some. Some people devils and some not. And some a little of both. But it ain't they blood or color makes 'em so. It just theyselves. Blood and color don't matter."

A look of pain distorted the old woman's features and she tried to push herself up in the bed but weakly fell back against the pillows. Henny lifted her forward and adjusted her pillows. Emma nodded her gratitude and continued.

"Mr. Lionel, he settles down and a good man when he gets Miss Lavinia. Miss Cornelia and me think he gonna turn out fine, like Mr. Edmund, after all." She paused as the hopefulness of her memory turned into disappointment. "But it never happen," she said sadly. "In two or three years, he right back at his old ways agin—drinkin' and gamblin' and causin' his mamma and Miss Livvy all kinds of grief. And the whores. He stay half the time in Richmond whorehouses and after that took up with your mammy."

Henny bristled and her cheeks burned at hearing her mother mentioned in the same category as Richmond prostitutes. She was almost ready to be sympathetic to the dying woman and now she was insulting her mammy. Henny knew about whores—bad women, hussies—and what they did. They were even talked about in the Bible. She tried to withdraw her hand, but Emma hung on with surprising strength.

"It warn't her fault, I knows now."

She looked at Henny with weary honesty. "A slave woman got to do what she got to do. But I hated her 'cause she was his wench and he brought her here. And Miss Lavinia not knowin' what she here far—thinkin' he brought her here to help with them precious little twin boys that died. Miss Livy never know about the lanterns he sets in his window for her to see from the quarters when he wantin' her to slip up to the big house after night fall to bed with him."

Henny's discomfort increased and she wanted to scream at the old woman to shut up. Henny could only remember the sweetness of her mother, and the tender, loving smiles she gave her even though her eyes were sad and her face drawn with weariness. Perhaps now she knew the reason why. Perhaps this was why her mother always seemed so weighed down by despair and sadness.

"And I was part of hidin' it from her. When he with her in the cabins and Miss Vinny looks for him, I tell her he in the fields, and...I covers up for him just like I do when he a child and do something bad. He so purty and I loves him so."

Once again, Emma paused, her breathing labored , and she struggled for the strength to continue.

"Don't talk, Mammy Emma. Rest," Henny said, more to prevent further revelations than for consideration of Emma.

"No! No! I gots to tell it. I goin' to meet my Jesus soon. I got to try and make right how I treat you all these years." Tears began to well up in the tired, rheumy eyes and spilled down the old woman's face, glistening in the lamplight like silver streaks against dark leather. Henny dabbed Emma's cheeks with her apron.

"When you born, I hated you, too, 'cause we all knowed you was his. Mr. Lionel see that Miss Vinny in Richmond 'bout that time. And when we see them blue eyes they wasn't no doubt. Miz Livy never knowed for a long time. Till you 'bout nine-years-old and come up here that day wantin' to be her maid. We done hid you out like we done that little sick baby Miss Vinny brought from the Barksdales way back yonder. Miss Vinny thought his women was all white-trash whores in Richmond, and them nasty widders and saloon sluts. Never knowed he had one here at Hawthorn Hill. But I knowed."

Once again, Henny felt her face burn with humiliation and anger. Yet suddenly, she didn't fear this helpless old crone any more. Seeing the nearly lifeless old skeleton, so thin and wasted she barely made a ripple under the quilt, she realized that Emma's threats were more frightening than anything she actually did. She was all wind and bluff, her power nothing more than angry words and promises—and always had been.

"I wrong to blame you and hate you all these years," she said, and then, with what must have taken the courage of a lifetime, she raised her head and struggled to push herself closer to Henny.

"I's askin' you to forgive me."

She looked pleadingly at Henny. Suddenly, all the ancient fear and bitterness Henny had stored up through the years of Emma's abuse vanished like fog under the rays of a hot sun. How harmless and unthreatening the pitiful old woman seemed to her now. And how strangely easy it was to grant her request.

"I forgive you, Emma," Henny said, and her old enemy broke into quiet sobs.

"Thank you, Jesus," she said. "I's ready to be took up now."

"Now, don't talk like that, Emma," Henny said. "You're going to get well and—" She felt a twinge of guilt at lying since Emma had been so honest.

"Now, you hush!" Emma stormed. The old Emma, angry and threatening, was not gone yet. "Ain't no need to lie."

She lay quietly staring at the attic's slanting rafters, relaxing her grip on Henny's hand but still holding it. Henny made no move and sat silently. Perhaps unburdened and exhausted by her efforts, Emma would sleep.

"Where that Reuben? He ain't been to see me lately."

"He's alright, Emma. He doin' most of the driving now. Right big help to Uncle Lemiel."

"He your feller?"

Henny lowered her head. "I don't know, Emma."

"Piney say so. She mighty jealous 'bout it. Say you done stole him like you done a lace dress off her onct. You remember that?"

"I remember, Emma."

"How old you now?"

"Fourteen."

"That old enough. You ax Miss Vinny if you can jump the broom with Reuben in a year or two if you wants to. She let you. Better hurry before that Piney try and nab him."

Henny said nothing, embarrassed at Emma's prying. Emma was quiet for a long time and Henny hoped she would drift off to sleep.

"They's something' else," she finally said. "Over by the chimney, over there in the corner." She struggled to raise herself on one elbow and pointed in the direction of her trunk beside the chimney. "Under the floor there. Move my trunk and raise up the board, the one with no nails in it."

Henny went to the chimney, pushed the heavy trunk aside, and examined the floor. She found an un-nailed floor board which she removed. In the cavity below, she found a small wooden box resting on the lathe of the ceiling of the room below.

"Bring it here."

Henny lifted the box from its hiding place and placed it beside Emma. She helped her in her struggle to sit up, adjusting her pillows for support. She moved the lamp nearer as the old woman opened the box and smacked her lips as if in anticipation of its contents.

Slowly, she removed an ancient paper, yellowed with age, and handed it to Henny.

As Henny took it and unfolded it, the old woman's eyes glowed with pride and she smiled triumphantly.

"These my freedom papers!" she said proudly. "Mr. Lionel done give me my freedom and nobody don't know nothin' 'bout it! I been free all these years. But I has to keep it secret or they make me leave Virginia and I don't want to leave my people."

"People?" Henny was unaware of any relatives Emma might have.

"My white people. My Hawthorn people—and the Harveys."

Savoring her triumph, Emma watched closely for Henny's reaction.

"But why have you stayed?" Henny finally asked. "Why not leave and—"

"Never had nowhere to go," Emma said, "and I needed here. Mr. Lionel done gone so much to that factory in Richmond, Miss Vinny not be able to run this place by herself without me. And she always treats me good. There wasn't no need to leave. Wherever I go, I be treated the same. Freedom don't change your color and I still has to work. At least here, I be in the house, not the fields or the tobacco factories. I guess I just pick out my misery ruther than lets others picks it."

Henny wanted to protest, to remind her that freedom was worth any misery and that slavery was an evil, inhuman existence. She felt a lessening of respect for Emma, almost contempt, that she would remain in bondage when she had papers granting her freedom. She wondered if the old woman—free because a piece of paper said she was—realized that even in that freedom, she had done nothing but take orders from white people all her life. Old blacks sometimes seemed so used to their condition that through the years, they lost the fire of youthful opposition and simply accepted their fate. But Henny vowed she never would. The whispered discontent in the quarters was not lost on her, even as she reconciled her state as a slave with the relatively easy life as a house servant.

"And looky here," Emma said, still digging through the contents of the box, a few old buttons, a comb, and a sack of coins. "I's saved two hundred twenty dollars in gold through the years. Bet I's the richest black woman in the whole county."

She shook the bag of coins enticingly at Henny, her eyes sparkling at the sound of its jingle.

"I wants you to have it. I is willin' it to you, but givin' it to you now so the others won't know. And don't you tell Piney nothing 'bout it. I givin' her my gold earbobs and my Bible. And Beck all them fancy shawls and head rags and gloves and lace collars and fancy aprons and things Master Lionel and them brings me through the years. They in my trunk. But the gold coins goes to you. Reckon I buyin' a clear conscience for the wrongs I done you."

She grinned widely, showing her toothless gums. Henny had so seldom seen Emma smile, it was a revelation.

"When I first started, I was savin' it to buy myself free. I goin' to look for my Zed then. Before I come to Hawthorn Hill, me and my husband, Zed—he Zed Johnson—we was at another plantation. Our masters sold us and somebody buys Zed at the auction in Richmond, but never wants me. I was expectin' my baby then and I reckon they never want nobody but workers. I grieve right much for Zed and I reckon I grieves so much it brings on my baby too soon and it die, too."

Henny was stunned. Emma once had a husband and baby. Henny had never considered that Emma had any life other than that as black matriarch of Hawthorn Hill.

"When my baby die, Mr. Edmund lookin' for a wet nurse for Miss Cornelia and buys me. Mr. Lionel been born and she never had no milk hardly at all. Titties dry as powder. So even if me and Zed's baby die, I get me another one in Mr. Lionel." A soft smile came to her lips and she closed her eyes. Henny thought she had drifted off to sleep. She was about to ease her hand out of Emma's relaxed grip and slip away when the old woman's fingers tightened and held her again.

"Zed. Done a lot of thinking' about my Zed all these years," she said. "Even now." She stopped, and her thoughts reached back over fifty years to the memory of Zed Johnson and her hopes for his emancipation and their eventual reunion.

"Mr. Edmund tracks Zed to Alabama after we sold, but he sold agin there and when he try to run off that place he shot. Reckon he might have been tryin' to get back to me in Virginia. And our little baby. Don't reckon he ever find out it die. I never know, but that the way I think it. When I gets to Heaven, the Lord will tell me. And maybe Zed and our baby be there waiting on me. You reckon that baby grow up in Heaven or still be little?"

"Still be little, Emma. Waitin' on its mammy to get there."

"That like I thinkin' and wantin' it to be."

She placed the bag of coins in Henny's hand. "It gold, too. Ain't no paper to it. Just gold. That one of the reasons I wants to be brought back to my old room. So I could shows you where the money hid. It yorn now."

"Oh, Emma." Henny felt her throat tighten and her eyes sting with the beginning of tears.

"They somethin' else."

"Yes, Emma?"

"I wants you to get me a piece of paper and a quill."

Henny looked at her blankly, not understanding her request.

"Do it, I say! And paper, too!"

Henny went downstairs and returned with paper, pen, and an inkwell.

"Dip it in. I wants to show you something."

As Emma struggled to a more upright position, Henny dipped the pen into the ink. The old woman took the pen and with a shaking hand painstakingly scratched something on the paper. Then, her eyes glistening proudly, she handed it to Henny.

On it she had written *Emma Johnson*.

Henny looked at the awkward scribbling and smiled at Emma, who looked back with a luminous sense of accomplishment. "Miss Vinny teaches me."

"That mighty good writin', Mammy Emma," Henny said.

Emma beamed with pride and angled the paper at different distances from her, studying her penmanship critically. "Might could have done better on that *J*."

She looked back at the paper for a long time and then fell back on the pillow. "I wanted to do it just one more time. Make me feel more like a person knowin' who I is and bein' able to write it for anybody to see. Most of our people can't do that."

She closed her eyes and sighed. She looked peaceful and relieved.

"Thank you for the money—"

"Hush, now. Don't say nothin'. I's feelin' a little easier now so you get on downstairs and lemme rest." She released

Henny's hand and soon her breathing indicated she was asleep.

"Thank you, Emma," Henny said. She watched the old woman for a long time before she silently rose from the bed and left the attic when she heard Piney's approaching footsteps.

Emma's condition worsened and Dr. Hunter predicted the end was near. Advised of the urgency by Lavinia, Lionel made arrangements for the family to leave at once by the next available train. Sensing that every hour was crucial, and the long horse-drawn coach ride would be too taxing on Mr. Edmund, even Cornelia consented to travel by train with the rest of the family. Ariadne pleaded ill health and did not join the others.

The morning they were to leave, Margaret and Alexander joined her parents for breakfast.

"And you might try to advance your own cause this time," said Margaret to her brother. "You've been to Hawthorn Hill twice since you were shot and done nothing to reinstate yourself with Lavinia."

"I barely had the opportunity to see Mrs. Hawthorn the last two times I was in the country, dear sister."

"Well, it's easy to see why."

"Oh, but she mentioned you in the last letter, dear," Cornelia said. "The first time in a year. She said you could sell the tobacco while you were there."

"Well, I suppose that means I shall not be fired upon from the front porch."

"Don't be flippant," his mother ordered. "This is too serious for jokes. And one bullet was enough, wasn't it?"

"Indeed," Margaret said. "You've got to try and worm your good-for-nothing self back into the family again."

"I? It is I who must get back in?"

"As far as I am concerned it is. Lavinia wasn't caught in a hotel room with another woman's husband!"

"Margaret!" Cornelia gasped. "You are a minister's wife and my daughter! I will not permit such talk—"

"Perhaps my son and daughter-in-law will be able to strike an accord without the assistance of his mother and sister," Mr. Edmund said.

"Thank you, Papa," Lionel said.

Told that the family would arrive soon, Emma struggled to hold on, "to see my babies one more time."

When the family had not arrived in what Emma deemed adequate time, she questioned Lavinia the next time she sat with her. Emma, propped up in bed on a small mountain of pillows, ate soup fed to her by Henny as Lavinia sat nearby knitting.

"Why he not come see me sooner?" Emma asked, watching Lavinia with eyes narrowed to half-slits, a sure sign she suspected something amiss. "He don't come near as often as he use to. And don't stay no time when he do."

"He's been so busy with the tobacco factory in Richmond, Mammy," Lavinia said, looking at her knitting to avoid the old woman's close scrutiny and exposure as a liar.

"They troubles back agin twixt you?"

"What makes you think so, Emma?" She looked at the old woman evenly.

Emma made a little snort of scorn. "You think I can't tell just by breathin' when they something not right in this house? Mr. Lionel not come here, ner you go out to Richmond since the plantin' to sees him, and you think I don't know?"

"Save your strength, Emma. And eat. You must be strong when Mr. Lionel gets here."

"Ain't got no time to fiddle. I hears them field hands movin' his room back downstairs. I knows what that mean. And Piney done told me all about it. She pick it up in the kitchen when Miss Margaret and Beck talks 'bout it. Now don't you lay her out for it. I done tricked her into tellin' me. Done threaten to has her sent to the fields."

Lavinia nodded and continued to knit. "Mr. Lionel seems to have interests in Richmond more important—"

"A woman?"

"It is...was..."

"They all like that, Miss Vinny. All the mens I ever knowed of 'cept Mr. Edmund and Mr. Alexander...and my Zed...and one or two others. Got to poke it in as many holes as they ken."

"Emma!"

"It the truth, and like the Bible says, 'The truth stand when the world on fire.' Don't care if it fine gentlemans or field workers, all mens the same." She looked at Henny and said, "But my Zed wasn't like that. He like Mr. Edmund and Mr. Alexander. With women's it's they tongues gets them in trouble, with men it they peckers—"

"Emma! Remember, we are in the presence of a child."

"Ain't no child. She done fourteen. Be wantin' to know why they different down there herself, 'fore long." The old woman turned her attention to Henny and narrowed her eyes suspiciously. "If she ain't already—"

"Henny, I'll finish feeding Mammy," Lavinia said, putting aside her knitting and moving toward the bed. Henny, embarrassed, handed her the soup and left the attic.

"Now eat and stop talking about men's parts," Lavinia said, sitting on the edge of the bed and extending a spoon to the old woman, who grinned mischievously. She took a noisy slurp of the soup and grew serious.

"You and Mr. Lionel wastin' a lot of time on foolishness," she said. "I knows about time 'cause I ain't got much. When he come, you think on it. Study it right out and see if I ain't right."

After a few more spoonfuls of soup, the old woman shook her head and her leathery eyelids grew heavy. She settled into a deep sleep.

Lavinia sat with her a long time, thinking of what the old woman said, even sensing the wisdom in her words. But weighed against the bitterness and disappointment that still lay so heavily in her heart, she thought as precious as time was, she would rather spend it in peace alone than with a man who had so often disappointed and hurt her.

When the family arrived, Lavinia met her in-laws with the same affection she always had. With Lionel her greeting was cold and indifferent, but out of respect for Emma and the senior Hawthorns, and aware of Piney's hungry ears, no hostile words were exchanged.

Lionel and his parents had a joyous reunion with his daughters, who at first shied away from the stranger known as Papa, but accepted him after only one day of his patient enticement and winning charm. He visited Emma at least twice a day, and spent time in the fields with Mr. Mudley or with his hounds and horses. Although Lavinia had months ago had his bedroom moved back downstairs, what seemed to concern him more than exile from his room was the absence of many of his hunting trophies.

"Where is my moose head? And my bear skin?"

"In the barn. Those things were never properly cured and the odor in there is terrible. It smells like a tannery and until they dry out, those skins are going to smell bad."

"Papa is too frail for the stairs—"

"Mr. Hawthorn can have your room—inhabitable now that the animal skin odor is gone. You can sleep in Randy's old room."

Lavinia was grateful that the presence of the Harveys and elder Hawthorns provided a buffer against being in Lionel's company alone. When her sons arrived, she was further provided with distractions to keep her well away from any close contact with her husband.

But everyone knew of Lavinia's enmity, even as it remained unexpressed. Now she had to deal with the discomfort of Cornelia's constant mournful expression as the old lady, ready to burst into tears, looked helplessly back and forth between Lavinia and Lionel, hoping to see a move toward reconciliation. And Margaret was ever ready to drop not-so-subtle hints that it was time to heal the breach as she and Alexander demonstrated the joys of a happy marriage by endless expressions of affection.

Lavinia was most touched by the kind, gentlemanly courtesies of the patrician Mr. Edmund as he tried to diplomatically invest the enforced suppers together with an atmosphere of harmony and tranquility, as if nothing was amiss between his son and daughter-in-law. Lavinia could always count on Mr. Edmund to come to her rescue from Margaret's blatant, and Cornelia's even more guileless, campaign to end the separation.

Margaret delighted in telling Lavinia of Ariadne's fall from grace in Richmond society.

"Margaret, you have become the biggest gossip in Richmond," Alexander Harvey said to his wife.

"It's not gossip when it concerns the family and told only within the family. Ariadne actually entertained Bithia

Clevinger privately at supper. And everyone in Richmond knows about it. That's how we found out the Clevingers have slipped back into town and are again residing at the Bird and Owl Hotel."

When Lavinia showed only indifference, Margaret pressed on, "But I know for a fact that Lionel has not seen her. Even when the hussy sent him a note hand-delivered by Ariadne's butler, Madison, I heard Lionel tell him he had no return message. And I spied the note: an invitation to her hotel!"

Margaret was so delighted at Ariadne's decline in Richmond society, she did not wait to tell Lavinia privately, but blurted it all out at supper with Lionel and Lavinia sitting stiffly and uncomfortably at opposite ends of the table.

Alexander Harvey shifted uncomfortably in his seat and cleared his throat loudly in an attempt to silence Margaret, but she would not be deterred. Although she left unmentioned the reason for Ariadne's recent snubs, referring to Lionel's shooting and subsequent separation from Lavinia as "other people's business," she left no detail unreported.

"Well, Ariadne fixed herself first with old Mrs. Robertson Carter when she started minding other people's business and told her all about things she had no business telling at a tea Mrs. Carter gave for her granddaughter's engagement. I was there, and Mrs. Carter said, 'Ariadne, if you had spent as much time trying to get a husband for yourself as you do gossiping about ladies who are having trouble with theirs, you'd be married by now and have your own marriage to worry about.'"

Margaret laughed and Lavinia only dabbed her mouth with her napkin. Lionel began a conversation with his father about the tobacco market.

"Margaret, perhaps this might be discussed later," Alexander said, sensing Lionel's and Lavinia's discomfort.

"This is within the family, Alexander," Margaret said testily. "I am not in a pulpit or speaking at the capitol telling it to all of Richmond."

"I really think Lavinia should know," Cornelia said to Alexander, who, sensing the uselessness of his diplomacy, withdrew into silence.

"Thank you, Mother," Margaret said. She continued, "Shortly after Mrs. Carter put her in her place, Ariadne was struck from guest lists all over the city. I know of two important fall weddings she has not yet received invitations for. I've already gotten mine and so have Mama and Papa, and she's so desperate she's spending gobs of money on wedding gifts and sending them to the brides-to-be before she gets an invitation to try and get one. She has no shame!"

Cornelia added to the news, whispering her contribution as if Ariadne were in the next room. "Ogletha told my Ibby that Ariadne was so upset when she wasn't invited to Abigail Harrison's garden party, when her roses were at their peak, she almost had another one of her episodes."

"Oh, Mama, tell it the way it happened. Ogletha told Ibby she threw another fit and threw things and had to be restrained and Dr. Rudd came and gave her bromides and the next day Madison had her sent to Baltimore."

"Not Warm Springs?" Lavinia asked, forgetting herself and her intention to maintain an appearance of stony disinterest.

"Oh, no. She's gotten too bad for Warm Springs," Margaret said.

"It's a hospital situation, dear," Cornelia whispered. "To...to regulate her medicine."

"You mean she's there now?" asked Lavinia.

"Yes. And I hope she stays the rest of the fall. Except she will use her health as an excuse for not being invited to anything. And no one goes to her teas except when forced to. Ogletha told Ibby she gave a tea for Georgiana Rudrum, Roseanna Fleming, Martha Willis, the Walford twins, and Suzie, and not a single one came! What was such a holler was that everyone had their maids send around notes of regret just an hour before the tea saying they had headaches. Six headaches! Isn't it delicious?"

Lavinia said nothing but noted that even Cornelia, her lips pursed with repressed pleasure, seemed amused that an epidemic of headaches seemed to strike so many Richmond belles at the same time.

"She blames you, dear," Cornelia whispered to Lavinia. "She actually told Elizabeth Edmundson you were a part of the Underground Railroad, says you stole that Jennie of hers. Her accusations are so outrageous, people laugh at her. Poor Ariadne," said Cornelia. "When Lionel—" But she did not finish.

In the succeeding days, Emma's breathing became more and more labored and Dr. Hunter visited her every day. Lionel spent a great deal of time with her and Alexander Harvey prayed and read the Bible to her each evening. Finally, Dr. Hunter gave the family the news that her demise was eminent and they quietly gathered around her in the attic to await her final breath.

She was in and out of consciousness as the end drew near, but occasionally opened her eyes to see the family to whom she had devoted her life gathered around her, their faces brave masks concealing their sense of loss and helplessness.

The old woman would smile faintly in satisfaction at seeing them, her eyes, and theirs, glistening with love and gratitude. Then her lids would flutter and close as she drifted into sleep. Finally, the labored breath became quieter and almost indistinct and Dr. Hunter, sitting with the group and joined by Uncle Lemiel, Aunt Beck, Henny, and Piney, announced that she was gone.

Folding her arms across her chest and closing her eyes, the old doctor left the attic. Tears flowed and Alexander Harvey led the family in prayer.

One by one, they left the attic until Henny found herself alone with only the lifeless old woman and Lionel.

Lionel sat beside his mammy, studying the still, wrinkled old face a long time. Finally, he extended his arm and reached out for Henny. As she moved toward him, he placed his arm on her shoulder. He had never touched her before.

"She told me last night to be good to you, Henny," he said. "If I'm ever not, you remind me that Mammy told me to."

"Yes, sir."

"And Miss Lavinia. She said I must not cause her any more heartache."

Before either could say anything else, for the second time that evening, the drone of Uncle Lemiel's bell tolled out the news of Emma's death to the people in the quarters. Just as it had earlier signaled the end of the Hawthorn Hill work day, this time the bell signaled the end of Emma's labor for life.

When the bell finally stopped and Henny and Lionel joined the family downstairs, they found most of the black population gathered just outside the fence of the backyard. Although a friend to few and a foe to many, Emma had been one of their own and too long a presence at Hawthorn Hill not to have been significant in all their lives.

When Lionel announced that she was gone, there were a few cries of grief and some of the women began a mournful wail. An atmosphere of sadness descended on the entire plantation.

As instructed by Lionel, Benjamin and Reuben brought Emma's coffin from the blacksmith shop to the house. The mourning blacks parted as they made their way past them with the pine box on their shoulders.

Unlike the usual pine boxes used for ordinary blacks, Emma's coffin had been prepared sometime earlier especially for her, and according to Mr. Lionel's instructions, been fitted with brass handles and lined with cotton padding covered by a good grade of white muslin. There was even a small, down satin pillow for her head.

Aunt Beck, Katie, and Nancy prepared the body, bathing it and dressing it in a freshly washed and ironed dress. With Lavinia assisting, they selected one of the innumerable scarves Lionel had brought her through the years and wrapped it around her head and another, her favorite, Aunt Beck said, was placed around her neck. Then her arms were folded across her chest and she was placed in the coffin which had been brought to the attic.

Reuben, assisted by Clevis and two other field hands, carried the coffin down to the first floor where Lionel ordered it be placed between two chairs turned inward as a bier in the front hall. A dozen candles in the candelabra brought from the dining room burned at the head and foot of the coffin as various members of the family and servants sat with Emma during her last night in the house she had ruled most of her life.

Toward morning, Henny approached the corpse and, unnoticed by Uncle Lemiel and Aunt Beck who were also in the hall, slipped the piece of paper on which Emma had so painstakingly written her name for the last time into the coffin.

"Jesus know who you is, Emma," Henny said softly to the old woman. "But this make certain everybody else in heaven know, too."

All work was canceled the next day and the entire slave population of Hawthorn Hill, as well as any blacks permitted by their masters on neighboring plantations, filed by Emma's casket in the front hall. Several whites attended, some of whom had known Emma for as long as fifty years and realized her importance to the Hawthorn family.

Although there were few blacks on Hawthorn Hill Plantation who had not fallen under the stinging tongue of Emma's reproach, and if they were field hands, felt her condescension as well, there was a grudging sense of respect for her as the black matriarch who ruled them all. The wrongs she had visited on them in her harsh judgments and swift punishments were forgotten and there was a suitable solemnity in the crowd that gathered for her funeral.

She had left detailed instructions for the performance of her rites and Lionel directed they be carried out to the letter. Her favorite passages from the Bible were read by Reverend Alexander Harvey, who conducted the ceremony, and no less than four of her favorite hymns were sung.

Piney, accustomed to the more emotional expressions of grief at funerals, began a loud wail, which Henny terminated with a firm pinch and warning hiss. "Emma never wanted none of that carrying on. She say it not dignified."

Other blacks were not as compliant, however, and in spite of Emma's request and to Henny's mortification, cries of grief and wailing punctuated the ceremony. Piney, already wearing her inheritance—Emma's gold earrings—joined in and between wails of sorrow, cast Henny withering glances of scorn and gloating sneers of victory in her defiant, emotional expressions of grief.

Reverend Alexander Harvey was eloquent in his comforting remarks and Lionel's eulogy, praising Emma's long service to his family and their love, respect, and gratitude for her, touched all their hearts. With tears drying on their cheeks, the graveside rites at last came to an end and Lionel gave the signal that his second mother finally be lowered into the earth. She was laid to rest in a place of honor in the black cemetery not far from the Hawthorn Family burying ground.

After several of their white friends expressed their sympathy and departed, the mourners began to disperse.

Lavinia, genuinely moved by Lionel's loss, felt her heart soften and she made no resistance when he clasped her hand as they left the burial ground. Certainly now was no time to continue their quarrel, and out of respect for Emma and her own sense of loss, Lavinia allowed him to walk beside her as he still held her hand. Somehow, perhaps because of the somber occasion, the old thrill of his touch was gone. It might as well have been old Mr. Hawthorn, or Alexander, or Margaret who held her hand. Something was gone forever and she added the lost magic to the sadness that already lay so heavily in her heart.

The blacks split into groups and returned to either the quarters at Hawthorn Hill or the waiting wagons that would take them back to other plantations.

Aunt Beck, Uncle Lemiel, Piney, and Henny followed behind Mr. Edmund, Miss Cornelia, the Harveys, and the other Hawthorns. The group paused when they reached the family cemetery where Hawthorns for over a hundred years had been buried. Here were the remains of Lionel's great-great-grandfather and members of generations on through his own, including his twin sons and his daughter, Oralee. Here, he and his father and mother would find their final resting places. After pausing a moment at the edge of the iron spiked fence, the group moved on across the field toward the house.

Walking at a slow pace to accommodate Mr. Edmund's feebleness, Margaret and Cornelia looked at each other with expressions of gratitude and hopefully looked heavenward as they saw the interlocked hands of Lionel and Lavinia. Cornelia nudged Edmund to look, too. Randy and Frederick exchanged smiles, heartened at the first sign of closeness they had witnessed in their parents in nearly a year.

But at the house, the temporary truce, if not suspended, returned to the old formal silence, as Lavinia's attitude of indifference returned. In spite of their prayers and gentle prodding, Cornelia's and Margaret's hope for a reconciliation was no closer than it had been months before.

Chapter Forty-Three

⊶═◉═⊶

In Richmond, a major slave escape was being finalized after months of covert, meticulous planning by the Underground Railroad.

South of Richmond on the James River, fifty runaway slaves huddled below deck in the steamship the *Thelma Lyle*, waiting to be transported down the James to the Atlantic Ocean. Crowded together in restless anticipation, the fugitives waited for the sound of the low-humming engine to increase and the ship to begin the journey that would transport them to freedom. It was a moonless, starless night, just after midnight, and the vessel had fired up its powerful engines an hour before. Kept at low steam to create as little noise as possible, the *Thelma Lyle* would shortly depart for the five-hour journey to Chesapeake Bay and continue north in the Atlantic to Boston Harbor in Massachusetts, where the human cargo would disembark, no longer as slaves, but as free citizens of the Commonwealth of Massachusetts.

The fifty runaways had been assembled after a massive effort coordinated by abolitionists in Richmond, Petersburg, other areas of Virginia, and the Carolinas in cooperation with those in Boston in what was hoped to be one of the largest single slave escapes in the history of the Underground Railroad. In the waters just above Norfolk Harbor, another hundred slaves, smuggled from North and South Carolina, were to join the steamer in its voyage to Boston. Also to be picked up en route to Norfolk were an additional fifty to seventy-five blacks assembled at a plantation on the James known as Fleur de l'Eau.

Those involved in the plan hoped the dramatic rescue of so many slaves at one time would score a major moral and political victory in the battle to end slavery in America.

Sixty-five-year-old Captain William Pierce, a man of generous spirit and largeness of soul, was a well-known Boston shipper of whiskey, tobacco, flour, and iron to Northern ports. Less known were his abolitionist sympathies and his occasional transport of runaway slaves to freedom.

For years, the corpulent, white-headed captain had smuggled small numbers of escapees on return journeys from ports in the South to the Port of Boston. His efforts in the past had been limited to one or two escapees and never more than six at one time. Because he was retiring after this trip, Captain Pierce wanted to make his final voyage at the helm of the *Thelma Lyle* a spectacular one. Over one hundred fifty blacks spirited to freedom in a single effort would be unprecedented; Captain Pierce wanted to be the man who did it.

Strutting back and forth on the pier as the human cargo was secretly taken aboard one and two at a time, the strapping captain beamed in pride at the thought of his soon-to-be realized achievement. Since sunset and darkness concealed the effort, Captain Pierce had greeted his cargo. His thick white hair and the long bushy sideburns extending halfway down his firm, prominent chin framed a ruddy face glowing with anticipation.

After learning that among his passengers was a young couple who wished to be married, the munificent captain offered his quarters on board as a site and performed the ceremony with great pomp in his capacity as captain.

"You'll begin your married life in freedom," he intoned expansively at the conclusion of the brief ceremony. In a further gesture of generosity, he offered the couple private quarters to consummate their marriage when the boat sailed.

The *Thelma Lyle* was scheduled to cast off an hour after midnight. But only minutes before the departure, a mysterious stranger, wearing a long black cloak and large hat pulled low on his forehead, approached the boat, and requested to see the captain.

"The escape will have to be aborted, sir," the stranger said. "The slave patrols are aware of the plan."

Captain Pierce tugged at one of his outlandishly large, bushy sideburns and looked over the narrow, oval lenses of his spectacles. His cheerful countenance turned into a frown as he listened to the bad news.

"But how do you know?" the captain asked the stranger.

"On good authority, sir. A man named Blassingame warned me only an hour ago."

"Blassingame? Jeremiah Blassingame, the whiskey wholesaler?"

"One and the same, sir."

"Why, I've transported liquor to Boston for Blassingame for years. And more than a few blacks, too. How did he find out?"

"Well, Mr. Blassingame sells whiskey all over Virginia—and elsewhere. He moves blacks as a side line. But he has to pay an occasional bribe to the patrols to do it. One of them warned him."

Captain Pierce drew back his shoulders and thrust out his large abdomen in surprise. "The patrols warned him?"

"Yes, sir."

"Mighty peculiar that the patrols would warn the very party they were trying to apprehend." The captain cocked his bushy eyebrows quizzically.

"With good reason, sir."

"Oh?"

"If Mr. Blassingame were arrested for assisting runaway slaves, it would put an end to future bribe money, which the informant would not want to lose."

The captain nodded his understanding, and once again tugged on his sideburns. "Greed, of course. It never ends, but perhaps it has served us well in prompting a warning. Did Blassingame know what they were planning?"

"A patrol boat will be down the river about three miles. They're planning to come aboard when you pass, find and seize the blacks, and arrest you and the crew. There would be serious charges, sir."

Captain Pierce's brow knitted with concern and he continued to tug at his sideburns. "Well, I can't have that. As much as I hate to tell you, they'll have to get off."

The informant's eyebrows rose in alarm. "But where will they go? How can we possibly hide fifty people?"

"Wish I knew, my man. But that is not my responsibility. I can't risk exposure and arrest. I had scheduled two more stops on my way down the James to pick up other runaways. I've taken too many risks already. I was told this plan was fool-proof and that there was no chance it could fail."

"Oh, my God." The man raised a hand to his head. "We're all doomed. Some of these people don't even know their way around Richmond. They come from all over Virginia and farther south, many of them country people who have never been beyond their owners' plantations. They have no familiarity with the city—they'll walk right into the hands of the patrols."

"I think I may be able to help," a deep male voice spoke from the darkness.

The captain and the informant turned to see a tall black man, impeccably dressed, step out of the shadows. He bowed stiffly to them and removed his hat. "If the people will be quiet and not panic, and do as they are told in an orderly manner, I know a place that they can hide for a short time—perhaps two or three days. If the captain could wait that long?"

"And who are you?" the captain asked the black man, looking him up and down. "You don't sound like a Virginia black. You don't sound like a black at all."

"I am called Madison, sir. But it is unimportant who I am. It is only important that I may be able to save this mission. And I am willing to take a certain amount of risk to attempt it."

"Madison!" the man in the black hat and long cloak said. "I...I had no idea."

"Reverend Harvey!" said Madison. "I am equally surprised, sir. I thought you were in the country."

The two men shook hands. "I just returned today," said Alexander.

"I gather you two are known to each other?" Captain Pierce asked.

"Indeed, Captain," said Alexander. "We have a long association."

"Then you can vouch for this man?" Captain Pierce asked Reverend Harvey.

"I can indeed, Captain."

"Then continue," said the captain to Madison. "Tell us what you have in mind."

"If the captain leaves the blacks here and proceeds down the river, the patrols will find nothing. If the patrols find nothing when you repeat your run down the river on two or three more evenings, perhaps they will abandon their surveillance and believe they were advised falsely. Or that it is another vessel they should be investigating. Then we can continue with the original plan."

"I'm not sure," Captain Pierce said, furrowing his brow and tugging at his sideburns.

"Excuse me, Reverend Harvey," Madison said, looking apologetically at Alexander. "But if I might speak to the captain alone, for just a moment. I would not want to compromise your position, Reverend, with information about the Underground that—"

"Say no more, Madison," Alexander interrupted the black man. "I understand that knowledge is dangerous in this business."

"Thank you, sir," Madison said. Alexander bowed to the captain and moved away into the darkness.

"Come aboard, my man," said the captain.

When they were alone in the captain's quarters, Madison said in a confidential tone, "Should the delay cause the captain to incur additional expense, as I am sure it may, I have a draft here for five thousand dollars."

Captain Pierce took the draft from the black man and examined it closely, holding the paper close to the lamplight of his cabin. He paused a long time before he spoke, as if asking himself, *Where would a black man, no matter how impeccably dressed, no matter how cultivated in speech and manner, get five thousand dollars?*

Madison anticipated the captain's doubts as the older man lifted his eyes from the draft and viewed him with skepticism. "I am the man who was to guide you to the first pick-up point on the James, sir: Fleur de l'Eau Plantation, thirty miles downstream. We are expecting fifty or more escapees to be picked up there, the people of Fleur de l'Eau Plantation and others."

"Why, I've been waiting for you all day," Captain Pierce said. "Wondered how I was ever to find this place with nothing but signals from lanterns on shore and in skiffs to guide me. I don't like to dock in unfamiliar waters at night."

"The people were to be already waiting in bateaux, sir," Madison explained. "Docking would not even be necessary. Only stopping to pick them up. I know where."

The captain's suspicions were lessened, but he cast another doubtful glance at the draft, which he still held in his hands.

"Drafts can be worthless. How about cash?"

"The draft will be made out to you, sir. Duly signed by a donor who wishes to remain anonymous. Present it to any bank in the city tomorrow and you will find it is quite legitimate and you will have your cash. If questioned, you can say the money is in payment for a delivery of furniture from Boston."

The captain hesitated only a moment before accepting the terms and agreed to the plan. With a pen and ink from the captain's desk, Madison wrote Captain Pierce's name on the draft and passed it back to him.

Captain Pierce, waiting for the ink to dry, examined the document again, turning it over in his hand. "Ariadne Carter Woodhull. Mighty generous lady. My thanks to her."

"I will forward them to her, captain," Madison said. "But at all costs, she would wish to remain anonymous. Even from Reverend Harvey. There are family connections, sir."

"I understand. And I'm not surprised. Many families in Virginia are divided over this slavery business. And at any rate, all Virginians seem to be kin to each other."

Captain Pierce chuckled, stuffed the draft in his coat pocket, and patted it. "And I see no reason for Reverend Harvey to know of our private transaction in this matter at all. I shall see that the negotiation of this draft is conducted in strictest confidence—for the delivery of furniture. I've been doing business in Richmond for years and am known personally at Miss Woodhull's bank. I anticipate no problems. I'll have to warn the fugitives waiting in Norfolk, but I will return tomorrow and run this draft then. If it is legitimate, and I am sure it will be, we are in business."

The captain sent a crewman for Alexander Harvey, who boarded the *Thelma Lyle* and joined the men for a final discussion of the plan.

"Our plan is afloat again," the captain said, his doubts removed and his enthusiasm restored.

"So many will be eternally in your debt," said Alexander Harvey.

The captain modestly brushed aside his gratitude. "But your people will have to get off the boat now. If I'm boarded and searched tonight, they will find nothing. But tomorrow night, and the boat again bearing nothing, they might get suspicious, think I'm waiting them out to pick up black cargo. Do you suppose Blassingame could load me some additional whiskey tomorrow I can deliver to Norfolk? It will look suspicious to find no cargo two nights in a row."

"I'll see Blassingame tomorrow," Alexander Harvey said. "He's got a warehouse full of whiskey. I'm sure I can get his cooperation."

Captain Pierce chuckled and shook his head. "A preacher arranging for the transport of whiskey."

"I prefer to think of myself as arranging the transport of souls, sir," said Harvey.

"Excellent!" the captain said. "Then, the third night, if they have not stopped me after I've gone ten or fifteen miles downstream, I'll turn back and make the run as planned."

With a little more discussion as to time, and warning signals from shore should it be necessary to abandon the plan, the three men went over every detail concerning the escape or "rescue," as Captain Pierce preferred to term the mission.

The details agreed upon, the blacks were addressed and informed by Madison that there would be a one or two day delay in their journey, but that with their cooperation, they would be safe until then.

A moan of disappointment arose from huddled blacks, but they had no choice but to follow the instructions Madison gave them to ensure they remained undetected by the patrols. The captain promised he would return for them in three days.

"We are not abandoning you," he said. "I will be back tomorrow and the next day and the day after that, if necessary. Besides," he threw Madison a wink and patted the pocket containing the five-thousand-dollar draft, "the delay is providential. I have certain banking business to conduct in the city tomorrow."

The passengers, who had been gathering in safe houses in Richmond and the surrounding area on both sides of the James River for days prior to the expected departure, had been assembled to board the *Thelma Lyle* in a rushed, coordinated effort of only five or six hours. It would be impossible to return them to the dozens of different safe houses they came from, but Madison had an alternative plan.

As the blacks streamed down the gangplank and huddled in the darkness, Reverend Harvey, his hat pulled low, directed them toward concealment in the space between two warehouses.

"You will be moved to a safer place soon," he said, "but silence and your cooperation is absolutely necessary."

Although the dock selected for the departure was seldom used—and deserted between midnight and the early hours of morning—it would be impossible to leave the blacks there once daylight exposed them.

"They can't stay here long," said Alexander to Madison once the blacks were all ashore and Captain Pierce had cast off. "Once they find that the boat is empty, they'll be here within the hour to check every warehouse from here to the falls."

"We'll have them transported by then," Madison said, "to another place—a safe house I know. Will you stay with the people and calm them until I can get them transported?"

"Yes."

"I have brought Miss Ariadne's coach. As you know, she is still in Baltimore receiving treatment for her...condition. I'll get a friend of mine and within the hour we will begin the first run. I'm sorry I can't confide in you where I am taking them, Reverend Harvey, but you are too valuable to our cause to endanger with knowledge making you culpable of our activities."

"I understand, Madison. And thank you."

Madison disappeared into the darkness and in a moment Alexander heard the rumble of Ariadne's carriage as it raced away from the dock toward the city.

The blacks huddled and whispered with fear among themselves. Reverend Harvey reassured them that they would be taken to safety as soon as possible and that the escape was only delayed, the plan firmly in place. Thus heartened, they grew less restless and patiently awaited their rescue.

Within an hour, the sound of approaching horses could be heard and as the blacks cowered in renewed fear, Ariadne's ornate carriage rolled out of the darkness, followed by a large wagon covered by a canvas tarpaulin and driven by a black man. The vehicles stopped in front of the space between the warehouses, where the blacks were quickly calmed by the information that these were their rescuers, not patrols.

"Alonso!" Alexander said, recognizing the man driving the wagon. "Good Lord! Is every household in my family involved in this?"

"I won't tell on you, Reverend Harvey, if you won't tell on me," Alonso said with a grin when he recognized Alexander under the large black hat.

"Agreed, Alonso," Alexander said.

Madison jumped from the carriage, and with Alexander began to organize the loading of the people. The two or three elderly blacks and three women with very young children were crowded into the carriage. Then about half of the people climbed into the wagon and lay down, pressing themselves together as close as possible. The smaller women and children piled on top of the lower layer of larger men. Madison, Alexander, and Alonso then covered them with a canvas tarpaulin.

Surveying the remaining blacks, Madison said, "I think one more load is all it will take to get everyone to safety."

"You've done well," said Alexander. "Thank God you've come to our rescue. And you're sure you have a safe place?"

"Quite sure, sir."

"And you can feed them for three days?"

"Yes, sir. But I must hurry. At this hour, there should be few patrols about and I think that by taking the back streets and alleys we can make it."

"God bless you, Madison," Alexander said, giving Madison's hand a firm shake. "I'll be here the night of the departure. And you know where to find me in the meantime."

Reverend Harvey disappeared into the darkness, and in a moment the sound of his horse could be heard galloping away.

Fortunately, because Ariadne's coach was often seen on the streets of Richmond at late hours, transporting guests to and from her late night entertainments, it aroused no suspicion from the patrols. They recognized Madison in full regalia driving the vehicle with drawn drapes at the windows through the streets at two o'clock in the morning. Another late night revel, the knowing patrols surmised, with Madison taking home the guests too inebriated to get there on their own.

In only two trips and three hours' time, Madison and Alonso had transported fifty-seven people from the warehouse on the James River to the cellar of Ariadne Woodhull's house on Marshall Street.

Quietly unloaded in the alley behind the house and slipped through the back garden to the cellar entrance, the people were safely out of sight in a matter of minutes after their arrival.

Told the necessity of remaining quiet, and that they would have to endure the cramped, uncomfortable cellar for as much as three days, the blacks, grateful for the efforts made on their behalf, cooperated and waited for deliverance.

When they were inside, Ogletha and several of Ariadne's servants who were among the runaways, were aghast at Madison's recklessness. It might have been acceptable to hide them there—it's where they came from, where they belonged, where their presence would arouse no suspicion at all. But bringing fifty-seven—Ogletha had counted them—runaways into Ariadne's house!

"Here I am, right back where I started," said Ogletha. "You are going to get us all killed. I thought I seen the last of this place."

"It is the only chance we have, Ogletha," Madison said. "I could think of no other plan. Besides, it may not be so risky after all with Miss Ariadne away."

"But what if she come back? What if we followed?"

"All of you have chosen to leave. Even I. I put no one at any risk I am not taking myself. Miss Ariadne has been at the hospital in Baltimore for only two weeks. Her treatment will take two more at the least. If all goes well, we will be safely in Boston and Canada by the time she returns."

Ogletha shook her head at the audacity of it all and bit her lip, fear and doubt distorting her features.

"Freedom is a precious thing, Ogletha. We must be willing to take great risks to achieve it."

"Well, I ain't stayin' in this cellar. I am goin' to my old room on the third floor."

Easter, the cook, spoke up. "What we goin' to do about food? And where this many people goin' to do they business? We ain't got fifty-seven slop jars! Fifty-seven people in one house—"

"We will discuss this later."

Upstairs, the protest continued. Returned to the location of their bondage of so many years, the house servants were abjectly disappointed to once again find themselves under Ariadne's roof.

"You're goin' to get us all hanged," said Velvet, a serving maid.

"You promised us we were goin' down the river to Boston!" wailed Polly, a kitchen girl.

"And how we goin' to bed down fifty-seven?" Esta wanted to know. "Crammin' all them folks in the cellar is worse than them slave boats my mammy's mammy tells us about."

"And what if she comes back? You know she never give us word. Ever year they take her to that place for not-right-in-the-head people, and she bobs up back here 'fore we expectin' her."

"It's just for three days," Madison explained patiently. "Now start cooking for all those people. The pantry is full. I'll get additional supplies tomorrow. We have plenty of meal and potatoes and—"

"I ain't goin' to do it," Easter said. "I done think I bound for freedom and ends right back where I always been. Only now I got to cook for fifty-seven! That worse than them big dinners Miss Ariadne gives and axes half of Richmond to."

"Indeed you can do it and you will do it," Madison said. "And we will either all hang together, or all hang separately. Your American statesman, Mr. Benjamin Franklin, said something like that. Now we know what he meant."

The spacious cellar was still inadequate for sleeping fifty-seven people, even after blankets and quilts from every source in the house were laid down. Finally, Madison had to allow some of the blacks to come up to the first and second floors. The plush carpets in the parlor, library, and other rooms were thick and luxuriant compared to the previous conditions provided by some of their masters, and even the runners in the halls were better than hard floors and thin pallets that had been the earlier bedding of many.

With the draperies drawn shut, and the minimum of lamplight permitted by Madison, the unexpected guests fumbled about in the darkness. Parents with infants who might cry and be heard by the neighbors or from the street were settled in the cellar. Those with toddlers were sent to the second floor, where the maids carefully removed all breakable items from tables and shelves to safety from curious, grasping little hands. The others were housed on the first floor. It had been decided that Ariadne's bedroom would be unavailable and closed-off to the fugitives.

Many of the runaways were house servants and Easter's stubborn refusal to cook changed when several volunteers willingly agreed to take over the kitchen. At the first whiff of baking bread, Easter quickly reclaimed her territory, informing Madison in no uncertain terms, "This is my kitchen and been so for thirty years. Them new folks can help, but I in charge!"

Under Madison's expert management, it seemed the plan would work. But even as he expressed the highest hopes for success, he had to warn the leaders that upon the first hint that Ariadne was returning, they would have to leave the house instantly. He would provide a wagon and cover of the tarpaulin to conceal the occupants, and the second of his mistress's coaches, but everyone would have to take immediate refuge in the cellar, prior to attempted escape in these vehicles.

On the night the slaves had been taken to Ariadne's, the *Thelma Lyle* was stopped, as Captain Pierce had been warned, three miles down the James River, boarded by a hoard of inspectors, and thoroughly searched. When nothing was found, the police apologized to the captain and sent him on his way.

The second night, with fifty crisp one-hundred-dollar certificates bulging in Captain Pierce's pocket, another raid was made on the *Thelma Lyle* just two miles beyond the site of the first, and again no fugitives were found. Disappointed that only a cargo of several kegs of whiskey—a late shipment from Kentucky, explained Captain Pierce—was on board, the police examined each barrel to make sure none contained human cargo, a smuggling device often used by the Underground Railroad to export escapees.

Captain Pierce expressed his irritation, embarrassment, and injured pride at being selected for a raid two nights in a row. When the leader of the patrols found no slaves and nothing suspicious, he apologized profusely at having offended the proud old New Englander.

Captain Pierce, with typical good will, magnanimously accepted the apology, but lamented the necessity of having to make another run for cargo.

"Now I'll have to make another run tomorrow," he fumed. "That liquor salesman didn't have half the casks of whiskey I wanted, but promises me a good supply tomorrow. Guess I'll just take these on to Norfolk and come back."

Finding nothing on two successive nights, the authorities began to suspect that they had been deceived and the information that the *Thelma Lyle* was being used to transport slaves was untrue, in error, or was a trick to divert their attention from the actual boat elsewhere.

Because the *Thelma Lyle* passed down the James unmolested for almost twenty miles on the third night, Captain Pierce decided to go through with the plan. He reversed the steamer and slowly piloted the boat back upstream to await his illegal human cargo as originally planned, with only the hour of departure adjusted for the false run. Five thousand dollars richer and seemingly free of suspicion by the patrols, the portly captain was anxious to return to Boston, blissful retirement, and the glowing praise and public esteem he was sure would be forthcoming when his daring, heroic rescue of over one hundred fifty slaves became known in the North.

Madison and Jeremiah Blassingame had planned a strategy by which the blacks would be loaded into wagons driven by Blassingame and Alonso and the carriage by Madison an hour before the departure of the *Thelma Lyle*.

"With the carriage, and by piling them two-deep in two wagons, we ought to be able to get all fifty-seven of them down to the dock in one trip without notice," said Blassingame. "I'll have my wagon waiting in the alley behind the house at precisely three o'clock. It will be there an hour before we load, so if it raises suspicion, it can be checked by the police and found empty well before we actually load her up."

The time of departure had been changed to four in the morning, when it was hoped that the movement of the wagons would create less suspicion as they blended with other vehicles in the normal early hour's congestion of traffic.

At the dock, the entrance blocked by a deliberately disabled wagon once the escapees had arrived, the blacks would be loaded on the boat and the plan would proceed as originally conceived.

But Madison's best intentions and careful planning of the fastest way to evacuate the house was not to be.

Ariadne returned in the middle of the night the runaways were to leave.

Chapter Forty-Four

Infuriated because her physicians in Baltimore diagnosed her medical problems, mental and physical, as the result of excessive use of opium and bromides, Ariadne steadfastly refused to abandon the drugs or accept a program of graduated lower doses. Denouncing the physicians as quacks, she left Baltimore to return to Richmond, where she could find any number of physicians more sympathetic to her medicinal needs. Doctors Rudd, Hall, and McGuire would not see her suffer—even as one physician was unaware she received the same medications from the others.

Unwilling to wait for Madison to come for her, and with her own supply of narcotics alarmingly low, she had taken the train from Baltimore to Fredericksburg, where she retained the services of a local driver and rented a horse-drawn coach for the rest of the journey. In great need of medication, she had refused to continue the journey by train, having calculated that a return by coach would arrive in Richmond sooner than waiting for the next train. Denying her driver more than a minimum of stops on the way, she ordered the exhausted coachman and horses to proceed, arriving in Richmond at two o'clock in the morning, only hours before the scheduled departure of the slaves hiding in her house.

Her driver, a white man, had been infuriatingly slow and showing some consideration for the exhausted horses, refused to race at the speed she demanded.

"I should have gotten a black driver, you fool!" she screeched at him. "A black would never refuse to obey me!"

So unnerved was the man that under the constant onslaught of Ariadne's unreasonable prodding, he had become confused when he entered Richmond, misinterpreted her directions, and mistakenly taken a street into an area of town Ariadne did not know until she recognized it as Slab Town, an area occupied almost exclusively by free blacks.

"You fool!" she shrieked at the driver. "We'll be murdered! Get us out of here!" Having worked herself into a state by the driver's error, Ariadne's ravings had the man in fear for his life as he quickly retraced his tracks through the quiet, sleeping section of town and at last brought her to her house on Marshall Street.

Once at her house, she paid the driver, told him he was more stupid than any black she had ever seen, and then told him to bring in her luggage. As he unloaded her bags and carried them up the steps to the stoop at her front door, her fingers nervously searched her bag until she found the large brass key. She chose not to ring but use her own key, not through any consideration for her servants, sleeping at that hour, but in response to the urgency of her need for medication, all the more acute from the frightening journey through the heart of a population she believed was determined to kill her.

"Put the luggage in here, you idiot," she ordered as she opened the front door. While the man carried in her trunks and valises, she felt her way through the darkness and found a lamp. Lighting it, she made a quick count of her luggage and dismissed the driver. "Now get out, you stupid fool!"

Only too glad to be rid of her, the driver left the house and hurried down the steps to the carriage, the sound of the slamming front door ringing in his ears.

In the house, Ariadne heard rustling from the deeper recesses of the darkened front hall. Startled by the sound, she muttered angrily to herself, "Those wenches have left that cat in the house again. If my rugs have been soiled—"

Trying to think of some particularly objectionable punishment for such a lapse, she removed her gloves and bonnet as the sound of the departing carriage on the cobblestone street faded into the night. She fired up a lamp, turned up the flame, and raised it before her. Exhausted and shaken from her trip through black town, she longed for the calming embrace of the Tincture of Opium in her room.

As she approached the stairs, the circle of light from the lamp fell on a black asleep on the floor of the large, cavernous front hall. Startled, she stepped aside, only to have her foot strike another prone form—a large black man, who, surprised by the nudge, raised up.

For a moment, she thought the blacks were her own servants, drunk in her absence, having helped themselves to her liquor. But as her eyes adjusted to the dim circle of lamplight, it fell on another, and then another, and then even others lying about and rising up from the floor all around her. She did not know these black faces looking at her with wide, astonished eyes reflecting the lamplight, and rising like specters from a mass grave. The gaping, open-mouthed stares, flinching in the light, peering close to identify her, frowning with lack of recognition and critical, stunned disbelief at her horrified expression, sent a convulsion of terror through Ariadne.

Standing in the middle of a dozen blacks leaping to their feet on all sides of her, Ariadne's mind seemed to explode in madness. Emitting an ear-splitting scream, she began to run toward the stairs, tossing aside the lamp as she went.

When the lamp crashed and broke, the lamp oil ignited and flowed across the floor, spreading the flame in a wide arc across the hall. Leaping to one side to escape the flames, a large black man lunged toward Ariadne, causing her to recoil into the path of another. Backing away, she tripped over another black struggling to get to his feet, and, falling on top of the man, found her face pressed against his as if in some grotesque embrace and kiss. She screamed again with revulsion.

As the flames flared higher, the light more completely illuminated the scene around her. Ariadne saw the circle of stunned, wide-eyed, shiny black faces staring at her. Her screams increased as she struggled out of the unintended embrace of the black man beneath her. Once on her feet, she backed away from the startled faces and ran up the steps, where she collided with another black rushing down the stairs.

It was to Ariadne as if she had been transported to hell—a hell more tormenting and horrible than any she could have imagined, with fire and blacks all around her. By now, the flames were spreading fast and a black woman's scream joined Ariadne's.

"Fire!" a man yelled in Ariadne's face as he blocked her path. She fell back against the banister and sank to the steps. Another black, trying to be helpful, reached out to help her to her feet, but she thought he was grabbing for her and screamed in terror, recoiling from his large, outstretched hands.

They're going to burn me! It will be just like Mama and Papa when I threw the lamp! I'll be killed by burning alive!

Fighting off the outstretched, clutching hands reaching to assist her, Ariadne struggled to her feet, and clinging to the banister, backed up the steps, her screams now more like the howl of an animal. In the hall below, one of the men quickly seized a rug and in an attempt to smother the flames, threw it across the blazing floor.

By the time Ariadne reached the second floor, having dodged one black after another as they bounded down the steps and into her path, someone had lighted a lamp and the terrified woman was again confronted by a wall of wide-eyed black faces. Some sat upright on the floor, others were struggling to their feet and some, already standing, blocked the path to her bedroom farther down the hall.

Her wails were a bellow now as she bumped into one black after another in her erratic, weaving path in the semi-darkness. Someone fired another lamp and more and more blacks fell within the faint glow, even bounding down the steps from the third floor.

It's happened! she screamed in her mind. *A revolt! They're going to kill us all. They've invaded my house. I'll be raped and murdered! And burned alive!*

The commotion brought Madison springing down the stairs from the third floor. Following Ariadne into her room, he tried to calm his mistress, but she would not be quieted, her hysteria having risen to a level even her past episodes had never equaled.

"An insurrection! I told you they would kill us!" she cried, recoiling from Madison, who rushed about the room lighting lamps.

"You're part of it! You've brought them here!"

"You are in no danger, ma'am."

When the room was illuminated, Ariadne sought safety in her bed as she saw more curious black faces looking into the room from the hall and smoke swirling from the floor below, fanned by the carpets smothering out the fire.

"They're everywhere! They've invaded my home!"

"Get out," Madison demanded. He went out into the hall, closing the door behind him.

"Get everyone in the house downstairs and into the cellar," Madison called out in the hall. "Now! And make sure the fire is completely out."

The startled blacks, only too anxious to escape the still bellowing wild white woman, rushed down the steps. Madison returned to Ariadne's room and closed the door against the sound of other stampeding feet rushing down the steps from the third floor.

"I'll prepare your medicine, madam," he said, searching her washstand for the Tincture of Opium. He lit an additional lamp and doubled her usual dosage while Ariadne scooted deeper into the recess under the canopy of her bed, her face still distorted with horror as she whimpered in panic and clutched the bedclothes under her chin like a frightened child.

"You're one of them—"

Suddenly, a new volley of shrieks reached Madison's ears. Swinging around, he saw that Ariadne had gotten into bed with the naked newlyweds, who had ignored his rule against entering her room. Struggling to both dress and escape at the same time, the young man leaped over Ariadne, tripped on the trousers tangled around his legs, and fell to the floor, naked from the knees up. His wife, also nude, scooped up her underclothes and dress at the foot of the bed and fled the room as the young man struggled to pull up his trousers and follow.

Ariadne glared at the sight, her large, liquid eyes so wide it seemed they would pop out of her head. Emitting a whimper, she looked at Madison with stupid desperation and promptly sank back on the pillows in a dead faint.

Taking advantage of her loss of consciousness, Madison placed her medicine beside her bed and rushed out into the hall.

"Out! Out!" he called. "Everyone to the cellar."

Shouting as he went, he rushed up the stairs to the third floor. "Everyone out! And check all the rooms! Everyone must go!"

He repeated the order on the second floor and the first and soon the cellar was full and he instructed the overflow to go quietly into the back garden.

Ariadne's screams had reached the house next door and lights appeared at the windows. The concerned neighbors, accustomed to Ariadne's outbursts in the past, were startled by this demonstration, more intense than any they had ever heard before.

Observing the blacks streaming out of the house into the backyard, it was apparent that their number exceeded that of Ariadne's servants. Knowing that Ariadne was supposed to be away, the sight of so many blacks being quickly loaded onto a carriage and two wagons waiting in the alley behind the house, the master of the house next door became alarmed.

"Oh, Lord have mercy," the neighbor's wife exclaimed. "Blacks are pouring out of there by the dozen!"

"I'll get the police," her husband said.

"Look!" his wife exclaimed, pointing toward the entrance to the cellar from which even more people rushed. "There's more of them!" Then, whimpering fearfully, she begged her husband not to leave her.

"Miss Woodhull always predicted this would happen," the frightened wife said, clinging to her husband. "It's the uprising she spoke of!"

The concerned neighbor, believing the unusual number of blacks might constitute some kind of uprising—at least an illegal assembly of some kind—finally convinced his wife the authorities would have to be alerted and left the house.

Afraid to leave by the usual exits, the neighbor slipped out a window on the other side of his house and ran for several blocks for fear he would be killed if discovered by the fleeing blacks. Unsure of what surveillance might have been set up around the house, the man cautiously avoided being seen on the main street by traveling over a block by way of several of his neighbor's back gardens. It was thirty minutes before he found a white man on horseback, blocks away, who assisted him in notifying the police.

Because of the urgency of the excited neighbor's report, many of those who would normally be patrolling the darkened streets of Richmond were sent to Ariadne's house on Marshall Street. Because of the "hundreds of blacks" the panicked neighbor reported seeing flow from Ariadne's cellar, reports of a slave insurrection on Marshall Street spread through the ranks, and far more policemen than necessary descended on the house. Patrols were even sent to Capitol Square and the Governor's Mansion not far from the reported disturbance to make sure adequate defenses were in place should an actual uprising be afoot.

By the time a large concentration of police surrounded Ariadne's house, the carriage and two wagons driven by Madison, Blassingame, and Alonso were well on their way to the docks. It was later agreed that the concentration of forces sent to Ariadne's had diverted proper attention from the streets closer to the James River and allowed the runaways to proceed unchecked to the seldom used pier where they were hurriedly loaded into the *Thelma Lyle*, which slipped silently into deep water and quickly began the journey down the James River. To the police, the "hundreds of blacks" seemed to have vanished in thin air.

Of the fifty-seven slaves concealed in Ariadne's house, all made the trip to the *Thelma Lyle* successfully, and by the time the magnitude of the escape was known, the ship was safely at sea, bound for Boston with an additional one hundred escapees picked up at a plantation on the James River known as Fleur de l'Eau, and almost a hundred more in Norfolk.

Over a week later, Captain Pierce's wildest expectations were realized when he anchored in Boston Harbor and delivered over two hundred fifty blacks to freedom.

Chapter Forty-Five

Within a week of the escape, Ariadne was arrested and jailed.

She was charged with harboring runaway slaves and aiding and abetting their escape.

Because they were still in the country following Emma's funeral, the Hawthorns knew nothing of Ariadne's arrest, and it was two days before they learned of the situation and Lionel was called back to Richmond to act as her attorney. To Lavinia's relief, his departure removed the strain his presence created and the annoyance of Cornelia's and Margaret's efforts to reunite them.

Still baffled as to Ariadne's crimes, the matter became clearer as the senior Hawthorns and Margaret extended their visit at Hawthorn Hill. Clarification arrived almost immediately as the newspaper clippings and correspondence from Aunt Priscilla began to arrive. Each delivery of the mail brought more and more shocking details of the nightmare, and the clippings from the *Richmond Whig*, *Richmond Enquirer*, and other publications detailing the bizarre case only confirmed as true what the family had earlier suspected was Aunt Priscilla's tendency to exaggerate.

At last convinced there was no mistake, the Hawthorns returned to Richmond. Margaret begged Lavinia to accompany them, but she declined.

In Richmond, the family discovered the worst they could have imagined was indeed true. The *Richmond Whig* reported the arrest the day after Ariadne's incarceration and the *Richmond Enquirer*, aware of the public's interest in the case, began a contest with the *Whig*, which prompted both papers to publish the most insignificant details.

According to the *Whig*, for some time Ariadne had been under investigation as being a supporter and activist in the Underground Railroad because funds supporting abolitionist activities in the North could be traced to her. Further inquiry revealed that she had, years before, transferred funds in excess of eight hundred thousand from Virginia to banks in Boston and New York.

Numerous drafts from her accounts to known Underground Railroad supporters, such as the free black Ezekiel Scott, a cobbler on Thirteenth Street, proved her financial support of the Underground Railroad. Scott, arrested for his association with the abolitionist movement, revealed that Ariadne had indeed made contributions to the cause, but his evidence would likely be discounted in any court in Virginia since he was black, even though a free man.

His testimony to the prosecutors, however, allowed them to trace the funds to white participants who agreed to testify in exchange for being allowed to leave Virginia quietly with no charges being brought against them. Although others acted as the principal participants in such transactions, Ariadne's signature was proof of her approval and support of the illegal activities.

It was discovered that in the past ten years, drafts for nearly twelve thousand dollars had gone out of her accounts in New York, Boston, and Richmond for abolitionist purposes, usually in small amounts to avoid suspicion. Her most recent contribution was to Captain William Pierce, to finance the spectacular escape of over two hundred runaways on his boat, the *Thelma Lyle*.

A search of her home also revealed abolitionist publications and pamphlets encouraging blacks to run away from their owners.

Because of her financial involvement, Ariadne's house had been watched for some time, but no evidence could be found that she actually harbored runaways until the evening when the house, crowded with escapees, caught fire.

According to the police, quoting respectable Richmond citizens who lived on either side of Ariadne, screams from the house alerted them to the fire and they saw "at least a hundred" blacks rushing from the house to escape in wagons and carriages in an alley behind the building. The investigation concluded that Ariadne, staging an alibi in an out-of-town hospital, had actually returned to Richmond to hide the blacks prior to their escape to Boston on the steamship the *Thelma Lyle*.

The papers reported that Ariadne denied the charges and would say nothing until her attorney, who was out of town, returned. She accused her servant, Madison, of tricking her into signing the drafts used for illegal purposes, but this was discounted since her signature had clearly authorized each and every withdrawal, all of which were to abolitionist groups and none to Madison. She also claimed the abolitionist literature found in her home belonged to Madison.

She was held in the city jail even though her physician, Dr. Thomas Rudd, protested that she was too ill to be incarcerated since she was under treatment for hysteria. Missing slaves from all over Virginia and farther South could be traced to the group fleeing Ariadne's cellar or one of her plantation properties, Fleur de l'Eau, farther down the James. Her ownership of this property, with a slave population of nearly a hundred—all safely in the North now—further incriminated her. As did the absence of her Richmond servants who had all disappeared.

In the interest of fairness, the *Whig* reported, "Miss Woodhull has denied all charges and said they are the invention of her enemies, namely her servant, Madison, a black in her employ for the past twelve years, who was among those who fled the same night."

Lionel quickly began to prepare Ariadne's defense. He avowed strenuously that she was innocent and the victim of a plot.

Among those most stunned to learn of Ariadne's involvement was the Reverend Alexander Harvey, who, confessing his involvement to Margaret, now understood why Madison was so reluctant to impart the location where the blacks would be hidden.

"He was protecting Ariadne!" he said to Margaret. "Ariadne is being punished for us all. And all she has done is support the movement financially. I should turn myself in."

"You shall do no such thing," Margaret said. "Your going to jail will help no one. Think of me and the children and the future of the movement. And I cannot for a moment believe that she would do anything to help a black."

Margaret further demanded that he cease all future involvement in such dangerous activities. "This is not some

frivolous adventure in a novel," she said, "but a real danger."
She understood now the reasons for his mysterious nocturnal
absences and begged his forgiveness for suspecting he was
being unfaithful.

Cornelia, Margaret, and Aunt Priscilla visited Ariadne in
the jail where even the usually unsympathetic Margaret was
moved to compassion for her cousin. She wrote Lavinia, "She
was wild-eyed and almost insane with rage and humiliation
at the indignity of the accusations. She had Mama and Aunt
Priscilla in tears as she described her horror in arriving
home and finding herself trapped and surrounded by savage,
violent blacks.

"She said there were even naked black men hiding
beneath the covers of her bed waiting for her!" Margaret
reported. "She is not even sure if the naked black man
violated her since she fainted when she saw him and did
not wake up until sometime later. Of course, she refused to
allow a physician to examine her, and we believe this is just
part of her mental instability. Both Mama and Aunt Priscilla
are certain this preposterous charge means Ariadne's mind
had been affected. Mama is particularly embarrassed that the
papers published Dr. Rudd's diagnosis suggesting Ariadne
was suffering from hysteria and afraid people will think
insanity runs in our family. There was no sign of violence
visited upon her, and we are confused by her insistence they
intended her harm. She says her screams frightened them
away, but the authorities seem to believe it was her fear of
fire that brought on her hysteria and that she knew the blacks
were being harbored there all along."

Aunt Priscilla's letter dismissed Ariadne's claims as
nonsense. "Now tell me how a lone woman could escape
the evil intentions of nearly a hundred blacks by simply

screaming? They could have snuffed her out like a candle if they were so minded. I hate to say it, but I was suspicious of her story from the very first."

Cornelia's more sympathetic, tear-stained missives mourned the paper's mention of Ariadne's "mental instability," and defended her with, "Ariadne's incarceration with trashy people is responsible for her nervous condition. And, of course, anyone should understand how fire would be particularly frightening to her since her parents died in a fire."

A later letter from Margaret added, "Dr. Rudd and Dr. Hall believe Ariadne should be hospitalized. She even admitted to Mother that the night it happened, she thought she was going mad and was certain that the great black insurrection she had predicted was beginning. Fortunately, she fainted and only awoke when she heard pounding on her bedroom door.

"That's when she shot the policemen. The newspapers have made a big to-do about that. Ariadne thought the stomping feet coming up the stairs were the blacks coming back. She got the pistol she kept for protection, and when they banged on her door, she fired. The shots went right through the door and struck two policemen. Thank heavens they didn't fire back or Ariadne might be dead."

Margaret's report continued, "One policeman was only grazed in the side. The other was shot in the knee and has a permanent limp. But he didn't die, either. Otherwise they would have charged her with murder."

The newspapers reported the shooting as further evidence of Ariadne's guilt, and the police charged she shot the officers in an attempt to escape.

"Now why," Aunt Priscilla said, "would Ariadne fire on her white rescuers if, indeed, she thought she was in danger from the blacks? And if she was truly frightened of the blacks, why didn't she fire on them?"

Lionel made every effort to get his client released on bail, but to no avail. Incarceration in a public jail increased Ariadne's humiliation. "I'm in the company of nothing but ill-bred trash and low-life criminals," she wailed to Cornelia..

Soon, the northern press was trumpeting the news of a successful slave run of over two hundred fifty slaves, although the details were vague and unspecified to protect the participants, particularly Captain Pierce, from legal action. Some reports even exaggerated the number as "over three hundred."

Many Richmond slave owners were outraged and humiliated at the gloating northern reaction. "This brings us even closer to war," some said.

To release her for such crimes was unthinkable, and Ariadne was held in jail without bail. "She's just a black-loving Yankee under the skin," said others.

Lavinia, stunned by the news, immediately wrote to Ariadne and tried to encourage her toward a more optimistic outlook. Lavinia felt both relief and guilt that it was not she in Ariadne's position. She had assisted runaways for years; she was sure Ariadne had not. Yet Ariadne had been arrested and suffered the punishment that rightfully should have been Lavinia's. She wrote, "Lionel will find a way to clarify the errors of the charges and until then, I know you will bear the ordeal with the dignity your aristocratic breeding provides."

But further developments in Ariadne's plight were less than encouraging.

The case was the most sensational topic of conversation Richmond society had to chew on in years. The scandal of Lionel's shooting was quickly forgotten, replaced by

Ariadne's troubles. Her friends and family quickly divided into two distinct groups: those who thought her innocent and those who did not.

"But she's always hated blacks so—and feared them," Cousin Gertrude said to her cousins Priscilla and Cornelia at tea with Iris Spencer and Evelyn Eppes.

"Covering up, dear," Aunt Priscilla said. "Trying to fool us all. And she did! The same way she has fooled Cornelia into believing she was such an innocent when we all knew she was cunning and deceitful."

"I'm not going to even visit her in jail. Are you, Iris?" Evelyn said.

"Indeed not. I've never visited felons and I shall not begin now."

"Why, she even hoodwinked me by accusing that lovely Lavinia Hawthorn of crimes she committed herself!" fumed Judge Addison Povall as his little pig eyes snapped with outrage. He refused Cornelia's pleas to use his influence to have Ariadne released on bail or be allowed to return to her home under house arrest.

Although he was careful to reveal nothing of his indirect and innocent contributions to her crimes, Judge Povall was incensed that his past highly confidential revelations to Ariadne of ongoing Underground Railroad investigations was the reason so many scheduled arrests, raids, and exposure of escape plots had been thwarted by prior warnings of inexplicable origin. Ariadne may now claim eavesdropping servants, Ogletha, Madison, and Jennie, had passed on the information, but Judge Povall knew better. It had to have been Ariadne herself.

He had even told her that spies had discovered a plan in which a certain Boston ship captain named Pierce planned to spirit a shipload of runaways to freedom and a raid on his steamship was scheduled. Ariadne's betrayal of this information was particularly galling to the old man when the plot succeeded and Captain Pierce was heralded as "the Boston Moses" by the Yankee press.

Ariadne, begging to be released on bail, wrote Povall insisting that Madison or her other servants had warned Captain Pierce. Povall would have none of it, citing occasions when only the innocent Jennie, who sang and danced so well, had been in service when he visited Ariadne. Jennie, having disappeared ages ago, no doubt with Ariadne's blessing, was now forever beyond Judge Povall's reach, which further infuriated the old man and explained why Ariadne would never sell the black woman to him.

The controversial case was fueled by fires from the North when the news reports of the *Whig* and the *Enquirer* were picked up by newspapers in Washington and Baltimore, then Philadelphia, New York, and finally Boston. As the news of the case spread, Ariadne became something of a heroine in the abolitionist North, where editorials referred to her as a "champion of freedom" and "a noble advocate of abolition" in one publication after another. These reports did little for her standing in Richmond, and as she was heralded in the North as a "martyr for the black man's freedom and the end of slavery," she was pilloried in the Southern press as far away as New Orleans as "a traitor to her class, the noble Commonwealth of Virginia, states' rights, and the entire South."

Even her staunchest defenders began to waver and many, fearing they would be labeled as abolitionists or "black-lovers," abandoned her defense and her support crumbled as opposition against her continued to build.

As news of her case spread, letters began to arrive from the North to the authorities, newspapers, and Ariadne herself, mostly from anonymous free blacks who had escaped by way of the Virginia Underground Railroad. These grateful souls wanted to thank their "unknown benefactress" for her efforts on their behalf and to wish her well under the "unfair system of justice in Virginia."

The police, impounding all of Ariadne's mail, reserved these letters as evidence, as well as those that appeared in the newspapers. News editors turned them over to the prosecution in exchange for any "inside" evidence they might publish before rival papers.

Two or three of Ariadne's former servants, knowing full well she was innocent of any intentional benevolence toward blacks, exercised long-delayed, long distance revenge on their former owner and tormentor. Writing to her as if she were a most benevolent mistress who had planned, encouraged, supported, and helped in their escape, they thanked her in loving terms and further incriminated her. Impounded by the police, these letters appeared in the Richmond papers and Ariadne's case sank deeper into hopelessness.

One letter, mailed to both the *Richmond Whig* and *Richmond Enquirer*, was unintentionally printed by both papers the same week, because each publication thought they were the sole recipient of the document.

It read:

To the Citizens of Richmond,

You must know of the generosity and benevolence of my former Mistress, Miss Ariadne Carter Woodhull, who has been arrested for assisting and supporting the Underground Railroad.

For so many years, my loving mistress treated me like a daughter, always recognizing my dignity as a human being and never subjecting me to the humiliation and degradation so many of my color have suffered under slavery. She encouraged and helped me plan my escape in every detail—providing me with funds, spiritual...

After several more paragraphs, which further incriminated Ariadne by listing groups to which Ariadne had contributed financially, the letter was signed: *Ogletha (Mrs. Madison) St. George Overton.*

Subpoenaed bank records provided proof that she had indeed supported these organizations. This evidence, along with the draft for five thousand dollars, negotiated in Richmond only two days before the escape arranged by Captain William Pierce, sealed her fate.

As the days went on and the mountain of evidence against Ariadne grew, Lionel saw his chances at winning acquittal for his cousin vanish, even as he consulted and sought the counsel of the most learned and skilled legal minds in the Commonwealth.

At Hawthorn Hill, Lavinia also received a letter mailed from Boston from Ogletha and Madison St. George Overton.

Dear Mrs. Hawthorn,

My husband is writing this for me. I have wanted to write to you for some time, but my husband thought it wiser to wait until we were safely North and we could freely express our gratitude to you.

Since arriving in Boston, we have learned that his former master has recovered from the financial losses he suffered in the West Indies, and his son, whom Madison tutored, has been searching for him for some time, and is currently living in France. We are leaving for France in one week, where my husband has secured a position as tutor to the grandchildren of his former master.

My husband was aware of your and the Barksdale ladies' efforts on behalf of our people and we wish to thank you and wish you well before we leave your country for France.

The letter was signed by both Ogletha and Madison St. George Overton.

As Ariadne's troubles spiraled toward almost certain conviction, Lavinia's guilt for her own illegal activities deepened. Finally acceding to Cornelia's pleas that, despite her troubles with Lionel, she must join the family in a show of unity at Ariadne's trial, Lavinia agreed to return to Richmond.

On her second day in the city, she joined Cornelia and Margaret for a visit to the jail to see Ariadne.

"I doubt she will be very happy to see me," Lavinia protested, but both Margaret and Cornelia insisted that Ariadne's ostracism was so extreme she would appreciate any sympathetic company.

"She'd probably welcome Nat Turner," Margaret said.

"No one visits," Cornelia said. "All her former friends have deserted her. Except that dreadful Clevinger woman, I'm told."

"Only one at a time," a bearded guard curtly said when Lavinia, Margaret, and Cornelia arrived at the jail to see Ariadne. Ashamed to be seen in so disreputable an environment, Cornelia shielded her face with a bonnet with wide layers of ruffles at the sides, a veil, and her fan, and drew a long black cloak about her.

"You go first, dear," she said to Lavinia. "We come so often—"

Lavinia followed the surly, bearded guard past a contingent of other men through a door while Margaret and Cornelia waited in an ante-room. In a corridor with numerous doors on each side of its unplastered brick walls, the guard stopped and turned to Lavinia.

"I'll have to examine that," he said, and he took the basket Lavinia carried and removed its contents. After carefully inspecting the items—during which he ruined the crust of a perfect apple pie by ripping through it with a knife—the guard seemed convinced that Lavinia brought no weapons and nothing more than the pie, some apples, and some freshly washed linen and hose.

"Goin' to have to start cuttin' back on this visitin'," the guard grumbled, returning the basket. "This is a jail—ain't no social hall."

He led Lavinia down the narrow brick corridor from which she could hear the occupants of the individual cells— some in loud quarrelsome conversations, others weeping. A few, upon hearing the approaching footsteps, rushed to press their faces close to the bars of the small windows at the top of the doors.

Lavinia was shocked at the variety of women she saw. Some seemed so young, others old; some had faces as innocent as children, others appeared hard and cruel. Although she tried to avoid looking at the women, some called to her, asking for help; others made rude comments, and one asked for her prayers.

When one wild-eyed, gray-haired prisoner shouted an obscenity at her, the guard only chuckled to himself and said, "Don't mind her. She kilt her husband and is half-idiot."

Some looked at her with such sadness, she was stung by their misery. Others glared with hostility and abhorrence. One even spat from between the bars, narrowly missing Lavinia and the guard.

As she proceeded farther down the corridor, the women began to call after her.

"She's here to see the black-lover!"

"All the fancy dressed ones is!"

"Don't reckon a slut like you'd be expectin' fancy, dressed-up sisters to pay you a visit would you, Leafy?" a voice called, followed by raucous laughter.

"See if you ken git the black-lover to send us to Boston!"

"Better git yerself out of here first."

Lavinia was relieved when they reached the end of the corridor and the guard produced a large ring of keys and opened a door. Lavinia entered and the guard followed, closing the door behind him. The room had a stale, fetid odor.

"Put the basket down and set here," the guard directed, gesturing toward a bench in the cell. "I have to stay with you. Since we don't search down the lady callers, we have to make sure you ain't goin' to slip her no weapon or nothin' you mighta hid on yourself."

Lavinia sat down and set the basket on the floor while the guard stood beside the door, his arms folded across his chest.

The small, narrow cell had but a single one-foot square window, which looked out on a narrow alley. Only muted light flowed through the small, barred opening. Lavinia strained to see the length of the cell and the huddled figure in the opposite corner lying on a wooden cot.

For a long time there was only silence, and then the guard barked loudly, "You got company, sister. Says she's your cousin and come with that old lady and the preacher's wife."

Lavinia, thinking Ariadne was asleep, gently called to her, "Ariadne, it's Lavinia."

"Come to gloat?" a surprisingly strong voice answered from the darkness, and the figure moved, sitting upright on the edge of the cot. "Come to see your victim vanquished?" A throaty chuckle followed, as mirthless and grim as the bitterness of the voice.

"I've brought you some fruit, and an apple pie."

"Baked by the girl of the mountains herself, no doubt? Probably gathered the apples. But I was so looking forward to 'possum pie, or groundhog, or pole cat—" Ariadne's laugh rose from the darkened corner.

"It's an apple pie. Ibby baked it this morning. And there's fresh linen and some stockings—"

Ariadne stood and approached her visitor. When the light from the single window fell across her face, Lavinia breathed a faint gasp of shock at the ravages the ordeal of the last weeks had wrought on Ariadne's features.

Her normally thin face was now puffed, and her large eyes were denuded of their liquid shine and looked out with dead, unfeeling coldness. Only hatred and bitterness showed above the dark pouches beneath her empty gaze. In her mouth alone could Lavinia detect any of the old familiar characteristics: the thin lips drawn in a line of contempt, bitterness, and withering scorn.

"I am so sorry—" Lavinia began, uncertain what to say but realizing that her visit had been misinterpreted and was a mistake.

"Sorry?" Ariadne's voice rose and she took a step forward. "Sorry to see your triumph achieve heights you could not imagine?" Then her voice became calmer, but no less vicious. "I assure you, were our circumstances reversed, I would not be sorry! And that is exactly what I hoped to see. You know I had nothing to do with those escapes, yet I am locked in a cage like an animal—with other animals. And you...you who have run slaves for years...are free."

She glared at Lavinia and waited, as if expecting her denial.

Lavinia, moved only by pity and guilt, rose from her chair. "I am so sorry for the misfortune which has befallen you, Ariadne," she said. "Mother Cornelia has spoken to Judge Povall and we hope we might secure you...house arrest. Senator Holmes and others are talking to influential friends in hopes that you might be incarcerated in your home. Lionel is doing everything possible to ensure—"

"Lionel? You are back with Lionel?" Alarm colored her voice.

"No. We are still estranged. Perhaps you have not gone without some measure of victory after all. In your campaign against me for the last twenty-five years, you might find satisfaction in knowing that we are still living apart."

For a moment Ariadne's eyes seem to recapture a spark of the old light when nefarious schemes brought her satisfaction. Her lips formed a twisted smile, but her voice was still cold and empty.

"No, Lavinia, you won that one, too. You may not share the same bed—or even the same roof—but he is completely yours and always has been."

Ariadne lowered her head and spat out the words of her greatest defeat. "He still loves you."

She turned toward the darkened corner of the cell, where she sat down.

Lavinia was silent and uncertain whether to leave or stay. There was nothing left to say, and any further words were pointless.

Finally, Ariadne spoke. "Now get out. And don't come back. And tell Margaret and Aunt Cornelia I'd rather not see them today."

"Goodbye, Ariadne," Lavinia said and, accompanied by the guard, she left the cell and headed down the corridor as the guard closed the door to Ariadne's cell and locked it.

As the date for Ariadne's trial drew nearer, Judge Povall, after a visit by Lavinia, whom he considered the maligned victim of Ariadne's poisonous campaign to divert suspicion from herself, at last relented to Cornelia's and Margaret's appeals and through other influential persons, it was arranged that Ariadne be permitted to return to her residence on Marshall Street. But the conditions of her transfer mandated that she never leave the confines of the property, and that guards be placed both inside and outside the house twenty-four hours a day.

Upon hearing that Ariadne was not even allowed the services of a personal maid, Cornelia, already in a state at her unfortunate circumstances, became distraught. Because all her servants had escaped along with Madison, Cornelia felt it unthinkable that Ariadne be forced to live in a prison without servants, even if it was her own home. She began a campaign to correct the outrage of so unjust an arrangement.

"Why, do they expect the child to wait on herself?" she asked tearfully. "Ariadne has never come closer to kitchen work than arranging place cards."

"I'm sure she won't starve, Mother," Margaret said. "Believe me, Ariadne's servant problems are the least of her worries at the moment. Besides, they have a dozen guards there swarming all over the house and grounds and their meals are prepared by some policeman."

"Oh," Cornelia moaned, "I know Ariadne will not eat a bite! It will be the same as that jail food. And I don't even believe they give her the dishes I send over; they're so afraid we'll try and smuggle her weapons. And it is so important that she keep up her strength. And who will help her dress? She's never dressed herself since she was a child!"

"We all should learn how to dress ourselves by the age of forty-four, don't you think, Mother?"

"You're just making fun of Ariadne—and me, your own mother. You should be ashamed!"

When Ibby and Lottie arrived at Ariadne's house, with papers written by Cornelia clearly instructing the policemen to install the black women as Ariadne's temporary servants, the men only laughed and promptly sent them home.

Outraged at the rebuff, Cornelia sprang into action. Along with Dr. Rudd's medical evaluation of Ariadne, and Cornelia's influence on her cousins Agnes Cabell, wife of retired Judge Powatan Goode Cabell, and senators Holmes and Wyatt, the circumstances of Ariadne's incarceration were improved. By channels of influence originating from Judge Cabell and Senator Wyatt, the court permitted one of the women be allowed into the house as Ariadne's maid— or nurse, since Dr. Rudd said she was ill. Searches of all items brought to the house by the servants, and the servants themselves, would be required.

With the oversight corrected, Cornelia triumphantly sent Ibby to the Woodhull residence on Marshall Street at once.

Lavinia delayed her return to Hawthorn Hill when Cornelia pleaded that she should remain with the family as a united front for Ariadne's trial. "We cannot desert one of our own now," Cornelia said. "And we need your strength, dear."

Lavinia agreed to return to Richmond for the trial after a visit with Randy and Sarah and her grandchildren. She wrote Margaret of her arrival by train, and although she would have preferred to reside with the Harveys, decided such arrangements might offend Cornelia and Edmund and agreed to stay with them.

She suspected that Lionel's involvement in the case, especially as the day of the trial drew nearer, would keep him well out of her presence and continue as such during the duration of the legal proceedings. When she arrived, Margaret, Cornelia, and Aunt Priscilla all met her at the train. To Lavinia's relief, she learned that none of them had seen Lionel for days since he was so occupied with the case.

"Bless you for coming," Cornelia said, her eyes red from days of tears. She clutched Lavinia's hand as she crowded into the carriage. "Your presence shall sustain us all."

"Is there no good news in all this? No evidence that would benefit Ariadne?" Lavinia asked as the carriage made its way toward Clay Street.

"Oh, yes," said Margaret. "The Yankees are defending her and making her Joan of Arc. The major abolitionist organizations are working on her behalf—by denying any connection with her!" She handed Lavinia several recent newspapers in which the anti-slavery groups disavowed any association with Ariadne.

"Clearly an organized effort to cover for her," Aunt Priscilla said. "They claim that other than her financial contributions, they had no knowledge of her!"

"I can take no more," Cornelia mourned. "First Lionel is accused falsely of involvement with that Clevinger woman, and now poor Ariadne is falsely implicated. It's just intolerance and bigotry against us, I know."

"Of course it is, Mama," Margaret agreed, rolling her eyes in exasperation. "It's all just bigotry and intolerance."

Aunt Priscilla grunted her disagreement and pursed her lips in disgust at Cornelia's gullibility. "Mark my word," she said. "It's just like the Bible says: 'Be sure your sins will find you out.'"

Lavinia said nothing, but a new wave of fear and guilt swept over her as the carriage rattled on through the streets of Richmond. She felt particularly uncomfortable since she had made freeing the blacks of Hawthorn Hill a determined commitment, even as she feared ending up like Ariadne. For the rest of the carriage ride home, Lavinia was particularly quiet.

Chapter Forty-Six

At three o'clock in the afternoon, three days before Ariadne's trial, two guards lolled at the wooden door in the brick wall surrounding the garden in the rear of Ariadne's house. It was a warm day and the boredom of the watch had lulled the guards into a listlessness from which they were roused by the sound of a knock.

The guard opened the door to reveal a woman dressed entirely in black.

"What do you want?" the older of the two guards asked the woman.

"My mistress—she out of medicine and Dr. Rudd say I have to go get her some," the woman said, barely above a whisper, and extended a paper to the guard. "Here my papers."

The guard snatched the paper, which read: "The woman bearing this paper is Ibby, a servant of Miss Ariadne Woodhull, and has been sent by me, Dr. Thomas Rudd, to Lawson's Apothecary on Main Street to secure medication for my patient, Miss Ariadne Woodhull." The document, appropriately dated and with a clear explanation of the woman's duties, specified that she was to return to Ariadne's home within one hour of her departure. The order was signed and dated by Dr. Rudd, who had called on Ariadne the evening before.

"Alright, Ibby. Now, what you got in that basket?"

"Nothing, sir."

She held out the basket, its handle bearing a bright red satin ribbon tied in a large bow. Finding it empty, he dropped her papers in it. Then he looked at the younger guard and grinned. "You wouldn't be hidin' no guns or knives on you, would you, little Ibby?" He cocked his head to one side in mock seriousness.

"No, sir."

"Now, how do I know that? That mistress of yorn a mighty dangerous woman, if you ask me. Looks like she helps just about half the black folks in Virginia to run off. How come she never heps you, Ibby? All her other blacks went." He glanced again at the younger guard and winked.

"I belong to Miz Hawthorn. I...I'm not hers."

He then ran his eyes critically up and down the woman's body. "I gotta check you out—see you ain't got no guns or knives on you."

The guard, towering above her, ran his hands up and down her body. Looking at the other guard and grinning, he allowed his hands to linger on her breasts. "Lift that dress, little Ibby," he ordered.

The woman hesitated. She rose to her full height as if in indignation but seeing the hardness in his eyes, her body seemed to shrink as she wavered in unsettling indecision and lowered her head.

"I said, lift that dress!"

Tentatively, she lifted her skirts to just below her knees and the man laughed. "Kinda modest, ain't you, Ibby? You right sure you ain't hidin' a gun under there?"

"I don't—"

"You what?"

"I don't have...weapons."

"I don't have no weapons, sir!" he bellowed, bending close to her. "Reckon I'll just have to see about that." He roughly lifted her skirts and petticoats and his hands ran up and down her black-hosed legs and, winking at the other guard, into her underclothes, around her body, until he clutched her crotch.

"Reckon I'll have to shake you down to see if anything hid up there and fall out," he said, and he laughed as he lifted the woman and bounced her up and down, rubbing her body suggestively against his own.

"Well, I reckon you ain't," he said, removing his hands. She stepped back from him as her skirts and petticoat fell back into place. "Now you make sure you're back here not one minute past four o'clock."

The woman turned and rushed down the alley.

"Hold it!" the guard said. "I said make sure you're back here not one minute past four o'clock, wench."

The woman stopped. "I heard you, sir."

"What?"

"I said, 'I heard you, sir.'"

"You turn around and face me when I'm talking to you, woman." The woman turned around and the man advanced toward her. He stabbed the air with his finger, emphasizing each word he spoke. "And you make damn sure you never turn your back on a white man before he dismisses you, you hear?"

"Yes, sir."

"Just because you been workin' in the house of a white woman that thinks you low-lifed blacks are as good as white people don't give you no right to not call your betters 'sir' and 'ma'am,' you understand?"

"Yes, sir."

"Alright. Now go on."

"Yes, sir," she said. When he had turned back to the other guard, she rushed on her way down the alley.

"You reckon we ought to follow her?" the younger guard asked. "Or tell that doctor we have to do the fetchin'?"

"Hell, no. I ain't doin' no black work for no black-lover. Let the wench do it for her. We'll just search that basket she's carryin' when she gets back. And it'll be your turn to feel her up and down right good. Her knobs ain't much, but she got a right smooth tail on her," he said, and the two guards laughed as they watched the retreating figure scurry down the alley.

After six blocks, the woman turned and headed toward Broad Street. Darting between the numerous vehicles on the wide, heavily traveled street, she was almost run over by a carriage in the heavy traffic.

"Out of the way, you damn—" the irate driver yelled, as a buggy bore down on her. "Damn fool!" the driver shouted, and he lashed her across the back with his whip.

The sharp impact of the whip stung like a hot iron across her back as she finally made it to the street and leaned against a lamp post to wait until the pain of the blow subsided. Recovering, she turned a corner and made her way down a connecting street toward Main Street where she seemed confused and looked about uncertainly. The sparsely traveled side street became a mob scene when it intersected with Main. People from all directions joined the confusion of wagons, carriages, and single riders in an uninterrupted procession of noisy congestion. The sting of the whip lingered as she rushed on, trying to decide which way to go.

She approached a group of black men talking on the corner and asked them how to get to Ninth Street. They told her and she was about to proceed when she felt a hand grasp her tightly by the arm.

"What you talking about here, woman?" the rough voice of a bearded policeman asked her above the din of traffic.

"I was asking the way to Ninth Street, sir."

The group of four black men stepped back and separated.

"Get on!" the policeman ordered with a wave of his hand and they dispersed, each rushing away in a different direction.

"Where's your papers?"

"Right here, sir." She handed her papers toward him but he waved them away with his hand.

"Don't you know the law says no more than four blacks can gather on the street in one place at one time? Can't you count to four, woman?"

"Yes, sir."

"If you can, then why did you make your little confab five by joining four black men? You planning a conspiracy of some kind? You blacks getting the word out to riot or burn or destroy or try to stage some kind of insurrection?"

"No, sir. I just askin' the way to Ninth Street."

"What for? What business you got on Ninth Street?"

"I got to get medicine for my mistress, sir."

The policeman dismissed her and she moved on. Her head held low, she almost ran until she came to the intersection of Main and Ninth Street. The throng on the street seemed even larger and the traffic heavier. Looking about, she searched the endless procession of carriages, wagons, and rigs, interspersed with mounted riders traveling up and down Main. She seemed to grow more agitated as she waited and rushed from one side of the street to the other, constantly scanning the traffic.

She almost ran into two white women, one of whom was outraged at the near collision and struck her over the head with her folded parasol. "You stupid, wall-eyed black fool!" she shrieked in a coarse voice. "You step aside when you see a white person approach! Don't you know the law?"

"Yes, ma'am," she said, shielding herself from the blows.

The woman went on, angrily talking to her companion. "Must be a free black. They're the worst, you know. Takin' over the entire city–"

The woman in black held the basket handle with the bright red ribbon just beneath her chin and searched the streets for the sign of a familiar vehicle. At the same time that she tried to remain as inconspicuous as possible, she seemed also to be displaying herself. She kept a foot off the curb to avoid other encounters and noticed that most of the blacks stepped aside when whites approached to give them the right of way.

Finally, a carriage pulled out of the flow of traffic, stopped at the curb, and the door flew open. The blonde head of a woman emerged.

"Is it you?" she asked.

The woman in black nodded and lowered the basket. A gloved hand extended from the carriage and motioned for her to get inside.

Once seated in the carriage, the woman saw the blonde-haired woman was accompanied by a barrel-chested, swarthy man with a black moustache.

"We've been around the block six times. Why are you late?" he asked in a distinctly Northern accent.

"I...I...the traffic was so thick. The people...I..."

The white woman stared with wide-eyed disbelief at the woman in black as the man asked a series of questions.

"Did you bring the money?"

The black woman removed one of her gloves to reveal a piece of paper folded tightly in the palm of her shaking hand. She unfolded it and handed it to the man.

After carefully examining the bank draft, he nodded his satisfaction and stuck it in the inside breast pocket of his coat.

"Bank of Boston," he said with satisfaction. He rapped on the roof of the coach. He ordered the driver to proceed. "Cross the Mayo Bridge and go on to Manchester." He sat back and joined the blonde woman in staring in incredulity at the woman across from him.

"We'll try and get to Petersburg by tonight," he said. "Tomorrow we'll go on to Norfolk. The next day you are booked on a steamer to New York."

Shifting uncomfortably under their gaze, the woman in black finally said, "It makes me sick to ride backward. Swap seats with me."

The white woman switched places and the woman in black sat beside the man.

At the Mayo Bridge, the coach was stopped by the police, who proceeded to make a cursory inspection of all traffic crossing the bridge. Wagons of tobacco entering the city were jabbed to see if any blacks were concealed beneath and any unusually large boxes were examined. Occasionally trunks, if they were large enough to contain a human being, were opened.

Looking inside the carriage, the inspector asked the driver his destination. He was about to wave the vehicle on when he suddenly looked at the woman seated beside the white man. "You," he said. "Step out of the carriage."

"She's my maid," the white woman said. The woman in black hesitated and the policeman once more ordered her to step outside. She obeyed and stood meekly before the policeman.

"And who are you, sir?"

"I'm Josiah Clevinger," the man said. He nodded toward the woman across from him. "And this is my wife, Mrs. Clevinger."

"And are you from Richmond, Mr. Clevinger?"

"No, I'm from New York. I do business here now and again."

"And you're the maid?"

"Yes, sir."

"Here in the South, a white man rides in a coach sitting beside his wife. Not beside his wife's black slave, sir. Just don't look right the other way."

The mustached white man's face darkened with anger. The policeman directed his attention toward the woman standing outside the coach.

"Hold your head up," he ordered her gruffly, his eyes narrowing.

Reluctantly, the woman lifted her head and the policeman's brow creased with suspicion. He looked at the woman a long time.

"You're not a black, are you?"

The woman was silent, but her large eyes filled with panic and she looked about wildly. Her hand reached under her basket as she raised it to her chest as if it would protect her.

The policeman extended his hand and ran his fingernails slowly down her cheek. A trail of white tracks remained where his fingernails had scraped off the cinnamon, lampblack, and bay rum mixture that had been applied to the woman's face.

The policeman looked from her face to his fingers, smudged with her blackness, and grinned in incomprehension. Taking her gloved hand, he raised it to her face and forced it down the side of her other cheek. Again, white skin was revealed under the smeared black coating. He looked at the woman in astonishment.

The woman, looking about her fearfully, took a step back from the policeman. He advanced toward her, still trying to understand.

"They usually does it the other way, white covering black. Who are you? And where are you going?"

Suddenly, the woman turned and started to run across the bridge.

"Hold it," the policeman called after her.

The woman stopped and turned around. She continued, walking backwards, as the policeman advanced toward her.

"Stop!" the policeman called.

"I...I got papers!" She reached in the basket, removed the papers, and thrust them out in front of her. "I got business for my mistress."

"White people don't need papers," he said, and he continued to move toward her. "Now you come back here and tell me what this is about."

"I'm not white!" she cried desperately as she continued to back away from him. "I'm black! Look at me! I'm black!"

"Black don't rub off, sister."

The policeman looked at his smudged fingers. When he reached her and snatched the basket from her hands, he ran his fingers inside and handed it back to her. "What business you got for your mistress, little white woman?"

"None of your business!" she shrieked. "You leave me alone!"

The policeman laughed. "Now is that any way for a black to talk to a white? But I believe you got white, too, ain't you now? Maybe you're both—part black and part white."

With a single swift movement, the woman reached under her bonnet and removed a Derringer, which she pointed at the policeman.

All signs of his amusement vanished and his expression changed to alarm. Backing away from her, he reached for the pistol holstered at his side but before he could draw, the woman fired the Derringer.

The bullet hit the policeman in the side and he lurched sideways, dropping his weapon beside him. His eyes widened and his mouth fell open with even greater amazement as he staggered forward, clutched his wound, and sank to his knees.

Tossing the basket aside, the woman bent down and swooped up the policeman's pistol. Holding it awkwardly in one hand, and the Derringer in the other, she pointed them both at the kneeling man. He continued to watch her as he clutched his side and blood seeped through his fingers.

Mrs. Clevinger, watching from the coach, screamed and covered her face with her hands. Another guard quickly approached the coach and ordered Mr. Clevinger, who was about to emerge, to stay in the vehicle.

Suddenly, the woman turned and started running across the bridge.

Another policeman drew his gun and rushed to the side of his wounded comrade. He fired in the air as the woman ran toward the center of the bridge. The policeman took aim for a second shot but an advancing carriage blocked his view. Once the carriage had passed, the policeman began to run after the retreating woman, who continued to race on, weaving her way between the heavy traffic of buggies, carriages, and wagons.

She turned and raised the Derringer to fire again but her pursuer fell to the ground before she wasted her last shot. The policeman drew one of the two pistols at his side and, having a moment of unobstructed aim, fired. Other riders and vehicles quickly snapped their horses to a greater pace or slowed, unsure of the gunfire's source or target. The shot missed the woman, who turned and resumed her flight across the bridge. At the sound of another shot, riders and drivers ducked and lurched to one side, attempting frantic adjustments in their horse's pace and direction to avoid hitting the woman as she twisted in and out of the traffic in her race across the bridge. The policeman pursuing her, with no chance of a clear target, fired into the air. "Stop that woman!" he yelled.

The woman continued to run, dodging the approaching horses and vehicles. When she reached the center of the bridge, she darted into the path of a quickly advancing coach. The driver was forced to draw rein so quickly the horses reared and veered to one side. For an instant, the horses' front hooves clawed the air before crashing down into an approaching team of horses coming in the opposite direction. The horses of both vehicles panicked and lunged forward in spite of the drivers' shouts and tightened reins.

The policeman fired another warning shot, which further frightened the horses and drivers. By now the traffic was in chaos, a jumble of wagons, coaches, and individual riders caught in a tangle of confusion. The snorts and neighs of horses, the shouts and curses of drivers, and the screams of frightened women filled the air as reins snapped and whips cracked.

Once more, the woman, still holding the policeman's gun and the Derringer, stopped and turned to fire at the pursuing policeman. The shot was wild and struck a wagon, which lurched in front of her target. The shouts, curses, and neighs increased as the woman tossed aside the Derringer and ran on.

At the center of the bridge, the woman climbed a wagon that was jammed against the bridge's railing and blocked her way. Waving the gun, she extended one foot to the railing as if contemplating jumping. Wobbling unsteadily, she looked desperately about her for some way to escape.

"I didn't do it!" she screamed. Her black face, with the exposed areas of her natural skin on each cheek, appeared as if painted with some kind of white tribal markings. "I hate them! I hate them! I hate them all, I tell you!"

Then, turning the gun on herself, she thrust the barrel into her mouth. Pulling the trigger, there followed a dull report as her head jerked back and her black bonnet flew behind her through the air in an explosion of blood, bone, flesh, and hair. For a split second, her body stood upright as her arms fell limply at her side and the gun clattered against the bridge railing. Then, still standing upright, she wobbled for a brief instant before falling over the side of the bridge and landing at the rocky edge of Mayo Island in the James River below.

A woman in a carriage screamed and a man at the reins of a wagon recoiled in horror as he looked into his lap at the bloody bonnet that had landed there, like a small sack, containing fragments of bone and blood and brain tissue. Placing one hand over his mouth to avert nausea, he dropped the gory pouch beside the wagon while the woman in the carriage continued to scream. Others jumped from their wagons and buggies and lined the bridge, looking over the railing.

As the scene of confusion and disorder continued, the body of Ariadne Carter Woodhull lay prone on the rocks below as a rivulet of red mingled with the flint-colored water of the James River.

When the identity of the body was discovered to be Ariadne, the newspapers headlined her suicide with the same sensationalism as they had her alleged crimes and arrest. The circumstances of her disguise, attempted escape, and eventual lurid death on the Mayo Bridge blared on the front pages of the papers for days. The people of Richmond, believing there was little more to say about the case until it was tried, found their interest awakened anew by the suicide.

That the New Yorkers, Josiah and Bithia Clevinger, were arrested and charged as accessories in Ariadne's attempted escape, added further interest to the matter: New York Yankees receiving their due.

"Trouble makers!" Cornelia said. "I knew it the first time I met them!"

Investigation revealed that the servant girl, Ibby, had been taken to the fourth floor of the Woodhull mansion by Ariadne and locked in a large chest. Then the desperate Ariadne darkened her skin and eluded her guards disguised as a black.

"Wasn't nothin' easy on me, neither," Ibby said to her mistress when she had been taken home by the police after being let out of the chest. "I knows what it like to be put in the coffin for dead when you ain't. I kick and scream half a day 'fore them guards hear me and gets me out."

Ibby related the details of the foiled escape not published in the paper to Cornelia, Margaret, and Lavinia.

"I think it mighty quar Miss Ariadne up so early that mornin'," Ibby said gravely. "She never up before noontime, and I sure surprised when she ring me at eight that morning and want me to go to the attic with her to fetch somethin'. She unlocks this great big chest up there on the third floor and tell me it her hope chest. She done got all kinds of linens, tablecloths, napkins, and fancy lace goods in there and 'bout a half a dozen dresses. She take all them dresses out and tells me they the ones she plannin' to wear when her engagement to Mr. Lionel was announced way back yonder when she a girl."

Cornelia erupted into fresh tears and Ibby offered to stop, but Margaret pressed for further details.

"Go on, Ibby. We should know."

"Well, she try on these dresses and sashay around in the attic like she a bride-to-be and tell me this dress her first-day dress and that dress her second-day dress and this the one she wear when she and Mr. Lionel leaves on they weddin' trip."

Ibby shook her head sadly. "Made me feel right sorry for her, bein' an old maid and all, and goin' on 'bout what she wear to teas and socials and things people goin' to has for her. She tell me she plan her weddin' to Mr. Lionel since she nine-years-old, addin' linens and lace to her hope chest all them years."

As Ibby continued her story of Ariadne's last morning, even Margaret felt a twinge of pity for her cousin. Her blue eyes became soft and moist as Ibby continued. "She finally get to the bottom of that chest and bring out the most beautifulest dress of all—her weddin' dress. It take you breath away it so purty—all white satin with lace and little bows. She act just like a girl again and she puts it on and I even pin back her hair to go with that fine white veil you could see through and she get in front of the mirror and say, 'Wait 'till Lionel sees me come down the stairs in this!'"

Cornelia seized a handkerchief and pressed it tightly to her lips as Ibby's voice softened with sadness.

"She even makes me go in the back garden and picks the last of them white roses she so proud of and mix it with ivy to make her a flower 'rangement. She spend just about the whole morning goin' up and down the front stairs wearin' that dress and carrying them flowers and hummin' weddin' music to herself. It right sad." She shook her head sadly and raised her apron to dab her eyes.

"She make me stands in the parlor by the fireplace where she say the preacher and Mr. Lionel be standin' when she come down the stairs, and say Mr. Edmund be waitin' for her at the bottom of the steps and she act like she take his arm and he 'scorts her up to give her to Mr. Lionel to take the vows."

Seeing the pain in her mistress's eyes, Ibby said, "I can stop, Miss Cornelia. Ain't no use gettin' you all tore up—"

"No," Cornelia said in a watery voice. "I should hear..."

"Well, it remind me right much of a little child playin' bride. And sorrowful sad. And Miss Margaret, she say when she stands at the top of the stairs and throws her flower bouquet, she goin' to aim it right at you and make sure you the one that ketches it."

Margaret pressed her eyes tightly shut and emitted a choked whimper.

"She keep goin' up and down them stairs most of the mornin' 'till she see them hateful policemen what was all over the house peepin' in the doors and sniggerin' and laughin' behind they hands at her. And then all at once, it like she remember she ain't never goin' to come down no stairs for Mr. Lionel ner anybody else and she look down at that lace dress and her face twist all up and she start tearin' at it.

"I says, 'No, Miss Ariadne, don't tears it,' but she want it off quick and she rip her veil right bad but I talks her out of ruinin' that dress, I reckon. Back up on the fourth floor, she get right quiet, and when the clock strike one, she tells me to see what else in the chest and I looks and 'bout to tell her it empty as a gourd when she push me in and slam that lid down 'fore I know what end's up and I hears the key turn and I think I goin' to smother—"

The Hawthorns and all branches of Ariadne's family immediately went into seclusion, and the notice of the private funeral in the parlor of the Woodhull house was sent to only close relatives and a few friends.

The servants of those invited spread the word, however, and a small crowd of the curious gathered outside the house before the eleven o'clock morning rites and had grown even larger by the time the brief Episcopal ceremony ended.

Lavinia, facing Lionel for the first time since arriving in Richmond, managed to keep her distance, the somber occasion requiring little conversation and no more comment from Lionel than his notice that she was once again wearing the familiar black, which had earned Ariadne's disdain for so long.

As the funeral procession followed the horse-drawn hearse, the crowd increased, joined by the curious as word spread as to the identity of the deceased. By the time the mourners reached the cemetery, between one hundred and two hundred huddled in respectful, curious silence and strained to see the final burial rites.

Alexander Harvey's eloquent concluding prayer of forgiveness, quoting Christ's admonition, "Judge not lest ye be judged," brought the spectacle to a close and Ariadne was finally lowered into the ground. When the relatives returned to their carriages, the crowd began to disperse.

As the Hawthorn carriage made its way home from the cemetery, Cornelia sobbed quietly into her handkerchief as Mr. Edmund helplessly patted her free hand. Lavinia, Lionel, Margaret, and Alexander were also in the coach, silent and dry-eyed, each reflecting silently on the tragedy of Ariadne's life and the sadness that prompted her to end it so ignominiously.

"Poor Ariadne," Cornelia said, finally breaking the silence and blowing her nose while the others waited for the conclusion of the familiar epigram. "I always wondered why, even when she was a child, she was so very, very mean."

Chapter Forty-Seven

Lavinia left Richmond the day after Ariadne's funeral. Already in a state of despair at the condition of her marriage and undecided about her future, she was grateful for a visit a week later by Richard and Ellie. But on the evening before their return to southwestern Virginia, she felt the beginning of the loneliness of having no one but the twins and Henny with her once they left.

As they sat on the front porch after supper, Lavinia contemplated her future at Hawthorn Hill in the enveloping darkness of the cool fall evening.

"I suppose I shall become like Aunt Lyla and Aunt Puss," she said, speaking of two spinster aunts who had no homes of their own. "Passed from relative to relative and living on the charity of my kin. Start saving up the darning, Ellie, here comes Aunt Lavinia for the winter."

"Now it's none of my business, Sis, but don't you think you've punished Lionel enough?"

"After all, he did get shot for his...wrong," Ellie added.

Lavinia sensed once more a well-intentioned family conspiracy to reunite her with her husband. Richard and Ellie had been reluctant to intrude in Lavinia's private problems and other than occasional subtle praise for Lionel's better qualities, they had said little regarding the matter.

"I do believe he's truly sorry, Sis. He even asked me if I ever thought... Well, he said, 'Do you think Lavinia's heart will ever thaw?'"

"And I told him it would," Ellie said, as if her prediction made it true. "And it will, won't it, Livy? You always took him back before. He's a good man."

"I've been through enough with Mr. Hawthorn, thank you. I'd just rather go home to Ma and Pa."

"But the Bible says you have to forgive seven times seven," Ellie said. "That's forty-nine. You know Lionel hasn't had forty-nine...ladies."

"Oh, I'm sure he's had far more. And they were never ladies."

"But you have more to stay for than just Lionel," Ellie persisted. "What about the boys? And the twins?"

Lavinia had thought of that, and it remained the most agonizing of the consequences her actions to free her slaves and abandon Hawthorn Hill would bring.

Saying little, they listened to the night sounds. Cold weather would come soon and they appreciated one of the last porch days. Finally, Lavinia broke the silence. "Old Sheba and Aunt Beck say many of our own people want to be free. They know I've helped so many others, they can't understand why I don't do the same for them."

"But how can you free your own slaves?" Richard asked. "Hawthorn Hill is dependent on slave labor. It couldn't operate without it."

"I don't know and I don't care," she said, but she was thinking of Hawthorn Hill only in its connection with Lionel. But at a deeper level, she knew she loved Hawthorn Hill with or without the man who had wronged her. It had been her home for nearly thirty years. Her children had been born there. Three of them had died there.

She thought of Hawthorn Hill's acres, abandoned and fallow, neglected, withered, and returned to the wilderness it had been before the labor of so many generations of blacks and whites had wrested it from nature to its present fecund, bountiful state of productivity. Then the image of bowed backs in the hot sun, struggling with ax, plow, and hoe came to her as she realized just whose labor it had been that had created Hawthorn Hill: generations of blacks. And the gratitude for what their labor had produced was still bondage, and nothing for themselves but what their owners chose to mete out to them. True, white masters had guided the toil, but plantations like Hawthorn Hill were created by slaves.

Again, she felt the shame of her own paltry, self-righteous efforts on behalf of abolition by merely clipping at the branches of slavery, while waiting for the politicians to destroy the root of the evil and rip it from the land. She knew the business of running a tobacco plantation as well as any man. The economics and social consequences of black liberation in the South would never permit a voluntary end to slavery. The politicians would only debate, compromise, argue, and threaten, and the results would be the same: slavery would continue.

Would she be responsible for the death of Hawthorn Hill? No. Lionel would simply buy more slaves, or draw them from the work force at the tobacco factory. She could not free every slave in the South, but she could those of Hawthorn Hill.

"Will you help me do it?" Lavinia asked Richard and Ellie. "We've got all winter to plan it. We'll even plant the crops—the final crop—next spring before we go...in a mass exodus."

Richard's eyebrows drew together in indecision. "I don't know, Sis. It takes on a whole different look when it's your brother-in-law's property. It's like stealing."

"What about the people's lives?" Lavinia said. "Weren't they stolen?"

He thrust his hands deep in his pockets and paced up and down the length of the porch. "I'll have to study on it, Sis. And God knows the trouble we'll all be in if we go through with it." He stopped pacing and looked at her. "And how can we do it?"

"The planting season is a week or two later in Washington County than here. Spring's slower coming in our hills and we can do what we have done for years, take some hands out to help Pa with his crops. For pay, of course, just like always. Everyone knows we do that, and have for years. Only this time we'll take the workers and their families. And this time we won't bring them back."

Richard leaned against the porch railing and listened as Lavinia continued.

"And when we get to Washington County—within striking distance of freedom—we'll tell them anyone who wants freedom can have it. Those who don't want to go will be returned to Hawthorn Hill."

"But you've got forty-four people, Lavinia. It would be like moving an army across Virginia. It can only attract attention and bring the law down on us."

"They are Hawthorn property. They are leased labor on the way to their new fields. There's no law against that. I'll have papers to prove it. And since the people themselves aren't to be told they don't have to return with us, we cannot be exposed."

Richard considered her plan and slowly nodded. "You may be right, Livy, but I've got to think about this."

Ellie, who had listened quietly, was immediately seized by enthusiasm for the enterprise. "Why, they'll be runaways and not even know it!"

Her eyes glowed at the possibility. "We...you and the brothers, Frank, Ed, and Witt, can come back in the spring, right after plowing, and bring extra wagons and anything else we'll need."

Lavinia and Ellie began to exchange ideas and knock down one obstacle after another as Richard presented them. Richard finally agreed to the plan and began to plot the logistics of transporting forty-four people from Hawthorn Hill to Washington County.

Through the winter, Richard and Lavinia corresponded at length and planned every detail. Often, Lavinia had only Henny to consult.

"Can't be lettin' any of them know before we starts, Miss Vinny," Henny advised. "Piney spread it all over and it get out to the people on the other plantations and soon their masters know, too, and the sheriff and Charles Hicks be on you like specks on a turkey egg."

Lavinia agreed: secrecy was essential. In many private conferences, Lavinia considered Henny's ideas as anticipation of problems.

"Might take a dog or two with us to warn us 'bout patrols," Henny suggested. "Gots to get old Mudley away from the place. Gettin' him drunk be good."

Lavinia had thought of this obstacle, but so far had come up with no solution.

"How we gonna feed them horses all that way?"

It was decided that some feed would be taken, the rest purchased along the way.

"Better get Old Sheba to packs us a medicine box. Might be sickness..."

Henny was assigned to the task.

"Better take some wagon grease so them slave patrols won't hear us at night squeakin' down the road."

Lavinia was amazed at Henny's forethought in anticipating such little-anticipated, but likely, situations, unaware of the girl's memory of the Stratchey brothers' wagon and its whining wheels.

"Might even puts one or two in chains so if we stopped, the patrols think we real slaves." Her eyes saddened as she remembered the origin of this idea, and she added in a quiet, distant voice, "They don't have to be jined to the wagon—just look that way." She quickly shook off the unhappy memory that prompted her suggestion and offered other ideas.

"Ought to have all the horses shoed mighty good. It sure ruin a good horse's hooves not to has good shoes. Ought to have papers like black folks has to have in Richmond if we needs them. I help you writes them."

And she did. By spring, every adult slave at Hawthorn Hill had carefully written emancipation papers and permission papers, each document bearing Lionel's name, expertly forged by Lavinia. Having been provided with Emma's emancipation papers by Henny, Lavinia used them as a guide and even forged the two-year-dead Judge Aaron Payne's signature to the documents.

They spent hours preparing the papers and Lavinia learned that the secret of successful forgery was like painting roses; it just took practice, doing it over and over again.

"Be mighty hard for old Jedge Payne to deny he signed these papers and he dead and in the cemetery," Henny said, inspecting her expert efforts in duplicating the deceased man's signature. "Couldn't write no 'count anyhow."

"Let's hope we won't have to use the papers. Except as a last resort."

"How about me, Miss Vinny? You goin' to fix me papers, too?"

"Of course, Henny. But you're only fourteen. You'll be my little girl for quite some time before you need to exercise the rights of freedom."

"Still, be mighty good to has 'em."

"Then, indeed, you shall."

"And...and Reuben?" she asked, looking at the floor. "He nineteen now."

Lavinia had watched with amusement as the childhood friendship between Henny and Reuben had changed to wary, juvenile antagonism, and occasional outright hostility in which Henny had asserted, "I don't like that Reuben no more at all. He all the time teases and makes fun of me."

But recently, the relationship seemed to lose some of its animosity and even showed signs of developing into an attachment of a warmer character. Lavinia had too often caught the exchange of sly smiles and signs of modest flirtation between them. And now, Henny's unusual display of embarrassment confirmed her suspicion that the girl's reticence in discussing Reuben might signal the beginning of her first experience with romance.

"Of course Reuben shall have his papers," Lavinia said.

Henny smiled to herself and lowered her head.

"Reuben's an awfully nice boy, don't you think?" Lavinia asked casually.

"He alright, I reckon."

Not wishing to embarrass her, Lavinia made no further inquiries, but she noticed the two talking in the stables and Henny often took Reuben servings of Aunt Beck's special desserts. The situation was confirmed when Piney, who had long coveted Reuben's attentions but finally became resigned to ignominious rejection, reported to Lavinia that she had seen them holding hands in church.

"It right shameful, Miss Vinny," Piney said. "I seen ever bit of it. They was settin' there like they 'sposed to and before the first hymn he had done slid down the pew-seat right beside her and durin' the prayin' he snuck his hand out and took hern in it and held it most of the next hymn and prayer and sermon and everything. And she never even snatched it back or slapped his face or nothin'!"

"Oh, dear," said Lavinia.

"Yes, ma'am! Right there in church. It just plain awful! I nearly die of shame and prays and prays 'bout it."

"I shall speak to Henny."

She never did, of course, believing the infatuation would duly run its course and wished to offer no encouragement through the slightest expression of disapproval. Besides, she did not disapprove. Reuben was perfectly acceptable and met all Lavinia's requirements as to politeness and good conduct. She had even included him in her occasional secret reading classes in the quarters and found him an adept student.

For Lavinia and Henny, the winter seemed to pass like an eternity.

Ellie and Lavinia kept a steady exchange of mail going. Through veiled, coded messages, "next spring's project" was analyzed from all angles and ideas were examined, abandoned, altered, and enhanced. Those of Lavinia's relatives in Washington County with abolitionist sympathies sufficient to be trusted with knowledge of the plan were already concealing food supplies for the "spring project's" arrivals.

Sheer nerves drove Lavinia and Henny to piece one quilt after another, and they even designed canvas covers for two of the wagons. Henny's schooling was intensified and her reading skills were so advanced she often read aloud to Lavinia from the works of Sir Walter Scott and Mr. Hawthorne. Her handwriting was exceptionally good, too, approaching the excellence of Angelica's penmanship.

"And I believe I done got you beat on old Jedge Payne's name, Miss Vinny," Henny said, holding up a sample of her excellent forgery.

"What a terrible mother I am, Henny," Lavinia said, looking at the child who was fast growing past childhood. "Teaching my child forgery!"

"Why, you the best mother in the world, Miss Vinny," Henny said. "And this ain't bad, Miss Vinny. This helpin' the people. Helpin' people one of the good things." She smiled and Lavinia reached out and touched the smooth, brown face.

"You've become a young lady," Lavinia said, noting the child-like features were taking on the beauty and maturity of her mother and father. Her sweet disposition and her wit and charm were given free expression by Lavinia, who had long ago stopped considering Henny a servant. She was her ward, charge—yes, even adopted daughter. She wondered, when Lionel had entered the record of Emma's death in the People Book, if he had come across the notice of Henny's adoption she had written so long ago.

He had appeared in the fall, following the marketing season, but otherwise only for brief visits with the twins or to pay taxes or transact other plantation business. Hawthorn Hill had been solely Lavinia's responsibility since their latest estrangement. She wondered if he would bother to come at all if it were not for his children.

Piney considered herself the new Emma as far as managing the house, and the assumption met with one rebuff after another as both black and white sought to shatter her illusion. She was perplexed that she neither generated the same fear nor commanded the immediate obedience that had been prerogatives of her predecessor. While threatening stares or the wag of a finger had brought instant subservience from Emma, shouts, screams, and the fiercest of threats from Piney brought only laughter and sneers and her requests were pointedly ignored. Only the younger children reacted with the desired fright and Piney realized it would take a generation to develop the same fear and domination Emma had engendered.

Piney's conflict with Henny also remained active, although mostly expressed with smirks and glares and in private skirmishes unheard or witnessed by Lavinia, who firmly ordered any outward demonstration of the ancient hostility desist. Nevertheless, the battle erupted anew from time to time.

Lavinia could often hear their squabbles and unless too heated, chose to ignore them.

"You done et the last piece of spice cake in this house!" Piney could be heard complaining.

"I never done it!" came back Henny's firm denial.

"You did so too. And I'm tellin' Miss Vinny. Mr. Lionel sometimes like a piece of cake 'fore he go to bed and you done et the last bite."

"Never done it. I took it to Reuben. Aunt Beck say I could."

"You ain't supposed to do that. He ain't house people and Miss Vinny have a fit if she find out you takin' all the food we got in this house to field people. I'm tellin' her soon as I can."

"You just mad 'cause Reuben won't eat nothin' you takes him. And he ain't field people, neither. Here lately he drive the carriage most as much as Uncle Lemiel do, and carriage people is house people."

"They is not. Uncle Lemiel the only one. I tellin' Miss Vinny."

With her pursuit of Reuben as a suitor ended, Piney seethed in silent jealousy as she observed Henny and the young man's relationship grow closer.

"And they somethin' else I'm tellin' Miss Vinny. I seen you settin' on the back steps with Reuben two or three times and he ain't even suppose to be up here unless he fetchin' company's horses or bring one to Miss Vinny from the stable. Aunt Emma have a fit if she knowed how this place done gone down since she die. Next thing you know, they be field blacks in the yard and settin' on the porch and in the parlor. And all 'cause of you. I tellin' Miss Vinny—"

"I done told you, Reuben ain't field people and if I wants to set with him on the kitchen steps, ain't none of your business."

"I tellin' Miss Vinny."

Usually such exchanges were brought to quick termination by Aunt Beck, but often Lavinia had to intervene. So rancorous was the girls' relationship that sharing in the care of the twins was almost impossible and only provided another area for argument and conflict.

"That ain't the way to bathe that child," Piney said.

"It is so too."

"Naw, it ain't. You git soap in its eyes. Give it to me."

"You touch this child and I knock you cock-eyed."

"I tellin' Miss Vinny."

In an effort to maintain peace, Piney was assigned to household duties, which kept her on the first floor and in the kitchen; Henny was given responsibilities in the nursery on the floor above.

Lavinia enjoyed her late motherhood and found the twins her greatest joy. They decided that Margaret was more mischievous than Cornelia, but that Cornelia was the fussier of the two. "Just like their namesakes," said Lavinia.

Nearly four-years-old, the curly haired, blue-eyed charmers soon learned they had control of almost everyone in the household. During his visits, Lionel frustrated Lavinia's efforts to discipline the girls. He always came bearing gifts and to make up for his frequent separation from them indulged the little girls shamelessly. After the brief, cold business conferences with Lavinia and his supervision of the fields and instructions to Virgil Mudley, he spent every moment with his daughters, romping with them on the bed like a child, running up and down the stairs, and playing hide-and-seek in the parlor where they were constantly in danger of overturning Lavinia's vases and lamps. Every activity Lavinia had forbidden he encouraged, and they delighted in the relaxed license their father's presence permitted.

"But Papa say we can!" became an unending litany from the upturned little blonde heads and pink, pursed lips as they responded to Lavinia's mild admonitions.

"Why, these are wonderful mud pies, darlings! Papa is mighty glad you brought him one," Lionel said, defending their efforts dripping on the parlor carpet.

The little girls squealed with delight when Lionel pretended to eat their creations and Lavinia's reminder that mud pies were forbidden in the house was met with trembling lips and blue eyes brimming with the tears of hurt feelings.

"But we brought you one, too, Mama," Maggie said, and Cordy held up a little fist dripping with mud, the hurt in the little girl's eyes and pouting faces as disarming to Lavinia as to Lionel.

"Now isn't that the sweetest thing," Lionel said. "Bringing your mama and papa nice mud pies you made all by yourselves. Now how about a kiss, too?"

The spoiled girls worshiped their indulgent father and Lavinia feared they would begin to regard her as a constantly scolding nag. She knew Lionel was deliberately undermining her authority and it was becoming like the old days: another subtle battle between them, unacknowledged but under the surface, being played through the children. He had done it before when their sons were young.

"Come, Mrs. Hawwthorn," he said. "Maggie and Cordy are very sorry they broke your vase, and Papa will replace it with a finer one when he is in Richmond." Then he winked at the girls and lifted them up into his arms, where hugs and kisses erased the consequences for their most recent misbehavior.

"I wish you would not allow the girls to behave like monkeys," she said, referring to their most recent transgression of jumping up and down on the feather tick and breaking two slats in the bed. "After your visits here, they are almost unmanageable and think they can do anything they please."

Lionel laughed. He thought his daughters' high-spirited disobedience was endearing and charming; Lavinia did not.

Edmund and Cornelia came for a long Christmas visit, extending their stay well into January to celebrate the twins' fourth birthday. Lionel came to Hawthorn Hill to deliver gifts but spent most of the holiday in Richmond with the Harveys and Sarah and Randy.

Frederick, having finished his schooling at the College of William and Mary, was now an attorney and proudly joined the family law firm in Richmond. His Christmas visit to Hawthorn Hill brought the news that his Williamsburg sweetheart, the mysterious Miss Frances Robertson, had finally agreed to become his wife and he hoped to be married within the year.

Frederick and the elder Hawthorn relatives were a welcome sight to Lavinia, who had seen little of them since her troubles with Lionel. Cornelia took up once more her campaign to reunite Lionel and Lavinia through numerous references to her son's model behavior and hard work.

"He even attends church occasionally," she reported.

But his mother's efforts fell on deaf ears, even as her awkward attempts moved and saddened Lavinia. She did all she could to lift the shadow Lionel's absence brought to the household and tried to ease the discomfort by carrying on as brightly as she had before.

Lavinia's sadness extended in areas of which they were not even aware, however. She knew when she absconded with the Hawthorn Hill slaves in the spring she would probably never see her family on friendly terms again. They would regard her action as an insult and betrayal and no explanation she could offer would ever justify her deed. Indeed, she would be as much a pariah as Ariadne. She anticipated only grief and disappointment in their reactions. Even Margaret would be loath to offer more than weak excuses for her treason.

By mid-January, the family had departed and Lavinia was once again alone. She longed to see Margaret and, to avoid Lionel, agreed to a brief visit in February at Randy's plantation rather than in Richmond. Taking Henny and the twins with her, she was reunited with Margaret and the doting grandmothers marveled at the beauty and accomplishment of their grandchildren, which had increased to three by now, with the addition of another Harvey son born to Sarah and Randy in late January.

"They're having one almost every year, just like Alexander and I," said Margaret with pride. "Isn't that wonderful?"

She wanted to tell Margaret of her plan to free the Hawthorn blacks but decided it would be unfair to place her sister-in-law in a position of knowing she planned to deceive and betray her family, yet expect her not to tell it.

She remained silent and the nagging guilt continued. But she had gone too far to turn back now. The plan was too far advanced to retreat.

Chapter Forty-Eight

At last the winter of 1858 released Virginia and spring arrived. The warmer-than-usual April prompted Lavinia to order the fields be plowed sooner than normal, and planting began as soon as the spring frosts were past.

With planting done, the escape would wait for the arrival of Richard and his brothers, Witt, Edward, and Frank, with additional wagons. Then the right moment would be selected and the plan set in motion. Lavinia's confidence rose each day. It seemed that even nature was in concert with the plot as the woods' spring growth flourished and thickened, providing a dense veil of foliage the wagons would seek for concealment in the forests along the way when the caravan of runaways was not traveling.

Even the problem of how to temporarily get rid of the Mudleys had been solved. On an earlier visit, Lionel, growing even more perplexed that Randy was becoming no more adept at managing a plantation than in the past, mentioned it to Lavinia. She immediately incorporated the problem of the Mudleys' presence into her suggestion of a possible solution.

"Perhaps Randy is trying too hard to please you. Perhaps if his guidance came from someone other than his father.

Maybe Mr. Mudley could be of help if we sent him to assist. In spite of his frequent inebriation and sloth, he has ability and—"

Lionel considered the idea and agreed to try her suggestion. Lavinia could not believe her good fortune when Lionel approached Mudley with the idea and the overseer readily agreed to the plan. It was decided that Mudley would be sent to assist Randy as soon as Hawthorn Hill's planting was under way.

By now, a cold indifference numbed her conscience and guilt, and she felt only a disturbing sense of satisfaction. Her only guilt was in her lack of guilt.

She revealed the plan only to Old Sheba, Uncle Lemiel, and Aunt Beck. With only these three aware of the real reason why the laborers' families were accompanying them across the Commonwealth while Mudley was miles away assisting Randy, it could be days before the world outside Hawthorn Hill learned of the mass exodus.

"We'll be safely halfway across Virginia or, with good fortune, even farther before we're missed," Lavinia said.

"But who goin' to raise the crops here, Miss Lavinia?" Uncle Lemiel asked.

"That will be Mr. Hawthorn's problem," Lavinia said.

"What we do if Mr. Lionel come back and you just left out?" Aunt Beck asked.

"We will leave within one or two days of Mr. Hawthorn's May visit. He never visits more often than once a month anymore and we'll be well beyond his reach by the time he returns."

As Lavinia expected, the three elderly blacks did not choose to go.

"Me and Beck mighty grateful, Miss Vinny," Uncle Lemiel said, "but we too old to head out on our own. We just stay and finish up our days here."

Aunt Beck shook her head with doubt. "Don't know who Master Lionel gets when our people gone."

"They won't all want to go to Ohio, Miss Vinny," Uncle Lemiel said. "And they be some wants to come back. They come back 'cause they scared of gettin' caught. Or scared of not gettin' caught and havin' freedom they don't know what to do with. Freedom be so new, they not know what it for. Hawthorn Hill blacks ain't got nothin' in Ohio and Canada. What good freedom when you got no land, or roof over your head, or food to eat? You think they goin' to give black folks them things in Ohio and Canada?"

"But they'll be given the money they've earned all these years. And I'll be adding additional funds—at least five hundred dollars a family—late payment for their labor at Hawthorn Hill. They will have enough for a start if they don't let some chiseler swindle it out of them. My brothers who will accompany them are in touch with organizations and abolitionists in Ohio who provide assistance to runaways. They will guide and protect our people against exploitation."

"You not gets away with this, Miss Lavinia," the old gentleman cautioned. "You been mighty lucky gettin' two and three out, here and there, now and then, but this mighty nervy."

"Remember, Uncle Lemiel," his mistress said, "I am only taking our people to help my father plant his crops. No one is escaping. We've done this for years."

"Not with the women and the children," said Aunt Beck. "They gonna think something 'bout that many goin' just to work hemp and wheat fields and put out a crop of tobacco."

Uncle Lemiel and Aunt Beck's doubts and protests were feeble and mostly kept in silence against Lavinia's determined resistance, but it was clear they did not approve of her mission.

The household servants' decision to stay prompted her to reveal her plan to a few of the older slaves for whom she felt the trip would be too arduous. She told the sickly John and Party, who chose to stay at Hawthorn Hill. Another elderly couple, Burkes and Elizabeth, also declined, as did one of their sons, Lacy, and his family, who chose not to leave his elderly parents. Lavinia offered Lacy the option of freedom later and gave him forged emancipation papers. She was relieved that at least one younger family would be at Hawthorn Hill to care for the elderly and assist them in the everyday chores.

"And I light two or three fires in the cabins ever day, even though ain't nobody there, so folks see the smoke and think they still people here," Lacy said.

Old Sheba declined to flee also, but she did not reject the offer of freedom. "Done too late for me," she said. "But if you could writ me some papers, I could be free here. Reckon Mr. Lionel keep me till the end like he done Emma."

Then the stooped old woman grinned. Lavinia felt she had finally earned Old Sheba's respect and she treasured the moment.

The remaining older blacks indicated a willingness to go because their sons and daughters were going. They were included ostensibly to cook and help care for the younger children while the adults worked the fields.

"I'm sorry I can't tell them all before we leave, Sheba. It's just too dangerous," Lavinia said.

The old woman nodded and narrowing her eyes, chuckled at some thought she chose not to share. "Can't have it gettin' out or it go sour," she said.

Even as Lavinia first revealed her plan to the old woman and obtained her promise of secrecy, Old Sheba's brain had begun to seethe and churn with a plan of her own. Like a cauldron of her mysterious medical concoctions, bubbling and distilling into its final formulation, each component came together as the old woman sat in the darkness on her cabin porch, smoking her pipe, swaying slowly back and forth in her squeaking rocker, planning and scheming every detail of her own private revenge against the white devils she had hated for so long.

Long into the night—and many more nights thereafter—she conspired, the squeak of her rocker and the occasional chuckle of her laughter mixing with the night sounds of birds, insects, and frogs. If her machinations went according to her carefully thought-out design, Lavinia would only learn of it days after she and the Hawthorn blacks had departed from Hawthorn Hill.

By May of 1859, the planting completed and the fields in unusually pristine condition, the days grew near for the migration from Hawthorn Hill.

Lionel made a brief visit just after planting season. The day after he returned to Richmond, Lavinia began putting into motion the mass exodus. She knew it would be two, possibly three weeks before he would return.

She immediately dispatched both Mr. and Mrs. Mudley, along with their two daughters, to the Hawthorn plantation Randy managed in Chesterfield County. With the enticement of extra recompense, Virgil Mudley jumped at the chance to assist and teach Randy plantation management. Lavinia flattered Mrs. Mudley into believing her presence was necessary as well, to instruct Sarah, her daughter-in-law, in the proper management of house, nursery, and wash house.

"Why, the poor girl doesn't even know how to make soap, Mrs. Mudley," Lavinia declared. "Throws away some of that good hog fat the plantation doesn't use for cooking. You'll have to get some lye and show her. And for heaven's sake, teach her how to make good sausage and to cure a ham properly."

"I'll larn her how," Mrs. Mudley said, beaming her toothless grin and, hands on her hips, rearing back to extend her abdomen with pride.

Within days, Richard arrived with his brothers Witt, Edward, and Franklin, along with two of Franklin's older sons, Fielding and Jacob, each driving large wagons which would transfer over forty men, women, and children and supplies.

Leaving her brothers to arrange the final details, Lavinia made a trip to Lynchburg and withdrew the money and accrued interest the Hawthorn Hill blacks had earned working for her father on their earlier yearly trips to Washington County. She also withdrew several thousand dollars of Hawthorn Hill's assets, and through forged drafts bearing Lionel's name, transferred funds to a bank near her home in Washington County. She would see that the people had at least enough money to start a new life in Ohio and Canada, even enough to purchase acreage of their own.

She had now added embezzlement to the list of her crimes.

The blacks, pleased at the prospect of being paid for their labor, were even happier when told that on this trip they would be accompanied by their wives and children. They worked doubly hard to ready the six wagons and coach for the long trip. The smokehouse was practically stripped of meat, the potato bin was emptied, and barrels of flour and corn meal and all other types of food to sustain the caravan were loaded for the massive movement west. Two milk cows were even tethered to the back of the wagons to provide fresh milk.

As the plans were made, a nervous sense of expectation and guardedness descended upon Lavinia and those who knew of the scheme. She saw it in Aunt Beck and Uncle Lemiel, even as they labored in baking bread and preparing other food and supplies for the trip. Although both had tried to discourage her, they saw the reckless plan become less of a dream and approach frightening reality.

Old Sheba, however, knew no fear and encouraged Lavinia every time she saw her. She always had the same request: "Just wants to know when you makin' the move. You tells me that, won't you? A day or two before?"

"I shall inform you myself," Lavinia said, although she wondered why having two day's advance notice was so important to the old woman. Perhaps she was reconsidering her decision not to go and at the last minute would, or she was planning a few quick, heartfelt goodbyes to those of the people with whom she was particularly close and knew she would never see again.

Just when Lavinia thought she was ready to proceed with the escape, a new problem arose. Mattie Rose Shankrall visited Hawthorn Hill seeking a diagnosis and remedy to treat her oldest child, four-year-old Grover Freel. (In the four years of her marriage to Freel Shankrall, Mattie Rose had borne four children and was in the advanced stages of pregnancy with the fifth.)

Mattie Rose would have preferred Dr. Hunter to diagnose the strange rash that appeared on the torso of the little boy with buck teeth and wild, unruly black hair sprouting in all directions, but the old physician was on the other side of the county delivering a baby.

Because Mr. and Mrs. Mudley were away, Mattie Rose had no one to turn to since she refused to speak with the new owners of the Barksdale property because they had given the house she had previously lived in to the new white overseer and moved the Shankrall family into a house previously occupied by Barksdale blacks. Mattie Rose would have left immediately had she anywhere else to go.

"What my little Grover Freel got, Miss Vinny?" Mattie Rose asked.

"It looks like chicken pox, Mattie," Lavinia said when she examined the child. She had seen the same skin lesions in her own sons when they were infected as children. "My boys had it and I don't think it's serious, but you must keep him from scratching the places or it will leave scars. Go to the cabins and see Old Sheba for some salve to stop the itching."

Mattie Rose was insulted. "My people don't go to coloreds for doctorin'."

"Then I'll get some for you," Lavinia said, anxious to have the girl and her sick child off the place before his malady spread to her own people and the twins.

"What will we do when she comes back every day?" Lavinia asked Old Sheba as the old woman dug into a jar with a wooden spoon and scooped an oily, sheep-tallow-based ointment of crushed camphor and mint into a jar.

"When she returns and finds all our blacks gone, she'll expose everything."

Old Sheba pondered the problem for a moment and finally said, "I look at that child."

Laboriously having made her way to the big house, she examined Mattie Rose's son and her eyes grew wide and she recoiled in horror as Mattie Rose looked at the old woman with an expression of haughty resentment.

"That child got leprosy!"

"Now, Sheba..." Lavinia wondered what the sly old woman was up to.

"Got to git that child back to you place and not leaves it for ten days."

Mattie Rose grew deathly pale. "You...you mean like leprosy in the Bible?"

"I reckon I does. They ain't but one kind."

Mattie emitted a whimper and her face collapsed into frightened anguish. "It that house we livin' in that give it to him. It where them blacks lived."

"Now, Sheba..." Lavinia said, unwilling to allow Sheba to continue her deception.

"Hit the truth!" Old Sheba interrupted, glaring at Lavinia. "I done seen it before. But I can cures it." Sheba raised her hand to still Lavinia's further protest. "I got special cures for leprosy and if you does what I says and not go outside the Holy Circle for ten days, it go 'way and not kill this boy and the rest of you youngins."

Mattie Rose began to whimper and looked fearfully at Lavinia.

"They live and be just fine if you does what I say," Old Sheba said. "I got special healin' powder you got to put all 'round you house and not go past it for ten days, and this child and your other youngins and you and your man all heals up and hit never come back."

"Oh, dear," Lavinia said, distressed that Old Sheba's obvious lie was frightening Mattie Rose. But she realized the old woman had a scheme that could keep the girl away from Hawthorn Hill until the people had time to be miles away before their absence was discovered.

Mattie Rose interpreted Lavinia's woeful expression and vocal protest as confirmation of Old Sheba's diagnosis, and began to bellow.

"I says I can cures it. Drives that leprosy right off. Ain't that right, Miss Lavinia? Didn't I cure your boys when they 'bout that size and gets it?"

"Of course you did," Lavinia said, noting the glimmer of satisfaction in Old Sheba's eyes that she had made her an accomplice in the ruse.

Mattie Rose immediately agreed to Old Sheba's treatment and the old woman returned to her cabin and soon emerged with a jar of ointment, her gourd, and a small sack of powder which she held up. "This drives it off. Just like Jesus did in the Bible."

Lavinia had Reuben drive Old Sheba and Mattie and her child to the Shankrall house and old Sheba began her rites, by circling the small dwelling and sprinkling the power in a wide circle around the house, all the while uttering mysterious chants and rattling her gourd.

Mattie Rose's husband, a balding, not-too-intelligent hulk of a man, emerged from the house holding one of the three other Shankrall children and listened in wary, slack-jawed silence as Mattie Rose tearfully explained the medical condition of their son, which threatened them all unless they did what Sheba said.

"Now I done make this Holy Circle big enough to go 'round you house. And I puts some holy powder at you privy and the spring house, but you can't go no war else for ten—"

"Twelve," hissed Lavinia under her breath.

"For twelve days—one for each of the Ten Commandments plus one for Jesus and Moses—or it come all the faster and you rots away with it. Put that salve I give you on the places of them that gits it and don't let nobody scratch them places. In twelve days, you be well and hit never come agin. If you don't, your flesh rot off and eyes fall out."

"What 'bout the workin' Mr. Moss 'pectin' me to do?" Shankrall asked.

"Workin' not matter when you pecker falls off," Old Sheba said defiantly.

Mattie Rose emitted a whimper and Lavinia sent Old Sheba a squelching glance. "I'll tell Mr. Moss that you are ill and that you can't work for some time."

"He runs us off, he hears we got leprosy!" Mattie Rose said miserably, and she began scratching her arm.

"I shall tell him it is something else. Chicken pox—but that you must be isolated. I promise you, I shall not tell him you have leprosy."

The Shankralls readily agreed to the treatment and promised to adhere to twelve days of isolation.

On the way back to Hawthorn Hill, Lavinia questioned Old Sheba about the mysterious powder she had sprinkled around the house.

"It idiot-powder, Miss Lavinia," the old woman said proudly. "It for folks like them half-wit Shankralls and ain't nothin' but wheat flour and salt." The old woman chuckled to herself and the carriage rolled on toward Hawthorn Hill.

Mr. Moss was only too happy to cooperate with the quarantine when Lavinia reported chicken pox afflicted the Shankralls. With Mattie Rose and her family isolated for as many as twelve days, there seemed to be no obstacles remaining to block the exodus of the Hawthorn Hill blacks.

As the wagons were being packed with food and the time of the move neared, Lavinia finally announced that the group would be leaving the following evening just after midnight.

"To avoid the heat of daytime travel," she said in explanation of the strange hour. "And so the children can sleep through the first miles."

As she had promised, she had told Old Sheba the day before. By sunrise the day after their departure, they would be in an uninhabited wooded area, noted by Richard in numerous past trips as an ideal location for concealing the caravan. There, the wagons could be hidden in the forest and remain until nightfall again concealed them and they could move on. Only after the third or fourth day, depending upon the condition of the horses and no unforeseen difficulties, would they risk travel during the day. All towns and heavily populated areas would be avoided whenever possible. Should they be stopped by patrols, Lavinia had the proper papers, and after many years of transporting workers to work for her father, she was known to many of the patrols and she anticipated no more problems than when these transfers had been legitimate.

"Don't worry about patrols, Livvy," Witt said. "On our way out with the empty wagons, we met many patrols, sheriffs, and deputies, and told them we would be coming back with a load of slaves hired out to work. They're already convinced this is a legal transfer."

The day they were to leave, Lavinia left Hawthorn Hill on horseback early to visit the Barksdale graveyard. It would be her last opportunity to keep her promise to her friends to visit their parents' graves. She also visited the Hawthorn cemeteries, black and white, and wept bitter tears as she said goodbye at the graves of Emma and her twin sons and Oralee. That evening, with only a few hours remaining until the midnight departure, Lavinia sat alone in Lionel's office. She now faced the most difficult task she had before leaving Hawthorn Hill, composing a farewell letter to Lionel.

As she sat at his large oak desk, the odor of his tobacco, leather, and hunting trophies was like the presence of Lionel himself. In spite of her efforts to rid the room of the smells, and her heart of his presence, it was as if he were there and she ached for his arms around her.

She suddenly realized that the enormity of the crime she was about to commit would preclude her from ever returning to Hawthorn Hill again. The thought brought her searing pain and she was overwhelmed by a sorrow matching all the grief she had ever experienced before. She was not only leaving Hawthorn Hill forever, but Lionel, her sons and grandchildren, all her family and friends, and her faithful servants, and—

For an hour she sat in the darkness, thinking, agonizing, reliving in memory the happy and unhappy thirty-six years that Hawthorn Hill had been her home.

Jolted back to the present by a timid knock on the door, she sat erect.

"Yes? Come in."

It was Richard. "It's almost time, Sis. We've finished loading the supplies and the horses are being hitched up and the people will be loading themselves soon. We'll leave in an hour."

"Have Reuben saddle Mercury for me," she said in a tight voice.

"He already has. We'll be waiting for you." He closed the door behind him and once again she was alone with the lonely task before her. When she fired a lamp, she noticed the taper quivered in her hand, and she wanted to weep and surrender to the crushing weight of grief that bore down on her. But tears would not release her from her sorrow now, nor turn back the clock, nor vent the pain and sadness that settled in her chest and would not diminish. It was too late. She had to press on.

She found paper and dipped her pen in the inkwell and wrote:

Dear Lionel,

By now you know of my ultimate betrayal. Believe me when I say that it has been only in the last hour that I have realized the full import of what I am doing and it has shaken me to the depth of my soul. And yet, even as I could stop the entire enterprise with a single word, I cannot.

I will not give you my reasons—you have accused me correctly of abolitionist sympathies for years—and like all of our kind, my reasons are the same as theirs. But I would ask you to understand that my crime is in no way perpetuated as a personal affront to you, my husband.

Our personal problems are not the stimulus for my motives, nor are my actions an attempt at revenge or retaliation or to punish you. I say this because I want you to know that although I cannot live with the pain and humiliation you have brought me, I cannot stop loving you.

It is difficult to admit this, but I have no more time for our dishonest contests anymore.

You once said you could forgive me anything. Do you remember? If you do, I hope that you will bless me with your forgiveness now. Just as I have forgiven you. Even though I do not believe I could ever be happy with you again and choose not to suffer the ordeal of any attempted reconciliation.

I am fully prepared to answer to the authorities and pay the consequences for my crimes and will be living with my father and mother in Williamsville should you seek my indictment.

Please understand I am not stealing your daughters, and you may see little Margaret and Cornelia whenever you wish. I shall write our sons and Mr. and Mrs. Hawthorn and Margaret when I get home.

Lavinia

She sealed the letter in an envelope on which she had written his name and left it on his desk.

The late night exodus generated a certain amount of grumbling and perplexed questions, but Lavinia and Richard again offered no explanation other than it would be cooler and the children could sleep during the beginning of the journey and be less irritable than they would during the day.

Uncle Lemiel, Aunt Beck, and Old Sheba were more emotional in their goodbyes than in past years when the slaves had left Hawthorn Hill to work for a month at Lavinia's father's property.

"Why, we be back soon as we get them fields plowed and planted, Aunt Beck!" Katie said, noting the old woman's sobs. "Ain't goin' to be forever!"

"Guess it just you takin' the little ones this time," Aunt Beck said, drying her tears on her apron. "Gonna miss them babies more than you!"

Lavinia concealed her own regret, even as she knew that for many, this would be their final farewell to Hawthorn Hill. Barely daring to look at Aunt Beck and Uncle Lemiel as she hugged them to her in the shadows of the passage connecting the kitchen and big house, she bit her lip and struggled to steady her voice as she bade them farewell.

"Take care of Mr. Lionel," she said, her voice wavering. "And Hawthorn Hill."

"We always has, Miss Vinny," Uncle Lemiel said. "You takes care of you."

"Make sure he finds the letter I've left for him on his desk in the office." Lavinia broke away and ran to the gate leading to the quarters. Not daring to look back, she reached the wagons, already lined up and waiting for Richard's order to depart. Reuben was waiting with Mercury saddled and ready to travel.

Only Old Sheba remained for Lavinia to see before she left, and she was surprised when she was not in her cabin or with the elderly blacks who were to remain and were making their goodbyes.

"Last time I see her, she headin' to the creek, Miss Livy," one of the elderly blacks told Lavinia. "That just after sunset and she movin' faster than I see her moves in nigh ten years. She in a mighty big hurry to get where she goin', wherever it was."

Puzzled by the old woman's disappearance, Lavinia returned to the duties of the escape and wondered what purpose prompted the trip to the creek. There was nothing at the creek and beyond it was only a meadow and the tobacco fields and beyond that the Wroughton property. Perhaps she dreaded the heartache of farewells as much as Lavinia and wished to avoid the sorrow of final separation.

As instructed earlier, Henny and Piney had carried the sleeping twins and put them on large down-filled pillows in the carriage, which would lead the procession, just ahead of the first wagon, which was driven by Richard. Once Lavinia mounted Mercury, and Reuben hoisted himself on Romulus, she nodded to her brothers, who snapped their reins and the wheels began to move.

Riding just in front of the caravan, Lavinia looked straight ahead through the tears that streamed down her face, never daring to glance back until she was miles past the boundaries of Hawthorn Hill. Grateful for the darkness and that no one could see her as long as she stayed a sufficient distance ahead of the caravan, Lavinia no longer attempted to suppress her sobs and allowed her anguish to pour out freely as they proceeded into the night.

It was miles later that she felt she had vented her distress and even as a persistent ache remained, she directed her attention to the strenuous, nerve-wracking journey ahead, the days of anxiety, fear, and uncertainty that awaited her at every turn in the road, shadow in the woods, or approaching stranger. She was grateful for Richard's confidence and Ellie's constant encouragement when her spirits flagged. The rightness of her action far outweighed the guilt, and she believed that her undertaking fell within divine protection. This was her greatest comfort, and she prayed again for safe delivery.

As the hours and miles slowly went by, Lavinia rode the length of the procession and back again numerous times, making sure they were proceeding in an orderly way and that the people were as comfortable as could be expected, considering they were crammed in at an average of eight to ten in a wagon, crowded along with the food and other supplies. It was, as Richard had said it would be, like moving a small army.

Lavinia became the self-appointed sentry of the group, extending her surveillance by riding a mile or so ahead of the caravan to check for patrols or circumstances that might impede their progress, and then dropping behind to make sure they were not being followed.

Reuben, in charge of extra horses brought along to alternate with the heavy work of pulling the wagons, shared with Lavinia the role of sentry. An excellent horseman, Reuben was permitted to ride either of Lavinia's favorites, Mercury or Romulus, and did so with such skill that even at a gallop, their tiny hooves stirred little dust and made almost no noise.

It was only after the six wagons and carriage had traveled for almost four hours that Lavinia suspected they were being followed. She had at first attributed faraway sounds of horses and creaking wagons as a peculiar echo created by her own group as they moved within a long, narrow corridor of tall pines and thick woods on either side of the road.

But the echo grew louder and more distinct. Bringing Mercury to a complete stop, she heard the sound of her own people's vehicles diminish as they moved past her.

Dropping back, she guided Mercury into the woods and waited. As she listened, the sounds of her own wagons and horses faded while those of others, coming behind them, grew louder. Certainly this was no echo, but another series of wagons and rigs. Within minutes there could be no mistake, as the ribbon of moonlit road revealed three or four wagons approaching. All were loaded with people.

Baffled by the strange coincidence of two separate groups of wagons, both going in the same direction, both loaded with people going down the same road in the middle of the night, she quickly prodded Mercury to return to her own wagons. As she rode away, she was sure she heard the rush of running feet on the road behind her and when she looked back she caught sight of a figure dashing from the road into the woods.

"Why, they have someone scouting ahead for them, too!" she said. "Richard," she called when she reached the lead wagon. "There are wagons following us."

Richard turned around in his seat but the road behind disappeared into darkness with no sign of any movement.

"You see it or hear it? I've been hearing our own wagons echo off the woods all night."

"I saw them!"

"Now, Sis. I know you're nerve-wracked and—"

"Hold up and go see for yourself!" She yanked Mercury to a halt and Richard raised a lantern and waved it as he slowly reined the wagon to a stop.

A sleepy Henny stuck her head out of the carriage and asked, "What we stoppin' for, Miss Vinny? We in Washington County already?"

"No, dear. Mr. Richard is only checking the other wagons. We may change drivers if they are tired." Lavinia dismounted and climbed aboard the wagon and took the reins. Richard, riding Mercury, rode off in the direction of the mysterious sounds.

Henny sighed and shook her head as she saw her mistress at the reins. "I sure glad we a far piece away from Hawthorn Hill, Miss Vinny," she said. "People at home see you riding a field wagon think you no lady at all."

After what seemed an eternity to Lavinia, Richard returned. When she started to alight from the wagon to remount Mercury, Richard stopped her and tied Mercury's reins to the wagon.

"Stay. We've got to talk."

He mounted the wagon, signaled they would be pulling out, and prodded the horses into action with a flick of the reins. For a long time he said nothing, just shook his head as if in disbelief and made a grunting noise. "Mmm, mmm, mmm."

"Well?" Lavinia demanded. Richard seemed reluctant to tell her what he had discovered or how to best reveal it.

"It's wagons alright. And over thirty blacks."

"But whose? Where are they going? Why are they following us?"

Richard did not answer, only made an annoying clicking sound with his tongue.

Lavinia fumed with impatience. "Where do they come from? Why are they following us?"

"Because we know the way, I reckon," Richard said. He chuckled to himself and again shook his head as if in disbelief.

"The way? For God's sake, Richard, tell me what you're talking about!"

"The wagons behind us are all runaways. They know we're going toward Kentucky and they need a guide, that's all."

Lavinia gasped in horror. "But don't you know they will only make us more conspicuous? The patrols will think they're with us! And where did they come from?"

"Not too far from...from Hawthorn Hill. Fact of the matter is, they came from right next to Hawthorn Hill. Looks like the entire slave population belonging to Mr. Horace Wroughton has decided to run off."

Chapter Forty-Nine

L avinia sat in stunned disbelief as Richard told her what
he had learned from the man driving the first wagon of
Wroughton escapees.

"I talked to a man named George, who seems to be their
leader," Richard said. "George told me Old Sheba had been
a friend of his mother's. Two days before we left, Old Sheba
sent one of our people over to Wroughton's after dark to
get George. She told him we were all going to escape to
Kentucky and if he could get the people ready and attend to
Wroughton they could follow us."

"Old Sheba!" Lavinia said. Now she understood why
the old woman had to know every step of the plan and had
disappeared prior to the exodus from Hawthorn Hill. "She's
been planning this all along."

"It looks that way," said Richard. "George liked the idea,
made a quick survey, and found every living black soul on
the Wroughton place willing to chance it. Even the old ones.
Seems they knew you helped Bingo and Jane and other
blacks, and...well, they think if you're leading the way, there's
nothing to fear."

He grinned as even under the diminished lamplight
Lavinia's face became visibly ashen and she grew rigid with
astonishment.

"Oh, my God!" she said. "Sheba knew I'd never agree to take them."

"Anyway, we're hours away from Wroughton, so I figure with luck we might as well just go ahead. Old Sheba told them step by step what we had been doing the last few days—packing food, makin' sure the wagons were in good working order—and they did the same thing. And in just two days. They said Wroughton was amazed at how anxious they were to mend broken reins and grease wagon axles and such. Of course, he had no idea why."

"But how did they get away? Why isn't Wroughton—" With an intake of breath, she gasped in horror. "Did they kill him?"

"Didn't have to. But they would have, I reckon. When he passed out drunk after supper two days ago, the kitchen woman sent for two field hands who carried him to the cellar. He's got a kind of dungeon down there: walls of solid stone and brick behind a two-inch oak door with a one-inch space at the bottom to slide a plate of food. Bolted from outside, and with no windows, there's no way to get out. George said he didn't even realize he was being carried down there."

"Bingo told me about that room," said Lavinia. "Oh, mercy! We'll have to...to send them back. We..." She sputtered helplessly. "He'll have an army after us. Wroughton's blacks threaten everything!"

"Well, maybe not. Seems like some kind of justice is at work here. Not a single one chose to stay! Amazing."

"That has nothing to do with the freedom of our people, Richard. They don't even know I'm giving them that option and Wroughton's people... We can't have them tagging after us. Their presence will destroy our entire effort!"

"It will be days before they're missed. Old Sheba, Aunt Beck, and Uncle Lemiel are going to feed Wroughton every day. He won't even know who is slipping a plate of food under the door. And Burkes and Lacy are going to keep fires burning and create other signs of life in the Wroughton cabins to give the impression there are still people there, just like they are at Hawthorn Hill."

Lavinia listened in mute horror as Richard justified the Wroughton slaves' presence and ensured her it did not disrupt the plan.

"They're going to wait two or three weeks before unlocking the cellar Wroughton's in. It will take longer for his slaves to be missed than those from Hawthorn Hill. Nobody ever goes there, and Hawthorn Hill and the mostly deserted Barksdale place are the nearest neighbors."

Lavinia saluted Old Sheba's cleverness and imagined the old woman's gloating smile and the chuckle of her triumph at her "private justice."

Because Lavinia's excited comments were attracting the curiosity of the blacks in the wagon, Lavinia and Richard waited until they had made the planned detour off the main road and were deep into the woods where they would camp during the day until nightfall again shielded their journey. Richard had used the same location in previous runs and he knew it was well isolated.

Within an hour, the second cluster of wagons, which had continued to follow them, came to a halt a few hundred feet away. They too began to set up camp.

Lavinia was still too numb to speak. She looked helplessly from one brother to another, still fearful but grateful for their presence and reassuring words. She smiled and nodded, making them grin with satisfaction that they mollified, if not entirely erased, her concerns.

Witt proposed dividing the caravan. "I'm thinking that if we can get as far as Wythe County, we can divide up there. I'll lead the Wroughton people through Tazewell and Mercer County and on to Ohio, which borders Virginia just north of there. The Hawthorn blacks can go on through Pa's in Washington County to Kentucky and Ohio that way." The plan was accepted.

Lavinia lowered her head and covered her eyes with her hand. Old Sheba's face rose before her, the sly old lizard's cunning smile reveling in her victory, confirming that her strategy had progressed too far to turn back and that her scheme would prevail.

"Don't worry, Sis. I think this can be our best run yet. Of course, we may have to leave Virginia. Brother Benjamin says Ohio isn't so bad a place to live."

"Oh, you're not being realistic. When Wroughton is free, he'll have the sheriff and county militia after us within hours. They may already be!"

She felt a wave of panic at the thought that Wroughton, the sheriff, Charles Hicks, and even the county militia might thunder into sight at any minute.

When the eastern sky warmed with the first sign of morning, the exhausted group settled down to sleep. Many could not, especially the children who had slept during the night in spite of the jolting wagon ride.

Lavinia and Richard decided that the two groups of blacks, hers and Wroughton's, should be kept apart, but by sunrise, the two slave populations were visiting as they did in the old days when they were allowed to congregate on

Sundays at church. The Hawthorn people were overjoyed that the Wroughton blacks were making a bid for freedom. Fearing resentment would settle in her own people, Lavinia told several of her own slaves that they too would have the opportunity to flee to Ohio if they chose. The joy was etched in unremitting smiles and faces glowed with the prospect of freedom in both camps.

With little to conceal, Lavinia and Richard had the opportunity to advise all the blacks of the dangers and cautions that would be necessary during the following days as they traveled across Virginia. Various strategies were developed to cover any number of emergencies, including encounters with slave patrols.

Lavinia's concern with a response from Wroughton was quickly dispelled.

"He not get out, Miss Hawthorn," a Wroughton black said. "That place solid rock and dark. Ain't no way he'll get out—'less he let out."

"But he'll have to be let out sometime. What if he dies there? Then we'd be charged with murder."

"He ain't gonna die, Miz Hawthorn," the Wroughton black assured her. "Old Sheba gonna tell your Beck and Lemiel what we done. They gonna takes him food and water ever day. He be took better care of than he ever did us."

"Wroughton will think I'm responsible for the entire enterprise," she said. "I'm an outlaw—a fugitive!"

"Not in Ohio, you won't be," Ellie said. "We'll all live with Witt if we have to—until we can find places of our own. And you can live with Richard and me."

"And the Barksdale sisters would take me in Philadelphia, I'm sure."

With the situation impossible to get worse, Lavinia decided to forge ahead. Lionel might not prosecute his own wife; she could expect no such leniency from Horace Wroughton. She was doomed but had no choice but to brashly proceed.

"I shall be as reckless as I have to be," she told herself. "I shall be guilty of the least and guilty of the whole. After all, if I go down, I might as well do it in a grand way."

The next evening the caravans, still separated, continued once darkness fell. It was decided that keeping a half-mile distance between the two groups might offer some protection from both ends. Warnings of trouble at either group would send a fleet-footed runner or horseman to warn the other.

The occasional lone rider or wagon they met merely looked at the passing group with curiosity as Lavinia, Richard, and Ellie greeted the strangers with calculated, conspicuous friendliness. With whites obviously in charge, no one suspected anything unusual. When the curious inquired, they explained they were moving slaves from one property to another.

It had been a week since Horace Wroughton had been carried drunk and unconscious and locked in the cellar. In the perpetual darkness, with only a sliver of light below the door of his cell a sign of day, he had lost count of time.

The eight-by-ten-foot room in which he was confined was escape-proof by Wroughton's own design. Realizing his only chance of escape would come from outside hands, Wroughton had yelled and beaten on the door helplessly for most of the first three days of his imprisonment. His voice, raspy from yelling, and his arms and fists sore from endless pounding, he nevertheless began hammering and bellowing again whenever he first saw a shadow cut the light at the bottom of the door.

As always, when he heard approaching footsteps or the scrape of the tin plate on the stone threshold as it was slid under the door with his food, Wroughton fell to the floor and pressed his face to the cold stone surface to better see beneath the door. Through the one-inch space, he sometimes saw the hem of a woman's dress, or the shoe or boot of a man. But the visitor was always there for the same purpose. A tin plate of food and another thin pan which was then filled with water were set down by hands wearing white gloves, obscuring the skin color of the wearer. Then the gloved hand or a foot pushed the pans within reach of Wroughton's fingers.

"I know who you are," Wroughton bellowed when he saw the black dress beneath the door. "You're that goddamn Hawthorn woman. You can take your white gloves off, you goddamned bitch. You can't fool me into believing you're a damn black coverin' your black hands. I know hits you!"

On the first day in the cellar, Wroughton had angrily thrown the plates across the room and cursed the unidentified bearers of the food and water. But after another day, he was so driven by thirst and hunger he seized the plates as soon as he could reach their edges when they were slid beneath the door.

Falling to his knees, he pressed his face into the plate and gobbled the contents like an animal, since he had not been given a spoon or fork. Likewise, he sucked up the water while kneeling over it when he found that attempting to lift the shallow vessel to his lips almost always spilled a portion of the precious liquid. Twice a day the deliveries of food and water were made, and each time he demanded to be released.

"Let me out, goddammit! You black-lovin' bitch! You'll pay for this!"

By the third day, he was begging for his freedom. Hunger, perpetual darkness, the lack of sanitation, the maddening silence—all caused him to think he was losing his sanity.

"Who are you?" he yelled. But silence and the soft sound of retreating steps was the only response.

"Wait! Don't go! I'll pay you to let me out! Just lift the bar on the door! I'll give you fifty dollars!"

Sometimes these requests were answered with a low chuckle. This only incited Wroughton's rage and he cursed and called his unknown captors vile names and threatened them with cruel punishments.

"I'll kill you myself! I'll pay to have you kilt!"

On the fifth evening of his imprisonment—he could tell it was night because the long, inch-high rectangle of daylight beneath the door had long since faded into the blackness of the rest of the cellar—he heard the approach of feet and the familiar low chuckle. Quickly lowering himself to the ground, he caught the flicker of lantern light beneath the door and, saying nothing, waited for the scraping sound that signaled the tin plate was being slipped across the stone threshold. As usual, the plate was filled with beans or corn and perhaps a thin crust of corn pone. Then another tin plate was put down and the sound of water being poured indicated it was being filled.

Wroughton immediately pulled the plates toward him and grunting like an animal, hungrily attacked the food and quickly slurped up the water. In only a matter of minutes, he had finished and licked clean the plates. In a broken voice he begged once again to be released.

"I won't do nothin'. Just let me out! I'll pay you good! I'll give you a thousand dollars! Just raise the bar and run on off and I'll wait and not even know who you are! I swear to God I won't do nothin' now or ever. Just let me out!"

His pleas only brought more of the despised chuckles, but this time the gleeful cackling was followed by another sound. It was a squeaking sound, familiar to him yet resisting precise identification. He knew he had heard it before, yet he could not remember where. But how could a man think or remember anything when nearly mad from eternal darkness and silence and confinement day after day?

The squeaking continued, like a gate on whining hinges in the wind, until at last Wroughton's heart was seized as if grasped by the vice-like grip of an icy hand. He recognized the sound now, and his mind was filled with horror at the implications it carried. His breath came in gasps as he waited and listened and watched the sliver of light at the bottom of the door.

Suddenly the faint lamplight beneath the door increased and as he watched it closely, something was slid beneath it. Touching it, it felt like paper. Pulling it toward him, he discovered the brightness of the light was caused by fire and the other end of the paper was burning. As the flame burned his fingers and flared before him he dropped it. But even as he did, and took a step back from the blazing paper before him, he recognized the document, the light of the flame permitting him to read certain words as it was being consumed. It was the deed to his property.

As his scream rose with the horror of what the presence of the deed meant, the chuckle beyond the door increased. The deed was nothing. Burn a thousand deeds and the property was still his. It could be rewritten; there was a copy on file at the courthouse. Burning a deed in no way threatened his ownership of his property.

But the deed had been in his strongbox, the box under his bed. The squeaking sound was the lid of the box being opened, held by the lid and swung back and forth so that he could hear and know that its contents had been pilfered. That squeak had preceded each deposit he had made in the box when he had opened and closed it himself to add to his profits, and on countless occasions when he had opened the box to lovingly count and re-count his growing wealth.

His money! They had found his money!

A rage greater than any he had ever experienced overwhelmed him and a howl tore from his throat as he beat his head and fists against the door and bellowed every vile and profane oath he could think of in wild, uncontrolled fury. Finally, he tasted his own blood as it streamed down his face from his head's repeated impact against the door. All for naught! It had all been for nothing! His years of labor, hoarding, miserliness, and self-deprivation had all gone to naught.

Wailing miserably, he fell to the floor and whimpered like a child, realizing that he had clawed the oak door until some of his fingernails were detached and turned back from their flesh.

He knew now that all his blacks were gone. And they had taken his money with them. Over one hundred thousand dollars—every cent he had accumulated during the years of personal denial—all the money he had in the world, his hoarded profits from as long as he had owned his property in Virginia. With that amount, his blacks would be able to bribe their way to any destination they chose. Even Charles Hicks and the local patrols would be unable to resist the temptation of such a bribe.

His loss nauseated him and he vomited, the bile of sickness and loss burning his throat. His stomach convulsed with pain. Holding his belly, he collapsed against the hard, cold walls of his dungeon and slid to the filthy floor, wailing at the loss of his fortune while he beat his fists helplessly against the resistant stone.

Finally, the squeaking lid of the cash box was hushed, its message successfully delivered. Then beneath the hated, gleeful chuckle, he heard the retreat of his torturer's steps as they faded away and there was only the sound of his sobs in the darkness, the odor of vomit and his own filth, and the acrid smell of the burned deed.

Far into the night, unheard by any ears except his own, the mournful, childlike whimper of Horace Wroughton's hopelessness and loss rose unheeded from the cellar.

Chapter Fifty

On the sixth day on the road, the Wroughton blacks drew suspicion from two white men who identified themselves as sheriff's deputies. The men ordered them to stop and questioned them extensively. A Wroughton slave, driving the first wagon in the second caravan, claimed to be behind the main group because of a loose wheel he had been forced to stop and repair.

"Our masters right on ahead of us, sir," the driver of the wagon said. "They knows we ketch up with them right soon."

"Why are you travelin' at night?"

"Master says it cooler on the horses and the little fellers less restless and we gots to make up time to get to the fields in Scott County in time to plant. Master wantin' to get that tobacco in the ground quick as we can."

The black's story was confirmed by Richard, who assumed the role of the master, when the men rode ahead to investigate further.

"Are they behaving back there?" Richard asked. "Did they talk respectful to you gentlemen?"

Convinced that everything was in order, the men proceeded on their way.

Other curious interruptions were handled with other ruses, devised in meetings with the Wroughton blacks the night before.

"The wagons following us may have a child or two with diphtheria," Lavinia lamented when stopped by patrols in Montgomery County. "They're from our second plantation and we want them as far away from the people from our other plantation as possible."

This story was not only believable but kept the curious at a safe distance from the possibly contagious group a mile or two behind them. By the time they reached Montgomery County, the diphtheria claim actually served to hasten their journey and they erected white flags to signify disease was in their midst. No one wanted an epidemic and they were rushed through, in one county even escorted by militia members to hasten their departure.

"They're not doing this as a courtesy," Lavinia whispered to Ellie. "They want us out of the county as soon as possible so we won't spread the epidemic."

Many of the blacks proved themselves superior actors and imitated the raspy cough and wheeze of diphtheria they had heard when the epidemic was real. Word that a fleet of sick slaves would be passing through preceded them and all but guaranteed roads free of travelers. They actually saw horses, wagons, and rigs turn and speed away in the opposite direction at the sight of the white flags heralding their approach. More than once, curious workers laboring near the road abandoned their hoes and plows and backed away toward the center of the field as the procession of obviously sick blacks passed, the workers recoiling fearfully as coughs and moans reached their ears.

Soon after crossing into Smith County, the caravan divided and the Wroughton slaves, led by Witt, headed for Ohio by the northern route; Lavinia's went on toward Washington County.

"But how will the Wroughton people ever survive in Ohio? What will they do? I'm giving our blacks money for a start, but they have nothing," Lavinia said.

Richard laughed. "I wouldn't worry about them, Sis. It's better that you not know how they got it, but they're probably the richest blacks in Virginia."

"Then they did kill Wroughton—and robbed him."

"They didn't kill him. They just got paid a little late, that's all."

Once the Wroughton blacks were gone, Lavinia finally relaxed, the tension of their presence lifted. She could actually breathe again and didn't start at the sound of every approaching horse or bark of a dog. At the same time, she still worried. In a way, she had become as much a fugitive as her blacks, but this only reaffirmed her commitment and her heart lifted.

Once in Washington County, by-passing the town of Abingdon and within thirty miles of her home, Lavinia began to believe the impossible: they were going to succeed. Now her prayers for deliverance became prayers of gratitude.

"Henny, we're going to make it. The Lord has seen us through."

"He does just about ever time, Miss Vinny. He one of the good things."

Even though the horses had been pushed far beyond what Lavinia would normally have tolerated, she persisted in driving them to the maximum. Home never before seemed such an urgent goal. Stops for the horses and cows to graze were shortened and hours on the road extended. At last they reached Williamsville and Lavinia wept as she saw her old home in the distance.

"Thank God," she murmured, hugging Henny, seated beside her, and looking at the radiant face of Ellie as tears streamed down both their faces.

Her mother and brothers Woodrow and Martin, and various nephews and nieces, were overjoyed at the sight of the procession of wagons, a carriage, and rigs, all loaded to capacity with blacks.

"My God, it looks like you've brought every black in Virginia!" shouted Woodrow as he ran to meet them. When he heard the total number, forty-four from Hawthorn Hill and thirty-eight from the Wroughton plantation who had gone on with Witt, he howled with laughter.

"Seventy-eight! Seventy-eight! It's a record, I tell you."

"A few over eighty, brother," Richard corrected. "The Wroughton blacks smuggled on three others we accidentally ran into back in Campbell County."

"And I wasn't told, of course," Lavinia said indignantly. She added with relief, "Thank you, Richard."

"We better get everyone into the barns," said Richard. "We'll have to keep the folks on the quiet until we can head out for Kentucky. The horses are about to drop and need to be fed and rest a few days. And the people are worn out, too."

"This isn't like the dozen or so we've sent before," said Lavinia, greeting her family with kisses and hugs. "We're almost certain to be pursued. We'll have to hide the people in the caves. Those caves we explored as children will come in handy."

"We'll deny ever having seen anything," Ellie said. "Lavinia has simply come to see Pa."

Mrs. Williamson and her daughters-in-law began immediately the endless cooking that would be necessary to feed so many additional people. Ovens would never cool, the meal and flour would be exhausted in a matter of days, but quickly replenished from nearby mills, and it would be necessary to kill a hog or cow. Wild turkeys, partridge, quail, and other game abounded in the nearby woods and there would be no shortage of food. And there would be enough to resupply the wagons for the journey when they continued on.

Because they were uncertain how long Horace Wroughton could be restrained in his cellar, it was decided that the slaves be moved out of Virginia as soon as possible. Two days was thought to be enough time to rest before continuing the journey. During that time, just as at Hawthorn Hill, the wagons were loaded with fresh supplies and readied for travel.

With fresh horses provided by the Williamsons, the Hawthorn blacks could leave before sunset on the third day. With continued good weather, seldom-used shortcuts, and recent improvements in the mountain roads, the travelers could make it to Kentucky in a day. There, Witt would lead them through the sparsely settled mountains. By staying on seldom-traveled routes, some little more than the vestiges of old Indian trails and buffalo runs, they would be able to elude anyone following them as they penetrated deeper and deeper into the mountain vastness.

The old ruse of moving a wagon-load of diphtheria or typhoid victims would guarantee unmolested passage should they encounter any of the few mountaineers who inhabited or hunted the area. Taciturn by nature, most of these mountain people wanted only to be left alone and would do little to interfere with those passing through as long as they minded their business and kept a respectful distance.

"If they like most white folks, they just be happy to sees us keeps on goin'," Paulina said. "They be more stirred up if we wanted to stay."

Lavinia felt safe at last. In only a few more days, her own blacks would be on their way to Ohio and then perhaps she could find at least a momentary peace before the inevitable consequences of her crimes fell upon her. She could do nothing but wait for the denouement of her great adventure to be played out.

Her offense was grave, and she knew she would be called to answer for it, but until then she would push thoughts of her day of reckoning out of her mind.

On the day they were to depart for Ohio, Henny and Reuben were in the barn helping to load the wagons with supplies. Only an hour before they were to leave, Henny's face was a study of misery and indecision.

"You told her yet?" Reuben asked.

Henny shook her head and looked at him helplessly, her blue eyes brimming with tears. The wagons were loaded and the people were slowly boarding, lifting the children to outstretched arms and waiting ticks and quilts. The passengers vied for choice positions in the smoother-riding wagons. Excitement filled the air as the expectant travelers knew they had passed the most dangerous part of their journey and would possibly be in Kentucky by the next day, and a week or so later in Ohio.

Only Henny's unhappiness was at variance with the euphoria that spread among the people as the departure neared.

"Stop lookin' at me like that," Reuben said. "I can't stand it when you does." He turned away from Henny's agonized, imploring gaze.

"But how am I going to tell her? I—"

"You just has to do it, that's all. I know it ain't goin' to be easy, but I been tellin' you since we decides, and you say you will. You know you has to."

Henny lay her head against the barn wall. "I'd heap rather be beat—"

"Hush. You just makin' it worser. Now go ahead and do it now."

"She goin' to be in such trouble when Mr. Lionel and ol' Wroughton finds out. She goin' to need me more than ever—"

Reuben extended his hand and she took it. Squeezing it tightly, he finally made himself look at her and she saw his own eyes were misty.

"I'll tell her," Henny said. "I'll do it now."

Henny found Lavinia in the kitchen wrapping a just-baked skillet of corn bread. It was the final one for the trip and she placed it on the table with a dozen other rounds waiting for transfer to the wagons.

"You may take this bread to Katie, Henny," Lavinia said, and then stopped. "Have you been crying, dear?"

Henny lowered her head and Lavinia, wiping her hands on her apron, approached her. Sitting down at the table, she drew Henny near and put her arms around her.

"We're all very sad to be saying goodbye to our people, aren't we? I understand. But we must be brave and—"

"Oh, Miss Vinny," Henny said, collapsing against her mistress and encircling her with her arms.

"Yes, dear?"

Pulling away from her, Henny looked at her through her tears and said, "I want to go too, Miss Vinny."

Lavinia smiled and sighed, understanding how Henny felt, but then she read something else, more frightening in the girl's eyes and quickly reappraised her words.

"You...you mean...really want to go?"

Henny nodded, and for a long moment the enormity of what the girl said and meant stunned Lavinia into silence.

"I want to go with my people."

"You mean...forever?" Lavinia managed to ask, her throat tight and the image of Henny blurring before her as tears flooded her eyes.

"Yes, ma'am. I don't want to leave you, but...but I want to go with my people and Reuben and...I want to be free, Miss Lavinia."

Lavinia's expression lost some of its anxiety. Uncertain hope eased her fears. She caught her breath and brought her hand to her breast in a gesture of relief.

"Reuben. Of course. I understand how fond you are of Reuben, but darling, you belong to me. And you are free. You know that. You're my little girl and—" She stopped short when she saw that Henny was not reacting with any sign of understanding nor had the seriousness of her expression lessened.

"It's not just Reuben, Miss Vinny. It's bein' free, mostly. Reuben say sometime we might get married. But that a far-off thing, if we ever does. I just on fifteen and bein' free in Ohio is what I want the most."

There was a long pause and Lavinia emitted a sob.

"Oh, but... Henny, you can't mean you'd leave me. And you are free...with me." Lavinia could not believe what she heard. Henny didn't mean it. How could she, a mere child? The idea angered her. "I forbid you. You're just a child."

How dare she? Lavinia thought. Her words caught in her throat and refused to come. *After all I've done for her,* she thought. *I will not permit it. She is mine—not as a slave but mine by right of my having taken her in as my own child and treating her so and rearing her as such and—*

"I'm right much grown up now, Miss Vinny," Henny said gently. "And I've been studyin' about this for a long, long time." Her imploring look, her eyes begging for understanding, struck Lavinia right in her heart. The terrible reality that the girl was sincere and her words indeed were her own shocked and twisted Lavinia into knots. But the moist blue eyes watching her did not glisten with the joy of starry-eyed romance but with the same sadness and suffering as Lavinia's. Henny's choice was not for love of a boy named Reuben, but for the love of freedom. And the girl grieved at its cost to her, just as Lavinia did.

"Go with me, Miss Vinny," Henny said. "If you goes with us to Ohio, we still be together."

Lavinia, so choked with grief she could not speak, shook her head and closed her eyes. She bit her lip and, finally finding her voice, said, "You're breaking my heart, you know."

"Oh, Miss Vinny, please don't make it any harder than it is. I'm tormented to pieces, too."

"But I...I always thought we'd be together. That—"

Henny closed her eyes as if to shut out her anguish, and struggled to find the words that would explain to her mistress how she felt.

"I's...I'm a black girl, Miss Vinny," she said. "I could be your little girl when it was just us, but not when it wasn't just us. When they others there, black or white, I was your maid. You know that, 'cause that how we had to do it. I'll always be black and you'll always be white and...and even though inside we know I'm your little girl and always will be, I don't think outside I can be... I'll always be black."

Lavinia looked at the girl before her and studied her for a long time. Then a glimmer of new understanding came to her eyes and she rose from her chair. Drying her tears and grasping a thread of what she thought Henny was trying to tell her, Lavinia decided to bury her pain with all the other suffering she held inside her. Henny wanted her freedom and she would not spoil her first steps toward that freedom by selfishly holding her back.

"What a wise child you are, Henny," she said at last, her voice soft as if in awe of the blue-eyed girl before her. She moved toward Henny and took her into her arms, holding her as the girl laid her head against her shoulder.

"You can always come back, you know."

"I know, Miss Vinny."

"And you must write me every week—"

"You know I will."

Smiling through the mist of tears she fought valiantly to restrain, Lavinia kissed Henny's cheek.

"I'll help you pack, if you haven't already."

"I just wants to tuck Maggie and Cordie in one more time," Henny said. "That one of the good things. I goin' to miss them 'bout as much as you, Miss Vinny."

Lavinia nodded her understanding, her words once again held back by the choking sense of loss lodged in her throat. Henny rose to go upstairs and say goodbye to the twins as Lavinia followed her into the front hall. Halfway up the stairs, she turned back toward Lavinia.

"Of all the good things, Miss Vinny," Henny said, "you is the best."

As time for the slaves' departure approached, Lavinia said goodbye to her brothers and sisters-in-law and her nephews who would be assisting in the journey. A lump of lead seemed to settle in her chest as she prepared for the more painful farewell to the people of Hawthorn Hill. She would see her brothers and their families again; in all likelihood this would be a final goodbye to her black family, many with whom she had shared life at Hawthorn Hill for over thirty years.

The wagons had been inspected, harnesses and gear repaired, the horses rested, and all was in readiness for the people to depart. After a final supper in the back yard, the people loaded their meager possessions, climbed aboard the wagons, and waited for Frank, who as driver of the first wagon, would lead the caravan. When the final sack of corn and bale of hay were loaded, the wagons waited in line for the order to advance. It was after six o'clock and the sun was lowering on the horizon, as if calling them to follow it beyond the hills westward to Kentucky and Ohio.

The farewells were bittersweet, and Lavinia's sadness in parting from them overrode her joy in their freedom. The tears she tried to suppress came, even as she tried to conceal her sorrow. Her strained smile made her face ache in its mask-like tableau of happiness in seeing the people begin the final steps in their journey.

The drivers picked up the reins, released the brakes on the wagons, and waited for Frank's call to advance.

Racing the length of the wagon train—now extended to seven vehicles by the addition of three other wagons, which would carry more food and supplies—Lavinia called to the people in each as she ran past them.

"You can come back, you know. I'll always find you a place either here or at Hawthorn Hill."

The grateful blacks extended their hands for her to shake and she saw glistening tracks of tears on many of the faces bending toward her and heard one voice after another offer her their thanks and prayers.

"We never forgets you, Miss Vinny..."

"We misses you..."

"Thank you..."

"You're more than just our people. You are family to me," Lavinia called, fighting back the tears as she touched one hand after another and heard their expressions of gratitude and sadness in saying goodbye. She wished she had more time to counsel and instruct them, for now they would be beyond her control and guidance.

"Benjamin, remind the people again what I told you about chiselers," Lavinia called up to Benjamin, who would be driving the second wagon. "They will try to exploit you. Tell them to spend their money wisely and not allow wicked people to cheat them. My brothers will guide them to honest men who can help them with deeds and purchases of property."

"I be watchful, Miss Lavinia."

"And encourage everyone go to church. And see the little ones are baptized."

"I do that, Miss Vinny," a voice called, and Piney's head appeared amid the faces toward the rear of the wagon. "I makes 'em all go to church and get baptized."

"You do that, Piney. And promise me you and Henny won't fight."

"I promises... And I make these youngins mind, too. All the way to Ohio." As if proving her intention, she turned toward some of the children in her wagon and said, "You all sets down and stop jumpin' 'round. You fall out of the wagon if you ain't keerful!"

"Ain't goin' to do it!"

"Miss Vinny, you tells 'em they gots to mind me!" Piney said.

"Ain't goin' to do it. We free now!"

At another wagon, she saw several of Nancy and Clevis's children whom she had taught the fundamentals of reading and arithmetic. "Don't stop reading. And practice your letters. And when you have children of your own, teach them to read and write, too, and..."

Her eyes fell on one grateful face after another as she went on to the next wagon, hearing their goodbyes and shaking their outstretched hands. So tight was the lump in her throat, she was unable to speak now and only nodded and waved to acknowledge the chorus of farewells and one expression after another of their affection and gratitude.

When she reached the fourth wagon, she heard Frank call out the order to pull out and saw the waving lantern he raised to signal their leaving. With the snap of reins and the drivers' orders to the horses to move echoing down the length of the train, the wagons started to roll.

Lest she be overwhelmed by sobs, Lavinia now only risked saying a few words, uttering choked goodbyes and nodding her head.

As the heavy vehicles lurched forward, Lavinia searched the faces for Henny. When she reached the sixth wagon, she felt a hand touching her shoulder and looked up to see Henny extending her arm, her blue eyes streaming with tears.

Behind her, Reuben stood with his head lowered. Lavinia stretched out her arm for Henny's hand and clung to it as the wagon moved forward. Unable to bear the sight of the black girl's sorrow and fighting to hold back her own, Lavinia directed her attention to Reuben.

"You take care of Henny for me, Reuben," she said. "And you make her write to me...and never let her forget me, and..."

"We both writes you, Miss Lavinia," Reuben said, his eyes moist and shining in the lantern light.

Still clutching Henny's hand, Lavinia walked beside the moving vehicle and increased her pace to a run as the wagon increased its speed. She was finally forced to release Henny's hand as the wagon passed through the yard's narrow gate, which blocked Lavinia's way and prevented her from going farther.

"I love you, Miss Vinny," Henny called.

"And I love you. And go to church and say your prayers and read—" Her voice stopped, her throat so tight she could say no more. Henny nodded, and the other wagons followed and lurched toward the setting sun.

Against the sunlit sky, she saw the silhouette of the wagons and the waving arms of the people as the caravan rolled on, with Lavinia struggling to follow as long as she could. The people called back their final goodbyes and promises to get word to her of their safe arrival in Ohio.

As the wagons receded into the distance, Lavinia found she was still following them, even as the distance between them increased. To her surprise, she found she had walked almost to the Johnson Springs Church.

She sat down on the top step of the stone horse stile, on which those riding horses dismounted when attending church. The last sound of the caravan faded into the deepening shadows as she watched the gentle lurch and sway of the wagons in the distance as they inched over the final hill that would take them out of her life forever.

She hoped the quiet of the evening, with only the cry of crickets, frogs, and night birds, would lull her into peace. But her thoughts could not be tamed and she could not keep from thinking of her people, especially Henny.

She knew she should be writing letters to her sons, Mr. Edmund, Miss Cornelia, Margaret, and so many others who would be stung by what she had done. But she would get to those unhappy duties in time. She also had to let Aunt Beck, Uncle Lemiel, and Old Sheba know that she had made it home and the others had but one state to cross before they were free men and women. In so many ways her—and her blacks'—ordeal was only beginning.

She was bone-tired but knew sleep would be impossible. As her thoughts weighed down on her, she felt the emptiness of Henny's being beyond the call of her voice for the first time in so many years. Never had Lavinia felt so alone.

Drawing her shawl around her against the cool mountain air, she surrendered to the fatigue that made every muscle in her body ache. She leaned against the top step of the brick horse-stile. Suddenly she remembered that it was here, on this very spot, over thirty years before that Lionel had asked her to marry him and she had accepted. How long ago it seemed, and how different she was now. That lovesick sixteen-year-old girl seemed like another person—a person she could not recognize.

A chilling wind stirred the tall pines nearby and she looked toward the cemetery just beyond the churchyard where so many of her ancestors were buried. Some of them had fought Indians, and died doing so. Others had perished before they had reached their thirtieth or fortieth year. All had lived lives of struggle, suffering, sadness, and happiness; anonymous and forgotten now, the earliest of them had only a field stone marking their final resting place. Other than their names written in the old Williamson Bible, they would pass into the past, forgotten and uncelebrated. And so it would be for Lavinia. But at least she was still alive. For all her struggles in the past, her wounds had not been mortal—yet.

She knew Henny was right, but the ache of surrendering her to a life of her own choosing still throbbed in her chest. How brave and true this little girl was, and how proud she was that her special insight had been recognized and given the right to its free expression.

How grateful she was to have been touched and blessed by the presence of this child if only for so short a time. She would mourn long and hard the loss of Henrietta Valentine Hawthorn, but she would never regret letting her go, even as it tore at her as no pain had since the death of Oralee. She knew she could not arrange Henny's happiness, but she could, by forcing her to stay, arrange the beginning of her unhappiness.

She remembered the letter she had received from Angelica describing the realities of being black in the North and prayed that Henny might meet with a more fortunate future. The world seemed so ugly, unfair, and cruel. She could only pray that someday it would be better.

The night closed around her and she shuddered as the breeze whispered secret messages in the rustle of the trees. She wanted to cry, but the lump in her throat stayed, stubbornly refusing to erupt into the release she so desperately needed.

She was drifting into despair and tried to cast off the pall of gloom. Self-pity would serve no purpose and the challenges she would face in the future would be a greater test of her character than any she had ever faced in the past.

She had no doubt that she would be implicated in the Wroughton slave disappearances. What Lionel would do was another matter. But whatever her fate, she knew that over eighty were free who would not have been otherwise— nearly one hundred if she counted all the others she had assisted through the years. She wished she had kept a count.

She wished she had the Barksdales to tell of her triumph. If they knew the consequences she faced, they would order her to come to them for protection. She could hide and evade capture indefinitely. But she chose not to run.

She would stay where she was, just as she had told Lionel in her letter to him, and face the consequences of her actions.

After a time, as the sun sank behind the hills, Lavinia rose to return home. Remembering the past had refreshed her and renewed her spirits. She inhaled the Virginia air and her heart was lifted. It was planting season in the mountains and there was much work to be done. There would be a genuine need for her here. She said a prayer of gratitude for her blessings and started down the hill for home. She vowed not to surrender to self-pity and melancholy. She would allow the future to unfold as it may. In the meantime, she would remember the happy times of her past.

In the midst of her misery a glimmer of light dawned: the realization that as unhappy as she was now, there was much in her forty-six years that had blessed her and brought her joy. She would remember those things and put aside the bad, like banishing shadows and gloom of a darkened room by letting in the sun or lighting a lamp.

She would remember happier times, those of her early years when as a girl she discovered horses and books, and made friends such as Margaret, who would never desert her. She would remember her babies, living and dead, and her grandchildren, and the people of Hawthorn Hill. She would remember the morning she saw a little black girl dressed in Alençon lace slip onto her side porch and into her heart. She would remember a sick baby in a basket she prayed would not cry out and reveal he was not a litter of kittens. She would remember the long procession of fearful, brave, and hopeful black faces, belonging to those she had helped escape the wretched scourge of slavery. She would remember a pair of indigo blue eyes lovingly watching her as she brushed aside the stray lock of blond hair she had countless times pushed back from a lined, deeply tanned forehead, and the dimpled cheeks that became even deeper pits when he grinned and erupted into raucous laughter. And another pair of indigo blue eyes, looking out from a little black face, pleading innocence to the charge of stealing.

Most of all, she would remember those two sets of indigo blue eyes. And she would be thankful for those things that had been the good things.

Made in the USA
Las Vegas, NV
05 May 2022

48419807R00418